select
editions

Reader's
Digest

Reader's Digest

www.readersdigest.co.uk

Published in the United Kingdom by Vivat Direct Limited (t/a Reader's Digest), 157 Edgware Road, London W2 2HR

For information as to ownership of copyright in the material of this book, and acknowledgments, see last page.

Printed in Germany
ISBN 978 1 78020 019 4

THE READER'S DIGEST ASSOCIATION, INC.

contents

author in focus

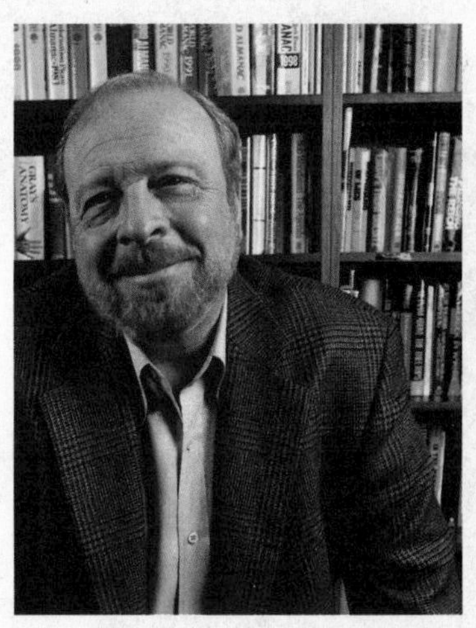

Nelson DeMille was born in New York City in 1943 and grew up on Long Island, where he still lives. He has written fourteen international best sellers, including *The Lion's Game*, which is the prequel to *The Lion*, and *The General's Daughter*, which was made into a film starring John Travolta, who played another of DeMille's series characters, Paul Brenner. 'I've decided to give Brenner a major part in my next John Corey novel,' says Nelson DeMille. 'So, for the first time, two of my main characters meet in a novel: John Corey and Paul Brenner. Two lovable egomaniacs. This should be interesting.'

in the spotlight

The fictional canine hero of *Finding Jack* is based on reality—military working dogs have been used by the United States since the Second World War. Originally a variety of breeds were utilised, but German Shepherds and Labradors soon emerged as the dogs of choice. In the Vietnam War, dogs served in three main capacities. Scout dogs, usually German Shepherds, would walk 'point' (out front) looking for tripwires and booby traps. Combat tracker dogs, often Labradors, tracked missing personnel by following body odours and blood trails. Sentry dogs were used by military police to help protect bases, ammunition depots, and many other vital areas. It is estimated that these Vietnam War dogs and their handlers saved more than 10,000 lives.

Nelson DeMille

THE LION

It's been three years since John Corey, a special agent for America's Anti-Terrorist Task Force, last traded words—and bullets—with Asad Khalil, one of America's most wanted terrorists.

Now, The Lion, with his dark and fearless gaze, is back on US soil, plotting vengeance on his old Task Force enemies. Corey, it seems, has one more chance to settle the score and put Khalil where he belongs . . .

CHAPTER ONE

So I'm sitting in a Chevy SUV on Third Avenue, waiting for my target, a guy named Komeni Weenie or something, who is Third Deputy something or other with the Iranian Mission to the United Nations. Actually, I have all this written down for my report, but this is off the top of my head.

Also off the top of my head, I'm John Corey and I'm an agent with the Federal Anti-Terrorist Task Force. I used to be a homicide detective with the NYPD, but I'm retired on disability—gunshot wounds, though my wife says I'm also morally disabled—and I've taken this job as a contract agent with the Feds. The ATTF is mostly an FBI outfit, and I work out of 26 Federal Plaza with my FBI colleagues, which includes my wife. It's not a bad gig, and the work can be interesting, though working for the Federal government—the FBI in particular—is a challenge.

Speaking of the FBI and challenges, my driver today is FBI Special Agent Lisa Sims, right out of Quantico by way of East Wheatfield, Iowa, or someplace—the tallest building she's previously seen is a grain silo. Also, she does not drive well in Manhattan, but she wants to learn. Which is why she's sitting where I should be sitting.

Ms Sims asked me, 'How long do we wait for this guy?'

'Until he comes out of the building.'

'What do we have on him? I mean, why are we watching him?'

'He is an Iranian military intelligence officer with diplomatic cover. As you know, we have information that he has asked for his car and driver to be available from one p.m. That is all we know.'

'Right.'

Lisa Sims seemed bright enough, and she knew when to stop asking questions. Like now. She's also an attractive young woman in a clean-cut sort of way, and she was dressed casually for this assignment in jeans, running shoes and a lime green T-shirt that barely concealed her .40 calibre Glock and pancake holster. I, too, wore running shoes—you never know when you might be sprinting—jeans, black T-shirt and a blue sports jacket that concealed my 9mm Glock, my radio, my pocket comb and breath mints. Beats carrying a handbag, like Ms Sims did.

Anyway, it was a nice day in May, and the big ornamental clock across the street said 3.17. We'd been waiting for this character for two hours.

The Iranian Mission to the U.N. is located on the upper floors of a thirty-nine storey office building off Third Avenue. Because of the U.N., Manhattan is home to over a hundred foreign missions and consulates, and not all of these countries are our buds. So you get a lot of bad actors posing as diplomats who need to be watched, and it's a pain in the ass. They should move the U.N. to Iowa.

I was the team leader today, which is a guarantee of success, and on this surveillance with me were four agents on foot and three other vehicles—another Chevy SUV and two Dodge minivans—all equipped with the whole police package: flashing lights, sirens, tinted windows. Inside the vehicle we have 35mm digital Nikon cameras with zoom lenses, Sony 8mm video cameras, handheld portable radios and so on. We all carry a change of clothes, a Kevlar vest, Nextel cellphones, even a little gadget that detects radioactive substances, which I don't even want to think about.

In any case, we are prepared for anything, and have been since 9/11.

When I was a cop I did a lot of surveillance, so I'm used to this, but Special Agent Sims was getting antsy. She said, 'Maybe we missed him.'

'Not likely.'

'Maybe he changed his plans.'

'They do that.'

Another fifteen minutes passed, and Special Agent Sims asked me, 'What is that place behind us? Au Bon Pain.'

'It's like a coffee shop. A chain.'

'Do you think I can run out and get a muffin?'

Well, she had running shoes, but the answer was no, though maybe if Ms Sims got out of the SUV, and if Komeni Weenie came out of the building and got into a car, then I could drive off and lose her.

'Well . . .'

My radio crackled and a voice—one of the guys on foot—said, 'Target exiting subject building from courtyard, out and moving.'

I said to Sims, 'Sure, go ahead.'

'Didn't he just say—?'

'Hold on.' I looked into the courtyard where two of my foot guys were helping to keep New York clean by collecting litter.

The radio crackled again, and Sweeper One said, 'Target heading east.'

I saw our target walking through the courtyard and onto the sidewalk. He was a tall guy, very thin, wearing a well-cut pinstripe suit. We give code names to the targets, and this guy had a big beak and moved his head like a bird, so I said into my radio, 'Target is henceforth Big Bird.'

All of a sudden another guy—who I profiled as being of Middle Eastern extraction—came up to Big Bird. Big Bird seemed to know him, and they shook hands, looking happy and surprised to see each other. I thought something was being passed. Or they were just shaking hands. You never know. Anyway, Big Bird has diplomatic immunity, and we're certainly not going to bust him for shaking hands with another Middle Eastern gentleman. In fact, now we have two people to watch.

Big Bird and the unknown separated, and the unknown began walking north on Third, while Big Bird stayed put.

I said into the radio, 'Units Three and Four, stay with the unknown and try to ID him.'

They acknowledged, and Ms Sims said to me, 'I don't think that was a chance meeting.'

I said, 'I think you're right.'

A minute later, a big grey Mercedes with dip plates pulled up near Big Bird. The driver, another Iranian gent, jumped out and ran round to the other side of the car like he was being chased by Israeli commandos. He bowed low—I should get my driver to do that—then opened the door, and Big Bird folded himself into the rear seat.

I said into the radio, 'Big Bird is mobile.' I gave the make and colour of the car and the plate number, and Unit Two acknowledged. Unit Two, by the way, was the second Dodge minivan, driven by Mel Jacobs, a NYPD Intelligence Unit detective. With Mel was George Foster, an FBI Special Agent who I've worked with before and who I like, because he knows from experience how brilliant I am.

The Mercedes headed north on Third Avenue. Special Agent Sims threw the SUV into gear and off we went, threading our way through heavy traffic. The Iranian chauffeur was an erratic driver. I couldn't tell if he was driving like that to lose a tail or if he was just a really bad driver.

The Mercedes made a sudden left on 51st Street and Ms Sims followed.

Unit Two continued on Third, where he'd hang a left on 53rd and run parallel to us until I could tell them what the Mercedes was doing. You don't want a parade following the subject vehicle; you want to mix it up a bit.

We were heading west now. I had no idea where Big Bird was going, but he was heading towards the Theater District and Times Square, where these guys sometimes went to experience American culture, like strip joints and titty bars. I mean, you don't get much of that back in Sandland. Right?

The Mercedes continued on 51st towards the area called Hell's Kitchen. Maybe Big Bird was headed for a Hudson River crossing. I said to Ms Sims, 'He may be going to Jersey.'

She nodded.

In truth, ninety per cent of our surveillances go nowhere. Abdul is just out and about, or he's trying to draw us off from something else that's happening. Or they're just practising their counter-surveillance techniques. Now and then, though, you get the real thing—like one of these dips meeting a known bad guy. These characters can tell us more by being kept under the eye than they'd tell us in an interrogation room. You can't question the dips anyway, and getting them booted out is left to people with a higher pay grade than mine.

The goal, of course, is to prevent another 9/11. So far, so good. But it's been too quiet for too long. Like over a year and a half since that day. So, are we lucky, or are we good? For sure, the bad guys haven't given up, so we'll see.

The Mercedes continued on towards Twelfth Avenue, which runs along the Hudson River and is the place where civilisation ends. No offence to New Jersey, but I haven't gotten my malaria shots this year.

There isn't as much traffic in this area of warehouses and piers, so the Mercedes picked up speed, continuing south towards Lower Manhattan, and Ms Sims kept up without being obvious. I could see Unit Two in my sideview mirror, and we acknowledged visual contact. By now, the Iranian driver should know he was being followed, but these guys are so dumb they can't even find themselves in a mirror, let alone a tail.

Maybe I spoke too soon, because the guy suddenly slowed up, and Ms Sims misjudged our relative speeds, so we were now too close to the Mercedes, with no one between us and him. I could see Big Bird's head in the back right seat. The driver must have said something to him, because he twisted round in his seat, looked at us, then smiled and gave us the finger. I returned the salute. Prick.

Ms Sims said, 'Sorry,' and dropped back.

Well, it's not the end of the world when the subject is on to you. It happens about half the time when you're mobile, though less on foot. There is a Plan B, however, and I called Unit Two and explained that we'd been burned. I told Ms Sims to drop further back, and Unit Two passed us and picked up the visual tail.

We all continued on, and I kept Unit Two in sight.

We got down below the West Village, and Unit Two radioed that the subject was turning on West Houston.

Then Unit Two said, 'Subject is turning into the entrance ramp for the Holland Tunnel.'

'Copy.'

In a few minutes, we were on the entrance ramp to the tunnel, following Unit Two.

Ms Sims asked, 'Where do you think he's going?'

'New Jersey,' I said, 'That's where the tunnel goes.'

She didn't respond to that bit of Zen, and instead she informed me, 'Iranian diplomats may not travel more than a twenty-five-mile radius from Manhattan.'

'Right.' I think I knew that.

We exited the tunnel, and soon we were approaching the interchange for Interstate 95. I said, 'Ten bucks says he goes south. Newark Airport.'

She thought a moment, then said, 'Well, he's been travelling south, but he has no luggage for the airport—unless it's in the trunk. I say he's going south, but not to the airport. To Atlantic City.'

'OK. Ten bucks.'

'Fifty.'

'You're on.'

Unit Two radioed, 'Subject has taken the southbound entrance to Ninety-five.'

'Copy.' So it was either Newark Airport or maybe Atlantic City. I mean, these guys did go down to AC to gamble, drink and get laid. I've followed Abdul down there on a number of occasions.

I could still see Unit Two, and they could see the subject vehicle, and Jacobs radioed, 'Subject passed the exit for Newark Airport.'

Ms Sims said to me, 'You can pay me now.'

I said, 'He could be going to Fort Dix. You know, spying on a military installation. He's a military intel guy,' I reminded her.

'And the chauffeur and Mercedes are cover for what?'

I didn't reply.

We continued on, hitting speeds of eighty miles an hour on Route 95, known here as the New Jersey Turnpike.

I said to Ms Sims, 'You know, maybe I should call for air.'

She didn't reply, so I further explained, 'We have an air spotter we can use. Makes our job easier.' I started to switch the frequency on the radio, but Ms Sims said, 'He's booked at the Taj Mahal.'

I took my hand off the dial. 'How do you know?'

'We got a tip.'

'And when were you going to share this with me?' I enquired.

'After I had my muffin.'

I was a little pissed off. Maybe a lot.

A few minutes later, she asked me, 'Are you, like, not speaking to me?'

In fact, I wasn't, so I didn't reply.

'But we've got to follow him down there to see that he actually goes to the Taj and checks in,' she said. 'We've got a team down there already, so after they pick him up we can turn round and head back to the city.'

I had no reply.

She assured me, 'You don't owe me the fifty dollars. In fact, I'll buy you a drink.'

No use staying mad, so I said, 'Thank you.' I mean, typical FBI. They wouldn't tell you if your ass was on fire. The concept of this joint Task Force is to create synergy by joining Federal agents and NYPD, who know the city intimately and do a lot of the street work. In practice, however, there is some tension among the men and women of these two very different cultures.

I radioed Unit Two with my new info, though I advised them to stay with us in case our info was wrong and Big Bird was heading elsewhere.

We continued on, and Ms Sims said, 'We have about two hours. Tell me all you know about surveillance. I'd like to know what you've learned in the last forty years.'

It hasn't been that long, and I'm sure Ms Sims was just making an ageist joke. She actually had a sense of humour, a rarity among her colleagues, so to demonstrate to her the spirit of joint FBI/NYPD cooperation, I said, 'All right. I talk, you listen. Hold your questions.'

She nodded, and I settled back and imparted my extensive knowledge of surveillance techniques, interspersed with anecdotal and personal stories of surveillances, even the ones that went bad.

Ms Sims, true to her word, did not interrupt as I held her spellbound with my stories. I really don't like to brag, but this was a teaching moment, so how could I avoid it? As I say, I was honest about the screw-ups.

On that subject, and on the subject of smart bad guys, in my three years with the Task Force I've run into only two truly evil geniuses. One was an American; the other was a Libyan guy with a very big grudge against the USA. Not only was he evil and smart, he was also a perfect killing machine, and there were times when I wasn't sure if I was the hunter or the hunted.

That episode did not have a happy ending, and the whole case was classified as Top Secret and 'need to know', meaning I couldn't share it with Ms Sims, or with anyone, ever. Which was fine with me.

But someday, I was sure, there would be a rematch. He had promised me that.

ABOUT THREE HOURS after Ms Sims did not get her muffin in Manhattan, we pulled into the long, fountain-lined drive of the Trump Taj Mahal. The Taj is topped with bulbous domes and minarets, so perhaps Big Bird thought it was a mosque.

Ms Sims had called ahead to let the team know the subject was on the way so they could get to Reception. She also described what he was wearing. I radioed Unit Two, who were parked a distance from the entrance, and told them, 'You can take off.' Mel Jacobs and George Foster volunteered to stay—above and beyond the call of duty—and I replied, 'Do whatever you want. You're on your own time.'

The thing that makes this Task Force work, in my opinion, is that it's free of a lot of the bureaucratic crap that keeps the job from getting done. About half the agents are retired NYPD, like me, which means we're not worried about our careers and not worried about crossing the line. Plus, we bring

NYPD street smarts to the table. Results may vary, of course, but mostly we get the job done.

The Mercedes driver pulled away without Big Bird, who went inside carrying an overnight bag. We couldn't give the fully equipped SUV to the parking attendant, so we just parked near the entrance. I flashed my creds and said, 'Official business. Watch the car.' I gave the parking guy a twenty and he said, 'No problem.'

We entered the big ornate marble lobby, and I spotted Big Bird at the VIP check-in. I also spotted two guys from the Special Operations detail. We made eye contact and they signalled they were on the case.

Great news. Time for a drink.

I didn't think Big Bird could recognise us from our brief, long-distance exchange of salutes, so I escorted Ms Sims past where he was checking in. I mean, he knew he'd been followed here and that he wasn't supposed to be this far from Third Avenue, but we don't make an issue of it unless someone in Washington wants us to.

Anyway, we each made a pit stop, then went into the casino area, and I asked Ms Sims, 'Would you like a muffin?'

'I owe you a drink.'

I headed directly for the Ego Lounge, which at night becomes the Libido Lounge. We sat at the bar, and Ms Sims ordered a white wine while I got my usual Dewar's and soda. We clinked glasses and she said, 'Cheers,' then asked me, 'Why are we here?'

'Just to be sure Big Bird is playing and not meeting someone.'

She reminded me, 'We have a team here. Also, B.B. could have a meet in his room and we wouldn't know.'

'The S.O. guys would know. And you want to be around if something goes down,' I advised her. 'You got someplace else to go?'

'Nope.'

'Good. We'll give it an hour.'

Actually, there was no reason to stay, except I needed a drink. Plus, I was pissed off at Big Bird for giving me the finger. That wasn't very diplomatic of him.

'Sorry I couldn't tell you about this, John. They wanted to run it as a standard surveillance so that the subject couldn't guess by our actions that we knew where he was going,' Ms Sims explained. 'Only I knew in case we actually lost him.'

'Right. Whatever.' I had no idea whose brilliant idea that was, but I could guess that it was the idea of Tom Walsh, the FBI Special Agent in Charge of the Anti-Terrorist Task Force in New York. Walsh loves the cloak-and-dagger stuff and doesn't quite get standard police work. I mean, this secrecy crap would never have happened when I was a cop.

To change the subject, I said, 'Call the S.O. team and ask that we be called if Big Bird leaves his room and comes down to the casino.'

So we chatted, mostly about her living and working in New York, which she didn't like personally but did like professionally. Lisa Sims reminded me in some ways of my wife, Kate Mayfield, who I met on the job three years ago on the previously mentioned case of the Libyan asshole. Kate, too, is from the hinterland, and she wasn't initially thrilled with the New York assignment, but after meeting me she wouldn't live anywhere else. And then there was 9/11. After that, she wanted us to transfer out of New York, but when the trauma wore off—we were both there when it happened—she rethought it and she realised she couldn't leave. Which was good, since I wasn't leaving.

I had a second drink, but Ms Sims—now Lisa—switched to club soda because I told her she was driving back.

Her cellphone blinged, and she took it and listened, then said to the caller, 'OK, we'll probably head out.' She signed off and said to me, 'Big Bird is alone at a roulette table.'

'How's he doing?'

'I didn't ask.' She paid the bill, but as she turned towards the lobby, I said, 'I just want to get a close look at this guy.'

We made our way into the cavernous casino and, within a few minutes, we spotted him sitting at a roulette wheel with a drink in his hand.

I observed, 'Satan has entered his soul. I need to help him. Let's get some tokens and hit the slots.'

Lisa hesitated. 'John—'

'Come on.' I took her arm and we went to the cashier, where I got a hundred one-dollar tokens on my government credit card—the accounting office would get a good laugh out of that—and we headed for the dollar slots, from where we could see Big Bird's back.

Lisa and I sat side by side at two poker machines. I divided up the silver coins and briefly explained the machine to Lisa, and we played slot machine poker. Soon Lisa was getting into it, hoping to retire early on the

Zillion Dollar Jackpot. Meanwhile, Big Bird was sinking deeper into the fires of hell with each spin of the wheel. I had to save him.

After about half an hour, Big Bird cashed out and got up.

Lisa got four kings and the machine chimed and disgorged a stream of coins into her tray.

I said to her, 'Big Bird is moving. Stay here and play my machine. Call the Special Ops team and tell them I've got him.'

She glanced round and said, 'OK . . .'

I headed across the casino floor, hoping that Big Bird would head to the men's room—or any place where we could be alone for a chat.

Sure enough he headed out to the restrooms. I followed him.

These guys don't piss at the urinal—they like privacy when they pull out their pee-pees—and Big Bird was in one of the stalls.

There were two guys at the urinals and one at the sink. Very quietly and diplomatically, I showed my creds and asked them to move out quickly, and I asked one of them to stand outside and keep people out.

They all exited, and I stood at the sink, looking in the mirror. The stall door opened and Big Bird gave me a glance. I could tell he didn't recognise me. But then he made his move. He suddenly rushed me and somehow managed to smash his balls into my fist. Well, that took me by surprise. I stepped back as he sank to his knees making threatening groans at me. Then he slumped forwards and lay on the floor, breathing hard, ready to attack again. I didn't want to cause an international incident, so I excused myself and left.

Out in the corridor, I released my deputy and went back into the casino, where I ran into Lisa, who was carrying a plastic container filled with tokens. She asked me, 'Where's Big—'

'Time to go.'

'What do I do with these tokens?'

'Give them to accounting.'

We got outside and headed towards the SUV.

Lisa asked, 'What happened? Where's Big Bird?'

The less she knew, the better for her, so I said, 'Men's room.'

She asked, 'Who's covering him? Is he moving?'

'Uh . . . not too much.'

'John—'

'Call the S.O. team and report his last location.'

We got to the SUV and I said I'd drive. She gave me the keys, we got in and I pulled away.

Lisa called the surveillance team and told them I'd left Big Bird in the men's room, which they already knew. She listened, then signed off and said to me, 'Big Bird . . . had a fall or something.'

'Slippery when wet.'

I headed out of town towards the Jersey Turnpike.

After a few minutes, she asked, 'Did you . . . have an encounter with him?'

'Hey, how'd we do? What do you have there?'

'I think we won ten bucks.'

'Not bad for an hour's work.'

She stayed silent, then said, 'Well . . . I suppose he's not in a good position to make a complaint.'

I didn't reply.

'They told me I'd learn a lot from you.'

'Am I a legend?'

'In your own mind.' She then observed, 'You seem like a nice guy and you're smart. But you have another side to you. You're into payback.'

'Well, if I am, I'm in the right business.'

She had no response to that, and we continued on in silence.

We got onto the Turnpike northbound towards the city, which was about 130 miles away, less than two hours if I pushed it. The sun was below the horizon and the western sky was rapidly fading into darkness.

A while later, she said, as if to herself, 'This is a tough business.'

And what was your first clue? I replied, 'And getting tougher.'

We took the Holland Tunnel into Manhattan, and I dropped her off at 26 Fed, where she had some work to do. I continued on to my apartment on East 72nd.

Kate was home, watching the news. 'How did it go?' she asked.

'OK. The target went down to AC and we followed. How was your day?'

'Office all day.'

We made drinks, clinked, smooched and sat down and watched the news together. I was waiting for a story about an Iranian diplomat who was found in the men's room of the Taj Mahal Casino with his nuts stuck in his throat, but apparently this was not going to be a news item.

We shut off the TV, and Kate reminded me that we were going upstate for the weekend—skydiving.

This was not my favourite subject, though she was excited about it.

Aside from the fact that I don't like trees and woods and bears and whatever else is north of the Bronx, I damned sure don't like jumping out of planes. I see no reason to put myself in danger for fun. I mean, I get enough danger on my job. And all the fun I want. Like tonight. But I'm a good guy and a good husband, so I've taken up skydiving.

I went out to my thirty-fourth floor balcony and looked south down the length of Manhattan Island. What a view. Gone from view, however, were the Twin Towers, and I held up two fingers in a V where they used to be. Victory and peace. Not in my lifetime, but maybe someday.

Meanwhile, the name of the game was payback.

ASAD KHALIL, Libyan terrorist, travelling on a forged Egyptian passport, walked quickly down the jetway that connected his Air France jetliner to Terminal Two of Los Angeles International Airport.

The flight from Cairo to Paris had been uneventful, as had the flight from Paris to Los Angeles, thanks to well-placed friends who had expedited his passage through the security checks. Now he was in America. Or nearly so.

Khalil walked with his fellow Air France passengers towards the passport control booths. Most of the people on board the flight were French nationals, though that included many fellow Muslims with French citizenship. Khalil thought he did not stand out among his fellow travellers and he had been assured by his Al Qaeda friends that this particular route would get him at least this far without a problem. All that remained was for him to get through American passport control with his forged Egyptian documents.

There were ten passport control booths operating, and he stood in the line with other arriving passengers. He glanced at his watch, which he had set to local time: 5.40 p.m., a busy hour, which was part of the plan.

Asad Khalil wore a blue sports blazer, tan slacks, loafers and a button-down Oxford shirt—an outfit that gave off the image of a man of the upper middle class who had attended the right schools and was no threat to anyone. He was a westernised Egyptian tourist by the name of Mustafa Hasheem.

He walked quickly to the next available booth. The passport control officer was a middle-aged man who looked bored and tired. He took Khalil's passport, visa and customs declaration form and stared at them, flipping through the passport pages. Then he returned to the photo page and divided his attention between the photograph and the man standing before him. Khalil smiled, as did most people at this juncture.

The man said to him, 'What is the purpose of your visit?'

To kill, Khalil thought to himself, but replied, 'Tourism.' He spoke English almost fluently.

The man glanced at Khalil's customs form and said, 'You're staying at the Beverly Hilton?'

'The Beverly Hills Hotel.'

'What is your next destination?'

Home or Paradise. Khalil replied, 'Home.'

'You have a reservation at the Beverly Hills Hotel?'

He did, although he knew not to offer to show it unless he was asked. He replied, 'Yes.'

The man looked into Khalil's deep, dark eyes, and Khalil could tell that he had a small doubt in his mind that could grow into a larger doubt in the next few seconds of eye contact. Khalil remained impassive, showing no signs of anxiety and no feigned impatience.

The man turned his attention to his computer and began typing as he glanced at Khalil's passport.

Khalil waited. The passport itself, he knew, looked genuine, but the information inside it was not. His Al Qaeda friends, who knew much about American airport security, did not, unfortunately, know much about what the computer databank was capable of knowing or detecting. As always, it came down to the man.

The passport officer looked again at the Egyptian tourist, then hesitated a second before stamping the passport. He said, 'Welcome to the United States, Mr Hasheem. Have a pleasant visit.'

'Thank you.'

Khalil collected his documents and moved towards the luggage carousel. There he assumed the pose and the blank gaze of the other tired passengers who stared at the carousel opening, for he knew it was here that people sometimes revealed themselves, forgetting that they were still being watched on video monitors.

Within five minutes he had retrieved his bag and wheeled it towards the customs counters. He chose a counter with a young man and handed him his customs form.

The man looked at it and asked him, 'Anything to declare?'

'No.'

The man glanced at the black suitcase that was behind Khalil and said, 'If I looked in there, would I find anything you're not supposed to have?'

Asad Khalil answered truthfully, 'No.'

The young man joked, 'No hashish?'

Khalil returned the smile and replied, 'No.'

'Thank you.'

Khalil continued on. The security doors were ten metres away and it was here, he knew, that he would be stopped if they intended to stop him, although the Americans did not often make pre-emptive arrests: they followed you, saw who you met, where you went, and what you did. A week or a month later they would make the arrests.

Asad Khalil walked through the security doors into the crowded terminal and followed signs to the taxi stand. Within a few minutes, he and his suitcase were in a taxi. He said to the driver, 'The Beverly Hills Hotel.'

As the taxi moved towards the airport exit, the driver asked him, 'First time in LA?'

'No.'

'Business or pleasure?'

Killing Mr Chip Wiggins would be both a business and a pleasure, so Khalil replied, 'Both.'

'I hope you have fun and make lots of money.'

'Thank you.'

Khalil took his guidebook from his overnight bag and pretended to read it, and the driver settled into silence as they entered the freeway and continued north towards Beverly Hills.

Within half an hour, they pulled into the long, palm-lined drive that led to the pink stucco hotel on the hill. Khalil paid the driver, and checked in under his assumed name. The receptionist, a young lady, assured him that all charges were prepaid by his company in Cairo, and that no credit card was necessary. He let the receptionist know that he might not be returning to the hotel that evening and that he did not require a wake-up call or a newspaper in the morning.

He was shown to his room, a spacious and sunny suite on the second floor overlooking the pool. He stood on the small balcony and looked out at the swimming pool, where men and women paraded and lounged. He wondered at men who would allow their wives to be seen half-naked by other men. Then he unpacked his suitcase and waited for his call.

When the phone rang, he answered, 'Hasheem.'

The voice at the other end said, 'This is Gabbar. Are you well?'

'I am. And how is your father?'

'Quite well, thank you.'

The sign and countersign having been given, Khalil said, 'Five minutes. I have a flower for your wife.'

'Yes, sir.'

Khalil hung up and went again to the balcony. Many of the men, he now noticed, were fat, and many of them had young women with them. Waiters carried trays of beverages to the lounge chairs and tables. It was the cocktail hour, the time to cloud one's mind with alcohol.

'Pigs,' he said aloud. 'Fat pigs to the slaughter.'

ASAD KHALIL, carrying a bird of paradise flower from his room, walked out of the lobby of the Beverly Hills Hotel and waited for the blue Ford Taurus that had been sitting nearby to move forwards and stop in front of him.

Khalil got quickly into the passenger seat, threw the flower on top of the dashboard and the car moved off. The driver said in Arabic, 'Good evening, sir.' Khalil did not respond.

The driver headed down the long driveway and said, 'I have taken a room under my own name at the Best Western hotel in Santa Barbara.'

Khalil nodded and asked, 'And what is your name?'

The driver replied, 'It is Farid Mansur, sir.'

Khalil enquired, 'Do you have my parcels, Mr Mansur?'

'I do, sir. They are in my hotel room, as instructed. Two locked luggage pieces for which I have no keys. Is that correct, sir?'

Khalil nodded and asked, 'Do you have the other items I requested?'

'Yes, sir. They are in the trunk.'

'And the card?'

Mansur handed Khalil a plastic card without comment.

Khalil examined the card, which had little information printed on it for security reasons—not even the name of the airport where it could be used, or the specific security gate that it would open.

Khalil asked, 'How did you get this card?'

Mansur replied, 'It was given to me by our mutual friend here. I was told to tell you that it is on loan from another friend, a man of our faith who will not be needing it for two days.'

Khalil put the card in his pocket.

As Farid Mansur turned right on Sunset Boulevard, Khalil glanced in the sideview mirror, but saw that no vehicles seemed to be following. He said to Mansur, 'This is a rental car, correct?'

'Yes, sir. I have taken it for three days, as instructed.'

'Good.' So the vehicle would not be missed until Monday.

Khalil stared out of the side window, and Mansur commented, 'The wealthy live here. Movie stars and those in the film industry.'

Khalil observed, 'Sin pays well here.'

Mansur replied, as was expected of him, 'Here, yes. But there is a higher price to pay in Hell.'

Khalil did not respond to that and asked, 'And your wife knows you will not be returning home for two or three days?'

'Yes, sir.'

Farid Mansur realised that this man made him nervous. He had seen men like this in Libya, and sometimes here, at the mosque. They shared with him the same faith, but in a different way. And this man . . . his voice, his manner, his eyes . . . this man was different even from the others who were different; this man frightened him.

Mansur turned right onto Wilshire Boulevard and headed west towards Santa Barbara. They continued on along the wide boulevard lined with shops. Traffic was heavy and moved slowly.

Khalil asked, 'Where in Libya are you from?'

Mansur replied, 'Benghazi, sir.' He was quick to add, 'My dream is to return to our country.'

'You will,' Khalil said. 'Were you in Benghazi when the Americans bombed the city?'

'Yes. I remember that night very well. April the 15th, 1986. I was a young boy.'

'Were you frightened?'

'Of course.'

Khalil said, 'I, too, was a young boy, living in the Al Azziziyah compound in Tripoli. One of their aircraft flew directly over the rooftop where I was standing and released a bomb. I was unhurt.'

Farid Mansur said, 'Allah was merciful, sir.'

'Yes. But my mother, two brothers and two sisters ascended to Paradise that night.'

Mansur took a deep breath, then said softly, 'May they dwell with the angels for eternity.'

'Yes. They will.'

They drove on in silence, then Khalil asked, 'Why are you doing this?'

Farid Mansur considered his reply. To say that he was doing this for his country or his faith was to admit that he knew there was more to this than assisting a countryman on his visit.

'I have been asked to do a favour for a countryman, and—'

'Have you ever come to the attention of the authorities?'

'No, sir. I live quietly with my family.'

'And your wife. What does she do?'

'What a good woman does. She tends to her house and family.'

'Good. So, a little extra money would be of help.'

'Yes, sir.'

Mansur took the Pacific Coast Highway north towards Santa Barbara. He informed his passenger, 'It should be less than two hours to the hotel.'

Khalil glanced at the dashboard clock. It was just 7.30 and the sun was sinking into the ocean.

Farid Mansur said, 'This is the more scenic route to Santa Barbara, sir. On Sunday, we can take the freeway back, if you wish.'

Khalil did not care about the scenery, and neither he nor Farid Mansur would be returning to Beverly Hills on Sunday. But to put the man's mind at ease, he replied, 'Whatever you wish. I am in your hands.'

'Yes, sir.'

'And we are both in God's hands.'

'Yes, sir.'

In fact, Khalil thought, Mr Mansur would be in God's hands within the next two hours.

As for Mr Chip Wiggins, who was one of the pilots who had bombed Tripoli seventeen years ago, and had perhaps been the one to murder Khalil's family, he would be in Hell before the sun rose again.

And then Khalil would go to New York to settle other unfinished business.

A FEW MILES NORTH OF Santa Barbara, Farid Mansur pulled into the entrance of the Best Western hotel. He drove round to the back of the hotel and parked in a space facing the building.

Khalil exited the car and said to Mansur, 'Open the trunk.' Mansur did so and Khalil peered inside. Sitting on the trunk floor was a long canvas carrying case, which Khalil opened. In it was a heavy crowbar, and also a butcher's saw. Khalil touched the sharp, jagged teeth of the saw and smiled. He slammed the trunk closed and said to Mansur, 'Lock the car.' Mansur locked it with the remote and Khalil took the keys from him and motioned towards the hotel. Khalil followed Mansur into a rear entrance that Mansur opened with his passcard. They turned down a corridor, and Mansur stopped at Room 140.

It was a pleasant room with two large beds, and on one of the beds sat two pieces of luggage—a black suitcase and a black duffle bag. Khalil walked to the bags and from his wallet he retrieved two small keys that had been given to him in Cairo.

Farid Mansur had moved to the window and was staring out at the parking lot.

Khalil unlocked and unzipped the duffle bag and saw that it had a few changes of clothing for him. Then he opened the suitcase. Inside were the other things he needed to complete his mission—cash, credit cards, forged passports and documents, plus a few maps, binoculars and a cellphone and charger. Also the instruments of death that he had requested—a Colt .45 calibre automatic pistol, a large butcher's knife and a few smaller knives. There was also a pair of leather gloves, a copy of the Koran and a garrote. And finally, there was the ice pick that he'd asked for.

Satisfied that all was in order, he glanced at Mansur's back, then slipped on the gloves and removed the piano wire garrote from the bag.

Khalil said to Mansur, 'Close the drapes.'

Mansur pulled the drapes shut, but remained facing the window.

Khalil came up behind him. Mansur said, 'Please, sir.'

Khalil quickly slipped the wire noose over Mansur's head and twisted the wooden grip. The wire tightened, and Mansur tried to pull it from his throat as a high-pitched squeaking sound came out of his mouth. Khalil tightened it further, and Mansur lurched about, finally falling facedown on the floor with Khalil on his back, keeping the wire taut. A line of blood oozed round the man's throat and neck where the wire bit into his flesh.

Khalil waited a full minute before he loosened the wire. He said to Mansur, 'The angels shall bear thee aloft.' Then he rolled the dead man over on his back. Farid Mansur's eyes stared up at Khalil and his mouth was open in a silent scream.

Khalil retrieved his garrote, then rolled and pushed the dead man under one of the double beds. By the time the body was found, he would be far from California.

Khalil removed the Colt .45 automatic from the suitcase. He checked the magazine, chambered a round and stuck the pistol in his belt. He opened the Koran and read a verse for the man under his bed. 'Wherever ye be, God will bring you all back at the resurrection.' Then he read a few more favourite verses, turned off all the lights and lay down fully dressed on the bed.

Asad Khalil did not sleep. Like the lion, after whom he was named, he rested his body but kept his senses awake. He recalled an old Arab proverb: 'On the day of victory, no one is tired.'

AT 2.30 A.M. Khalil went out into the cool, dark morning, got into the car, and drove out of the parking lot. There was no traffic on the roads, and within ten minutes he was approaching the northeast corner of Santa Barbara Airport, the part reserved for private aircraft, charter companies and air freight.

He drove through the open gate into a long, narrow parking lot where several low buildings backed onto the aircraft parking ramps. He saw not a single person or moving vehicle at this hour. So far, his information had been correct. Al Qaeda had not made his mission possible, as they believed, but, he admitted, they had made it easier. Asad Khalil, The Lion, had killed the enemies of Islam all over Europe and America without help from anyone, but Al Qaeda had made him an offer of assistance in exchange for his carrying out a mission for them in New York. For security reasons, the target would not be revealed to him until he had completed his personal mission of revenge.

Most of the buildings were dark, but one of them had a lighted sign that read ALPHA AIR FREIGHT—Mr Chip Wiggins's place of employment. Khalil saw a dark Ford Explorer parked near the freight office that matched the photograph he had been shown. Mr Wiggins was apparently working this evening, as scheduled. Today was Friday, and Mr Wiggins, who lived alone, was not scheduled to work again until Sunday night.

Khalil parked the Ford Taurus in a space opposite Alpha Air Freight, next to Wiggins's vehicle. He got out and checked the licence plate of the Explorer, confirming it was Wiggins's vehicle. Then he opened the Taurus's trunk and removed the canvas carrying case that contained the crowbar and the butcher's saw, and slung the case over his shoulder.

Khalil walked quickly across the parking lot towards the open space between the freight building and the building beside it. There was a high security fence and gate between the two buildings that led to the airport ramps. Khalil used the access card that he'd received from Farid Mansur, opened the gate, and slipped into the secured area.

The space between the buildings was not well lit, and he walked in the shadow close to the Alpha building, then knelt beside a trash container at the corner of the building and scanned the area around him.

Close to the rear of the Alpha building were two small twin-engine aircraft with the Alpha markings on their tails. These aircraft, he'd been told, were two of the three aircraft that Alpha operated. The third aircraft in the Alpha fleet was a white twin-engine Cessna piloted by Mr Wiggins, whose pick-up and drop-off route would not usually get him back here until three or four in the morning. Khalil looked at the luminous dial of his watch and saw it was now 2.58 a.m.

Khalil stared out at the airport. In the far distance he could see the lights of the main terminal and also the lights of the runways. There were not many aircraft landing or departing at this hour, but Khalil did see the lights of a small aircraft as it came in low over the closest runway.

The aircraft touched down and, a few minutes later, Khalil saw the beams of two white landing lights cutting through the darkness and illuminating the taxiway that led to the ramps.

He had waited a long time for this moment, and he was now very close to Mr Wiggins, the last of the eight pilots who had dropped their bombs on the Al Azziziyah compound in Tripoli where he had lived, and where his family had died.

As the twin-engine aircraft taxied towards him, he opened the canvas carrying case and took out the heavy crowbar. Within moments, the aircraft had come to a stop, its lights extinguished, both engines shut down, and the night was again dark and quiet.

Khalil watched and waited. Then he saw the airstair door on the left side of the fuselage swing down, and a moment later a man stepped out and descended the stairs. There was little illumination in the ramp area, and Khalil could not be certain that this pilot was Wiggins, but this was the aircraft he flew and his arrival time was correct.

The pilot was carrying wheel chocks on ropes and he bent down to wedge the first chock behind the aircraft's left tyre.

Khalil grabbed the canvas carrying case and sprang forward, covering the ten metres between him and the aircraft in a few seconds.

Hearing a sound, the pilot turned. Khalil was right on top of him. In an instant he recognised the face from photographs as that of Chip Wiggins.

Wiggins stared at the man and said, 'Who—?'

Khalil had dropped the canvas bag and was now holding the crowbar in both hands. He swung the heavy steel bar around in an arc and smashed it down on top of Wiggins's left shoulder, shattering his clavicle. Wiggins let out a bellowing cry of pain, staggered backwards, then fell to the ground.

Khalil swung again and again, shattering Wiggins' right kneecap, smashing his left shin bone, breaking his right shoulder. He could see that the man was passing into unconsciousness. Khalil looked round quickly, then threw the crowbar and the case with the saw up into the plane's cabin. He hefted the semi-conscious man over his shoulder, then made his way up the stairs, which he closed behind him.

The freight cabin was dark and the ceiling was low, so Khalil moved in a crouch towards the rear bulkhead, where he dropped Wiggins into a sitting position, the man's back against the wall.

Khalil retrieved his butcher's saw, then knelt astride Wiggins's legs. Wiggins moaned and his eyes opened.

Khalil put his face close to Wiggins and said, 'It is me, Mr Wiggins. It is Asad Khalil, who you have been expecting for three years. You escaped me once, but now I have a very unpleasant death planned for you.'

CHAPTER TWO

Skydiving.

I've done a lot of stupid things in my life, and it would be hard for me to list them in order of stupidity. Except for number one: skydiving. What was I thinking?

When I married my wonderful wife, Kate, three years ago, I didn't know she was a skydiver. When she confessed this to me about six months ago, I thought she said 'streetwalker', which I could forgive. What I can't forgive is her getting me to agree to take up this so-called sport.

So, here we were—Mr and Mrs John Corey—at Sullivan County Airport, which is basically in the middle of nowhere in upstate New York.

If you're into nature and stuff, the Catskill Mountains look nice, and it was a beautiful Sunday in May with clear skies and temperatures in the mid sixties. Most important for what lay ahead, it was a nearly windless day, a perfect day to jump out of an airplane.

Kate, looking good in a silver jumpsuit, said to me, 'I'm excited. This is my first time jumping from a Douglas DC-7B. It's a fabulous addition to our jumper's logbook.'

'Fabulous,' I said.

'This is the last flying DC-7B in the world.'

'I'm not surprised.' I looked at the huge, old four-engine propeller aircraft taking up most of the blacktop ramp. It had apparently never been painted, except for an orange lightning bolt running along the fuselage, nose to tail. The bare aluminium had taken on a blue-grey hue, sort of like an old coffee pot. I asked my wife, 'How old is that thing?'

'I think it's older than you. It's a piece of history. Like you.'

Kate is fifteen years younger than me, and when you marry a woman that much younger, the age difference comes up now and then, like now, when she continued, 'I'm sure you remember these planes.'

In fact, I had a vague memory of seeing this kind of aircraft when I went to Idlewild—now JFK—with my parents to see people off. Huge thrill. Reminiscing aloud, I said, 'Eisenhower was president.'

'Who?'

When I met Kate three and a half years ago, she showed no tendency towards sarcasm, and she has since indicated to me that this is one of several bad habits that she's picked up from me.

Kate was born Katherine Mayfield in some frozen flyover state in the Midwest, and her father was an FBI agent. Mrs Corey still uses her maiden name for business, or when she wants to pretend she doesn't know me. Kate's business, as I said, is the same as mine—Anti-Terrorist Task Force—and we are actually partners on the job as we are in life. One of our professional differences is that she's an FBI agent, like her father, and I'm a cop. Or as I said, a former cop on three-quarter disability—a result of me taking three badly aimed bullets up on West 102nd Street almost four years ago.

Kate turned her attention to the sixty or so skydivers who were milling around aimlessly in silly coloured jumpsuits, giving each other dopey high fives or checking one another's pack and harness. I felt for my Glock 9mm, in a zippered pocket. As per regs, we couldn't leave our weapons in the motel, or even in the trunk of our car. If you lose a weapon, or it's stolen, your career is in trouble, so both Kate and I were packing heat.

Anyway, while Kate was checking out our fellow skydivers, I looked at the pilot standing under the wing of the DC-7B. He was peering up at one of the engines. I don't like it when they do that. I observed, 'The pilot looks older than the plane. And what the hell is he looking at?'

Kate glanced towards me. 'John, are you getting a little . . . ?'

'Please don't question my manhood.' In fact, that was how she got me to agree to skydiving lessons. I said to her, 'Be right back.'

I walked over to the pilot, who had a close-cropped beard the colour of his aluminium plane. He looked even older up close. He turned his attention away from the possibly problematic engine and asked, 'Help ya?'

'Yeah. How's your heart?'

'Say what?'

'Do you need a part?'

'Huh? Oh . . . no, just checking something.' He introduced himself as Ralph and asked me, 'You jumpin' today?'

'You tell me.'

He got my drift and smiled. 'This was once an American Airlines luxury liner. I bought it for peanuts and converted it to haul cargo. Don't let the looks of this old bird fool you.'

I pointed to some puddles on the tarmac. 'There's oil dripping out of the engines.'

Ralph agreed, 'Yep. Oil. These old prop planes just swim in oil. When it's time to add more, we just pump it up from fifty-five-gallon drums. Problem is when you don't see oil.'

'Are you making that up?'

'Hey, you people have parachutes. I don't. All you got to worry about is getting up there. I got to land this damn thing.'

'Good point.'

An even older guy ambled over, and Ralph and he spoke for a minute about things I couldn't understand. The older gent then shuffled off, and Ralph said, 'That's Cliff. He's my flight engineer.'

I thought he was Ralph's grandfather.

'Cliff works the engine throttles, the mixture controls and all that stuff. He's a dying breed.'

I hoped he didn't die after takeoff.

I wanted to ask him if he and Cliff had new batteries in their pacemakers, but walked back to Kate instead. She was in a conversation with one of the guys in our so-called club, a putz named Craig who fancies his chances with my wife.

His stupid smile faded when he saw me, and Kate said, 'Craig and I were discussing the scheduling for our jumps in the next few weeks.'

'Is that what was making Craig smile?'

After a moment of silence, Craig said to me, 'Kate was just telling me that you had some concerns about the plane.'

'I do, but I could reduce the takeoff weight by sending you to hospital.'

Craig thought about that, then turned and walked away.

Mrs Corey said to me, 'That was totally uncalled for.'

'Why did you tell him I was concerned about the plane?'

'I . . . he asked why you were talking to the pilot, and I . . .' She shrugged, then said, 'I'm sorry.'

I was really pissed off, and I said, 'We'll discuss this after the jump.'

She didn't respond to that but just said, 'We're starting to assemble for boarding.'

I saw that our group was drifting towards the aircraft. A guy from the skydiving club was standing on the tarmac marshalling people into their jump groups. As I understood it, there would be two large groups exiting en masse to attempt a prearranged join-up formation. They were trying for some sort of record. Like Biggest Circle of Flying Fools. Kate had enough experience to join either of the groups, but I did not, so Kate and I would be jumping together, along with some single jumpers.

The guy from the skydiving club was now standing at the rolling stairs that led to the big cargo opening in the rear of the fuselage. He was holding a clipboard, checking off names as the jumpers assembled.

I announced, 'Corey. Mr and Mrs.'

He consulted his chart and said, 'OK. Go all the way forward. Row two. Have a good and safe jump, Mr Corey.'

I followed Kate up the stairs, and into the dark cavernous cabin.

The interior had been stripped bare and the windows covered with an aluminium skin to convert this airliner into a cargo plane. Apparently we would be sitting on the floor, like cargo.

Other than a few dim light fixtures, the only light in the cabin was sunlight coming in from the cargo opening and from the cockpit windscreen up ahead. I noticed that there was no door leading to the cockpit—just an open passageway through the interior bulkhead. The required anti-hijacking door was not there—and why should it be? If we got hijacked, we could all jump out of the plane. On the floor I saw cargo rings, which I guessed were used to secure pallets but now secured nylon straps for us to hang on to.

The first four skydivers had already boarded and were sitting abreast in row one facing us, packed together across the full width of the cabin. Kate sat near the wall on the left side. I sat beside her, with my hand on the cargo strap, and said, 'Fasten your seat belt.'

'Are you done with the stupid remarks?'

'Seat in the full upright position for takeoff.'

I looked round the cabin. The cargo opening, as I'd noticed when we entered, was very wide, but now I also noticed that there was no door—just that large opening. I brought this to Kate's attention, and she explained that they had to remove the big cargo door for this jump because it couldn't be operated in flight.

I said, 'It's going to be cold and noisy in here without a door.'

'Very noisy.' She added cheerily, 'I won't be able to hear you.'

The jumpers continued to board. My thirty-five-pound parachute rig was making my back ache in this position, and my butt, which is all muscle and no fat, was starting to feel the hard floor. This totally sucked.

I saw Craig coming towards us, walking between the skydivers. As some sort of officer in the club, he was checking to see that everyone was OK.

I wanted to make amends to Craig—and to Kate—for my uncalled-for remark, so I shouted out to him, 'Hey, Craig! Let's get this bird airborne. We're gonna have a helluva jump today, bro!'

Craig gave me a weak smile and continued on into the cockpit.

I looked at Kate, who had her eyes closed. I made a mental note in my logbook: *Have Craig followed. Possible terrorist.*

The guy with the clipboard came into the cabin to check names and groupings. As he got to the front rows, Craig came out of the cockpit and asked him, 'How's it look, Joe?'

Joe replied, 'We've had two jumpers drop out, and one last-minute sign-on, so that's a total of sixty-three jumpers.'

'OK,' said Craig. 'And we'll probably lose a few for the second jump.'

What?

Craig turned to me and said, 'I assume you will be making all three jumps today, John?'

'Hey, Craig, I'm here to *jump*!' I replied enthusiastically. 'I'm buying you a beer tonight.'

Craig glanced at Kate, then turned and found his place on the floor near the cargo opening. He wasn't wearing his helmet, and I noticed he had a big bald spot on the back of his head.

In fact, most people weren't wearing their helmets at this point. One guy, in an all-black jumpsuit, had his helmet on and instead of goggles, which most skydivers wear, he had a tinted helmet shield that was pulled down. As a cop, things like motorcycle helmets with tinted face shields automatically grab my attention. But I wasn't in full cop mode and I made little note of it.

There was an undercurrent of babble in the cabin. I noticed that Craig was chatting up a pretty lady sitting next to him. He probably made up the jump order so he could hold her hand on the way down.

I had been a bachelor most of my adult life, and I really didn't miss it—well . . . sometimes maybe just a little. But Kate has really made my life . . . more . . . very . . . incredibly . . . totally . . .

'John.'

'Yes, sweetheart?'

'I love you.'

'And I love you.' I squeezed her hand.

Kate had never been married, so she had no way of knowing if I was a normal husband. This has been good for our marriage.

I heard one of the engines firing up, then another, then the last two. The noise of the engines was deafening, and the aircraft seemed to be squeaking and squealing as it taxied to the end of the runway and stopped. Then the old plane vibrated and strained forwards, gathering momentum and, before I knew it, it nosed up and we were airborne.

As the aircraft gained altitude, it began a wide corkscrew turn. The drop zone, which was a big, hopefully bear-free meadow, was not far from the west side of the airport, so most of this thirty-minute flight would be vertical until we reached 14,000 feet.

The aircraft droned on, continuing its slow spiral climb.

'John?'

'Yes, darling?'

She put her mouth to my ear and said, 'Review the manoeuvring sequence we discussed. Ask me any questions you might have.'

'What colour is your parachute?'

'When you stabilise, you need to watch me.'

'I love watching you.'

'You weren't watching me last time.'

'Have we done this before?'

'We don't want to collide in free-fall.'

'Bad.'

'We'll do some relative work, as agreed, then I will initiate the separation.'

Same as my last wife did. Divorced in six months.

Kate continued, patiently going over the manoeuvre and other details having to do mostly with safety and not dying.

She was, I understood, very brave to jump with a novice. New guys caused accidents. Accidents caused certain death. I assured her, 'I got it.'

We both retreated into silence as the aircraft continued climbing. I glanced at the digital altimeter on my left wrist. Nearly 10,000 feet.

How the hell did I get here? Well, I went to skydiving school, which was my first mistake. That was last November, when Kate and I were on vacation in Florida. It was there that I discovered that Kate actually holds a United States Parachute Association 'C' licence, which qualifies her to be a jumpmaster. I wish I'd known that before I slept with her.

As for me, I took a two-week basic course that started, thankfully, in the classroom but progressed rapidly to 14,000 feet and something called the accelerated free-fall, which is two big guys named Gordon and Al jumping out alongside me, and the three of us falling through the open sky together with them holding on to my grippers. I've made maybe a dozen weekend jumps since that wonderful two weeks in Florida, and I've earned my USPA 'A' licence, which allows me to make solo skydives and begin some basic relative work with a jumpmaster, who today would be the lucky lady next to me.

The prop engines changed pitch, and I looked at my altimeter. We were at 14,000 feet.

The loadmaster shouted for those in the first group to get ready. There was a flurry of activity in the cabin.

The aircraft seemed to slow, then with a loud command from their leader, the first group of about twenty skydivers began to quickly exit the aircraft and disappear silently into the deathly void of space. Or, one could say, they jumped merrily into the clear blue sky. Whatever.

As the aircraft circled back to the drop zone, the second large batch of skydivers jumped to their feet, and the process was repeated.

Kate said, 'There is a cameraman on the ground, and one in each group. I can't wait to see those jumps on tape.'

Neither could the personal injury lawyers.

Again, the aircraft began to circle back over the drop zone and the loadmaster gave us a two-minute warning. The last group, who were all solo and small-group jumpers, got to their feet, including me and my jumpmaster. There were about ten people in front of us, lined up to make their two- or three-person jumps, and behind us were four people who were making solo jumps. We all put on our goggles or lowered our face shields and did a final equipment check.

By now the two big groups were on the ground. In a rare moment of empathy I sincerely hoped that my fellow club pals had set whatever hookup record they were trying for, and that they had all landed safely. Even Craig. You hear that, God?

The loadmaster shouted, 'Ready!' Then 'Go!'

The skydivers in front of me began to exit in their pre-arranged groups of two and three with a brief interlude between them.

I stepped up to the opening and I could feel the whirling wind and see the green-and-brown field three miles below. I could see a few people in free-fall, which is a very strange sight. I also saw a few brightly coloured chutes deploy, and suddenly I wanted to jump—to fly through the sky at the speed of a diving eagle and then to float gently down to earth.

I felt a hand on my shoulder and I turned my head to see Kate smiling at me. I smiled back.

I noticed now that the solo jumper directly behind Kate was crowding her more than he really should. He needed to let her clear the airplane before he jumped. Maybe he was nervous.

The loadmaster said something, and I realised I was holding up the show.

I turned back to the cargo door and, without thinking too much about what I was about to do, I dived face-first, leaving the solid floor of the aircraft behind me.

THERE I WAS, falling through the sky. But my mind was back in the aircraft, and I had two split-second thoughts: one, Kate had yelled something just as my feet left the airplane; two, the guy behind her was the same guy I'd noticed earlier in the black jumpsuit and the full-tinted face shield. He had sat in front of us, so he should have jumped ahead of us. Why was he behind us?

Even with the helmet covering my ears, the roar from the wind stream sounded like a freight train going through my head. I forced my body into a medium arch, then extended my arms and legs, and the airstream began to stabilise my fall. I was dropping now at about 110 miles per hour, which was terminal velocity for the position of my body.

I expected to see Kate appear on my right, as we'd planned, but when I didn't see her, I twisted my head to the right and upwards, but still I didn't see her. This move altered the aerodynamics that were steering me, and I began to rotate away from the direction I'd turned. I quickly went back to my fully stabilised position with my arms and legs extended and symmetrical, and I began to stabilise again. Where the hell was Kate?

Just as I was about to attempt another look, I saw in my peripheral vision that Kate was catching me up. She was about fifty yards off my right shoulder, but I saw that the skydiver in black, who I'd thought was too close to her in the plane, was actually hanging on to her. *What the hell . . . ?*

He had his right arm wrapped round her body, and he appeared to be holding on to the gripper on the left side of her jumpsuit with his left hand. I saw, too, that he had his legs wrapped around hers.

They were falling faster than I was because of their combined weight and because of how their bodies were positioned. Within a few seconds, they were below me and falling further away.

My heart started to race. What was this? Maybe, I thought, one of them had a problem of some sort and had grabbed on to the other. Maybe the guy had panicked. I couldn't understand this or make sense of it.

Kate and the guy were now a few hundred yards below me, free-falling at an accelerating rate. It hit me that this guy might be trying to commit suicide and for some sick reason he was taking Kate with him.

Then I saw the small pilot chute stream out from Kate's pack, blossom into an open position and lift the main canopy out of its container. Her parachute began to fill with air and her drop speed reduced.

Thank God.

Kate's white canopy with red markings was fully extended, and her rapid free-fall ended in a jerk that reduced her drop speed to about 1,000 feet per minute. As I continued my free-fall, I could see that the hitchhiker was still attached to Kate, and they both swayed under her canopy. Why had she deployed her chute so soon?

I grabbed my ripcord, arched my body and looked around to be sure I was clear of any other chutes—then I pulled it. I felt a jerk as the pilot chute filled with air, then another jerk as my main chute was dragged out of its container and deployed. I now had full control.

I scanned the space around me and spotted Kate and her hook-up guy about 200 feet above me, and about 100 feet to my front. The noise of the airstream had been reduced considerably now, so I shouted, 'Kate!'

She seemed not to hear, but the guy with her looked towards me.

I needed to get closer before Kate's faster rate of descent caused her and the guy to drop too far below me—but canopy relative work is inherently dangerous, and a wrong move would get the two chutes tangled, which results in everyone falling like a rock.

Just as they came abreast of me, I pulled on my front risers, which caused me to match their rate of descent and allowed me to manoeuvre my chute closer to theirs. In less than a minute, only about fifty feet separated our parachutes, which was almost too close.

'Kate!'

She looked at me and shouted something, but I couldn't hear her.

I carefully manoeuvred closer, and now I could see that there was a short cord between them, attached to Kate's gripper and to the guy's gripper, and that explained how he'd stayed with her from the time of the jump. What was going on? Who was this idiot?

Kate called out to me again, but all I could hear was 'John,' and then something that sounded like 'Eel.'

I shouted at the guy, slowly, distinctly, 'What—are— you—doing?'

He seemed to hear me—he reached up and pulled Kate's left riser, which caused her chute and them to slip towards me on a collision course.

Good God . . . I let go of my risers and my rate of descent slowed as theirs continued faster, and Kate's chute passed under my feet with only about ten feet separating us. This guy was crazy. Suicidal.

Using my risers again, I increased my rate of descent, and within a minute we were again within fifty feet of each other.

I let go of my risers, pulled off my right glove and unzipped the pocket that held my Glock. I had no idea who this guy was or what he was up to, but he'd done a very dangerous thing, and he was strapped to my wife. If I could get a shot off safely, I was going to kill him.

I shouted, 'Get—away—from—her! Now! Unhook! Unhook!'

The guy turned towards me, then lifted his face shield. He was grinning at me. He shouted, 'Hello, Mr Corey!'

I stared at him.

Asad Khalil.

My heart started to race again.

I heard Kate shout, 'John! It's Khalil! Khalil! He's got a—'

Khalil punched her in the face and her head snapped back.

I drew my Glock and took aim, but I was swaying under the canopy, and Khalil had twisted himself and Kate so that she was between me and him. I could not fire safely, but I *could* fire, and I squeezed off two rounds, wide to the right.

That got Khalil's attention and he positioned himself yet closer to Kate.

I worked the risers until about fifty feet separated us.

Asad Khalil. Libyan terrorist. Known in anti-terrorist circles as The Lion. It had been my misfortune to cross paths with him three years ago, when I was new with the ATTF. I never actually met him, though Kate and I did have some interesting cellphone conversations with him while we followed his trail of blood and death.

Khalil pulled on Kate's risers, and again they drifted towards me. He called out, 'I promised you I would return, Mr Corey!'

I looked at Khalil and we stared at each other. Seeing him hanging there, floating in the clear blue sky, I recalled that Asad Khalil had demonstrated a high degree of showmanship and originality in committing his murders—in fact, he'd pushed it in our faces—and I was not surprised that he'd chosen this method of reappearing.

He shouted, 'Your wife seems unhappy to see me!'

Come on, Kate. Get on this. But I could see she'd been stunned by the blow to her face.

Khalil shouted, 'I want you to witness this!'

I now noticed a glint of reflected sunlight coming from Khalil's right hand. A gun.

As they got closer, I raised my Glock again.

I could see Khalil's face peeking over Kate's left shoulder, and that's all I could see of him. I had no shot, but he had an easy shot at me dangling from my parachute. I kept my gun trained on his face, wondering why he didn't fire at me.

Khalil flashed me another smile and answered my question. 'Today she dies! And you will live to see it! Tomorrow, you die!'

I steadied my aim at his face, but before I could squeeze off a round, he ducked his head behind hers. Then I saw his right hand go up, and I realised that the metallic object in his hand was not a gun. It was a knife.

I saw the flash of the blade as Khalil brought it down in a slashing motion. Kate made a quick movement, and I could see her left hand go towards Khalil's face. Then she screamed and, almost immediately, I saw blood shooting into the airstream.

My God . . . I had no shot, but I fired over their heads.

Khalil made a sudden movement, and I saw that he'd cut the cord that attached them, and in a second he'd released his hold on Kate and was in a head-down free-fall.

I could have gotten off one shot, but Khalil was not the problem now. I shoved my gun into my pocket and pulled on my risers to get closer to Kate. Khalil's push-off had caused her to rotate, so she was facing me, and I could see blood gushing from her throat. I shouted out, 'Kate! Pressure! Pressure!'

She seemed to hear me and her hands went to her throat, but her blood kept flying into the air.

I glanced at my wrist altimeter: 6,500 feet. Seven more minutes until we reached the ground. She'd be dead by then. I needed to do something, and there was only one thing that might save her.

I steered my parachute towards hers, then, just as the two chutes were about to touch, I swung my body in an arc. As the chutes collided I reached for her gripper with my left hand and got hold of it. I caught a glimpse of her face, and saw the blood gushing through her fingers from the right side of her throat where he'd sliced into her.

'Kate!' She opened her eyes, then closed them again, and her hands dropped from her throat.

The tangled chutes were collapsing, and we were starting to fall rapidly, so I did the only thing I could do: I yanked the emergency release on her main chute and it immediately flew away, pulling me and my entangled chute with it, and putting Kate into a free-fall. I yanked my own main chute release and now we were both in a feet-first free-fall.

I looked down and saw her dropping away below me, with her arms above her head. She was either unconscious or close to it, and she was unable to stem the bleeding or control her free-fall. I did a forward roll so that my head was pointed straight down, and I tucked my arms and legs in so that I could accelerate to maximum speed. We were both rocketing at terminal velocity towards the ground, and there was nothing I could do now except wait.

The barometric devices on our chutes were supposed to pop the reserve chute if the skydiver fell through 1,000 feet at a high rate of descent and didn't pull the ripcord because of panic, malfunction or unconsciousness. The damned barometric devices should have deployed Kate's reserve chute, and mine too, but so far nothing was happening except a fatal, high-speed fall to the ground.

I could have manually pulled my ripcord and deployed my reserve chute, but I wasn't going to do that until I saw Kate's chute open.

My altimeter read 2,000 feet, and I knew that these chutes had to open now. I stared at Kate falling a few hundred feet below me, and just when I gave up all hope, I saw her reserve chute stream out of its pack and begin to fill with air. Yes!

Before I could pull my ripcord my barometric device kicked in, and in a few seconds my own small reserve chute was fully deployed.

I watched Kate as she fell, her arms hanging at her sides and her head slumped against her chest. She was definitely unconscious.

Her chute drifted towards a thick wood, and I steered towards her. She had about thirty seconds before touchdown, and I prayed that she'd land in the open field before she hit the trees. In either case, her touchdown would be uncontrolled and she might break some bones—or worse.

Below, everyone had realised that something was very wrong, and people were running towards Kate's drifting parachute. I saw, too, that the standby ambulance was racing across to her. Where was Khalil?

Kate hit the ground hard, without any movement to make a controlled landing.

I hit the ground near by, shoulder-rolled, then jumped to my feet and released my reserve chute as I sprinted towards Kate. I barrelled through the gathering crowd, shouting, 'Let me through! Get back!'

Within seconds I was kneeling beside my wife. She was on her back, her eyes closed. Her face was deathly white, except for the streaks of blood from her lips and nose where he'd hit her. Her neck wound was still bleeding, which meant her heart was still pumping.

I pressed very hard against her carotid artery below the wound and the flow of blood stopped. Another minute or two and there would have been no blood to pump.

I lowered my face towards hers. 'Kate!'

No response.

I put my hand on her chest and felt her heart racing, and also saw her chest rise and fall in shallow movements. Not good.

I looked around and saw the ambulance pull up and stop ten feet away. Two guys jumped out with a stretcher and medical equipment and raced towards us. I shouted to the paramedics, 'Severed artery!'

I turned back to Kate and said to her, 'It's all right. It's OK, sweetheart. Just hang in there, Kate. Hang on.'

The two paramedics sized up the situation very quickly. One said to me, 'Keep the pressure on.'

The other paramedic got a breathing tube in Kate's throat, while the first guy took her blood pressure and checked her breathing, then started a saline drip in one arm and another drip in her other arm. The second guy attached a bag to the breathing tube and began squeezing it to force air into her lungs. They log-rolled her to her side and the ambulance driver slid a back-board under her. Then they rolled her back and immobilised her with straps. They quickly transferred her to a rolling stretcher while I kept the pressure on her artery.

Within a minute we were all in the ambulance and it was moving as quickly as possible across the rough field. The paramedics—Pete and Ron—looked grim, which confirmed my own prognosis.

I stood over Kate, my fingers pressed on her throat, as the two paramedics cut away her jumpsuit and quickly examined her for other injuries, but found nothing external. When they seemed satisfied that she was stable, they put EKG leads on her chest and turned on the monitor. Pete said to his partner, 'Normal sinus rhythm . . . but tachycardia with a rate in the one-forties.'

I didn't ask what that meant, but I did ask, 'How far is the hospital?'

Pete replied, 'We should be there in ten minutes.'

I flashed my creds and said, 'Federal law enforcement. In my wife's jumpsuit you will find her FBI credentials case, her gun and cellphone. I need those items.'

Pete went through Kate's jumpsuit and retrieved her creds case, which he gave to me, saying, 'There's no gun and no cellphone.'

I put the creds case in my pocket. Maybe she hadn't been carrying her cellphone. But she would have been carrying her gun.

As soon as we got onto a farm road the driver hit the lights and siren and we accelerated.

Pete asked me, 'What the hell happened?'

I replied, 'This is a knife wound. Did you see the guy in the black jumpsuit who was hooked up to her?'

Ron replied, 'Yeah, he steered his chute over on the other side of the woods. I couldn't figure that out . . . now I get it. Do you know who that was?'

I did. This was our worst nightmare. The Lion had returned.

CHAPTER THREE

As the ambulance raced to the hospital, I used my cellphone to call 911. I identified myself to the dispatcher as a Federal law officer and explained that I was reporting the attempted murder of a member of the service. Then I asked to be transferred to the State Police.

A few seconds later, I was speaking to a desk officer at the State Police station in Liberty, New York. I described the incident to him and added, 'I am also the husband of the victim, who is an FBI agent. The assailant is still at large.' I gave him the location of the incident and told them to get some troopers over there to see if they could locate the assailant. But I knew he would have had a vehicle parked on the far side of the woods and would be long gone. Then I asked to be transfered to the back room, where I used to work.

About thirty seconds later, a man came on the line and said, 'This is Investigator Harris. My desk man has explained the situation to me.'

We spoke, cop to cop, for a minute, and Investigator Harris said, 'We've dispatched troopers to the scene to look for the perpetrator, and a senior homicide investigator will meet you at the hospital.'

'Thank you.'

'How is your wife?'

I glanced at Kate and replied, 'Critical.'

'Sorry . . . Can you describe the perpetrator?'

'Yeah. He's a Libyan national, aged about thirty, name Asad Khalil, tall, dark, hooked nose, armed and dangerous. Call the FBI duty officer at 26 Federal Plaza in New York, and they'll email you a photo. This man is an international terrorist, wanted by INTERPOL and half the world.'

There was a silence, then Investigator Harris said, 'OK . . . wow. OK, I'll get Senior Investigator Miller to meet you at the hospital.'

I kept my fingers pressed tight against Kate's artery, aware that by keeping her from bleeding to death, I was also reducing blood flow to her brain. I pushed back her eyelids and looked into her blue eyes. I thought that the life in them was dimming.

A trauma team was waiting for us at the emergency entrance, and they took Kate directly into the trauma room. I quickly filled out some paperwork, then a nurse led me into a small waiting room and said, 'The surgeon will be Dr Andrew Goldberg. He's the best vascular surgeon on staff. He will see you when he comes out of surgery.'

In the waiting room, I unzipped the pocket that held my Glock. I didn't know if the State Troopers were here yet, and I would not put it past Asad Khalil to know that this was where Kate would be taken, dead or alive, and that this was where victim number two, John Corey, would be. Regardless if Kate lived or died, Asad Khalil still had some unfinished business—with me.

A nurse came into the waiting room, and I was sure she had bad news. But she handed me a plastic bag, saying, 'These are your wife's personal effects. When you get a moment, please stop at the nurses' station and sign for them.'

'OK . . . How is she?'

'Being prepped for surgery.'

I nodded and the nurse left.

I looked at the items in the bag and saw Kate's wallet, a comb, tissues, a tube of lip gloss and her wedding ring. I put the bag in a zippered pocket of my jumpsuit. I had to assume that Khalil had her gun. But what about her cellphone? Had it fallen out of her pocket? Or had she left it in the car? I wouldn't want to think that Asad Khalil had her cellphone, complete with her phone directory.

Pulling out my own phone, I went into the corridor to call my office and report the attempted murder of a Federal agent by a known terrorist.

I made a full and hopefully intelligible report to the FBI duty officer of all that had happened, up to and including me now standing in a corridor at the Catskill Regional Medical Center. I concluded by saying, 'Call Walsh and Paresi and tell them The Lion is back. I've asked the State Police here in Liberty to call the FBI Ops Centre and request email or fax photos of Asad Khalil. Make sure this was done.'

'Will do.'

'And we want a news blackout. This is classified.'

I hung up and my heart skipped a beat when I saw a nurse walking towards me. She said, 'There's a State Trooper here to see you.'

I followed her to the nurses' station, where a man was speaking to one of the nurses and making notes in a notebook. He saw me, glanced at my bloodstained jumpsuit, then walked towards me, extending his hand.

We shook and he introduced himself as Senior Investigator Matt Miller, Bureau of Criminal Investigation.

'Thank you for coming.'

Investigator Miller had secured a small coffee room for us, and we sat on plastic chairs with a table between us. An intelligent-looking man, he began by saying, 'I'm sorry about your wife.'

'Thank you.'

He then politely asked to see my identification and also asked some preliminary questions.

The State Police are a good organisation, highly trained and disciplined, and I was sure they were up to this task. I was also sure that the FBI would descend on Sullivan County and take over. But for now, what I needed was for the State Police to flood the area with troopers and look for Asad Khalil before he got away. Or before he showed up here.

On that subject, Investigator Miller said, 'The troopers who went out to the scene found tyre tracks at the edge of the woods. The tracks led to a road. We didn't find a jumpsuit or a parachute, but we're still looking.' He filled me in on the manhunt, concluding, 'If those tyre tracks were from the perpetrator's vehicle, then he has about a twenty-minute head start on us, and we don't even know what kind of vehicle we're looking for. But we are setting up roadblocks and looking for a guy who fits the description. Or who maybe has a jumpsuit or a parachute in his vehicle.'

I said, 'You're not going to find those with him.' Asad Khalil would have planned his escape with at least as much care as he had planned his attack. Still, it wasn't so easy getting out of a rural area when the State Police were tightening the net. 'Tell your troopers this guy is armed and very dangerous, and he wouldn't hesitate to kill a cop.'

He replied, 'He's already tried to kill an FBI agent—your wife. So we know that.' He added, 'I remember the Khalil case. This is the guy who arrived at JFK under armed escort and killed his two escorts and some people on the ground. The same day as the arrival of that airliner with the toxic fumes that killed everyone on board.'

'Right.' It was, in reality, the same flight: Khalil had personally arranged for the 'toxic fumes' that killed everyone on board except himself. But that case had been so tightly wrapped in national security that few people knew what really happened. I was one of the few who did, but I had to give Investigator Miller only enough information to do his job. I said, 'The suspect was thought to be working for Libyan Intelligence. He's a professional assassin.'

Investigator Miller was not overly impressed. The word 'assassin' didn't appear in his mental dictionary. The suspect was simply a killer.

Miller got down to specifics. 'We've stationed uniformed and plainclothes troopers in the lobby and on this floor. We've received two photos of the alleged perpetrator, which we are electronically circulating to all state highway patrol vehicles and local police in this county. Your office also emailed a wanted poster. I see he is a fugitive from Federal justice and wanted for the murder of Federal law enforcement agents. I assume that would be his armed escorts on that flight.'

'That's right.' Plus three more on the ground. I added, 'There are to be no details of the attack issued—no names, no medical reports issued. No nothing.'

'Your office has made that clear.' Investigator Miller was probably wondering how this had landed in his lap on a quiet Sunday afternoon up in God's country.

'I can't give you any details, but I—and my wife—worked the case that involved the murders referred to on the wanted poster.'

'So . . . this guy attacked your wife because she worked that case?'

'Apparently.'

To change the subject and to interject a personal touch into our interview,

I said, 'She actually wasn't my wife then. We met on that case.'

And now, he was thinking, she may have been murdered on this case.

I said to him, and to myself, 'She'll be OK.'

He looked at me, wondering, I'm sure, why I thought that. This wasn't what the nurses had told him, and he'd already figured this was probably a homicide. He asked, 'Do you think he had any accomplices?'

'He's a loner. Last time he was in the US, he had a few unwitting and unwilling accomplices, but he killed them. So you may get a body or two turning up in the area.'

He made a note of that, then asked a few more standard questions, which I answered. I wanted to be cooperative, but they weren't going to apprehend Khalil using standard detective work. If they did catch him, it would be the result of a lucky car stop by State Troopers, or because some local citizen had reported a strange-looking guy in the 7–Eleven asking for a camel burger.

Also, it was possible that he was actually in this hospital right now.

I said, 'We're dealing with a professional, highly trained killer who doesn't make the usual mistakes that we count on when we're looking for killers. He is very goal-oriented, and his goal today was to kill my wife and let me live to see it. He failed in that goal . . . which he may or may not know. So I'm requesting that you maintain round-the-clock police protection in the hospital and outside her room until I can get my wife moved back to the city.'

He nodded and said, 'Do you want protection as well?'

'I can protect myself.'

I'm sure he thought, 'Famous last words', but again, he was polite and courteous. 'All right. You carrying?'

'I am.'

'Good.' He then asked, 'Where is your wife's weapon?'

'The perpetrator may have it, or it may have fallen out over the drop zone. It's a .40 calibre Glock 22, FBI issue.'

Investigator Miller made a note of that and said, 'We'll get a citizens' search team out to the drop zone.'

'The skydiving club had a video camera on the ground, so maybe this incident was captured on film,' I suggested.

He noted that too, and enquired about the skydiving club.

I replied, 'It's a loose organisation, and I'm sure that Asad Khalil is not a dues-paying member. Get hold of a guy named Craig Hauser. He can fill you in. They'll be staying at the High Top Motel in Monticello.'

He asked, 'Where are your wife's creds?'

'I have them. But her Nextel phone seems to be missing.'

He thought about that and said, 'If the perpetrator has her phone, he has her entire phone directory. Unless you need a code to access it.'

'There is no code for the phone directory, or the push-to-talk directory, or for text messages.'

He raised his eyebrows, but said only, 'We'll have the search team look for the cellphone, too.'

'Good. And could you do me a favour? I don't think I'll be returning to the motel, so could you have someone check Mr and Mrs Corey out of the motel and retrieve our personal things?'

He nodded, and added, 'We'll place a surveillance team there to see if anyone comes looking for you.'

'Good thinking,' I said. 'Another favour. My car is parked at the airport—'

'We'll get it for you.'

'Thanks. Look in the car for her phone,' I suggested. I gave him my keys and registration and asked him to have the vehicle, a Jeep Cherokee, delivered to the hospital with my and Kate's luggage.

We discussed a few more details of the incident. In truth, Asad Khalil was most probably long gone from Sullivan County—unless he was in the corridor now, wearing scrubs.

The thing that had impressed me most about Khalil, aside from his intelligence and his resourcefulness, was the speed of his attacks and escape. Khalil had also used private charter aircraft the last time he was here, so he may well have flown into and out of Sullivan County Airport. I passed on this thought to Investigator Miller, and he said he'd send an investigator to the airport.

I could not give Investigator Miller any details of Asad Khalil's previous murders, which were partly classified, but I filled him in on the suspect's M.O., including Khalil's ability to assume many identities to get close to his victims. 'This morning, for instance, he was a skydiver. Now he may be a hospital orderly. His compatriots call him The Lion because of his fearlessness. But it goes beyond that—he has the instincts of a cat. A big, nasty cat. The killing is secondary. The ritual is primary.'

He nodded and observed, 'Which is why he didn't go for you this time, and probably means he'll come for you next.' He added, unnecessarily, 'He'll find you.'

I always knew this day would come. I recalled the last words that Asad Khalil had said to me on Kate's cellphone three years ago. '*I will be back and I will kill you and that whore you are with, if it takes me all of my life.*'

He had apparently developed a strong personal dislike of me and of Kate as well. And, to be frank, we didn't like him, either.

I WENT TO the nurses' station to sign for Kate's personal effects.

The hospital staff knew by now that Kate was not an ordinary accident victim, and they knew who I was. The supervising nurse, Mrs Carroll, assured me that there were uniformed troopers outside the operating room, in Kate's ward and at the elevators. Everyone on duty, including hospital security staff, had been briefed to be on the lookout for a man whose photograph they'd been given by the State Troopers.

As for Mrs Corey's condition, the nurses had no new information, but Mrs Carroll strongly suggested that I stay in the surgery waiting room, because that was where Dr Goldberg would look for me.

I promised to return to the waiting room, but I needed to be a cop while I waited, so I went instead to the elevators, where two uniformed State Troopers stood, one at each elevator.

I showed them my creds, identified myself as the husband of the victim and asked to see the photo they had of the suspect.

The colour photograph had been taken in the American Embassy in Paris three years ago, when Asad Khalil had shown up one day and declared himself a fugitive from American justice. He was surrendering, he had said, and wished to cooperate with American intelligence agencies, insisting on being flown to New York for interrogation. Kate and I had been part of the team sent to JFK to meet Khalil and his two on-board escorts. Someone should have smelled a rat, but Khalil was such a high-value defector that the CIA, FBI and everyone else let their giggles get in the way of their training and common sense.

I looked closely at Khalil's photo. He was a swarthy man in his early thirties with a hooked Roman nose, slicked-back hair and deep, dark eyes. He had been able to pass himself off as Egyptian, Italian, Greek and even Israeli in the past. He also spoke fairly good English. His core identity, however, was killer.

I handed the photograph back to the trooper and said, 'This man has killed people all over Europe and America, including law enforcement people. He is very dangerous and very smart. His facial features are distinctive, yet he has successfully changed his appearance in the past.' I advised both troopers, 'What doesn't change is his eyes. If you see those eyes, that may be the last thing you'll ever see. Be very alert.'

They looked at me as though I was off my trolley, but nodded politely.

As I was walking to the surgery waiting room, my cellphone rang, and I saw it was the home number of the boss, Tom Walsh, FBI Special Agent in Charge of the New York Anti-Terrorist Task Force.

I answered, and Walsh said, 'John, I'm so sorry. How is Kate doing?'

'Still in surgery.'

'My God . . . I can't believe this.' Then he got down to business and said, 'I heard the tape of your report to the duty officer. We will devote all the necessary resources to apprehend this individual.'

Tom Walsh is an OK guy, though he's a political animal who tests the winds from Washington about four times a day. His worst fault, however, is underestimating the cops who work for him. He demonstrated that now by asking, 'John, are you sure that this person you saw was Asad Khalil?'

'I'm sure. And Kate ID'd him by name. Is that positive enough?'

'In your report you suggest that Asad Khalil has returned to the US with the intent of exacting revenge on the people in our Task Force who worked on the original case three years ago.'

'That's right. I think that's a very logical assumption.'

'Right . . . but . . . that seems like a very elaborate plan. You know?'

'Psychopaths engage in elaborate rituals, Tom.'

'I know . . . but . . .'

Tom Walsh knew he needed to be more patient with me than he usually was. My wife was in critical condition, and I was distraught. He actually didn't care about my emotional state, but he did care about Kate, who was one of his own. He liked her personally and professionally. He changed the subject and said, 'You reported that Kate's duty weapon is missing, and so is her cellphone. The Glock in Khalil's hands is a problem, but most likely he already has his own weapon. The real problem is the cellphone.'

'Agreed. But it could be an opportunity.'

'Correct. The Communication Analysis Unit is busy running a trace on its signal.'

'Good. But I'm sure Khalil will have turned it off. He's not stupid. The opportunity comes if he turns it on to use Kate's phone directory.'

'Right. But assuming he's savvy, he knows he can't keep the phone on for more than a minute or two before CAU pinpoints the signal.'

I resisted telling Walsh I understood the technology and reminded him, 'If Kate's cellphone is actually in Khalil's hands, Khalil is now able to read all our text messages.'

There was a short silence on the phone, then Walsh said, 'Damn it.'

I took out my cellphone and saw that I had a text message, sent to all agents. I retrieved it and read: NY ATTF—FBI Agent Kate Mayfield criminally assaulted in Sullivan County, NY. Possible suspect, Asad Khalil, a known terrorist, Libyan national. Her medical condition classified. See your email for full details, updates and operational instructions. Walsh.

So Asad Khalil had most probably read that, right from the boss.

At least Walsh had correctly withheld Kate's medical condition, leaving Asad Khalil wondering if he'd had a good day or a bad day.

Walsh said, 'We'll cut off the service to that phone immediately.'

'Good idea. But before you do that, send her phone a text saying, "Two Libyan informants in NY metro have come forward with info on suspect Khalil. Check email for details and operational instructions regarding apprehending suspect."' I added, 'Or something like that.'

'OK. I'll do that,' Walsh said.

I said, in case he didn't fully get it, 'That should spook him, and maybe keep him away from his resources here.'

'Right. Good.'

I had a thought that I should have had an hour ago. 'You should also alert George Foster. Khalil is here for revenge, and George was on the original team with Kate and me assigned to meet Khalil at the airport three years ago. George also worked the case.'

'OK.'

Tom Walsh wasn't around when Khalil was here with a long list of must-kill people. I wanted to impress on him the serious nature of this problem—and also ruin his day—so I said, 'You should not think that Asad Khalil hasn't considered killing you as well.'

There was silence on the line, then Walsh said, 'We have no idea what his intentions are. And, by the way, I'm wondering, why didn't Khalil just pull a gun and blast both of you on the ground? This skydiving knife attack really doesn't make much sense.'

'Not to you. But it does to him. When you get to the office, pull up the Lion file and see what he did last time he was here,' I suggested.

'All right.' Then he informed me, 'We're managing the news on this, John. Also, there are some agents from Washington on their way there, and I'll assign a detective and an FBI agent from the Task Force.'

'The guy who is handling the case here is Senior Investigator Matt Miller of the Bureau of Criminal Investigation.' I gave Walsh Miller's cell-phone number. 'He seems competent, and he's got the troopers out looking for Khalil.'

'Good. We will assist in any way we can.'

'And there's a guy you need to locate. His name is Elwood Wiggins, a.k.a. Chip Wiggins. He was one of the pilots on the Libyan air raid back in eighty-six, and he was on Khalil's original hit list, but we got to him before Khalil did. He needs protection.' Actually, I was certain that by this time what Chip Wiggins would need was an undertaker. I said to Walsh, 'But we may be too late for that.'

Walsh stayed silent for a moment, then said, 'All right. I'll let you get back to Kate now. And if you feel you need to take leave time—'

'I will, after we find Khalil.' On that subject, I said, 'I assume I am the case agent on this investigation.'

There was a silence on the phone, then Walsh said, 'Well—'

'Tom. Don't mess with me.'

'Excuse me, Detective. I believe I am still in charge of this Task Force.' He paused, 'The thing is, John, if Kate . . . takes a turn for the worse, or whatever, then you will want some time off, and I need to assign this case to someone who can stay with it.'

'I will stay with it. I am very motivated.'

'Yes, but to be quite honest, you may be too emotionally involved to . . . Look, I promise you will be assigned to the case, but I can't promise you that you will be the lead case agent. I'll think about that. Meanwhile, George Foster will lead the FBI end. End of subject.'

No use arguing and pissing him off, so I said, 'All right.'

'Good. Meanwhile, I'll have Captain Paresi call you. I've asked the hospital to keep me updated. My prayers are with Kate.'

'Thank you.'

'I've got one more thing to say to you. If the State Police apprehend him, and if we don't have any agents there yet, you are not to speak to the suspect or do anything that might compromise our case against him.'

'Why would I do that, Tom?'

He didn't respond to that directly. 'I know you're angry, but don't get yourself in a bad situation. We don't do revenge—we do justice,' he reminded me.

Is there a difference? I replied, 'Right.'

We hung up, and I walked back to the waiting room. I went to the window and looked out at the mountains. The sun was still high above the distant peaks in a blue, cloudless sky. The morning of September 11, 2001 had been a perfect day, like this.

What had motivated me for most of my police career, I confess, was my own ego—I was smarter than any killer who had the audacity to murder someone on John Corey's beat. Then came the Anti-Terrorist Task Force, and I got a little patriotic buzz going, especially after 9/11.

Now it all came down to personal revenge and me asking God to help me kill Asad Khalil. And I was sure that Khalil was right now asking God for the same favour.

Only one of us was going to have his prayers answered.

I STOOD in the empty waiting room, watching the clock on the wall. It had been over an hour since Kate was wheeled into surgery, and I was beginning to think that this might be a good sign. How long does it take to bleed to death? Not very long. How long does it take to repair a severed artery? Maybe two hours.

My phone rang, and I saw that it was the cellphone of Captain Vince Paresi. I answered, 'Corey.'

'John, how is she?'

'Still in surgery.'

'Mother of God . . . I can't believe this. How are you doing?'

'OK.'

He said, 'We're gonna get this scumbag, John.'

I allowed myself a small smile at the familiar NYPD profanity. Captain Paresi was in command of the NYPD detectives assigned to the Task Force, and he was my immediate supervisor.

Paresi continued, 'We're waiting for the go-ahead to pull in the usual suspects for questioning, and we'll be contacting our sources inside the Muslim community, with special emphasis on the Libyans.'

He went through the standard response drill. Terrorism aside, an FBI agent had been attacked, and she was married to a retired cop. That made a subtle difference in the response—sometimes not so subtle.

Paresi asked me for some suggestions based on my past encounter with Asad Khalil. I had to think about what I could tell him, and what was still classified or on a need-to-know basis.

The file on Khalil had never been closed, of course, and after he had disappeared three years ago, the then Special Agent in Charge of the Task Force, Jack Koenig, had formed a special team consisting of Kate, me, George Foster, and our only Arab-American on the Task Force, Gabriel Haytham, an NYPD detective, to follow every lead to do with Asad Khalil. Koenig had given us the not very clever code name of Lion Hunters, and we reported directly to him.

Well, Jack Koenig was dead, as was Captain Paresi's predecessor, David Stein, both killed in the collapse of the North Tower, and over the years the leads and tips from domestic sources and various foreign intelligence agencies had gone from a trickle to a dry hole. Neither I nor Kate had ever believed that this silence meant Khalil was dead or retired. Unfortunately, we were right.

I said to Paresi, 'The ATTF file on this guy is pretty thin. There is another computer file that contains a complete report on what happened three years ago. That file, however, is highly classified and Washington won't give you access to it. But three years ago, Koenig and Stein assigned me, Kate, George Foster and Gabe Haytham to stay with this case. No one ever cancelled that assignment, and we have a paper folder on Khalil. Gabe can give it to you.' I continued, 'Khalil worked for Libyan Intelligence, and his contacts here were all Libyans. Our folder contains the names, addresses, photos and particulars of Libyans living in the New York metro area who we've spoken to over the years. That's a good starting point for surveillance.'

Paresi said, 'I assume Tom Walsh has a copy of this folder.'

I didn't reply, which means no.

Captain Paresi asked me a few more questions about what happened three years ago, and while I was answering, another thought popped into my head.

'If Khalil knows that Gabriel Haytham, an Arab-American, is on the Task Force, he may consider him to be a traitor, and target him.'

'Yeah . . . that's a thought. OK, I'll give Gabe a call.'

I took the opportunity to say, 'I'd like you to speak to Walsh about making me the case agent.'

He seemed prepared for that. 'I have to agree with Walsh that you may not be the best man for that job. And between us, you may be better off not being the case agent. You'll have less bullshit to deal with and more freedom to . . . do your own thing. Understand?'

There was a logic to that, and a subtext. I said, 'OK. I understand.'

'Good.' Paresi changed the subject. 'Do you think this asshole has any other mission here? I mean, is this all a personal revenge thing with him? Even if he's not working for Libyan Intelligence, somebody has to be backing him, like Al Qaeda. Maybe his deal with his backers is that he gets money and resources to come here to settle some personal scores, and in exchange he's got to spread anthrax or blow up something.'

'That's a thought. What does Walsh think?'

'We didn't discuss theories. Basically, he just wants me to call out the troops and put these people under the eye.' He paused, thinking for a moment. 'What's Khalil's beef?' he asked. 'I don't know how this started.'

I replied, 'It started on April the 15th, 1986, when Reagan sent a bunch of fighter-bombers to blow the shit out of Libya. Khalil lost his whole family.'

'No shit? I guess he's still pissed off.'

'Apparently. Did Walsh mention Chip Wiggins?'

'No. Who's that?'

Apparently Walsh didn't want to share this information with his junior partner. And to be fair to Walsh, Khalil's first visit to America was, as I said, mostly classified information. Nevertheless, I said to Paresi, 'Wiggins was one of the F-111 pilots who bombed Tripoli. Khalil came here three years ago with a list of those pilots and he began murdering them.'

'Jeez . . . Do we know where Wiggins is?'

'His last known address is Ventura, California.'

'I'll bet Khalil knows. Wiggins is already dead,' Paresi concluded.

'Probably.'

Paresi said, 'OK. I'm headed right now for the office. I'll call Gabe and have him meet me there and we'll look at your folder.'

'Tell him to watch himself. Also, maybe his family wants to take a vacation. He's got a wife, and I think one daughter.'

'All right . . .'

I said to him, 'I'll get to the office as soon as I can.'

'John, don't worry about it. Take care of Kate.'

'There is a chance she won't make it.'

There was a short silence, then Paresi said, 'She'll make it. She's in my prayers.' He added, 'She's tough.'

SHORTLY AFTER he'd hung up, the door opened, revealing a middle-aged man in green scrubs.

'Mr Corey?'

'Yes.'

We walked towards each other, and he put out his hand and introduced himself as Dr Andrew Goldberg. He put his other hand on my shoulder and said, 'She's resting comfortably in ICU.'

I closed my eyes and nodded.

'Her vital signs are stable. Blood pressure and breathing are good.' Again, I nodded. He steered me towards some chairs, and we sat side by side, while he reported in a soft voice, 'The surgery was successful in closing the laceration to her right carotid artery. There were other contusions as a result of her fall, but I don't believe there were any internal injuries, and no internal bleeding, though there may be bone fractures.'

I asked him, 'Prognosis?'

He stayed silent a second too long, then replied, 'Guarded.'

'Why?'

'Well . . . she lost six units of blood, and we—and you, I understand—needed to stem the flow of blood . . . which goes to the brain . . .'

I knew this was coming, and I waited for the verdict.

Dr Goldberg continued, 'It may have caused some oxygen deprivation before the paramedics got a breathing tube down her throat. We just don't know if there will be any neurological impairment.'

'When will we know?'

'Shortly after she recovers from anaesthesia. An hour or two.'

I did not reply.

He hesitated, then asked me, 'Any more questions?'

'No.'

Dr Goldberg stood, and I stood also. He said, 'She'll get a complete evaluation as soon as possible. I assume you'll want to stay here until she regains consciousness.'

'That's right.'

We shook hands and I said, 'Thank you.'

He patted my shoulder. 'Take a break in the cafeteria. It will be a while before we have any further news for you. She's in good hands.'

Dr Goldberg left the waiting room, and I went into the corridor and followed the signs to the ICU.

At the nurses' station I identified myself as John Corey, the husband of Kate Mayfield, who had just arrived from the OR. I told the ICU staff not to disclose the patient's location or condition to anyone except an authorised medical person or a law enforcement officer.

A nurse, who identified herself as Betty, a supervisor, made a note of that and escorted me towards the ICU. On the way she said, 'Don't be alarmed by her appearance, or all the monitors and infusion tubes. Dr Goldberg is a wonderful surgeon.'

But no one, including Dr Goldberg, knew what was going on, or not going on, in Kate's brain.

We reached Kate's bed, and I stood over my wife and looked at her. Some colour had returned to her face, and her breathing, aided by a ventilator, seemed steady. There was a thick dressing round her neck, tubes in her arms, and wires that connected to three different monitors. I looked at the screens and everything seemed normal.

Betty glanced at the monitors and assured me, 'Her signs are good.'

I took a deep breath and stared at Kate. I could see the swelling round her mouth where Khalil had hit her. *Bastard*. I bent over and kissed her on the cheek. 'Hi, beautiful.'

No response.

Betty advised me to sit in the bedside chair, which I did. 'Press the call button if you need anything.' She turned and left.

I took Kate's hand, which was cool and dry, and I could feel her pulse. I kept looking at her face, but it remained expressionless.

I prayed that she would come through this, against all medical odds. But if there was some impairment, then I'd quit the job and take care of her.

After I killed Asad Khalil.

I CONTINUED MY VIGIL beside Kate's bed, holding her hand and looking for signs of her coming out of anesthesia. After half an hour I left to pick up my cellphone messages.

The first was from Tom Walsh, who said, 'I spoke to Investigator Matt Miller about his search for Khalil. No news there. I called George Foster, and he understands the situation.' Walsh paused, then said, 'We can't seem to locate Gabe.' Another pause, then, 'Or Chip Wiggins in California.' He ended with, 'Call me.'

The next call was from Investigator Miller, who informed me that my vehicle and luggage were in the hospital parking lot and the keys were at the ICU nurses' station.

He also said, 'The vehicle and the luggage are clean. We did not find your wife's cellphone in the room or in the vehicle, and the search of the drop zone hasn't yet turned up anything. We checked Sullivan County Airport, and we found an Enterprise rental car in the parking area, rented to a man named Mario Roselini, but nothing in his rental agreement checks out. The tyre treads might match the treads we found near the woods. We're trying to do a match. The car is under surveillance. Also, we checked with the airport, and a Citation jet landed there Saturday evening, then took off Sunday about thirty or forty minutes after the incident, destination and passengers, if any, unknown. No flight plan filed. We're following up on this.' He ended with, 'The hospital tells me your wife is resting comfortably. Some good news.'

I put the phone back in my pocket and went back to Kate. I tried to see if there was anything in her face that would give me a clue about her mental condition, but her expression revealed nothing.

There are different degrees of mental impairment, as I knew, and I had to prepare myself for anything from mild impairment to . . . whatever.

Another half-hour passed; a few nurses came by and one of them brought me a cup of coffee. I was about to get up and take a walk in the corridor, when I thought I saw Kate move.

I stood near her bed and watched her closely. She moved her head, then her right arm. I decided to wait.

Every few seconds, she moved an arm or a leg, and her head rolled from side to side.

I leaned closer to her and touched her arm. 'Kate?'

She opened her eyes, but kept staring up at the ceiling.

'Kate? Can you hear me?'

She turned her head towards me and we made eye contact.

The breathing tube kept her from speaking, so I took her hand in mine and told her, 'Squeeze my hand if you can hear me.'

After a few seconds, she squeezed my hand. I smiled at her and asked, 'Do you know who I am?'

She stared at me, then nodded tentatively.

'Squeeze if you know why you're here and what happened to you.'

She pulled her hand away and made a shaky movement with her right hand that looked like the beginning of a seizure. I reached for the call button, but then I realised she was pantomiming holding a pen.

I grabbed a pen and pad from the nightstand and put the pen in her right hand and the pad in her left hand.

She held them both above her face and wrote something, then turned the pad towards me. It said, *Why are you asking me these stupid questions?*

I felt my eyes get moist and I bent over and kissed her cheek.

CHAPTER FOUR

Asad Khalil looked across the aisle at the west-facing window of his chartered Citation jet as it began its descent into Long Island's Republic Airport. In the distance, about sixty kilometres away, he could see the skyline of Manhattan Island. He checked his watch. The flight from Sullivan County Airport had taken twenty-six minutes.

As the aircraft made its final approach, Khalil reflected briefly on his interesting parachute jump. He had two thoughts: one was that he could not be absolutely certain that he had killed the woman; his second thought was that he should have taken the opportunity to shoot the man named Corey.

The woman—Corey's wife—had struck his hand, and he had not been able to complete the cut across her throat. He was not accustomed to women who used physical force against a man, and though he knew this was possible, it had nevertheless taken him by surprise. Still, he had severed her artery, and she undoubtedly bled to death before she hit the ground. As for Corey, the plan had always been to leave him until the end.

The Citation touched the runway and the aircraft began to decelerate, as the co-pilot announced, 'Welcome to Long Island's Republic Airport, Mr Demetrios. I hope you have a successful business meeting.'

To which Khalil, the Greek businessman, replied, 'I am sure I will.'

The Citation taxied towards one of the hangars and Khalil looked out of the window, trying to determine if somehow the authorities had discovered his means of transportation and his destination. When he had landed at Sullivan on Saturday evening, Khalil had told the pilots that he would be flying to Buffalo on Sunday, so he was certain they had filed a flight plan for that city. But when he had returned from his business of killing Corey's wife, he had announced a sudden change of plan and asked to be taken to Long Island's Republic Airport. The pilots had had no problem with this—he was, as they kept telling him, the boss. They had also informed him that no flight plan needed to be filed because it was a clear day, and because they would avoid the New York City restricted airspace zone.

Khalil knew all this, of course. The lack of official paperwork in private flights had amazed Khalil when he was here three years ago. Even more amazing, he thought, was that a year and a half after the martyrdom of his fellow jihadists on September 11, it was still possible to fly around this country in private aircraft and leave little or no evidence of the journey. All that was required was a credit card that ensured the payment to the charter company.

An image of Corey again came into his mind. This man was clever and had caused him some unexpected problems the last time he was in America. But he had not caught up with Asad Khalil the last time, and he would not do so this time. In fact, it would be the other way around.

The aircraft came to a halt near one of the hangars and the twin jet engines shut down. Khalil scanned the tarmac again for activity. His mentor in Libya, Malik, had recognised in his protégé a sixth sense that alerted him to danger. Malik had said, 'You have been blessed with this gift, my friend, and if you stay true to your purpose and to God, it will never leave you.'

And it had never left him, which was why he was still alive.

The co-pilot swung open the door, which caused a set of steps to descend, and the pilot came into the cabin and asked, 'Do you know how long you'll be here, sir?'

'Yes. I need to leave here tomorrow for my meeting in Buffalo, which has been rescheduled for one p.m.'

The pilot replied, 'OK, then we can leave at, say, ten a.m., and that will give you plenty of time.'

'Excellent.' Khalil unbuckled his seat belt, retrieved his overnight bag from under his seat and moved into the aisle.

The pilot led the way out of the cabin, and Khalil stayed close to him, one hand in the side pocket of his blue sports jacket that held the .40 calibre Glock pistol of his victim, whom he had known as Miss Mayfield, and who had become Mrs Corey during his three-year absence.

And now she was the late Mrs Corey.

The pilot and co-pilot and their customer, Mr Demetrios, began walking towards the nearby hangar. The pilot asked, 'You got a place to stay tonight?'

'I assume my colleagues here have arranged that.'

'Right. Well, Jerry and I will meet you here about nine-thirty tomorrow. If there's any change of plans, you have our cell numbers.'

There was already a change of plans, Khalil thought. He was not going to Buffalo with these men. But it was not their business to know this. In fact, as they would learn, they were lucky to be alive.

They arrived at the entrance of the fixed base operator's office, which would take care of their aircraft, and the pilot asked, 'Where are your people meeting you?'

Khalil did not want the pilots to see that he had no business colleagues here, and that in fact he had booked a livery vehicle with a driver to meet him in the parking lot. He replied, 'My colleagues are most likely in the parking area.'

'OK. Any problem, call us.'

'Thank you.'

The pilots entered the office, and Khalil continued to a wide paved area between the hangars.

If a trap had been set for him, it would be at this point—with the pilots safely out of his control—that it would be sprung. He would not be able to escape the trap, but he could send some of his enemies to Hell. He kept his hand on the butt of his pistol, his finger on the trigger.

He continued between the hangars to the parking area, which was nearly empty. Close to the rear of the hangar he saw a black limousine. A driver of enormous proportions sat sleeping in his seat. A white cardboard sign stuck in the windscreen said MR GOLD.

Khalil looked round the parking lot, satisfied now that there was no danger. He moved away from the car and the sleeping driver, then opened his bag and retrieved the cellphone that had been in the luggage given to him by the late Farid Mansur in Santa Barbara. Khalil knew this was an untraceable throw-away phone with 200 prepaid minutes. He dialled a number.

A man answered, 'Amir.'

Khalil said in English, 'This is Mr Gold.'

After a pause, Amir replied, 'Yes, sir.'

Khalil switched to Arabic and asked, 'Can you tell me if my friends are at home?'

Amir replied in Arabic, 'Yes, sir. I have passed the house several times and their two vehicles are still in the driveway.'

'Good. I will call you again. Watch the house closely, but do not arouse suspicion.'

'Yes, sir.' He added, 'My taxi would not arouse suspicion.'

Khalil hung up and approached the vehicle, which he recognised as a Lincoln Town Car, and knocked hard on the window. The driver sat up quickly, then lowered the window. 'Mr Gold?' he asked.

'Correct.'

Before the driver could get out, Khalil said, 'I have only this bag,' and he got in the rear seat behind the driver.

The driver removed the sign from the windscreen and started the vehicle. He handed Khalil a card and said, 'My name is Charles Taylor. There's water in the seat pocket and I've got the Sunday papers up here if you want one. The *Post* and *Newsday*.'

'Thank you.'

The driver asked, 'Where we headed?'

Khalil gave him an address in the Douglaston section of Queens, a borough of New York City. It was not the actual address of his next victim, but it was very close. The driver programmed his GPS, pulled out of the parking lot, and within a few minutes they were on the Southern State Parkway, heading west.

Khalil's Al Qaeda friends had shown him a photograph of the Haytham house, and told him that the house was located in a residential area of private homes and middle-class people. They advised him that a stranger might arouse suspicion, but assured him that residents and visitors did arrive by taxi from the train station, and that if he dressed well and acted quickly, he should be able to finish his business and leave without trouble.

Khalil's only concern was that someone from Haytham's agency would come to a conclusion that Jibral Haytham—who called himself by the Christian translation of Gabriel—was also on Khalil's list of victims.

The last time Khalil was here on his mission of revenge, he'd had no direct contact with Haytham, though he had known of this traitor who had chosen to work for an anti-Islamic league of Christian crusaders and Zionists, and would have killed him then if he had been able.

But, according to Amir, who was watching the house, there was no evidence that the FBI were waiting for him.

The one person who the FBI would know for certain was on Khalil's list was the late Mr Chip Wiggins. The last time Khalil was here, the FBI—or perhaps it was Corey—had made some conclusions, and they had been waiting for him at Wiggins's home in California.

This time, however, they were too late to save him.

AFTER ABOUT twenty-five minutes, the vehicle's GPS sounded a verbal command and the driver exited into a residential area.

Khalil noted that the homes seemed substantial, many made of brick and stone, and that the trees were large and the vegetation was lush and well tended. The traitor Haytham lived well.

Khalil said, 'Stop the vehicle, please.'

The driver pulled in to the kerb.

Khalil retrieved the dead woman's cellphone from his overnight bag and turned on the power. His Al Qaeda colleagues had told him that he would have one minute, perhaps two, to access any information on an agent's cellphone before the signal was traced. The chime sounded and he saw on the screen that a text message had been sent. He pushed the button and read: NY ATTF—FBI Agent Kate Mayfield criminally assaulted in Sullivan County, NY. Possible suspect, Asad Khalil . . .

So, Khalil thought, when they sent this message, they did not know that he had possession of the woman's cellphone, and this message had been delivered to all Federal agents, including the dead one. Or they knew he had her cellphone and hoped he would be so stupid as to use the cellphone so they could track his movements.

He thought about the words 'criminally assaulted'. Could that mean she was not dead? Or would they not announce in a text message that she was dead? This troubled him, but he put it out of his mind and turned his thoughts to his next victim: would this message alert Haytham to the possibility that he was in danger?

Khalil's instincts, which he knew never failed him, told him to ignore the possibility that there was a trap set for him at the Haytham house. He could smell danger, but what he smelled now was Jibral Haytham's blood.

Khalil dialled a number on his own cellphone.

A voice answered, 'Amir.'

Khalil said in Arabic, 'Mr Gold. How are things looking there?'

Amir replied, 'The same, sir.'

'There is nothing at the house that disturbs you?'

'No, sir.'

Khalil hung up and said to the driver, 'A small change of plan. I must meet someone coming from the city at the Douglaston train station.'

'No problem. It's just a few blocks from here.'

Within three minutes, the driver had pulled into the eastbound side of the small parking lot of the Long Island railroad station.

Khalil said, 'Park there, beside that van.'

The station was deserted and the driver pulled into a space beside a large van that blocked the view of the limo from the road.

Satisfied that he could do his business here, Khalil dialled from his cellphone again. When Amir answered, Khalil said, 'Meet me in the parking lot of the Douglaston railroad station.' He hung up.

The driver asked, 'Did he say how long?'

'A few minutes.' Khalil took a bottle of water from the seat pocket, opened it, and drank all but a few ounces. Then he retrieved Mrs Cory's Glock from his bag. The other advantage of private air travel was that one could carry firearms on board aircraft without anyone knowing, or for that matter, even caring.

He pressed the water bottle against the back of the driver's seat, lining it up with the obese man's upper spine, opposite his heart. He then placed the muzzle of the Glock against the bottle's open neck.

Charles Taylor said, 'I'm gonna step out for a quick smoke.'

'You can smoke here.' Khalil pulled the trigger, and the Glock bucked in his hand as a muffled blast filled the car.

Taylor pitched forwards, then his seat belt snapped him back, and his head rolled to the side. Khalil fired again into the smoke-filled plastic bottle to be certain. He drew a long breath through his nostrils, savouring the smell of burnt gunpowder, then put the pistol in his pocket.

He pushed the two shell casings and the smoking bottle under the seat, retrieved his overnight bag, exited the car and opened the driver's door.

The two .40 calibre rounds had passed through the driver's immense body and lodged in the dashboard, but the bullets had stopped his heart quickly, and there was no excessive bleeding.

It would be good when the ballistic test showed the bullets were from an FBI weapon.

Khalil found the seat control and lowered the driver's seat to its maximum reclining position. He then reached across the dead man's body and retrieved the two Sunday newspapers from the passenger seat. He laid the pages of *Newsday* over the driver's face and took the keys. It could be many hours or even the next morning before anyone noticed a sleeping livery driver waiting for his customer at the railroad station.

Khalil walked towards the road at the edge of the small parking area. When he saw a yellow taxi approach with its off-duty light illuminated, he dropped the limousine's keys through the grate of a drain and walked towards the taxi. The driver lowered his window and asked, 'Mr Gold?'

Khalil nodded and got into the taxi behind the driver. He said in Arabic, 'Take me to the house.'

'Yes, sir.' Amir glanced at his passenger in the rearview mirror. The man's eyes were black like night, but nevertheless seemed to burn like coal. He did not know this man, except as a fellow Libyan, a friend of a friend. And this friend had made it clear to Amir that this man, who for some reason was posing as an Israeli Jew, was a very important man.

They drove slowly, and Amir made a few turns through the quiet neighbourhood. His mentor, Malik, had told Khalil that the Christian Sabbath was a quiet day in residential areas. Perhaps the Americans went to church in the morning and then they observed the secular aspects of the Sabbath—shopping, or going to the park or to the beach where men, women and children paraded half-naked in front of one another.

Khalil turned his thoughts back to the taxi driver sitting in front of him. He asked Amir, 'Have you remained observant here?'

'Of course, sir. And my wife and my six children. We answer the call to prayer five times each day and read from the Koran each evening.'

'Why are you here?'

'For the money, sir. The infidels' money. I send it to my family in Tripoli. Soon, we will all return to our country, Allah willing.' He turned onto a tree-lined street of brick houses and said, 'The house is up ahead, on this side of the road.'

Khalil asked, 'Do you have my gift?'

'I do, sir.' Amir took a black plastic bag off the floor of the cab and handed it to his passenger.

Khalil opened the bag and extracted a bouquet of flowers wrapped in cellophane. He took from his overnight bag an eight-inch carving knife and stuck it into the bouquet. He said to Amir, 'Stop at the house, then park where you can see the whole street. Call me if you see anyone approaching.'

'Yes, sir.' Amir stopped in front of a two-storey house with a blue front door, which Khalil recognised from the photograph Malik had shown him.

Khalil scanned the area around him, but saw nothing to alarm him. Yet that text message would certainly have reached Haytham's cellphone.

A more cautious man would not have come, but caution was another word for coward.

He exited the taxi quickly with the flowers in his left hand, the Glock in his right jacket pocket, and his Colt .45 stuck in his belt under his jacket.

Khalil walked straight up the driveway of the house in which two vehicles were parked. If anyone saw him, they would not be suspicious of a man in a sports jacket carrying flowers to a friend's house. He could thank his former trainer, Boris the Russian, for the contrivance of the flowers which, according to Boris, was a tried-and-tested KGB ruse. A man with flowers and a smile on his face is not perceived as a dangerous man.

He would thank Boris in person—before he cut out his heart. He smiled.

At the end of the driveway was a garage, connected to the house by a white fence with a gate. According to Malik, Khalil could expect that the family would be in the backyard, eating outdoors. Khalil now heard music coming from there, Western music, which was not pleasant to his ears.

He took a step beyond the concealment of the house and peered over the low fence. But there was no one on the patio. He opened the gate and moved quickly towards the back door of the house. Then he realised that the music was coming from behind him, and he turned towards a garden lounger that was facing away from him. On it was a girl of about fifteen, lying asleep in the sunlight, wearing only a small white bathing suit. On the ground beside her he saw the radio that was playing the music.

He stepped towards the girl, Haytham's daughter. As he moved towards her, he kept glancing back at the house, but saw no one. He stopped beside the girl and looked down at her body. In Libya, she would be whipped for her near nakedness, and her mother and father, too, for allowing this. He withdrew the knife from the bouquet.

The girl must have sensed his presence or that something was blocking the sun on her body, and she opened her eyes. She did not see the knife; she saw only Khalil's face and the bouquet that he extended towards her. She opened her mouth, and Khalil thrust the knife into her chest between her ribs, deep into her heart. The girl stared at him, but only a small sound came from her mouth. Khalil twisted the knife and let it go, then threw the flowers on her chest.

He spun round, drew the Glock, and moved straight towards the back door. He turned the door handle and stepped into a small room that was cluttered with shoes and jackets. To the right was an open doorway through which he could see the back of a woman at a sink, preparing food. She was wearing shorts and a sleeveless shirt.

Moving towards the opening, focusing on an open doorway that led towards the front of the house, Khalil heard the cheer of a crowd—a sporting event on the television.

He pocketed the pistol, stepped into the kitchen, and took two long strides towards the woman.

Turning her head over her shoulder, the woman said, 'Nadia?' Khalil clamped one hand over her mouth and the other on the back of her head, pushing her hard against the sink with his body. He saw a knife in her hand, but before she could raise it, he twisted her head until he felt her neck snap. The knife fell.

She began twitching, and Khalil let her slide gently to the floor.

Khalil drew the Glock again and walked through the open door, which led into a hallway. To the left was a large opening, through which he could hear the sporting event, which he identified as the American national game of baseball. He entered the living room and saw on the couch opposite him a man who he was sure was Jibral Haytham, lying facing the television. On the coffee table beside Haytham was a can of beer. Haytham was asleep.

Khalil thought he should put a bullet in his head and move on to other business. But he had been anticipating some conversation if it were possible—and now it seemed possible.

He walked towards the sleeping man and satisfied himself that there was no gun nearby, though he saw a cellphone on the coffee table—a Nextel, such as he'd taken from Corey's wife. He picked it up, pushed a button and a message appeared—the message from Walsh that he had seen on the phone of Corey's wife. The alert had come in time for Jibral

Haytham, but unfortunately for him, he had been sleeping, or he had not appreciated the nature of the message in regard to himself.

Khalil put the phone in his pocket. Then he sat down in an armchair that faced the couch. He watched his victim for a few seconds, then looked round the room.

In his country, this house of two levels with its own garden would be the home of a man of some means. Here, such houses belonged to common people, with vehicles in the driveway, televisions and good furnishings. He understood why so many believers from the poorer nations of Islam had emigrated to America—the land of the Christians and the Jews—and he did not condemn them for it so long as they retained their customs and their faith. Haytham, however, had been corrupted to the extreme by this morally debased nation, selling his soul to the enemies of Islam. Khalil recited aloud a Sutra from the Koran. 'Believers, take neither Jews nor Christians for friends.'

Gabriel Haytham stirred on the couch.

Khalil noticed a remote control on the low table beside the can of beer, and he reached for it, examined it, then shut off the television.

Gabriel Haytham stirred again, then yawned, sat up, and stared at the blank screen. He seemed confused, then reached for the remote control and noticed Asad Khalil in the nearby chair.

Haytham sat straight up and swung his legs off the couch. 'Who the hell are you?'

Khalil pointed his gun at Haytham. 'Do not move or I will kill you.'

Gabriel Haytham focused on the gun, then looked at the intruder. 'Take whatever you want—'

'Shut up. You will know what I want when you know who I am.'

Haytham stared at the intruder's face, and Khalil could see recognition seeping into his brain. Gabriel Haytham nodded, then said in a quiet voice, 'Where is my wife?'

Khalil knew from experience that if he said the loved one was dead, then the intended victim became irrational and sometimes aggressive, so he replied, 'Your wife and daughter are safely secured.'

'I want to see them.'

'You will. Soon. But first you will answer some questions. Has your agency contacted you with the news of my return?'

Haytham nodded.

'If you are telling the truth, why are you sleeping?' He smiled and extracted Haytham's phone from his pocket and read the text message to him. Then he said, in Arabic, 'If you had been awake to read this, then perhaps you would not now be waiting for death.'

Gabriel Haytham did not reply, and his eyes darted around the room.

Khalil knew that the man was looking for a way out of his situation, judging the distance between them and thinking of an aggressive move. Khalil stood, but before he could back away, Haytham thrust the coffee table towards him, then charged.

Khalil deflected the flying table as Haytham lunged at him, and he fired a single round into the man's chest, missing his heart. Before he could fire again, Haytham got his hands on Khalil's right arm, and they struggled for a few seconds before Khalil felt the wounded man weakening.

Khalil broke free and stepped away. Gabriel Haytham stood unsteadily on his feet, his left hand over the bleeding chest wound. Blood began running from his mouth.

Khalil knew the battle was over and all that remained was to deliver a final damnation that the traitor could take to Hell with him. He said in Arabic, 'You have turned away from your faith and sold your soul to the infidel. For this, Jibral Haytham, you will die and burn in Hell.'

Haytham's knees buckled and he knelt on the floor, staring at Khalil.

Khalil then said, 'Your wife and your whore daughter are dead, and you will join them soon.'

Haytham cried out in a surprisingly strong voice, 'You bastard!' and tried to stand, but fell back to his knees, coughing up blood.

Khalil aimed the Glock at Haytham's forehead, but before he pulled the trigger, the cellphone in his pocket rang. He took Haytham's phone from his pocket and looked at the display window. It read ATTF-3.

He looked again at Haytham, who was still kneeling, now with both hands pressed to his wound, which continued to seep blood.

The phone stopped ringing, and a second later a beep sounded.

So, Khalil thought, perhaps this call to Haytham was to warn him, and if that was the case, the police might not be more than minutes away.

He put Haytham's cellphone back in his pocket, then used his own cellphone and called Amir, saying to him, 'Come quickly.'

He ended the call, raised the Glock, and fired a single shot into Haytham's forehead.

A YELLOW TAXI stopped at the kerb. Khalil left the house through the front door, moved quickly down the path, and got into the taxi. 'Go.'

Amir accelerated up the street. Khalil said, 'Do not speed. Continue on this street.' Within a few minutes they were on the entrance ramp to the Long Island Expressway, westbound towards Manhattan.

Khalil and Amir rode in silence, then finally Amir cleared his throat and asked in Arabic, 'What is your destination in Manhattan, sir?'

'The World Trade Center.'

Amir did not reply. Khalil instructed, 'I do not want to pass through a toll booth.'

'Yes, sir. We will take the Brooklyn Bridge across the river.'

Amir exited onto a southbound expressway. Khalil looked out of the window and saw the skyline of Manhattan Island in the distance. He inquired of Amir, 'Where were they?'

'Sir? Oh . . .' He pointed in a southwesterly direction and said, 'There.'

Khalil gazed out the window. He now recalled from his last visit where he had seen the Twin Towers while riding in this same vicinity in a taxi that had been driven by another compatriot—a man who had suffered the same fate as Amir would suffer.

Khalil knew he needed to watch his driver carefully; if the man began to suspect his fate, as Farid Mansur had, he might attempt to flee—instead of accepting his fate as Mansur had.

Khalil said to Amir, 'You are performing a great service to our cause, Amir. You will be rewarded, and your family in Tripoli will profit greatly from your service to our Great Leader, Colonel Khadafi, and to Islam.'

Amir stayed silent for a moment too long, then said, 'Thank you, sir.'

Khalil recalled that Malik had always warned him about causing too many incidental deaths. 'A murdered man or woman is like leaving your footprints on your journey. Kill who you must kill and who you have vowed to kill, but try to be merciful with others, especially those of our faith.' Khalil respected Malik's advice. He was an old man who had seen much in his life and killed his share of infidels. But he was sometimes too cautious with the Americans, and that was because of the bombing raid.

Asad Khalil's mind returned to that night of April 15, 1986. He could see himself as a young man on the flat rooftop of the building in the old Italian fortress of Al Azziziyah in Tripoli. He had been with a young woman, but he could not remember her. All he could remember was the blur of the aircraft coming towards him, the hellfire spitting from its tail . . . and then the world had exploded.

Had the night ended there, it would still have been the worst night of his life. But later . . . later, when he returned to his home after the bombing, he had found rubble . . . and the bodies of his younger sisters, Adara, aged nine, and Lina, aged eleven. And his two brothers, Esam, a boy of five years, and Qadir, aged fourteen, two years younger than himself. Then he had found his mother dying in her bedroom, blood running from her mouth. She had asked him about her children . . . then died in his arms.

'Mother!'

Amir was startled and hit the brakes. 'Sir?'

Khalil slumped back in the seat and began praying silently.

Amir exited the expressway and drove towards the nearby Brooklyn Bridge. Asad Khalil gazed out the window and noted a food shop whose sign was in Arabic. He also saw two women walking, wearing head scarves. He asked Amir, 'Is this a district of Muslims?'

Amir replied, 'There are a few here, sir, but many more south of here, in the district called Bay Ridge.'

Khalil asked, 'Where is Brighton Beach?'

'Further south, sir. That is the Russian district.'

Khalil knew that. That was where Boris lived, and where Boris would die.

Amir drove onto the Brooklyn Bridge. Khalil looked across the river to the towering buildings of Manhattan Island. Truly, he thought, this was a place of wealth and power, and it was easy for the jihadists to become discouraged when they gazed on this scene. But Khalil sensed that the American empire was past the height of its power and glory and, like Rome, it had begun its long journey of sickness and death. The children of Islam would inherit the ruins of America and Europe, completing the conquest that had begun with the Prophet thirteen centuries before.

Khalil looked towards where the Twin Towers had been. That moment when they fell, he knew, had been the beginning of the end.

The taxi left the bridge and, as Amir continued south, he said, 'Straight ahead, sir, is where the towers once stood. There is an observation platform from which you can see the site. If you wish to see the hole in the earth, I will stop near this platform.'

Khalil replied, 'Yes, good. But first I must go to see the building of the Internal Revenue Service, which I am told is on Murray Street.'

Amir did not ask why his passenger needed to see that building, and he turned right on Church Street, beside the observation platform, and left into Murray Street, a one-way street of dark office buildings. Khalil noted that there were a few vehicles parked at the kerbs, but no moving vehicles except his taxi, and no pedestrians.

Amir pointed to the left and said, 'There is the IRS building.'

'Stop across the street.'

Amir pulled into the kerb opposite the building.

Khalil said, 'I will walk back to the observation platform from here.'

'Yes, sir.' Amir put the vehicle in park and asked in a carefully worded sentence, 'Will I be continuing my service to you, sir?'

'I think not.'

'Yes, sir . . . Our mutual friend mentioned a compensation—'

'Of course.' Khalil leaned down to the floor and took from his overnight bag a long ice pick, and also an American baseball cap that said 'Mets' on the crown. He assured Amir, 'You did an excellent job.'

'Thank you, sir.'

Khalil gripped the wooden handle with his right hand, looked around to be sure they were alone, then brought the ice pick around in a wide, powerful swing. The tip of the pick easily pierced Amir's skull and entered the top right portion of his head.

Amir's right hand flew back and grabbed Khalil's hand, which still gripped the ice pick. Amir seemed confused about what had happened, and he was pulling at Khalil's hand. 'What . . . ? What are you . . . ?'

'Relax, my friend. Do not upset yourself.'

Amir's grip on Khalil's hand started to loosen, but Khalil had to wait for the internal bleeding to do its work in the man's brain. He looked around impatiently and saw a young man entering Murray Street.

Amir said weakly, 'What has happened . . . ?'

Khalil extracted the ice pick, slipped it into his jacket pocket, then pushed the baseball cap over Amir's head and said to him in Arabic, 'The angels shall bear thee up to Paradise.' He reached over the seat, took Amir's cellphone from his shirt pocket and then, grabbing his bag, he exited the taxi.

The man on the sidewalk was now less than thirty metres from him. The man had obviously not noticed anything that had happened in the taxi. Khalil passed the man and looked back at him as he approached the taxi. The man glanced at it but kept walking.

Khalil continued towards the corner of Church Street. He looked back again and was startled to see Amir out of the taxi, still wearing the baseball cap, his arms flailing and his legs trying to propel him forwards. The man continued on, unaware of Amir, who now collapsed in the street.

Khalil carried on, cursing his choice of the ice pick. He knew that Amir's death would not be immediate, but it should have been quicker and relatively painless. He recalled that it was Boris, many years ago, who had encouraged him to choose an ice pick in certain circumstances because it was quick and silent. Khalil would have to tell Boris what happened with Amir. Perhaps he would even demonstrate the problem to him.

As he turned the corner onto Church Street he dropped Amir's cellphone into a drain. Following a young couple dressed in shorts and T-shirts, holding hands—he wondered if anything was sacred to these people—Khalil continued towards the platform that overlooked the place where the jihadists had achieved their great victory over the Americans. He climbed a set of stairs and saw that the platform held perhaps fifty people, most of them dressed as disrespectfully as the young man and woman ahead of him.

He walked to the railings and looked down at the vast excavation below him. He was surprised to see that no rubble remained, and the earth was bare, though the sides of the excavation were lined with concrete. A large earthen ramp led into the excavation, and he saw trucks and equipment sitting motionless at the bottom of the pit.

Khalil looked into the sky where the two towers had risen, and he recalled the images he had seen of people jumping from the burning buildings, hundreds of metres to their deaths.

A middle-aged man standing near him said to his wife, 'We ought to wipe out those bastards.'

'Harold. Don't say that.'

'Why not?'

The woman seemed to be aware that the man standing close to them might be a foreigner. Perhaps a Muslim. She nudged her husband, took his arm, and moved him away.

Khalil smiled.

He now noticed a small group of young men and women kneeling at the rail, praying silently, and Khalil had no doubt that they were praying not only for the dead but also for their enemies and asking that God forgive them. Some of them, Khalil thought, only dimly understood why this had happened. Most of them, he was certain, saw this event as a single incident, without context and without meaning. The Americans' ignorance and their arrogance, and their love of comfort and their disobedience to God, were their greatest weaknesses.

The sound of sirens brought him out of his thoughts. He glanced back at Church Street and saw two police cars moving rapidly in the direction of Murray Street. He assumed they were responding to a call regarding a dead taxi driver. Perhaps it was time to leave.

Khalil uttered a silent prayer for the fallen martyrs and ended with a verse from an Arab war song: 'Terrible he rode alone with his Yemen sword for aid; ornament, it carried none but the notches on the blade.'

ASAD KHALIL sat alone on a bench in Battery Park, so named, he understood, because this southern tip of Manhattan Island once held forts and artillery batteries to protect the city. Now it was a pleasant park with views across the bay, and the enemy was inside the city.

He opened a bottle of water that he had bought from a street vendor and took a long drink. Then he put the bottle in his bag and retrieved the cellphones of the two dead Federal agents. He turned them on and saw they still had service, which surprised him. It was possible, he thought, that the police or the FBI had not yet noticed that the phones were missing. The Americans, in true cowboy fashion, always worried first about the guns.

He accessed the text messages on Haytham's phone and saw one new message, from Paresi, Capt., ATTF/NYPD. This man, he knew, was the superior of Corey. Khalil read the message and saw that it was a short command, calling the police detectives to duty, and instructing them to begin surveillance of the Muslim community with special emphasis on the Libyan community.

This was to be expected and it did not cause him any alarm. His potential contacts in America were not all Libyans; there were his Al Qaeda friends from other Islamic nations. His only Libyan contacts so far had been Farid in California, and Amir here in New York, and both of them were now in Paradise, far beyond American surveillance.

He shut off Haytham's phone and accessed the text messages on Corey's wife's—he still thought of her as Mayfield—phone. A new text from Walsh read: To all FBI agents and NYPD detectives: two Libyan informants in NY metro have come forward with info on suspect Khalil. Check email for details and operational instruction regarding apprehending suspect. Walsh.

Khalil shut off the phone and thought about this. If it was true, it presented some problems to him and to his mission. In fact, he would not know who to trust.

He realised, though, that if this message from Walsh had been sent to all agents and all detectives, then it should have appeared on Haytham's screen. But it had not. And why was it on Mayfield's phone? The woman was dead when the message was sent.

Therefore, he thought, this was a false message, sent only to Mayfield's cellphone, which Walsh must now suspect was in the hands of Khalil. And this was why Mayfield's phone was still in service.

He sat back on the bench and stared out at the sunlit water. So perhaps they were being clever. But not clever enough.

In any case, this message had all the tell-tale signs of disinformation, and that was how he would regard it, which would please Boris, who had spent days teaching him about this. 'The British are masters of disinformation, and the Americans have learned from them,' Boris had said, concluding his lecture with, 'But the best disseminators of disinformation in the world are the KGB.'

Khalil had reminded Boris that the KGB no longer existed, so perhaps the word 'are' should have been replaced with 'were.' Boris had only laughed at Khalil's insults. Malik had advised Khalil to be easier on the Russian, saying, 'He is a lost soul from a lost empire. Use him, Khalil, but pity him. He will never leave here alive.'

But Boris had left Libya, with the assistance of the CIA, and sold himself to the Americans and done for them what he had done for Libyan Intelligence: betrayed secrets for money. And nearly betrayed Asad Khalil. But the day of judgment was now at hand for Boris.

Khalil opened a bag of peanuts that he had purchased from the street vendor, realising he hadn't eaten since before dawn, and ate the nuts. Pigeons soon began to congregate, and he threw a few nuts to them.

He threw more nuts, these still in their shells, and observed that the birds understood what they had to do to get the nuts and pecked at the shells—but they kept cocking their heads from side to side, looking for the nuts that had been shelled for them. Their birds, too, were lazy.

He smiled, extending an open hand filled with nuts, and a pigeon approached cautiously. As the bird lowered its head and took a kernel, Khalil wrapped his hand round the pigeon's head and crushed its neck.

CHAPTER FIVE

I slept in the chair in Kate's room, and at dawn I went out to the parking lot, found my Jeep, and collected some clothes from my luggage. Back in ICU, I dressed and sat beside Kate's bed and watched her sleeping.

When she woke up she looked remarkably well for having been at death's door. The attending physician wanted to keep the ventilator going, so she still couldn't speak, but she wrote me notes. One said, *Find Khalil before he finds you.* I assured her, 'I will.' But in fact, I had not been his next target, as expected. Vince Paresi had telephoned me yesterday afternoon to say that Gabe Haytham and his wife and daughter had been found dead.

The death of one of our own, along with his family, had completely changed this case from an attempted murder of a Federal agent to . . . well, something quite different. I knew Gabe, I liked him and respected him, and he had been very helpful to me the last time Asad Khalil was in town. I guess Khalil knew that, too, and had decided that Gabe was a traitor and deserved to die. But why did he kill Gabe's wife and daughter?

I suppose I could blame myself for not thinking of Gabe Haytham sooner . . . but I wasn't going to beat myself up with this. I was going to find Asad Khalil and bring him to justice.

I decided not to tell Kate about the murder of the Haytham family yet. As for media coverage, the Feds were keeping a tight grip.

Dr Goldberg arrived to check on his patient and he was all smiles. It must be kind of neat saving someone's life, and it probably makes you feel good inside. As a homicide detective, almost every crime victim I've seen was on the way to the morgue, not the hospital. And to be up front, I've put a few perpetrators in both places, and it never felt good. Well . . . sometimes it did.

Dr Goldberg assured us that Kate could be moved by medical helicopter to the city in about two days, then a few more days in the hospital, then home, and back to duty within a month.

After he left, she wrote, *I want to be back to work next week.*

I replied, 'I need to evaluate the extent of your mental impairment first.'

She tried to flash me the peace sign, but in her weakened condition, she only managed to raise her middle finger.

I spent another half-hour with her. She scribbled a lot of questions regarding what was going on with the case, and I told her what I knew, except about the Haytham family. I also didn't tell her that her cellphone and gun were probably in the hands of her assailant. That kind of thing really gets to a cop or an FBI agent. Neither did I want to get into exactly what happened after we stepped out of the aircraft.

I certainly didn't want to blow my own horn and tell her how I had bravely risked my own life to get her into free-fall so she wouldn't bleed to death. And how I had expertly stopped her bleeding for a crucial minute before the EMS arrived. I was sure, however, that she would want to read my full incident report, in which I was obligated to recount all these things in some detail. Then she would draw her own conclusions about her husband's heroic actions.

I said to her, 'Well, I really have to get to the office so I can write my incident report. I'll keep in touch with the hospital and we'll get you out of here as soon as possible. Meanwhile, you get some rest and follow doctor's orders.'

I kissed her on the cheek and she grabbed my hand and squeezed it. Then wrote, *Be very, very careful.*

Indeed.

I WENT FIRST to the nurses' station and reminded them to be security conscious, though in truth I thought the immediate danger had passed; Asad Khalil was obviously in the New York City area, where he'd murdered Gabe and his family. Anyway, I arranged a code phrase—Crazy John—that would allow me to get medical updates.

Down in the lobby, I went into the gift shop, where I bought a cute stuffed lion that growled, for Kate, and asked them to deliver it to her room. I'm a thoughtful guy. And, speaking of growling, my stomach was making noises, so I bought some snacks and a coffee, then went out to the parking lot and got into my Jeep.

I began the two-hour drive back to Manhattan. It was another perfect day, and the mountains in May are really nice. I could see why Kate sometimes spoke about getting a place up here.

My cellphone rang, and I took the call. It was Captain Paresi, who asked, 'How's Kate?'

'On the road to recovery.'

'Good. Where are you?'

'On the road to New York.'

'OK. Look, a body was discovered by a commuter early this morning at the Douglaston train station, near Gabe's house. The victim was a livery driver, Caucasian, mid-thirties, name of Charles Taylor. He was found behind the wheel of his Lincoln Town Car, with two bullet wounds fired through the back of his seat. Forensics recovered two bullets from the dashboard, and they were .40 calibre. Ballistics is comparing them to the ballistic file on Kate's weapon.'

'OK. We won't be surprised to discover a match.'

'No, we won't. Ballistics confirms that Gabe was killed with Kate's gun.' He continued, 'They lifted lots of prints from the limo and from the Haytham residence. Do we have Khalil's prints on file?'

'They printed him at the US Embassy in Paris three years ago.'

'Good. So, if we get a match, that nails it all down. They also found two .40 calibre shell casings under the driver's seat and a plastic water bottle with two holes in the bottom.'

'The water bottle is Khalil's M.O. from last time,' I said. 'It's not the best silencer, but it's better than nothing, and he seems happy with it.'

Paresi speculated, 'If the bullets are from Kate's weapon, that could mean Khalil has no weapon of his own.'

I replied, 'If Khalil has contacts in this country—and I'm sure he does—then he has his own gun. He used Kate's gun to give us the finger.'

'Yeah . . . I guess . . .' He continued his briefing. 'We contacted Charles Taylor's livery company on Long Island and discovered that Mr Taylor was to pick up a passenger at Republic by the name of Mr Brian Gold and take him to a destination as directed by the customer. The livery company was prepaid by credit card, and we're trying to track down the cardholder, which is a corporation in Lichtenstein called Global Entertainment.'

'Tell Walsh not to waste too much time on the money trail,' I advised. 'OK, so did Charles Taylor take Asad Khalil, a.k.a. Brian Gold, to the Haytham house?' I answered my own question and said, 'Not likely. Khalil met up with someone else, probably at the train station after he whacked Taylor. Look for a dead Libyan cab driver.'

After a few seconds of silence, Paresi informed me, 'We got one. How did you know?'

'Excellent. So where did this body turn up? How was he killed?'

Paresi ignored my question and said, 'Next subject. The medical examiner confirms that Gabe's daughter died of knife wounds. The wife died of a broken neck.' He stayed silent a second, then said, 'He left flowers on the daughter's chest . . . This guy is a very cold-hearted killer.'

'Right.'

Captain Paresi went on, 'Based on what the medical examiner said about the time of death, and what the two responding officers discovered, I think we just missed Khalil by . . . maybe minutes. I wish I'd gotten a patrol car there sooner. Maybe we could have . . . headed this off.'

I advised him, 'Move on, Captain.'

Paresi did not reply, but took the opportunity to remind me, 'You are likely to be the next person who interacts with him.'

'Right. He wants to *interact* with me next.'

Paresi also reminded me, 'Washington wants him alive.'

'Well, they think they do. But what are they going to do with him? Do they want this guy being tried in Federal court where he can say things that the public shouldn't hear? His whole file is classified.'

Paresi asked, 'Where is the file that you and Gabe kept on Khalil?'

I replied, 'I'll find it when I get to the office.'

'OK. Where are you now?'

'I'm on scenic Route 17. Maybe an hour and a half away.'

'Let me know when you get here. We're booked in to have a meeting at noon in Walsh's office.'

'Who's at the meeting?'

'Your other "Lion Hunter", George Foster; you; and me. Walsh wants to keep it small and focused.'

Meaning quiet and restricted. Kate and Gabe would have been there, too, but the Lion Hunter team was getting smaller.

Paresi confided, 'Walsh thinks you're a loose cannon. So watch yourself at this meeting.'

Loose cannon? *Me?* 'At the moment, I'm just lion's bait.'

'Or his next meal.'

He hung up, and I used the driving time to think about Gabe and some of the insights he'd given me about Asad Khalil three years ago.

Gabe had never met Khalil, until yesterday, but he had been able to come up with a sort of psychological profile on his co-religionist. He'd explained to me about the blood feud—the obligation of an Arab male to avenge the murder of a family member. This, more than political ideology or religion, was what drove Khalil; the Americans had killed his family and he was honour-bound to kill those responsible, and those who tried to keep him from his duty. Like me.

Gabe had also mentioned the Arab tradition of the lone warrior, the avenger who is a law unto himself, not unlike the American cowboy hero. He recited a verse that sort of summed it up: 'Terrible he rode alone with his Yemen sword for aid; ornament, it carried none but the notches on the blade.'

It was therefore very possible that Khalil intended to meet John Corey alone, man to man, with no accomplices, and no purpose other than to see who was the better man—the better killer. And that was fine with me.

My cellphone rang, and I answered, 'Corey.' It was Investigator Matt Miller who, after enquiring about Kate, told me, 'We spoke to Craig Hauser, the president of the skydiving club. He really didn't know much about the new sign-on who turned out to be the suspect. But we also confiscated the videotape of your skydive as evidence.'

'Good.'

He hesitated, then said, 'Incredible. You're a damned brave man, Detective Corey.'

This is true, but I replied, 'You saw what Khalil was capable of.'

'I did. But he's not brave—he's psychotic.'

I agreed: 'He's a little over the top. Where is the videotape?'

'The FBI has possession of it. They've put half a dozen FBI agents in my headquarters.' He added, 'I've also been advised that you are not the case agent and that in future I need to speak only to whoever is assigned to this case.'

'OK. But let's stay in touch.'

'That's not what I just said.'

'You just called me,' I reminded him.

'This was a one-time courtesy.'

Right. Cop to cop. I said, 'Well, I hope the FBI extends you some courtesies. For instance, do you intend to interview the victim?'

He didn't reply, and I knew that the FBI had already told him to forget about talking to Kate.

He did say, 'My new FBI friends in my office say they're moving your wife tomorrow morning.'

That was news to me. Obviously, they wanted her out of the jurisdiction of the State Police and back in Manhattan where they could keep a tighter lid on the case.

We seemed to have run out of things to speak about, so I said, 'I appreciate the call.'

'Let me know how this turns out.'

I couldn't promise that, but I said, 'If I find him, I'll let you know.'

Investigator Miller added, 'And if he finds you, I'll see it on the news.'

Not funny, Investigator Miller.

We hung up, and I continued along the state highway, then exited onto the New York State Thruway, whose sign promised NEW YORK—50 MILES.

AS I APPROACHED the Holland Tunnel, I thought about what Paresi was saying to me. It occurred to me that this noon meeting in Walsh's office might actually be less about Asad Khalil and more about John Corey. Apparently I had become a problem.

I don't usually get paranoid about my career because, one, I'm good at what I do, and two, I don't need the job. But for now, I really needed to stay with the Feds until Mr Khalil and I interacted one last time.

I exited the tunnel and made my way through the busy streets of Lower Manhattan. Using Kate's parking permit, I parked in front of 26 Federal Plaza.

As I was looking to see where Kate hid the parking permit—glove compartment? Under the driver's seat? Behind the sun visor?—a uniformed cop sauntered over and knocked on my window.

I rolled down my window, and he said, 'Official business only.'

'Right. I'm looking for my permit.' I handed him my Fed creds and flashed my NYPD detective shield while I rummaged under the passenger seat. Why the hell does she pick a different place every time?

The cop handed me my creds and said, 'Thank you, Detective.'

He was about to move off, but I took a shot and asked him, 'Hey, do you know anything about the murder of a cab driver? Libyan guy.'

'Yesterday afternoon on Murray Street?' The cop, whose name badge said 'Timmons', let me know, 'We got a "be on the look out" on the suspect.'

'You got a suspect?'

'Yeah. An Arab guy.'

'Good. Hey, if you were a woman, where would you put the permit?'

I thought he was going to say, 'You're the detective,' but he said, wisely, 'I don't even want to go there.'

'Right. How'd this guy get clipped?'

'Something like an ice pick in his head.'

'Ouch.' Then I asked, 'What was the victim's name?'

He was wondering, I'm sure, why I didn't ask my boss these questions, and I thought he was going to ask to see my creds again, but he replied, 'His name was Amir . . . some Arab name.'

I asked Officer Timmons, 'Any particulars on the incident?'

He replied, 'Homicide Squad says it wasn't a robbery, so it looks like Abdul A knew Abdul B and maybe they had some sort of disagreement. I got a photo of the suspect. You want to see it?'

'No.'

'It's on the floor,' Timmons said.

'You should have that photo on your dashboard.'

'No, your parking permit. It's on the floor behind you.'

'Really?' I twisted round and sure enough, there it was.

Anyway, the cop moved off. I retrieved the permit and put it on the dashboard, locked the car and began walking towards 26 Federal Plaza.

AS THE NAME suggests, 26 Federal Plaza is a US government building, and its forty-four floors house various tax-eating agencies, most of them filled with civil servants who agonise over how best to serve the American public. Floors 22 through 29, however, are where the FBI and the Anti-Terrorist Task Force are located, along with other law enforcement and national security agencies that will go unnamed. OK, I'll name one—the CIA. Actually, most of their offices are across Duane Street at 290 Broadway, but we are fortunate to have a few of our comrades in arms here at 26 Fed. Conversely, we have some ATTF personnel at 290 Broadway. The purpose of this, I assume, is to not put all our eggs in one basket in case a plane or a truck bomb takes out one of the buildings.

Inside the big lobby, I went up to the thick Plexiglas walls that surround the elevators and punched in my code to open the door. An elevator arrived, and I climbed aboard and pushed the button for the twenty-eighth floor, where Tom Walsh has his big corner office.

On the way up, I thought some more about Asad Khalil. The guy was a unique individual, possessed of some native intelligence and good primitive instincts. I needed to give him credit for his dedication to his mission and his ability to operate in an alien and hostile environment. I mean, the guy was a friggin' camel jockey, who probably couldn't tell the difference between an ATM machine and a condom dispenser, yet here he was in America jumping out of planes, chartering flights, whacking people in their homes and cars, and making us look stupid. None of this was computing.

True, he had some resources here, like the late Amir guy whose head Khalil mistook for a block of ice. But local Libyans were only part of the reason for Khalil's success; he had smarts and balls. Worse, he believed God was on his side. Still . . . that didn't explain his James Bond savvy and sophisticated M.O. Then it hit me.

Boris.

I stepped off the elevator and stood into the hallway. Boris. A former KGB guy, hired by Libyan Intelligence to train Asad Khalil.

Boris had not only trained Khalil in the art of killing, deception, escape and evasion; he'd also briefed him on how to get by in the Western world—practical things like making airline reservations, checking into a hotel, renting a car. Plus, Boris spoke nearly flawless English, and he'd tutored his motivated student in the finer points of the language.

And this brought me to my next thought: *Khalil wanted to kill Boris.*

The first and only time I met Boris was at CIA Headquarters in Langley, Virginia, three years ago, after Khalil had given us the slip. Boris had indicated that the Libyans intended to terminate his employment—and his life—after he gave Khalil his last lesson. But Boris had gotten out of Libya alive, with a little help from the CIA, and when Kate and I met him, he was spilling the beans about Libyan Intelligence to his new CIA friends. In return, Boris would be getting an American passport and some other considerations, like maybe a lifetime supply of Marlboros and Stoli, which I recalled he seemed to enjoy.

Boris (no last name, please) was an impressive man, and I would have liked to have spent more time with him, but he had been surrounded by his CIA keepers, which put some restrictions on the conversation. But I did remember Boris saying of Asad Khalil, 'That man is a perfect killing machine, and what he doesn't kill today, he will kill tomorrow.'

I'd kind of figured that out for myself, but to be contrary, I had replied, 'He's just a man.'

To which Boris had replied, 'Sometimes I wonder.'

Apparently, Asad Khalil, The Lion, had taken on mythological proportions in the minds of his friends and his enemies, and Boris had ended our tea-and-vodka hour with these words: 'I congratulate you both on your survival. Don't waste any of your days.'

Thanks for the advice. I hope Boris has taken his own advice. Bottom line on Boris: I liked him, but I didn't like that he'd created a monster. And I was sure that Boris was going to regret this himself.

If Boris was alive, I needed to find him and warn him that his former student was back in the USA to settle some old scores. I also wanted to speak to him about how best to find Asad Khalil.

And finally, if Boris was not yet dead, then he would make good bait.

TOM WALSH'S secretary, Kathy, greeted me and said, 'Mr Walsh will be arriving shortly. Go right in and have a seat.'

'Thanks.'

Captain Paresi was sitting at the round conference table across from FBI Special Agent George Foster. They looked grim.

I shook hands with both men, and George asked, 'How's Kate?'

'Resting comfortably, thank you.'

He remarked, 'This is unbelievable.'

I replied, 'George, you more than anyone know this is not unbelievable.'

He nodded. George was present at this meeting because he'd been a participant in the events at JFK three years ago, and had been part of the ad hoc Lion Hunter team.

I exchanged a few words with Captain Paresi, and he was a bit cool, which meant that his boss, Tom Walsh, had set the tone regarding John Corey.

I said to Paresi, 'I am not being taken off this case.'

He didn't respond directly, but said, 'We value your dedication and your prior experience with the suspect.'

To further set the tone, I replied, 'Bullshit.'

I went to one of the big windows. From here on the twenty-eighth floor, I could see most of Lower Manhattan. I tried to guess where Khalil intended to hide out: I didn't think he would hole up in a Muslim neighbourhood in the outer boroughs where someone might figure out that this new guy was worth a million bucks to the Feds. I mean, Khalil couldn't kill them all, the way he'd killed Amir the taxi driver. Hiding out in a hotel would be a problem because of security cameras. A better bet would be a hot-sheet hotel or a flophouse that offered daily rates, cash up front, no questions asked.

More likely, though, he would be holed up in an apartment that had been rented under a corporate name by his backers. That was standard procedure in the well-financed world of international terrorism and, unfortunately, despite our best efforts, we rarely discovered these safe houses unless we happened to follow some bad guy to the building.

I looked to the southwest where the Twin Towers once stood. I couldn't see the observation platform from here, but I could picture the visitors—people from all over the world—staring into the big hole that had been the temporary mass grave of close to 3,000 human beings. If you were one of the tens of thousands of survivors who had been in the towers that morning, or were on your way there, as Kate and I had been, not a day went by that you didn't wonder why you were spared.

On Walsh's office window was a transfer that showed a black silhouette of the towers, and the words: 9/11—NEVER FORGET!

Also a few blocks from here was Murray Street, where Amir the taxi driver had dropped off his last customer. Assuming the fare-beater was Asad Khalil, what was he doing in Lower Manhattan on a Sunday? What was in Manhattan to attract him?

Well, the Coreys lived on the Upper East Side, as did Tom Walsh. Vince Paresi and wife number three lived on Central Park West. All worked right here and followed a somewhat predictable routine.

Which brought me to the thought that Asad Khalil had some very good intel about Mr and Mrs John Corey. How else could he know that we'd be jumping out of an aircraft on Sunday morning? This guy had a big supporting cast here in New York. Like maybe Al Qaeda.

As I turned from the window, Tom Walsh walked into his office. We all shook hands, and Walsh said, 'Please sit.'

He threw a thick folder on the table and began, 'There's no good news, so I'll start with the bad news.'

BEFORE TOM WALSH got to the bad news, he suggested a moment of silence for Gabe, his wife and his daughter. It was a nice gesture and we all bowed our heads.

I don't know too many Muslim prayers, but I knew what Gabe would want me to pray for, so I prayed that I'd find Asad Khalil and make him pay for what he'd done. Amen.

A brief word about Tom Walsh. He is young for this job—maybe mid forties—and Kate tells me he's good-looking, though in my opinion he looks like one of those coiffed pretty boys you see in men's clothing ads. I've seen his significant other, a lady lawyer, at a few office social functions and they seem like a good fit—cool, detached, ambitious and narcissistic. They don't live together, but if they did, they'd need separate bedrooms for their egos.

The moment of silence ended, and Walsh began, 'We have located Chip Wiggins.' Since there was no good news, that wasn't good news.

Walsh informed us, 'As we suspected, he's dead.'

As Walsh gave us some background on Wiggins, which I already knew, I exchanged glances with Paresi and Foster. Paresi already knew Wiggins was dead, of course, but George Foster looked surprised, and more pale than usual.

I took the opportunity to remind everyone that I'd worked this case. 'Wiggins was also flying for Alpha three years ago and we strongly suggested then that he move, or get another job.' Which was my way of saying that we had done all we could to get Wiggins off Khalil's radar.

Walsh commented, 'Well, he should have taken that advice.' He filled us in on the FBI's search for Wiggins, who was eventually found in the aircraft that he flew.

Walsh took three photos from his folder and slid them across the table.

I looked at one. A man was sitting on the floor of the aircraft's cabin with his back against a wall, wearing black pants and a white shirt, which was red with blood, though you should not make assumptions from a photo. Neither should you assume the subject of the photo is dead, but Walsh said Wiggins was dead, and the face looked like Wiggins. The clincher, though, was that Chip Wiggins's head was sitting in his lap.

I heard Paresi say, 'Jesus . . . That bastard.'

I glanced at George, who was staring blankly at the photo. His face looked whiter than Wiggins's.

Walsh let us study the photos for a few seconds, then reminded us, 'This is all highly sensitive. Nothing we discuss leaves this room unless I say so.'

I said to him, 'I do intend to brief Kate on this meeting.'

He hesitated, then said, 'Of course. But you should speak to her off the record in the event she's called to testify in any future proceedings.'

Tom Walsh was thinking down the road to some end-game scenarios. He and his bosses at FBI Headquarters were lawyers. Therefore, everything had to be legal and correct, even in the war on terrorism. The police and the CIA, on the other hand, were cowboys. One could argue the merits of lawyers and cowboys forever but pre-9/11, the lawyers were in charge. Now the cowboys were getting a little more room to ride.

Walsh said, 'There was another murder in California that is most probably related to this case.'

The body count had just gone from six to seven.

Walsh consulted his folder and said, 'Before we get to that, let me just say that we don't know how Asad Khalil entered the country, but it's probable that he flew into LAX, using a false passport and visa from an Arabic-speaking country. A man like this could easily pass muster at passport control. We are checking video security tapes at a number of airports. And our office in Santa Barbara paid a visit last night to Sterling Air Charters at Santa Barbara Airport, the company that owns and operates the Citation jet that Khalil used to fly from Sullivan County Airport to Republic Airport on Long Island.'

He scanned an email in his hand and said, 'At about seven a.m. on Saturday morning, a man who identified himself as Christos Demetrios showed up at the Sterling office. He had a reservation made by his company in Athens, Hydra Shipping. He met his pilot and co-pilot, and they departed on time, landing at six thirteen p.m. local time at Sullivan County Airport. Mr Demetrios—who the Sterling pilots identified from our photo as Asad Khalil—rented a car, and the two pilots went to a local motel with instructions to be ready to fly out the next morning, Sunday, sometime after ten a.m., to the stated destination of Buffalo.'

Walsh paused for a moment and then said, 'When Khalil re-boarded the aircraft in Sullivan County next day, he'd just . . . attacked Kate, and the pilots said he appeared quite at ease . . . he was smiling. The only thing the pilots noticed out of the ordinary was that their passenger no longer had his duffle bag, which we assume held his skydiving gear. Also, he changed the flight plan from Buffalo to Republic.' Walsh concluded, 'He knows how to keep the authorities off his tail.'

It's a fact that serial murderers gain more confidence after about the third murder. They also get better at it. But then the learning curve starts to flatten and the level of confidence turns into carelessness. I wasn't sure where Asad Khalil was on this curve. So far, the only real mistake that he had made was not killing me when he had the chance.

Walsh looked at us and said, 'Victim seven. The Ventura County Police reported a body found with no ID under a bed in a Best Western hotel near Santa Barbara Airport. The room was registered to a Farid Mansur, a Middle Eastern immigrant. The police put this together with a missing person report filed by a Libyan-American lady, Mrs Hala Mansur, whose husband went missing on Friday, and she ID'd the body.'

He continued, 'We can assume Farid Mansur passed on the usual false IDs, money, weapons, and maybe the skydiving gear to Asad Khalil. We must also now assume that Khalil is poised to strike again. Based on his attack on Kate, his murder of Gabe, and his threat to John, let's recognise that the Task Force has become his target.'

George Foster went from white to grey, and even Paresi, who's usually cool and macho, looked a little unsettled.

Walsh looked at me and said, 'You are definitely a target. So maybe you should lie low. Like, stay home while Kate recuperates.'

I had seen that coming and replied, 'That's not what I had in mind. Look, Tom, I'm willing to act as bait—if we can come up with a good plan.'

'We can discuss that later,' Walsh said, remembering to add, 'I appreciate the offer.' He changed subjects. 'We have another murder that may be connected to Asad Khalil.' He looked at me and said, 'Captain Paresi told you about the Libyan taxi driver.'

'Correct.'

Walsh asked me, 'How did you anticipate that?'

I replied, 'The last time he was here, Khalil used a Libyan taxi driver to take him from JFK to New Jersey, where he murdered him the same way as he murdered'—here was my moment—'Amir on Murray Street.'

Paresi said, 'I never mentioned the name of the murdered taxi driver, or where he was murdered. How did you know that?'

I wasn't going to tell him I had had a chance chat with a cop on the beat; I wanted to stay on this case, so I needed to maintain my aura of being informed and connected in high places. 'I have my sources.'

That did not go over well with my two bosses, but Walsh let it go and continued, 'No murder weapon was recovered, but the medical examiner says that he found a puncture wound in the deceased's skull consistent with the type of wound made by an ice pick.' He added, 'Death was not instantaneous. In fact, the victim exited his taxi and died on the street.'

That didn't sound like the Asad Khalil that I knew. I mean, you really don't want your victims doing the zombie walk in the middle of the street while you're trying to put some distance between you and them. If I was seeing Boris's training here, you'd think Boris would have remembered to tell Khalil, 'We love that ice pick, Asad, but you gotta give them two or three pokes.'

Walsh continued with his crime scene briefing. 'The police found no cellphone on the driver's body or in his taxi. We then discovered that he had no house phone, and if he had a cellphone—which he undoubtedly did—it was either not in his name, or it was the paid-minutes type and no records exist.' He concluded, 'Dead end.'

Poor choice of words, perhaps, but not surprising. As I've discovered, most Middle Eastern immigrants come from places where it's not a good idea to create records of your existence—and that mentality had carried over to America, which made my job a little more difficult.

Walsh filled us in on a few odds and ends, including the not-surprising discovery that Global Entertainment in Lichtenstein and Hydra Shipping in Athens were sham corporations. INTERPOL was investigating.

In police work we always say, 'It's important to know who fired the bullet, but it's more important to know who paid for it.' And when you know that, you can guess at the bigger picture. Who was backing Asad Khalil? And why? He could not have pulled all this off by himself. My knowledge of geopolitics is limited, but I did know that Libya and its president, Colonel Muammar Khadafi, had been quiet since the bombing in 1986. And since 9/11, they'd gotten even quieter. So they wouldn't risk backing their former psychotic terrorist—there was nothing in it for them except more bombs.

The next usual suspect was Al Qaeda, but I didn't see their fingerprints on this—unless there was something in it for them. Asad Khalil's mission was his, and not very significant in terms of what it would accomplish in the war against the US. I mean, whacking Mr and Mrs Corey was not high on Al Qaeda's agenda. Therefore, if Al Qaeda had provided funds, passports and intel about his intended victims, Khalil would have to return the favour; maybe take out a big target for his sponsors—a building or monument, or an important person or persons.

I was thinking about all this while Walsh was going on about this and that. I was waiting for him to get to the question of who might be behind Asad Khalil, and the possibility of a major attack. But that didn't seem to be on Walsh's agenda memo. Maybe later.

Walsh said, 'I'd like you all to see this.' He took a remote control from the table and clicked on the television in the corner. In a few seconds, we were watching a bunch of assholes jumping out of an aircraft.

The first scene was obviously taken by a skydiver as he was free-falling, and it was a bit jumpy, as you can imagine.

Walsh asked me, 'You do that?'

I replied, 'Kate and I love it. You should try it.' *I'll pack your chute.*

Walsh fast forwarded. This shot was taken from the ground with a telephoto lens, and I could clearly see Kate free-falling with Khalil hooked up to her. Then I saw myself free-falling towards Kate and Khalil, and then Kate's chute opened, and then mine opened.

Walsh froze the picture and said to me, 'You don't have to watch this.'

I didn't reply and he continued in slow motion. As the scene unfolded, Walsh asked me to provide a commentary, but I said, 'I'll put it in my report.'

Even with the telephoto lens, it was difficult for the people on the ground, or in this room, to comprehend what was happening, though it was clear something was wrong. But I knew the moment when Khalil cut Kate's throat, and I did bring that to everyone's attention.

Then you could see Khalil going into free-fall, and I saw his chute opening, and I could see that he'd steered himself towards the woods.

Khalil was now out of the frame, and the cameraman had centred his shot on me steering towards Kate. Then our chutes collided and collapsed, and someone on the ground screamed.

Next you could see Kate's collapsed chute sailing away after I jettisoned it, then my chute, too, when I released it. Then there we were in free-fall again. To the uninitiated, it appeared Kate and I were falling to our deaths.

Paresi asked me, 'What the hell is happening?'

'I had to get rid of our main chutes to get us on the ground quickly before she bled to death. Our emergency chutes will open.'

Paresi mumbled, 'Jesus . . .'

Kate and I were free-falling for what seemed a very long time before Kate's emergency chute popped, followed by mine. Kate hit the ground first, then before I hit, the cameraman must have stopped filming, because the next scene was of the ambulance racing towards where we'd landed. Walsh shut off the TV.

We sat there for a few seconds before Walsh said, 'You did a good job.'

I didn't reply.

Paresi said, as if to himself, 'I can't believe that asshole did that.'

Walsh suggested, 'Let's take a fifteen-minute break.'

I stood and walked out of the room and headed to the elevators, my heart pounding in my chest.

You bastard. You arrogant bastard, I thought. You only get one chance at me, asshole. You had it, and you blew it. Payback's a bitch.

I SAT AT MY DESK and stared out over the expanse of low-walled cubicles. It was lunch hour, quiet and empty in Fedland—very unlike an NYPD squad room at any hour of any day.

Captain Paresi appeared and walked over to my desk. He sat down in my side chair and asked me, 'How you doing?'

'Fine.'

'I think you're experiencing post-traumatic stress.' Apparently Walsh had come up with a good reason for me to ask for some leave time. I didn't respond.

He assured me, 'No one here will think any the less of you if you ask for time to be with your wife. That's what a husband does.'

I wasn't sure if I should take marital advice from a man who's been married three times.

He changed the subject and said, 'I'll take your Khalil file.'

I unlocked the file cabinet beside my desk. In the bottom drawer was a folder marked 'Islamic Community Outreach Programme'. I pulled out the folder and handed it to Paresi, who glanced at the index tab and smiled. He opened the folder, flipped through the pages, and asked me a few questions. I briefed him on the efforts of the Lion Hunter team over the past three years and explained, 'His father, Captain Karim Khalil, was a big shot in the Khadafi government. Captain Khalil was assassinated in Paris, supposedly by Israeli agents, making him a martyr for Islam.' I added, 'Actually, it was Khadafi himself who ordered the hit.'

'Why?'

'The CIA says that Khadafi was sexually involved with Mrs Khalil.'

'No kidding?'

'It's complicated, but the CIA tried to turn Asad Khalil with this info and have him whack Khadafi.'

Paresi thought about that, but did not comment.

I continued, 'Prior to Karim Khalil's residence in paradise, he and his family lived in a former Italian military compound in Tripoli called Al Azziziyah, where the Khadafis also had a house. On the night of April 15, 1986, four US Air Force F-111s bombed the compound, killing, among others, Khadafi's adopted daughter and, as I told you, Asad Khalil's entire family—his mother, two sisters and two brothers.'

Paresi processed that, then asked, 'How did that bastard survive?'

'I don't know. But Khalil would tell you he was spared by God to seek revenge; for himself, and for his Great Leader, Muammar Khadafi.'

'So, Chip Wiggins was the last of those eight pilots.'

'He was,' I replied.

'So, time to go home.'

'Well, I would. You would. But you know, he's in town anyway, so why not whack a few more people on the way out?'

Captain Paresi observed, 'He's got a big hate eating his guts.'

'You think?'

Paresi and I kicked around a few thoughts, and the subject came up regarding where Khalil might be hiding out. I said, 'As we can see, Khalil is well-funded and he has some sophisticated backing—apparently a network or cell here in New York. Whoever these people are, they probably have a few safe houses in Manhattan—they'll be apartments rented by XYZ Corporation for visiting colleagues. We know of three safe-house apartment buildings in Manhattan, and you should have round-the-clock surveillance on those buildings.'

'We do.'

'But I'm fairly sure his sponsors have a never-used place for him to hang out.'

Paresi considered all that and concluded, 'It won't be easy to find this guy in the usual way.'

I said to him, 'Maybe we should discuss now your thoughts about what else Khalil is doing here to pay back his sponsors.'

He didn't reply for a few seconds, then said, 'That would be a very speculative discussion. We have no information on that possibility.'

Apparently Captain Paresi did not want to pursue the subject that he himself had brought up. At least he didn't want to pursue it with me.

He glanced at his watch and said, 'We're a minute late.' He stood and walked towards the elevators, carrying my folder with him.

I waited a few minutes, then followed.

TOM WALSH didn't comment on my lateness or on the fact that George Foster, who apparently had been made case officer, was not there.

Walsh looked at me. 'John, let me begin by saying that we appreciate your dedication to duty, especially in light of Kate's serious injuries, and the stress'—stress on the stress—'that you've been under—'

'Thank you.'

'After thinking about this situation, and after consulting with Captain Paresi, I strongly suggest that you ask for a month's traumatic leave so that you can be with your wife during her convalescence.'

I didn't respond.

He sweetened the deal by saying, 'This will be paid leave. But I would advise you to stay in your apartment, except for necessary errands and such.'

'Can I see a Yankees game?'

'No.' He went on, 'You'll have ample time at home to write your incident report and to write me a confidential memo regarding everything you know about Asad Khalil and about what happened three years ago.'

I glanced at Paresi, fully expecting him to say, 'Tom, I have a whole folder that John just gave me on that very subject. I'll make you a copy.' But Captain Paresi did not say that. In fact, Captain Paresi had been screwed so many times by the FBI that he was keeping this to himself. Why share information? No one else does. Paresi's fantasy, of course, was that he and his detectives would find Asad Khalil without help from the FBI.

Walsh assured me, 'Your request for leave will have no negative impact on your career.'

This was getting a little tedious, not to mention silly. I just wanted to get out of there, so I said, 'I appreciate that.'

Walsh reminded me, 'This case, like all our cases, is classified and on a need-to-know basis. And I would ask you not to discuss this case with anyone in this office—or anyone from any other law enforcement or intelligence agency, unless authorised by me personally.'

'Right.'

Walsh reminded me, 'Kate is under the same restrictions as you are.'

I glanced at my watch. 'OK. Are we done?'

Walsh continued, 'I've asked Captain Paresi to arrange for protection for you and for Kate.'

Paresi informed me, 'There will be S.O.G. personnel in your apartment lobby around the clock.'

The Special Operations Group are the people I worked with last week on the Iranian diplomat surveillance. They're part of the Terrorist Task Force, and their speciality is not only surveillance but also protective details. They're good at what they do, but I let Paresi know, 'I do not want surveillance people tailing me. I can take care of myself.'

He said, 'Look, John, we don't want to lose another agent.' He smiled. 'Not even you. We'll all have S.O.G. personnel assigned to us. That's how we may catch this guy.'

On that subject, I said to Walsh, 'I'm still willing to act as bait.'

Walsh replied, 'I think we're all bait now.'

'Good point.' In fact, Walsh had finally come to the unhappy conclusion that he had no clue about how to find Asad Khalil—except for letting Khalil find us. Thus I was authorised to leave my apartment to go on 'necessary errands and such'. In reality, Walsh and Paresi didn't care where I went—if I agreed to not lose my protective detail.

'It's like the spy who came in from the cold,' said Walsh. 'You're fired—officially off the case, but unofficially, you're bait.'

'Got it.'

'Good.' He asked, 'Agreed?'

Better half a loaf and all that. I said, 'Agreed.'

Paresi informed me, 'You'll wear a vest when you go out, and we'll give you a GPS tracking device to wear.' He added, 'You know the drill.'

I nodded.

'You can pick those things up at Tech before you leave.'

That seemed to be the end of that subject, and Walsh said to me, 'We have requested the NYPD ambulance helicopter to pick up Kate tomorrow a.m. and bring her to Bellevue Hospital.'

'Good.'

Walsh glanced at his watch, then asked me, 'Any questions?'

'Yes. It seems to me that Asad Khalil needs to pay back the people who financed his trip here and who have provided him with information and logistical support. Would you agree with that?'

He replied, 'I agree that he has backers. And you can be sure you're not the first person to think of this, Detective. Washington is aware, and Counter-intelligence is investigating.'

'Good.' I asked, 'Is Homeland Security going to raise the alert level?'

He replied, 'I have no idea,' and advised me, 'Check the news tonight.'

Walsh was trying to put me in my place, of course. The Big Picture, if there was one, was none of my business, unless and until Tom Walsh or someone higher up made it my business.

I looked out of the window to where the towers used to be and I said, 'I felt I should mention this.'

'Thank you. You're on the record. Anything further?'

Well, yes, Tom. I want to tell you about Boris, who could be an important resource for us in apprehending Asad Khalil. But you're such a scumbag, Tom, that I'll keep that to myself. Or maybe you already know about Boris and you're keeping it to *your*self. Either way, screw you.

'John?'

'Nothing further.'

'Good.' He stood, I stood, and Captain Paresi stood.

Walsh said, 'Thank you, gentlemen, for your time and your thoughts. I have no doubt that we, working together with our colleagues in the war on terrorism, will bring this man to justice.'

We all shook hands, but as I raced Paresi to the door I heard Walsh say, 'John, I just need a minute more of your time.'

Paresi said to me, 'See me before you leave.'

I returned to Walsh's desk, but did not sit.

He said, 'I have an unofficial complaint forwarded to me through the State Department, regarding an incident that allegedly took place last week in the Taj Mahal Casino in Atlantic City.'

I replied innocently, 'I'm sorry. I used my government credit card to buy gambling tokens.'

'This has to do with someone assaulting an Iranian U.N. diplomat.'

'Let me check my notes and I'll get back to you.'

He looked at me a moment, then said, 'You have demonstrated in the past a tendency towards rough justice. Payback is not what we do here. Neither is personal revenge.'

'Right.'

Walsh walked me to the door and reminded me in an almost offhand way, 'If you find him, and if you kill him—and if you can't prove self-defence—you will face murder charges.'

I didn't say anything.

He also reminded me, 'We don't murder people. Or even punch them in the groin. We try them in Federal court, as common criminals.' Then he got to the heart of the matter. 'I want you to promise me that if you receive any knowledge of Khalil's whereabouts, or if he contacts you, you will inform me immediately. If you can't promise that before you leave here, then I promise you that I'll do everything in my power to get you put in protective custody. Ankle bracelet, house arrest, the whole nine yards.'

I think that was a bluff. He wanted me out and about with back-up people following me. I was his best chance to grab Khalil. On the other hand, I shouldn't call his bluff if I wanted to stay free.

'John?'

I looked him in the eye and said, 'I understand that this is not about me. You can count on me to keep you fully informed, to coordinate with the Task Force, to stay close to my surveillance team, and if I should somehow come into personal contact with the suspect, I will follow all the rules regarding the use of deadly force.' I added, 'I promise.'

That seemed to make him happy. 'Good. That's the right thing.'

We shook on the deal, and I left his office, thinking that what I'd just said was right, and the best thing for everyone. Revenge is not justice.

But by the time I got to the elevators, I was back to where I was when I saw Khalil cut Kate's throat.

It's really scary when you have a moment of temporary sanity.

CHAPTER SIX

I went down to the twenty-sixth floor to gather a few things from my desk, but before I did that, I went to Gabe's desk to look for his copy of the Khalil folder. In a file storage box I found his folder labelled 'Islamic Community Outreach Programme'.

I noticed another box marked 'Haytham—Personal' and opened it. There wasn't much in the box but I saw a book of Arab proverbs in English, with tabbed pages. I opened the book to a marked page and read an underlined sentence: 'Death is afraid of him, because he has the heart of a lion.' I put the book back and saw a framed photograph showing two smiling, attractive women who must have been Gabe's wife and daughter—murdered by Asad Khalil in cold blood. Even after a decade of homicide work, I was still shocked by motiveless murder—sport killing. And they wanted this guy taken alive?

I went to my desk and played my voicemails, listening for a message from Asad Khalil. He had Kate's cellphone and Gabe's cellphone, so he now had all my phone numbers, and I was certain I'd hear from him. I logged on to my computer, checked my emails, and put into a folder ten copies of the NYPD Be On The Lookout photo of Asad Khalil.

People were starting to drift back in from lunch and I didn't want to get involved in conversations with my colleagues, so I locked up and headed to the elevators.

I was supposed to go to Tech to pick up my tracking device and wire, but I forgot. I think I was also supposed to see Captain Paresi, but I was under a lot of stress, which made me forgetful.

Out on the street, I got into my Jeep and headed uptown, towards my apartment on East 72nd Street.

My apartment building is a 1980s high-rise, nondescript but fairly expensive, like most apartments on the Upper East Side. As I pulled into my underground garage I also pulled my Glock. I don't normally arrive at my assigned parking space with a gun in my hand—unless some asshole is pulling into my spot—but things had changed recently.

I checked out my surroundings, parked and walked towards the lobby elevator, my right hand in my pocket with the Glock.

I got out in the lobby and immediately noticed a guy sitting in a chair against the far wall. He was wearing jeans and an orange shirt that had a logo on it—deliveryman. In fact, there were two pizza boxes on the side table. From where he was sitting, he could see the front doors and the garage elevator, and he could also see the door to the fire stairs, the freight elevator and the apartment elevators—but where he was looking was at me.

Alfred, the doorman at the front desk, greeted me, but I ignored him and walked towards the pizza delivery guy, who stood as I approached. I was ninety-nine per cent sure he was a cop.

As I got closer to him—hand in my pocket—I asked, 'On the job?'

He nodded and asked me, 'Detective Corey?'

'That's right.'

He said, 'I'm Detective A. J. Nastasi, Special Operations.' He added, unnecessarily, 'I've been assigned to your protective detail.'

'Right—glad to hear it.' I selected one of the Khalil photos from my folder and asked Detective Nastasi, 'Do you know who this guy is?'

He replied, 'I have that photo. I was told that he's a professional hit man, foreign-born, armed and dangerous, and that he may be disguised.'

'Right. He's also the biggest scumbag on the planet. You got a vest?'

'Never leave home without it.'

'Good. You got real pizzas in those boxes?'

He smiled. 'No.'

This was not turning out to be my lucky day.

We chatted a while about procedures, how many shifts there would be, the layout here, my anticipated comings and goings, and so forth. He advised me, 'I have some written instructions and contact numbers for you.' He handed me a sealed envelope, which I put in my pocket.

I walked over to Alfred, who had remained behind his desk. He greeted me again and asked, 'Is there a problem, Mr Corey?'

'Mrs Corey had a minor accident upstate so she won't be returning here for two or three days.'

'I'm sorry to hear that.'

'She's fine, but we'll both be working at home for a few weeks.'

'Yes, sir.'

'We are not expecting visitors or deliveries. Has anyone been in my apartment? Phone company? Electrician?'

He checked his visitors' log and said, 'I don't show any visitors while you're out.' Alfred is not stupid, and he's been doing this for twenty years, so he's seen it all—cheating spouses, domestic disturbances and God knows what else. Bottom line on Manhattan doormen, they know when to be alert and when to look the other way.

I said to Alfred, 'I have luggage in my Jeep. Please have the porter bring it to my apartment.'

'Yes, sir.'

I also said to him, 'Be certain my Jeep is locked and have the garage attendant give you my keys. I'll get them later.'

'Yes, sir.'

There are a number of small but important things to remember regarding personal security, and I've advised many witnesses, informants and others at risk of these common-sense precautions. Now I needed to take my own advice. I mean, if someone really wants to get you, they'll get you; but you don't have to make it easy for them.

I went to the elevators and rode up to my thirty-fourth floor apartment.

Key in my left hand, Glock in my right, I entered my apartment. I know my own place very well, and within five minutes I'd cleared every room and closet. Fortunately for Asad Khalil, he wasn't there.

I also looked for signs that anyone had been in the apartment, but nothing appeared to be disturbed, though it's hard to tell with Kate's closet and dressing table, which always look like they've been burglarised. My next priority was the bar, where I poured myself a little lunch.

I sat at my living room desk and called the Catskill Regional Medical Center. I enquired about Kate then said, 'Please tell her that Crazy John loves her and that I'll be there to sign her out.'

I hung up and opened the envelope that Detective Nastasi had given me. It was basically an ATTF memo informing me of my status as a protected person, plus phone numbers and email addresses of people to contact regarding my obligation to report my departures and my intended destinations. In addition to the person or persons in my lobby, there would be a surveillance team outside my building, but they wanted at least an hour's notice in order to get a mobile detail in place to follow me. I was to carry my tracking device, wear my wire and vest, and establish wire and cellphone contact with my mobile detail.

My cellphone rang and I saw it was Vince Paresi.

I answered, 'Corey.'

He skipped the pleasantries and said, 'You were supposed to see me before you left the office.'

'Sorry. I'm so stressed—'

'And you were supposed to go to Tech Support.'

'Today?'

'I'll have those items sent over to you.'

'Great. I'm at home.'

'Have you met your S.O. guy in your lobby?'

'Detective Nastasi, Mario's Pizza delivery. You guys all protected?'

He informed me, 'I don't believe we're targets. But, yes, we are taking necessary precautions.' He paused, then continued, 'I am your immediate supervisor,' he reminded me. 'I am responsible for you. Do not screw up.'

I'm the target of a psychotic terrorist and all my boss is worried about is his career. I replied, 'We're a team.'

'Good.' There was a short silence, then he said, 'John, we may ask you to visit some locations. Places that you can walk to, or get to by bus—'

'Yeah? Oh, I get it. Places where Khalil could follow me and where you've already positioned a SWAT team.'

'Something like that.'

I said to him, 'Look, I don't mind being the bait in the trap, but if I'm overprotected, and they assign too many people to the job, you'll spook The Lion.'

He assured me, 'The chances are very good that the surveillance team will spot Khalil before he spots us.'

I thought about that and replied, 'Well, I don't think it will be Asad Khalil himself who will be waiting under the lamppost for me to leave my apartment. It will be people who have prepped his mission here and who will be in communication with Khalil. Then when the opportunity arises, Khalil will show up for his date with John Corey.'

'I know, but we're better and smarter than they are. And the counter-surveillance team will be on the lookout for anyone who seems to be shadowing you.'

When you do these kinds of things—tailing people, setting traps and all that fun stuff—you never know how it's going to go down. But rather than argue with him I said, 'My offer to be red meat stands.'

He moved on to a happier subject. 'The NYPD helicopter to pick up Kate will leave the East 34th Street heliport at seven a.m.'

'Good.'

'Don't hesitate to call me with any questions, thoughts or information that you may recall or receive.'

'I will do that.'

'And be careful.'

'Yourself as well.'

We hung up and I refreshed my beverage. I also retrieved a fully charged paid-minutes cellphone from the kitchen counter. It's important to have one of these if you're a drug dealer, a cheating spouse, a terrorist, or just an honest guy like me with a government phone who doesn't want the taxpayers picking up the charges for his private calls.

I keyed in a number on my prepaid cellphone and a female voice answered, 'Kearns Investigative Service. How may I help you?'

I replied, 'This is John Corey. I'd like to speak to Mr Kearns.'

'He's not in. May I take a message?'

'Yes, I'm Mrs Kearns's boyfriend. I need to speak to him.'

'Uh . . . you are . . .?'

'Mr Kearns's old friend.'

'Oh . . . I thought you . . .' She gathered herself and said crisply, 'Please hold,' and the rousing theme song from *Bonanza* came on, which made me confident I'd called the right people.

Retired NYPD Detective Dick Kearns, my old bud, worked briefly for the Anti-Terrorist Task Force, where he learned, among other things, how the Feds operated. He then left the ATTF and started an agency that performed background investigations on people who had applied for work with the Federal government. More importantly for me, Kearns has built up a large database, and he has good contacts in various government agencies, including the FBI.

Mr Kearns himself came on the line. 'How long has this been going on for?'

'Since you had the midnight-to-eight shift and I had the four-to-midnight shift.'

'How's Kate?'

Rather than get into that now, I replied, 'She's good. How's Mo?'

'Still putting up with my crap.'

The opening remarks concluded, I said, 'Hey, Dick, I need a favour.'

'Hello? John? You're breaking up.'

Everyone's a friggin' comedian. I said, 'This is important and highly confidential. Are you bug-free there? Phone and office?'

'Uh . . . yeah. I mean, I check.'

'OK. Here's the deal. I'm looking for a guy named Boris. Russian born, former KGB, aged about fifty, last known—'

'Hold on. Boris who?'

'I don't know. I'm asking you.'

'Don't you, like, work for the FBI?'

'I'm outsourcing this.'

'The last two times I did this for you, I was sweating getting caught and losing my licence.'

'You're licensed?'

'And my government contract.'

'Last known living in the D.C. area three years ago. Are you writing this down?'

'You're an asshole.'

'After leaving the KGB, this man worked for Libyan Intelligence. Then he defected—actually, escaped from Libya—with the help of the CIA and wound up in Washington, where I met him three years ago—'

'I don't want to touch anything that has to do with the Company.'

'I'm not asking you to. Once Boris got through debriefing, he went into this post-Soviet resettlement programme run by the FBI. So he is registered with a local FBI field office somewhere. I think we have two possible locations: Washington metro area and New York metro. That's where half these Russians wind up. So call your FBI sources.'

'What the hell am I supposed to tell them?'

'Wing it. You're doing a background check for a security clearance. That's what the government pays you to do, Dick.'

'They usually give me the person's last name, John. I need more. I do background checks on people—I don't find people.'

'What happened to the old can-do Dick Kearns?'

'Cut the shit. OK, here's what I can do. I can give the Bureau the name of a Russian guy I'm actually doing an FBI background check on, and I can say this guy seems to be in contact with a Russian guy named Boris who I need to check out. Maybe the FBI'll come up with a Boris who fits the known information.'

'See? Simple.'

'Long shot.'

Dick did not ask me what this was about because obviously he did not want to know. But he did know that I was off the reservation again, so to give him a little motivation, I said, 'Kate is actually not good. She was attacked by an Islamic terrorist. Knife wound to the neck.'

'What? Holy—'

'She's OK. She'll be back home under house protection in a few days.'

'Thank God. So . . . the assailant is still at large?'

'He is.'

'And this guy Boris, who worked for Libyan Intelligence—?'

'It's related.'

'OK. If Boris is in the US, I'll find him for you.'

'I know you will.' I gave him my prepaid cellphone number and said, 'Thanks, Dick.' I hung up and finished my drink.

Dick Kearns had about a fifty-fifty chance of finding Boris. Maybe less.

The odds of Boris still being alive were less than that. But if Dick found him alive, then maybe Boris and I could talk about how to solve our common problem.

THE FOLLOWING MORNING there was a different Special Operations guy in my lobby, Detective Lou Ramos, who had chosen to be a bagel deliveryman—a good choice at 9.30 a.m. and, better yet, he had real bagels and a black coffee for me.

I was supposed to stay in the lobby until my car arrived, so I chatted to Detective Ramos, who seemed a little in awe of me for some reason. He confided, 'If something happens to you on my watch, my ass is O-U-T.'

'How do you think I'd feel? D-E-A-D.'

I sipped my coffee and thought about yesterday afternoon. A package had arrived from Tech Support, and I was now wearing my wire and GPS tracking device. I was also wearing my Kevlar vest under a sports jacket that had been tailored to look good over my bulletproof undershirt. I'm not vain, but it's important to look good when you're wearing a gun and armour, in case your picture gets in the papers.

I had used the remainder of the afternoon to read through the Khalil file. There wasn't much in there that I didn't recall, but seeing the notes and memos about our worldwide search for the elusive Libyan asshole made me realise how hard we'd tried for three years, and how completely this bastard had disappeared. But I knew where Khalil was now, and I knew what he thought he was going to do. I'd then called the hospital around six to check on Kate—resting comfortably—and then spent some time at my computer, sending emails to friends and family informing them of Kate's 'minor accident' and that we'd be going away for a few weeks, and be unable to access email.

I had gone to bed, and for the first time in a long time, I had slept with my gun. Now here I was in the lobby of my apartment building, eating my bagel and waiting for my ride to the hospital.

I was looking forward to seeing Kate, but not happy that she was going to another hospital rather than coming home.

A marked Highway Unit SUV pulled up, and Detective Ramos and I went out to the sidewalk. A uniformed officer, who introduced himself as Ken Jackson, was behind the wheel, and another uniformed officer named Ed Regan opened the rear door for me. I slid in, Officer Regan got in the passenger seat, and off we went.

Bellevue Hospital, where Kate had been taken by helicopter earlier that morning, was on the East River. Bellevue handled what we called sensitive cases—sick and injured prisoners, as well as injured witnesses and victims who were thought to be at further risk, like Kate.

The NYPD had stationed a uniformed cop directly outside the door of Kate's private room. Actually, half the floor is a secured zone, and most of the patients are guests of the FBI, the NYPD, or the Department of Corrections.

Kate had no IVs attached to her and no ventilator, which was a good sight.

I went over to her and said, 'Hi, beautiful.'

We kissed and she said, 'It's good to see you.'

Her voice was a little raspy, but I didn't mention it. I said, 'It's good to see you. You look great.' And she did look well. Her lip and cheek were still a little puffy where Khalil had hit her, but she had good colour. There was only a small dressing over her wound, though I could see black and blue marks around the dressing.

Kate and I chatted awhile. Her voice was weak and I urged her not to talk too much. Then I said, 'I've been put on traumatic leave, so I'll be home while you convalesce.'

'That's not necessary.'

'This leave is not voluntary.' Then I reminded her, 'No business talk until you're home.'

'OK.' Then she said, 'I'd really rather be going home. I feel fine.'

'You'll be home in a few days.'

Kate didn't bring up the subject of Khalil's attack on her, but I was sure it was on her mind. It's best not to repress the trauma, but rather to talk about it, so I said, 'I saw the videotape of the jump.'

She stayed silent, then asked, 'What could you see?'

'You need to see it yourself. And read my report.'

She advised me, 'Don't puff yourself up like you usually do.'

'I can tell you're getting back to your old self.'

She smiled, took my hand, and said, 'I know you saved my life.'

I said, 'We can talk about all that when you're home.'

Kate had noticed my extra bulk, and we discussed some of what was happening in regard to my status—and her status—as a protected person, though I didn't mention that I might be taking some long walks at night.

She thought a moment, then said, 'Has anyone done anything about Chip Wiggins?'

'Actually, yes. Khalil has.'

'Oh . . . my God . . .'

'Right. Last week, in Santa Barbara.' I told her about the murder of Chip Wiggins, and then I told her about the Libyan-American, Farid Mansur, and the cab driver knocked off in Murray Street.

She nodded, and correctly concluded, 'Khalil is in the city.' Her next thought was that I, John Corey, was the man most likely to next see Asad Khalil—assuming I saw it coming. 'John, I hope they have you completely covered. Be careful . . . and don't volunteer to trap Khalil.'

'Of course not.'

It was time to tell her about Gabe, but first I said, 'We're thinking that Khalil may be targeting the Task Force, so there may be others on Khalil's list—like George Foster, or even Paresi or Walsh.'

Kate nodded and said, 'I suppose Khalil does have some knowledge of the command structure of the Task Force.' This brought her to another thought. 'Also Gabe. He's on the Lion Hunter team.'

I took her hand and said, 'Gabe is dead.' I told her what happened to Gabe and his wife and daughter. I also filled her in about the murder of the limo driver near Gabe's house.

She stared up at the ceiling with tears in her eyes. Finally, she said, 'What did those poor women do to . . . die like that?'

She seemed tired and her voice was getting weaker, so I said, 'I'm going to let you rest.'

She looked at me and said, 'Get me out of here tomorrow.'

'I'll try.'

We kissed again and I went to the nurses' station and told the duty nurse that Mrs Corey wanted to be discharged the next day. The nurse consulted her chart and informed me that Mrs Corey first needed to be medically evaluated. Also, there was a flag on her discharge.

'Meaning?'

'Meaning it is not purely a medical decision. We need to notify certain people before she can be discharged.'

Meaning that Walsh had decided to keep Special Agent Kate Mayfield in Bellevue, away from her husband whom she loved dearly, but who the FBI needed to borrow for a special assignment, namely, live bait.

The people at 26 Fed and in Washington sometimes impressed me with their thinking. I say that whenever they think like I do.

BACK IN MY APARTMENT, I sat in front of my computer writing my incident report—being careful not to embellish the facts—until cocktail hour. I had time for a small one before I was picked up by my chauffeur and shotgun rider for my evening hospital visit. As I was trying to decide if I wanted vodka (odourless) or Scotch (my usual), my prepaid cellphone rang. Not many people had the number. I picked up the phone and answered, 'Corey.'

Dick Kearns's voice said, 'May I speak to the man of the house?'

Dick obviously had good news. I replied, 'Yes, ma'am. I'll get him.'

He laughed and said, 'Hey, John, I think I found him.'

'Alive?'

'Yeah . . . I guess. The guy I got this from in the New York field office didn't say he was dead. You ready to copy?'

I had a pad and pencil on the table and said, 'Shoot.'

'OK. Boris Korsakov.' He spelled it out for me and said, 'He fits your description of age and former KGB employment. The FBI guy I spoke to said that Boris was here under the post-Soviet resettlement programme. I've emailed you the photo the FBI emailed me.'

'Hold on.' I retrieved Dick's email, and staring back at me on the screen was Boris. My Boris. 'That's him, Dick. You're a genius.'

'I am a total bullshit artist. I had this FBI guy in the palm of my hand.'

Dick went on a bit, and while I listened politely and patiently I kept staring at the photo of Boris. This was a tough-looking hombre. Could Asad Khalil have gotten the upper hand on this guy? I wouldn't have thought so three years ago when I'd met Boris, but . . .

'He lives at 12-355 Brighton 12th Street, Brighton Beach—along with half the Russians in New York. Apartment 16A.' Dick added, 'He's been there almost three years.'

'OK.' Boris had picked a neighbourhood where ex-KGB guys got together over a bottle of vodka and reminisced about the good old days when they were young and hated.

'I couldn't get Boris's cell or home phone from the FBI, but I did get his business phone. And here's the part that could be a little fun for you, so I saved it for last. Boris owns and operates a Russian nightclub in Brighton Beach. It's called Svetlana. It's right on the boardwalk at Brighton 3rd Street.'

'OK . . . and this place is owned by Boris?'

'Well, with these Ruskies, who knows who the silent partners could be? It's all Russian Mafia. Right? Maybe Boris is the front guy.'

'Maybe. But maybe the CIA gave him a loan.'

'Yeah? Hey, let me know how this turns out.'

'OK. I owe you big time for this.'

THE HIGH-SECURITY FLOOR at Bellevue is the worst of two bad worlds—a hospital run like a prison. My name was on the authorised visitor list, and my Fed creds got me through the security checkpoint with only minor hassles. On the positive side, Asad Khalil was not getting onto this floor.

Actually, Asad Khalil should have no idea that Mrs Corey was alive, well, and here. I wondered, though, if his friends in New York were checking the public records for Kate's death. I made a mental note to tell Walsh to get a phony death certificate issued and recorded. Sitting now beside Kate's bed, I let her know that she needed to stay in the hospital for a while, but she'd already discovered that, and she wasn't happy about it.

I noticed that she had the stuffed lion hanging by its neck from the window-blind cord, so I asked her, 'Have you had your mental evaluation yet?'

She smiled. 'I'm trying to get into the nut ward so we can be together.'

We chatted and then Kate said, 'I feel so helpless here . . . so useless.'

I tried to make her feel better by saying, 'You may be the only person on this planet who fought back against Khalil and lived to tell about it.'

She forced a smile, then asked, 'Why didn't he . . . try to kill you, too?'

Kate was obviously starting to think about all this. I said, 'He had his hands full with you.'

She looked at me. 'I think he wanted you to see me die.'

To get her off unpleasant subjects, and to put her mind at ease, I told her about how I was surrounded by Special Operations teams wherever I went, and that our apartment building was under tight security.

An orderly came by and dropped off a dinner menu. Kate checked off some items, then passed the menu to me and suggested, 'Get something.'

I saw that it was fusion cooking—prison and hospital—and decided to pass on the dinner. We watched a little TV and talked until her meal came.

I would have stayed with Kate until visiting hours were over, but she said she was tired so I kissed her goodbye and said, 'Try to get some rest.'

'What else can I do here?'

'Think about what else Khalil might be up to.'

'I'm thinking.' She asked me, 'Where are you going now?'

'The only place I'm allowed to go. Home.'

'Good.' She smiled and said, 'Don't go out clubbing.'

Funny you should say that.

'Be careful, John.' She squeezed my hand and said, 'I love you.'

'Me too. See you tomorrow morning.'

I left her room and chatted with Kate's NYPD guard, a lady named Mindy who assured me that she was aware that Kate's assailant was not a common, dumb criminal, and that not even Conan the Barbarian could get past Mindy Jacobs.

I said good night and took the elevator down to the lobby, where I met my escorts—still Officers Ken Jackson and Ed Regan. Within fifteen minutes, I was back at my apartment building.

There was a custodian in the lobby who looked very much like Detective Louis Ramos, the bagel deliveryman. I stopped and chatted with Ramos a moment, then went to the desk where Alfred was reading a newspaper.

He put down his newspaper and enquired, 'How is Mrs Corey?'

'Much better, thank you,' I said. 'I forgot to pick up my car keys.'

'I have them right here.' He opened a drawer and produced my keys.

I told him, 'I need to get some things out of storage, so if you don't mind, I'll borrow the key for the freight elevator.'

'Yes, sir.' He retrieved the key to the freight elevator and put it on the desk. I picked up the keys and walked to the apartment elevators.

The other way out of here without going through the lobby was the fire stairs, but each staircase had surveillance cameras, and the monitor was sitting on the doorman's desk. The freight elevator was not monitored, and was sort of an express to the underground garage.

I rode up to my apartment, where I'd already picked out my Russian nightclub outfit.

I HAD LAID OUT a dark grey suit and grey tie that I usually wear for weddings and funerals, plus a silk shirt and diamond cufflinks. My shoes were Italian Gravatis and to complete my outfit, I slipped into my Kevlar vest, though this time I forgot my wire and tracking device. I finished dressing, not forgetting my Glock, and checked myself out in the mirror. Russian Mafia? Italian Mafia? Irish cop dressed funny?

I put one of the photos of Asad Khalil in my jacket pocket, left my apartment, and walked to the freight elevator, located in a far corner of the thirty-fourth floor. I used the key to summon the elevator. The doors opened, and I got into the big, padded car and pushed the button for the garage level.

I stepped out of the elevator into the underground garage. So far so good. Or was I now trapped in the garage whose entrance would be under surveillance by the Special Operations team on the street? Obviously, I couldn't walk up the parking ramp or drive my green Jeep out onto 72nd Street without getting busted.

I walked over to the parking attendant's window, and there was an old gent in the small office who I didn't recognise. He was watching TV—a Mets game—and I said, 'Excuse me. I need a ride.'

He looked away from the TV and asked, 'What's your number?'

'No,' I explained, 'I don't need my car. I need a ride.'

'I think you got the wrong place, Bub.'

'I'll give you fifty bucks to take me down to 68th and Lex.' I explained, 'I have a proctologist appointment.'

He looked at me and asked, 'Why don't you walk?'

'Hemorrhoids. Come on—what's your name?'

'People call me Gomp.'

'OK, Gomp. Sixty bucks.'

'I don't have a car.'

'You have two hundred cars. Pick one.' I assured him, 'You can listen to the game on the radio.'

Gomp looked me over, silk shirt and all, and decided I was a man to be trusted—or Mafia—and he said, 'OK. But we gotta move fast.'

I threw three twenties on the counter, and he snatched them up, then picked a key off the board, saying, 'This guy ain't used his car in two months. Needs a run.'

Within a few minutes I was in the passenger seat of a late-model Lexus sedan, and Gomp was driving up the ramp. He confessed, 'I do this for the old people once in a while—hey, whaddaya doin'?'

'Tying my shoes.'

'Oh . . .'

I stayed below the dashboard and felt the car turn right onto 72nd Street. I waited until we stopped at the light on Third Avenue before sitting up. I looked in the sideview mirror and didn't see any of the usual models that the Task Force used.

Gomp asked me, 'You live in the building?'

'No.' I volunteered, 'I live on East 84th.' I put out my hand and said, 'Tom Walsh.'

Gomp took my hand and said, 'Good to meet you, Tom.'

'My friends call me Tight-ass.'

'Huh?'

God, I hope the FBI interviews this guy tonight.

The light changed, and he continued on 72nd, while tuning in to the Mets game. He asked me, 'Are you Mets or Yankees?'

'Mets,' I lied.

Gomp was an old New York icon, accent and all, and I realised I was missing the old days when life was simpler and stupider.

When we reached the corner of Lexington and 68th Street, I said, 'I'll get out here.'

He pulled over. 'Anytime you need a ride, Tom, look for me in the garage.'

'Thanks. Maybe tomorrow. Urologist.'

I got out of the car and descended the stairs to the Lexington Avenue subway entrance. I consulted the transit map, saw that the B train went to Brighton Beach, and found my platform.

The train came, and I got on, then got off, then got on again as the doors closed. I saw this in a movie once.

To make a long subway ride short, less than an hour after I'd boarded the train, I was travelling on an elevated section of the line, high above the wilds of Brooklyn. I got off at the Ocean Parkway stop and descended the stairs onto Brighton Beach Avenue, which ran under the elevated tracks. After all this escape and evasion, Boris had damned well better be alive and at his nightclub.

I haven't been to Brighton Beach in maybe fifteen years, and then only a few times, with a Russian-American cop named Ivan. Of all the interesting ethnic enclaves in New York, this is one of the most interesting.

I walked east along the avenue and checked it out. Lots of cars, lots of people, and lots of life on the street. A guy was selling Russian caviar from a table on the sidewalk for ten bucks an ounce. Great price. No overheads and no middle man. No refrigeration either.

I got to Brighton 4th Street and headed south towards the ocean. The people seemed well fed. No famine here. As for how they were dressed . . . well, it was interesting. Everything from expensive suits to old ladies who'd brought their clothes with them from the Motherland. Despite the balmy weather, a few guys wore fur hats.

As I approached Brightwater Court, I could see the lighted entrance to Svetlana in a huge old brick building that ran a few hundred feet back to the boardwalk. I continued past the building and onto the boardwalk, where I saw, as I'd expected, a boardwalk entrance to Svetlana. There was a cloud of grey smoke outside the nightclub, and if I looked through the smoke I could see tables and chairs, and lots of men and women puffing on cigarettes. It's good to get out into this healthy salt air.

I went over to the railing and looked out at the beach and the Atlantic Ocean. It was a little after 10 p.m., but there were still people on the beach, walking or sitting in groups, and I'm certain drinking some of the clear stuff from Mother Russia. The night, too, was clear and starry, and a half-moon was rising in the east.

I turned and looked up and down the long boardwalk. There were hundreds of people promenading on this warm evening: parents pushing strollers, families walking and talking, groups of young men and women engaged in pre-mating rituals. Indeed, it was a good world, filled with good people, doing good things. But there were also the bad guys, who I dealt with, and who were more into death than life.

I slipped off my wedding band—not so I could pass as single to the babes at the bar, but because in this business you don't give or advertise any personal information—and took a last look around to be certain I was alone. Then I walked across the boardwalk towards the red neon sign that said SVETLANA.

How can I describe the place? Well, it was an interesting blend of old-Russia opulence and Vegas nightclub, designed perhaps by someone who had watched *Dr Zhivago* too many times. There was a big horseshoe-shaped bar in the rear with a partial view of the ocean and a better view of the patrons. I made my way through the cocktail tables and squeezed myself in at the bar between a beefy guy in an iridescent suit and a bleached blonde lady who was wearing her daughter's cocktail dress.

I don't think I look particularly Russian, but the bartender said something to me in Russian. I know about six Russian words, and I used two of them: 'Stolichnaya, *pozhaluista*.' He moved off and I looked around the cocktail lounge. Aside from the slick suits, there were a lot of guys with open shirts and multiple gold chains around their necks, and a lot of women who had more rings than fingers. The predominant language being spoken seemed to be Russian. My Stoli came and I used my third Russian word: '*Spasibo*.'

I could see the huge restaurant section through an etched glass wall, and nearly every table was filled. Boris was doing OK for himself. At the far end of the restaurant I could see a big stage where a four-piece band was playing. The dance floor was crowded with couples, young and old, plus a lot of pre-teen girls dancing with each other, and old ladies out on the floor giving their hip replacements a workout. I should say, too, for the sake of accurate reporting, and because I am trained to observe people, that there were a fair number of hot babes in the joint.

The lady next to me, who might have been a hot Russian babe fifteen years ago, seemed interested in the new boy. I could smell her lilac cologne heating up. She said to me, in a thick accent, 'You are not Roosian.'

'What was your first clue?'

'Your Roosian is terrible.'

Your English ain't so hot either, sweetheart. 'Come here often?'

'Yes, of course.' She then gave me the correct pronunciation of '*spasibo*,' '*pozhaluista*,' and 'Stolichnaya,' and made me repeat after her.

Apparently, I wasn't getting it, and she suggested, 'Perhaps another voodka would help you.'

We both got a chuckle out of that, and we introduced ourselves. Her name was Veronika—with a k—and she was originally from Kansas. No, Kursk. I introduced myself as Tom Walsh.

I bought us another round. She was drinking cognac, which I recalled the Ruskies loved—at twenty bucks a pop, what's not to love? And I couldn't even put this on my expense account.

Anyway, recalling Nietzsche's famous dictum—the most common form of human stupidity is forgetting what one is trying to do—I said to her, 'I need to see someone in the restaurant, but maybe I'll see you later.'

Veronika pouted and said, 'Why don't you dance with me?'

'I'd love to. Don't go away.' I told the bartender, 'Give this lady another cognac when she's ready, and put it on my tab.'

Veronika raised her glass and said to me, '*Spasibo*.'

The tab came, and I paid cash, then made my way through the cocktail lounge and into the restaurant. It really smelled good in here and my empty stomach rumbled.

I found the maître d's stand and approached a gentleman in a black suit. He regarded me for a moment, decided I was a foreigner, and addressed me in English, asking, 'How may I help you?'

I replied, 'I'm here to see Mr Korsakov.'

He seemed a bit surprised, and asked, 'Is he expecting you?'

So, Boris was alive and here, and I replied, 'I'm an old friend.' I gave him my card, and he stared at it. I assumed he didn't like what he was reading—Anti-Terrorist Task Force and all that—so I said, 'This is not official business. Please take that to Mr Korsakov and I will wait here.'

He hesitated, then made his way towards the back of the restaurant, where he disappeared through a red curtain.

I looked around the cavernous restaurant. The tables were covered with gold cloths on which sat vodka bottles, champagne buckets, and tiered trays filled with mounds of food. The diners were doing a hell of a job getting that food where it belonged.

The wall behind the stage where the band was playing rose up about twenty feet—two storeys—and I noticed now that in the centre of the wall near the ceiling was a big mirror that reflected the crystal chandeliers. This, I was certain, was actually a two-way mirror from which someone could observe the entire restaurant below. Maybe that was Boris's office, so I waved.

Three female singers had taken the stage. They were all tall, blonde and pretty, of course, and because my attention was focused on them, I didn't see the maître d' approaching. With him was a crew-cut blond guy wearing a boxy suit that barely fitted over a weight lifter's body.

The maître d' said to me, 'This is Viktor'—with a k?—'and he will take you to Mr Korsakov.'

I followed Viktor through the crowded restaurant. He parted the red curtain, and I found myself in a hallway that led to a locked steel door, which he opened with a key. We entered a small plain room that had two chairs, another steel door on the opposite wall and an elevator. The only other item of note was a security camera on the ceiling that swivelled 360 degrees.

Viktor used another key to open the elevator doors and he motioned me in. As we rode up, I said to him, 'So, are you the pastry chef?'

He kept staring straight ahead, but he did smile. A little humour goes a long way in bridging the species gap. Plus, he understood English.

The elevator doors opened into an anteroom similar to the one below, including another security camera, but this room had a second steel door—with a fisheye peephole. Viktor pushed a button, and a few seconds later I heard a bolt slide and the door opened.

Standing in the doorway was Boris, who said to me, 'It is so good to see you alive.'

'You too.'

CHAPTER SEVEN

Boris motioned me to an overstuffed armchair, and he sat in a similar chair opposite me. He was wearing a black European-cut suit and a silk shirt, open at the collar. He looked like he was still in decent shape, but not as lean or hard as I remembered him.

Viktor remained in the room, and he took a drink order from the boss—a bottle of chilled vodka.

Boris poured into two crystal glasses, raised his glass and said, 'Health.' His English was nearly perfect, and I'm sure he'd learned a lot more words since I'd last seen him—like 'profit and loss statement', 'working capital' and so forth.

I replied, '*Nazdorov'e*,' which I think means 'health'—or does it mean 'I love you'? Anyway, the vodka travelled well.

Boris then said something to Viktor, who walked to the door, but did not open it until he had looked through the peephole. Maybe this was normal precaution for a Russian nightclub. Or paranoia. Anyhow, Viktor left and Boris bolted the door.

I stood and looked out of the two-way mirror that took up half the wall and had a sweeping view of the restaurant below, and also the bar beyond the glass wall. Veronika was still there. On the rear wall of the restaurant above the maître d's stand were high windows that offered glimpses of the beach and the ocean. Not bad, Boris. Beats the hell out of Libya.

Boris asked me, 'Were you enjoying the show?'

Obviously, he'd seen me waiting at the maître d's stand.

I replied, 'You put on a good one.'

'Thank you.'

I turned and looked round the big room. The place was filled with a hodgepodge of Russian stuff like icons, a porcelain stove, a silver samovar, and lots of Russian *tchotchkes*. 'You've done well,' I said.

He replied, 'It is a lot of work and worry. I have many government inspectors coming here—fire, health, alcohol—and I have to deal with cheating vendors, staff who steal—'

'Kill them.'

He smiled and replied, 'Yes, sometimes I miss my old job in Russia.'

'The pay sucked.'

'But the power was intoxicating.'

'I'm sure.' I asked him, 'Do you miss your old job in Libya?'

He shook his head. 'Not at all.'

I didn't care what Boris had done for a living in the Soviet Union. But it bothered me that he'd sold himself to a rogue nation and trained a man like Khalil. I'm sure he regretted it, but the damage was done.

Since I was standing anyway, I took the opportunity to walk around the room and check out the goods. Boris was happy to tell me about the icons, the lacquered boxes, the porcelains and all his other treasures.

He said to me, 'These are all antiques and quite valuable.'

'Which is why you have such good security,' I suggested.

'Yes, that's right.' He saw me looking at him, so he added, 'Of course, the most valuable thing here is me.' He smiled, then explained, 'In this business, one can make enemies.'

'As in your last business,' I reminded him.

'And yours as well, Mr Corey.'

I suggested, 'Maybe we should both look for another business.'

He laughed and I continued my walk around the room. On one wall was an old Soviet poster showing a caricature of Uncle Sam holding a money bag in one hand and an atomic bomb in the other. His feet were planted astride a globe of the world, and under his boots were the necks of poor native people from around the world. The Soviet Union—CCCP—was surrounded by American missiles, all pointing towards the Motherland.

The iconography was perhaps a bit subtle for me, but I think I got it.

'Some of my American friends still find that poster offensive.'

'Can't imagine why.'

He reminded me, 'The Cold War is over. You won. Those posters are expensive. That one cost me 2,000 dollars.'

I pointed out, 'Not a lot of money for a successful entrepreneur.'

He agreed, 'Yes, I am now a capitalist pig with a money bag in my hand. Fate is strange.' He lit a cigarette and offered me one, which I declined. He asked, 'How did you find me?'

'Boris, I work for the FBI.'

'Yes, of course, but my friends in Langley assured me that all information about me is classified.'

I replied, 'This may come as a shock to you, but the CIA lies.'

We both got a smile out of that one.

Then he got serious again and said, 'And any information about me is on a need-to-know basis. So, what is your "need to know", Mr Corey?'

I replied, 'Please call me John.' I changed the subject and my tactics and said, 'Hey, I'm drinking on an empty stomach.'

He hesitated, then replied, 'Of course. I have forgotten my manners.'

'No, I should have called.' I suggested, 'Don't go out of your way. Maybe call for a pizza.'

He went to the phone on a side table and assured me, 'No trouble. In fact, you may have noticed this is a restaurant.'

'Right.' Boris had a little sarcastic streak, which shows intelligence and good mental health, as I have to explain often to my wife.

Boris spoke on the phone intercom in Russian, and I heard the word *zakuskie*, which I knew from my cop pal Ivan means appetisers. He hung up and said to me, 'Why don't you sit?'

So I sat, and we both relaxed a bit, sipping vodka and enjoying the moment before I got down to what he knew was not going to be pleasant.

Boris said, 'I have forgotten to ask you: how is that lovely lady you were with—Kate. Correct?'

In this business, as I said, you never reveal personal information, so I replied, 'I still see her at work, and she's well.'

'Good. I enjoyed her company. Please give her my regards.'

'I will.' It was time, I thought, to move the ball down the field, so I asked him, 'Have you heard from your friends in Langley recently?'

He asked me, 'Are you now here on official business?'

'I am.'

'Then I should ask you to leave, and I should call my attorney.'

'You can do that anytime you want. This isn't the Soviet Union.'

He ignored that and said, 'Tell me why I should speak to you.'

'Because it's your civic duty to assist in the investigation of a crime.'

'What crime?'

'Murder.'

He enquired, 'What murder?'

'Well, maybe yours. Asad Khalil is back.'

That called for a drink, and he poured himself one.

I said to him, 'Are you surprised?'

'Not at all.'

A few musical notes sounded—Tchaikovsky? Boris went to the door, and looked through the peephole. He opened the door, and a waiter entered pushing a cart heaped with food, with Viktor bringing up the rear.

Viktor closed and bolted the door, and Boris seemed to forget my bad news as he busied himself with directing the waiter to set the table with linens, silverware and crystal.

Boris said to me, 'Sit. Here.'

I sat, and Boris followed the waiter and Viktor to the door and bolted it after them, then sat opposite me.

He asked me, 'Do you enjoy Russian food?'

'Who doesn't?'

'Here,' he said, 'this is smoked blackfish, this is pickled herring and this is smoked eel.' He named everything for me, concluding with 'the pièce de résistance—pigs-in-a-blanket', which were actually chunks of sausage—*kolbasa*—wrapped in some kind of fried dumpling dough. I put a few of them on my plate along with some other things that looked safe, and we dug into the chow.

As we dined, Boris asked me, 'How do you know he is back?'

I replied, 'He's killed some people.'

'Who?'

'I'm not at liberty to tell you, but I will say he completed his mission from last time.'

Boris stopped eating, then said, 'I want you to know that I did not train him for a specific mission. I simply trained him to operate in the West.'

'And to kill.'

He hesitated, then said, 'Well . . . yes, to kill. But if the CIA believed I knew that Khalil was going to kill American pilots, would they have got me out of Libya? Would they have let me live?'

That was a good question, and I had no good answer. What I did know was that the CIA and Boris Korsakov had struck a devil's deal: they saved his life, and he spilled his guts. There may have been more to the deal, but neither Boris nor the CIA was going to tell John Corey what it was.

'I assume the CIA briefed you on what Khalil did three years ago.'

'Not fully.' He added, 'I had no need to know.'

'But you told me then you knew he murdered American pilots.'

'Yes . . . they did tell me that.'

'Right.' I wasn't trying to get at any truth with these questions—I just wanted to put him on the defensive, which I'd done, so I said, 'All right. Let's move on.' I pushed my food aside and said, 'Khalil has been in this country for maybe a week. He killed the last pilot who had been on the Libyan raid—a nice man, named Chip—then he killed a few more people. So, yeah, we know he's here. In fact, right here in the city.'

Boris stopped chewing.

I continued, 'It has occurred to me that Khalil has some scores to settle with you. If I'm wrong, tell me, and I will get up and leave.'

Boris poured me some mineral water.

So I went on, 'Quite frankly, I didn't expect to see you alive.'

He nodded, then said to me, 'I'm surprised you are alive.'

'You're lucky I'm alive. Look, I know we're both on his must-kill list, so we need to talk.'

Boris nodded. 'And perhaps your friend Kate is also in danger.'

'Perhaps. But to give you more information than you need to know, she is now in a location that is more secure than yours.' I gave him the happy news. 'So I think it's just you and me left.'

He took that well and joked, 'You can sleep on this couch tonight.'

I said, 'You should also stay here. Your wife will understand.'

'I assure you, she will not.' He thought a moment, then said, 'In fact, she will be going to Moscow tomorrow.'

'Not a bad idea.'

Boris poured himself a cognac and poured one for me, then said, 'I assume you have a better plan than hiding.'

'Actually, I do. My plan is to use you as bait to trap Khalil.'

He didn't respond. Then he asked me, 'Do you have any actual information that he knows where I am?'

I replied, 'We don't. But why don't we assume he does know? He had three years to find you. Plus he has friends in America.'

Boris nodded, then smiled and informed me, 'I have actually been mentioned in some publications that write about food, or about the Russian immigrant community.'

'I hope they didn't use your photo, Boris.'

He shrugged. 'A few times. It is part of my business. And to be truthful, I didn't mind the publicity.'

'And that's your real name?'

'It is. The CIA urged me to change my name, but it is all I have from my past.'

'Right. So let's assume that Khalil knows you are the proprietor of Svetlana, and that you have a wife and an apartment on Brighton 12th Street. You can run, you can hide, but you can also sit here and wait for him, and I'll have people waiting with you.'

'Well, I will think about that. In the meantime, you and your organisation should think about some other way to capture him—or kill him.'

I pointed out, 'I think you know him better than the Feds.'

He thought a moment, then said, 'He will be difficult to find. But he will find you.'

'Boris, I know that. The question is, How do I find him?'

Boris sat back in his chair and lit another cigarette. He stared at a point in space and said, almost to himself: 'The Soviet Union, for all its faults, never underestimated the Americans. Khalil, on the other hand, is from a culture that underestimates the West, and especially the Americans. This perhaps is his weakness. They call him The Lion because of his courage, his stealth, his speed, and his ability to sense danger. But in this last regard, he often misses the signs of danger because of his belief that he is strong—physically, mentally and morally—and that his enemies are weak, stupid and corrupt.' He looked at me and said, 'I warned him once about this, but I did not bother to warn him again.'

He thought a moment, then continued, 'Khalil had a mentor, an old man called Malik, who was somewhat of a mystic. Malik convinced Khalil that he was blessed—that he had special powers, a sixth sense for danger, for knowing when his prey was close. Nonsense, of course, but Khalil believed it, and therefore he does stupid things. He seems to get away with his stupidity, but perhaps his luck is running out.'

Not so you'd notice, but I said, 'Maybe.'

Boris took a drag on his cigarette and said, 'He was an excellent learner—very quick, very intelligent. And also very motivated—but what motivated him was hate.' He looked at me. 'Hate clouds the judgment. He will want to attack you in a personal way—the way a lion attacks, with his teeth and his claws. He needs to taste your blood. And like a cat playing with a mouse, he often plays with his victim before killing him. This is important to him. So if you survive the initial assault, you may have a chance to respond. This is all I can tell you that may be of help.'

Well, aside from Malik the mystic, there wasn't too much there that I didn't already know. But it was good to have my own thoughts confirmed. I said, 'So we should bend over and kiss our asses goodbye?'

Smiling, he complimented me by saying, 'I feel that you can handle the situation, if it should arise.' He added, 'And so can I.'

Maybe I shouldn't have cancelled my gym membership. I returned to my previous suggestion. 'Another way to kill a lion is to leave bait in a trap.'

He'd apparently given some thought to my suggestion. 'Yes. If you want the lion alive, you put a live goat in a cage, and when the lion enters the cage, the door closes. The lion is trapped, but the goat gets eaten. Or if you want the lion dead, the goat is tethered to a tree, and as the lion is killing him, the hunter shoots. In either case, the goat is dead.'

'Good point. But we will ensure your safety,' I assured him.

He wasn't so sure of that. 'You try it first.'

'OK. I'll let you know how I make out.'

'Yes, if you can.' He did say, however, 'It is an interesting idea, and it may be the only way you will capture or kill him. But be advised, John, even as you are setting a trap for him, he may be doing the same for you.'

'Right. I'll remember that. And if you don't want to be actual bait, we can still work out some sort of protective detail for you.'

He had another thought. 'You know, I am very safe here, and I have no plans to leave . . . until Khalil is killed, captured, or flees . . . so I am not sure I need your protection. In fact, I pay very good money for my own protection.'

There was a subtext here, and I thought that Boris was realising he did not want the NYPD or the FBI hanging around Svetlana for a variety of reasons, some legitimate, and some maybe not so. It occurred to me, too, that Boris was coming to some of the same conclusions that I had come to—he wanted to kill Asad Khalil without police or FBI interference. And his reasons went beyond my simple reasons of revenge and permanent peace of mind. Boris, I suspected, wanted Asad Khalil dead because what

Khalil knew about Boris did not comport with what Boris had told the CIA three years ago. Boris would not be the first defector to be shipped back to the old country.

I said, 'Come on, Boris. I know what you're thinking. If anyone can capture—or kill—Asad Khalil, it's you. But don't get overconfident. Khalil hasn't spent three years running a nightclub and drinking vodka.'

This annoyed him, as I knew it would, and he leaned towards me and said, 'I have no fear of this man. I taught him all he knows, and it would be a good thing if I was able to teach him one last lesson.'

I said, 'Well, I'll pass on your statement that you don't want protection. It is your right to decline police protection, and you certainly don't have to volunteer to act as bait. But if you should somehow capture him alive, call me first.'

'If you wish.'

Boris was getting less talkative and it was time for me to leave. The next thing I had to do was report this meeting to Walsh and Paresi. I could get away with what I'd done so far—cops and agents often take a shot at something without telling the boss. But if you don't make a quick and full report of something like this, you are in big trouble.

On the other hand . . . I wasn't even supposed to be here. I mean, I think Walsh was pretty clear about my limited duties. And Boris and I seemed to be on the same page with this. Khalil did not need to be apprehended—he needed to be killed.

Boris was deep in thought. He looked at me and said, 'Give me a week. Give yourself a week. One of us, I think, will resolve this problem in a way that is best for us.'

I replied, of course: 'This is not just about us. It is about the law, and justice and national security.'

Again, he shook his head and said, 'No. It is about us.'

I didn't want to continue on this subject, so I changed it. 'Here's my card.' I stood and said, 'I need your phone numbers.'

He took his card and a pen from his inside pocket, wrote on the card, and handed it to me, saying, 'Please keep me informed.'

I took Khalil's photograph from my pocket, handed it to him, and suggested, 'Copy it and give it to your people.'

'Yes, thank you.'

I moved towards the door and said to him, 'I can let myself out.'

'I am afraid not.' He stood, went to his phone, hit the intercom and said something in Russian.

A short burst of Tchaikovsky filled the room, and Boris walked to the door, looked through the peephole, then unbolted the door and opened it. Viktor stood aside for me, but as I walked to the door I said to Boris, 'If you look through a peephole, you can get a serious eye and brain injury if there's a gun muzzle looking back at you.'

He seemed annoyed at my critique of his security procedures and said, 'Thank you, Detective.'

'And thank you for your time and your hospitality.'

The taxi from Brighton Beach let me off in my underground parking garage, and also left me forty bucks poorer—cheap for life insurance. I took the freight elevator up to my apartment; no one from the surveillance team seemed to have noticed my absence.

WEDNESDAY MORNING and I was getting ready to visit Kate at Bellevue. My cellphone rang and it was Paresi. I answered, 'Corey.'

Captain Paresi enquired, 'What did you do last night after you got back from the hospital? The surveillance guy in your lobby, Ramos, reported that he called your apartment phone and your cellphone and also had the doorman buzz your intercom, but you didn't answer.'

Uh-oh. Time to come clean. I replied, 'I was dead to the world by ten p.m. What did Ramos want?'

Paresi replied, 'Nothing. Just a commo check and a situation report.'

Bottom line here, Paresi had no evidence that I'd actually gone out, so I got a little huffy and said, 'Captain, I'm a cop, not some Mafia informant who needs watching twenty-four, seven.'

There was a silence, then Paresi said, 'All right. So how is Kate?'

'Well enough to get out of the hospital, but Walsh is keeping her there. By the way, you need to have a death certificate issued and recorded in Sullivan County ASAP, and have the Catskill Medical Center alter their records accordingly.'

'All right. Will do. Have you received or recalled anything I should know about?'

This was basically my last chance to come clean about Boris, and I'd weighed the pros and cons of reporting my contact with him. Boris had asked me for a week of no police or FBI interference—a week to see if

Khalil attempted to whack him on his protected turf. Boris's purpose, of course, was to silence Asad Khalil for ever, and his best interests might coincide with mine. On the other hand, Boris might call me and say he'd changed his mind and please send the police to protect him. Or for all I knew, Boris, the devious KGB man, might now be hightailing it to Moscow with his wife. This was a tough call.

'Hello? John?'

'I can't think of anything.' I changed the subject and asked him, 'Has Special Operations seen anything unusual at the bad guy safe houses?'

'No. We're checking with rental agents about corporate rentals that they may have thought were suspicious—but that's very time-consuming and a very long shot.'

I said, 'I had a thought that if I was Khalil's pals in New York, I'd have rented a place on my street and I'd be keeping an eye on my front door from a monitor located in that office or apartment. You should get some manpower on that.'

'That's a thought . . . You should stay off your balcony,' he advised me.

'I was going to invite you over for drinks on it.'

Paresi sometimes appreciated my dark humour, but this was not one of those times. He said, 'I have to tell you, we're spread pretty thin, but I'll see if I can get the FBI field office and the NYPD to give us some people.'

Recalling my unproductive surveillance of the Iranian diplomat, I suggested, 'Pull people off the U.N. assignments. This case is high priority.'

'I know. But you have no idea how many tips, threats and leads we've gotten in the last few months that we have to follow up on.'

I thought about that and said, 'It's possible these are planned distractions. Any hits from the Communication Analysis Unit on Kate's cellphone or Gabe's cellphone?'

He replied, 'We've discontinued service on both, but CAU is watching to see if anyone turns them on to use their phone directories.'

'OK. I assume you've cancelled all leave and that everyone is putting in extra hours.'

'Goes without saying. Let me assure you that despite personnel shortages, the Task Force, the FBI and the NYPD are on top of this. And let me remind you, you are not part of the investigation. You are on leave.'

Well, I had been wavering about telling him about Boris, but I wasn't wavering anymore. Hey, I'm not part of the investigation.

I said, 'My car and driver are waiting. Anything else?'

'Yes, the reason I called. You're going trawling tonight.'

That was exciting news. 'Good. What's the plan?'

He began, 'At about ten p.m., you will leave your apartment and go on foot along 72nd Street and enter Central Park—'

'I could get mugged.'

He ignored that. 'We're using the park because we all know it and we've all trained there for surveillance and counter-surveillance. You'll meet a Special Operations Group supervisor in your lobby at ten, and he will give you your route and your various destinations in the park. Then you will establish communication with the surveillance teams outside your building, and off you go.'

'Sounds like a plan.' Then I reminded him, 'I don't want a parade behind me or a brass band in front of me.'

'Right. You're covered, but not overprotected.' He went on with his mission briefing. 'At your various destinations in the park, there will be back-up people—SWAT teams—concealed with night-vision devices and sniper rifles.'

'Don't forget to tell them what I'm wearing.'

Without even a chuckle, he continued, 'The places where you will stop and linger are waterside spots—the Kerbs Boathouse, then a pre-arranged spot on Belvedere Lake, and then maybe up at the Reservoir. The SWAT teams want to use waterside locations because that limits the possible avenues of approach for Khalil. In other words, you're covered on one side by the water.' Then a joke. 'Can you swim?'

'No. But I can walk on water.' I asked, 'What am I supposed to do at these locations at that hour, other than look like I'm bait in a trap?'

'Good question. And I don't have a good answer, but I'm thinking you just lost your wife . . . and you can just be taking a long walk. You know? Head down, sit on a bench, put your face in your hands . . .'

'Maybe I should look like I'm going to drown myself in the lake.'

'Yeah, you can do that, I guess. Anyway, you'll walk slowly, follow the planned route and listen to instructions in an earphone.'

'Right.'

'And remember, John, as you said, if anyone is watching your building and waiting for you to come out, it could take some time for them to get hold of Khalil. The most critical part of this, if it's going to work, is that they pick you up as you leave your lobby. The counter-surveillance team will pick up anyone tailing you. Right? So, linger without being obvious.'

'Obviously.'

'Any questions?'

'Nope.'

Then the pep talk. 'This is above and beyond, John, and we appreciate your willingness to put yourself in harm's way. Rest assured Tom and I, and everyone on the Task Force, will be thinking of you and praying for your safety and your success.'

'Thank you. Where will you be thinking of me and praying for me?'

'I'm home on call.' He reminded me, 'I'm on Central Park West, and I can be in the park within minutes.'

'Good. We can both pose for photos with the dead lion.'

He also reminded me, 'We want to take him alive, if possible.'

'Of course.' We seemed to have covered all the points, and I said, 'I'm off to the hospital.'

'Give my regards to Kate.'

ALFRED WAS ON DUTY. I wished him good morning and confessed, 'I can't find the freight elevator key.'

'Oh . . .'

'I'll keep looking, but in the meantime . . .' I pushed five twenties across the counter. 'If you need to have one made . . .'

'Yes, sir. I do have a spare, but if you can't find it, I'll see a locksmith.'

'I'm sure I'll find it, but you keep that for your trouble.'

'Thank you, sir.'

'Don't mention it.' And I meant don't mention it. I saw there was a new surveillance person in my lobby, a female this time, sitting in an armchair reading the *Times*. I went over and introduced myself. She was an attractive, well-dressed woman in her mid-twenties, maybe older, who introduced herself as Kiera Liantonio. I asked her, 'FBI?'

'Does it show?'

'I'm afraid it does.' Where do they get these kids? Right out of law school and Quantico. I suppose this kind of assignment was good on-the-job training for a rookie FBI agent. Why assign a pro to guard my life?

I said to Special Agent Liantonio, 'Stay alert. This is a very bad guy.'

She nodded.

I left the building and stood under the canopy with my shotgun rider—Ed Regan again—while the Highway Unit SUV pulled up closer.

I got in the vehicle and off we went. The driver was someone new, and now and then he did some weird things, but I knew he was trying to see if we had a tail.

We got to Bellevue without mishap, and I got out and said, 'I'll call you.'

Kate's physical appearance was better, but she told me she was going a little stir crazy and wanted out.

'You should talk to your jailer.'

'Has Tom asked you to . . . go out and see if Khalil follows you?'

Good question, and I needed a nuanced reply. I said, 'Well, we've discussed that with Paresi. But only as a last resort—if we can't find Khalil using standard methods and procedures.'

She stayed silent for a while, then said, 'You don't have to do that. That's not in anyone's job description.'

I reminded her. 'We have a personal interest in apprehending Khalil.'

She stayed silent again, then said, 'Why don't you wait until I get out of here? Then I can be part of that operation.'

She's a big girl, and she's in the business, so I said, bluntly, 'Why do you think you're still here? You're here so you're safely out of the way while Khalil and I see who finds who first.'

Again she stayed silent, then asked me, 'Do you have a good plan?'

Well, I thought the plan seemed OK, and I trust the surveillance teams. But as an old army guy once told me, even the best battle plans rarely survive the first contact with the enemy.

I said, 'It's a standard and safe surveillance and counter-surveillance, with a SWAT team added in case an arrest is not possible.'

She asked, 'When are you doing this?'

I really didn't want her losing any sleep over this, so I lied, 'I told you—when we've exhausted everything else.'

She nodded and said, 'Let me know.'

'I will.'

It was lunchtime and Kate insisted I have lunch with her. I looked at the menu and said, 'I'll have the bass with the stir-crazy vegetables.'

She smiled, which was a good sign.

Over lunch, which wasn't too bad, she said, 'I've been thinking. Khalil will go for Boris. Have you told Tom about him?'

I knew I couldn't lie because she'd check with Walsh, so I replied, 'I have not.'

'Why not? We could use him to entrap Khalil.'

Good follow-up question. I couldn't finesse this, and I didn't want to tell her the truth, so I retreated into the last refuge of husbands and boyfriends and said, 'Trust me.'

'What is that supposed to mean?'

'Trust me.'

We made eye contact and after a few seconds she said, 'Tell me about Boris, John.'

I took a deep breath, and told her about my trip to Brighton Beach. I concluded with, 'Boris convinced me to give him a week, and I agreed. And now I want you to do the same.' I added, 'He sends his regards.'

She processed all this very quickly and asked me, 'Are you crazy?'

'Yes, but that's not relevant.'

She retreated into some deep thinking, then said, 'I did not hear this.'

I nodded.

She advised me, 'Call Tom.'

I stood and bent over to kiss her, and she took my head in her hands and gave me a long, hard kiss. 'I know you'll be looking for Khalil tonight. Be careful. Please. We have a long life ahead of us.'

'I know we do.' I squeezed her hand and said, 'I'll call you later.'

I SPENT THE REST of the afternoon doing paperwork in my apartment.

I spoke to Paresi again, who didn't have anything new to say except, 'Everyone is revved up about tonight. Good luck.'

'Let's not get too excited.'

'Yeah . . . but at least we're doing something—not just reacting.'

I'd noticed that Tom Walsh wasn't calling me, and I guessed that he wanted to distance himself from this operation, in case it went south. If, however, I nailed Khalil tonight, Walsh would be waiting in his apartment with a car running outside so he could share the moment with me.

At 5 p.m., I cleaned my Glock and took three extra magazines of 9mm rounds. I also cleaned my old .38 Smith & Wesson police special. The high-performance automatics like the Glock sometimes jam, so the second weapon should be a basic revolver, which is less likely to go click, click when you want to hear bang, bang.

I rummaged through my closet and found some clothes for my walk in the park. Then I found an old Marine K-bar knife that needed sharpening, which I did with a honing stone from the kitchen drawer. While I was sharpening the big knife, I understood a little of how ancient warriors must have felt on the eve of battle. The sharpening of the steel was less about the cutting edge of the blade than it was about the cutting edge of the soul and psyche; it was an ancient communion with every man who ever faced battle and death, and who stood with his comrades, but stood alone, with his own thoughts and his own fears, waiting for the signal to meet the enemy, and to meet himself.

AT 10 P.M., I went down to the lobby, where a Special Operations supervisor, FBI Special Agent Bob Stark, was waiting for me. I knew Bob, and he was one of the good guys.

I was wearing khaki trousers, running shoes and a white pullover. It was drizzling on and off, so I had on a tan windbreaker and a tan rain hat. It was kind of a dorky outfit, designed to be seen in the dark, and I hoped I didn't run into anyone I knew. Except, of course, the Libyan guy.

Stark and I went over the assignment, and I did a commo check on my wire, making sure my GPS was up and running. I had my Glock in a hip holster and the S & W stuck in my gun belt on the left side for a quick crossover draw, plus the K-bar knife on my gun belt.

Satisfied that I was good to go, Bob said, 'OK, I'll be in a commo van. I'm S.O. One, and you are Walker—'

'Hunter.'

'It doesn't . . . OK, you are Hunter. As you know, the wire is an open channel, so when you speak, the surveillance teams can hear you. But to keep wire traffic at a minimum, my teams will speak to me via cell radio, and I will relay to you.'

'Understood.'

He said to me, 'Good hunting, Detective.'

I said to him, 'If it gets late and the weather gets bad, will you let me know when the FBI guys go home?'

He smiled. 'This is not a good time to make FBI jokes.'

'Good point.'

So off I went.

I stepped outside and stood under the lights of the apartment canopy for a moment, feigning indecision. This was the only place where I could be picked up by the bad guys, so I lingered, without being obvious.

East 72nd Street is a wide, busy street, so it would be hard for me to tell if anyone was watching me from the street or from a vehicle—but the surveillance team would have picked that up by now. My best guess, as I'd told Paresi, was that Khalil's friends had rented an apartment or an office on this street, and were keeping my front door under 24/7 surveillance.

I turned to my right and walked slowly along the crowded sidewalk towards Central Park.

Bob Stark's voice in my earphone said, 'Hunter, S.O. One here—you read?'

I spoke to my condenser mic under my shirt, 'Hunter five by five.'

'OK, we're with you, but I think you're alone. Stop at the park entrance and we'll see if anyone seems interested in you.'

'Right.' FYI, if you're walking along the street in New York talking to yourself, no one notices—except maybe other people who are talking to themselves.

I crossed Fifth Avenue and stood near the wall that surrounds the park. There were still a few pushcart vendors at the entrance, and remembering that I needed to linger here, I took the opportunity to buy a chili dog. In fact, two. Hey, this could be my last meal.

I sat on a bench and ate my hot dogs, trying to look like a dejected widower, which is not easy when you have two magnificent dogs in your hands. When I'd finished, I walked into the park.

I spotted the surveillance couple sitting on a bench, looking for all the world like lovers. They did not look at me, and I sensed they were pros.

As I walked deeper into the park, I was struck by how the mood changed—it was almost as though I'd stepped back in time to when Manhattan Island was all forest, meadows and rock outcrops. You can, however, see the lighted skyscrapers around the park, and in the park are paved paths lined with ornamental post lights. I followed one of those paths north towards my first stopping point, the Kerbs Boathouse. The drizzle had kept the crowds away, so there weren't many people around and this was good.

I tried to spot my surveillance people, but other than the couple, who were now walking fifty yards behind me holding hands, I couldn't ID anyone.

I got to the boathouse and stood on the stone patio between the house and the pond, looking out over the water.

Somewhere across the pond was a SWAT team with sniper rifles, who could shoot the chewing gum out of a guy's mouth and not chip his teeth. But it seemed that I was the only one here.

There were benches near the shore and I sat on one of them, looking despondent, which isn't hard to do when your ass is wet and the rain is getting colder.

I gave it ten minutes, and headed towards another body of water, Belvedere Lake, which was in a heavily treed area about a third of a mile further north and west, a good place for an ambush.

When I reached the lake, Stark said to me, 'Take a walk around the lake.'

So I took a slow walk around Belvedere Lake, also known as Turtle Pond, or perhaps tonight as Sitting Duck Lake. I completed the walk without meeting anyone interesting, and I stopped near a building called Belvedere Castle, where I sat on a wet bench.

I said, 'Hunter at rest.'

Stark replied, 'We have visual. No one followed you. But sit a while.'

So I sat for fifteen minutes, then Stark said, 'We're thinking that if you had company, we'd know by now. So maybe we'll cancel the Reservoir.'

'I'm having too much fun. Maybe I'll jog around the Reservoir a couple of times.'

I heard a few loud groans in my earpiece and said, 'Hey guys, I'm the one trying to get mugged by a terrorist.'

Stark said, 'Your call.'

I stood and replied, 'Hunter mobile.'

I got on the jogging track and began running in a counterclockwise direction, which is the rule. My running shoes and socks were wet, and I could hear squishing coming from my feet.

The track is about a mile and a half around, and after about five minutes I was starting to enjoy it, which is the first creepy step towards becoming a jogger zombie. I circumnavigated the Reservoir in about twenty minutes, which is not too bad, and I was so jazzed, I took a deep breath and said to Stark, 'I'm going to do that again.'

Stark replied, 'Hold on—I'm trying to talk the SWAT team out of shooting you.'

'Come on. Just one more—'

'It's over. The operation is over. Surveillance and counter-surveillance all report no sightings. Time to go home.'

'All right . . . but I'll walk back through the park.' I gave him my route along the east side of the park and began walking. I felt disappointed, but also strangely elated. It was like Paresi said—we were doing something, which was better than doing nothing. Tonight's operation was over, but I was game to do it again, tomorrow night, and every night for as long as Walsh and Paresi believed this could work, and as long as they wanted to commit manpower to it. This was all we had. The only other way that we'd find Khalil was to wait until he sprung his own plan on us.

I said, 'S.O. One, Hunter here. Do me a favour—call Bellevue, have someone on the security floor go into my wife's room and tell her I'm heading home.'

'Will do.'

I exited the park at Fifth Avenue and 72nd Street. The street was quiet at this hour, and the rain was a little heavier.

Stark said, 'We'll try another location tomorrow night.'

I said to everyone, 'Thanks. Good job.'

About eight or nine voices acknowledged.

I WALKED INTO MY LOBBY, and Special Agent Lisa Sims, of all people, was on duty. She asked me, 'How'd it go?'

'A good trial run.'

She smiled. 'You look like you need a good night's sleep.'

'Yeah.' I wished her a good evening, walked to the elevator, got in, and drew my Glock.

I entered my apartment, gun in hand. I'd left all the lights on and they were all still on. I swept the rooms, returned to the door, and bolted it. The bolt itself was good, but not great. If someone had a door ram with them, they could take out the lock with one or two hits, so I dragged the couch over and shoved it against the door.

Then I changed into dry clothing and sat in my La-Z-Boy. I turned on the TV and found a great old John Wayne movie—*Danger Rides the Range*—and when the Duke got into a gunfight, I aimed my revolver at the screen and helped him out. Bang, bang. Watch out, Duke! Bang.

At about 2 a.m., I went to bed. I was completely pissed off that I had to live like this; it went against my training and my natural instincts to be the guy playing offence. But sometimes you just had to wait for the other guy to make his move, and when he did, the game would be over quickly.

CHAPTER EIGHT

Thursday morning. I spoke to Captain Paresi and we discussed the previous night's operation. There wasn't much to say except that it had run well. The target of the operation, however, Asad Khalil, did not show up.

Paresi said he had got some manpower to check the apartment houses and office buildings on East 72nd Street, starting across the street from my building. He informed me that it would take at least ten days to accomplish this—unless, of course, they got lucky before that.

Then he said, 'Are you up for another night of walking?'

'Anything that gets me out of the house.'

'OK, we're going to try something different tonight. I want you to come to 26 Fed at about six p.m. We're going to assume, or hope, that 26 Fed is being watched. At about nine p.m. you will leave the building and proceed on foot to the area of the World Trade Center construction site. It's pretty quiet down there after dark and you'll just wander the area—sad, lonely, contemplating life and death. Then at some point you'll walk down to Battery Park. We'll play it by ear and see what looks good as the hour gets later.'

'OK,' I said. 'But I want to pick the place for tomorrow night.'

He replied, 'We're not running this operation over the weekend. Too many people out and about. But we'll use the manpower we save on you this weekend to knock on doors in your neighbourhood.'

'All right, but I need to make myself available to him.'

He pointed out, 'You're also available at home. Maybe he'll try that this weekend.'

I didn't want to argue with him. I was already thinking about giving my protective detail the slip and going out on my own to see if The Lion was stalking me.

I CALLED KATE and she said, 'A nurse came in last night about one and said she had a message for me. I thought you were dead.'

'I wouldn't leave you a message like that.'

'This is not funny.'

'Sorry, but I can't get through the switchboard after midnight.'

I told her I would be going out again tonight and we chatted for a bit.

When we'd finished the call, I started work on my incident report again. Then I began drafting a long memo about the case, starting from the beginning. The memo contained all I knew that was classified, and also my own thoughts about things like the CIA's involvement in the original case. I had no idea who this memo was addressed to; maybe it was addressed to whoever worked this case in the event of my death.

Under the heading 'Khalil II,' I revealed my recent meeting with Boris Korsakov, which reminded me that I hadn't heard from him since I'd left him contemplating a reunion with his star pupil. This might mean that he was dead, but it was more likely that Boris had nothing more to say to me. Or he'd skipped town, which would have been the smart move.

I used my ATTF cellphone to dial Boris, hoping he'd recognise the number that I'd given him and that he'd take the call. Or another voice would answer, 'Khalil here.'

Boris Korsakov answered. 'Good afternoon, Mr Corey.'

'And to you. Where are you?' I asked him.

'Where I was when I last saw you.'

'So, what have you been up to?'

'Nothing. And you?'

'Same. And where is Mrs Korsakov?'

'Moscow.'

'Lucky girl. Look, I'm rethinking what I said to you about not having your place put under surveillance. What do you think?'

Without hesitation, he replied, 'You promised me a week.'

'Boris, I made no such promise. Or if I did I've come to my senses. Look, you don't have much chance of killing or capturing Khalil. I'm thinking you need my help. I want to put your place under surveillance, and I want you to let me set up a trap.' I explained, 'You leave your fort there, go about your normal business, and I'll have people around you who can protect you and also grab Khalil if he makes an attempt on your life.' I assured him, 'I've done this a thousand times. Haven't lost anyone yet.' Not even myself.

He didn't respond to that and said, 'May I ask you a question?'

'Sure.'

'Why did you come here alone?'

Good question. I replied, 'Well, I was on my way to Coney Island, and out of the blue I had this thought that Boris Korsakov could be living in Brighton Beach.'

He didn't respond to that and said, 'You came alone . . . unofficially, I believe . . . because you want to kill him. Not capture him, but kill him.'

'Boris, I think you were in the KGB too long.'

'Long enough to know how to solve a problem. We are both men who have seen something of the world, and we understand how things are done. In Langley, they told me a little about your involvement with Khalil when he was here last, and I have concluded that you have some personal reasons for wanting Khalil dead. And he feels the same about you—as he feels about me. So why don't we leave our conversation where it was when you walked out of my office?'

I thought about that. I mean, what was the downside to letting Boris try to kill Khalil? None. There was a big downside for Boris if Khalil killed him instead. That, however, was not a downside for me—in fact, hate to say it, but Boris would get just what he deserved at the hands of the creature he had created.

'OK. I said a week. That's Tuesday.'

'Good. That is the correct decision for both of us.'

I asked him, 'Have you thought about what else Khalil might have planned, aside from whacking me and you?'

He stayed silent awhile, then replied, 'Well, I think he must need to repay someone for his trip to America. But I can tell you that when Khalil was last here, he had not been trained in explosives or in handling chemicals or biological materials.'

'Well, that's good news. But he could have learned something new in the last three years.'

'Of course. But he did not learn from me. That is not my area of expertise.'

'Right. So if we all start keeling over from nerve gas or anthrax, or there's a large explosion, you had nothing to do with that.'

'Correct.'

'OK, but . . . do you have any thoughts about a possible target—is there anything this asshole might have said to you?'

'I wish I could be helpful in guessing a possible target . . . but this man has so many hates. He did not like women, though he is not gay. He rejected all comforts and material objects, except his clothing and his weapons.'

'Not a fun guy.'

'No. In fact, a rather boring man. But his biggest hate was simply America. He considers America corrupt, decadent and weak. So he has many targets.'

'Right. Maybe he needs a night in Svetlana.'

Boris laughed. 'Khalil had a favourite expression—"The Americans know too much of gold, and they have forgotten steel."'

Well, there could be some truth there. But rather than tell Boris that, I said, 'Let me ask you one more question. Did your friends at Langley have any involvement with Asad Khalil?'

No reply.

I waited.

Finally he said, 'I have no idea if Khalil and the CIA had any sort of understanding then—or now. But I will tell you this: when a country has not been attacked in . . . let us say almost two years, people forget. And perhaps they become critical of the government, and critical of the methods used by the government in fighting the enemy. Correct? So what is the solution of the government? The solution is another attack.'

Again, I didn't respond, but I understood what he was saying. But Boris was . . . well, a Russian. KGB. These guys loved conspiracies.

'Mr Corey?'

'Sorry, I was making notes for a movie script.'

'Is there anything else I can help you with?'

'Not at this time,' I assured him.

'Thank you for your call. And for the week.'

'You're quite welcome, and don't forget to call me if you should happen to kill him in self-defence.'

'My attorney first, then you.'

'You're a real American, Boris.'

'Thank you.' He stayed silent a moment, then said to me, 'Whatever he has planned for you, Mr Corey, is not going to be pleasant.'

'Right. You too. And probably you first.'

He didn't reply to that and we hung up.

Well, I wasn't any closer to finding Khalil. And I wasn't any closer to figuring out what else he had planned here. But I was a little more certain that he had something planned—maybe something chemical, biological, or, God forbid, nuclear.

As for Boris's CIA conspiracy theory . . . well, he wasn't the first person to think there were people who'd welcome another attack. But welcoming an attack and conspiracy to instigate one were very different things.

My other thought was that I shouldn't be conspiring with Boris Korsakov, former KGB assassin. But as the Arabs say, the enemy of my enemy is my friend. Plus, by partnering up with a bad guy, I doubled the chances that Khalil would wind up dead before he could set off a weapon of mass destruction. Or kill me.

I'd worry later about explaining all this to Tom Walsh, if I had to.

AT 5.30 P.M., I TOOK a taxi to 26 Federal Plaza. I spent a few hours at my desk, catching up on emails and listening to voicemails. There was nothing pertaining to Khalil, which reinforced my conclusion that this was a very tightly controlled case. I didn't see Tom Walsh, which reinforced my suspicion that he was distancing himself from me and from the operation. As for all the other cases that I had been working on, it appeared that they'd been parcelled out to other agents.

At 8 p.m., I met with Paresi and Stark, and we went over the operation in detail. At 9 p.m., I left 26 Federal Plaza and made the short walk down to the Trade Center site, which was deserted at this hour.

I did a complete walk around the site, which was about a third of a mile on each side, stopping a few times to look down into the huge excavation. At the bottom of the brightly lit pit was construction equipment and piles of building material. Virtually all the rubble was gone, but now and then human remains still turned up. Bastards.

On the Liberty Street side of the big hole was the long earthen ramp that went down into the construction site. The ramp was blocked by two high chain-link gates, which were locked. On the other side of the gates I could see a house trailer that was a comfortable guard post for the Port Authority Police who manned this single entrance to the excavation.

Well, I didn't expect to see Asad Khalil here, so I moved onto West Street, which runs between the World Trade Center site and the buildings of the World Financial Center site. This had been so heavily damaged by the collapse of the Twin Towers that the area was blocked off by security fences. This place was like a war zone—which it was.

Stark's voice in my earpiece said, 'You are alone.'

'Copy.'

I walked down to Battery Park, half a mile south of Ground Zero. It was a nice evening, so there were a few people looking across at the Statue of Liberty, including the surveillance team couple I'd seen in Central Park, sitting on a bench again, holding hands. I hoped they at least liked each other.

I said into my mic, 'This is not promising.'

Stark replied, 'Maybe it's too early. Let's take a walk on some dark, quiet streets. Then we'll come back here later.'

I liked the way Stark used the plural pronoun as though he was walking. No, I was walking, and half the surveillance team was walking, and the other half was in unmarked vehicles, along with the SWAT team.

As I walked through the quiet streets of the Financial District, I called Kate to put her mind at ease. She answered and said, 'I've been waiting for your call. Where are you?'

'Stepping over drunk stockbrokers.'

'Be careful, John.'

'Love you.'

Being married to someone in the business has its advantages. You worry about the other person, but it's informed worrying.

I continued the walk through the nearly deserted streets of Lower Manhattan, then back to Battery Park, then back to the Trade Center.

At about midnight, we all agreed that no one was following me, and I found a taxi near 26 Fed and headed home.

On the way, I called Kate and said, 'No luck. I'm heading home.'

'Good. Don't do this again. I don't think my nerves can take another night of this.'

Well, there goes my theory about being married to someone in the business. I said, 'I've got the weekend off. I'll see you tomorrow.'

Me being lion bait did not seem to be working. Which could mean that Khalil and his local contacts had no idea I was out and about. Or they knew, but they smelled a trap. Or Khalil was gone.

No. He was here. I knew he was here. He hadn't come this far with that much hate in his heart to let me live.

FRIDAY MORNING. The sun came through the balcony doors and it looked like it was going to be another nice day. Today would be a good day to kill Asad Khalil.

I visited Kate at Bellevue. She was determined to break out today.

'I am *not* spending the weekend in this place,' she said.

I really didn't want her back in the apartment yet, so I said, 'Tell you what. If something doesn't happen by Monday, you and I will fly out to . . . where your parents live . . .'

'Minnesota.'

'Right. But just hang in here a few more days.'

She didn't reply.

I really didn't want to go to East Cow Meadow, Minnesota, but maybe I could deposit Kate with her parents and get back here. Khalil didn't know Kate was even alive. To the best of my knowledge. Even so, I took my revolver out of its holster and slid it under her pillow. I said, 'You'll sleep better with Mr Smith and Mr Wesson.'

She nodded, but didn't reply.

I stayed for lunch—broiled stool pigeon with plea bargain peas—and after we'd dined, Kate asked me if I was going out again on Monday night.

I replied, 'I haven't heard.'

She said, 'It's a waste of time. Khalil's not going to fall for an obvious trap. Plus, you just never know.' She took my hand. 'John . . . Khalil has obviously thought this out. He has his own trap. For you.'

'Look, Kate, I can spot a trap, too.'

'I know you can. And I also know that you'll walk right into it because you think you can turn it around. You have a big ego,' she suggested.

Leading cause of death among alpha males.

She said, 'Monday, two tickets to Minnesota. I'll book the trip.'

'Great.' Actually, of course, I wasn't going with her. Unless Asad Khalil was dead by Monday. And if I was dead by Monday, then I certainly wasn't going to Minnesota. I stood up to go. 'Remember you have a revolver under your pillow.'

'Maybe that will improve the service here.'

'See you tonight.'

She suggested, 'Take the night off, John. I'm fine here.'

'Are you sure?'

'I'll see you in the morning. And don't try to give your protective detail the slip and go out to see if Khalil is waiting for you.'

Wives become mind readers. Or maybe I was predictable. I replied, 'I wouldn't do anything that dangerous.'

'Of course you wouldn't.'

I SPENT THE AFTERNOON on paperwork and thinking, and also working out. A sound mind in a sound body. The body is easier to work on.

At 6 p.m., I called down to my protective detail and ordered a pepperoni pizza, which is good for the soul.

At seven, my intercom buzzed and the S.O. guy said, 'Pizza coming up.'

I unlocked the door and left it ajar, then drew my Glock and moved back, away from the door. If the pizza had anchovies, the delivery guy was dead.

There was a knock on the door, then it opened, and there was Vince Paresi carrying a pizza box. I wished I had a camera instead of a gun.

Paresi noticed me holstering the Glock, but didn't comment.

He said to me, 'I thought I'd keep you company tonight.'

That sounded like it could have been Kate's idea. Or Walsh's. Or Paresi had the same idea himself—Corey needed to be watched.

I said, 'That's very thoughtful of you.'

'Yeah. Take the pizza.'

I took the box and noticed that Paresi also had a bottle of red vino under his arm. 'Let's dine al fresco,' I suggested.

'You're not supposed to go out on your balcony,' he reminded me.

'Live dangerously.'

I took the pizza out to the balcony and set it on the table, then went back and collected a corkscrew, glasses and a bottle of Scotch.

At my urging, Vince joined me on the balcony, and we shared his wine and my pizza. It was a nice night, and below on the street the city was coming alive on this Friday evening. But he kept looking at the buildings up and down the street and the conversation was sort of strained. Vince was not a good date.

Finally, he said to me, 'Those bastards could nail both of us up here.'

'Don't be paranoid. If Khalil wanted to whack me with a sniper rifle, he'd have already done it.' I added, 'He has something else planned for me.'

Paresi replied, 'I was thinking about me.'

He poured himself the last of the wine and informed me, 'CAU got a hit on Kate's cellphone just a few hours ago. A seven- or eight-second signal lock, like someone was accessing the phone's directory.'

'Where did the signal come from?'

'Well, the cell tower that logged in her phone has coverage between 44th and 43rd streets.'

'OK . . . did you send cars there?'

'We did, but I'm guessing the signal came from a moving vehicle.'

'Well, at least we know that Kate's cellphone is in Manhattan.'

'Right.' He nodded towards the city below and said, 'He's out there.'

I looked at the towering apartments and office buildings up and down my street. Some windows were lighted, some were dark, and I suspected one of those windows was looking back at us.

I asked Paresi, 'How's it going on 72nd Street?'

He glanced out at the buildings and replied, 'Lots of doors to knock on. Half the doors we bang on don't even answer. I think we've cleared about half the apartments and maybe eighty per cent of the offices.' He then said, 'It would have been good if that cell signal came from across the street.'

'They're not that stupid.'

He disagreed. 'They are.'

'They were, but they're getting smarter.' I advised him, 'Don't underestimate them. And do not underestimate Asad Khalil.'

Kate called and was very happy to find me home with my date. She enquired, 'Have you been drinking?'

'No. We're still drinking.'

'Good night, John. I love you.'

'Love you, too.'

Paresi and I finished a half bottle of Scotch, and he left before midnight.

I went to bed. It was a quiet night. But I had that feeling I sometimes get when nothing happens that something is going to happen.

ON SATURDAY I called for my government vehicle at 10 a.m., and visited Kate at Bellevue. She seemed in a good mood, knowing she'd be out soon. I asked her, 'Is Tom OK with you leaving?'

'He is,' she informed me, 'as long as I go to my parents' place.'

'OK. Does he know that you want me to go with you?'

'Yes. He's fine with that.' That was a surprise. She informed me, 'I had a very frank talk with Tom. And I told him that, one, he couldn't keep me here against my will, and two, Washington might not approve of him using you—a contract agent—as live bait to trap a terrorist. If something happened to you—'

'Hold on. I volunteered for this.' I seem to remember my life and job being simpler before I got married—both times.

Kate also informed me, 'Tom doesn't believe this is working, anyway.' And then the clincher. 'In fact, if something happened someplace in the city, and it came out that half the surveillance teams were watching our apartment and following you around, Tom would have a lot of explaining to do in Washington.'

Kate is a smart lady. She knew how to play Walsh better than I did.

'Don't sulk. I'm doing this for us.' She took my hand and said, 'If you love me, you won't want to put yourself in danger—'

'Of course I love you. But I don't want us looking over our shoulders for the rest of our lives.'

'John, there are hundreds of people, here and around the world, who are now looking for Asad Khalil. They will find him without your help.' And more bad news. 'I also called your parents and told them we'd be visiting them in Florida, right after our visit to my parents. Plan to be gone for two months. We're on administrative leave.'

'Two months? With your parents and mine? Can I borrow your gun?'

She took my hand again and looked at me. 'You've become obsessed with this, and that's not healthy. You need to get away.'

I didn't reply.

'Tom wants me to stay in the hospital until Monday. He feels I'm safer here, and he doesn't want anyone to see me in case it leaks out to the wrong people who think I'm dead.' She switched to the honey trap. 'John, I love you. You saved my life, and this is how I'm repaying you.'

I must have missed a link in that chain of logic, but I said, 'OK. Monday to Indianapolis.'

'Minneapolis, John. In Minnesota.'

'Right. OK, I have to go.'

'I feel so much better knowing you won't be out tonight.'

'Me too.'

'And before we leave, you will call Tom and tell him about Boris.'

'Yes, ma'am.'

'See you tonight.'

We kissed and I left.

Well, I'd been boxed in by the boss and the wife—the perfect one-two punch. This sucked.

I had less than forty-eight hours before I was on my way into exile. I might have one, maybe two plays left before then.

Back in my apartment, I called Tom Walsh, but it was Saturday and apparently Tom wasn't taking business calls—not mine, anyway. I left a message that made a convincing argument for continuing the operation, or at the very least letting me back into the office to work the case. I would have told him about Boris if he'd taken the call, and if he agreed with me that I needed to stay here, on the case. In any event, I'd tell him Tuesday, when Boris's time was up to see if Khalil tried to whack him. Unfortunately, I might be making that call to Tom from a cow pasture.

Later, as I was getting ready for my evening visit to Bellevue, my house phone rang. Caller ID said 'Blocked.'

I answered and said, 'Corey.'

Silence. I knew who it was.

A voice with an accent said, 'It is me. Asad Khalil.'

I replied in an even tone, 'I've been expecting your call.'

'I know you have. I found your number on your wife's cellphone, so I am calling to express my condolences on her death.'

'That is really sick.'

'And the death of your friend and colleague, Mr Haytham.'

'You also killed his wife and daughter. What kind of man are you?'

'I don't understand your question.'

'You are going to burn in hell.'

'No, you are going to burn in hell. I will live for ever in Paradise.'

I didn't respond. There was a silence on the phone, and I could hear traffic noises in the background. Then he said, 'I told you three years ago that I would return, and you saw that I kept my promise.' He added, 'When I promise to kill someone, I kill them.'

Again, I didn't respond.

He reminded me, 'You had more to say to me the last time I was here. I know you are mourning the death of your wife, and that makes one . . . less talkative. And perhaps less arrogant and less insulting.'

Again, I didn't respond, and let the silence continue.

CAU was not listening in on my calls, but they were monitoring my number, and they could trace any incoming calls to their source.

As if he knew what I was thinking, he said, 'I am in a moving vehicle and soon this phone will be out of the window.' He added, 'I have many phones, Mr Corey. You will not find me that way.'

'But I will find you. And kill you. I promise.'

'You are not clever enough to find me. Nor are you man enough to kill me. But I will find *you* and kill you.'

'You know where I live, and where I work. If you had any balls, you'd have already tried. Instead, you kill defenceless women, and murder your countrymen who trust you. You're a coward.'

He didn't respond to that, and I thought he'd hung up, but I could still hear background noise.

Finally he said, 'Did you think I was a coward when we all jumped from that aircraft?'

'You looked scared shitless when I popped off a few rounds at you.'

He replied in a less cool voice, 'I told you I would kill that whore, and I did. And you watched her die, bleeding like a frightened lamb with her throat cut.'

I took a deep breath and said, 'Enough of this. We need to meet and finish this. Now. I will come alone—'

'Please. You are not speaking to an idiot. When we meet, I will pick the time and place, and I will be certain you are alone.'

'You should have tried to kill me when you had the chance, stupid.'

'It is you, Mr Corey, who is stupid if you think I would kill you so quickly, as I killed your wife. I have a more interesting death planned for you. First, I intend to cut off your genitals, and feed them to dogs. Then I will cut off your face. I will peel it from your skull, as the Taliban do in Afghanistan. Have you seen the photographs? That, Mr Corey, is what I intend to do to you. The next time we meet. So, until then—'

'Hold on. I want to remind you again that your mother was a whore, and she was screwing your great asshole of a leader, who you know had your father killed so he could keep screwing your mother.'

I could hear him breathing, and I think he was a little pissed off at me.

Finally he said, 'We will meet,' and the phone went dead.

Well, that was a good conversation. No beating around the bush. That's what I like about psychopaths. They give it to you straight.

I was now supposed to call Walsh or Paresi, but . . . I dialled Svetlana to see if the place was closed because of the death of the owner.

A man with a Russian accent answered, and I could hear music and loud talking in the background. I asked for Mr Korsakov, and the man said he was not available, but he would take a message. I told him, 'Have him call Mr Corey. It's important.'

I hung up. Well, Boris was still alive. But Boris, I thought, was the canary in the coal mine. Once he was dead, could John Corey be far behind? Bottom line here was that I had to wait for Khalil to make his move, on his terms and at his time.

SUNDAY MORNING. My Special Operations keepers offered to accompany me to church if I was so inclined. Last Sunday, I was threatened with death by a skydiving terrorist, so I gave this some serious consideration before opting to watch a little of the televised Mass, in my bathrobe. But I was there in spirit.

Kate was in a jolly mood, and I was reminded of prisoners I'd seen on the eve of their release date. She asked me, 'Have you packed yet?'

'All packed and ready to go.' Not.

Because it was Sunday, the ward was busy with chaplains making their rounds, offering Communion and God's message of love to those who needed it most—murderers, rapists, drug dealers and other felons capable of salvation, except convicted politicians, who have no souls to save. I was not in as jolly a mood as Kate, and she sensed this, but dealt with it by ignoring it.

I stayed for Sunday lunch, which was actually not bad, especially the pat-down de foie gras. The visit ended on a bittersweet note, with Kate saying to me, 'You are a brave man, John, and I know you don't want to leave this problem for others to solve. But if something happened to you . . . my life would be over. So, think of me. Of us.'

If something happened to me, my life would also be over, but I replied in the spirit of the sentiment, 'We have a long life ahead of us.' Unless I drop dead of boredom at a Mayfield family dinner.

I left Kate still in a good mood—hers, not mine—and met my driver in the lobby. His name was Preston Tyler, and I wasn't sure he was old enough to drive a non-farm vehicle. Anyway, we got on the road, and he asked me, 'Did Captain Paresi get hold of you?'

'Nope.'

I looked at my cellphone and there was a text message from Paresi that I'd missed, which said: *A new development. Call me ASAP.*

I called Paresi's cellphone and asked, 'What's up?'

He replied, 'Well, we may have found the safe house—or a safe house.'

'Where?'

'Where we thought—across the street from you.'

We? I thought that was my idea.

Paresi continued, 'The command centre got an anonymous phone call early this morning from a male who said he had observed suspicious activity in an apartment at 320 East 72nd Street—suspicious-looking people, coming and going at all hours. Where are you now?'

'I'm about five minutes from there.'

'Good. I'm here. Apartment 2712.'

I hung up and said to Preston, 'Drop me at 320 East 72nd, between First and Second Avenues.'

The address was a nice pre-war building, about thirty storeys high. I'd passed it a million times, but for some reason it had never occurred to me that there could be terrorists in Apartment 2712.

I entered the foyer of the building and the doorman buzzed me in.

There were four NYPD detectives in the ornate old lobby—in case the terrorist tenants showed up—and we did the ID thing. Then one of them escorted me to Apartment 2712. He rang the bell for me, and the door was opened by Captain Paresi, who said, 'Wipe your feet.'

The joke here was that the apartment was not neat—it was, in fact, filthy, as I could see and smell from the doorway. I walked in, and Paresi, who was the only person in the room, asked me, 'How's Kate?'

'Happy and healthy.'

'Good. The country air will do her a world of good. You too.'

I put that subject on hold for later and asked, 'What do we have here?'

He replied, 'As you can see, we have a squalid apartment—a one-room studio leased to the Eastern Export Corporation, with headquarters in Beirut, Lebanon. They've had the lease for two years.'

I asked, 'And we've never seen any bad guys coming or going here?'

'No. It's not a safe house on our list. And we actually knocked on this door twice in the last two days, but no one answered.'

I also asked, 'What does the doorman say?'

'He says there were three or four guys—he can't be sure—foreign-looking, and they showed up only about two or three weeks ago. He barely saw them and they were quiet.'

I pointed out, 'That doesn't square with the tipster who said there were suspicious-looking people coming and going at all hours.'

'No,' he agreed, 'it doesn't.'

I looked around the studio apartment, which had a galley kitchen and two doors—one that led to the bathroom, and one for a closet that was empty. The only furniture was three ratty-looking armchairs, four unpleasant-looking mattresses on the floor and a big television on a cheap stand.

Paresi said, 'There's some stuff like food and toiletries, but there's no clothing or luggage, so it looks like they pulled out.'

'Right.' I asked, 'Any camel milk in the fridge?'

'No, but it's mostly Middle Eastern-type food.'

'When do we get forensics here?' I asked.

'Soon. I'm waiting for a search warrant.' He added, 'We entered under exigent circumstances with the super's passkey on the suspicion that there could be a dead or dying person in here.' These days you need a search warrant even if the lease says 'Al Qaeda Waste Management'.

I looked around again. There was nothing in the apartment to suggest that it was anything but a crash pad for illegal aliens.

I walked around the mattresses and opened one of the two windows. I looked to the left, saw my building, and spotted my balcony. It would be no problem for a sniper to shoot my cocktail glass out of my hand. Also, close enough to mount a video surveillance camera here, pointed at my front door.

Paresi said, 'Over here.'

I went to the second window and looked at the wide, painted sill. In the centre was a spot where the dust had been disturbed. I speculated, 'This is where they set the wine bucket down.'

'Yeah. And the lead wire from the wine bucket ran to the TV.'

We both walked to the television, a fairly new model, and though there were no video wires attached, the TV was equipped to accept a video camera input. *The John Corey Show*. Reality TV.

Paresi said, 'So, these guys watched us having wine and pizza.'

'Right.' And they chose to do nothing about that. Because Khalil has his own plan. Also, they saw me getting in a vehicle a few times a day, but I couldn't know if I'd ever been followed to Bellevue. The trail vehicle didn't pick it up. It was kind of disturbing and creepy.

Paresi was thinking aloud. 'OK, we got three or four foreign-looking guys who enjoy Middle Eastern cuisine, and they happen to have a view of your building, and we know that Asad Khalil is trying to kill you. So can we assume that the people who were living here were Arab terrorists watching you? Or is this just a coincidence?'

'The coincidence,' I agreed, 'is suspicious. And here's another coincidence: the tip came just before these guys pulled out. Therefore—follow me on this—the tipster was one of Khalil's guys.'

'And now we're supposed to believe that Khalil and his pals have gone back to Sandland?'

'Correct. Or at least they have put some doubts in our minds.'

This might have been the time to tell Captain Paresi that I'd recently chatted with the scumbag in question. Just as I was supposed to report my contact with Boris Korsakov. But, if I came clean now, I'd be removed from the case immediately for not reporting the contact in a timely manner. And I still had about twenty-four hours before I was exiled.

We poked around the apartment awhile, being careful not to touch or disturb anything that would throw the forensic people into a fit.

A few minutes later, a Task Force detective showed up with a search warrant and a few minutes after that the NYPD forensic team arrived and kicked everyone out.

Down in the lobby, Paresi said to me, 'You know, John, Khalil really may be gone. So don't feel too bad about going on vacation.'

I replied, 'I'm fairly certain this is a ruse to make us all drop our guards and scale down our manhunt. So don't drop your guard, Vince.'

He had no reply to that, but he did extend his hand and say, 'Have a good trip. We'll stay in touch.' He added, 'See you in a few months.'

BACK IN MY APARTMENT again, with my Sunday afternoon Bloody Mary in hand, I went out to the balcony. They were gone—right? But a stupid ruse is often a cover for a smart ruse.

Asad Khalil came halfway round the world to cross names off his list, and he hadn't gotten to my name yet. Or Boris's.

And what happened to that big finale we were expecting? Have they already poisoned the water supply? Is there a bomb ticking somewhere?

This was one of those cases where the silence is deafening.

I looked down the street at the window that had looked back at me for two or three weeks. Where were they? Where was Asad Khalil?

I spent the late afternoon packing.

Time was slipping by, and I thought about calling Boris again on the theory that if he was still alive, it would mean that Khalil hadn't begun his final clean-up operation.

Boris didn't answer his cellphone—but neither did Asad Khalil nor a homicide detective—so I left another message with the maître d' for Boris to call me. This time I said 'urgent.' I pictured Boris with some girl, plying her with champagne and impressing her with his KGB exploits while the Red Army Chorus set the mood.

At 6 p.m., I called for my ride to Bellevue.

CHAPTER NINE

Asad Khalil sat in a taxi in front of Svetlana. A text message appeared on his cellphone, and Khalil read it, then got out of the taxi and said to Rasheed, the Libyan driver, 'Wait here.'

Khalil, wearing a suit and tie, and also a drooping moustache and glasses, entered through the front door of the Brooklyn nightclub, where he was greeted by a maître d', who asked him in Russian, 'Do you have a reservation?' Khalil replied in the passable Russian he'd learned from Boris, 'I am going only to the bar.' The maître d' took him for a native of one of the former Asian Soviet Republics—a Kazakh, perhaps, or an Uzbek. The maître d' did not like these people, but it was difficult to turn away someone who only wanted to sit at the bar to watch the floor show, so he motioned wordlessly towards the open doorway behind him and turned his attention to an arriving group. Khalil walked through the doorway and down a long corridor that opened out into the big restaurant.

Khalil had never been here, but he felt he knew the place from the photographs and information given to him a few days earlier by a fellow Muslim, a man named Vladimir, a Russified Chechen who had been instructed a month ago to find himself a job here.

At 6 p.m. on this Sunday evening, the restaurant was only half full. Khalil stood at the entrance for almost a minute, knowing that a security person would notice him. Then he walked deliberately to a red-curtained doorway at the rear and entered the short corridor that led to a locked door.

Almost immediately, he heard footsteps behind him, and a man's voice in English said, 'Stop,' then in Russian, '*Stoi!*'

The man put his hand on Khalil's shoulder, and Khalil spun round and thrust a long carving knife into his throat, severing his windpipe. The man slid into a sitting position against the wall, and Khalil withdrew the knife. He went through the dying man's pockets and found a keychain, a Colt .45 automatic pistol and a radio phone.

Khalil glanced at the red curtain. No one had followed them. He hefted the dying man over his shoulder, then went to the locked door, tried a key, then another, and the door opened. Khalil found himself in a small room that contained an elevator and a steel door that Vladimir had told him led to the staircase. Vladimir had also texted Khalil that the other bodyguard, Viktor, was now sitting in the anteroom above, outside Boris's office, and that Boris was expecting a lady to arrive shortly.

Khalil relocked the door to the corridor, then unlocked the steel door to the staircase and threw the bodyguard, who now appeared close to death, onto the stairs. He relocked the staircase door and made his way quickly up the stairs.

At the top of the stairs was another door. Putting the key in the lock with his left hand and holding the long carving knife in his right hand, Khalil opened the door quickly and burst into the small room.

Viktor jumped to his feet and his hand went inside his jacket for his gun, but Khalil was already on him, thrusting the long knife into Viktor's lower abdomen while pulling him closer in a tight hug with his left arm so that Viktor could not draw his gun. He withdrew the knife quickly, then brought it round and thrust the blade into Viktor's lower back, puncturing his diaphragm and leaving him unable to make a sound.

Viktor tried to break loose, but Khalil held him tightly. He could hear the man's breathing becoming more laboured and shallow. He also felt the warm wetness of Viktor's blood on his skin. Then Viktor's body arched and shook in a series of death throes, before going limp.

Khalil lowered the dead man back into his chair and retrieved Viktor's gun from his shoulder holster, noting that it was also a Colt .45 automatic. He stuck the gun in his belt, next to the gun of the other dead bodyguard.

Khalil looked at his watch. It had been just nine minutes since he'd entered this place. He dialled Vladimir's cellphone.

BORIS KORSAKOV sat in his armchair, sipping a cognac, smoking and reading a local Russian-language weekly. The busboy, Vladimir, was taking his time setting the table with chilled caviar and champagne for two. A lady would be arriving at 6.30 p.m. It was already 6.15, and the stupid busboy—who was only a few weeks on the job—seemed nervous or unsure of what to do.

Boris said to the busboy in Russian, 'Are you not done yet?'

'I am just finishing, sir.'

Vladimir knew that for all appearances he was an ethnic Russian, but in fact his name, speech and Russian ways had been forced on him from birth by the Russian occupiers of Chechnya—and in his heart he hated everything and everyone who was Russian, especially this former KGB man sitting with his back to him, drinking, smoking and giving him orders.

Vladimir felt his cellphone vibrate in his pocket. It was time.

Boris put down his newspaper and said to Vladimir, 'Just leave everything and go.' Boris stood to show the busboy out.

But Vladimir was already at the door, his hand on the bolt.

Boris shouted, 'Stop! You idiot! Stand away from that door!'

Vladimir slid the bolt open, stood aside, and the door swung open. He left quickly as Asad Khalil entered with a pistol in his hand and bolted the door again.

Boris stood absolutely still, his eyes fixed on the man who stood less than twenty feet from him, looking at him. The man had a moustache and glasses, and his hair was not combed back as he recalled, but he knew who his visitor was.

Boris also noted, almost absently, that the man's dark suit and white shirt were covered with fresh blood.

Khalil took off his glasses and peeled off his moustache, then said in Russian, 'Are you not happy to see your favourite student?'

Boris took a deep breath and replied in English, 'Your Russian is still as bad as the stench of your mouth and your body.'

Khalil did not respond to that, but said, 'I would advise you now to reach for your gun so that I will be forced to give you a quick death. But if you prefer to live a few minutes longer, we can share a few words before you suffer a painful death. The choice is yours.'

Boris reverted to Russian and said, '*Yob vas*.' Fuck you.

Khalil smiled and said, 'Where are your CIA friends? They used you like the whore you are, and they put you here in this place filled with other whores and drunken pigs. Are they not protecting you?'

Boris's eyes darted round the room, looking for a way to save his life. He said, 'What did I teach you? Kill quickly. You talk too much.'

'I enjoy the talk.'

'I assure you, your victims do not.'

Khalil seemed annoyed and said, 'I had to listen to you for one year insulting me, my country and my faith.' He stared at Boris. 'And look at you now. Who are you? Who is holding the gun? Not you. And how clever are you? You should be more careful who you hire. Vladimir is a Chechen and he would pay me if I let him cut your throat. And you should also know that your two bodyguards are now waiting for you in Hell.'

Boris's mind was racing, thinking of a way to save himself. The girl, Tanya, would be escorted here by a security man, and that man would notice . . . something. A body. Blood on the floor . . .

Khalil, who knew exactly what his old teacher was thinking, said, 'Vladimir has called downstairs to have the girl sent away—on your instructions. You will not be having champagne and caviar tonight, and you will not be fornicating after I cut off your testicles.'

Boris did not reply, his mind still searching for a way out. Finally, he realised that there was only one move he could make—he had to go for his gun. That would either save him, or end it quickly. He looked at Khalil for a sign that the man's attention was not fully focused, but all he saw was Khalil's black eyes staring straight at him, and the black muzzle of the gun aimed as accurately as Khalil's eyes.

Again, Khalil seemed to know what Boris was thinking, and he said, 'Show some courage. Do something.'

Boris took another deep breath and in his mind he was reaching inside his jacket for the gun on his hip as he dived to the side, rolled and fired. But he realised that no matter what he did—rolled, dived, even charged at Khalil—this man would shoot to wound him, then he would finish him off in a way that Boris did not want to think about.

Maybe if he could keep Khalil talking, someone would come up the stairs or the elevator and see that something was not right. He waited for the doorbell to ring—a few notes of Tchaikovsky that would distract Khalil for half a second. That's all he needed to draw the gun concealed in his jacket.

Boris cleared his throat and said in a confident voice, 'This building is under surveillance by the police and the FBI.'

Khalil replied, 'They do not seem to be any more competent or alert than your stupid bodyguards.'

'You will not get out of this building alive.'

'It is you who will not get out of this building alive.'

Khalil had not moved far from the door, and now he stepped back and put his ear to it, then turned to Boris and said, 'Someone is coming.'

Boris prepared himself to go for his gun.

Then Khalil smiled and said, 'Perhaps I was hearing things.' Then he laughed, and Boris understood that this man needed to torment him and mock him before he killed him.

Boris shouted a string of half-remembered Arabic obscenities, then yelled in English, 'You bastard! You piece of shit! Your mother was a whore!'

Khalil aimed his gun at Boris's midsection, and Boris could see that Khalil's arm was shaking in rage. Boris waited for the bullet, hoping it would either miss him or hit his heart.

Then Khalil reached under his jacket and pulled out the carving knife that he'd used to kill the two bodyguards. He gripped the blade in a throwing position, cocked his arm back, and flung the knife towards Boris.

Boris flinched as the knife stuck in the carpet at his feet. He understood what was coming.

Khalil said, 'You may have the knife—in exchange for your gun.'

Boris looked at Khalil, but did not respond.

Khalil said, 'You have chosen not to draw your gun, so I am offering you this instead. This is very generous of me—though it will be more painful for you. Have you been practising with the knife since I last saw you?' He smiled. 'Or perhaps just the knife and fork.'

Boris weighed his options, which were reduced now to two—go for his gun and hope for a quick bullet in the head or heart, or engage Asad Khalil in a knife fight.

'You seem to be unable to make a decision today. So I will make it for you.' Khalil crouched in a shooting stance and steadied his aim.

Boris shouted, 'No!' He raised both hands, then slowly lowered his left hand and pulled back his jacket, revealing his gun and holster on his belt.

Khalil nodded.

Boris grasped the gun butt with his thumb and index finger and pulled the gun out of his holster, then slid it across the rug towards Khalil.

Khalil stepped forwards and retrieved the gun, which he saw was a Browning automatic. He removed the magazine and dropped the gun into a glass bowl heaped with black caviar.

He said to Boris, 'I would take your word that you have no other gun—but perhaps you can show me.'

Boris nodded and pulled up his trouser legs to show he had no ankle holster; then he turned his pockets inside out. He slowly removed his jacket and turned completely around and faced Khalil again.

Khalil said, 'I am surprised you have not taken your own advice about a second gun.'

'Even if I had a second gun, I would prefer to cut your throat.'

Khalil smiled and said, 'That is also my preference for you.'

He drew the two Colt .45s from his belt, removed the magazines, and stuck both guns in the champagne bucket. Then he removed the magazine from his own gun, and laid the Glock on a table napkin. He then drew a short, heavy hunting knife from his belt and flung it to the floor, where it stuck in the carpet.

He looked at Boris and asked, 'Are you ready?'

Boris did not reply, but he took off his tie, shoes and socks, then wrapped his jacket around his left arm.

Khalil smiled approvingly and did the same.

Both men stood about fifteen feet apart and stared at each other, the knives stuck in the floor a few feet in front of them.

For the first time since Khalil had walked into the room, Boris believed he had a chance to kill this man. He knew that he could have a second gun, but it didn't matter—he would prefer a bullet to losing this fight.

They stood watching each other, waiting for the other to make a move.

Boris made the first move, running straight at Khalil and snatching the knife as he continued towards him.

Khalil lunged forwards, grabbed his knife and rolled to the right, then sprang up and went into a crouched defensive position with his wrapped arm in front of him and his legs spread wide.

Boris stopped short, wheeled round and came at Khalil.

Khalil held his position, and Boris feinted left and right, stepped in, then stepped back, then in again. He remembered Khalil's major weakness was impatience, which often led him to an impulsive and ill-timed attack. But now, Boris saw, Khalil had apparently learned when to defend and when to attack.

Boris decided on another strategy and he backed away, putting nearly twenty feet between them.

Khalil came out of his defensive position and strode directly at Boris, and the two men circled each other in the middle of the large room.

Boris watched Khalil's movements. He knew that the Libyan was more agile and in far better shape than he was, but Boris believed he was still physically stronger than Khalil.

Khalil again dropped into a half-crouch, with his legs spread and his coat-wrapped arm in a horizontal position that made Boris think that he was becoming anxious. It made Boris more confident.

He moved in quickly—a feint that he hoped would cause Khalil to backpedal and lose his defensive posture. But instead, Khalil unexpectedly charged forwards to meet Boris's forward movement in mid-stride.

Khalil came in low under Boris's knife hand and wrapped arm and delivered an upward thrust that caught Boris below his left rib cage.

Boris let out a startled cry of pain, then pivoted away from the probing knife and delivered a high kick to Khalil's lowered head.

Neither man pressed the attack and both of them retreated to safety.

Khalil nodded and said, 'Very good.'

Boris cautiously felt his wound and determined that it was a narrow puncture wound, perhaps deep, but not bleeding profusely, and not mortal. But he also determined that he wasn't going to win this fight—he was already out of breath, and the wound would eventually weaken him. He admitted too, that Khalil was the better knife fighter, and possessed the will and the courage to face a man with a knife. Boris was not sure that he himself possessed that will any longer.

Out of desperation, Boris said to Khalil, 'It is over. You have won.'

Khalil laughed. 'Yes? I had hoped you would be good practise for the other who is going to die in this way tonight. Now I see you are a poor opponent—too old, too slow and too frightened.'

Boris took a deep breath. 'You have made your point.' He lowered his knife and said, 'I have done nothing to you. I have taught you—'

'Shut up.' Khalil took a few steps towards Boris, and as Boris moved back, Khalil said, 'We have not finished this lesson. Do you not want to show me how you will disarm me and throw me against the wall as you did once? Do you think I have forgotten your knee in my testicles?'

Despite everything, Boris suddenly felt his anger rising. He pulled the jacket from around his arm and snapped it at Khalil as he moved forwards, his knife extended in his right hand.

Khalil stepped back and lost his footing on the loose rug, then fell to the floor, losing his knife.

Boris charged him, and realised too late he'd been drawn into a ruse, as Khalil raised his legs and caught Boris in the abdomen and hurled him headfirst into a china cabinet, which shattered in a loud crash.

Khalil snatched up his knife, jumped up quickly, and watched as Boris pulled himself unsteadily to his feet, his face bleeding from glass cuts and his eyes blinded with blood. He had lost his knife, and he wiped his eyes with his hands as Khalil moved in for the kill.

Boris, his back to the shattered china cabinet, sidestepped along the wall, and Khalil followed him, then realised what Boris was doing.

Boris seized a floor lamp with both hands and swung the heavy base at Khalil's head.

Khalil ducked, and Boris missed, but then Boris pivoted in the direction of his swing and came around again, with the base of the lamp now lower. He caught Khalil's outstretched arm in a glancing blow that knocked the knife from Khalil's hand.

Khalil backpedalled quickly, and Boris, knowing this was his last and only chance to kill this man, charged forwards with the floor lamp.

Khalil feinted right, then moved left and kicked Boris's legs out from under him. Boris crashed to the floor, losing his grip on the lamp, and Khalil was on Boris's back, his knees straddling the big Russian and his right arm locked round Boris's throat, constricting his airway.

Boris lay perfectly still, not wanting to provoke the man. Khalil's head was close, and Boris could feel his warm, steady breath on his neck. Then Khalil whispered into Boris's ear, 'You taught me well, Mr Korsakov, so I will not mutilate you or cause you a painful death.'

Boris tried to nod his head, but Khalil tightened the pressure round his neck.

Khalil said, 'But you gave me some bad advice . . .'

Boris saw something in front of his blurry eyes, and he could not identify it at first, though he could see Khalil's free hand gripping something.

Then he knew what he was seeing—the long, thin shaft of an ice pick.

'No!'

Khalil put the tip of the ice pick into Boris's left nostril and pushed it back into his brain. He withdrew the pick, then pushed it up into Boris's brain again. He kept pushing until the ice pick came up through Boris's skull.

VLADIMIR WAS WAITING for Khalil in the basement at the elevator and escorted him through the dark storage area to a flight of concrete steps, which they both ascended.

Vladimir pushed on a metal door that opened to an alleyway between the buildings, filled with trash cans and plastic garbage bags, two of which now contained the corpses of the bodyguards.

Vladimir said to him, 'God has blessed you, my friend.'

'And you.'

Khalil pulled his hand out of his pocket, and Vladimir thought he was extending his hand in friendship, but as he reached for Khalil's hand, he saw that the hand was wrapped in a bloodstained table napkin, and he hesitated.

Khalil fired a single bullet into Vladimir's forehead.

The man fell back into a pile of garbage bags. Khalil tossed the smoking cloth on his face, pocketed the gun, then covered his body with more garbage bags.

Khalil walked up the alleyway to an iron gate, which he unbolted and exited onto the sidewalk of Brightwater Court.

There was a number of pedestrians on the sidewalk, and Khalil moved through the crowd towards his taxicab. He opened a rear door and jumped in, pulling the door shut as Rasheed moved away from the kerb.

Rasheed asked in Arabic, 'Where now?'

Khalil replied, 'The Brooklyn-Battery Tunnel. Hurry, but do not speed.' Then he sat back, looking out the window, and said to himself, 'And now for Mr Corey.'

RASHEED DROVE HIS TAXI through the long Brooklyn-Battery Tunnel and exited in Manhattan at West Street, near the site of the World Trade Center. Asad Khalil made a cellphone call, spoke for a few seconds, then hung up and said to Rasheed, 'Rector Street.'

Rasheed continued on for a minute, then turned into the narrow one-way street. Parked on the short and quiet street, near the large Battery Parking Garage, was a tractor-trailer. Khalil said, 'Wait here.'

Khalil exited the taxi and walked towards the large truck.

Painted on the side of the long trailer was CARLINO MASONRY SUPPLIES, with an address and phone number in Weehawken, New Jersey.

Khalil approached the tractor, and he saw a man's face looking at him in the large sideview mirror. Khalil held up his right hand and made a fist.

The door opened, and Khalil climbed up the step and swung into the rear compartment of the big cab.

This large windowless compartment appeared to be a sleeping area, and in it was a burly man with a crew cut, dressed in jeans and a green T-shirt with the masonry company's logo on the front. In the driver's seat was another man, wearing a baseball cap, and in the right front seat was the man who had opened the door for him, who also wore a cap, jeans and a blue team shirt that said 'Mets.'

These three men, Khalil understood, were European Muslims, Bosnians, and they had all fought in the war against the Christian Serbs, so they were not strangers to danger or killing. Khalil would have preferred to be meeting Arabic speakers, whom he could fully trust. But this part of his mission was controlled by others, who felt that these Western-looking men were well suited for what needed to be done.

Each man introduced himself in English by his first name, and Khalil said to them, 'You may call me Malik,' using the name of his spiritual advisor in Libya—a name that meant 'master' or even sometimes 'angel', though these men would not know that.

He gestured to the rear of the truck. 'Tell me what you have here.'

Tarik, in the passenger seat, replied, 'We have fertiliser.' He laughed, and the other two men laughed with him. Khalil did not laugh, and the men became quiet. None of them enjoyed working with Arabs. The Arabs were almost without humour, they did not enjoy a drink or a cigarette, as Bosnian Muslims did, and they treated their women—all women—very badly.

Khalil asked again, 'What do you have?'

Tarik replied, this time in a flat tone of voice, 'Ammonium nitrate fertiliser, liquid nitromethane, diesel fuel and Tovex Blastrite gel, all mixed in fifty-five-gallon drums—eighty-eight of them.' He added, 'It took us two years to amass these chemicals in this quantity without arousing suspicion.'

Khalil asked, 'How do you know you have not aroused suspicion?'

It was Edis, the driver, who replied, 'All of these chemicals are legal for their intended use, and they were purchased in small quantities by others who had legitimate uses for them, and then resold to us at a criminal price.' He smiled and said, 'What is not legal is mixing them together. Or attaching blasting caps to the mixture and blowing it up.'

Khalil smiled then, so Edis added, 'The most expensive ingredient at today's prices was the diesel fuel.'

Tarik and the man in the back of the cab, Bojan, laughed at this, and Edis said to Khalil, 'The Arabs are going to bankrupt this country with these oil prices.'

The three Bosnians all laughed, and Khalil thought they were idiots—but useful idiots who had apparently accomplished their task. He asked, 'How large is the bomb?'

Tarik, who seemed to be the expert, answered, 'The explosion that will result from this quantity of chemicals will be the equivalent of 50,000 pounds of TNT. This explosion, if it was detonated in midtown Manhattan, would cause death and destruction for a mile in all directions, and it would be heard and felt for over a hundred miles.'

Khalil thought about that, and he wished that the bomb would be detonated in midtown Manhattan, among the skyscrapers and the hundreds of thousands of people on the streets. But those who had planned this operation had decided on something else—a symbolic act that would shake American confidence, strike a blow at their arrogance and re-open a large and recent wound.

Khalil asked Tarik, 'How is this detonated?'

Tarik replied, 'It is electrical. There are fifty blasting caps in the drums, which I have connected by wires to a standard twelve-volt battery. The current from the battery must pass through a switch, and the switch will make the electrical connection when the electronic timer reaches the hour I have set it for.' He asked Khalil, 'Do you understand?'

In fact, Khalil did not fully understand. His experience with explosives was limited, and he would have preferred a martyr in the back of the trailer to detonate the bomb, as he thought this would be a more trustworthy method than a timing device. But this idea for the bomb was not his. He was in America to kill with the knife and the gun, the way a mujahideen kills. His jihad, however, needed to be paid for, and so he had agreed to assist his Al Qaeda backers with the bomb.

Khalil looked at his watch and said, 'I have much work to do tonight. You will hear from me at approximately ten p.m., and I will assist you in the killing of the guards. Until then, you will move this truck every half hour and you will do nothing to attract attention or arouse suspicion.'

No one replied, and Khalil continued, 'If a policeman is inquisitive, and he asks you to open the trailer, you will do as he asks. If he becomes more inquisitive, you must kill him.'

This time, each man nodded.

Addressing each of them by name, Khalil said, 'Edis, Bojan, Tarik, are you all armed?'

Each man produced an automatic pistol with a silencer.

Khalil nodded and said, 'Good. You are being paid to kill anyone who is a threat to this mission. I will be with you later. Then you are free to leave.'

In fact, they were not going to leave—they were going to die. But Khalil did not think they suspected this. And even if they did, they were stupid and arrogant enough to believe that three former soldiers with guns would be safe from harm. 'In the name of Allah—peace be unto Him—the most merciful, the most compassionate, I ask his blessing on you and your jihad.' He ended with, 'May God be with us this night.'

The three men hesitated, then responded, 'Go in peace.' Tarik opened the door, and Khalil climbed out of the cab.

As soon as he was out of earshot, Bojan said in Bosnian, 'Go to hell.'

The men laughed, but then Edis said, 'That man frightens me.'

No one had anything to add to that.

CHAPTER TEN

Bellevue. I'm gonna miss this place.

I'd brought Kate some clothes that she'd asked for, plus make-up and whatever so she'd look good when they wheeled her into an ambulette the next day. She asked me, 'Anything new?'

Just the usual, so I replied, 'Nope.'

She asked me, 'Have you spoken to Walsh or Paresi?'

'Nope.'

Kate and I watched some TV—a History Channel documentary about the earth being wiped out by a meteorite, which, if it happened tonight, would put the Minnesota trip on hold for a while. God?

Visiting hours ended at 9 p.m. Kate and I kissed goodbye, and she said, 'I'll see you tomorrow. Get here an hour early and get me checked out.' She added, 'This is the last time we have to say goodbye here.'

'Get some recipes before you go.'

My FBI driver was still Preston Tyler, who was putting in a long day.

He informed me that there would be no driver on duty until morning, but he assured me, 'Your surveillance and protective detail is still in place.'

'Terrific.'

There were no messages on my home phone, no email, and my cellphone was silent. I thought about calling Boris again, but then I thought about just sneaking out of here and making another unannounced visit to Svetlana. I decided to wait half an hour, and if Khalil didn't turn up here, I'd go and see Boris.

At 10.15 p.m. my cellphone vibrated. It was a text from Paresi that said: *Urgent and confidential. Meet at WTC site, Port Authority trailer. ASAP.*

I stared at the text. I wasn't sure what Paresi meant by confidential. Maybe he was finally getting his head on straight. Was this the break I'd been waiting for?

I texted him: *20 minutes.*

I called down to the parking garage and was happy to get Gomp on the phone. I said, 'Gomp, this is Tom Walsh.'

'Hey, Tom, how ya doin'?'

'Swell. I need a ride down to 68th and Lex again.'

'Sure thing.'

'Meet me at the freight elevator in two minutes. And mum's the word.' I added, 'Fifty bucks.'

'Sure thing.'

I hung up and strapped on my gun belt and hip holster. On the belt, in a sheath, was my K-bar knife, which I'd taken with me on all my walks in the park. I put on a blue windbreaker and left my apartment.

As I was speed walking towards the freight elevator, I realised my vest was packed in my luggage. I don't normally wear a vest, so it's not second nature, like my gun. I hesitated and looked at my watch. The hell with it. I got in the freight elevator and hit the garage button.

The elevator doors opened, and there was Gomp sitting in a nice BMW SUV. I was glad he hadn't stolen my green Jeep.

I came round the car and said to him, 'I need help with something in the elevator.'

'Sure thing.'

He got out of the BMW and moved towards the freight elevator as I jumped in the driver's seat. He shouted, 'Hey! Tom! Where you—?'

I hit the accelerator, drove up the ramp, and turned right onto 72nd

Street. I caught the green light at Third Avenue and continued on.

I looked in the rearview mirror. There wasn't much traffic at this hour on a drizzly Sunday night, and I didn't see any headlights trying to keep up with me. That was easy.

I drove through Central Park at the 65th Street Transverse Road, then got over to the West Side Highway and within fifteen minutes I was on West Street, driving between the dark, devastated sites of the World Financial Center and World Trade Center. Pre-9/11, a footbridge spanned West Street at Liberty, and I saw the remnants of the structure and turned left. I parked the BMW near the chain-link gates and got out.

I walked to the gates, and saw that the heavy chain and lock were in place, but there was a lot of slack in the chain. I squeezed through and walked quickly to the Port Authority trailer.

I knocked on the door, then tried the handle. The door was unlocked, so I opened it and called, 'Federal agent! Hello? Coming in.'

I stepped up into the trailer and saw that the front area—an office with two desks, a radio, and maps—was empty. An electric coffee maker was on in the galley kitchen, but the TV on the counter was turned off.

I called out, 'Anybody home?' but no one answered.

My cellphone buzzed. I looked at the text message, which was from Paresi: *We're down in the pit. Where are you?*

I replied: *PA trailer. 1 minute.*

I left the trailer and started down the long, wide earthen ramp that went into the deep pit.

The excavation site was huge, covering sixteen acres, and it would have been pitch-dark except for a dozen or so stadium lights that illuminated some of the desolate acreage. Pieces of equipment were scattered around—mostly earth-moving equipment and a few cranes. I also saw a big tractor-trailer parked near the centre of the site.

About halfway down the ramp, I stopped. I looked into the pit, but I didn't see anyone. I texted Paresi: *Where?*

He replied: *Centre, big semi.*

I looked at the big tractor-trailer I'd seen, about 200 yards away, and I saw someone pass from light to darkness.

I continued down the hard-packed earth ramp. Why did Paresi want to meet here? And where were the Port Authority cops? Down in the pit?

The drizzle had stopped, but at the bottom of the ramp the softer earth had turned muddy, and I wished I'd changed out of my loafers. I also noticed deep, fresh tyre marks made by what was probably an eighteen-wheeler that had come through not too long ago. Assuming these were made by the big semi in the centre of the site, I followed the tread marks.

I was passing in and out of darkness, and the banks of stadium lights to my front were shining in my eyes.

I saw the tractor-trailer—CARLINO MASONRY SUPPLIES—about fifty yards ahead, but I didn't see Paresi or anyone else.

I took another few steps and stopped. I was getting a weird feeling about this . . . the stadium lights . . . the shadows . . .

I pulled my Glock and stuck it in my belt, then moved more slowly towards the tractor-trailer.

I stopped and looked to my left. About ten yards away, I could see something moving in the half-light. As my eyes adjusted, I could see an object swinging from the cable of a crane, and it took me a few seconds to realise it was a person . . . Then I realised I was looking at the face of Vince Paresi.

I grabbed my gun out of my belt and, as I was dropping to one knee, I heard a high-pitched scream from the top of the dump truck behind me, and a fast-moving shadow flitted across the light. Then something slammed into my back with such force that I was driven face-first into the wet ground. The wind was knocked out of me, and I saw my gun lying in the mud a few feet in front of me. I lunged for it, but something hit the back of my head, and then a foot kicked the gun away.

I jumped to my feet and realised I was wobbly. As I caught my breath and tried to get my bearings, I saw someone in dark clothing standing about ten feet from me. I took a deep breath and stared at The Lion.

Asad Khalil had a gun in his hand, but it was at his side.

Finally, he said, 'So, we meet again.'

He wanted to talk, of course, so I replied, 'Fuck you.'

He informed me, 'That is the second time tonight someone has said that to me. But the last man said it in Russian.'

Well, I knew who that was, and since Khalil was standing here, I knew that Boris was not standing anywhere. And Paresi . . . my God . . . I felt a rage rising inside me, but I knew I had to keep it under control.

He said to me, 'I want you to know that I am alone. It is just us. I saved you for last, Mr Corey.'

I replied, 'I saved you for myself.'

He smiled, and it wasn't a nice smile. 'I didn't feel a bulletproof vest when I knocked you to the ground.'

I didn't reply.

'No matter. I am not going to shoot you in the heart.' He held up his gun and said, 'This is the gun of your deceased wife. I am looking forward to shooting off your manhood with this gun.'

He had a few more things to say before he did that, and I thought about a few moves I could make, but none of them seemed promising.

Without my head moving, my eyes darted around at what was nearby. My gun was too far away, and there was nothing close by that I could use. I quickly scanned the top of the distant foundation walls. The observation deck was closed, and even if someone was walking by at street level, they couldn't see this far into the dark pit.

Khalil said, 'There is no one here to help you. They are all dead. The two policemen in their trailer are dead. And as you can clearly see, your superior officer cannot help you.' He held up a cell. 'His final message to you is this—Asad Khalil has won.'

Again, I felt the anger taking over—this cold-blooded, murdering—

'Did it not occur to you, Mr Corey, that this was not as it seemed?'

I thought about that. Maybe it did occur to me, deep down, but I'd just left it there because it hadn't mattered to me if it was Paresi or Khalil.

He looked at me and said, 'It was fated that we meet.' He glanced around. 'Here we are, where 3,000 of your countrymen died.'

I reminded him, 'Hundreds of Muslims died in the towers.'

He ignored that, and said, 'This, I think, is a good place for you to die as well. Did I choose well?' I didn't reply, and he continued, 'But I will not kill you unless you force me to. I will, however, shoot you in the groin, then slice off your face as I promised.'

I had no reply to that, either.

He reached behind his back and produced a long knife. He said, 'You will be alive to feel it and to see your face being pulled from your skull.'

He was into taunting, which was part of the ritual for most pleasure killers. Then he asked me, 'Do you have another gun?'

Well, I did, but I'd loaned it to Kate. I didn't reply.

He looked at me, then stuck his knife back in his belt, and then his gun, too. 'Is your gun hand faster than mine? Please. Reach for your gun.'

If I had one, asshole, the first and last thing you'd see would be the flash of the muzzle.

He said, 'You either have no gun, or you are a coward.'

I had no gun, but I did have a knife he didn't seem to know about. I said, 'I can't hear you. Step closer.'

He drew his knife again and moved towards me, a big smile on his face, saying, 'I once flayed a man's flesh from his chest, and I could see his ribs, his lungs, and his beating heart.'

As he came closer, I could see his face looked exactly like the photograph in the wanted poster—deep, dark, narrow-set eyes, separated by a hooked nose that gave him more the appearance of a bird of prey than a lion.

'If you turn and run, I will shoot your legs out from under you, then butcher you.' He was really having fun.

'I'm not running.'

'No, but you are stepping backwards. Come to me. Fight like a man.'

'You have the knife, asshole. Put it down.'

He flipped the knife into the air, then caught it and smiled again.

He was enjoying this and, to be honest, I was not. I knew this guy could slice me up if I made a move towards him, so I again backed off.

It was time to end his fun, so I reminded him, 'Your mother was a whore.'

He screamed something and charged at me.

I turned, took a running step, pretended to slip in the mud, then drew my knife and spun around on my knees and let him run into the K-bar knife, which caught him in his groin.

He let out a surprised scream and backed away as I charged in for the kill before he went for his gun.

He had his knife hand over his groin and his other hand was reaching for the Glock as he backpedalled, and he lost his footing in the mud and fell backwards. The only move I had was to dive on him to keep him away from the Glock, and I made a running jump and landed full on his chest as he was starting to raise his legs to catapult me into the air. I saw his arm coming round, and I felt his knife cutting into the back of my shoulder blade, scraping across the bone. Then his arm was rising again for another stab, and I grabbed his wrist. I kept the full weight of my body on him as he struggled to get me off him and get his knife hand free.

My knife hand was free, and his left hand was free, but instead of reaching for his gun, he made the right decision to grab my arm before I got my blade into his face or throat. He got a tight grip on my wrist, then lifted his head and got his teeth into my cheek and bit down hard on the maxillary nerve, which sent flashes of pain through my head.

He was still holding my wrist, but I managed to get my arm up, and I brought the butt end of the heavy K-bar down on the top of his head.

He released his bite on my cheek, and I twisted my hand to bring the business end of the knife into the top of his skull, but he was incredibly strong and he pulled my arm away and held it.

So we were locked together, neither of us able to use our knives, and this would go on until one of us weakened, or did something unexpected—or desperate. He was in very good physical shape, and he didn't seem to be tiring as we each tried to break free from the other's grip.

He tried a few times to get his knee in my groin, but he had no leverage, and I kept my full weight on him. Then he tried to get his teeth into my face again, but I kept my head tilted back.

I had no idea where I'd stuck him. Genitals? Thigh? Lower abdomen? But I knew the wound wasn't bleeding enough to weaken him.

My cheek wound felt warm and wet, but I didn't think he'd done too much damage.

We made eye contact and I said, 'You're going to die.'

He shook his head and said, 'You.'

His voice was still baritone so I guess I'd missed his nuts.

As we struggled, I realised he wasn't weakening at all, but I was. Time to do something.

I gave him a head butt, but it didn't cause him any more pain than it did me. He retaliated by trying to get his teeth on my face again, which is what I wanted him to do. I clamped my teeth on his big hooked nose, and I bit down as hard as I've ever bitten on anything. He screamed in great pain, and with adrenaline-charged strength, arched his body up with me on top, which gave him the leverage he needed to go into a rolling motion, trying to reverse our positions and get on top of me. I lost my grip on his knife hand, and he immediately brought his knife down into my back again, slicing into my rib cage.

He would have stabbed me again, but I suddenly relaxed my muscles and he found himself going through the rest of his twist and roll without resistance. This put him unexpectedly face-first into the ground with me on his back. His knife hand was free, but he couldn't use it from that position. He tried to scramble away, but I came down heavily, and he collapsed on his chest and stomach. Both my hands were free now. I pulled his bleeding head back by his long hair and slashed his throat, then pushed his face into the mud. He didn't make a move or a sound, but my instincts said he wasn't finished.

In fact, his arm slid under his body, and I knew he was going for his gun. I got there first and snatched the gun out of his belt, and because you don't want a gun in play this close, I jumped off him and stepped back.

I stood there, breathing hard, keeping my eye on him.

The stadium lights were shining in my eyes. A worse problem was that the wetness was spreading over my back. I realised that the second stab had gone deeper than I thought and I was losing blood. My head was getting light, and I felt my knees giving out. Then I found myself kneeling on the ground.

Khalil was moving now, and I watched as he rose slowly to his feet.

His back was to me, but I saw him wiping his face with his hands. Then he turned round and looked at me. His face and clothes were covered with mud, but I could see the blood on his throat and his shirt. I realised, however, that the blood wasn't gushing the way it should have if I'd hit his jugular or carotid.

He spotted his knife on the ground, picked it up, and came towards me.

Die, you sonofabitch.

I stood too quickly and felt light-headed again. I thought I was going to pass out, but I took a few deep breaths and kept still so my heart wouldn't start pumping more blood out of me.

Khalil kept coming, holding his knife in front of him.

When he was less than ten feet from me, he said, 'Your face.'

Well, I didn't want him to deface me. So I raised Kate's Glock and pointed it at him. Again I thought I was going to black out.

I said, 'Drop the knife.'

I noticed that the Glock was totally covered with mud, and I wasn't sure it was going to fire, and neither was he. I said, 'Drop it, asshole.'

He took a few more steps, then sank to his knees.

It was over, but it's not over until it's over—and he was still holding his knife pointed at me.

I would have waited it out, but I was starting to get that bleeding-to-death feeling that I knew too well, so I had to put the final nail in this bastard . . . I aimed at his head and started to squeeze the trigger, but then I stopped and looked at him. I lowered the gun and shoved it in my belt.

Again Khalil stood, and he did the zombie walk with his knife pointing the way towards me.

I took a deep breath, then lunged at him with my knife, parrying his arm away as I brought the K-bar up in an underhand motion. The blade sliced through the bottom of his chin, through his mouth and into his palate, where it stuck. I let go of the knife and stepped back.

His eyes widened, and he tried to speak or scream, but he just made a few unintelligible sounds, blood running out of his mouth.

He started choking, then amazingly he took another step towards me, and we made eye contact, not three feet apart.

I looked into his eyes, and they were bright and burning.

I said to him, 'My wife is alive. I am alive. You are dead.'

He kept staring at me. Then he clumsily shook his head. As we both stood there, a few feet apart, our eyes fixed on each other, I had the sense that this was a contest of wills—who was going to drop first?

It wasn't going to be me. I managed to keep standing, even though my head was starting to spin.

Khalil suddenly seemed aware that he had a problem, and his right hand came up and grabbed the handle of the knife stuck under his chin.

Well, nobody but me touches my combat knife, so I smashed him in the face.

He went down, and I knew he wasn't getting up again. I let myself fall to my knees. Then I crawled over to Khalil and dropped my head and shoulders on his chest to keep my wounds elevated.

I found my cellphone and called 911. I said to the dispatcher, 'Ten-thirteen . . .' Officer in trouble. I ID'd myself and gave her my shield number, then used cop lingo to make it sound urgent: 'I need a bus, forthwith,' an ambulance—now. I gave her the location, then I said, 'Look for the . . . big semi . . . Carlino Masonry . . . yeah . . . let's be quick.'

I closed my eyes and tried to control my breathing and my beating heart. This was going to be close.

Within five minutes, I heard sirens up on Church Street.

I turned my head and looked at Vince Paresi dangling from the big crane. I took a deep breath and said to him, 'It's over, Captain—we won.'

Early morning sun was coming through the window, and hanging from the window cord was a stuffed lion. I was pretty sure this wasn't a dream, and the room definitely looked familiar.

Someone was squeezing my hand, and I turned my head to see Kate standing beside my bed. She was wearing the white blouse and blue skirt I'd brought her, and it took me a few seconds to process that.

She smiled and asked me, 'How are you, handsome?'

I didn't know how I was, but I replied, 'Not bad.' I added, 'You should see the other guy.'

She forced a smile and said, 'You're going to be fine.'

'Good.' But I can't go to Minnesota.

She had tears in her eyes, and she bent over and kissed me.

I found the bed control and raised myself into a sitting position.

I had tubes and wires attached to me, and I checked out the monitors, which looked OK. I was starting to experience that euphoria you get when the Grim Reaper has just missed you. I leaned forwards and said, 'I want to get out of here.'

Kate said, 'The doctor said three or four days—but I told him a week.'

Not funny.

She held a cup of ice water to my lips and I took a sip. I noticed now that her bed was still in the room, and I asked her, 'You staying?'

'No, you're staying. I'm leaving.'

'Yeah?' I lay back, and even with the painkillers, I could feel where I'd taken the two knife cuts. In fact, my whole body ached.

I stared up at the ceiling for a while, then I said, 'Khalil's dead.'

'I know.'

'Vince Paresi is dead. Khalil killed him.'

A silence, then, 'I know.'

She was crying, and to be honest, I felt a lump in my throat. I had no idea how Khalil had killed Vince, but I hoped it was quick.

She pulled up a chair and took my hand. 'When you're ready to talk about it . . . I want to know what happened.'

I was ready to talk about it now, but I knew I'd be telling the same story at least twenty times to half the Justice Department, so I said, 'When I get home. You can help me with my incident report.'

She smiled and said, 'Don't puff yourself up.'

Kate and I agreed that I needed a few weeks at home so I could recuperate quietly. I expressed my deep disappointment that we couldn't see her parents in the foreseeable future, and she knew I was full of crap, but she couldn't say that to a man in my delicate condition.

I asked her, 'Have you heard anything about Boris?'

She shook her head and said, 'Why do you ask?'

'I think Khalil killed him.'

She didn't respond, but she was probably thinking what I was thinking—I should have reported my contact with Boris to Tom Walsh. Not only would Boris probably still be alive, but if the surveillance team had grabbed Khalil in Brighton Beach, I could have saved myself some excitement at the WTC site—not to mention a few days in the hospital.

Also, Vince Paresi would still be alive.

Well, in this business, you call it like you see it and, as I said, you live—or die—with the consequences.

I asked Kate, 'Did you hear anything about the Port Authority cops? The ones who were in the PA trailer?'

She replied, 'Tom mentioned that there were two of them, but they haven't been found. He's at the crime scene.' She added, 'I don't want to talk about this now.'

I nodded, but it was still on my mind. I tried to focus on something that was bothering me about this.

It was certainly possible that someone like Khalil could get the drop on two cops who weren't expecting trouble. But if he did have accomplices, to kill the cops or hang Vince from the crane, where were they? Disposing of the bodies? Or did Khalil, true to his M.O., kill them, too?

All of this brought me back to what had been on my mind all week. Based on what I had seen in the apartment on 72nd Street, Khalil obviously had accomplices and resources here, so he probably had a favour to repay. Did Khalil have something else planned? What was it? And was it still in the works?

I raised my bed a little more and could feel the sutures pulling in my back. I closed my eyes and got my brain in gear. Something had struck me as odd at the WTC site, and it was now coming back to me.

The tyre marks. They had been fresh.

That semi had been driven into that site sometime on Sunday. Why would the PA cops have let this tractor-trailer through the gates on a Sunday night?

Maybe because they were dead.

I thought of the signage, too—CARLINO MASONRY SUPPLIES. The masonry supply thing wasn't quite right either. They weren't pouring concrete yet, and there were no cement mixers on the site. So what was in that big trailer?

And why did Khalil choose the WTC site to meet me? Well, for the symbolism? I get it . . . but . . .

I sat up. 'Holy shit.'

'John? Are you all right?'

I was pretty sure I knew what was in that trailer—and I knew, too, it hadn't blown yet, because if it had, I'd have heard it, and even felt it, here, three miles away.

I reached for the phone on the nightstand. Kate asked me, 'Who are you calling? What's the matter?'

Walsh's cellphone went into voicemail. I was about to dial the Ops Centre, but I got into crazy mode and pulled the tubes and wires out of me. Kate went a little nuts and started yelling, but I slid out of bed, and said to her, 'Let's go.'

'What—?'

I took her arm, and as I moved her towards the door, I said, 'You're getting me out of here.'

She pulled her arm back and said, 'No. John—'

'Trust me. I'll explain. Come on.'

She looked at me, then said in a calming voice, 'Stay here, and I'll get you some clothes.'

I looked at my watch, but it was gone. I asked her, 'What time is it?'

She glanced at her watch and said, 'It's 8.05. You stay here—'

'Kate, at 8.46 a.m., the time when the first plane hit the North Tower, a very large bomb will detonate at the World Trade Center site.'

She looked frightened then—not about the bomb, but about me.

So to get this moving, I lied, 'Khalil told me this when he thought he was going to kill me.'

'Oh my God . . .'

'Let's go. You got your cellphone?'

She grabbed her handbag, and we hurried out of the door. We got to the security checkpoint and almost got through, but a big Department of Corrections guy stopped us. Kate went into full FBI mode, flashed her creds, and made it clear to the guy that this was none of his business. He backed off, and we were out in the corridor.

We got in an elevator. I said to Kate, 'When we get outside, commandeer an ambulance.'

She nodded.

The elevator reached the lobby, and Kate moved quickly towards the First Avenue exit as I dialled Walsh.

Tom answered, 'John . . . good to hear from you. Kate told me you were resting comfortably and I just want to say—'

'Tom, shut up and listen to me.' That shut him up, and I said, slowly and clearly with calm urgency in my voice, 'Asad Khalil, when he thought he was going to kill me, told me a bomb was planted at the WTC site—'

'What?'

I could hear engine noises in the background. 'Are you still there?'

'Yes.'

'I think the bomb is in the big semi there—Carlino Masonry Supplies. Do you see it?'

'I'm . . . standing next to . . .'

'You might want to move. But before you do that, call the Bomb Squad ASAP. Then get everyone the hell out of there—that is a very big truck.'

Silence.

I walked out of the lobby, and a guard shouted, 'Hey! Where're you goin'?'

Walsh asked, 'John . . . are you sure about this?'

Very good question. And the answer was no, but I said, 'Yes.'

The guard was speaking to me, but I waved him off.

I said to Walsh, 'It's set to go off at 8.46 a.m.'

He didn't ask why I thought that, because that time is burned into everyone's mind. The guard had another guard with him now.

There was another silence on the phone, and I thought I'd lost him, but then he said, 'That's thirty-one minutes . . . We can't evacuate this—'

'Try. Meanwhile, get the area cordoned off. Call the Bomb Squad.'

I hung up, and the guards had me by both arms, so I told them, 'I've got stage one leprosy.'

They backed off, and one of them made a call on his radio.

An ambulance pulled into the pick-up lane with Kate in the passenger seat. I went to it, opened her door and said to her, 'Get out.'

'No. I'm going with you. Get in the ambulance. Now! Or I'm going without you.'

She meant it, so I climbed in as quickly as I could and knelt between the two front seats.

Kate said to the driver, 'Ground Zero. Liberty Street. Lights and sirens.'

The driver, a young black woman, hit the bells and whistles and off we went. She asked Kate, 'What are we responding to without EMT personnel, and why are we taking a patient to Ground Zero?'

Kate explained, 'It's complicated, Jeena. And really urgent.'

Jeena knew how to weave and bob and blow the lights, and I estimated we'd be at Ground Zero in about five or six minutes.

I said to Jeena, 'As soon as you drop us on Liberty Street, turn around and get out of the area.'

She thought about that and said, 'Sounds like you might need an ambulance down there.'

'Yeah, but . . .' I tried to think about how big this bomb could be. Like everyone in this business, I compared it to the Oklahoma City bombing. That was a small truck with about 5,000 pounds of explosives that did massive damage. This trailer, if it was full of the same stuff, could take out twenty city blocks—basically all of Lower Manhattan. Holy shit.

Kate turned back to me. 'John, maybe we don't need to be there.'

No, we didn't need to be there, but I didn't respond to that logical statement. I looked out of the windscreen, and I could see we were already well within the blast zone.

I called Walsh and asked him, 'What's happening?'

He replied, 'We got all the construction guys out of here, and we've cleared the streets. There's no way to evacuate this area so we're trying to get people underground.'

'Where's the Bomb Squad?'

'I see the trucks coming down the ramp.'

'We'll be right there,' I said.

'What? Where are you?'

'Just speeding past your corner office in an ambulance.'

'Get the hell out of here. That's an order. OK, here's the Squad.'

The phone went dead, and Kate asked me, 'Where's Tom?'

'Still there.'

Jeena had put it all together and informed us, 'You guys got about twenty minutes.'

Up ahead at Murray Street, Broadway was blocked off with police cars.

They saw the ambulance coming, and one of the cruisers moved aside and we shot through.

The streets around the site were nearly deserted, except for police cruisers with their lights flashing, and warnings blasting out of their bullhorns saying, 'Get away from the windows! Go into your basement!'

Well, I wasn't an expert on bombs, but I did know that a massive explosion would suck the breathable air out of underground spaces. Not to mention ruptured gas lines, falling debris and collapsing buildings. I hoped to God this day didn't make 3,000 dead look small by comparison.

Jeena snapped a hard right on Barclay, a left on West, and within two minutes we were at the open gates to the ramp. Jeena headed down into the pit.

I said to Jeena, 'That big tractor-trailer over there. Thanks.'

As we moved quickly down the ramp, I could see one Bomb Squad truck and two guys in blast suits—which weren't going to help them at all—and Tom Walsh. And that was it. Except for three idiots on the way.

I could also see the yellow crime scene tape that encompassed about an acre around the tractor-trailer. The Bomb Squad guys were standing with Walsh at the rear of the trailer, but I could see that the doors were still closed.

Come on, guys. I said 8.46 a.m.—not p.m.

Kate also noticed and asked, 'Why are they just standing there?'

Coffee break? I said hopefully, 'Maybe they're finished.'

The ambulance was fishtailing in the soft earth, pulling up to the big semi. Kate and I jumped out, and Kate yelled to Jeena, 'Get out of here! Go!'

Jeena made a quick U-turn and gunned the vehicle back up the ramp.

Tom was speaking to the Bomb Squad guys, and I could tell they were a little tense—so this was not over.

I looked at the time on Kate's cellphone—8.31—then it changed to 8.32.

I said to Kate, 'They don't look happy.' She nodded.

I watched Tom and the two guys speaking quietly, as though a loud noise would set off the bomb. Bomb Squad people are, by definition, nuts. They volunteer for this. And I knew from past experience that they have a weird sense of humour about getting blown up. But they're highly trained and cool, and these two guys didn't look panicky yet, though Tom was a bit pale.

But . . . well, I give him my brass balls award for this.

Finally, Tom turned his attention to us, checked out my pyjamas, gave me an annoyed look, then said to Kate, 'Get in that Bomb Squad truck and get out of here. Now!'

Kate replied, 'I'm not leaving unless we all leave.'

There wasn't much time left to argue so Tom said, 'OK . . . here's what's happening—we sent the other Bomb Squad team away with the dog, who gave a positive reaction. Also, Dutch'—he indicated the older guy—'and Bobby say they can smell ammonium nitrate, diesel fuel and whatever. So we have a bomb.'

Right. I could smell it, too. I noticed now that the doors were open just a crack, and Bobby was looking inside with a flashlight.

I suggested, 'Maybe they should think about defusing it now.'

It was Dutch who replied, 'Sometimes these things are rigged with a booby-trap detonator.' He added, 'If we had time, we'd use the robot, but the robot is slow and you're telling me it could be set for 8.46—so Bobby is the robot.'

In fact, Bobby was now standing on the rear bumper rail with his flashlight, and he called out, 'I don't see any indication of a booby-trap detonator.' He added, 'But you never know until you try.'

He turned and said to Dutch and to Tom, 'Your call.' He asked, 'Do we open it?'

Tom and Dutch looked at each other, then Dutch looked at his watch and said, 'If it is set for eight forty-six, we have about ten minutes to defuse it, or ten minutes to get in our truck and get ourselves into a bank vault or something.'

Tom Walsh looked at the towering buildings around us, which we all knew were still filled with people, despite the warnings to clear the area.

Dutch informed us, 'We're talking about a mile, mile-and-a-half blast radius . . . depending on what they have in that fifty-three-footer.'

Tom nodded, but didn't respond.

Dutch also let us know, 'If it's a simple detonator—without any tricks—I can defuse it in a few seconds, by cutting some wires or interrupting the power source.'

I asked, of course, 'And if it's not so simple?'

He replied, 'If it looks like it's rigged with a current interruption switch, or maybe a second power source or some other sneaky detonating device . . . then . . .' He shrugged and said, 'If I had more time, I could dope it out . . . but we don't have a lot of time, so I just start cutting wires and see what happens.'

He went to school for this?

Dutch also let us know, 'And maybe it's command detonated. Like, someone is going to make a cellphone call and that trips the switch.'

No one had anything to say about that, so Dutch reminded us, 'Meanwhile, we've got to decide if we're going to open that door—that's step one. I can't defuse it from here.'

Bobby, who I thought had shown a lot of patience, said, 'I think our time is almost up to get out of here.'

Kate said to Tom, 'Open the doors.'

Tom glanced at his watch.

To help Tom with his decision I said, 'I'm guessing that Khalil stashed the PA cops' bodies in there, so the doors have already been opened.' Recalling that Boris had told me he'd never trained Khalil to work with bombs, I concluded, 'I don't think Khalil would risk disarming or re-arming a booby trap.'

Tom looked at me, then at Dutch, and said, 'Open the doors.'

Dutch said to his partner, 'Bobby—do it.'

Bobby grabbed the handle on the left door, and Dutch put his hands over his ears. What the *hell* is wrong with these people? This was *not* funny.

The big door swung open, and, just as I predicted, nothing happened. Or I was in heaven now. But Walsh was here.

Dutch was already in motion, and he jumped up into the trailer where a stack of cement bags formed a wall almost to the roof. Bobby gave him a boost, and Dutch scrambled up the bags, lay on the top row, and shone his flashlight into the trailer. For a second, I thought he was going to say, 'Just cement,' but he said, 'Mother of God . . .'

Oh, shit.

Bobby called up to him, 'What do we have, Dutch?'

Dutch replied, 'Well, for starters, five bodies. Two PA cops—male and female—and three males in civilian clothing.'

Bobby made the sign of the cross, which these guys probably did a lot.

Dutch said, 'Also, about eighty . . . ninety fifty-five-gallon drums . . . with wires running to them.'

Bobby asked Dutch, 'Do you think it's a bomb?'

I looked at Tom, who was looking at me. And he thought I was nuts?

Meanwhile, Dutch had some bad news. 'I don't see the power source or the timer or the switch.'

They're definitely in there, Dutch. Look hard.

Dutch gave Bobby a hand, and Bobby scrambled up to the top of the cement bags and shone his light into the trailer. He said, 'It's gotta be over there. See where the wires are running?'

'Yeah . . . but . . . it's tight in there . . .'

Tom called out helpfully, 'Four minutes.'

Dutch said to Bobby, 'OK, let's walk on barrels.'

They both dropped behind the wall of cement bags and disappeared. I didn't want to rip my stitches, but in about four minutes that would be the least of my problems, so I hopped up onto the bumper, followed by Kate and Tom. We boosted and pulled one another to the top of the cement bags and poked our heads into the dark trailer.

Tom had a flashlight. Below us was a two-foot space between the wall of bags and the first row of drums, and in that space were five bodies piled on the floor. In fact, I could smell them over the chemical smells. The three civilians looked young and burly, and I could see blood on their faces as though they'd each been shot in the head. I assumed, too, that these guys had something to do with the truck and with Khalil.

Tom was shining his light around, and I looked into the trailer and saw the tightly packed rows of fifty-five-gallon drums, each one covered with a lid. I could now see the wires running into the centres of the lids.

Neither Kate nor Tom said anything for a few seconds, then Kate said, 'That bastard.'

Dutch and Bobby were walking carefully on the rims of the drums, making their way towards the front of the trailer, shining their flashlights between the drums as they walked.

Tom asked them, 'Is there anything we can do?'

Neither man replied, and I had the sense that even these two were getting a little tense. I didn't want to look at the clock on Kate's cellphone, but I was estimating about two minutes until eternity.

Dutch said, 'Here it is.'

Good news.

'Hard to reach.'

Bad news.

Dutch flattened himself on top of the drums in the far right corner, and Bobby squatted beside him and kept his light trained into the dark space.

Dutch said, 'I see the twelve-volt . . . but I don't see the timer or the switch.'

Bobby agreed and added, 'They could be any place.'

I strongly suggested, 'Take the fucking cable off the battery.'

'Yeah,' Dutch replied, 'that's what I'm trying to do . . . thanks for the tip . . . tight in here . . . this vice grip was made by the lowest bidder . . . hope there's not a second battery somewhere . . .'

Kate, Tom and I lay there on top of the wall of concrete bags, peering into the dark, waiting for some positive statement from Dutch. Also, I was trying to remember why I thought I needed to be here. On that subject, I said to Kate, 'Sorry.'

She replied, 'It's OK, John.'

Right. I already saved her life once—so I was allowed one fatal mistake.

Tom was staring at his cellphone and said, very calmly, I thought, 'It is now 8.45.'

No one had anything to say about that.

It got very quiet in the trailer. I could actually hear the metallic sound of Dutch's vice grip trying to loosen the nut on the positive cable lead.

Then Dutch said, 'Got it.'

Bobby said, 'Hey dude, that's the wrong one.'

They both laughed.

I shut my eyes, and I could hear the bells of nearby St Paul's Chapel, which chimed every morning at 8.46.

nelson **demille**

American author Nelson DeMille is a no-nonsense kind of guy who sets himself a goal and goes for it. He gets impatient with overbearing rules and bureaucracy and he likes life to be served up with a strong dash of humour, refusing to take anyone or anything (and certainly not officialdom) too seriously.

As you get to know his hero, John Corey, who first appeared in *Plum Island* in 1997 and then in *The Lion's Game* in 2000 and now in *The Lion*, you realise that there's probably a strong dose of DeMille himself in his most popular character. Does the author agree that there are similarities? 'My wife thinks so,' he answers. 'Some other victims of my sharp tongue might think so, too. It's always in good humour, though. I think you see that with Corey. He has a good heart, even though he may be obnoxious at times. Maybe I share some of his traits. I don't suffer fools gladly; I get annoyed with stupid people and that's not good. John Corey's sarcastic. That's the way that he and I deal with the world—through sarcasm and wit and a little bit of irony sometimes.'

DeMille started life in New York City in 1943, although his family later moved out to Long Island, where he attended Hofstra University, before signing up with the military and attending Officer Cadet School. As a first lieutenant in the US Army from 1966 to 1969, he fought as an infantry platoon-leader in Vietnam and came out of that conflict with an Air Medal, a Bronze Star and the Vietnamese Cross of Gallantry. Jobs in construction followed, before he finally settled on a career in insurance fraud. 'Most of my life before I started writing was physical,' he says, looking back. 'Sports in high school and college, three years as an infantry officer, hunting, deep-sea fishing, construction jobs and lots of time in the gym. My other interest was girls . . .'

He originally wanted to write a great American war novel. 'I never really wrote the book, but it got me into the writing process.' He dabbled for a few years, seeing five of his earliest novels appear in paperback ('they're pretty awful, long out of print') until, finally, in 1976 he decided to take the writing seriously and give up the day job. At about the same time, Arab terrorism was a brand-new threat, capturing the world's attention. Taking up that theme, DeMille wrote *By the Rivers of Babylon*, which soared into the charts, was snapped up by book clubs, and sold worldwide.

It's a reasonable assumption that DeMille's past military career and the fact that he has forged great contacts in many of New York's top-flight institutions have aided him hugely in writing about John Corey, hero of *The Lion*, and a man brave enough to face up to the world's scariest terrorist. Corey works, for example, for the (fictional) Anti-Terrorist Task Force, an organisation that DeMille admits is very much based on America's real-world Joint Terrorist Task Force.

'*The Lion's Game* began with the Joint Terrorist Task Force in New York City. I knew somebody on it, which was my entrée into it. I think maybe writers always look for organisations that not everybody knows about,' DeMille says. 'The Task Force is an organisation that was really only formed after the World Trade Center bombing on February 26, 1993. An Arab terrorist group, for the first time, struck in America . . . and after the September 11, 2001 attack, more Americans had been killed than in the Korean War.' DeMille explains that the Force was meant to get the New York City Police Department, the CIA and the FBI collaborating closely. 'It was a good idea on paper, but the reality was that they didn't always work well together. So, it gives me a chance to have this conflict. Corey's not politically correct. They are. If you are a federal government worker, you watch your Ps and Qs. John Corey doesn't care about that, he just lets it rip . . . It was fun for me and that's how I knew it was going to be fun for the reader.'

And if DeMille had not succeeded in writing books? 'Archaeology has always fascinated me,' he says, 'and I touched on it in my first novel, *By the Rivers of Babylon*. I'm sure I'll probaby return to the subject one day in one of my books, so that I can become an archaeologist, vicariously.'

Ground Zero

Almost ten years on, the Ground Zero Memorial, *Reflecting Absence*, is nearing completion and will include the footprints of the former Twin Towers as recessed pools, with the largest man-made waterfalls in the country, where the victims' names are inscribed around the edges of the pools. Built alongside the commercial structures that will occupy the new World Trade Center site, the message is clear: to move on with confidence, but never forget.

CE PIER

Where the
Truth Lies
Julie Corbin

Claire Miller's husband has been keeping secrets. About the whereabouts of the key witness in the murder trial he's prosecuting. And about the emails he's been getting, threatening to kidnap and kill their four-year-old daughter, unless he reveals where the witness is hiding. With their daughter's life at stake, it is left to Claire to uncover the identity of the blackmailer.

And to stop them.

Before it's too late.

PROLOGUE

I didn't see it coming.

No black cats crossed my path. No clear-eyed crows cawed alarm from the trees. There was nothing to warn me.

An invisible clock was ticking, each beat drawing my family closer to danger, and I was oblivious. Busy with normal, everyday things, I didn't know about the threats or the blackmail, or about the brutal turn our lives were soon to take. I didn't know that someone close to me was on course to devastate my family. I thought my home was safe, that danger kept its distance.

I thought wrong.

1

It's the first of June, Bea's fourth birthday. The party's over and the other mums have arrived to collect the children. I move between the kitchen and the back garden, handing juice to children, tea or coffee to mums, catching snippets of conversations. My stepmother, Wendy, is tidying up the remnants of wrapping and streamers that lie across the kitchen floor.

'I can't believe she's four already,' Wendy says, as she arranges Bea's cards on the dresser. 'It seems like only yesterday she was learning to walk.'

'I know.' I look through the big picture window to where Bea and another child are hanging on to my husband, Julian, one on each arm. He's twirling them round. I lean my head against the window frame and smile, then laugh out loud as they drag him to the ground and start to pummel him with their small but persistent fists. They stop when he pretends to cry.

'It's such a pity Lisa can't be here,' Wendy continues, coming to stand beside me. 'Her scan results will be out tomorrow, won't they?'

My heart squeezes as I nod. The last round of chemotherapy has left Lisa weak, emptied out, drained of almost everything that makes her my sister, and we're all praying it's been worth it.

'When I visit her tomorrow, I'll show her the party photos,' I say, putting my arm round Wendy's shoulder.

'Give her a hug from me,' Wendy says, moving to one side as my friend Jem comes in from the garden, her arms loaded with a couple of discarded sweaters, a miniature cricket set and two Frisbees.

'Julian's going beyond the call of duty out there,' she says, dumping all the stuff on the table. 'They're running him ragged.'

'He's enjoying it,' I say, looking at my watch. 'He has to leave for Sofia in an hour. He can nap on the plane.'

'What's he going there for, then?' Jem asks.

'It's the case he's working on. He needs to double-check some details with the Bulgarian police.'

'He's prosecuting Pavel Georgiev,' Wendy says. 'You'll have heard of him, Jem. There's been a lot about him in the papers.'

'Yeah, I have.' Jem looks from Wendy to me. 'I didn't realise he was working on that case.'

'It's really very serious,' Wendy says, her voice hushed. 'Georgiev and the men who work for him . . .' She shakes her head at both of us. 'Shocking stuff. It's hard to believe that people can be so evil.'

'And that's not the half of it,' I say. I think of some of the things Julian has told me, details I've avoided discussing with friends and family: young girls trafficked and used for sex, men tortured and then killed because they refused to hand over a percentage of their earnings. I shiver. 'I'll be glad when the trial's over and he's locked up for good.'

Jem gives me a quick hug. 'You'll want some family time before Julian leaves.' She tilts her head in the direction of the garden. 'I'll get the ball rolling on the goodbyes.'

One mother and child after another come inside. Shoes and sweaters are found, goodbyes are said, and Bea hands each of her friends a party bag. She takes this very seriously, peering into each bag before handing it over.

'That one's for you, Adam,' she says. 'It has the red water pistol.' She looks up at me. 'He likes water pistols.'

'OK, sweetheart.' I stroke my hand across her forehead, bringing wispy blonde hair away from her eyes and tucking it back under her Alice band. She's wearing a white party dress with a turquoise ribbon round the bodice. It exactly matches the colour of her eyes, still turned up towards mine.

'I'm four.' She touches the badges pinned to her chest, each one shouting out the same number.

'You are.' I kiss her pink cheeks. 'But you'll always be my baby.'

'I'm not a baby, Mummy.' She stares at me earnestly. 'I'm four now.'

'Well, you'll always be my precious baby girl.' I tickle her middle.

The corners of her mouth twitch in a smile and then she hands out the next party bag. It's been a long day and I expected her to be over-wound by now, but she's taking all the attention in her stride. I feel proud of her.

Almost everyone has gone when I leave Bea at the door with Wendy and find one of the mums a spare T-shirt for her daughter, Jessica, who has spilled juice down the front of hers. We talk in Bea's room for a few minutes, and by the time we get back downstairs, Bea has left her post and the last remaining party bag is lying on the floor. I give the bag to Jessica and say goodbye to them both with a promise to arrange a play date soon.

I walk back to the kitchen and find Julian taking a glass from the shelf.

'That went well.' I cuddle into his back. 'Thank you for being chief entertainer. When the clown didn't turn up, I thought we were in for trouble.'

He holds the glass under the running cold tap until it's full to the brim. 'Couldn't have done it without Charlie.'

'You're right. It's great having him home.' I look outside into the garden but can't see our elder son, Charlie, or his girlfriend, Amy. Wendy is the only one there. 'Being away at university has helped him grow up.'

'It has.' He swallows down the water, then stretches out his spine. 'I'm getting too old for children's parties.'

'Fifty is the new forty, you know.'

'Tell that to my knees.' He collapses onto a chair and eases off his shoes.

'There's grass all over you.' I brush it off his upper back, then let my hands slide round his neck and rest my elbows on his shoulders. I put my mouth next to his ear. 'Do you really have to go to Sofia today?'

'I do.' He pulls me round onto his lap. 'I have a meeting early tomorrow.'

'It's been so nice having you home on a weekday.' I rest my head close to his neck. 'I hope the trial's over before the summer ends. We could go to Dorset, take Lisa with us and have a family holiday, all of us together.'

I feel his body tense ever so slightly.

'We're not going to get a holiday?' I say.

He doesn't answer me. I sit back so that I can see his expression.

Almost twenty-five years of looking at his face and I've yet to grow tired of it. He has good bone structure: high cheekbones and a straight nose. His mouth is wide and made for smiling. His eyes are the colour of rich mahogany; his hair is jet black and curly with a smattering of grey at his temples. Not for the first time I think that he's far too handsome to be a barrister. But today the way he's looking at me—staring, in fact—is puzzling.

'Are you OK?' I say.

The phone rings, high-pitched and intrusive. I reach behind Julian and take it from its cradle on the dresser.

'Hi, Mum. It's me.'

'Jack!' I automatically smile at the sound of my younger son's voice. 'Bea's had a great party. She loved the present you sent. How's the revision going?' Jack is at boarding school and in the throes of his GCSEs.

'Getting there,' he said. 'I just called to wish Bea a happy birthday.'

'OK. I'll pass you over to Dad while I find her.' Julian takes the phone and I go to the bottom of the stairs. 'Bea!' I call. 'Jack's on the phone.'

No answer. There's no way she'd want to miss out on a call from him. Although separated in age from Jack and Charlie by twelve and fifteen years, Bea loves both her brothers with a blind, full-on passion. Perhaps the excitement of the day has caught up with her and she's fallen asleep somewhere. I have a quick look in the sitting room—empty—then climb the stairs to her bedroom, calling her name as I go. I push open the door, but she isn't in there either. I check the master bedroom—it wouldn't be the first time she's decided to raid my make-up or try on my shoes. I go into our en suite bathroom. I even open my wardrobe, but there's no sign of her.

The shower is running in the family bathroom and I can hear Charlie singing quietly. Our house is on four floors and I go quickly up to the top floor, where we have two spare rooms. I don't expect to find her here and I don't.

'Jack's on the phone!' I call, going down the stairs again. 'Bea, if you're hiding, you have to come out now.'

I go all the way down to the basement, where there's Jack's bedroom, Julian's study and the utility room. There's nobody here. The utility room leads out onto the back garden and I shout to Wendy, 'Bea's not out there with you, is she?'

'No. I last saw her in the sitting room.'

I climb the stairs again and am almost back in the kitchen when I remember: Bea has a den under the stairs, where she keeps her soft toys and a pile of cushions. I pull aside the curtain that conceals the space. She isn't there.

I go back to the kitchen. 'I can't find her,' I say, fully expecting Julian to smile and remind me of some obvious place that I've forgotten to look.

He doesn't. His eyes hold mine for a split second, then he's out of his seat so quickly I lurch back against the work surface. He slides his feet into his shoes and speaks curtly into the phone. 'Jack, we'll call you back.' He puts down the handset and looks at me. 'What do you mean you can't find her?'

'I've called her, but she isn't answering. I think I've looked everywhere.'

'She couldn't have gone off with one of the mothers?'

'No, of course not.' I shake my head. 'Nobody would take her without asking.' I look around helplessly. 'She must be in the house somewhere.'

He moves past me and goes to the stairs. 'Bea!' He calls her name several times, his voice so loud it's almost a roar.

'Julian! That will frighten her.'

He ignores me and, taking the stairs two at a time, goes up to the first floor. 'Charlie!' He bangs on the bathroom door.

Charlie comes out onto the landing, a towel round his waist. 'What?'

'Have you seen Bea?'

'Amy's taken her to the park. Didn't she tell you?'

'No.'

'There we are, then.' I relax my shoulders. 'Whew! Panic over.'

But Julian isn't reassured. He goes into our bedroom, looking through the front window. We live in a terrace of white town houses in a crescent in Brighton. The road curves round a grassy play area with swings, a slide and a wooden climbing frame. I follow Julian's eyes and see at once that Bea isn't there. The park is empty apart from Jem, who's pushing her son, Adam, on the swing. Without looking at me, Julian goes down the stairs again.

I follow him. 'Julian?'

He's not listening. He's out of the front door and crossing the road. He shouts to Jem, 'Have you seen Bea?'

She shakes her head and Julian starts to pace in front of the iron railings. I try to catch his arm, but he doesn't even register I'm there. His expression is strained, his pallor strangely grey considering the speed of his breathing and the heat of the afternoon sun. But worst of all is the frantic look in his eyes, as his gaze trawls from one end of the street to the other. I have only one coherent thought: for some reason, Julian thinks Bea is in danger.

I grab his shirt. 'Julian!' I jerk him towards me. 'What's going on?'

'Where are they?' His eyes scan the street again.

'I don't know, but surely . . .' I take a deep breath. 'Surely you don't think Amy's going to harm Bea?'

'I don't know, Claire.' His lips, his face, his whole body is tight with tension. 'But think about it. What do we actually know about this girl?'

'Well . . .' I pause. 'Charlie's been going out with her for about nine months. Her parents live in Cyprus. She is—'

'Mostly unknown to us,' Julian says. Then he holds my shoulders and shakes me gently. 'Where else could she have taken her?'

'The corner shop. But—' He's gone before I can finish the sentence. 'Bea normally only goes there with one of the boys,' I say quietly to myself. The truth is that Bea isn't particularly fond of Amy and has told me that she likes it better when Charlie comes home on his own. I can't say that I've warmed to Amy either. She is abrasive, direct to the point of being rude.

I put my hands to my cheeks, close my eyes and allow myself to visualise Bea's face. If she were in danger, I would know. How could I not? She is my child. I spend most of every day with her and often the night too, when she climbs into our bed. There is an invisible cord that binds us together. If she were in danger, I would know.

'What's happening, Mum?' Charlie comes down the steps behind me.

'They aren't in the park,' I say. 'Can you think of anywhere Amy might have taken Bea?'

'I dunno.' He shakes his head. 'But she'll be OK. Why's Dad panicking?'

I follow Charlie's gaze to the end of the street. Julian has come out of the corner shop and is running towards us. I don't remember ever seeing him move with such urgency.

'Your dad has been tense recently . . . with the trial and everything.' I believe this, because it's the only explanation that makes sense. Before a trial begins, Julian is unusually preoccupied, his mind packed full of evidence and witness statements and arguments for the prosecution. This is the most high-profile case he has ever been involved in. What's more, twice in the last fifteen years Julian has been involved in trying to bring Georgiev to justice and both times the case fell apart because of problems with witnesses—one mysteriously disappeared and another retracted his statement at the eleventh hour. This time, the main witness is being protected by the Witness Anonymity Act and this is the best shot that Julian and his team at the Crown Prosecution Service will ever have at convicting Georgiev.

'The corner shop's empty and the girl serving hasn't seen them.' He stops in front of us. 'I'm going to call the police.'

'Dad, chill!' Charlie says. 'I'll call Amy and find out where they are.'

'Quickly, then,' Julian says.

'OK.' Charlie takes out his mobile and presses two buttons.

Seconds tick by.

'She's not answering?' Julian asks.

'Give her a chance.'

More seconds and Julian loses patience. He takes his own phone from his back pocket. I watch his fingers move over the buttons.

'Look! Look!' Charlie shakes his father's arm. 'They're coming.'

He's right. Amy, Bea and Mary Percival, Bea's nursery teacher, are walking along the pavement towards us. Bea is skipping between the two women, holding on to their hands. Relief surges through me. I watch Julian walk towards them and swing Bea up into his arms. He says something to Amy. She gives a careless shrug and he turns away.

Amy is tall for a girl, around five feet nine, and has a loose-hipped walk, accentuated by the way she dresses: floaty skirts with leggings and short, tight tops. When she's within earshot, she shouts, 'What's with Julian?'

'He was worried. We didn't know where Bea was.'

'She asked me to take her out. She saw her teacher through the window.'

'It's my fault,' Miss Percival pipes up.

'It's OK.' I half smile at them both. 'But next time, Amy, if you could just tell me before you take her ou—'

'I did.' Her brow furrows with indignation. 'I called up the stairs. You were there with another mother.'

'I'm sorry—I didn't hear you.'

She gives another careless shrug. 'I thought you had.'

'Nothing happened, Mum,' Charlie says, his arms protectively encircling Amy's shoulders. 'Dad seriously overreacted.'

'Perhaps he did, Charlie,' I say evenly, 'but next time'—I look at Amy—'you need to make sure I've heard you before you go off with Bea.'

'I was only trying to be helpful,' Amy says, making wide eyes at me.

I hold my tongue. Amy spends most of the university holidays and at least one night a week during term-time living in our home and eating our food. Not that I grudge her this, or expect any thanks. But her persistent I'm-right-and-you're-wrong attitude grates on my nerves.

However, I can already see that the incident is dividing Charlie's loyalties. He gives me an imploring look over her shoulder while drawing her still closer into his chest. I manage a smile and he smiles back, then leads Amy up the stairs and they both return indoors. I'm left with Miss Percival.

'All's well that ends'—she sees my face and hesitates—'well.'

'Yes.' I take a deep breath. 'That's true, but you can imagine . . . It was alarming to find that Bea had disappeared from the house.'

'I completely understand,' she says, taking my hand, then dropping it almost at once as if shocked by her own temerity. Not much more than five feet tall, she has unremarkable grey-blue eyes, and her brown hair is cut short. She comes across as someone who is more comfortable with children than adults, and is either shy or overly formal when talking to me. But with the children she relaxes into another part of herself and is clearly great fun.

'Bea just loves coming to nursery,' I say. 'She's very fond of you.'

'Well . . .' She blushes. 'She's a lovely little girl. She brings so much enthusiasm to the class. That's why we were at the end of the street—she wanted to show me where the men are building the new crossing. We've been talking about road safety at circle time.' She blushes again. 'I'm sorry to have caused you concern. It's the last thing I would want to do.'

A taxi pulls up alongside us and the driver winds down his window. 'Taxi for Julian Miller.'

'He's inside,' I say. 'I'll tell him you're here.'

Miss Percival smiles her goodbye and I go indoors. Julian is on the phone in the kitchen.

'The taxi's here,' I tell him.

He holds up a hand. I tap my watch and give him a significant look. He smiles distractedly and turns away from me, still talking into the phone, the fingers of his free hand drumming an impatient rhythm on the table.

The taxi beeps its horn from the front of the house. I get Julian's suitcase and leave it in the hall. Outside, I find the driver on the pavement, leaning against the side of the car. 'I'm sorry—could you wait just another minute or two? My husband's on the phone.'

He gives me a resigned look and lights up a cigarette as I return indoors.

Julian is coming along the hallway from the kitchen and I turn to meet him. 'Julian.' I throw my arms round him and feel the familiar weight and tilt of his body as it leans in to mine. 'That was a bit scary, wasn't it?'

'I overreacted.' He kisses me slowly. 'I'm sorry.'

'It's OK.' I rub his cheek. 'I know the trial is looming and that makes for a stressful time.'

He looks away, but not before I see a dark shadow move across his face. My spine straightens and I take a step back. 'What was that?' I say.

'What?'

'That look on your face.'

'What look?' He throws out his arms and smiles, innocence personified.

I'm not convinced. 'Julian? Everything's all right, isn't it?'

'Listen—' His attention strays as the driver sounds his horn again. 'I'll be back in no time.' He lifts his suitcase off the floor. 'I have my BlackBerry with me, but in case the signal is poor, I've left contact numbers on the pinboard.' He runs his hands up and down my back. 'I love you, you know.'

'I know.' I hold his eyes for a moment, warmed by the sincerity in them, and then I let him go.

I'M STILL STANDING on the step when Jem walks across from the park and shouts, 'Everything OK?'

'Yes.' I realise I'm holding my breath and I exhale with a loud sigh. 'Just a bit of a mix-up with Amy and Bea.'

'Oh . . . OK.' She looks at me uncertainly. 'Is Friday fine for me to finish off the room?' Jem is more than just a good friend. She runs her own painting and decorating business and has been helping me fix up a room for my sister, who's going to move in with us.

'Friday's ideal. Lisa should be coming out of hospital on Saturday.'

'How's she doing?'

'She's finished her second round of chemotherapy. We'll find out tomorrow whether it's done any good.'

She gives my upper arm a squeeze. 'Fingers crossed it's good news.'

Back inside, Wendy is getting ready to leave. 'What was happening with you and Julian earlier?' she says. 'I caught the tail end of Amy saying something to Charlie about neither of you trusting her.'

I explain about Amy taking Bea to the end of the street. 'She said she called up the stairs to me and she probably did, but I didn't hear her and—' I lower my voice. 'In all honesty, I haven't warmed to her. I know Charlie is bowled over by her, but she's not the easiest girl to like.'

'She made quite a play for him, didn't she?' Wendy says.

'She did. He couldn't believe that a third-year with as many friends as she has would be interested in him.'

'She comes in quite a package.'

'You're absolutely right.' I sigh. 'Step into the body of a nineteen-year-old boy and she's practically irresistible.' I give Wendy a kiss on the cheek. 'Thank you for all your help today.

'Always welcome. You know that.'

NEXT MORNING I wake up late. I spend a few minutes in the bathroom, then pull on some underwear and a track suit, and go downstairs. It's already eight o'clock: breakfast time. Charlie is sitting on a high stool at the kitchen island with Bea on his knee. When she sees me, she slides off him and runs to me. She is wearing a pink corduroy pinafore with embroidered flowers round the hem, a white T-shirt and her *Finding Nemo* wellingtons.

I lift her up to hug her. Her blonde hair is soft and wispy and smells of shampoo. 'Have you had a bath this morning?'

'She had chewing gum stuck in her hair,' Charlie says through a mouthful of cereal.

Normally in student accommodation, Charlie's living at home during exam week. He is in his first year at the University of Sussex, studying ecology and conservation. As the university is based in Brighton, he often pops home between lectures, so in some ways it feels as if he hasn't really left. Perhaps I should have encouraged him to go farther afield, but the course was perfect for him and I'm the first to admit that giving my children up is not something I'm good at. Sending Jack to boarding school was difficult enough, but as he had been offered a sports scholarship I could hardly stand in his way. And Julian felt that the set-up would improve Jack's self-discipline. For two years it did. Only recently has Jack's behaviour started to slide.

I sit Bea down next to Charlie, then walk behind her to put the kettle on. 'What time did you get up, then, young lady?'

'About half past six,' Charlie says.

'I'm sorry, love. You should have woken me.'

'You were out for the count. I didn't have the heart to disturb you.'

'Look, Mummy!' Bea holds up strands of her hair. A whole section is shorter than the rest. 'We had to cut it.'

'It was the only way,' Charlie says.

'The only way,' Bea echoes, nodding her head wisely.

I look at them, Charlie with his mop of curly black hair contrasting with her blonde one. They are such opposites, an almost grown man and a small girl, and yet they have a deep connection. I always wanted to have a large family, but I only fell pregnant three times. I had the two boys three years apart and then a twelve-year gap before Bea came along, a gift for the whole family and just at a time when we needed it most. My father had died unexpectedly of a heart attack and a year later Bea was born, a reason to celebrate and get back on with living. I feel proud to be their mother.

As if on cue, my mobile rings. It's Jack. My signal is weak in the kitchen, so I go out into the hallway.

'Morning, love. Sorry we didn't ring you back yesterday afternoon. Dad went off to the airport and then time ran away from us.'

'Dad sounded a bit weird when he hung up.'

'It was nothing,' I say. 'What are you up to today?'

'Revision. Sport . . . and stuff.' He sounds subdued. 'I just called to wish Bea happy birthday for yesterday.'

I call to Bea and she sits on the bottom stair, clutching my mobile to her ear as she starts telling Jack all about her party. I go back into the kitchen, where Charlie is rinsing the breakfast dishes.

'Is Dad OK now?' he asks. 'He's normally Mr Cool and he was acting like disaster had struck.'

'He's only human, Charlie,' I say. 'He has a lot going on with the case.'

'He'll get Georgiev this time, though, won't he?'

'The odds are in the prosecution's favour, but Georgiev's crafty. I wouldn't be surprised if the defence have something up their sleeve.'

I take a bite of a leftover crust of toast. Suddenly the kitchen door flies open and Bea comes running back in, a look of concentration on her face. She pulls the heavy fridge door open and stands on tiptoes to reach last night's leftover chicken, then she crams pieces into the pocket in her pinafore.

'What are you doing, Bea?' Charlie and I say at the same time.

'Miss Percival says I can give Douglas a treat if he sits nicely.'

'Ah!' Charlie hunkers down beside her. 'Miss Percival's little West Highland terrier?'

'He comes on Weds-days and we take him for a walk. He likes chicken.'

I open a cupboard and find a small plastic box. 'Look!' I hold it out to her. 'We can put it in this.'

Charlie helps her transfer the chicken from her pocket into the box.

'Douglas is having puppies,' she tells him.

'I thought Douglas was a boy,' he says.

'He made friends with a lady dog and *she* is having puppies.' She looks up at me. 'Miss Percival says I can have one.'

'Does she now?'

'Well, she didn't say, but she says . . . she says'—she jumps in the air a couple of times as she thinks—'I'm good with animals.'

'And she's right—you are.' I kiss the top of her head. 'And we need to get going otherwise we'll be late.'

She follows me into the hallway. 'So can I have a puppy?'

'Let's ask Daddy when he comes home, shall we?' Bea has been asking for a dog for as long as she's been able to talk.

I look through the window out onto the street. The morning began with a summer rain shower, but this is now long gone and the sun is warming the pavements, steam rising lazily upwards.

'I have to bring Bertie.' Wherever Bea goes Bertie goes too. He is a brown, furry, bedraggled creature with one ear beginning to fray and the stitching at his foot coming away, but she won't let me fix him. He doesn't like needles, she told me. They make him cry.

I put on a pair of sandals and open the door into the porch. I help Bea slide on her backpack, Bertie's head poking out of the top, and we set off down the steps. She skips along beside me, interested in everything around her. Suddenly she veers off the pavement to peer at a dead frog in the gutter.

She pokes it with the toe of her boot. 'Is it dead, Mummy?'

'Yes, it's dead.'

We are standing between parked cars and the one directly in front of us has two men inside. One is on his mobile and is looking through the side window towards the park. The other man is watching us and gives me a polite smile. I smile too and try to persuade Bea back onto the pavement.

'Poor frog.'

'Yes,' I say. 'Now let's get going. Douglas will be waiting.'

She drags her eyes away and we walk to nursery. Miss Percival is standing at the door of the classroom waiting to welcome in the children. Bea and I are the first to arrive. When Douglas sees Bea, his tail starts to wag and he strains on his lead to reach her. She runs to greet him, crouching down beside him to stroke his head.

'Look, Mummy!' She is giggling. 'His tail is polishing the floor.'

'So it is!'

'He wants some chicken.' She stands up and swings off her backpack.

'I hope you don't mind,' I say, looking at Miss Percival. 'She has a treat box for Douglas.'

'Not at all. But, Bea, perhaps you might fill up his water dish first? He's thirsty after the walk over here.'

'Yes, Miss Percival.' She wends her way across to the big sink.

'Did your husband get away OK yesterday?' Miss Percival asks me.

'Yes, thank you.' I'm watching Bea as she climbs up onto a little wooden stool so that she can reach the taps.

'There's a lot going on for you and your family at the moment,' Miss Percival says, and then she clears her throat. 'Bea has mentioned the trial.'

'Has she?' I stare at her, surprised. 'In what context?'

'Children talk as they play. About their lives and what's going on at home. Parents don't always realise how much their children pick up on.'

'I'm sure.' In fact I'm well aware that Bea is in the habit of listening in on adults, absorbing snippets of information here and there. But both Julian and I try hard to prevent her from hearing anything that might upset her, especially if it relates to his work or to Lisa's illness. 'What has she said?'

'That her daddy was putting a bad man in prison.'

I raise my eyebrows. 'That's the nub of it, I suppose.' I pick Bea's backpack up off the floor and hang it on her peg. 'But she didn't seem worried by it, did she?'

'Not exactly.'

'Not exactly?' I repeat.

'I was just anxious about the effect her father's job and her aunt's illness might be having on her,' she says stiffly.

'That's kind,' I say, 'but I think we're managing to shield her from the worst of both those things.' I turn and look along the corridor, mindful that other mothers are arriving. 'But if you have specific concerns, please tell me.'

'Of course.'

She gives me a tight smile and turns away. I feel like a child who's been dismissed and I almost leave there and then, but Bea is walking towards me, her face solid with concentration. She has filled the water dish to the brim and is taking small steps to ensure it doesn't spill onto the floor. I give her a kiss goodbye, then walk towards the door, my skin prickling.

When I talk to Miss Percival, I'm often left feeling that there's a subtext I'm not tuning in to. This isn't helped by the fact that we haven't yet made it to first-name terms. She's younger than I am by a good ten years and several times I have asked her to call me Claire, but she persists in being formal. It feels like she wants to keep her distance from me, but then she breaks this by asking me quite specific questions about Julian and Lisa.

I walk away, shaking my head. I don't know what to make of her and I don't see any point in dwelling on it.

2

We moved to Brighton from London just over five years ago and it took me a while to appreciate the flavour of the city. Just as the Thames adds colour and history to London's identity, the sea brings a similar sense of power and timelessness to Brighton's. Today, as I walk back from nursery, the sea is slate grey and calm, its glassy expanse spreading as far as the eye can see.

On the way home I stop at the wholefood shop in Western Road to buy some provisions. For the last month I've employed a cook, a young Turkish woman called Sezen Serbest, who has been a godsend. When Lisa was diagnosed with cancer, our lives changed. Like Wendy, Lisa had been an almost daily and much-welcomed visitor to our home. But the last year has seen her spending more and more time in hospital. Just when she needed food that was nutritious and health-affirming, Lisa was eating the worst diet she'd ever had. At first I cooked for her, taking food in at lunchtimes, but I soon realised that, although I knew the principles of good nutrition, I needed to up my game. After looking on the Internet, I found out about macrobiotics. With its emphasis on whole grains and vegetables, macrobiotic cooking was shown not just to encourage good health but to have therapeutic benefits. That was enough for me. I found Sezen, an experienced macrobiotic cook, through an agency, and she comes in for four hours every day.

When I reach the house, I go straight through the hallway and into the kitchen. Sezen is standing at the island in the middle of the kitchen using a spatula to move biscuits from a baking tray onto a wire rack.

'I could murder a cup of tea. And those biscuits.' I breathe in the smell. 'Can I steal one?'

'Of course!' She laughs. She is small and neat with dark hair tied in a plait that hangs halfway down her back. 'I thought you could take some to Lisa when you visit her at lunch, and I have made some soup.'

'Wonderful!' I say appreciatively. 'It smells of cinnamon.'

'It is warming,' she says. 'Charlie has gone out. He told me to let you know he will collect Bea at one o'clock.'

'Great.' I make myself a cup of tea, take another biscuit and sit down on the sofa by the window. 'So it's the big day tomorrow, Sezen.'

'Our move down from London? Yes. Lara and I are both looking forward to living in Brighton. The air here is fresher. Being close to the sea will be a joy. And it will make coming to work for you so much easier. Also I start maternity cover for a café in Hove next month.'

'How are you travelling?'

'We will manage on the train.'

I shake my head. 'I can collect you. I didn't think to offer sooner.'

'No, no, no.' She shakes her right index finger at me. 'You must not.'

All her worldly goods, plus her young daughter, on a train? The mind boggles. 'Really, Sezen. I want to come for you. Please let me.'

She pushes out her bottom lip, half thinking, half doubtful. I reassure her that it's the least I can do after all she has done for me. She gives in.

I look at my watch, then stand up. 'I should get going to the hospital.'

'Here is Lisa's lunch.' Sezen hands me the bag she has prepared. 'I put some of Bea's birthday cake in there too. I know it is not macrobiotic, but treats every now and then do not do any harm.'

THE WARD IS particularly quiet today. Often there are nurses bustling in and out of Lisa's side room, but not at the moment. I stand at the door and watch her through the glass. She is fast asleep, her cheeks the colour of the bed sheets, in stark contrast to the blood that's running from a bag on a drip-stand into a vein in her left arm.

'She's washed out today.' One of the nurses has stopped beside me. 'Her haemoglobin is low—that's why she has the blood up.'

'And the rest of the test results?' I turn to face her, apprehension filling the space in my throat.

'The scans, well . . .' She looks behind her to where the ward sister has just come out of the treatment room. 'Lynn can give you the details.'

'Claire.' Lynn puts an arm round my shoulder and guides me into the relatives' room, closing the door. My heart sinks. If the news had been good, she'd have told me in the corridor. 'We have the results back now.'

'The cancer?' My mouth is dry. 'It isn't gone, is it?'

She shakes her head. 'Unfortunately not.'

'Right. I see.' I take a couple of steps backwards. I want to be sick. I feel disappointment, heavy as concrete, lodge in my chest. No miracles, then. The cancer is still in her liver, and could still be travelling in her bloodstream, making up its mind where to settle next. 'Does Lisa know?'

'Yes. Dr Doyle told her.'

'How did she take it?'

'She took it well. She was more worried about you.'

'Right.' At once I feel ashamed. My sister, facing the prospect of premature death at forty-seven, is more concerned with my reaction than her own.

Lynn strokes my hands. 'All is not lost, Claire.'

I nod. I want to cry but know that, if I do, Lisa will notice the telltale signs and will worry about me. So I grit my teeth and spend ten minutes with Lynn discussing taking Lisa home on Saturday and what community support staff will visit. When I go into Lisa's room, she is just beginning to wake up, but she looks far from rested. She's painfully thin, her skeleton barely covered by anything more than a layer of skin.

'How are you today?' I kiss her cheek. She feels cold, so I pull her blanket up over her shoulders.

'Hello, Claire.' She gives me a tired smile. 'This is a nuisance.' She points to the line going into her arm.

I stroke her arm near where the cannula slides under her skin. 'The blood will perk you up a bit, though. Put some colour back in your cheeks.'

'For a little while,' she acknowledges.

'I spoke to Lynn about your results.'

She frowns. 'Let's not talk about that now. But tell me'—she widens her eyes—'how was the birthday party?'

'Great fun.' I tell her about the clown not turning up and how Julian stepped in to organise party games. 'Charlie was a big help.'

'He's such a good brother.' She shifts her head on the pillow.

I bring the soup, homemade spelt bread, biscuits and cake out of my bag. 'I have some butternut-squash soup to tempt you with.'

'How wonderful.' She starts to haul herself up into a sitting position and I help her. Her arms feel like spindles; each vertebra in her back is a raised knuckle of bone. 'I'll start with half a cup.' I pour some out for her and she takes a sip, smiles. 'It's good. Tasty.'

'Sezen's recipe,' I say. 'She's a real find. And in just a few days you can come home and experience her cooking first hand.'

'Do you think?' She throws a weak arm outwards to take in the clutter of medical equipment, dressing packs and creams. 'I don't travel light.'

'I've already discussed it with Lynn. The nurse will come in to administer your drugs and check on you. The rest we can work out between us.'

'Are you sure?'

'Sure?' I give a short laugh. 'You're my sister. I want to look after you. And we're all set up for it. Jem's almost finished decorating the room. Wendy will come round every day to help out with Bea.'

She leans forward to hug me. 'I'm so tired of these four walls. I can't wait to come home with you. Family is just what I need. I might not be able to join in, but I'd still love to be a part of it.' She takes hold of my hand. 'So did Julian get away OK?'

'Yes.' I hesitate as memories of yesterday flood back. 'After a bit of a do.'

'What happened?'

I tell her about Jack phoning and me going to look for Bea and Julian's reaction when I told him I couldn't find her. 'I've never seen him react so strongly. He went from perfectly normal to distraught.' I shake my head. 'We found out she was with Amy, but still . . . It was like he really believed Bea was in danger. He was really freaked out.'

'It's not like Julian to be alarmed without good reason.'

As she says this, I have a sudden, clear picture of the expression that crossed his face when we were in the hallway, just before he left. It was a shadowy look. A secretive look. A significant look. Shit. Something's wrong.

'You're right,' I say to Lisa, then stand up and walk a few paces, thinking. My heart begins to pound, and bubbles of anxiety spawn in the pit of my stomach. 'The taxi arrived before we had the chance to talk.' I rub my forehead and look across at my sister. 'What do you think I should do?'

'He calls every evening when he's away, doesn't he? Talk to him about it.'

She gives me a reassuring smile. 'There's probably a simple explanation.'

'Yes, probably.' I take a big breath. 'I'm sure it's fine.'

'Now, here.' She pats the space next to her. 'I was promised party photos.'

I take my digital camera out of my bag and plug the cable into Lisa's laptop. A happy hour passes as we look at the photographs. Lisa has had several long-term relationships but never married or had children of her own. She is a doting aunt who loves my children almost as much as I do.

When it's time for me to go, I'm careful not to hold her for too long as I hug her goodbye. Although I feel a crushing disappointment over the scan results, I keep it to myself.

On the drive home, Lisa's words about Julian nag away at me. More so because she was only voicing what in my heart of hearts I already knew—Julian would never go off at the deep end without good reason. Pretrial stress makes him quieter and often short-tempered; it doesn't make him overreact. He believed Bea was in danger. He believed it.

I shift in my seat and force my hands to relax their grip on the steering wheel, hoping to dissolve the bubbles of anxiety that have clumped together in the hollow of my stomach. I drive home faster than I should, parking haphazardly outside the house, running up the steps and bursting in through the front door. Holding my breath, I stop at the bottom of the stairs and listen. I hear Bea's laughter coming from her room, Wendy and Charlie's voices as they talk to her. All is well.

I gulp in some air and call up the stairs, 'I'm home!'

'Come and see me, Mummy!' Bea shouts.

Wendy appears on the landing above me. 'How's Lisa?' She comes down the stairs. 'And her scan results?'

I tell her the news and watch tears gather in her eyes. I hug her to me and we stand like that for a moment until she pulls away and becomes her practical self again. We talk about arrangements and then she heads off home.

Bea calls for me again, but first I go into the kitchen and use the house phone. I'm itching to speak to Julian. I don't want to wait until this evening, so I call his mobile number. It rings twice, then goes through to the answering service. I don't leave a message. Instead, I stand in front of the pinboard. My eyes scan the board, seeing takeaway menus, school and university phone numbers, postcards, but no sign of where Julian's staying. And yet he made a point of reminding me that the contact numbers were on the board.

I go upstairs and find Charlie reading a story to Bea. 'Where's Amy?'

'In my room, finishing off an essay.'

'Did either of you see Dad's hotel details? He usually puts them on the pinboard in the kitchen.'

'I haven't seen them,' Charlie says. 'I'll ask Amy.'

He goes next door and Bea slithers off the bed. 'Look, Mummy, I have all my toys here.' She points to the floor, where she's arranged her birthday presents in a line against the wall. She holds up the soft toy Jack gave her. 'I'm going to call him Douglas because he's the same as Miss Percival's dog.'

'He is,' I say, sitting down on the bed. Charlie comes back. I look up at him. 'Has Amy seen the details?'

'No.' He shakes his head. 'Is there a problem?'

'Not really. Dad will call soon anyway.'

'Charlie!' Amy's voice shouts from the bedroom and he goes at once, pulled by an invisible thread.

'She wants him again,' Bea says with a sigh. 'She always wants him.'

I hide my smile—Bea isn't happy with Amy's power over Charlie.

The thumb of her left hand goes in her mouth, while her right hand reaches up, seeking the ends of my hair. She moves the strands through her fingertips and sucks harder on her thumb. We stay like this for a couple of minutes, Bea growing ever more relaxed, her body leaning into mine.

I kiss her forehead. 'Are you hungry?'

She takes her thumb out of her mouth. 'Grandma Wendy gave me food.' She pats her tummy. 'We had eggs and strawberries.'

'That's a funny combination!' I tickle her cheeks and she grins up at me. 'Well, let me know if you get hungry. I'm going downstairs.'

Before I have the chance to slide her off my knee, she sits up straight and looks at me wide-eyed because she's just thought of something. 'Is Daddy going to see the man?'

'What man is that?'

'The man what sends the emails.'

'What emails are those, sweetheart?'

'On Daddy's 'puter.' She looks at me and shakes her head so that her hair falls into her eyes. 'I didn't go on Daddy's 'puter. It was Daddy.' She frowns and shakes her head again. 'Daddy doesn't like the email man.'

'I see,' I say, not really seeing at all. I think of Miss Percival's comment this morning about the things children pick up on. Bea is in the habit of squirrelling herself under tables or in the corner of rooms and she often does this in Julian's study. Sometimes he forgets she's there and it's not unusual for her to report back to me snippets of what she's heard. I think, in this case, that she must be talking about Georgiev. But Georgiev is in prison. It seems unlikely that he would be sending Julian emails.

'Megan doesn't like the man,' Bea continues. 'She said to Daddy he has to be careful.'

The anxiety-lump in my stomach shifts, releasing a tremor that ripples through my body. Megan is one of the instructing solicitors with the CPS. She and Julian have spent hundreds of hours working on the Georgiev case. If she is urging Julian to be careful, it's because there's something wrong.

'I'm sure Daddy will sort it all out,' I say lightly, easing Bea off my knee. 'I'm just going downstairs. Why don't you make a bed for Douglas?'

'I can put him in beside Bertie.' She pushes her hair out of her eyes, then runs to the corner of the room where Bertie has a real dog bed, complete with a cosy sheepskin and an extra blanket. 'Bertie will look after him.'

I leave her to it and go downstairs. The inside of my skull feels as if it's expanding. I stand in the living room and look through the window. Mary Percival is walking the real, live Douglas in the park opposite our house. She looks up at the window, sees me and gives an acknowledging wave. I wave back. My eyes are looking at her, but my thoughts are elsewhere.

I go through to the kitchen and have one last search of the pinboard. I'm not imagining it. The details aren't there. OK. There are other ways to find out where he's staying. I scroll through the numbers on my mobile phone and stop when I get to Megan Jennings. She'll know the name of the hotel. And judging by what Bea might have heard, she'll know quite a bit more than that. I call her number. She answers almost immediately.

'It's Claire Miller,' I say.

'Claire, hi! Did Julian get away OK?'

'Yes. It's just'—I take a breath—'he left the number for his hotel for me but I can't find it and I thought you might be able to help me out.'

'Of course. I have the details on my computer. I'm not in the office at the moment, but I'll be back there in a few hours and will call you then.'

'That's OK,' I say quickly. 'Why don't you stop by here on your way home?' Like Julian, Megan commutes to London. She lives in a small flat round the corner from us, the proximity a mixed blessing, as work often stretches into the weekend. 'I can even rustle up some supper for you. It will save you cooking when you get in.'

'Sure.' A slight pause. I can almost hear the gear change in her brain. 'I'll be with you just after eight thirty. Is that OK?'

'Perfect.' Enough time to put Bea to bed. 'I'll see you then.'

I know that Megan will be wondering why I'm asking her to come round when she can easily give me the details over the phone. She is every inch the professional and won't want to breach confidentiality, but I don't intend to let her leave without her shedding some light on Julian's mood. I want to know whether she can make sense of what Bea's just told me and whether it's linked to the way Julian reacted yesterday afternoon.

And then it occurs to me—why wait for Megan when I can check for emails myself? Julian isn't here, but his laptop is. I can log on and see whether there are any suspicious emails in his inbox.

I go down to his study and switch on his laptop. The system begins to load and then I click the icon to log on to his server at work. Almost at once a box appears asking me to type in the password. I'm confident I know this. Less than two months ago, Julian was in Durham when he called and asked me to log on to the server at his chambers. His password alternated between numbers and letters—J1A9C9K4—Jack and the year he was born.

I type it in. 'Incorrect password' comes up on the screen. Damn. He's changed it. I try the same pattern with Bea and Charlie and their birth years. It doesn't work. I try with Julian's and mine. Nothing.

I stand up and take a deep breath. Think. Be logical. When Julian changes his password, he keeps it personal. Not as obvious as a single name, but obvious enough to him and surely, therefore, to me. I pace up and down, running names and numbers through my head, then sit back down and try some combinations: our wedding anniversary, the date he took silk, the date we moved to Brighton.

The door to Julian's study opens. I look up. It's Amy. She starts back in surprise. 'I didn't realise you were in here.'

'Well, I am.' I try for a smile. 'Did you want something?'

'I came down to make Charlie and me some tea.'

I point to the ceiling. 'The kitchen's upstairs.'

'Yes, but I heard a noise down here and thought that maybe Jack was home. Are you on Julian's laptop?'

'Yes.'

'Something wrong with yours?'

'Why?'

'Nothing.' Her hair is long and wavy and is a luxurious copper colour. Normally she ties it up under a thick multicoloured hairband, but today it falls over her right shoulder and she is holding the end of it, swinging it from side to side. 'It's just that I'm pretty good at diagnosing problems.'

As she reaches my side of the desk, I minimise the window. She's looking at the screen but the only thing she can see is Julian's desktop photograph of Bea and the boys taken at Easter.

'Oh! You're not doing anything much, then?'

I turn my head to look up at her. 'What I'm doing is private.'

'Sorry.' She gives a stifled giggle. 'I'll leave you to it, then, shall I?'

'Yes, please.'

She is wearing patchouli, a strong, heavy scent that lingers in the room after she's gone. She heard a noise? She heard me typing from the top of the stairs? Not possible. So what's she playing at? Was she snooping? I don't know what to make of it, so I decide that I'll think about it later.

I stare back at the screen. The interruption has allowed time for guilt to creep from the back of my mind to the front. This is Julian's work email. I shouldn't be doing this. And then, just as my mind's made up to go back to the kitchen, it comes to me—Lisa—the sixth member of our family. My fingers move over the keys: L1I9S6A3. At once the system fires up. I click on the icon that opens Julian's email. I scroll down through his inbox but can't see anything suspicious. He has lists of folders down to one side, most of them case names. I click on 'Georgiev'. There are over two hundred emails, but all the addresses are from other solicitors.

I start clicking on the folders titled with numbers and letters. The first three folders contain admin and account emails. The fourth has eight emails in it, all from the same address. What's unusual is that none of them has been replied to. I open the first one.

I'll be blunt. You have information I want and I'm willing to go to extreme lengths to get it. The witness in the Georgiev trial—I want his name and his whereabouts.

I sit back in my seat. Apart from the laptop's low hum, the room is quiet. A blackbird sits on a branch of buddleia in the garden, beyond Julian's window, singing a summer song. I feel strangely clear-headed. There are seven more emails in the folder. I decide to print them out and take them upstairs where I'm less likely to be disturbed. I shut down Julian's laptop, collect the sheets from the printer tray and fold them in half. I climb the stairs, tiptoe past

Bea's bedroom, walk through my bedroom and shut myself in the en suite bathroom. I lay the pages out on the floor in the order they were sent.

The first one is dated Monday, 24 May, nine days ago. I read it again. There isn't a name at the end, but it's clear that, whoever's written it, Georgiev is behind it. He wants to silence the main witness. He's done this in the past and that's exactly why the judge granted Julian an anonymity order in the first place.

I move on to the second email, which arrived a day later:

> There are two ways for me to come by this information. At the pretrial hearing, you support the defence counsel's request to lift the anonymity order. Or you tell me who and where the witness is. Simple.

Julian has already mentioned to me that the pretrial hearing is scheduled for Monday, 7 June, five days from now. It's unimaginable that, as prosecuting counsel, he would agree to lifting the anonymity order. His case has been built around this man's evidence; without it a conviction is unlikely.

The third email arrived at midday a week ago:

> Leaking the name and the whereabouts of the witness will be easy—by letter, email, phone call or text. You choose. We can arrange it.
>
> I'm sure you'll make the right choice. For Bea.

I feel as if my heart has stopped beating. My body is still, spellbound. Only my eyes are moving, flicking around the everyday mess in the bathroom. Bea likes to bathe in here because we have a corner bath. Her yellow ducks and boats sit around the tub.

I look back at the emails. The fourth is dated 27 May, last Thursday:

> I watched Bea and Claire this afternoon as they walked back from nursery. Bea was wearing a pink dress with a white flower pattern on the hem and pale green sandals with two buckles across each foot. She was carrying her stuffed dog, Bertie. They stopped at the Italian delicatessen on Western Road. Claire bought mozzarella cheese, Parma ham and a chocolate treat for Bea.

I think back. The email is accurate. We were being followed. Someone was watching us, listening to us. The walk back home is almost a mile and not once did I suspect we had a stalker. No hairs rose on the back of my neck, no gut feeling that something was amiss.

My eyes shift to the fifth email:

This morning Bea played in the sandpit. She was told she had to wear her sunhat. She doesn't like the elastic under her chin, so she wore a boy's cap instead. I could have taken her then. I could take her still. And you'd never see her again.

I imagine a stranger's hand reach out to catch hold of my daughter's shoulder and I wonder why I'm not screaming.

The sixth email came on Monday, just two days ago:

How will Claire react, I wonder, when she finds out you're sacrificing your own daughter in order to protect the witness, a criminal out to save his own skin? This isn't a straightforward case of good versus evil. But then again, Julian, is it ever?

Julian. For the past nine days, he has been reading these, and Bea has already told me that Megan knew about them. He told her, but he didn't tell me. Bea is my daughter and yet he has kept me in the dark about this. I feel the merest swell of anger rise up through my rib cage. I don't grab hold of it. Not yet. I let the feeling trickle away and then I read the seventh email:

You doubt me? Have I mentioned that I've killed before? Mostly I favour the knife—a five-inch blade with a serrated edge. Last time, I pushed it in just below the fifth rib. It sliced through the muscle in her heart. She died quickly. Sometimes I enjoy making it slow.

I sit back on my heels. I notice a small tremor in my hands and press them firmly down on my knees. I wait a moment and in that space of time my mind hauls me back to before I had Bea, when I was employed as a solicitor with the CPS. The last case I worked on was a young woman called Kerry Smith, murdered by her ex-partner. She had been stabbed in the chest. I saw her body; I saw the damage a knife can do.

I force myself to finish what I have started. Email number eight:

Let me refer you to a couple of unsolved crimes: Carlo Brunetti, Rome, 2006, and Boleslav Hlutev, Sofia, 2008.

That's it. I read it several times, memorising the names, places and dates. Then I collect the emails into a pile, go into the walk-in wardrobe and slide them under a row of sweaters.

I move silently from my room along the carpeted hallway. I can hear Charlie and Amy laughing in his bedroom. I stop at the entrance to Bea's room and watch her from the doorway. She's lying on the floor, playing with Douglas and Bertie. The magnitude of what I've just read is sinking in and my impulse is to grab Bea, pack our bags and drive away. Drive and keep driving until we are beyond the blackmailer's reach. But I have to talk to Julian, find out whether he has a plan. Has he spoken to the police?

I go downstairs to the kitchen and take a bottle of wine from the fridge. I pour myself a glass, then sit at the table and face the back garden, where shadows lengthen as the sun slips lower in the sky. I sip the wine and think about the tone of the emails, the fact that we were followed and that the blackmailer watched Bea at nursery. He has to be someone who blends in or is pretending to blend in. A policeman or a lollipop man, or a postman.

'I've got grumbles in my tummy.' Bea comes running into the kitchen.

'I'm sorry, poppet!' I jump to my feet. 'Let's make dinner together, shall we?' I scoop her up into my arms, kiss her cheek and hug her tight.

'You're squeezing me, Mummy!'

I make myself set her down on the work surface, between the sink and the hob. 'Let's have some of this lovely soup Sezen made.'

She peers into the pot. 'I like fish fingers.'

'We'll have fish fingers too, then.'

AFTER BEA has eaten, we go upstairs. I help her with washing and brushing her teeth, read her a story and sit on her bed. It takes next to no time for her breathing to settle into the rhythm of sleep. I sit beside her, stroking her hair, soaking up the essence of her, until I hear the doorbell.

Leaving the bedroom door ajar, I go downstairs to let Megan in. She's about five eight, slim, neither pretty nor plain. Her dark hair is pulled back in a ponytail, and she's dressed in a tailored black trouser suit and a white blouse. She has a sharp, incisive intelligence. Top of her class at her girls' school, she achieved a double first from Balliol College, Oxford. She is an ambitious solicitor and is out to impress—not that I hold that against her. I was a solicitor myself once. I know that it takes focus and a healthy dose of ambition to make the grade, and for all her brisk efficiency, she always takes the time to chat to me and the children.

'Come on through,' I say.

She follows me into the kitchen and sits down on the window seat. She crosses her ankles and smiles at me. 'Did Bea enjoy her party yesterday?'

'Very much.' I offer her some wine, which she refuses, and then I gesture towards the pot on the hob. 'I know that it's more salad weather, but this soup is very good.' I give it a stir. 'Butternut squash. Sezen made it.'

'How's she working out?' She picks up a magazine and flicks through it.

'Great. She cooks all sorts, but she specialises in macrobiotic food.'

'This is a wonderful resort.' She holds up the magazine so that I can see the photograph of wooden chalets nestling in the snowy hillside. 'I spent my gap year working in the Alps.' She smiles. 'Absolutely loved it.'

She continues reading the article as I place bread, cheese and tomatoes on the table, then I sit down and we eat. Megan asks me how Lisa is doing and I tell her, keeping it short as I want to steer the conversation elsewhere.

'So, this business of the emails,' I say.

She tilts her head. 'So Julian told you?'

'You're not being threatened too, are you?'

'No, I'm not.' Her eyes cloud with sympathy. 'But I don't have children.'

I tear off a piece of bread and chew it slowly. 'How worried should I be?'

'Julian is taking the threats seriously and so are the police.'

'The police?'

'Didn't Julian mention that the police were involved?'

'We haven't had much of a chance to discuss it.'

'They're trying to trace the emails.' She cuts a slice of Cheddar and transfers it to her plate. 'Not easy, as the emailer is using a proxy server.'

'Georgiev hasn't become this powerful without being one step ahead.'

'Well, he's no longer powerful. He's in prison, pending trial. A trial that will be won by the prosecution. Of that there is no doubt.' She says this with an uncompromising straightening of her back. 'As long as we have the witness, Georgiev doesn't have a hope of being acquitted.'

I think she means to reassure me, but it has the reverse effect. If the witness is so crucial, then Georgiev won't stop until he has the name.

'The trial will go on, of course,' Megan continues. 'It's just unfortunate that Julian has had to resign'—her fingers move through the air, putting quotation marks round 'resign'—'when he's worked so hard on the case.'

Julian has resigned? I try not to show that this is news to me. I take a spoonful of soup and force it down my throat. 'Yes,' I hear my voice saying. 'It's been difficult for him.' So difficult that I didn't notice. And so concerned was he that he didn't feel the need to tell me he has resigned from a case he's spent almost a year working on. Two hulking great secrets that for nine whole days he's successfully kept to himself. I'd never have believed it.

'He's a fantastic barrister and a great teacher,' Megan continues. 'I've learned such a lot working with him.'

The undisguised hero-worship in her voice is both touching and hurtful. Megan knew about both the emails and his resignation. So why didn't I? My head scrolls through a thousand different reasons, but the only one that fits is that he feels closer to Megan than he does to me, that somewhere along the line she became his confidante. It feels like a betrayal.

'So what's the plan?' I say.

'Well, clearly there's a conflict of interest for Julian and so he's been obliged to step back. Gordon Lightman is now lead counsel.'

'I don't mean with the case. Bea's safety is what concerns me.'

'Hasn't Julian told you himself?'

'He had to go off in the taxi. The conversation was cut short.'

'Well, why don't I find you his hotel details?' She stands up to fetch her laptop bag. 'I have the address and phone number in here.' She sits down, takes out her laptop and switches it on. 'Won't take a moment.'

'I understand that he needs to resign,' I say. 'His position is compromised. I see that. So why, then, has he gone to Sofia?'

'He's taken Gordon with him for a handover. He's introducing him to Iliev, the chief of police out there, so they can review the evidence together.' She takes some paper and a pen from the side pocket of her laptop bag and writes. 'Here.' She holds the paper out to me. 'Address and phone number.'

'Thank you.' I take it and put it in my pocket.

'The soup was delicious.' She stands up again. 'I need to head off.'

I walk with her to the door.

'Nothing will happen until after the pretrial hearing on Monday,' she says, setting off down the steps. 'There's still time to find out who's sending them. It doesn't have to turn nasty.'

'Turn nasty?' My feet follow her down onto the pavement. I catch hold of her arm and another question occurs to me. 'Those two cases that the blackmailer quotes, Brunetti and Hlutev . . . what happened with them?'

'I don't know,' she says quickly. Too quickly. She puts her arms round me and gives me a brief, awkward hug. 'I'm sorry this is happening, Claire. Truly I am. Call Julian. He has more information than me.'

I go inside and lean my back against the closed door. My head spins with a jumble of half-questions and incomplete answers. And then, in the midst of it all, I see Bea's face: smiling, uncomplicated, safe. My hands start shaking again. I push the palms together to make them stop. I try to think my way forward. I need information and I need a plan. I take the piece of paper from my pocket and go into the kitchen. When I'm a few steps away from the phone, it starts to ring. I lift it and press the green button.

'Claire?'

The relief at hearing his voice sets up an ache inside me: part fear of what's to come and part hope that lying in his arms would make it go away.

'I was just about to call you,' I say. 'Julian, what's going on?'

'I've been meeting with Iliev, the chief of poli—'

'I don't mean that. I mean . . . I know about the emails.'

Silence.

'I know about the emails and I know about the fact that you've resigned and I feel scared and I feel hurt.' My voice cracks. I try to take a breath, but I feel as if I have a lump the size of a walnut in my throat. 'And I can't for the life of me come up with a good reason why you wouldn't have told me that our daughter's life was being threatened.'

More silence.

'Aren't you going to say anything?'

His voice when it comes sounds more distant than mere miles could account for. 'Who told you about the emails?'

'Bea told me.' Anger flares in my stomach. 'Because for some reason you were unable to.'

'Bea? How did she—?'

'She listens. She picks up snippets of conversations. You know that.'

'I'm sorry.'

'And Megan told me you resigned.'

Across the distance I hear him sigh.

'Why didn't you tell me?' I hear the puzzled tone in my voice and try for a firmer one. 'Julian, I'm your *wife*. You should not have kept either of these things from me.'

'Sweetheart'—he takes a quick breath—'let me explain everything face to face. I'll be home by four tomorrow. Can we leave it until then?'

'Bea and I have been *followed*. Someone has been watching her at nursery. Doesn't that bother you?'

'Of course it bothers me. It hasn't been easy keeping this from you.'

'Then why did you?'

'Because we thought we had a lead on the blackmailer and I thought it could all be resolved without worrying you.'

'Yet you had no difficulty telling Megan, and in front of Bea.'

'I had no idea that Bea was listening.'

'So that makes it OK?'

'Claire . . . please. Trust me on this. Will you? Nothing will happen before the pretrial hearing on Monday.'

'But yesterday you clearly thought Bea had been taken.'

'Yes, I did. And as I said yesterday, I overreacted.'

'So what are the police doing? Have they traced the emails?'

'Not yet. But I think you'll be reassured to know that Andrew MacPherson's running it.'

I hope I've heard wrong. I clear my throat. 'Who?'

'Andrew MacPherson. You worked with him, didn't you?'

I'm not breathing.

'He's with Serious and Organised Crimes. Has recently had a promotion to DI. Everyone calls him Mac.'

I know what everyone calls him.

'He'll come to the house and talk to all of us after the pretrial hearing.'

My mind is reeling. As if the threat to my daughter's life isn't enough for me to cope with, now Mac has been thrown into the mix. There must be a dozen senior policemen who could have been assigned this case and it ends up being him. I drop my head into my hands.

'Claire? Are you still there?'

'I'm thinking,' I say.

'You had a lot of respect for Mac, didn't you?'

'He's a good policeman,' I say flatly. 'Efficient, patient, intelligent.' *Dangerous*. 'He's as good as they get.'

'I feel that too. I think we're in good hands with him. I'll be home by four tomorrow. Sweetheart, we'll get through this.'

'I know,' I tell him. 'I'll see you soon.'

'I love you, Claire.'

I hesitate for a second and then say with complete conviction, 'And I love you.' I end the call and stand up. Today is Wednesday. I have no intention of waiting until Monday before I speak to the police. To Mac.

Mac. I sit down on the window seat and rest my elbows on my knees. It's been five years since we've been in each other's company, since I deleted his mobile number from my list of contacts and erased all thoughts of him from my mind. But half a dozen times in the last five years he has texted me. The last time only a month ago and I'm sure I've yet to delete it. I take my mobile from my handbag on the dresser and scroll through the messages until I find it: *You ever coming back to work or what?*

I don't know why he's kept up these intermittent communications with me. Guilt? Friendship? Or something more? I don't know, and I've never given it serious thought. Neither have I ever replied to his texts, but now I access his number and call it. It rings twice and then he answers.

'Claire?'

'Yes.'

'How are you?'

'How do you think?'

'Has Julian told you?'

'I found out.'

'How?'

'That doesn't matter. I understand you're running the case.'

'That's right. I know what's happening is awful, but we will do everything we can to keep you all safe.' He sounds exactly the same, his Scottish accent a melodic, comforting lilt. It almost makes me smile. 'I know you must have loads of ques—'

'I do. I want to talk to you. Do you have any free time tomorrow?'

'Sure. What suits you?'

'Any time.' And then I remember—Sezen is moving from London down to Brighton and I offered to help her with the move. 'No. Sorry. In the morning I'm driving up to Tooting. I could meet you there, at about ten?'

'Can do.' He names a café in Tooting, on the High Street.

'See you then.'

At once I make another call. It's almost eleven, but I know that Wendy turns in late. I tell her that Bea isn't going to nursery tomorrow and ask if she would mind looking after her for me. She agrees at once. I go down to the basement and make sure that every window and door is locked. I do the same on the ground floor, coming into the sitting room last. The sky is navy blue and starless; street lamps shed light on what little activity there is outside. And it's under the nearest streetlight that I see two men standing on the pavement talking to one another. One is smoking; the other is drinking from a metallic flask. They are dressed in suits, and the smoker is leaning on a Ford Mondeo. I recognise them. When Bea stepped off the pavement to examine the dead frog, these men were the ones sitting in the car. Surely they haven't been here all day? I go through to the kitchen to get my mobile.

I'll ask Mac to find out who they are. But by the time I come back into the living room, there's no sign of them or their car.

I close the curtains and go into the porch to set the burglar alarm. I know that until the blackmailer is caught, this is the way it will be. I'll be suspicious of every stranger, every unknown car or curious passer-by. Someone is watching us and until I know who that someone is, I'll have to be vigilant.

I climb the stairs. The house is quiet. I go into Bea's room. She is asleep, lying on her side under the duvet. I pull it back and see that she still has her arms round Bertie. Being careful not to wake her, I lift her from her bed and take her into mine. I slide into bed beside her and turn off the light, only to lie awake staring at the ceiling. I have never felt more afraid.

3

I wake up early the next morning with my arms round Bea. Like a new mother with her first baby, throughout the night I found myself reaching out to make sure she was safe. And whenever I did drift towards sleep, the words from the emails haunted me—*Have I mentioned that I've killed before? Mostly I favour the knife*—razor-sharp phrases that jerk me awake.

I slide out of bed quietly, leaving Bea asleep, and go into the shower. The warm water is invigorating, stinging my skin into life. I think about the day ahead. I'm meeting Mac at ten and don't have to collect Sezen until around twelve, so that gives Mac and me a good hour and a half to talk.

Mac. I don't relish the thought of seeing him again. Five years ago I was a solicitor with the CPS, and Mac was a detective. The last case we worked on prompted my decision to re-evaluate my life, to stop work altogether and concentrate on being a wife and mother. It was the murder of Kerry Smith. She was a good person who had, as a teenager, got in with the wrong crowd. She wasn't well spoken, her education had been intermittent, but she was trying to better herself and make a future for her kids. Becoming a mother had changed her. The only mistake she made was to become involved with the wrong man—Abe—a harmless-sounding name for such a violent criminal. The father of her children, he was wanted for aggravated assault, burglary and drug-dealing. She was prepared to give evidence against him, and she was given accommodation in a safe house. All was fine for a week and then Abe found her, and knifed her nine times in the chest.

Mac and I tormented ourselves with the realisation that we should have better protected her. We operated within the law, but perhaps we should have, could have found a safer safe house. Had we pulled out all the stops?

We both knew we hadn't.

To try to make up for it, we put all our energies into catching Abe, breaking down his alibi and convicting him. At the backs of our minds we knew it was too little too late. Her two young daughters were motherless, their grandparents out of their depth. And this made us push harder. We skated a fine line between what was lawful and what was not, but there was no way either of us could let him walk free.

And then there was Kerry's funeral.

I turn off the shower and start to dry myself, knowing that I'll have to remember what happened at the funeral sooner or later. Just not right now.

'Mummy!' Bea shouts through from the bedroom. 'Look at me!'

I open the bathroom door and call out, 'I'll be there in a minute.' I finish drying myself, go into the walk-in wardrobe and select a pair of fitted jeans and a red crossover top that flatters my figure. The shoes I wear with it are wedge sandals I bought only four weeks ago. Comfortable and stylish, they give me an extra few inches, and as I'm only five feet three, I immediately feel more confident. I blast my blonde hair quickly with the hair dryer, flicking out the ends and running some wax through it to help it hold its shape. Then I go into my bedroom and sit down at my dressing table.

'I can do tumble-overs,' Bea says. She is bouncing on the bed, and, with Bertie under her arm, she throws herself into a perfect forward roll.

'Hooray!' I clap. 'That's very good, Bea. No nursery today. Grandma Wendy is coming to look after you.'

By the time Wendy arrives, Bea is wearing her favourite shorts and T-shirt and has eaten a huge bowl of cereal.

'Hello, you,' Wendy says, when Bea opens the door to greet her.

I glance beyond Wendy and am shocked to see that the same two men are back in the street. One is stretching his legs; the other is leaning up against the side of the car, talking on his mobile and looking straight at me.

I slam the porch door. A heavy coldness sweeps through me and for a moment I'm numb. Could these be Georgiev's men? I stare straight ahead, seeing and hearing nothing, and then I look at the wall to one side of me.

The burglar alarm. And not just any old alarm, a state-of-the-art one that has CCTV cameras on the front and rear doors. When we were having it installed a couple of months ago, Julian was quite specific, twitchy even, about us making the house more secure, checking the locks on the windows and doors, priming the boys on personal safety. 'You can't be too careful,' he said. Did he know then that Georgiev was likely to threaten our family?

'Surely not,' I say out loud. 'Bloody, bloody hell.' I come in from the porch and close the inside door behind me.

'I'm going to get my dogs, Grandma!' Bea is running up the stairs, tripping over her feet in her haste.

Wendy gives me an uncertain smile. 'Everything all right, Claire?'

'Fine.' I try to smile back.

'So is nursery closed today, or . . . ?'

'No. I just thought Bea could do with some downtime. She's had a busy couple of days.' I kiss Wendy on the cheek. 'I really appreciate you dropping everything to come and look after her.'

'No trouble.' She walks towards the kitchen. 'I thought we'd bake some cakes, and while they're in the oven we could pop out for a bit.'

'I don't want you to take Bea out,' I say abruptly.

She turns to me. 'Why ever not? We won't go far. Just across to the park.'

'I'd feel happier if Bea didn't go further than the back garden.'

Her grey eyes stare back at me, first confused and then accepting. 'No problem.' She nods her head. 'We have lots to do in the vegetable plot.'

'Thank you.' I start off along the hallway. 'I'll just get myself organised. Charlie and Amy are still asleep.'

'I won't disturb them.'

I go downstairs to log on to Julian's email account. I need to see whether another email has arrived. Within minutes I see that there's nothing new. I've already put into my handbag the ones I printed out last night. I want to discuss them with Mac, to hear his theories and put forward some of my own.

As I'm leaving, Bea is halfway down the stairs with most of the animals from her toy chest. 'I'm bringing them for tea and cakes,' she tells me.

'You be a good girl.' I hug her tight. 'I'll be back soon.'

'You go and collect Sezen,' Wendy says. 'And take your time.' She gives me a gentle nudge. 'We'll be fine here.'

I come outside onto the pavement and stop in front of my car. The two men are still there. Still looking at the house. Still looking at me. I make a snap decision and, ignoring the possibility of danger, walk towards them, smiling as warmly as I can. 'Do I know you?'

'Mrs Miller.' The older one slides his mobile into his back pocket and holds out his hand. 'DS Baker, and this is DC Faraway.'

His handshake is solid and warm. 'Policemen?' I say.

'Indeed.' DS Baker takes his wallet from his trouser pocket and shows me his ID. 'Your safety is our priority.'

'Are you going to be here all day?'

'We are.'

'I'm going out now.' I fold my arms across my chest. 'I'm not sending my daughter to nursery this morning.' I look at Baker, then Faraway. 'She won't be leaving the house unless I or my husband is with her.'

'Understood,' Baker says. 'Hear you're meeting up with the boss.'

'Yes.' I try to smile. 'I need to get a handle on what's going on.'

'Rest assured we're doing our best this end.' His expression is sympathetic. 'Our very best.'

'Thank you. I really appreciate your presence here.'

I shake their hands again, then walk to my car. Once again Julian has kept me out of the loop. This must have been the result of the call he made before he went to the airport. I climb into my car and set off.

The traffic is light and soon I'm heading up the A23 towards London. When I arrive in Tooting and find the café, I'm fifteen minutes early. I sit in a quiet corner near the back of the room, order a coffee and wait.

Mac and I haven't been alone in each other's company since after Kerry's funeral, when we gathered at her parents' semi in Gravesend. That morning, my breakfast had been a muesli bar on the Underground and I hadn't eaten any lunch, so two quick, large whiskies and the alcohol ran through me, leaking into my bloodstream, into my limbs and my head. I climbed the stairs to the bathroom. When I came out, Mac was in the hallway and I lurched into him. He had his jacket off and his tie was loose.

Before Kerry's burial, we had spent two weeks together building the case against Abe. We worked all hours sifting through the evidence, living on coffee and muffins and the odd takeaway. Our thoughts were in sync, our closeness professional. It didn't feel sexual, but it did feel meaningful. I liked and respected him. I recognised that he was attractive, but I wasn't aware that I wanted him until the moment outside the bathroom.

I was drunk and exhausted. At that moment my family were in a parallel world, cared for by another me. Mac, on the other hand, was slap bang in front of me. He looked familiar and foreign and overwhelmingly desirable. He held my hand. I examined his fingers, then kissed them. He walked us into the bathroom. I locked the door behind us. He undid my blouse. I undid his trousers. He wrapped his arms round my waist. I leaned in to him. He kissed me slowly, teasingly. I pulled back to look into his eyes. He smiled at me. I smiled back. He sat on the edge of the bath and pulled me onto his knee. He slid a hand up my skirt. We didn't speak. We held eye contact throughout. It was a perfectly erotic, electric episode.

Afterwards I rested my head on his shoulder. My limbs were soft; my insides felt profoundly relaxed. We stayed like this for several long seconds before somebody tried the door handle.

'I'll be a minute,' Mac said.

I stood up, gasped—my legs were unsteady. He buttoned his trousers. I pulled down my skirt and buttoned my blouse. He straightened his tie. I tried to unlock the door. My fingers weren't working. He covered my hands with his, unlocked the door, turned me towards him and hugged me.

'We should go back down now,' he said. He opened the door. The hallway was clear. 'You first.'

He pushed me gently forwards. I went downstairs, my whole body zinging with energy. I felt more vital than I had in years. I ate four sandwiches one after the other and then I had a cup of coffee. I was just finishing up when Mac came back into the room. We had travelled here together, but I already knew that he was driving back to Scotland Yard, while I had accepted the offer of a lift to the station and then home. I watched as he said his goodbyes to Kerry's parents, held Mrs Smith while she cried into his shirt. He promised to ensure that Abe was locked up for as long as possible. Then he moved around the room, saying a quick goodbye to the rest of us. He gave me a casual hug, as he usually did, and then he left.

Mac didn't call me; I didn't call him. I saw him at work and there was nothing in his face to suggest that he knew me any better than he had before. I didn't know what to think, what to feel. I knew I didn't want him—not really, not the way I wanted Julian—but still there was something about him that made me feel both ashamed and exhilarated.

I finish my coffee. In a small, dark corner of myself I feel a flicker of excitement at the thought of seeing him again. And when, at just after ten, the door to the café opens, that flicker becomes a flame.

MAC SEES ME at once. He walks towards me and I stand up. Unlike Julian, he's not conventionally handsome. He is tall and broad as a rugby player and has a receding hairline, a nose that's too large for his face and brown eyes that are slightly too close together. What makes him attractive is the powerful charisma he exudes.

We kiss cheeks. He hugs me. He feels warm and solid.

'So . . .' He smiles. It's not just about his mouth or his eyes. It comes from deeper than that. And I remember that he uses his smiles sparingly. Must be why they're so effective. 'Long time no see. You look well.'

'Do I?' I half smile, ignoring the way my spirits lift as soon as I saw him and lift further with his compliment, because this isn't about me. It's about Bea. 'What I feel is afraid.' I breathe deeply. 'I have a lot of questions.'

'Fire away.'

'Why were you assigned this case?'

'Someone had to be.'

'It was just a bit of a shock.' I shrug. 'Of all the policemen in London . . .'

'There are three teams working this aspect of serious crimes. Makes it a one-in-three chance of it being me.'

'I heard you're a DI now. Congratulations.' I smile fully, then lean towards him. 'Is there a chance the blackmailer could be bluffing?'

'I don't think so. Georgiev is known for this sort of intimidation. Sofia and Rome are proof of that.'

I remember the email—*Carlo Brunetti, Rome, 2006, and Boleslav Hlutev, Sofia, 2008.* 'What happened with those two cases?'

'Both of them involved blackmail. And family members ended up paying the price,' he says quietly.

I swallow quickly. 'Did either of them involve children?'

'The Italian one. A little boy.'

'Was he—?' I stop abruptly, thinking about the blackmailer spying on Bea as she played in the sandpit. *I could have taken her then. I could take her still. And you'd never see her again.* 'Was the little boy kidnapped?'

Mac nods. 'I believe so. We don't have all the details at the moment.'

'Whose idea was it to keep me out of the loop, yours or Julian's?'

'It wasn't a case of keeping you out.' He shakes his head at me. 'It was more about not worrying you unnecessarily.'

'Was it your decision or Julian's?'

He sighs. 'It was Julian's. I have to accept that he knows you better than I do. He's only trying to protect you, Claire. And anyway, there really was nothing to be gained by you knowing earlier.'

'Because the threat will only be realised after the pretrial hearing?'

'Exactly.'

Anger simmers inside me, against both these men who have made decisions that affect Bea's safety and yet have neglected to include me. I rub my forehead. 'I want to know everything you know.'

He gives me a prolonged look as if checking to see how much I mean this. 'All right,' he says. 'But some of it makes for uncomfortable listening.'

'I understand that.' I reach down to the floor and bring my handbag up onto the table. 'I've brought copies of the emails with me.' I lay the pages out in front of him. 'I'd like to go through them. Hear your thoughts.'

He cocks his head on one side. 'Who gave you them?'

'No one. I logged on to Julian's email. I didn't feel good doing it,' I acknowledge, 'but I couldn't just sit on my hands until he came home.'

'OK.' He weighs this up. 'Firstly, I want you to know that we're giving this top priority.' I listen to everything he has to say, hearing words like 'imperative' and 'risk assessment' and 'profilers'. My brain hasn't felt this engaged since I gave up being a solicitor, and I realise that the person I thought I left behind was just waiting for the chance to show her face again.

'And are you having any luck tracing the emails?' I say.

'No, it's nigh on impossible. But we're bringing in for questioning all known criminals and informants who work or have worked with Georgiev.'

'And at one point you thought you had a lead?'

'Turned out to be a dead end.' He stands up, takes off his jacket and puts it over the back of the chair. 'You want another coffee?'

'Please.' I watch him as he goes up to the counter, the waitress tripping over herself to serve him, smiling for all she's worth. He comes back with two coffees and a packet of biscuits.

I dredge up a polite smile. 'So how's life been treating you?'

'Much the same.' He offers me a biscuit. I shake my head. 'Got married a couple of years back.'

'You're married?' Mac's a lot of things, I think, including intelligent and sexy, but he's not a man to marry. 'What's she like?'

'She's pretty. Interesting. She has long legs.' He thinks for a bit. 'She has a liking for tiger prawns and holidays in Crete.' He dunks a biscuit in his coffee. 'And country walks. She teaches yoga.'

I smile. The Mac I knew was always exercise-resistant unless it involved a football. I rest my hand on the copies of the emails. 'Do you think the blackmailer will leave us alone because Julian has resigned from the case?'

'We're hoping.'

'Isn't Georgiev able to work out who the witness is?'

'It's harder than you might think. He's had a lot of criminal associates over the years, most of whom would rather slit their own throats than give evidence against him. But this man . . .' He shrugs. 'He's got balls.'

'The blackmailer wants to know his whereabouts. Julian knows this too?'

Mac nods.

'Who else knows the details?'

'In this country, there's me, James Alexander at CPS, a couple of others. In Bulgaria, there's Iliev, Sofia's chief of police, and a couple of his men.'

'Do any of them have children?'

'No, they don't.'

I gesture towards the pages of emails. 'So what did you think of these?'

'This approach is subtle for Georgiev. Often he favours the heavies turning up with their Kalashnikovs. I think they're very deliberately going for the gradual build-up of fear in the hope that Julian will crack.'

'And will he?'

He stares at me. 'No, I don't think he will. Do you?'

'He's not easily intimidated.'

'Would you like him to give in?'

'Yes. If you can't find this emailer in the next couple of days, I would.'

'Claire—'

'I know all the arguments. But these people are talking about kidnapping my child.' I press my chest. 'My four-year-old daughter, Mac. The world's population is almost seven billion, and I have given birth to three of them. How can I not put their welfare ahead of other people's?'

'Every person is someone's child.'

I take a deep breath. 'For the past five years I've been having a quiet time at home with my family. I don't see criminals round every corner. I don't presume people are lying. That's not my world any more.' I take a deep breath. 'Or it wasn't until now. Fucking hell.' I make a face. 'That's another thing—I haven't said "fuck" since I worked with policemen.'

'You're softer now.'

I smile. 'Well, I feel the old me coming back. I'm toughening up again.' I look down at the emails, and say what's been slowly crystallising since I first read them. 'I think there's a good chance that whoever's writing these is a woman. The detail about Bea's shoes and dress. The shopping we bought.'

'You think a man can't notice these things?'

'I think it's less likely. But what really strikes me is this.' I read from the fourth email. '"She was carrying her stuffed dog, Bertie."'

Mac sits back in his chair, his arms folded. 'You think that the fact Bea's toy is named makes it more likely to be a woman?'

'Yes, I do, and more than that, I think it's someone who knows us and I think Julian thinks that too, otherwise he wouldn't have been so afraid when Bea was with Amy.' I also sit back in my seat. 'He told you about that, didn't he?' I say. 'Isn't that why the policemen appeared?'

He nods. 'We're not ruling out the possibility that someone close to you could be the blackmailer. But Georgiev uses people he knows, mostly fellow Bulgarians. Do you have any friends who are Bulgarian?'

'No.'

'Do any friends have criminal records or criminal links of any kind?'

'Not that I know of.'

'Are you suspicious of anyone you know?'

'No. Not exactly!' I throw out my hands. 'But still . . .'

'The information in these emails could be got in a brief observation from a passer-by. I'm not ruling out your idea and I will speak to the profilers about it,' he says, his tone placatory, 'but we have to keep an open mind.'

'OK,' I concede. 'But I've been thinking. If the witness protection order is not overturned at the hearing, then I'm going to take the children away—all three of them—because if I only take Bea away, then the spotlight could fall on Charlie or Jack. I'll take them to France or America, I don't know where, but I'm not letting them stick around here when they could be in danger.' And then I remember Lisa. 'I can't take Lisa abroad.' Even somewhere in the UK would be difficult. 'Shit, shit, shit.'

'I have a solution to that,' Mac says. 'Julian has already told me about your sister. We can arrange specialist nursing in the UK.' He looks uncomfortable suddenly. 'I have suggested to Julian that on Tuesday you all move to a safe house. We're making one ready.'

'A safe house?' Dread seeps into my mouth. It tastes of metal, of blood. 'No,' I say tersely. 'Absolutely not.'

'The best option is to get right away from where they expect to find you.'

'You're forgetting that the last time I had anything to do with a safe house, Kerry Smith ended up dead.'

'That was more of a women's refuge than a safe house.'

'Well, she thought—in fact we *promised*—that she and her children would be safe and yet she was knifed to death in front of them.'

'Claire, I know how badly that case affected you.' He cradles his coffee mug in his hands. 'But you didn't make a mistake.' He leans across and takes my hand, a comforting gesture. 'It wasn't your fault.'

'Well, it wasn't not my fault,' I say quietly. 'It's on my conscience, Mac. I felt uneasy, but I ignored the feeling when I should have acted on it. There's no excuse for that.' And there's nothing I can do about what followed either—our no-holds-barred investigation to get Abe convicted and then my slip-up with the man opposite me. I look at him. There's the merest flicker of acknowledgement that one event followed another: Kerry's death, Abe's conviction and then our coming together in the bathroom.

'Julian knows that I had sex with someone,' I say quietly. 'He just doesn't know who. I think he assumed it was another solicitor.'

'I guessed as much. He showed no reaction when I met him.' He pauses and looks at me sideways. 'You're not going to tell him, are you?'

'No.' I grip the edges of the table. 'Please, Mac. The focus has to be on keeping my family safe. We have to get this right.'

'And we will. I promise you. My priority is your family's safety. End of.' He stands up. 'I have to get back to the station. I'll be coming to see you all on Monday after the pretrial hearing. Better not say anything before then.'

We walk to the door together. 'What about my stepmother, Wendy?'

'We've included her in the plan.' He holds the door and I walk out onto the pavement. 'Julian thought you might want her along for support.'

'Yes,' I say. 'And then there's Sezen.' Julian will have told him our set-up.

'The more people involved, the more likely there is to be a leak.' He looks regretful. 'She has a child. Always complicates things.'

It's true, and anyway, how could I expect her to be cooped up with us, unable to get in touch with friends or even take her daughter to the shops without looking over her shoulder?

'Where are you parked?'

I point along the street. 'That way.'

'I'm the other way.' He hugs me tight. 'It's been good seeing you again. You take care.' He crosses the road and shouts back, 'I'll be in touch.'

I WALK TO my car, climb inside, close my eyes and let my head flop back against the headrest. In the space of twenty-four hours, life as I know it has hurtled into a dark and ominous place. It's every parent's worst fear that harm could come to their child and this is what's happening to us. Bea's safety is under threat, and every time I think of someone hurting her, fear creeps through me, deep into every muscle, every organ and every bone.

The only silver lining in this threatening cloud is that the blackmailer is giving us time to react. Today is Thursday and the pretrial hearing is on Monday. Time enough to catch the blackmailer.

I open my eyes and type Sezen's address into the sat nav. I watch the route pan out on the display and I'm about to start the engine when my mobile rings. The screen tells me it's an unknown number. I answer it, knowing it could be Julian, and it is. He's ringing from the airport in Sofia.

'I called the house just now. Wendy told me you're up in Tooting.'

'I offered to help Sezen with her move to Brighton.'

'And Wendy's looking after Bea?'

'I kept her out of nursery.'

'I understand. It doesn't do any harm to play completely safe.' I hear apology in his voice. 'Claire, I'm sure you're not very happy with me.'

'An understatement if ever there was one,' I say, under my breath.

'Let's make time tonight for us to talk about what's been happening and what the police are doing.'

It's my chance to say that I logged on to his computer and printed off the emails and that I've just spent the last hour and a half with the policeman in charge. If Mac is to be trusted, and I'm ninety-nine per cent sure that he is, then I'm as up to date with the details of the case as Julian is.

But I don't tell him this. We talk about the children and about arrangements and then say our goodbyes. I wish him a safe journey before tossing my phone onto the passenger seat. Talking to Julian, the man I love and cherish, should make me feel better, but it hasn't. It's made me feel worse. Until yesterday, I would have bet my life on the fact that our marriage is as honest as they get. But now secrecy has its foot in the door, wedging it open, allowing doubt and duplicity to creep inside. Why didn't he tell me about the blackmail? Could it be as simple as him not wanting to worry me, or is it something more? This question nags at me, and now here I am, doing the same. I am holding back on my meeting with Mac.

Ironic, when five years ago it was sex with Mac that almost cost us our marriage. For two whole weeks after Kerry's wake I lived with my infidelity, my stomach in knots, my heart heavy with shame. I hadn't told Julian about what I'd done, partly because I was afraid of his reaction, and partly because it felt unreal, as if I'd dreamed it.

Over those two weeks I realised that my job was incompatible with my life. It was time to reassess. I was married to a man I loved. We had two children together, but our lives needed an overhaul. Julian and I were both working too hard. While we were professionally linked and often shared lunch, at home we passed each other on the stairs and in the bathroom, hardly came together in the bedroom. Any energy we had left we gave to the boys at the weekend. It was one of those moments of clarity when I knew that if I didn't put my marriage and my family first, pretty soon I wasn't going to have a marriage or a family.

Julian deserved the truth and so I sat him down when the boys were in bed and I confessed. I told him I'd had sex with another man, that it had only happened once and would never happen again. Before I had the chance to tell him how much I loved him, he stood up and left the room. When I followed him, he held me at a distance with one arm, packed a case and left. For over a week he stayed away. I could barely sleep, barely breathe, terrified that he might have left me for good.

On the ninth evening he came back. I'd told the boys he was away on a case. They were delighted to see him and we spent an almost normal evening eating and chatting. When the boys were in bed, he started to talk.

'I don't want to know his name. I don't want any details,' he said. 'But I do want to know whether you love him.'

'No.' I shook my head. 'I don't. I don't know what possessed me to do it. But what I do know'—I dropped onto my knees in front of him—'is that as long as I live, I will never do anything like that again.' Perversely, having sex with Mac had made me realise just how much I loved Julian and my family. 'I love you, Julian. I love you more than I can express.'

'Do you see us growing old together?'

'Yes.' I took his hand. 'I can't imagine my life without you.'

He looked at me for a long time and then agreed that we could put it behind us. On one condition. 'You have to promise never to see him again.'

'Absolutely.'

I promised and then asked him how he felt about me giving up work to become a full-time mother and wife. We could move to Brighton. My father, Wendy and my sister were all living there. We could spend more time as a family. At first he was sceptical, but when we talked further, he could see that as a family we needed a change, and so we shed the bulk of our mortgage and moved to the coast. The boys settled easily. Julian managed the commute by reading through documents on the train, and I quickly settled into life as a stay-at-home mum. A choice I have never regretted.

But now the parameters have shifted. Bea's life is under threat and Mac is back in both our lives. Somehow Julian and I have to negotiate a way through this without losing our trust in each other.

4

Sezen and her daughter, Lara, live in a flat, in one of three unimaginative blocks of grey, each about ten storeys high. The balconies are a dirty blue colour, the paint chipped and worn. What little green there is around the buildings is trampled on and strewn with litter. Sezen is waiting for me outside, and as soon as my car pulls up she comes across to meet me. Her normally serene amber eyes are troubled.

'Everything OK?' I ask.

'Yes. We can be quick.' She glances around as if expecting to see someone lurking behind a lamppost. 'This is not a good place for you to come. I have packed all our belongings. Lara is upstairs.'

I follow her into the tower block. Lara is on the third floor, sitting on top of a black bin bag just inside the front door of one of the flats. She stands up as soon as she sees us coming. She is seven months older than Bea but about six inches shorter. She is petite, with thick black hair that falls in ringlets past her cheeks. Her eyes are amber, like her mother's.

'Hello.' I squat down in front of her. 'I'm Claire. You and Mummy are coming to live close by.'

Her eyes are solemn. She offers her right hand to me. 'I am happy to meet you,' she says.

I give her a hug and then I look around. Apart from the bin bag, there is a small child's pull-along case and one other suitcase tied in the middle with a scuffed leather belt. 'Is there anything else?'

'No.' Sezen is whispering. 'We share the room and already the others are sleeping. They work night duty. We have all our belongings here.'

I know from her references that her last position was a well-paid one, so I wonder why they've been living in such run-down, cramped circumstances, but I don't ask. I want to get home.

'THIS IS THE STREET.' Sezen points to the left. 'Number seventeen is about halfway along.'

We're back in Brighton now, close to where Sezen and Lara will be living. I indicate left and pull into the nearest spot. The three of us climb out and go to the front door. The house looks tired—the external walls are stained, and the window frames could do with being rubbed down—but the windows themselves are clean, and the curtains inside are hanging neatly.

Sezen rings the bell and within a minute the door opens. The man standing there looks about sixty. His moustache is a silver-grey colour, his eyes and skin a deep caramel.

'Mr Patel?' Sezen says.

'I am he.'

'I am Sezen Serbest.' She holds out her hand and he shakes it. 'This is my daughter, Lara, and my employer'—there's a split-second hesitation—'and friend Mrs Claire Miller. I spoke to your son about renting the small apartment on the top floor. I have my belongings in the car.'

'We are not expecting you this week. Mrs Patel and I are expecting you in twenty days when our tenant Mr Archibald has moved out.'

Sezen looks at me and then back to Mr Patel. 'But we arranged for me to move in on 3 June. I spoke to your son and—'

'I am so sorry. There is nothing to be done.'

Sezen clutches her chest and turns to look at me.

I take her hand. 'Don't worry,' I say. 'There has been a mix-up, but we can fix it.' I look at Mr Patel. 'So Sezen definitely has a place when?'

'On the 23rd of June, when Mr Archibald is leaving for Sheffield.'

'Thank you.' I hold out my hand. 'We will return then.'

'I am a man of my word.' His handshake is warm and firm. 'And I am most sorry for the misunderstanding.'

When he closes the door, Sezen is still looking confused. 'I am sure he said the 3rd of June. I am sure he did. I gave his son my deposit.'

'You have a receipt for that and a tenancy agreement?'

'Yes.' She digs around in her pocket. 'Here.'

She hands me the paperwork. I read it. Everything looks above board, and what's more the starting date is 23 June, just as Mr Patel said. I point this out to Sezen and she shrinks back into her jacket, then murmurs something under her breath. 'I am so stupid.' Her face is flushed, and she pushes back a tear. 'I am so sorry this has inconvenienced you.'

'These things happen.' I manage to smile. This whole time Lara has been standing silently, barely making her presence felt. I lift her into the back seat of the car and strap her in. 'It's nobody's fault.'

'You went out of your way to come for me and help me with my things. Your journey has been wasted and now we will have to go back to London.' She is pacing the pavement, her fists clenched by her side. 'I will talk to someone in . . . I may be allowed back.' Her face betrays her doubt. 'And if not, the neighbour was . . . may be willing . . .'

She goes in and out of my earshot as she strides back and forth along the pavement. Lara is watching her pace, her eyes large and liquid. Although she doesn't say much, I can see that her mother's distress is worrying her. I recognise the signs. My childhood wasn't always a bundle of laughs. After my mother died when I was just four, and for the two years before Wendy came along, Lisa and I were often left to fend for ourselves while my father drank himself into a stupor. I don't know much about the particulars of Sezen and Lara's background, but I do know something about the weight of uncertainty, and I see it fill Lara's small frame until she begins to tremble.

'You can't go back to Tooting,' I say. I make a quick decision. 'We have a room in the top of our house you can stay in for a couple of days.'

I watch her do battle with herself. I know that she is independent. Accepting help is difficult for her.

'For Lara,' I say. 'It's the least disruptive solution for her.'

Sezen glances quickly at her daughter and reluctantly agrees. We get in the car and set off again, round the corner and into my street. Lara spots the park opposite our house and points and shouts, 'Look, Mummy! Swings!'

'Yes.' Sezen turns round. 'Later, Lara. You can go on the swings later.'

In the rearview mirror I watch Lara deflate back into her seat. 'You can go now,' I say, my eyes seeking out Baker and Faraway and finding them exactly where I left them this morning. 'I'll get Bea and come and join you.'

Sezen and Lara cross the road to the park and I go inside. The house is completely quiet. I walk through to the kitchen and look down into the garden. Bea is playing outside, hopping first on her left foot and then her right, round and round in circles until she grows dizzy.

I hear the flush of the downstairs toilet and Wendy comes out. 'Oh! You're back!'

'Sorry I took so long.' I hang my car keys up on the hook. 'And thank you for looking after Bea.'

'No problem at all. How's Sezen? Is she pleased with her new rooms?'

'There was a mix-up.' I summarise our conversation with Mr Patel. 'So she and Lara will be staying with us for the next couple of days.'

I open the patio door to shout to Bea, who runs in to give Wendy a hug. Bea and I follow her to the front door to wave goodbye, and then I tell Bea that we are going to the park to play with Lara.

'Who?'

'Sezen's daughter. She told you about her. Remember?'

She thinks. 'Why is she here?'

'Because she's coming to live in Brighton.' I kneel down in front of her. 'In fact, for a couple of days she's coming to stay with us. You'll like her.' I pin back her hair and she winces as the grips rub against her scalp. 'She loves to play outside, just like you do.' We move out onto the front step. 'Look! There's Lara.' I point to where Lara is climbing the ladder on the slide.

Bea holds my hand while we cross the road, then runs off to join her. They find common ground instantly and play together for some time. Sezen and I sit down on a bench and chat. Out of the corner of my eye, I notice that the two policemen are watching us, their presence reassuring.

When the girls have had enough, we unpack the car and go inside. When I show Sezen where she and Lara will sleep, she exclaims with delight at the view. It stretches over the rooftops and out to the sea.

'I grew up on the coast,' she says. 'I love to be close to the sea.'

We join the girls downstairs, and Sezen offers to prepare dinner. I accept, knowing that I couldn't concentrate on making a meal. I look at my watch. Just under an hour until Julian gets home.

I go down to the basement and check his email—nothing new from the blackmailer. I wander next door to busy myself with laundry, building mounds of dirty and clean clothes. As I stand there, I hear steps in the corridor. I expect whoever it is to be heading for the garden and to walk through the room I'm in, but they don't. The door to Julian's study opens and closes. I wait for a couple of seconds and then it occurs me that it will be Bea, sneaking Lara into Julian's study so that she can have a turn on Julian's swivel chair and show her the wig Julian wears when he's in court.

I leave the laundry and open the study door. 'Now, young lady—' I stop short. It isn't Bea; it's Amy. She has her bag slung over her shoulder and is rummaging through a drawer. 'Amy?'

'Yeah?'

'What are you doing?'

'Looking for some plain paper, to do some drawing with Bea and Lara.'

'The paper is over there.' I wave my arm towards the printer on the corner of Julian's desk. Next to it there is a stack of paper.

'Oh.' She raises a languid eyebrow. 'So it is.'

'So what were you really looking for?'

'Excuse me?' Her stare is bold.

'You said you were looking for paper, but it's sitting on the desk, as large as life.' I give a short laugh. 'Instead, I catch you going through a drawer.'

'It's not a problem.' Her tone isn't aggressive; it's perplexed. Her fingers trail over some books as she walks across to stand in front of me. 'Is it?'

'You know, Amy, yes . . . I think it is.' I hold her gaze. Her eyes are the navy blue of stormy seawater. She blinks twice in quick succession. 'I'm sorry but it's not acceptable for you to come into Julian's study like this. He has confidential files stored here.'

She snorts again and her bag swings forward on her shoulder. A piece of paper is sticking out of the top and something is written on it. I do a double-take. Even from a few feet away I recognise Julian's handwriting.

'The paper on top of your bag, would you pass it to me, please?'

'What?' She looks down at the bag, then back at me. 'Why?'

'Because I don't think it belongs to you.'

With what seems like deliberate nonchalance, she takes it out of her bag and looks at it. 'It's scrap paper. I found it in the kitchen.'

'Let me see it, please.'

She sighs, rolls her eyes, then passes it to me. At the same time Charlie comes into the room and I glance at him briefly before reading it. On one side Amy has scrawled an address, and on the other are the details I was looking for—the name and phone number of Julian's hotel in Sofia.

'This piece of paper was on the pinboard,' I say quietly. 'Julian left it for me, and Charlie specifically asked you whether you'd seen it.'

'I didn't know he was talking about that piece.'

'Airhead.' Charlie gives her an affectionate slap on the backside.

'I wrote Bug's address on it,' she tells Charlie, 'but your mum thinks I'm up to no good.' She says the last four words with wide, mock-scary eyes and a humorous tone. Charlie laughs.

'Charlie, I need to have a word with you,' I say tersely. 'A private word.'

'Well . . . OK, yeah.'

I turn away as they kiss each other and then Amy saunters upstairs.

'Charlie.' I twist my hands in front of me. 'I don't know quite how to put this.' I hesitate. 'I'm not sure I trust Amy.'

'Eh?'

'This is the second time I've caught her coming into your dad's study. None of your other friends has ever done this.'

'Well.' He looks sheepish, shifts from one foot to the other. 'She probably doesn't realise it's private. I'll ask her not to.'

I remember Mac's question earlier—*Are you suspicious of anyone you know?* Am I suspicious of Amy, or is it just that I haven't warmed to her? Under normal circumstances I'd give her a second chance, but having her to stay while all this is going on with Bea doesn't feel right.

I move across the room and pull open the drawer that she was rummaging through. It's full of unimportant bits and pieces: batteries, screws, golf tees, a spare calculator and a stash of keys. Most of it needs binning. But still.

I turn back to Charlie. He's staring at me expectantly.

'Is Amy going to be staying much longer?' I ask.

'What do you mean, Mum? Isn't she welcome here?'

'No.' The word is out of my mouth before I can stop myself.

'Mum!' Charlie starts back. 'She's my girlfriend.'

'I know and I'm sorry I'm saying this, but—'

'That drawer doesn't having anything important in it!'

'I know, but that's not the point.' He's looking at me with such naked hurt that for a moment I falter. Then I think about what we're facing as a family and know that I can't leave any room for doubt. 'I'm so sorry, Charlie, but I really would like Amy to leave.'

'But she—'

'Not for ever.' I hold my hands up and go to place them on his shoulders, but he moves backwards. 'Just until . . . life is more settled.'

'What's that supposed to mean?'

'Well . . .' I give myself a couple of seconds to think. Mac said it would be better to keep this quiet until Monday, when he comes to talk to the family, but Charlie is nineteen and I think that keeping him completely in the dark is unfair. 'We have to be careful of security because of Dad's trial.'

His neck cranes forward in disbelief. 'You think Amy's a security risk?'

'Not exactly. But she doesn't behave the way most people would if they were in someone else's house.'

'Bollocks to this.' He stomps past me to the bottom of the stairs. 'Am I welcome here, then?' he shouts back. 'Or should I go as well?'

He takes the stairs two at a time. I call after him, but he ignores me. I lean my head against the wall and shut my eyes. I didn't handle that at all well. But I really don't want Amy here. Despite Mac's scepticism, I feel in my gut that the blackmailer is a woman. A woman who knows our family. And as Julian pointed out, what do we really know about Amy? Sezen has come into our home with cast-iron references, but the boys' friends and girlfriends are invited in on trust. I know that Amy made a play for Charlie. It was just around the time Julian was asked to represent the Crown against Georgiev. A coincidence? Probably. But it's not a risk I'm willing to take.

I stay in the laundry room until ten minutes before Julian is due to arrive home. Charlie and Amy have left the house, the door slamming loudly behind them. I ask Sezen to keep the girls busy in the kitchen so that I can have some time alone with Julian. The taxi pulls up outside the house and I open the door as he's paying the driver. He comes up the steps, drops his suitcase in the porch and holds out his arms. I am taken aback by how happy I am to see him, even with all that's going on.

'How was Sofia?'

'Hot and sticky.'

'Cup of tea?' I ask without thinking, and immediately hope he says no. If we go into the kitchen, Bea will monopolise him until bedtime.

'I'll have a shower first, I think. All that waiting around in airports has left me feeling grubby.'

I follow him up the stairs. I feel I should give him a couple of minutes to acclimatise before we start to talk about the emails.

When we reach our en suite, he says, 'How's Lisa bearing up?'

'The same. You know how stoic she is. Results weren't good and now . . .' I shrug. 'It's a case of waiting and seeing . . . and hoping.'

'I'm sorry, love.' He leans towards me, gives me a kiss, leaves his hand on my hair. 'I know this is difficult for you.'

'I want everything sorted for her when she comes out of hospital. Jem's coming tomorrow to finish painting the room.' I hold his eyes, wait for him to mention the safe house, but he doesn't. 'Are you ready to talk?' I ask.

'Let me have a quick shower first?' A question rather than a statement.

I nod and go back through to our bedroom, sit down on the bed and wait for him. I count the seconds—all three and a half minutes of them—and then he's standing in front of me drying himself.

'Where's Bea?'

'In the kitchen with Sezen and Lara, her little girl.'

'How are Bea and Lara getting along?'

'Really well. Bea even let her play with Bertie.'

He raises an eyebrow. 'She must like her.' He drops the towel on the bed and finds boxers, a T-shirt and a pair of jeans. He puts them on, then sits on the bed beside me and takes my left hand, staring at my wedding and engagement rings as if it's the first time he's ever seen them. 'I'm sorry, Claire.'

'You should have told me.'

'I know.'

'From now on will you talk to me?' He tries to pull me into his chest. I lean away from him. 'Let me know what's going on? Will you?'

He looks into my eyes. 'Yes.'

'Good.' I take a breath. My chest feels tight. 'When I found out about the emails, I was shocked and confused and afraid for Bea. I invited Megan round and she told me you'd resigned and . . .' I feel my lips trembling.

'Claire—'

'Do you know how that made me feel?'

He rubs his hand across his forehead.

'Really. You should think about it,' I say. 'I had to ask your instructing solicitor for details that affect our family's safety.'

He keeps his eyes averted.

'Two months ago, when you had the burglar alarm installed, was it because you thought something like this might happen?'

'Yes.'

Anger swells inside me. 'Why didn't you tell me *then*?'

'At that point I hadn't received any emails. I did it as a precaution.'

'So why not tell me that? Forewarn me?'

'I felt you had enough on your plate with Lisa. I didn't want to add to your worries when there was a chance that nothing would come of it.'

'Don't make this about my sister,' I warn him. 'You should have told me.' My cheeks are burning up. I go to the bedroom window, open it and let the sea air cool my face. 'How do you see me, Julian?' I frown back at him. 'As some sort of flaky, weak-willed woman who can't cope with reality?'

'Of course not.' He comes and stands beside me. 'I know how strong you are. I was trying to protect you.'

'Protect me?' Anger spikes again. 'You went off to Sofia without a word of warning!'

'There are two policemen ou—'

'Yes, I know,' I snap. 'Two plainclothes policemen in a beat-up Ford Mondeo, parked in our street, sticking out like tarts in a nunnery.'

'Claire—'

'Big bloody deal,' I shout. 'Fat lot of use they'd have been if a couple of gunmen turned up at the front door and me none the wiser.' I pace across the floor. 'How dare you? How fucking dare you waltz off to Sofia and leave me and the children with no knowledge of what was going on?'

'I was trying to protect all of you.'

'By keeping us in the dark?'

'I didn't feel . . . *We* didn't feel there was any point in worrying you before it was absolutely justified.'

'*We?* Who's "we" exactly?'

'The police. Andrew MacPherson. He's taking this extremely seriously.'

Another moment to confess that I printed out the emails, that I met up with Mac this morning and that, in doing so, broke the promise I made to Julian five years ago. But I don't say any of these things. Instead, I say, 'Have you considered giving in to the blackmailer's demands?'

'Claire'—he gives me a puzzled look—'you know that isn't an option.'

'Of course it's an option,' I say. 'Are you willing to consider it?'

'Apart from the fact that giving in to someone like Georgiev goes against everything I believe in, I would be disbarred and imprisoned.'

'So we spend months living in fear?'

'Our witness will be called to give evidence first.'

'And if the defence manages to think of reasons to delay?'

'They have no more options open to them.'

'You can't possibly know that! They could have anything up their sleeves.' I feel agitated. I pace back and forth. 'If we make it impossible for the blackmailer to get close to Bea, she will be forced to go after one of the boys.

We can't let Charlie go back to university or Jack to school.'

'She?' He starts back. 'Why did you say "she"?'

'I think the blackmailer's a woman.'

'But you haven't read the emails.' He pauses. 'Have you?'

'This is *me* you're talking to, Julian.' I bang my fist against my chest. 'After the way you reacted when Bea was missing with Amy . . .' I look down at the floor and then back into his eyes.

'You logged on to my laptop?'

'If you'd been honest with me,' I say quietly, 'I wouldn't have had to.'

'I know,' he says. 'Perhaps, in your shoes, I would have done the same.'

'You would never have been in my shoes,' I say, keeping my voice low. 'I wouldn't have kept this from you. And another thing.' I fill my lungs with air. 'I called Andrew MacPherson this morning and met him in a café.'

'I see.' He purses his lips and turns away from me.

'I would rather we had been together but'—I shrug—'you weren't here and I didn't want to wait.'

He sits down on the edge of the bed. 'You know . . . Claire.' He looks weary, his eyelids dropping low over his eyes. 'I'm not the enemy here.'

The kitchen door slams. Next thing, Bea lets out a delighted shout. I know she'll have seen Julian's case by the front door. Within seconds she's in our bedroom, launching herself at him. She screams with delight as he throws her up in the air, then tosses her onto our bed and tickles her. I leave the room. I help set the table, hoping that Sezen's calm demeanour will rub off on me, but it doesn't, and when Julian joins us, carrying Bea, my heart is still sore. He says hello to Sezen and she introduces him to Lara.

Sezen speaks to her daughter in Turkish and Lara looks up at Julian.

'Thank you for my room,' she says.

'And I would also like to thank you,' Sezen says. 'It is very kind of you to offer us a home.'

Julian looks across at me.

'Sezen's accommodation in Brighton isn't ready yet. I invited her to stay with us for a couple of days until she can organise somewhere else.'

He nods and smiles at me, with his mouth but not with his eyes. Then he looks at Sezen and says, 'Glad we could help.'

We take our places at the table—apart from Sezen, who insists she be the one to serve. Bea stays on Julian's knee, cosying in towards his chest, one thumb lodged in her mouth while the other hand twirls her hair.

'We start with miso soup,' Sezen says. 'Very refreshing on the palate.'

'Charlie not around?' Julian says.

'We had a bit of an argument.'

'Over what?'

'Amy.' Bea has slithered off Julian's knee to fetch Bertie, and I check that Sezen is out of earshot at the hob. 'I told Charlie she had to leave.'

'Why?'

'I don't trust her. I couldn't find your hotel details. She had taken the paper from the pinboard and written something on the back of it, and yet when Charlie asked her whether she'd seen it, she said no.'

'She is a bit scatty.'

'Maybe. But I found her in your study—twice—nosing around.'

'In my desk?'

'She was standing by the corner shelves, looking through a drawer. She said she was looking for paper.' I throw my hands out. 'I just didn't buy it.'

'Do you think she could have taken anything?'

'I don't think so.' I breathe in. 'I think it's extremely unlikely she has anything to do with Georgiev, but I don't want to take any chances.'

'Fair enough.' He leans back to allow Bea to climb onto his knee again. 'Is Charlie angry?'

'Yes.' I sigh. 'He may not talk to me for a while.'

Sezen brings full bowls over to the table. Pieces of spring onion and cubes of tofu float on the surface of the pale brown soup. We start to eat.

The doorbell rings and I get up to answer it.

'It'll probably be Megan,' Julian shouts after me.

It is Megan. She is standing on the step clutching bundles of documents to her chest. I know she will be keen to catch up with the latest developments. We kiss each other on both cheeks and I ask her to join us for supper.

Julian introduces Megan to Sezen and she helps herself to soup. I say nothing for the rest of the meal, preferring to order my thoughts. I want to go through the emails again, and to check whether another one has arrived. But now Julian will be taken up with Megan. I'll have to wait until she leaves, and that probably won't be for a couple of hours. When everyone's finished pudding, Julian excuses them both and they go down to his study, Bea still with him, to bring Megan up to date with what's happened in Sofia.

I hang back in the kitchen with Sezen, tidying up and planning food for tomorrow, and when she takes Lara upstairs to bed, I go into the sitting room and switch on the television, half an ear listening out for Megan leaving. I pick up a novel that I'm partway through and then put it down again when the phone rings. It's Jack's housemaster.

'Unfortunate incident this evening, Mrs Miller.' Without preamble, he goes on to tell me that Jack and three other year elevens stole some whisky from the staff common room and are 'suspended herewith'. 'Obviously this is a serious offence and one that ordinarily results in expulsion, but with GCSEs still to be completed we're going down the road of suspension.'

My initial thought is a desperate *Can't anything go right?* Why does Jack have to pick this moment to get himself suspended? 'I'm so sorry, Mr Schreiber,' I say. 'I'll come for him now, shall I?'

'Excellent. The boys are packing for home as we speak.'

I go downstairs and open the door to Julian's study. Bea is fast asleep on his knee. Megan is reading aloud from a document in the bundles.

'I'm going to school to fetch Jack,' I say. 'He's being sent home.'

'What's he done?'

'He and some others stole some whisky.'

'Did they drink it?'

'I expect so. I'm not sure.'

Julian sighs heavily, then shifts Bea across one arm and attempts to stand up without waking her. 'I'll go, Claire.'

'No, no.' I wave him down again. 'You've been travelling all day.' I kiss his cheek, say goodbye to Megan and head off feeling dismayed that several more hours will pass without another opportunity for Julian and me to talk.

THE SCHOOL IS over an hour's drive north, along country lanes, motorway and more lanes. When I arrive at Jack's house, the four boys are waiting on chairs in the corridor, surrounded by their belongings. I don't speak, suddenly realising that I can't, without unleashing a barrel-load of anger and frustration, not all of which should be directed at Jack. When he sees me, he sighs, stands up and balances his bags over his shoulders and arms. He has more stuff for one term than Sezen owns for herself and her daughter.

Mr Schreiber comes out of his flat and fills me in on the details. Not only did they take the alcohol and drink it, they used a permanent marker to graffiti the French teacher's workspace. I make repeated apologies, promise punishment and urge Jack ahead of me out of the school. A small crowd has gathered at the exit and Jack grins at some of them. I grab his arm.

'I am ashamed of you,' I say sharply as I propel him to the car. 'You have let yourself down. And Mr Schreiber. And your family.'

We put his bags in the back, then climb into the car. He reaches for the radio, changes the station and ups the volume.

'I'm not listening to that all the way home. Change it back, please.'

He does so and I then proceed to give him a lecture on respect. Halfway through he slumps down into his jacket and surreptitiously tries to put his iPod earphones into his ears.

'Don't even think about it,' I warn him. 'And sulking won't help you. You will write a letter of apology to Mr Schreiber and the French teacher, and you need to work for the money to replace the alcohol you took, and—'

'Jeez, give it a rest, will you? It was just half a bottle of whisky. And I didn't even do the graffiti.'

'Well, you were with the boy who did. You need to pick your friends more carefully. And I have yet to hear an apology.'

'Sorry,' he mumbles into his collar. 'Is Dad home?'

'Yes.' I look at the clock. 'But he's tired. He'll most likely be asleep by the time we get back.'

'Well, that'll stop him having a go.'

'Do you ever think about anyone other than yourself?' I accelerate into the outside lane. 'I am *so* disappointed in you. Not one more word.'

It's gone eleven o'clock when we get home. There's no sign of Sezen or Lara, and I'm relieved to see that Charlie's shoes are by the front door. I was worried that he might stay away to punish me. And for all Jack's teenage cheek I'm glad to have him home too. I set the burglar alarm and go upstairs. Bea is fast asleep in her bed. I tuck in her covers, kiss her forehead and go through to my bedroom. The bedside lamp is on. Julian is lying fully clothed on the bed, dozing. I go into the en suite and get ready for bed.

When I come back, Julian is still asleep. I bend down and kiss his cheek. At once his eyes open. They focus on mine and stay there. I see inside him as if seeing inside myself: love, anger, level-headedness and a burgeoning, visceral fear. We are no different. He swings his legs over the side of the bed and hugs me to him. I soften at once. His arms are too tight round me, but I don't complain. I hold my breath and kiss the top of his head, wait until the shaking has gone from his body, then pull back a little.

He looks up at me. 'We will get through this.' His tone is urgent.

I stroke his hair. 'I know.' I kiss his lips and smile. 'Now get undressed.'

He starts pulling off his clothes and then my nightdress and then we make love. It feels healing, like we are fixing each other, restoring blood and oxygen, honesty and love to each other's hearts.

Afterwards we lie together, arms and legs entwined. I feel as light as candyfloss, young and carefree, until I remember we are up against a greater crisis than we've ever faced before. I lean up on my elbow, propping my head on my hand. Julian is lying with his eyes shut. His jaw is relaxing open. I watch him for a few seconds—not thinking, just feeling.

Suddenly he opens his eyes and says, 'Did you collect Jack OK?'

'Yes.' I fill him in on the details.

'Is he sorry?'

'Not particularly.' I nuzzle my face into his neck. 'I think we need to have a serious talk with him.'

'We can do that over the weekend.' He closes his eyes again.

I close my eyes too and allow myself to wallow. This works for about ten minutes and then a thought starts to intrude. At first I ignore it and then it grows louder until I speak the words: 'Did another email come today?'

Julian's body jerks as my voice breaks into the stillness. 'Yes. It came a couple of hours ago.' His right hand feels around my neck and rests on the crest of my collarbone. 'I printed out a copy. It's on the chest of drawers.'

I climb out of bed to get it and don't look at it until I am back under the covers. Like all the others, there is no preamble. I read it aloud:

> Bea's birthday party didn't go to plan, did it? How did you feel when you realised she was gone? I think it's time we copied Claire in on these emails, don't you?

'Jesus!' I stare at Julian. 'So it was someone who was at Bea's party.'

'It looks that way.' His eyes are wide open now and he pulls himself up into the sitting position. 'But I've just run it by Mac and he agrees that it's hard to imagine it could be any of the people there.'

'Amy?' I say. 'Now that I've asked her to leave, she could be throwing caution to the wind.'

'But do you really believe Amy could be working for Georgiev?'

'Maybe she isn't directly working for him. Maybe she's just earning money by feeding information to a person who is part of his organisation.'

'Still. The blackmailer could just as easily have got the information about the party second hand.'

'From whom? I mean'—I come up onto my knees—'the blackmailer doesn't have to be a killer. She only has to be in a position of trust in our family.' My mind immediately thinks of Sezen. Earlier this afternoon I invited her to stay with us. But how can Sezen be involved in this? She was employed through an agency, a reputable one. I checked her references. They were genuine. 'And she wasn't at the party,' I say out loud.

'Who wasn't?'

'Sezen. And all Bea's friends' mums had left by then. So if it isn't Amy, it has to be Jem or Miss Percival.' I shake my head. 'And it can't be Jem. We've been friends since Bea and Adam were born. I'd trust her with my life. I'd trust her with Bea's life.'

Julian makes a face. 'Miss Percival doesn't strike me as a valid suspect.'

'Me neither, but then she could be playing the part of a shy, slightly awkward nursery teacher. And she's often quite strange with me.'

'Strange how?'

'When I collect Bea, I have the feeling she's staring at me, trying to listen to what I'm saying to the other mothers.'

'That hardly makes her our emailer.'

For the moment, I let it drop. 'So did Mac have anything else to say?'

'Just that he holds you in high regard.' He reaches across, takes my hand and kisses my fingers below my knuckles. 'I'm sorry I didn't tell you about the emails straight away.' He shakes his head. 'It was wrong of me.'

I smile, glad that we're finally getting somewhere. 'I've been preoccupied with Lisa. I don't blame you for thinking it might all be too much for me.'

'Mac also mentioned your reluctance over the safe house.'

I can't help but stiffen. He feels it and slides down until his face is level with mine. 'Apart from ourselves only three people will know where we are: Mac, Lisa's nurse and an armed policewoman who will live with us.'

'Mac's not going to notify the local police?'

'Not about us, no. But where we're going is normally the home of a senior member of the Foreign Office. If the alarm does go off, the police response time is less than two minutes.'

'Is the house in London?'

'No. Further north. I'm not sure exactly where.'

It all sounds perfectly sensible, but my gut isn't convinced. 'Let's just see how the next few days go,' I say. 'With any luck the police will have a breakthrough. Maybe that last email will help.' I put out the light, relax onto Julian's chest and close my eyes.

He falls asleep immediately. I don't. I lie awake thinking about what little information we have and trying to make connections. It sounds like the blackmailer intends to copy me in on the next email. That alone will narrow the field because I'm not a regular emailer. I don't belong to social networking sites; I rarely shop on the Internet. Few people know my email address.

Finally my limbs grow heavy and I fall asleep. I dream about car chases along badly lit streets and Bea, always ahead of me, being taken away into the darkness.

5

Friday morning and I wake just before seven. The curtains haven't been pulled completely shut and a shaft of light cuts its way across the carpet. Julian's side of the bed is empty. The smell of freshly brewed coffee and burnt toast drifts up the stairs. I grab my dressing gown and pop my head round Bea's door. She's still fast asleep. I go down to the kitchen, keen to see Julian, stopping short when I spot Megan sitting at the table. I make a beeline for Julian, who is taking the final bite of a piece of toast.

'Claire.' He gives me a wide smile and kisses me.

I look over at Megan. 'Do you mind if I borrow my husband for a minute?'

She shakes her head and her ponytail swings. 'Of course not.'

I take Julian's elbow and he doesn't resist as I pull him out into the hallway. 'I hoped you'd be in bed when I woke up.'

'You looked so peaceful.' He slides his hands under my dressing gown. 'I didn't have the heart to wake you. What are your plans for today?'

'Nothing much. I'll visit Lisa over lunch, but otherwise I'll stay at home. Will you call me if you hear from Mac?'

He nods.

'I'll be checking my emails every five minutes to see whether she copies me in, like she said she would.'

'Don't let it dictate your day, Claire. I'll be in touch if another one arrives.'

Megan comes out from the kitchen and Julian pulls his hands away from me, his eyes lingering on my face as we say our goodbyes. I watch from the sitting room window as they begin their walk up the hill to the station. The after-effects of making love still resonate, but seeing him walk away makes me feel vulnerable and twice I whisper his name. It's not until I turn round that I realise Sezen is behind me and I jump.

'I didn't hear you come down,' I say. 'Did you sleep well?'

'Yes.' Her eyes are large in her face. 'I hear the girls,' she says. 'I will make them some breakfast.'

I get dressed and potter about. Twice I pull the emails from their hiding place in my wardrobe and pore over them, and over a dozen times I check my email inbox, but there's nothing new. By eleven thirty Wendy has arrived and is in the kitchen with Sezen. I take the food parcel that Sezen has prepared for Lisa and go off to the hospital. Lisa is on good form and we spend a happy couple of hours together. It's on the tip of my tongue to tell her what's going on, but I don't. She'll find out soon enough and then my problems will become her problems. There's no way to save her from that.

When I return home, Jem is there. 'How was Lisa today?' she asks.

'Good. The thought of leaving hospital has perked her up no end.'

'Talking of which, I've finished the room. Do you want to see it?' We stand for a moment admiring her work. Under the picture rail, the walls are now as yellow as the yolk of a corn-fed chicken's egg, while above the rail the colour is creamy, like freshly churned butter. She's put the curtain pole and pale blue velvet curtains back up, the ends just skimming the floor.

'It's perfect, Jem,' I tell her. 'Sunny, fresh and upbeat.'

'The paint smell will be gone by the morning.' She picks some dust-sheets up off the floor. 'What time's she coming home?'

'I'll probably collect her around eleven.' I drag my eyes away from the black-and-white photograph of my mother that's on the cabinet beside the bed. It's the only one we have of her. She is standing on Brighton Pier, her hand shielding her eyes from the sun. 'Thank you for all your hard work.'

'There's something else I want to show you.' She takes me out onto the front step. 'Don't make it obvious, but behind you, about thirty yards away, this side of the pavement, there are two men sitting in a Ford Mondeo. I noticed them when I was passing by yesterday too.'

I look along the street. Baker and Faraway are parked in their usual spot.

Jem swings me back round to face her. 'I think they're policemen.'

'What makes you say that?'

'They give off a certain aroma.'

'You speaking from experience?'

She shrugs. 'Misspent youth. You know how it is.'

'You don't have cause to worry, Jem.' I smile. 'The car isn't expensive enough for them to be from the Inland Revenue.'

She gives me a weak smile and we go back inside. Bea and Lara come rushing up from the basement. They are both in pink dresses with angel wings on the back. They are flushed and screaming. Jack is chasing them, holding a battered wooden sword and wearing a pirate hat that is far too small for him and is attached to his hair with paperclips.

'Mummy! Mummy!' Bea hangs on to my leg and jumps up and down at the same time. 'Jack is a bad sparrow and he wants to kill us.'

The kitchen door opens and Wendy comes out. 'What's all the commotion? I thought you girls were washing your hands for tea.' She shoos them towards the bathroom, then glances at me. 'How was Lisa?'

'Good.' I nod vigorously. 'She's having a good day.'

'Jack has been doing a sterling job,' Wendy says.

Jack treats us all to one of his butter-wouldn't-melt grins. 'Can I go off duty now?' He gives a dramatic sigh. 'I'm exhausted.'

'Tea first, my dear.' Wendy unclips the pirate's hat from his hair. She looks at Jem. 'I hope you're staying too, Jem. There's plenty of food.'

Sezen and Wendy have prepared more food than we could eat in a week. There are at least a hundred jam tarts with decorated pastry tops, coconut creams, chocolate-chip cookies, star-shaped lemon biscuits, two fruit cakes and a treacle tart, not to mention the savoury dishes.

'Once we got started, we just couldn't stop!' Wendy says.

'And I have not forgotten macrobiotic treats,' Sezen says, pointing to a tray of small chocolate-coloured balls, lined up in neat, glistening rows. 'These are made with carob and amazake, brown rice syrup.'

'It all looks fantastic.' I'm holding Bea too tightly. She wriggles out of my arms. 'A veritable feast!' I say loudly.

The doorbell rings and I go to answer it. It's Miss Percival.

'Good evening, Mrs Miller. I'm sorry to disturb you, but Bea left this at nursery on Wednesday. And as she didn't come yesterday or today . . .' She trails off and hands me a small knitted gnome with pointed hat and bushy beard. 'I didn't want her to miss him over the weekend.'

'That's kind,' I say. 'Come in and join us. We're having a bit of a tea party.'

Her face passes through a range of emotions: discomfort, anxiety and then a tentative hope. 'I don't want to interrupt . . .'

'The more the merrier,' I say. 'Wendy and Sezen have been cooking. There's enough food to feed an army, and Bea would love to see you.'

'And your sister.' She bites her bottom lip. 'How is Lisa?'

'Soldiering on,' I say. 'She's coming home to stay with us tomorrow.'

'The chemotherapy was a success?'

I hang her light summer jacket on a peg by the door. 'Not really, no.'

'I'm so sorry.' Her eyes fill up and I wonder who she's thinking of, whether she's watched something similar happen to someone she loves.

We go into the kitchen and everyone says hello. Miss Percival sits between a delighted Bea and Lara, and then Jack comes up from the basement and we gather round the table.

Jem is trying the tempura: pieces of vegetables and fish covered in a light batter and deep-fried. Small bowls of tamari and Japanese sweet-chilli sauce are on the table. She dips some tempura into it, then puts it in her mouth. 'Wow!' She smacks her lips. 'If this is macrobiotic food, I'm sold.'

We're all quiet for a few minutes as we sample the dishes.

'Here you are!' Wendy says as Charlie walks into the kitchen. 'Amy not with you?'

Charlie helps himself to two pieces of tempura. 'A certain person asked her to leave.' He throws a sullen look my way.

'Oh.' Wendy pats his hand.'Well, never mind. A couple of days apart won't do you any harm. Now, why don't you try some of this chilli sauce?'

'But is it only a couple of days?' He glares at me across the table.

'Let's talk about this later, love, shall we?' I say.

'Why not now?' He throws his fork down. It clatters onto his plate.

'What's going on?' Jack has arrived at the table carrying some pickles.

'Mum has thrown Amy out,' Charlie shouts, so loudly that Lara and Bea both look round at the adults, their small faces fearful.

'Charlie, please.' I move to the other side of the table and take his elbow. He allows me to pull him into the hallway.

'You can't stop me seeing her. I'm nineteen.' He presses his chest. 'You can't control me. You can't tell me what to do.'

'I'm not saying you shouldn't see her. I'm asking you to trust me.'

'Trust you how? Trust you why?' He takes several steps away from me, then walks towards me again. 'Amy means a lot to me.' I see tears in his eyes.

'I know.' He allows me to touch his shoulder. 'Somebody is sending threatening emails to your dad. It's serious, Charlie.'

'And you think it's Amy?'

'I think we have to consider every possibility, no matter how unlikely.'

'Jesus! What is this? Have you completely lost it?'

'You started going out with her soon after Dad accepted the case against Georgiev.'

'You base throwing her out on *that*?'

'I've caught her in Dad's study twice now.'

'Oh, let that go, will you? It wasn't the way it looked.'

'She's two years older than you and you said yourself that she was the one who made a play for you.'

'She can't have just fancied me, then?' He gives a bitter laugh. 'Gee, thanks, Mum.' He turns away and heads towards the stairs.

I return to the kitchen and find the mood is subdued. 'Sorry about that,' I say. 'Charlie and I had a disagreement earlier and it's been festering a bit.'

'Glass of wine, Claire?' Jem is in the fridge and holds out the bottle of white towards me. 'Knock the edge off things?'

I nod and she pours me some. I excuse myself and take my wine into the sitting room, wishing I'd kept my mouth shut. Bloody hell. That's twice I've handled Charlie badly. I stand by the window and look out across the park. Half a dozen children are playing tag, some shouting and laughing their way across the grass, others serious as they sprint from one spot to another.

Jem comes in and stands beside me. 'Charlie will come round.'

'I hope so.'

'You have a lot on your plate with Lisa being so ill.' She nods in the direction of the street. 'And that one.' Megan and Julian have just walked down from the station and are approaching the steps leading up to our house.

'What do you mean?' I say.

'It can't be easy when Julian spends so much time with another woman.'

I don't know what she's driving at. 'I'm not with you.'

She shrugs. 'Attractive woman, working together . . .' She trails off.

I start back. 'You think Julian's having an affair?'

'Well, no, but . . . I saw you watching them and I thought . . . Well, isn't that what you were thinking?'

'I wasn't watching them!' I spin round to face her. 'I was watching the children in the park.'

Her face flushes. 'I need to keep my big mouth shut.' She looks genuinely remorseful, her eyes dipped, her head to one side. 'Shoot me now.'

'Apology accepted.' I lean my head against her shoulder. 'But really, Jem, Julian and Megan are colleagues, nothing more.'

'Of course.' Her smile is relieved. 'And now I'm going to love you and leave you.'

Before I have the chance to reply she's off. I hear the door slam and watch her say a quick hello to Megan and Julian before she climbs into her van and drives away. I expect Julian to come straight inside, but he doesn't. Megan is still talking to him. He listens, every now and then making a comment himself. This goes on for almost five minutes.

Finally Julian climbs the first step and Megan raises her head, says something that makes him laugh. The look that passes between them is one between good friends: frank, uninhibited, not lustful or sexually knowing, but there is a sense of sharing and commonality between them that sets off alarm bells. It reminds me of myself and Mac, and I know that although they haven't slept together yet, they may not be far off. She knew about the emails from the start; she knew about his resignation. Julian has shared his concerns with her. Not me. I haven't been his confidante, not for some time.

The realisation is a painful one. I hold the wineglass tight in my hand, so tight that the stem snaps and I cry out as wine spills and mixes with the warm blood that trickles from my palm.

I GO BACK INTO the kitchen and grab some paper towels to wrap round my hand. The girls and Jack have gone to their rooms. Sezen and Miss Percival are tidying up. They both hover around me as I apply pressure to the wound. It takes three minutes before it stops bleeding.

'It looks deep,' Miss Percival says, concerned. 'Do you think you should visit the hospital? It might need stitching.'

'I don't think so,' I say. 'A tight dressing will be good enough.'

I try to use my elbows to open a kitchen cupboard and Sezen steps forward to do it for me. She looks pale and her hands are shaking.

'Are you OK?' I ask.

'I do not like the sight of blood,' she says through gritted teeth. The white paper towel is now deep scarlet.

'Let me help,' Miss Percival says. She puts a dressing and then a bandage over the cut, while Sezen stands back, her eyes averted.

I hear the click of the front door closing and Julian's footsteps along the hallway. He comes straight into the kitchen and takes in the work surfaces laden with food. 'Wow! There's been some cooking going on in here today.'

Sezen immediately steps forward to offer him something to eat, and Miss Percival finishes clearing the dirty dishes from the table.

'Glad it's nearly the end of term, Miss Percival?' Julian asks her.

'Yes.' She looks down as she draws together crumbs with a wet cloth.

'Going anywhere for the summer?'

'No, I . . . em . . .' She finds my eyes. 'I must be heading off. Thank you so much for tea.'

'I'll see you to the door,' I say, but she's out of the kitchen before I finish.

Julian raises his eyebrows and says quietly, 'Was it something I said?'

'I told you,' I whisper. 'She's odd.'

I find her at the front door taking her jacket off the peg. I decide to probe a bit to see if I can find out anything more about her. 'Do you live alone?' I ask.

'Yes. I do. I am.' She hurries into her jacket, her fingers shaking as she does up the buttons. 'I have for some time now.'

'Do you have family?'

'Yes . . . well, no. Not really.' She reaches for the door handle. 'Thank you for inviting me in.'

'Wait! Bea will want to say goodbye to you.' I call up the stairs. Lara comes to the top and looks down at me. 'Is Bea up there?'

She nods. I climb the stairs and call Bea's name again.

'I'm in here,' she says, her voice coming from the bathroom.

I try the door, but it's locked. 'Do you need any help?' I say.

'No, Mummy. I'm four now.'

'OK.' I go back down the stairs and find Miss Percival still in the porch. 'Bea is on the loo. She may be a while.'

'He's not a man to be messed with.' She has a magazine in her hand and I look over her shoulder to see to whom she's referring. I recognise the article. It's one of the Sunday supplements from about a month ago. The story is about organised crime in Europe. The picture shows Georgiev and a couple of his heavies standing bare-chested, covered in tattoos.

For a moment I don't know what to say.

'A monster, by all accounts,' Miss Percival says.

'What do you mean by that?'

Her head jerks up. 'Nothing . . . I was just making conversation.'

'So you don't know this man?'

'Of course not.'

'Call me paranoid'—I fold my arms—'but Pavel Georgiev features large in our lives at the moment and it seems an unlikely coincidence that you've brought this magazine to my house.'

'I didn't!' She drops it on the table. 'It was lying here. Open at this page.'

'No, it wasn't.' I shake my head. 'There was some unopened junk mail on this table and nothing else.'

Colour spills across her cheeks like red wine across a tablecloth. 'I assure you I did not bring this magazine into your home.'

I stare her down. It doesn't take much—just my eyes looking into hers and she capitulates almost at once, turns on her heel and is through the door before I can say anything more.

I rejoin Julian, who is on his own in the kitchen, finishing off the rice. I show him the magazine. 'Did you bring this home?'

He glances at it and shakes his head.

'It was on the hall table. I just accused Miss Percival of bringing it here, but she denied it. Went scuttling off.'

'Parting shot from Amy?' he says.

'She's been gone for twenty-four hours.' I think. 'Could Charlie have put it there to wind me up?'

'Would he do something like that?'

'Well, he really is in a mood with me. He caused a bit of a scene while we were all eating. I really think we should tell him properly about the threat before Monday. He's very het up about Amy having to go.'

Julian weighs this up, his head tilting from one side to the other.

'We don't want him just disappearing off to be with Amy,' I say, leaning in closer to Julian. 'If the blackmailer can't get to Bea, do you think there's a risk that one of the boys might be taken?'

'It's much harder to kidnap someone adult-sized, and anyway'—he takes a sip of wine—'after Monday's pretrial hearing we'll be moving to a safe house.' He pauses. 'Won't we?'

'I hope not.' I clear away his empty plate. I'm not discussing this again. I rinse the plate, being careful not to wet the bandage, then turn back to Julian. 'No more emails today?'

'Not so far.' He spots the bandage. 'What happened to your hand?'

'I broke a wineglass.' When I was watching you and Megan. 'Silly, really. And poor Sezen. She hates the sight of blood. She went really pale. Looked like she was about to pass out.'

He finishes the last of his wine and stands up. 'I haven't seen Jack since I came home. Shall I speak to him while you put Bea to bed?'

We agree on the way forward for Jack, and I go to persuade Bea into bed. Sezen is already organising Lara, so she comes willingly enough, after extracting a promise from Julian that he will take her to the Sealife Centre so Lara can see the Nemo fish.

When I've settled Bea, I come out to find a note from Wendy saying that Charlie's accompanying her to her house to help her move some furniture and that he'll be back later this evening. I smile. Good for Wendy. Keeping Charlie busy and no doubt slipping him a twenty-pound note in the process.

I find Julian in Jack's room, just as Jack is agreeing to write a letter of apology to Mr Schreiber and to the French teacher. What's more, he promises to begin sixth form with a better attitude.

'Does that mean I'm not grounded?'

'In a week you can go back to school and finish your GCSEs. After that you can meet up with your friends. Until then you can study and make yourself useful here.'

He thinks about this, less inclined to argue with Julian than with me. 'OK, then.' He throws himself back onto his bed. 'Could be worse, I suppose.' He sighs. 'But don't blame me if I die from boredom.'

'And show me the letters before you seal the envelopes,' Julian says. 'No half-hearted attempts. You need to mean it.'

'Yeah, yeah. Pile on the pain, why don't you.'

We close the door on his grumblings and go upstairs to our room. Julian is about to put the main light on when he notices that Bea is in our bed, the muted light from the bedside lamp casting a golden glow over her sleeping form. 'Wouldn't she settle in her own bed?'

'I think she should sleep with us now. Just in case.' I bend down and kiss the top of her head. 'If she stays close to one of us, she'll be safe.'

He stands beside me and puts one hand on Bea's head and the other round my waist. 'No one will take her, Claire. I'd never let that happen.' He holds my eyes. 'I mean it. We can do this. No one will take her.' He leans against me and I feel some of the weight he's been carrying seep into my bones.

'We need to check for another email.' I stroke his hair off his forehead. 'I'll go.'

Sezen is reading in the sitting room. She doesn't look up as I pass. I log on to my own laptop this time and feel my blood freeze when I see the now familiar address in my inbox. I connect my laptop to the printer and print it off without reading it.

When I get back, Julian is in the shower. There's a second door from the en suite that leads into our walk-in wardrobe. I put the light on and sit down with my back against the wall. I take a deep breath, then read the latest email.

> Let me tell you what you're thinking. You're thinking that everything will be fine when you move to the safe house. Wrong. You're thinking that even the worst sort of criminals don't kill children. Wrong again.
>
> And, Claire, it took a while for him to tell you, didn't it? And yet you think you can leave all this to the police and to Julian to fix. Think again.
>
> There's not much time left. I'm ready. Are you?

I put the sheet of paper on the floor. I'm interested, almost heartened, to see that she's got me completely wrong. I don't think the safe house is a good option. I know there are people out there who kill children. And there's no way I would ever leave Mac and Julian to decide what happens next.

Julian comes through and stands behind me. 'Another one came?'

I read it out to him while he gets dressed. He sits down on the floor beside me. 'So what do you think?' I ask.

'I think he—'

'Or she.'

'Or she,' Julian acknowledges, 'is trying to influence your thinking. He wants you to lose confidence in the plans we're making.' He shrugs. 'He, or she, wants you to lose confidence in me.'

'What gets me is the information she has.' I sit forward. 'For example, how did she know that you didn't tell me about the emails straight away?'

'Because it would have affected your behaviour. It was only yesterday that you kept Bea home from nursery.'

'And how did she know about the safe house?'

'Standard police procedure,' he says. 'It's pretty obvious, isn't it?'

'So who else knows about the emails?'

'Only those who need to.'

'And of course Megan knows. Did she know from the beginning?'

'Not quite.'

'Do you unburden yourself to her?'

He frowns. 'It's not a case of un-bur-den-ing.' He stresses each of the four syllables. 'She's my instructing solicitor and I have had to resign.'

'I'm a solicitor.' I bring my fist into my chest. 'And I'm your wife and Bea's mother. Plus I'm mentioned by name in the emails. I would have thought that gave me a vested interest that at the very least equals Megan's.'

He sighs. 'I thought we'd moved past this.' He stands up and takes a sweater from the cupboard. 'I've apologised several times for not telling you about the emails sooner. Or . . . is this about Megan?'

I rub my sore palm and think about the way they looked at each other when they were outside. 'She clearly has a crush on you.'

'A crush? That's for teenage girls. She's almost thirty.'

'You spend a lot of time together.'

He pulls the sweater over his head. 'Working.'

I stand up too. 'Late evenings, weekends.'

'Am I about to be accused of full-blown adultery?'

'Well, now you mention it.' I make an effort to say it lightly. 'Have you had sex with Megan?'

'No.'

'But you've thought about it?'

'Not really.'

My stomach tips sideways and I stifle a gasp. 'So you have, then?'

'About three months ago she started coming on to me. Nothing too strong, just hints here and there.'

'And did you take her up on those hints?'

'Claire!' He looks at me as if he thinks I'm being deliberately obtuse. 'I can't believe you're even giving it a passing thought, never mind voicing it.'

'I watched you from the window. You looked at each other with . . .' I can't think of the right word and settle for 'fondness.'

'Fondness?' He laughs. 'If I never saw Megan again, it wouldn't matter to me. That's the truth.'

'Couldn't you have asked for another solicitor?'

'Why?'

'To eliminate temptation.'

'There was no real temptation.' His expression is closed. 'Most adults can work with members of the opposite sex without sleeping with them.'

The implication is clear. When I breathe in, my chest aches.

'I am happily married. I love you,' he says. He takes hold of my elbows and I look up into his face. 'I'm committed to you and to our family. I would never jeopardise that for a cheap affair.'

Put like that, my fear seems ridiculous, but my heart is slow to catch up with my head. I briefly rest my lips against his chest. 'I'm sorry.' I bend down and pick up the email, pushing it in with the others under a pile of sweaters.

I let him lead me into the bedroom. Bea is still fast asleep, her head almost completely covered by the duvet. 'I'm going to get a drink of water,' I say. 'Do you want anything?'

'Not for me.'

I go out onto the landing. I feel sad, ashamed, achy inside. I've always known that Julian is a better person than me. And much better than my father, who cheated on Wendy more than once. Julian has enough integrity and honour for ten men. He didn't have to spell it out for me to know that he found my suspicions about him and Megan insulting.

When I'm at the top of the stairs, I hear the front door close. Sezen comes in from the porch and goes into the sitting room. I'm not wearing anything on my feet. I make hardly any sound as I go down the carpeted stairs and she doesn't realise that I am behind her. When I reach the entrance to the sitting room, she is standing in front of the bay window, staring at a man's retreating back as he walks along the street. She leans right into the glass, her palms flat against the pane, so that she can catch the last sight of him as the pavement curves round the corner. Then she stands back and sighs, closes her eyes and turns her face up to the ceiling.

I don't want her to find me watching her like this, so I tiptoe along the hallway to the kitchen. Jack is taking some leftovers out of the fridge.

He holds up a cold chicken leg. 'Is it OK if I eat this?'

I nod. 'Do you know who that was at the door?'

He shrugs. 'Some friend of Sezen's.'

'Did you speak to him?'

'Not much. I answered the door and he asked if Sezen was here and I said I'd get her.' He uses his teeth to tear off some meat. 'That was it.'

'Did he speak English with an accent?'

'Yeah.'

'What did he look like?'

'Unshaven. Serious fish.'

'Meaning?'

'He didn't smile.'

'Did Sezen bring him in?'

'They stood outside for a minute or two.'

'What did they talk about?'

'I dunno!' He looks exasperated. 'What's with the twenty questions?'

'I'm interested.'

'Then ask her yourself. Maybe he's her boyfriend.'

'Is Charlie back from Wendy's yet?'

'He's in his room listening to music.'

I pour some water into a glass. 'Don't you stay up too late, now. You need your beauty sleep.' I take my glass of water and head to bed.

My foot is on the bottom stair when I decide to have a word with Sezen. She's still in the sitting room, her book unopened on her lap.

'Was that someone at the door?' I say lightly.

'It was just a man.'

'A friend of yours?'

'No.'

'Oh!' I take a sip of water. 'Jack thought you knew him.'

'I met him before.'

'And you gave him this address?'

She stands up, walks towards me and stops a couple of feet away. Her expression is sombre but her eyes are bright. 'He will not come here again.' And then she adds, 'He is nothing to me.'

I can't read the expression in her eyes, cloaked as it is by a fierce self-control. I take a step back. 'I'm off to bed,' I say. 'See you in the morning.'

'Sleep well.' She smiles. It has none of her usual warmth.

Julian has turned out the light. Bea is on my side of the bed. I climb over her and lie down between them.

'There's just been a man at the door for Sezen,' I tell Julian.

'Did she invite him in?'

'No. She denied he was her friend.' I shift my position, try to relax into Julian's side. 'And yet she stood right up close to the window and watched him all the way to the end of the street, like she couldn't get enough of him.'

'A secret lover?'

'Not one she's willing to admit to. Maybe he's someone from her past. Lara's father even.' I come up onto one elbow and look into Julian's face. There's just enough light for me to make out his features. 'Julian?'

'Mmm?'

'Under what circumstances would you consider giving up the witness's name and whereabouts?' I say it lightly, but my heart is hammering in my chest. That's the simplest way to end all this, isn't it? For Julian to just give the blackmailer the witness.

'You know I can't consider doing that.' He takes my hand and brings it up to his lips. 'We can't bend to this sort of intimidation.'

'But, Julian . . .' I can't say the words. I can't say 'Bea' and 'dead' in the same sentence. 'If the worst comes to the worst, you would put our family first, wouldn't you?'

'It's not going to happen.'

'But if it did,' I persist. 'Would you put Bea's safety before the interests of this case?'

'Claire, I will do everything in my power to protect our family.' He turns and puts his arms round me. 'I'm surprised you even have to ask me that.'

I believe him. I trust him. He is always there for me and for the children. He's my husband, solid and true—he has never let me down.

So why am I not reassured?

6

Saturday and I wake early. Julian and Bea are still asleep. I climb over Bea, go into the walk-in wardrobe, take all the emails out from underneath my sweaters and sit down on the floor to read them again. By the time I get to the final one, I feel the intensity of the threat tightening, like a snake coiling round a human body. But the fact that the blackmailer has copied me in on the emails should make it easier for me to track her down. Few people know my email address. Miss Percival is one of them. And the more I think about it, the more suspicious she seems. She's often walking Douglas in the park opposite my house when there is a larger, far more dog-friendly park near her house.

I put the emails away and have a shower. The cut on my hand has stopped bleeding, the edges of the wound pulling together nicely. I stand under the water, directing the flow onto my shoulders, where tension has tightened them into knots. My mind loops back to last night. Sezen. What was that all about? How could she not know the man, when he found out where she lives, and asked for her by name?

By nine o'clock everyone apart from Jack and Charlie is up and dressed and at the breakfast table.

'How is your hand?' Sezen says to me.

'Feels much better.' I show her my palm and the smaller plaster now covering it. 'It'll be healed in a couple of days.'

Bea has reminded Julian of his promise to take her and Lara to the Sealife Centre. We have season tickets. It's her favourite place to visit. She is fascinated with fish and crustaceans and anything that lives in the sea.

I stand up. 'I have to go now. You girls have fun!' I kiss the tops of their heads and then Julian's cheek. 'I'm off to get Lisa.'

'Need a hand?'

'No, we'll be fine. Could you have a word with Charlie before you go out?'

'Will do.'

'What would you like me to do this morning?' Sezen asks.

'It's Saturday,' I say. 'Take some time off. It'll give you a chance to look for somewhere to stay between now and moving into Mr Patel's place.'

'But would you like me to make some food for when you return.'

I tell her it isn't necessary. There's enough food left over from yesterday's cooking session. She follows me into the hallway.

'Claire. About last night. I hope you did not find me rude.' I can see she's choosing her words carefully. 'I am very appreciative of this job.'

'Sezen, you know that you can talk to me, don't you?' I see a moment of uncertainty flit across her face. I smile. 'I'm fairly unshockable, you know. If there's anything you need to tell me . . . something from the pas—'

'No!' she says forcefully, and at once I know there is something in her past.

'The man who came last night?'

'I will not see him again.' The shake of her head is emphatic.

'Sezen.' I reach for her hand. She lets me take it. 'I'm a good listener.'

Her expression softens. Her eyes fill with tears. 'You are a good person, Claire.' She hugs me quickly and then backs away.

'You will talk to me?' I say.

'Yes.' She smiles her thanks. 'I will.'

She closes the door after me. Feeling like I might have made some progress, I'm about to climb into my car when Jem calls me on her mobile.

'Only me,' she says. 'I didn't leave my Stanley knife in Lisa's room, did I? I woke up this morning with a horrible feeling I had. I don't want Bea to get hold of it and hurt herself.'

'Hang on.' I go back in the house and look around the room. 'Can't see it.'

'Oh well, must be in the van somewhere. How's things?'

I tell her about Julian taking the girls out to give me space to collect Lisa, walking into the sitting room as I talk. I look through the window and spot Mary Percival heading towards me through the park opposite, Douglas trotting beside her. She looks up at the house and I automatically pull myself back and to the side so that she won't be able to see me at the window. She stands at the bottom of the steps, looks at her watch, then back at the house. She climbs three steps and stops, looking nervous, scared even. She climbs one step higher, then does an about-turn and ends up back in the park.

'Are you listening?' Jem's voice is suddenly loud in my ear.

'I've got to go, Jem,' I say. 'Talk to you soon.'

I run out through the front door and across the road. Miss Percival looks up as I approach and smiles tentatively. Without pause for thought I say, 'Every time I look out of the window, you're there.'

She steps back, startled. 'I'm sorry. I . . . I want to . . .'

'You want to what? Why are you so strange with me? You've made a favourite of Bea and yet you can barely look me in the eye.' I try to soften my tone. 'If you have something to say, then you should say it.'

'I do have something to say. I do have something to tell you. I haven't been able to up till now. I never intended to tell you, but then Bea came to the nursery and I made the connection and—'

'What connection?'

My arms are folded; I'm tapping my foot. Not conducive to her coming clean with me and I'm not surprised when she says, 'When you're less . . . busy.' She's clutching the dog's lead with both hands. 'I won't bother you now.'

'No.' I hold her upper arm. She makes no attempt to shrug me off. 'We need to clear this up now. Or else I'll have to give your name to the police.'

'*What?* Why?'

'The magazine article you were reading. The one about Pavel Georgiev. Do you know him?'

'Of course not.' She stares at me, incredulous.

I drop my voice. 'My husband is being blackmailed by someone who intends to kidnap Bea unless he gives her the information she wants.'

'My God, I'm so sorry.' I'm taken aback as I watch her face collapse with horror. Her jaw hangs open and tears slide from her eyes. 'So very sorry. If there's anything I can do . . .'

'Yes. There is. You can eliminate yourself from the enquiries. Because someone in my life, and in Bea's life, is feeding information to this blackmailer and I need to be sure it isn't you.'

The sun chooses that moment to come out from behind a cloud and shine down upon us both as if we have been singled out for extra light and warmth. I hold my hand up to shield my eyes so that I can see Miss Percival's expression. She looks crushed. It doesn't make sense. Most people, guilty or innocent, would have come back at me by now with 'How dare you!'

'Miss Percival, Mary,' I say, more gently now, 'this is clearly upsetting you. Will you please tell me what's going on?'

She glances down at Douglas. He has lain down on a patch of grass and rolled onto his side. He looks a picture of contentment. She unclips the lead from his collar and walks over to a bench, positioned in the shade under an oak tree. I follow her and sit down beside her.

'The timing for this can never be right,' she begins. 'I don't want to upset anyone or to change the view you have of your father.'

'My father?' I almost laugh. 'What does he have to do with this?'

She takes a huge breath. 'I am an only child. I was brought up near Brighton by my mum and dad—or at least for thirty years I believed he was my dad. But then, six years ago, mum told me that in fact she'd fallen pregnant to someone else. I got in touch with this man—your dad. I took a DNA test and the result was positive. He was very kind to me, but I was confused and angry that I'd been lied to all my life and I left Brighton for a while. I came back a couple of years ago, made up with my parents but discovered that your dad, my biological father, had passed away.'

She says all of this in a deadpan tone as if she is repeating these words by rote. I, on the other hand, feel as if I've landed slap bang in the middle of an episode of *The Jeremy Kyle Show* and I'm shaking my head so quickly that I can feel blood swish in my ears.

'You're telling me you're my *half-sister*?'

'Yes.'

'You've been Bea's teacher since September and you never said a word!'

'I know. It took me a while to get my head round it. I knew that you and Lisa existed—your father was very proud of you both—but we were a couple of weeks into the term before I put two and two together and realised we were related.'

'So why not tell me then? October? November? Christmas?'

'Lisa had been diagnosed with cancer. I didn't think it was the right time.'

I stare at her, still shaking my head. My mind is reeling. My father had another daughter. *My father had another daughter?* I find it impossible to comprehend such enormous news.

'Why didn't my dad say something?'

'I asked him not to, and when I returned to Brighton, he'd passed away.'

'I'm sorry, but I don't believe you. You bear no resemblance to my father, or me, or Lisa.'

'I take after my mother.' She digs around in her bag. 'This is a letter your dad sent to me. It's the only thing I have of him.'

I don't touch it, but I can see that it's been repeatedly read. The paper is fraying at the edges and the two pages are heavily creased. And it is my dad's handwriting. No mistaking the long strokes on the 'f's and the 't's and the flourishes at the end of each sentence. It begins with 'My dear Mary, I was so delighted to meet you . . .' I have a sudden sense of him standing in front of me, smiling with that hundred-watt, winning enthusiasm that always made me feel special. Yes, he had his faults—not least his infidelity to Wendy—but he was my dad and I loved him.

'I don't want to read it.' I hold my hands up and back away from her. 'I can't deal with this now.'

'I understand.' She composes her face. 'You need time to think about it.'

'I have to go.' I walk away. My ears are ringing and I feel nauseous. When I reach the car, I sit in the driving seat and hold my breath while a powerful shake flows through my body, beginning in my stomach and ending in my toes and fingertips. *What the hell just happened?* I can't believe it. I have another sister. A younger sister. I'm already calculating that Mary would have been born a couple of years after my dad married Wendy. Wendy, who, two years after my mother's death, defied all step-mother stereotypes and came into our lives, bringing generosity and caring for two small girls and a grieving man. I wonder whether she knows that my father had another child. And should I tell her? Should I tell Lisa?

It takes me only a second to decide that I'll do nothing. I won't tell anyone. I'll pretend that it hasn't happened. I've known Mary Percival for nine months without her giving me so much as an inkling of her relationship to us. This is something that doesn't have to be dealt with now. Another few days or weeks are not going to make any difference.

I take a few deep breaths, start the engine and head to the hospital.

Lisa is sitting in an easy chair, her belongings in several bags arranged around her feet. When she sees me coming, she smiles wider than I've seen her smile in weeks.

'My rescuer!' she shouts, then leans in for a hug. 'Who needs a knight in shining armour when I have you?'

Lynn comes into the room to brief me on Lisa's medication regime. She has it all written up on a chart—some need to be taken with meals, others an hour before or after food.

'As if I'm not capable of working it out for myself,' Lisa chimes in.

'Little sister's in charge,' Lynn says, playfully nudging Lisa's shoulder before turning back to me. 'The community nurse will call on Tuesday, but if you need her before that, here's the number.' She points to it on the chart. 'And if Lisa gives you any trouble, Claire, you bring her straight back.'

'Not in a month of Sundays.' Lisa stands up and gives Lynn a hug. 'Much as I love you all, I have no intention of coming back.'

When we're outside, Lisa takes a huge breath of air. She throws her arms up above her head and then lets them fall back down to her sides.'It's great to be outdoors again.'

My heart skips a happy beat.

'I can sit in the shade and watch Bea playing and you can bring me jam sandwiches and homemade lemonade.'

I smile. The food of our childhood. Wendy would make us up a tray and we'd take it to the bottom of the garden and lie on our backs munching on squares of sandwich while sticky lemonade dribbled down our chins.

'Happiness is all about small moments and simple pleasures,' Lisa says, climbing into the car. 'Those are the things we remember in the end. Do you remember Dad used to always say'—she deepens her voice—'"You have to live life to the full, girls. No regrets."'

Dad. My eyes slide away from Lisa. Do we really have another sister? If so, when she came to see him six years ago, why on earth didn't he tell us?

'He was all about seizing the day.'

'From what I remember, the rest of us had to accommodate his seizing of the day,' I say, negotiating my way out of the hospital grounds and onto the main road. 'All those affairs. I mean, honestly! Who does that?'

'He never had an affair while Mum was alive.'

'It was Wendy who copped the brunt of it.' I shake my head. 'And why didn't he comfort us when Mum died? He acted like she'd never existed.'

'Some people don't do well with loss. They can't cope with the grief.'

'I suppose,' I say. 'But we were only kids, Lisa. You were six, and I was four—Bea's age. We were practically babies.'

'We had each other, Claire. Dad must have felt very alone. We had all our little games and imaginings and that made it easier.'

Our mother is a subject Lisa and I haven't spoken about for a while. She died of a brain haemorrhage. One sunny September day she dropped down in front of us, passing from life to death in the space of one ordinary moment. An extreme, abrupt ending that my child's mind found impossible to absorb. Every morning I woke up expecting her to have come back to us, but every morning the house was cold, breakfast unmade, our clothes lying where we'd dropped them.

My dad put everything that was left of her in the wardrobe in their room. Piece by piece, crawling commando style, Lisa and I sneaked some of Mum's belongings out of her old room and into ours. We kept a box under Lisa's bed. Inside were a silk scarf, some slingback shoes, a bottle of perfume and a pair of pearl earrings. We had one photograph of her. We took turns placing it under our pillow. For years we believed she would come home. We lived in a kind of limbo and said things to each other like 'When Mum comes back, we'll ask her if we can have riding lessons' or 'We should eat an apple every day because Mum said that keeps the doctor away.'

I must have been twelve before it really hit me that, of course, she wasn't coming back. I cried then, for her and for myself.

'The secret with grief is, don't fight it,' Lisa says. 'Let it wash over you. And when the next wave comes, bend your back and take that too.'

I know that she's partly talking about our parents and about herself and coming to terms with her illness. And I know, too, that she's partly talking to me, helping me see a way through it.

Lisa reaches over and squeezes my knee. 'Did you hear me?'

'I heard you.' I look sideways to give her a quick smile.

'Do you mind if we stop by my flat? I want to pick up some stuff.'

Before she was diagnosed with cancer, Lisa taught biology in a girls' school in Brighton. Her flat is between my house and the hospital. Parking is a nightmare, so I risk stopping in one of the disabled bays close to the entrance to her flat. It's on the first floor. We go inside. She stops halfway up the stairs and leans on the banister while she catches her breath.

'Take your time,' I say. 'There's no rush.'

'I don't want you getting a ticket.' She sets off up the last half a dozen steps. 'You know what the traffic wardens are like around here.'

'I'll sit at the window and watch out for them.' I unlock her front door, pick up the letters on the mat inside and hand them to her.

She lives on a busy corner, almost on top of a small roundabout where seven roads branch out: to the station, to the seafront, others inland. I sit at the window to watch for wardens. I've been sitting for five minutes when I notice a man approaching the roundabout. He has a distinctive style of walking, leaning over to one side, not quite a limp, but there is a definite tilt to his gait. Exactly like the man who came to see Sezen yesterday evening.

I go through to Lisa's bedroom. She is emptying the contents of her bedside drawer into a bag. 'Do you have any binoculars?'

'In the living-room bureau. They're Dad's old ones.'

I find them at once. The casing is scratched and heavy, the leather strap torn, but there's nothing wrong with the lenses. I lift them up to my eyes and turn the knob until the street is in focus. I home in on the man. Swarthy and unsmiling, he waits on the corner. His eyes dart anxiously down towards the right—Monkton Terrace—the street a person would walk up if they were coming from my house.

He sees her just before I do and I watch a slow smile spread across his face. I move the binoculars to the right, following his gaze along the street. My hands shake as I focus on Sezen walking towards him. When she spots him, her feet quicken, almost to a run. She reaches him and they embrace.

'And this is a man who is nothing to you?' I hear myself say out loud.

Sezen and the man step back and hold hands, their eyes fixed on each other. They stand like this for more than twenty seconds and then he says something. She smiles and replies. She hands him a piece of paper and he reads it, asks her questions. He pulls something out of his trouser pocket. I refocus the binoculars. It's a wad of cash, held together with an elastic band.

My heart lurches. I'm witnessing an exchange. Payment for information or services rendered. It's too much. This woman has access to my house. I've trusted her with Bea. And here she is meeting a man she said she would never see again and giving him information for money.

I call Julian. No answer, so I leave a message. 'Julian, don't let Bea go anywhere with Sezen. I think she may have something to do with all this.'

I put my mobile back in my pocket and lift up the binoculars again. They're still standing there, talking and smiling.

'What are you up to?' Lisa has come up behind me.

'I'm watching Sezen.' I hand her the binoculars.

She holds them up to her eyes, steadying them on the sash window. 'She's with someone she loves, by the looks of it. Have you met him?'

'He came to the house last night. She told me he meant nothing to her.'

She puts the binoculars on the windowsill and searches my face. 'Why do you look so worried?'

'Because she lied to me. Why did she tell me he wasn't her friend?'

'Maybe she doesn't see him as a friend. And anyway, you're her employer, not her priest. She's entitled to her privacy, isn't she?'

'Yes, but . . .' I shake my head. I'm trying to add it all up. Sezen knows my email address; we ordered macrobiotic ingredients on the Internet. She wasn't at Bea's party, but she could have found out about it from Wendy.

'Isn't she?' Lisa is waiting for me to say something else.

'It's complicated.' I briefly consider not telling her, but what's the point in prevaricating? It hasn't worked with Charlie and I feel even less inclined to lie to my sister. 'Julian has been receiving emails. We're being threatened,' I say flatly. 'By someone who works for Pavel Georgiev.'

'What?' She steps back and sits down hard on the arm of the couch. 'Why? Who?' Her head is shaking. 'What do you mean?'

'It's the case he's working on. The Bulgarian gangster.'

'What are they threatening him with?'

'The children's safety: most specifically Bea's.'

I fill her in on the details. She looks increasingly worried as I talk and then, when she can bear it no more, she bursts out, 'This is awful!' She grabs hold of both my hands. 'Claire, you should take the children and leave the country. Get right away from the danger.' She gives a sharp intake of breath. 'You're not still in this country because of me, are you?'

I look her in the eye. 'It has nothing to do with you,' I say.

Her face flushes. 'I could always tell when you were lying. You're no better at it now than you were when you were five.' She shakes me. 'You mustn't put me before your children's safety.'

'I'm not.' I hug her to me, feel her ribs jutting out, curved sticks beneath her skin. I stroke her hair. She didn't lose it with the chemo, but it feels coarse under my hand. 'I admit it was my first impulse to take them away, but then, when I had time to think about it, I realised it was a bad idea.'

'Are you sure?'

'Lisa, Georgiev is powerful. His reach extends further than England. Being in another country, waiting for that knock at the door or disturbance in the middle of the night would be far more stressful than staying here. I don't want you and me to be apart, and I don't want Julian and me to be apart. This is a time for us all to stick together. Safety in numbers. The thing is'—I take a breath—'the police are organising a safe house. If we have to go, you will come with us, won't you?'

'Of course!' She doesn't hesitate. 'Of course I'll come with you all.'

'They're arranging a live-in nurse.'

'Will Wendy come?'

'I hope so. She doesn't know about it yet, but on Monday the police will come to the house to brief us on what happens next.'

'What does Julian think?'

'He goes along with the police, but'—I breathe in—'he hasn't exactly been keeping me in the loop. He kept the emails a secret for over a week.' I tell her about Bea letting slip about the emails. 'Julian said he was going to tell me, but'—I blow air out through my mouth—'he didn't.'

'Why not?'

'Because he didn't want to worry me. And I do believe him.' I pause. 'He told Megan, though.'

'His assistant?'

'The instructing solicitor who works for the CPS.' I think of Megan with her privileged background and top-of-the-class ambition. 'The more modern, up-scaled version of me.'

She catches my tone, which I know sounds sullen and not just a little bit sour. 'Are you regretting giving up work?'

'No, but I'm regretting the effect it seems to have had on my marriage. I thought we were close, but now I just don't know. At the moment it feels like he's closer to Megan than he is to me.'

She recoils back a step. 'You're not saying . . . ?'

'That he's having an affair?' I shrug. 'I asked him and he said no.'

'Look, Claire, you've just had the most awful shock. You've found out your family is under threat and that's frightening. In fact it's beyond frightening. But Julian is your husband and your greatest ally.'

I want to believe her, but . . . 'Do you remember the policeman Andrew MacPherson? Mac?'

'Of course.' Apart from Julian, Lisa is the only person I told about my extramarital sex. And unlike Julian, she knew it was Mac. 'He was the reason you moved to Brighton, wasn't he?'

'He wasn't so much the reason as the catalyst, the final straw.'

'OK.' She inclines her head. 'If you say so.'

I let that go. 'Well, the thing is, Mac's been promoted since I knew him last. He's running this.'

'Mac?' Her eyes fix on mine. 'And have you seen him?'

'We hadn't spoken for years, but I met him, on my own, just after I found out about the emails. We discussed the case.'

'And does Julian know?'

'Yes.'

'And does he know that Mac was the man you slept with?'

'No.'

'This is dangerous, Claire.' She tilts her head to one side, eyebrows raised. 'You have history with this man and if Julian finds out—'

'He won't find out. But Mac's a good policeman and I'm glad he's on the case. I feel like he's on my side.'

'*Julian* is on your side.' Her voice is firm.

'I know.'

'So why didn't you include him in the meeting?'

'Because he was still in Sofia! And I didn't want to wait. And because I was hurt and angry, and he'd been keeping a hefty great secret from me for long enough.'

'Evening up the score?' She looks washed out suddenly. 'Claire, tell me you're better than that?'

Her look says it all and at once I feel guilty: small-minded and cheap.

'This is not about me and Mac. And it's not about me and Julian.' I try to regain some ground. 'It's about protecting my family. And Mac will do the best for us. I know he will.'

'Good.' She turns away. 'I'm going to get the rest of my stuff together.'

I watch her slowly make her way back to her bedroom. I know she's disappointed in me and it hurts. I go back to the window and lift the binoculars in time to catch Sezen and the man coming out of the café on the corner. They part on the pavement after he kisses her, on the mouth, confidently, like he knows she wants it.

'Lovers, then,' I say out loud. 'And we all know what lovers are willing to do for each other. Look at Myra Hindley.'

'You really think she might have something to do with this?' Lisa is back. She is holding a couple of bags.

'Let me carry those.' I put the binoculars down and she passes the bags to me. 'Yes, I really think she might. Details in the emails prove that the blackmailer either is or knows someone who has access to our family.'

We head for the door. Out on the street, I can't see any sign of Sezen or the man. I look out for them as I drive home, but they must have gone in another direction. When we arrive back at the house, only Jack is home. He comes forward to give Lisa a hug and lifts her off her feet.

'We have another man in the house!' she says.

He flexes his muscles and rolls up the sleeves of his T-shirt so that she can see. 'I've been working out.'

'Haven't you just!' She hugs him again.

They are both grinning like mad and I realise afresh that bringing Lisa home will be a good thing for her and also for the children, who love her dearly. Jack helps bring Lisa's stuff in from the car and I go into the kitchen to put the kettle on. Sezen has left a tray of food, beautifully prepared, and alongside it are pale pink tulips in a vase. All this before she went off to meet the man who means nothing to her.

I hear the front door open and Bea shouts, 'Mummy!'

'In the kitchen!' I shout back.

She comes running in and throws her arms round my legs. 'I won a twirly thing and Daddy lifted me and Lara up high and we saw the men juggling.' She pushes her stomach out, leans back on her heels and puckers her lips. 'The juggling man looked like that. And he had plates on the end of a stick and he let me hold one.'

'Did he, now? Lucky you.' I hunker down to her height and hug her tight. 'But guess who's come to stay?'

'Who?'

'Auntie Lisa.' Her eyes light up. I give her a gentle nudge. 'Go and tell her all about the good time you had.'

She's off again, knocking into Julian on the way.

'The girls had fun, then,' I say.

'Great time.' He unzips his jacket. 'They had special events on.'

'Where's Lara?'

'Sezen called me earlier. She met us down on the pier. They've gone off to see friends. She won't be back this evening.'

'Did you get my message?'

'No.' He takes his BlackBerry out of his pocket. 'Sorry. Left it in the car.'

'I saw her with the man who came to the door last night. At the roundabout by Lisa's flat. They were hugging like long-lost lovers.'

Julian looks unperturbed.

'Don't you think that's a problem?'

'In what way?' He walks into the pantry and I follow him.

'The emails.'

He moves aside a jar of pickles, some tuna fish and a tin of peaches. 'Why would Sezen have anything to do with the emails?'

'She might be feeding Georgiev's men information. It would be a good way to infiltrate our family, wouldn't it?'

'But you employed her, didn't you? You approached her? Her references checked out?'

'Yes, but you know how clever people can be.'

'Is it the fact that she hasn't shared the details of her relationship with this man that's bothering you?'

This irritates me, but I stay calm. 'No. It's the fact that she *lied*. I think that's cause for concern. An unknown man turns up at our house. Sezen denies he means anything to her and yet next day I see her kissing him. She gave him a piece of paper; he passed her a wad of cash. How can that be fine?'

He rolls his head from side to side. 'The two events are not necessarily linked. So she has a secret? It doesn't make her Georgiev's accomplice.' I go to protest and he holds up a hand. 'But you're right. Why risk it? We should ask her to leave.' He pours water into the kettle and switches it on. 'But it was only yesterday that you felt it couldn't possibly be Sezen. Mary Percival was definitely in the running, though.'

'Don't talk to me about her.' I put my hands over my face. 'It's not her.'

'How do you know?'

'I had it out with her in the park earlier and . . .' I shake my head. I don't even consider telling him. The thought of forming the words on my tongue—*she's my sister*—feels too alien. 'It's not her.'

'OK. So Sezen is now prime suspect?'

'Julian. Please. I feel in my bones that there's more going on here. If you'd seen her at the roundabout, I'm sure you'd feel the same.'

'Well, why don't we ask her when she gets back?'

I can't leave it at that. She won't be back until tomorrow and that's a long way off. Something inside me wants to get to the root of this now. Next thing I know I'm on the top floor, pushing open the door into Sezen's bedroom. I stand in the middle of the room and look around me. The space is neat and tidy. My fingers want to start poking through her stuff; my head tells me it's an invasion of privacy. I should ask her when she comes back.

A compromise is reached. I decide that I won't go through everything. I won't read letters or diaries. All I will do is see whether there is anything obvious that might give me a clue as to why she's been lying to me.

I open the drawers one by one, carefully moving folded blouses and underwear to look underneath. I don't really know what I expect to find, but I keep on looking anyway. The bottom drawer is heavy and stiff. I pull hard and see that she has stored papers and books in this one. Right at the back there is a pouch containing passports—three of them. I bring them out. One is made out to Lara, one to Sezen and the third to a Sylvia Cyrilova, a Bulgarian national. I look at the photo. I compare one with the other. Her hair is shorter and she's two or three years younger, but it's definitely Sezen. She has two identities. She is Turkish and she is Bulgarian. Or perhaps she is just Bulgarian. Like Georgiev.

'Should you be snooping in here?' It's Julian. He's standing at the door.

Wordlessly, I hold out the passports.

'You've found something?' He steps into the room and takes them. I watch his face register two different names, two different nationalities, same woman. He looks back at me and I see fear in his eyes. 'I'll call Mac.'

7

I stand to one side and listen as Julian calls Mac. He explains that we've found the passports, indicating that Sezen is far from what she seems. Mac tells Julian he should call him as soon as Sezen comes back tomorrow and that she will be taken in for questioning. In the meantime, he would like to come and see us this evening. He has the case files for the two murders quoted in the email—Carlo Brunetti, Rome, 2006, and Boleslav Hlutev, Sofia, 2008. We arrange for him to come round at eight thirty.

By eight o'clock Lisa is tired. I help her shower and then we go through the routine that Lynn has taught me. I organise all the medicines for the next day in a dosette box and put it on top of the cabinet. Then I stand in front of Lisa with a glass of water and half a dozen coloured pills.

'Who knew?' she says between swallows.

'Who knew what?'

'That you could be such a good little nurse.'

'Be thankful I haven't starched the sheets.' I take her elbow and we go through to the bedroom. I help her swing her legs round into the bed, where Bea, washed and pyjamaed, is lying with her head on one of the pillows.

'Are you sure you're OK with her in your bed?' I ask Lisa. 'She might kick you in her sleep.'

'I really don't mind,' Lisa says. 'I've missed her.'

I kiss them both on the forehead, close the door and look at my watch. Mac should be here any minute. I pour myself a glass of wine and go to wait in the sitting room. Breathing space. Time to think and reflect. For tonight, the family is settled. Jack is watching television in his room, still complaining about being grounded. Julian had a word with Charlie. I'm not sure what was said, but although he's still not talking to me, he isn't avoiding me any more, so I think a truce is in sight.

A few minutes before nine the doorbell sounds. I open the outside door and Mac comes into the porch. 'Sorry I'm late,' he says. 'Lost my car keys.'

'You're still doing that?'

'At least once a week.'

I usher him into the hallway and call Julian from his study. In the sitting room, Mac and Julian shake hands.

'Take a seat.' Julian gestures towards an easy chair. 'Something to drink?'

'Coffee would be great,' Mac says.

I make coffee, pour Julian a whisky and a glass of Merlot for myself. My mind is whirring. Mac is here. He has information on the two cases. I can't help but feel this might be the turning point. From here we could start to make progress.The safe house may not be necessary after all.

I give out the drinks and sit down on the sofa next to Julian.

'So.' Mac takes a breath. 'I came tonight to talk about Sezen but also to give you both an update on the two cases: Brunetti and Hlutev. It's taken a bit of piecing together, but we think the blackmailer is giving us a clue to the pattern of events.'

'How so?' I ask.

'In both cases, in Rome and in Sofia, the blackmailer infiltrated the family.' He looks at Julian then back at me. 'The blackmailer in these two cases was a woman. Our profilers feel that there's a good chance the same MO is happening here. As was your hunch all along, Claire.'

'OK.' I try not to feel too pleased. 'Do you know this woman's name?'

'There were two women. The similarities lie in the way Georgiev gained access to the victims. Both times it was through a trusted young woman.'

'Was either of them caught?'

'One was. She's in prison in Italy. She was Georgiev's girlfriend. He's had a few over the years.' He brings a sheaf of photographs out of the folder, then gives us both a sober look. 'These don't make for comfortable viewing.'

He lays the photographs out on the coffee table, dividing them into two sections. They are from crime scenes. Mac's index finger rests on the group of photos to his right. 'This murder was committed two years ago in the Alexander Nevski Cathedral in Sofia. The man was a priest. His brother repeatedly spoke out against Georgiev's crime syndicate.'

I examine one of the photographs.The man is young, no more than forty. He is lying on his back on a patterned rug. His throat has been cut. 'Was there any sign of a struggle?'

'None. It seems she caught him completely unawares.'

'How did the police know it was a woman?' Julian says.

'The priest had an appointment that morning. Every week for three months a woman who called herself Lucia Ivanova had been coming to him for spiritual guidance. She was described as around five feet six, slim, regular features. In this case she had blonde hair and blue eyes, but'—he shrugs—'doesn't count for a lot. She's never been caught.'

He turns to the other set of photographs. They show a child, a boy not much older than Bea. His hair is black and curly; his dark lashes lie on cheeks that are unnaturally pale and waxen. They would feel cold to the touch. I shrink back from the sight of him. 'Shit.' I grip the edges of the sofa.

'Sweetheart,' Julian says. 'If you'd rather not see this, Mac and I can—'

'No. No,' I say forcefully. 'I need to know what's happening. I'm fine.' My blouse feels as if it's constricting my throat. I try to undo the top button but find it's already undone. 'I can do this.'

'The boy was five. He was murdered four years ago,' Mac says flatly. 'His father was an Italian businessman, funding an organisation that tracked and rescued girls who'd been trafficked. Again the killer was a woman. She had been hired as an au pair and had been working there for almost a year. Her references had been checked and double-checked and they were genuine.'

'And she's in prison now?'

'Yes.'

'Was this woman willing to testify against Georgiev?' I ask.

'Not even close. She insisted the whole thing was her idea.'

Mac looks at Julian. 'Your witness has told us that Georgiev has several people working for him who have infiltrated government organisations.'

'Like the police service?' I say.

Mac nods. 'They gain people's trust. They're patient. They plan for months, sometimes even years.'

I stand up. 'So some woman has infiltrated our lives.' I start to tremble.

'The emails are warnings, Claire,' Mac says, standing up too. 'The blackmailer is letting us know that she can get close to you. That's why we need to look again at everyone who's in your life at the moment.' He takes a sheet of paper from his file. 'Julian already gave us some names.They've all been checked out and there are no direct links to Georgiev, but there might be something we've missed, especially with Sezen.'

'I only found the passports because I went looking,' I say. 'She hadn't been telling me the truth. A man came to our front door last night, and when I asked her who he was, she wouldn't give me his name. She said he was nothing to her, but then I saw them together at the roundabout today. They were kissing. He handed her a wad of cash.'

'Did you take a photo of him?'

'No. I didn't have a camera, just my dad's old binoculars.'

'We have photos of a number of Georgiev's men on file. If there is a link between Sezen and the blackmailer, then that might be the way to prove it. Will you come along to the station and look at them there?'

'Of course.'

'It's unlikely to be Sezen,' Julian says. 'She has a child.' He looks up at me. 'And you told me she's afraid of the sight of blood.'

'She could be a good actress.'

'You told me her face was pale when you cut your hand,' he replies, standing up alongside me. 'You can't act a pale face.'

'Then she could be giving the blackmailer information.' I look at Mac. 'Sezen might simply be doing it for the money. She has a child to bring up and no dad around.'

'Was she pushing for you to hire her?' Mac asks.

'No. I got her through an agency. Her references were excellent. But still. Apart from the man at the roundabout, there was something else not right. She's been working for years, in well-paid jobs, and yet she was living in such a run-down place, as if she had no money to pay rent.'

'What's your gut feeling?' Mac asks me.

I think for a moment. 'My gut says she's honest, but my head tells me there's a chance that she's so skilled at deception she can look me in the eye and make me believe she's innocent.'

'As soon as she's back tomorrow, call me and I'll send someone to pick her up.' He sits back down and reads another name on his list. 'Mary Percival.'

I shake my head. 'It's not her.'

'I thought she was behaving strangely around you?' Julian says, also retaking his seat.

'She was and then I saw her outside and I spoke to her and . . . Anyway'—I let out a big breath—'I now have an explanation for her strangeness.'

There's a silence. I'm looking down at my feet.

'What's the reason?' Mac says.

'Well, apparently . . .' I start to laugh. I know it's inappropriate and I try to squash it down under my rib cage, but it won't stay there. It rumbles up into my throat and erupts from my mouth. I keep this up for about thirty seconds, aware that both men are staring at me. 'Apparently . . .' I dig my fingernails into the palm of my hand, where the cut is still tender. The pain is enough for me to be able to hold my face straight. 'She's my sister.'

Neither of them says anything. They are both frowning as if they're in the process of translating what I've just said.

'On my father's side.' I widen my eyes. 'Obviously.'

'What?' Julian's expression is incredulous. 'How has this come about?'

'Well, you know what my father was like.'

'I don't mean that. Why did she tell you this now?'

'I all but forced it out of her. I still think it's possible she's making it up, but then'—I sigh as the post-hysterical low hits me—'she had a letter my dad had written to her.'

'When are you planning to have her meet everyone?'

'Julian, apart from the fact that I haven't even begun to get my head round it, how can you imagine we can invite her here with this going on?' I pretend to open a door. '"Welcome to our happy family! In three days we'll be moving to a safe house. Don't open the door to men with guns, will you?"'

Julian's face stiffens. 'Have you told Lisa about her?' he asks.

'No.'

'But you will tell her?'

'At the moment all I'm able to think about is getting through this crisis,' I say sharply. 'So could we please stop talking about this now?'

'I think it needs to be handled carefully and now is not a good time to do that,' Mac says.

'Exactly,' I say. 'Apart from anything else, there are Wendy's feelings to consider. Mary is my father's infidelity made flesh.'

Julian shakes his head at this. I know he thinks I'm being overly dramatic. He's about to say something else, then changes his mind and pats the space on the sofa beside him.

'I'm better standing,' I say. I feel like I'm about to cry.

Mac clears his throat and looks back at his list. 'Amy Barker.'

'She's gone back to her university accommodation.'

'Did you ask her to leave?'

'She was snooping around in Julian's office . . .' I shrug. 'I don't know whether it's just that I don't much like her or whether she's a possible threat.'

'Well, let's keep her out of your home in the meantime,' Mac says. 'Is Charlie on board with that?'

'I had a word with him,' Julian says. 'He understands the need to keep everything simple around here.'

'OK.' Mac gives us both an encouraging smile. 'Jem Ravens. She also comes in and out of your house a lot?'

'She's a friend,' I say. 'Although she's done a lot of work for us too.'

'She has a police record.'

'Does she?' I frown. 'What did she do?'

'She spent five months in prison for grievous bodily harm.'

'What?' I start back.

'The victim's head was stoved in with a golf club. I think she'd have been given a longer sentence if he hadn't fully recovered. That and the fact that bystanders gave evidence to support her assertion that she was provoked.'

I think of all the coffees Jem and I have had, the lunches, shared child-care. 'When was this?'

'It was back in 2002.'

Eight years ago. She has been with Pete for seven of those years. He works for the council. He's a burly, good-natured bloke. Everybody's mate. I suppose he must know about this.

'She knows almost everything about me,' I say. 'Apart from Lisa there's no one I confide in more.'

'She could have met anyone when she was in prison,' Mac says. 'I'll have a chat with her, just in case.' He stands up and puts a comforting hand on my shoulder. 'I know this is hard, Claire. You're doing really well.'

I give him a tight smile.

'We will catch this woman.'

'The Bulgarian police never caught the killer, and the Italians caught her too late.' I shrug. 'What chance do we have?'

'A good chance. Systems grow better all the time. Exchange of information. Forensic evidence. And sheer, dogged, old-fashioned police work. We will get this right.'

I nod my thanks, but inside I feel desolate. I think of Bea asleep in the room along the hall, Lisa on one side, Bertie on the other. Her life thus far has been about love and laughter. She completely trusts her parents and her brothers to protect her. My mind flashes to an image of her standing in a room, rigid with fear, asking for me, for her daddy, being ignored, being told to shut up, being denied a drink or a blanket. Being tortured.

'And your neighbours, Claire,' Mac says. 'Julian told me—'

'Our neighbours on the right are about a hundred and five,' I say flatly. 'Their groceries are delivered. They don't go any further than their back garden. And the ones on the left work for a children's charity. They've been living in Brazil for the past nine months. They haven't rented their place out.

'It's more likely there's a leak within the police or the CPS,' Julian says. 'I think there's something else, someone else we're not seeing.'

Mac sits down opposite him again and they go through a long list of thirty or so names of everyone who's involved in the case.

As I watch them both try to work this whole thing out, I have a moment of clarity. I won't allow either of these men to render me powerless. They know who the witness is and where he is being kept. I need to know that too. I'll get the information and then, after the pretrial on Monday, I'll email the blackmailer. She'll have what she wants and she'll back off.

'Claire?' Julian says.

I smile at him. 'Yes?'

'Is there anything else you wanted to ask?'

'No.' They both stand up and I step forward so that I'm between them. 'Thank you for everything you're doing, Mac,' I say, holding out my hand. 'It's much appreciated.'

There is a questioning expression in his eyes when he says, 'You're clear about the best way forward?'

'Perfectly,' I say. I walk ahead of him to the door. 'Let's stay in touch.'

SUNDAY. LISA IS TIRED today and decides to spend the morning in bed. The rest of us have a late breakfast together: porridge with Hunza apricots, pancakes with blueberries, and scrambled eggs. It's only ten o'clock but already I'm on tenterhooks anticipating Sezen's arrival back in the house.

Charlie has stopped being frosty with me. He sits down next to me and I put my hand on his. 'I'm sorry,' I say.

'Me too, Mum.'

'I'm sure it won't be long before you and Amy can be together again.'

'Yeah. I've told her we just have to be extra careful until Dad's trial is over. I think she gets it.'

Julian starts to talk about repairing the summerhouse—a grand name for the dilapidated shed that sits at the bottom of our garden. 'The roof is collapsing inwards,' he says. 'We need to think about fixing it up.'

We all look out of the window. The garden is about forty metres long. Most of it is laid over to grass, apart from the wildflower borders and Bea's vegetable patch. There are three elderflower trees at the bottom of the garden next to the summerhouse, which desperately needs a facelift.

'What do you think, Mum?' Jack is saying.

'Well . . . I'll mention it to Jem.'

Jem, who, twenty-four hours ago, was a trusted friend. The idea that she could be anything other than honest was ludicrous. She was the epitome of what you see is what you get. But now I don't know what to think.

The front door slams. 'That's Lara,' Bea says, her eyes lighting up as she pushes her chair back from the table and runs out of the room.

Julian, already on his feet, follows her. I hear him chatting to Sezen and they both come into the kitchen. Her cheeks are glowing; her eyes are sparkling. There's no doubt in my mind that she spent last night making love. And I'd bet my life it was with the man she met at the roundabout.

The rest of the family drift off to their rooms. Julian urges Sezen to share the last of the breakfast with us. She says yes to coffee but no to food and goes to the sink to wash her hands. I give Julian a questioning look. Does he want to talk to her, or is he leaving it to me? His face is non-committal.

Sezen dries her hands, then goes to the fridge and brings some ingredients back with her to the table. 'This evening I will make a special dish with tofu,' she says to me. 'It should be marinated for a few hours first.' She begins shredding ginger into a bowl. I stop her hand with mine.

'We need to talk. Please sit down.'

'OK.' She pulls out a chair.

'I have some concerns.'

'About my work?'

'No, no, no.' I shake my head. 'Your work is faultless. Sezen, we need to know more about you. We need to be able to trust you.'

She tips back. 'You feel you cannot trust me?' Her surprise seems absolutely genuine. 'I do not understand.'

'I'm not saying that you can't have your own life, but yes, at the moment I . . .' I look at Julian. 'We don't feel like we can trust you.'

She turns to Julian for help.

'Tell me again why you came to live in Brighton,' he says.

'Because London is busy and crowded.' She shrugs. 'I have this job here with you, and another one starting in July. I love to be beside the sea.'

'You were brought up in Turkey. The Dardanelles?'

'Yes. My father was a fisherman. My brothers are still there, but I came to northern Europe for work and . . . to live.' She falters. 'Is that a problem?'

'No.' He shakes his head and smiles. He has a way of smiling that seems to be non-threatening. He does it when he's cross-examining a witness. He encourages them with a nudge here and a gentle prod there to paint themselves into a corner. 'Your family must miss you?'

'Yes, but I am keeping the language alive with Lara and I hope to take her home soon for a visit.'

'To Bulgaria?'

'Yes, I have—' She realises her mistake and stops.

'Not Turkey,' Julian says. He is smiling, a relaxed and interested host.

Sezen is neither relaxed nor smiling. Her jaw is tight and she is staring down into her coffee. 'Turkey and Bulgaria share a border,' she says at last.

Julian lets that go. 'Your name is Sylvia Cyrilova,' he says.

She lifts her cup and tries to drink, but her hand is trembling. She puts it back down on the table and looks at me. Her eyes are pleading.

'It's a Bulgarian name, isn't it?' I say.

Moments pass and finally she turns her eyes to Julian's. 'Serbest,' she says. 'My name is Sezen Serbest.'

'And yet you have a passport that says your name is Sylvia Cyrilova.'

'It is not who I am.'

He brings the two passports out of his pocket and places them on the table. Then he stands up and leaves the kitchen. As he does, I see him press buttons on his BlackBerry.

'You went into my room?' she says to me.

The hurt in her eyes seems real and for a second my resolve wavers. I break eye contact, and when I look back at her, I say firmly, 'The man who came here on Friday night. You told me you didn't know him.'

'That is . . .' She shrugs. 'I . . .'

'I saw you with him,' I say. 'At the roundabout. I watched you embrace.'

She lets out a cry. 'You are following me?'

'No. Lisa's flat is there and I was looking out for traffic wardens. But I saw you, Sezen. I saw you. It was the same man.'

'With respect, Claire'—she takes an audible breath—'this does not concern you.'

'We have a situation here,' I say. 'The case Julian is working on, there are complications. We need to be absolutely sure that our children are safe.'

'You asked me to come here and now you are accusing me of wanting to harm your children?'

'You live in my home, Sezen. This man you said was nothing to you came to our front door.' I lean towards her. 'You have two passports, one of them Bulgarian. You know that Julian is prosecuting a Bulgarian criminal.'

She bites her lip.

'I don't mind you having a relationship. What I mind is the fact that you have lied to me. That makes me suspicious and it makes me afraid.'

She is looking down at her feet.

'Are you in trouble? Is someone asking you to do something dishonest?'

Her eyes flash towards me.

'Sezen.' I lean across the table some more. 'I saw him give you money.'

Her cheeks flush and the muscles in her jaw tighten. She looks down at the floor again. Her hair swings across to cover her face. I wait. Her fingers pick at the hem of her cardigan. A minute passes and then she looks back at me. 'I will leave.' She stands up, her expression blank. 'I am sorry.'

'Before you go'—I stand up too—'the police want to speak with you.'

She gives a small gasp of fear. 'The police are coming here?'

'Yes.'

'Then I will wait.'

She sits back down again, crosses her ankles and settles her hands on her lap, perfectly serene and composed. I join Julian in the hallway.

'Mac is sending a couple of officers over,' he says. 'They'll take her to the station for questioning.'

I know that she'll be worried about Lara. Sezen is clearly involved in something illegal, but that doesn't alter the fact that she's a good mother.

I go back into the kitchen. 'Sezen, the police officers will want you to return to the station with them. We are happy to look after Lara.'

She says nothing. She is staring straight ahead at the wall.

'I'm sure that if you're able to give the police an explanation, you'll be back in no time.'

Still nothing. I glance over my shoulder at the sound of the doorbell.

'Sezen?' I say.

She turns her face up. She looks hurt and puzzled, but mostly she just looks resigned. 'I thought you were different.'

'And I thought you were truthful,' I say, angry now. 'I believed you when you told me you were an honest person. It cuts both ways, Sezen.'

'Thank you for looking after Lara.' Her expression is blank again. It makes me want to shake her. 'I will come for her as soon as I can.'

There are two officers: one male, one female. They come into the kitchen with Julian. While they talk Sezen through what happens next, I go upstairs to Bea's room and ask Lara to come and say goodbye to her mum.

'Why?' Bea says.

'Sezen has to go out for a bit,' I say.

Both girls come to the front hall with me. Sezen bends down and speaks to Lara in what I always presumed to be Turkish but now I'm wondering whether it could be Bulgarian. Lara nods. As ever tranquil and self-possessed, she doesn't make a fuss. She stands on the front step and waves to Sezen, who goes with the officers to the car.

'That was awful,' I say to Julian when the door is closed and the girls have gone back to their game.

'Mmm.' He leans against the wall. 'She's not a practised liar. I expect that what she's hiding has nothing to do with this.'

I put my arms round him and rest my head on his shoulder. 'I'll be so glad when this is all over.'

He pulls me in to him and comforts me with his hands, stroking my hair and my back. It feels good, but my intention is not so much to be comforted as to make this a prelude for later, because if Sezen isn't the blackmailer, then I need to get the witness's name and whereabouts out of Julian and I won't get it through argument. The best chance is through closeness. I need to let him see we're both on the same side. Then I think he'll tell me.

His phone rings. 'Megan.' He looks apologetic. 'She wants to come round. Is that OK?'

Normally I might grumble—*On a Sunday?*—but I'm working hard to strengthen the good feeling between us and I won't jeopardise that.

'No problem. I know you need to be prepared for tomorrow.' I kiss him. 'I think I might go for a jog. Work off some of the tension.'

I STRETCH OUT my hamstrings on the front step, my eye automatically drawn to where the policemen are parked. They are both out on the pavement in conversation with a woman—Megan. She's flirting with them, flicking her hair, leaning in towards them, laughing at everything they say. I'm surprised to see her like this. It makes a change from her usual strictly professional manner. But then I remember—three months ago she made a play for Julian. When she sees me, she waves like we're best friends and I wave back.

I set off in the other direction, making my way down the hill until I reach the prom. With the sea on one side and the wind behind me, I find my stride and start to enjoy the feeling: one foot after the other, a steady rhythm of feet and pavement and pulse. I run for over a mile before I have to start dodging people: a couple up ahead of me are eating chips from a paper bag; some boys are meandering along slowly, five abreast on the pavement; dads are out in force with their children. I run as far as the pier and then stop, resting my hands on my knees for a minute or so.

And that's when I see Amy. She's standing close to the fast food stall, energetically snogging a young man in blue jeans and a hoodie. Initially I have a sinking feeling that it's Charlie, but the boy in question has lighter hair and is shorter than Charlie. I walk towards them.

'Amy?'

She turns round, slowly wiping the back of her hand across her mouth. She looks neither guilty nor apologetic. 'It's you,' she says. 'Everything running smoothly in the Miller household now that you've got rid of me?'

'Well, you don't seem to be suffering for it.'

'I'm a survivor. I move on.'

'Does Charlie know you've moved on?'

She looks momentarily thoughtful. 'He'll get the message.'

'Amy.' I shake my head in disbelief, feeling hurt for Charlie. 'You've been going out with him for nine months. Don't you think he deserves better than this?' I gesture towards the boy she's been kissing.

'Well, he should have taken my side, shouldn't he?'

'Over what?'

'Being thrown out!' She pauses for effect. 'There was a reason I was in Julian's precious study. I lost an earring in there last week and I thought Julian might have tidied it into one of the drawers.'

'Really?' I fold my arms. 'So you were standing in Julian's study and suddenly your earring fell out?'

'Are you dense or what?' She gives me a withering look. 'We had sex down there. Your perfect boy shagged me on the rug.'

I look down at my feet while I collect myself, realise that I can't, look back at her and say, with venom, 'Go to hell, Amy.' I turn and start making my way through the crowd.

My jog home is more of a run, anger fuelling my pace. I feel angry at Amy for her careless, selfish attitude, and I feel hurt on Charlie's behalf. Teenage heartbreak is hard to bear and it seems that Amy has no intention of sparing his feelings. As far as the sex goes, I'm not annoyed with Charlie. I'm surprised that he did it in Julian's study, but I'm sure it was Amy's idea. And I can understand why he didn't want to tell me.

A fine rain is beginning to fall. I jog faster, but within seconds my anger evaporates and an intense paranoia creeps over me. My back prickles with discomfort. I have the impression of eyes boring into me. I stop running and abruptly turn round. Most people have their heads down and are walking purposefully, carrier bags in each hand. I scan faces, but no one is looking my way. I start to run again, but the feeling doesn't lift. I feel as though someone, somewhere, has singled me out for attention. I stare up at the sky, and, as if waiting for just such a moment, the cloud above me rumbles. Then it empties a stream of water down onto my face. It feels personal.

I clench my fists and shout upwards, 'You took my mother. You took my father. You're taking my sister and now my daughter's in danger too? Bastard!'

'Oi! Mind your language!'

There's a man behind me. He is red-faced and miserable-looking. He has two little girls with him. Their heads are bare, their faces pinched with the unseasonably cold weather. 'Not in front of the kids.'

'I'm sorry.' I hold up my hand. 'I'm having a bad day.'

'You need to watch your mouth.' He is pointing a finger at me now. He comes closer and waves it in my face. 'This is a public place.'

He's right up close. He smells like he needs a wash and I move back a step. 'I've said I'm sorry and now I'm heading off.'

'I'll be watching out for you.' The finger waves in my face again. 'You keep it clean next time.'

'Go fuck yourself.' I say it under my breath, but like the best of busybodies his hearing is extra sharp.

'What did you say?' His face is a snarl; his shoulders are back, chest thrust forward, hips a cocky swagger; he's transformed into a hard man.

'You heard me,' I say, facing up to him, happy to fight, angry enough for ten men. 'Now back off or I'll make sure you regret it.'

He raises his fists. The two little girls look scared. One is pulling at his jacket. 'Daddy, stop now.'

A crowd is gathering and I see a couple of men deliberating about whether or not they should step in. The rain is increasing and umbrellas are going up. As good a weapon as any. I go to grab one from a woman behind me when a voice says, 'Show over. Break it up.'

It's Mac. He flashes his ID and the hard man backs off, shouting, 'She needs to watch her mouth.'

Mac takes my arm. 'I think you could do with a lift home.' He marches me to the edge of the pavement.

'I was fine,' I say, trying to shake him off. 'I was dealing with him.'

'You and whose army?' His car is parked on a double yellow line and already there are cars sounding their horns. He opens the door for me, then goes round to the driver's side. 'It might have turned nasty.'

'He was all bluster.'

'Since when did you go around picking fights?' He starts the engine. 'Don't add to your troubles, Claire.'

'I just feel so fucking angry. About Lisa. About Bea. About everything.'

'Anger without focus isn't a strategy,' he says. 'Put your seat belt on.'

I ram the belt into the clip. 'Were you following me?'

'Julian told me you were jogging along the prom. I have some photos for you to look through. You still OK with that?'

'Of course.' My temper subsides to a simmer.

'Any cafés you know around here that we can go to?'

'There's one just up here on the left.'

He stops the car on a single yellow line, then stretches behind him to take a folder off the back seat. The café is dense with steam and chatter. He walks us through to a free table at the back. A waitress comes over, all eyes for Mac. He orders the cooked breakfast for himself and two teas.

I point to the folder of mugshots at his feet. 'Shall I look through it now, before the food comes?'

'Yup.' He places it on the table. 'You know the drill. Don't focus on hair or clothes. Look at the shape of their eyes, their nose, bone structure.'

I open the folder. There are A4-size photographs of men, one after the other, about fifty of them. I take my time. Sezen's lover had a distinctive hooked nose and high cheekbones. Many of the photos I discount at once. They are of heavy, thickset men with small eyes and tattoos. The man I'm looking for is slight, and his features are Middle Eastern, not Eastern European. I get to the end of the folder without being able to pick him out.

'He's not there,' I say, disappointed, passing the folder back.

'OK.' He thinks for a moment. Our mugs of tea arrive. 'Let's wait and see what Sezen has to say for herself. Then we'll take it from there.'

I take a drink of my tea and watch Mac put two spoons of sugar in his. He sees me watching him and pats his small but evident belly. 'I know. Donna's working on me. I have to use sweetener at home.'

'Andrew MacPherson tamed by a woman.' I take another drink of tea. 'Who would have thought it?'

He laughs. 'Marriage,' he says. 'The sharing and the caring.'

He gives me a look, one that could lead me into saying all sorts of things I should keep to myself.

'Are you and Julian managing to hold it together?'

I'm not about to answer that. 'Do you know Megan Jennings? She works for the CPS. She's assigned to Georgiev's trial.'

He nods. 'Posh bird? Likes to think she's a bit superior?'

'That's her. Does she have a boyfriend?'

'Nobody seems to have shagged her, and a couple have tried.'

'She was chatting up Faraway just now, but she had designs on Julian.'

He shakes his head. 'Nothing's going on. I'd know about it. You know what a goldfish bowl that place is.' He takes a long drink of tea. 'Anyway, Julian would be a fool to take her over you, and he's no fool.'

I raise my mug up to his. 'Cheers for the vote of confidence.'

The food arrives. He takes a forkful and finishes chewing it before saying, 'Seriously, Claire. How are you holding up?'

'Well . . .' I almost laugh. 'It's not easy. I don't feel like I can trust anyone. I thought Sezen was genuine—she isn't. Mary Percival turns out to be my half-sister.' I make a face. 'I haven't had time to think about that yet. And then there's Jem.' I throw my arms out. 'I knew she was a bit fidgety around the police, but GBH? That's a serious crime. And these are three people I previously trusted with my child.'

'I agree that they're all hiding something, but there are no direct connections to Pavel Georgiev or organised crime of any sort.'

'Even Sezen?'

'We'll see what turns up today, but thus far her life looks transparent enough. She lived in Paris for four years. She worked for the Dutch Embassy as a chef. They were extremely sorry to see her go.'

'I wonder whether the mystery man is Lara's dad.'

'Could be.'

'Perhaps he's the one who knows Georgiev. Perhaps Sezen's only job was to open my front door. When the time came. I need to change the code for the burglar alarm. Just in case.' I finish the last of my tea.

Mac uses his fork to point at his plate. 'Want some?'

'What?'

'You're staring at my food.'

'Am I?' I use my fingers to break off a piece of his toast. 'Actually, I am quite hungry.' I take a bite. It's soggy but warm from melted butter and egg yolk. 'You drumming much?'

'Still doing the rounds of the clubs.'

'Is that how you met Donna?'

He nods. 'She's a yoga teacher, but she trained as a singer. Jazz mostly.'

'So are you in a band together?'

'Of sorts. We have a few gigs coming up at the end of June. I can email you details.' He sees my face. 'Or maybe not.'

'No offence, but I don't think I'll be allowed out of my safe house. Talking of which,' I say lightly, 'if you just gave me the name and whereabouts of the witness, we could skip the safe house. Save all that taxpayers' money.'

He stares at me, trying to gauge whether I mean it. 'It's putting away a man like Georgiev that makes this job worth it. You know that. For over fifteen years police have been gathering evidence against him and finally we have a rock-hard case that even the smartest defence won't be able to break. This is . . .' He searches for the right word.

'Exciting?' I say.

He looks uncomfortable.

'Well, pardon me for not sharing your excitement, but my daughter's safety is not a fair trade for a successful conviction.'

'No, it isn't,' he agrees. 'We will keep Bea safe. You know that. You know we'll do everything we can.'

'And if that isn't enough?'

'It will be enough.'

'I'm not so sure.' I stand up. 'I may have to persuade you to my way of thinking.' I look down at him. I hold his eyes. It's a warning shot across the bow. I watch him pull his arms into his sides. 'Thank you for the tea.'

As I walk away, I'm aware of his eyes on my back. I don't turn round.

8

By the time I get home it's two o'clock. The first thing I do is change the four-digit code on the alarm. Then I go inside to check on Lara and Bea. They're in the kitchen with Wendy and Charlie.

'Do you need any shopping, Mum?' Charlie asks.

'Just milk and bread . . . and bananas. Take some money from the jar.'

Fortunately, he doesn't have to go farther than the end of the road. I don't intend to tell him that I saw Amy kissing someone else. His feelings will take enough of a bashing as it is without me wading in.

Wendy gives me a tray with a pot of tea and spelt toast and honey, and I take it in to Lisa. She looks rested. I tell her that Sezen is with the police, and about finding the passports. I tell her about seeing Amy.

I don't say that at the moment life feels tougher than it has ever felt. That I'm terrified of something happening to Bea and that losing her is worse than unthinkable. It sets up an ache inside me that feels cataclysmic. I will never be able to forgive myself or Julian if she is taken. We have to act in her best interests. And if Julian won't, then I will.

By nine o'clock in the evening all I can think about is engineering some space where Julian and I can be on our own. Sezen still isn't back. Mac called to say they would be keeping her overnight. She isn't talking. She's being very polite but is refusing to say who the man is or how she knows him. We still have Lara. Bea has persuaded her to sleep in her bed with her and I settled them down about eight o'clock.

I know that Julian won't come to bed before midnight. Even though he has officially resigned from the case, he's still involved in making sure it all comes together smoothly for the pretrial hearing tomorrow. That means I'm going to have to tempt him upstairs. I rummage in my underwear drawer looking for something special. Last year we had our twentieth wedding anniversary, and he bought me expensive silk underwear. I haven't worn it since. I find it at the back of the drawer and put it on. A basque, it has upwards of thirty clips down the front. By the time I've attached the stockings to the suspenders, I'm almost puffing. I look at myself in the mirror: front, sides and back. I don't look bad, all things considered. Better if I had some height, though. I slip my feet into heels and automatically my legs grow longer. I cover up with a short silk robe, a swirly pattern of pale blues and pinks. Pleased with myself, I open the bedroom door and then close it again. I'm forgetting that it's not a normal weekday; there are several other people in the house. I cover the whole lot up with a large towelling dressing gown. It looks incongruous with the heels, but it'll have to do.

I walk down the stairs, feeling faintly ridiculous. I go to the kitchen, have a slug of wine, then take two glasses and a chilled bottle of sauvignon blanc down the next flight of stairs. I go into Julian's study. He's sitting behind his desk, papers laid out in front of him.

I put the wine and glasses on his desk, pour us both some and stand behind his chair, leaning my elbows on his shoulders and resting my face against his neck.

He pats the side of my head absent-mindedly. 'So what's on your mind?'

'Just thought I'd come down and see if you want to come to bed.'

'Is Bea in our bed?'

'No. We have a temporary reprieve. She's sharing a bed with Lara.'

He pulls me round onto his knees.

'Julian, I was thinking . . . you know when we met?' I run my fingers through his hair. 'When we were stuck in the lift? Do you remember?'

He laughs. 'Of course I remember. I bet I can tell you the whole conversation, word for word.'

'OK. Let me think. I'll tell you where to start.'

I look up at the ceiling and cast my mind back. We met in the university library. I was a first-year law student; Julian was a third-year. The library building covered four floors. The first floor was not so much for studying as for eating and chatting. The higher up the building you climbed, the more serious it became. The fourth floor was dense with law books and heavy with disapproval should anyone make the mistake of so much as whispering. Julian and I had already noticed each other and were at the stage where we acknowledged one another with a smile. I was struggling with an end-of-year assignment and decided to ask him a question. I wrote him a note. He answered me by walking over to a shelf, finding the correct volume of *Halsbury's Statutes*, bringing it to me and opening it up at the right page. He pointed out the Act of Parliament I needed. I mouthed a thank-you and he smiled, held my eyes for a second or two and then went back to his seat. Suddenly I couldn't concentrate. My face was hot. I needed air.

Leaving my papers behind, I headed for the lift. Just as the doors closed, Julian stepped inside. 'Giving up?' he said.

I'm brought back to the present as Julian's hands find their way inside my dressing gown. 'Well, well, well! Is this for my benefit?'

'Maybe. But first you have to prove you remember what we said to each other when we met.'

'No problem. Are we going from when we were in the lift?'

I nod.

'I said, "Giving up?"'

'And I said, "No. I just need a drink."'

'I said, "I'll buy you a coffee."' He pulls the towelling dressing gown off my shoulders. 'That's better,' he says, and kisses my throat.

'And I said, "That would be great."'

'Actually, it was more of a stammer,' he reminds me. 'You were tripping over your words. You were blushing.'

His kisses are making me tingle. I hold him away from me. 'Then the lift started to make those grinding noises,' I remind him. 'And you said—'

'"Doesn't sound very healthy."'

'And then the lift juddered to a stop.'

He laughs and leans forward to kiss me again.

'Not so fast,' I say. 'We haven't got to the best bit yet.'

'OK.' He leans back but keeps one hand on my thigh and the other round my waist. 'So we used the phone to call the janitor and he said—'

' "We'll have you out in a jiffy." '

'We sat down on the floor and then—'

He was kissing me when the janitor prised open the door. We went down to the café in the basement. We drank coffee and we talked and then we collected our books from upstairs and I invited him back to my shared flat.

'I remember when we went back to my flat, we made a promise.'

'That we would always be honest.' He's kissing the tops of my breasts.

'Exactly.'

I lift his head so that I can see the expression in his eyes. 'We've come a long way, Jules. Haven't we?'

'We have.' He stands us both up. 'And now I'd like to go a bit further.' He drinks back his wine, keeps hold of the glass, puts the bottle under his arm and grabs my hand. 'Bring your glass. We're going upstairs.'

I pull the dressing gown round me. He takes my hand and I run to keep up with him as he climbs the stairs two at a time. He closes the bedroom door behind us, puts a chair against it—he's not completely forgetting about children, then—and undresses with the speed of a teenager. He sits on the bed and pulls me to him. 'Am I allowed to unwrap you now?'

I manage a flirty smile and let the dressing gown and the silk robe fall behind me onto the carpet. 'Only if you take your time.'

He undoes the basque clips one by one, kissing his way down my breasts and then my belly as he goes. I shiver but not in a good way. This isn't me. I'm not someone who pretends or manipulates. I've never pretended to want him. I've never had to. I've never even faked an orgasm. But if I'm going to do it, I might as well attempt to enjoy it, so I shut my eyes and try to let go to the feeling rising inside me. He lays me back on the bed.

Fortunately, he's in the mood for doing all the work. Nothing is expected of me except that I moan in the right places and move my hips at the right times. When at last he's lying beside me, sated, I give him a few minutes to enjoy the feeling as I work out exactly how to approach this.

'Julian, we've never had any trouble being straight with one another, have we?'

He pretends to frown. 'This isn't going to get serious, is it?'

'I don't mean it to. But we're coming up against the biggest problem we've ever faced and I need to know we're being honest with each other.'

He takes a moment to consider. 'You're not still thinking I might be having a scene with Megan?'

'No.' I kiss the soft spot behind his ear. 'But I wonder if she's the reason you didn't tell me about the emails before now.'

'She's not. The decision was entirely mine. I didn't ask for her opinion, but if I had, I expect she would have told me to tell you.'

'OK.' I believe him. 'Thank you.'

'Anything else?'

'Yes.' I keep my tone light. 'Will you please tell me what the witness is called and where he is?'

He gives me a questioning look.

'I won't use the information. I won't.' I find I can look him straight in the eye and lie. 'But I'll have it if I need it. It's like giving me a life raft so that if the sea is choppy, I can bail our daughter out.'

'I can't give you the name.'

'I understand that you can't be the one to communicate with the blackmailer, but I can. I'm not saying I'd do it now. But if for some reason we are separated or there is an emergency of some sort, I may be the only one who can help Bea. Our daughter, Julian. *Our child.* You have information that could help me care for Bea—save her life even. You need to trust me.'

I'm getting through to him. A shadow of doubt flickers across his eyes.

'Do you love me, Julian?'

'Yes, I love you. You're my wife. I love you more than I can say. You are my soul mate, my best friend and my lover all rolled up in one package.' He strokes the small of my back. 'One very lovely package.'

At another time such a declaration would have warmed my heart, but now I see it as the green light to take me right where I want to be.

'Then prove it. Please.' I bring my face close to his and whisper, 'Prove that you love me. Tell me who the witness is and where he's being kept.'

Seconds pass and in those seconds I watch tears form in his eyes. His lips are trembling. He looks more upset and conflicted than I have ever seen him and I draw back. Anxiety climbs into my throat.

He gives a monumental sigh. 'I can't tell you, Claire,' he says quietly.

'You can't, or you won't?'

'I can't.' He looks regretful. 'I asked for the witness to be moved and that I shouldn't be told where. I emailed that to the blackmailer this morning.'

A noise comes out of my throat. I feel like I'm choking.

Julian puts a steadying hand on my shoulder. 'I had to, Claire. It's the best way to protect Bea.'

I am filled with complete and utter disbelief. All I can do is stare at him.

'If I have nothing she wants, then she has no reason to come after Bea. It was the best solution,' he says. 'You do see that, don't you?'

The shock of his revelation is beginning to dissipate. I breathe in and feel anger mix with the air that fills my lungs. 'No, I don't see that.'

'Claire, we had to do something.'

'Damn you, Julian!' I shout. 'If anything were to happen, it was the only bargaining chip we had. You seriously think she'll just back off?'

'It's a calculated risk, but yes, we do.'

'Crossing the road is a risk. Swimming in the sea is a risk. But this? This is madness! It's asking for trouble.' I stand up and lift my nightdress off the low stool at the end of the bed. 'Have you forgotten that we make decisions concerning our children together. *Together*, Julian.'

'I hoped that you would see the sense in this.'

'Damn you for excluding me and for treating this like some sort of game.'

'I am not treating this like a game.' He grabs my arm and swings me round to look at him. 'I love our daughter just as much as you do. This is exactly the sort of emotional, knee-jerk reaction that is unhelpful.'

'You think our daughter being kidnapped isn't something to get emotional about?'

'Claire, you of all people should understand that it's for this sort of intimidation that Georgiev is being brought to justice in the first place. The law can't buckle and fold in the face of threats, no matter how extreme.'

'There's a mother in Italy who's living with the memory of a murdered son. I will not be her.' I move close to his face. 'I am not interested in rhetoric. I am not interested in what's right. I want our daughter safe, and if you have it in your power to keep her safe and you don't exercise that power, then I will not live with you any more.'

He doesn't have an answer to that and in his eyes there is an acute sadness. It doesn't make me retract my threat and it doesn't make me feel sympathy for him. I want to hurt him like he is hurting me. I want him to see that he's putting his work before his family. I'm just about to reiterate this when our bedroom door is pushed. It moves only a couple of inches before it hits the back of the chair. I pull the nightdress on over my head and take the chair away from the door. Bea is there. Her eyes are barely open. She moves automatically towards the bed. She is holding one of Bertie's legs, the rest of him trailing on the carpet behind her.

She whispers loudly, 'I not wake Daddy. I just climb in velly quiet-y.' In seconds she is under the covers, her head hardly denting the pillow.

I point towards the bed. 'Bea trusts us to do what's best for her.' I pause. 'Can you honestly tell me that's what you're doing?' I wait a couple of seconds, watching him wrestle with an answer.

When none is forthcoming, I go downstairs and into the kitchen.

I pour myself a glass of wine, my hands shaking so much that some spills onto the work surface. I sit down at the table and drink the wine quickly as if it's medicine. I hadn't expected this. I'm horrified by Julian's decision.

Within five minutes he follows me into the kitchen. He's wearing pyjamas now, his expression cloudy with tension. 'Was that what the sex was for, Claire? So you could find out about the witness?'

I flick my eyes towards his. 'Yes.'

Julian is rarely lost for words. 'The . . .' He clears his throat. 'Claire, I . . .' He leans his back against the wall and sighs. Then he walks away.

Two glasses of wine later and I'm coming to terms with what I have to do next. Mac. He knows the witness's name and he'll also know where he's been moved to. Mac is a rarity among policemen. He's not all about rules and payback, black and white crime and punishment. He is compassionate. I've seen that side of him and I'm sure I can make him understand my position. If not one way, then the other. Put simply, I have information that could ruin his career. A whisper in the right place and he'd be discredited.

I go into the sitting room, stand at the bay window and pull the curtain a little to one side. The police have stepped up their security. One of them is standing at the bottom of the steps. The porch light is on and he is alert, looking out into the darkness, his head moving from side to side as if waiting for someone to materialise. Feeling reassured, I slide the curtain back and go back upstairs. I climb into bed. Bea is lying between Julian and me.

Julian's voice whispers into the almost darkness, 'This is going to work out,' he says softly. 'I'm confident we can beat her.'

'Well, I don't share your confidence. I have a horrible, sinking feeling she's going to get Bea.'

'How, Claire? How?'

'I don't know *how*,' I say, my voice rising so that Bea stirs beside me. I compose myself and then say much more quietly, 'But I do know that she's smarter than us and that's why we should have given her what she wanted.'

'I can't agree with you.'

'Then we've nothing to say to each other.'

I spend what's left of the night drifting in and out of sleep. Each time I wake up I check that Bea is still there.

COME SIX O'CLOCK, I decide to get up. It's Monday, the day of the pretrial hearing. The judge will decide whether to grant the defence's request for full witness disclosure. Julian's already up and I know he'll leave for work early. I get dressed. Lisa and Julian are in the kitchen. They look up as I walk in.

'I've made some porridge,' Lisa says, standing up.

I wave her down again. 'I'll get it.'

I see her look at Julian, waiting for him to say something. He doesn't speak. He doesn't acknowledge my presence. Fine by me. I ladle some porridge into a bowl and join them at the table.

'What has to be established are not so much the rights and wrongs of it,' Julian is saying to Lisa, 'but whether the defendant has broken the law.' He takes a spoonful of porridge. 'It's about proof. In an ideal world justice would always prevail, but we don't live in an ideal world.'

'But with witness anonymity,' Lisa says, 'there must be some problems.'

'There are credibility issues. Does the witness have motive to lie? That's the main one. But in a case like this, with Georgiev as dangerous as we know he is, anonymity is the only way to stay alive.'

'Do you have forensic evidence?'

'Criminals like Georgiev can't be caught with direct evidence: fingerprints, DNA, blood, CCTV. Useless. He has other people doing his dirty work. We need a witness to testify. To give names, dates, details that tie in with police intelligence.' He finishes his porridge and pushes the bowl across the table. 'Finally we have a chance to get him.'

'And your family is paying the price for that,' I say. And then compound it by adding, 'Or hadn't you noticed?'

He glances across at me. 'What's happening is inconvenient, Claire, I grant you, but in the grand scheme of things, having to live in a safe house for a month or so is hardly the greatest of hardships.'

'It's not just the safe house, though, is it? It's the incipient danger and the fear that it generates.' I bang my chest. 'I am afraid, Julian. *Me*. Your wife.'

'Claire, there are young girls being trafficked and murdered out there.'

'And you have brought your children, *our* children into that world.'

'Like it or not, this is the world we live in.'

'Well, I don't like it, and it isn't my world.' I stand up. 'And for me, my family comes first.'

'And it doesn't for me?'

'You're sacrificing your family's safety for your principles.'

'I am not.' He stands up and leans towards me. He is angry; it simmers in his eyes. 'When did you lose your principles, Claire? What happened to the girl who went into law to make a difference?'

'She woke up!' I slam my bowl down on the table and it breaks into two halves; left over milk spills onto the wooden surface. 'I don't have the luxury of principles, not when my daughter's life is at stake.'

'I can't talk to you when you're like this.' He turns away from me. 'You need to calm down.'

'Fuck you, Julian. And fuck your principles.' At once Lisa is beside me, gripping my elbow, urging me to sit. I shake her off and follow Julian across the kitchen. 'If something happens to our daughter, I will cry every day for the rest of my life. I won't be able to live; I won't be able to breathe.' I follow him into the hallway. 'It will never be bearable. We will never have peace. We will never be a family again. We will never be a couple again.' He's on his way downstairs to his study and I step in front of him to block his path. 'I am not ready to lose my sister, I was not ready to lose my mother or my father, and I will never, *never* be ready to lose a child. Do you understand that?' His expression is stony. 'If we lose our child because of your principles, then God damn you to hell, Julian.'

I move out of his way and he goes off down the stairs. I'm shaking from anger and from the realisation that I meant every word I said. Julian and I are moving further apart. Our outlooks are irreconcilable. I am sacrificing my marriage to ensure my daughter's safety. That's the way it has to be.

The doorbell rings and I answer it straight away. Megan. I bring her into the porch but no further.

'Big day,' I say. 'Are you all ready for it?'

'I have butterflies.' She presses her stomach and gives me her busy-but-interested smile. 'We're well prepared.'

'What do you know about the witness?'

'Sorry?' She looks around as if she thinks I might be talking to an invisible someone behind her.

'The witness,' I say. 'Do you know who he is and where he's being kept?'

'No, I . . .' She clears her throat. 'That's not the sort of information I'm given. This one's top secret. You know how it is.'

'Yes, I do.' I move a step closer. She keeps her gaze away from mine. 'Woman to woman, I am asking you whether you can help me.'

'I don't know anything, Claire. Trust the police. Trust Julian.'

The inside door opens and Julian is standing there. Megan immediately straightens up and steps away from me. I open the outside door for them both and they start off down the steps. When they're almost at the bottom, Julian glances back at me. 'I'll be in touch after the pretrial ruling.'

Why bother? I almost shout, but don't want the two policemen and Megan as an audience. Instead I pretend he hasn't spoken and close the door.

I look at the clock. It's only just after seven. A bit too early to ring Mac. I fill the sink with hot soapy water and start cleaning the kitchen surfaces. I've been at it for twenty minutes or so when Bea comes in with Lara, who has dressed herself and even managed to brush her hair and put on a hairband. She is as composed as ever, and it makes me wonder how often Sezen has left her and with whom. When Lara sits at the table to have breakfast, I ask her whether Mummy often has to leave her with a friend.

'Mummy has to work.' She nods into her bowl of porridge. 'She has to make money to help Jalal.'

'Of course.' I give her a smile. 'And did you meet Jalal yesterday?'

'Yes, but he has to do work for the men. To make them leave him alone.'

'Right.' My pulse rate begins to climb. I stand up and lift my mobile from the dresser. 'I'm just going to make a phone call, girls. I'll be next door.'

I go through to the sitting room, select Mac's number and wait for it to connect. The two policemen outside see me at the window and I raise my hand by way of a hello.

'Mac.'

'It's me. Claire.'

'Morning.' He takes a big breath. 'We're still questioning Sezen. She's a tough nut. Whoever she's protecting, he either means a lot to her or she's afraid of reprisals.'

I tell him about my conversation with Lara. 'I think you could get more out of her. She's a bright little button. She might even show you where he lives.'

'Well, if nothing else, the threat of questioning her daughter will be more power to our elbow with Sezen.' I hear the rustle of cellophane. 'Officers have questioned Jem Ravens but couldn't find anything suspicious.' He's speaking through a mouthful of something doughy. 'She was shocked and upset and appeared genuine in her assertion that she knew nothing about this.'

'Well . . . honestly, Mac, I never believed it would be Jem. And let's face it, we still don't have a lot to go on, do we?'

'No, but soon we will have ruled Sezen either in or out and that's what police work is all about—finding the clues, following them to see where they might lead, fitting together the pieces.'

'Can we have a chat on our own today, Mac? Please.'

There's a split second of hesitation before he says, 'Of course. Later this morning? I'll come to you. Around eleven?'

'Great. I'll see you then.'

I put my phone into the back pocket of my jeans and think about what I will need to say, or do, for him to give me the witness's details. I'll promise. I'll plead. I'll beg. I'll flirt. Whatever it takes, I'll do it.

I'll get the details and I'll give them to the blackmailer. And in the meantime, if Julian can email the blackmailer with his intentions, then I can surely do the same. I log on to my laptop and open my email. I click on 'New message' and type her address into the first box.

Subject: Witness Details

Please do not attempt to take my child. I will get you the details. I will have them to you by midnight. Claire Miller

WHILE I WAIT for Mac to arrive, I keep myself busy in the kitchen. The girls are under the table, playing house. When the doorbell rings I expect the postman, but Jem is standing on the step. Her hands are in her pockets. Her clothes are grubby; her hair is unkempt.

'I spent the night in the van.' She moves from one foot to the other as if the step is hot. 'I hadn't told Pete about prison. I should have done.' Her face flushes and I see she's close to tears. 'I'm hoping he'll cool off.'

'It was quite a secret you were keeping, Jem.'

'I know. I was ashamed.' She purses her lips. 'Pete's too good for me.'

'Oh, come on! That simply isn't true.' I give her a hug. 'I'm sorry that my troubles brought this out, but Pete will forgive you. Give him time.' I hesitate. 'I'm sorry I can't offer you a place to stay.'

She shakes her head. 'So the cops were watching out for you?'

'Yeah.' I hesitate again. 'What happened, though? Back then, I mean.'

'I was saving up for a deposit on a house and worked two jobs: daytime with a builder and evenings in a pub. There was a bloke there, a regular bully, who had been harassing me all evening. I went to change a keg and he caught me in the cellar, hands everywhere, stinking breath in my face. The golf club was handy and before I knew it I'd thumped him over the head with it. Hard.' She shakes her head. 'It was absolute bloody madness and I deserved every minute of the five months I served. He spent three weeks in intensive care. To be honest, I was just grateful I hadn't killed him.'

'Sounds like he deserved it.'

'Maybe. But tell me, what's going on with you? The police wouldn't give me any details. Just that someone was threatening your family.'

'Yes . . . it's to do with Julian's case. Hopefully, it will all be over soon.'

'Well.' She sees I'm not going to say any more and goes down a couple of steps. 'If I can do anything . . . help in any way . . . get in touch.'

I stand on the step and watch as she climbs into her van, then drives off. I hope our friendship hasn't been damaged beyond repair.

The postman's van has stopped close to the kerb. I'm expecting some of the macrobiotic ingredients Sezen and I ordered on the Internet, so I wait. He comes up the steps with three parcels, which I sign for and take indoors. Charlie is beside the kettle making coffee. The girls are still under the table.

'You're not forgetting that later today we're having a family meeting, love, are you?' I say.

'Nope. Four o'clock, wasn't it?'

'About then. Whenever Dad gets back from the pretrial hearing.'

'So is it some big bombshell?'

'Yes.' I pick up the smallest parcel. It's an oblong shape about six inches long and four inches high. There's no company logo on the box, and the postmark is local. I slice the packing tape with the end of a pair of scissors, being careful not to go too deeply into the box.

Charlie is staring at me, his arms wide. 'Well, what is it?'

Inside is a black plastic bag. I lift it out. It fits the shape of my palm and feels as if it weighs a couple of pounds. I frown. 'I'm not sure what this is.'

'Not *that*! The bombshell.'

'You'll find out later.' I look straight at him. 'I have been tempted to tell you, but I think it's something your dad and I should tell you together.'

His lips tremble. 'You're getting divorced?'

'No! Heavens above!' Still holding the plastic bag, I walk across and give him a hug. Then I point with my free hand under the table and put my finger to my lips. I don't want Bea announcing to all and sundry that we're getting divorced. 'It's to do with Dad's trial.'

'So what is it, then?' he whispers.

'Charlie, honestly, I can't say.'

'Fine, then.' He turns away, just a bit disgruntled, mumbling to himself.

I go back to the table and check the box for a delivery note. Nothing.

The bag is made of tough plastic and is secured at one end with tape. I put it on the table and pull off the tape. As soon as the seal is broken, I notice a smell: earthy, metallic, sharp. Something in my head says, *Stop now! Don't open it. Don't go any further*, but my hands keep unwrapping. I slide it out of the bag onto the table and stifle a scream. It's a piece of meat shaped like a fist. There are thick, rubbery, tube-like vessels coming out of the top. I know without anyone having to tell me that it's a heart. My jaw clenches tight against the nausea rising into my throat.

Charlie takes control. He guides me to the sink, squirts liquid soap on my hands, holds them under the hot tap and says, 'What the hell, Mum? I didn't know you were ordering body parts.'

He goes over to the table and peers at it. 'I'm not sure what animal it's from. We dissected hearts in biology once. Oh, look!' Inside the black plastic bag there is a cellophane envelope. He holds it at the edge so as not to get blood on his fingers, brings it to the sink and runs it under the tap. 'There should be a delivery note inside.' He dries it with a paper towel and slits the packet with a knife. Inside is a piece of paper folded down the centre. He hands it to me. I take a breath and then I read it. There are seven words printed in a regular font: *Next time it will be your daughter's.*

A scream resounds inside my head, insistent as a police siren. I clamp my mouth shut to stop the sound escaping.

'Mum?' Charlie looks panicked. 'What does it say?'

I slip the note into my pocket. 'Charlie, I need you to take Bea and Lara downstairs.' He goes to protest. 'Please. Please do this for me. Don't let them see what's on the table. Ask Jack to stay with them, and then when you come back, I will try to explain what's going on.'

'OK.'

I wait until he's crawled under the table to speak to the girls and then, without looking at the heart, I go to the front door and down the steps. I'm still holding my hands away from me. They're scrubbed clean, but the smell clings inside my nose. I stagger towards the police car. They see me coming and are out of the car before I get that far. I don't trust myself to speak. I point towards the house and then turn so that they can follow me inside. I lead them into the kitchen and point at the table.

'What the . . . ?' Faraway, the younger of the two, visibly shivers.

DS Baker looks at the heart, then back to me. 'This was just delivered?'

I nod. My hands are shaking as I hand them the note. They both read it and then everything happens quickly. Faraway calls Mac and within ten minutes he arrives. He takes a statement from me and from the policemen and then from Charlie. The forensic team arrive to deal with the heart. They take photographs, then they dust the packaging for prints, taking fingerprints from all of us to exclude us from the investigation.

The whole thing takes over three hours. In the middle of it all Wendy turns up. 'Claire, what on earth is going on?'

The kitchen out of bounds, we've all congregated in Jack's room. Lisa and I are on beanbags on the floor; Bea and Lara are lying on their fronts on the bed watching television; Charlie is pacing up and down. I've told him that this is the emailer taking the threat to the next level.

Jack, sitting cross-legged on his bed, has brought milk and cereal down from the kitchen. He is eating one bowl after the next, his noisy munching punctuated with questions: 'Why would someone send a heart to us?' 'How come that cop already knows you, Mum?' and 'What's this got to do with Dad's case?' To every question I say the same thing: 'When Dad gets back from London, we'll give you all the details.'

I answer Wendy's questions in the same way. She sits down on the chair at Jack's desk and looks around at us all. 'And where's Sezen?'

'She's . . . out.' I stand up. I know that Wendy will have questions lining up on her tongue, none of which I'll be able to answer to her satisfaction. 'I'm going upstairs to see how things are progressing.'

Mac is at the top of the stairs finishing off a phone call. 'That was Julian. He's on his way back. The judge has upheld the anonymity order.'

It's what I expected but still it feels like another blow and I slump against the wall. 'Well, that's that, then,' I say.

'The trial date has been set for two weeks' time.'

Fourteen whole days. Unless I can put a stop to this we will be in a safe house, wondering at every footstep on the pavement or knock on the door.

'We finally got something out of Sezen. This bloke she's been protecting is called Jalal Khatib. He's an illegal immigrant, and he owes money to a couple of heavies who live in North London.'

'But at the roundabout, he was the one who gave her money.'

'She puts a certain amount in a bank account. As well as paying off the heavies with cash, she sends money back to his parents in the Middle East.'

'What about the business of her having two passports?'

'She was born Sezen Serbest, Turkish but living in Bulgaria. In 1984 all Bulgarian nationals who were ethnically Turkish were ordered to exchange their names for Bulgarian ones or be forced to leave. Sezen translates to Sylvia and her father had to choose another surname. He chose Cyrilova.'

'So she was telling the truth when she told us she was Turkish?'

'In effect, yes.'

'It can't be legal to have two passports in two different names, surely?'

'No.' He raises his eyebrows. 'But I'm in no mind to pursue it.'

'This business of the safe house . . .' I say.

'It'll be ready tomorrow. Is that what you wanted to talk to me about?'

'No.' I hold his eyes. 'I want to ask you for something.'

We're both leaning against the wall, sideways on to each other, our faces close. His eyes tell me that he gets my meaning. I feel the connection between us tighten a notch. 'I wondered whether we might get to that.'

One of the forensic team, dressed in a white boiler suit, comes out of the kitchen. Mac and I move apart.

'You almost done in there?' Mac asks him.

'Two minutes,' he says, and looks at me. 'Then we'll be out of your hair.'

'Thank you,' I say.

Mac moves back towards the kitchen. 'Later?' he says.

I nod and go downstairs again.

Charlie is standing at the bottom. 'So Dad's on his way?'

'Yes.'

We go in to tell the others. More questions that I can't answer, but I do reiterate that we'll be having the family meeting as soon as Julian is home.

'Should I be staying for that?' Wendy asks.

'I'd like you to.'

'Right . . . Well, in that case, how about I make some sandwiches?'

'Great idea.'

We all troop upstairs again. I'm hanging back. Since the heart was delivered I've felt dizzy. I know I'm breathing too quickly, but I can't seem to stop. I stand outside on the step, holding on to the railings, and try to take slower, deeper breaths. I know my body is experiencing the flight-or-fight response, my blood pumped full of adrenaline and oxygen. But I have nowhere to run, and the person I'm fighting is still invisible to us.

The forensic team are now packing their equipment into their van. Baker and Faraway have been joined by another half a dozen policemen, all milling around on the pavement. Several passers-by look up at the house to try and work out what's going on. Another police car pulls up outside and Sezen climbs out. It's the first time I've ever seen her looking tired and unkempt. She comes up the steps, her face tight.

She stands in front of me. 'I have come for Lara and for our things.'

'Of course.' I take a breath. 'I'm sorry for what you've had to go through.'

'Are you?' Her expression is defiant. 'You are not the one who has spent the night in a police cell.'

Her tone is vicious and it makes me recoil. 'You know what, Sezen? Keep your pride; keep your anger.' I raise my hands. 'I don't have time for this.'

I step out of her way and stay at the front door while she marches inside.

Wendy appears. 'What's happening with Sezen? She seems very upset.'

'Wendy, please.' I fold my arms. 'It will all be explained soon.'

'Increased security,' Mac says, appearing at just the right time. He introduces himself, holding out a hand for Wendy to shake.'And you must be the lovely Wendy. Claire tells me you're indispensable.'

'Well, I . . .'

He explains that the imminent trial has meant extra precautions. He manages to make it sound both serious and manageable. There's no question of Sezen and Lara being turned out, but not only is it better for them to go somewhere less hectic, it will keep things simple in this household too. A quiet B&B has been organised for them.

I go back indoors. Bea is playing under the stairs. I give her a bowl of her favourite snack foods: a small bunch of grapes, slices of apple and cubes of cheese. She settles back on the cushions.

Mac introduces me to a female officer called Pam. She can't be more than twenty-five, dark hair, dark eyes. She is to be our family liaison officer. I shake her hand. She is sincere, polite and sympathetic. Mac takes her through to the sitting room, where everyone is gathered: the boys, plus Lisa and Wendy. I hold back in the hallway, knowing that any second now Julian will walk through the front door. I start counting the seconds and only get as far as fifteen before his key is in the lock.

'So no more emails today?' I blurt out straight away as he comes in. Of course, he doesn't know that I've sent my own email, but I wonder whether the blackmailer would tell Julian I had written, just to further divide us.

He takes off his jacket and hangs it on one of the pegs inside the porch, his face turned away from me when he says, 'No.'

'Why do you think she hasn't replied to the one you sent her? The one that told her you no longer know where the witness is.'

'I don't know.' He throws me a look. 'Are you and the children OK?'

'A heart was delivered to the house today, Julian. *A heart*.'

'I heard.' He looks tired. Worse than that, he looks anxious, scared even.

'I don't suppose there was any need to send an email,' I say. 'The heart said it all. That was her reply.'

'According to the postmark, the heart was posted first thing yesterday morning. Before I sent the email.'

'The note she sent with the heart.' I give an involuntary shiver. 'She's not giving up, Julian.'

He puts his arms round my waist and pulls me close. I see a glimmer of the old Julian, the one I can trust. It gives me hope.

'Mission accomplished!' Wendy appears with a tray of tea and sandwiches. She gives us an appraising glance, then goes into the sitting room. I pull the door shut behind her.

'Julian, time is running out. We have to do something ourselves.'

'You're out of your depth with this, Claire.'

'I'm out of my depth?' I give a short laugh. 'We're all out of our depth! It's just that I'm the only one who can admit it.'

'I want Georgiev convicted.'

'I see.' I take a step back. 'Now we're getting to the nub of it.'

'Public office brings with it responsibility. You know that!'

'You are Bea's *father*.'

'Will you stop this!' he hisses. 'Keeping Bea safe and winning the trial are not mutually exclusive. We can have both.'

'Are you two coming in?' Wendy appears again. Sensing the atmosphere, she looks uncertainly from me to Julian and back again. 'Everyone's waiting.'

Julian gives me a dismissive glare and we go into the sitting room. I sit down on the sofa next to Lisa. The mood is expectant. Nobody is talking apart from Wendy, who is passing around the plate of sandwiches. 'Your tea is on the table over there, Claire.'

I try to catch Julian's eye, but his elbow is on the mantelpiece, his chin is in his hand, and he is looking through the window. He is tapping his foot on the fire surround. I walk over for my tea and on the way back to my seat I place my hand on his back. No response. I sit down again.

'So.' Mac smiles around at us all. 'I'm going to kick off this meeting. As you all know, Julian'—he looks at the boys—'your dad, is working on an important case.'

'Pavel Georgiev?' Jack says. 'The Bulgarian Mafia guy?'

'Exactly,' Mac says. 'The prosecution has a watertight case, but much of their evidence rests on a key witness. The identity and whereabouts of this witness are being kept a secret.'

'Because Georgiev's men might get to him?' Jack says.

'That's right.' He glances across at Julian before he says, 'There's no easy way to tell you all this. Georgiev's men have been sending threatening emails and, as a precaution, you're going to be moving to a safe house tomorrow.'

A second of silence and then several people speak at once.

'What sort of threats?'

'For how long?'

'Did you know about this, Claire?' Wendy says, her eyes wide and fearful.

'I haven't known for long,' I say.

Mac starts talking again. He explains about the emails. He says they haven't been able to trace whoever is writing them, but their suspicion is that she is a woman.

'So what's some woman going to do to us?' Jack says.

'It's likely this woman is a professional,' Mac says, 'but if she isn't, she will have help.'

'But what would she do if she got in?' Charlie asks. 'Does she carry a gun?'

'Probably a knife,' I say. 'The emails indicate she carries a knife and—'

'Claire!' Julian's voice is loud and almost everyone jumps.

'What?' I challenge his stare. I know he thinks I'm about to give gory details from the Italian and Bulgarian cases. I'm not, but at the same time I think we need to be more direct. 'If we don't tell them the truth, they won't realise how serious it is,' I say. I look at both the boys. 'We know Georgiev has engineered at least two situations like this before where young women who were working for him infiltrated people's lives and committed murder.'

Wendy lets out a cry. Her lips move as she works it out and then her attention turns to Mac. 'DI MacPherson, are the children, and Julian and Claire'—she takes a breath—'are their lives in *danger*?'

Mac nods. 'Possibly.'

'How? Why? What would someone gain from it?'

'The emailer wants information, Wendy. If she doesn't get it, she has threatened to kidnap Bea.' It's my voice again and this time Julian doesn't interrupt. 'Bea will be the easiest to take.'

'Little Bea?' Wendy's breathing is loud and fast as she struggles to take it in. 'She's just a baby.' She starts to cry.

Pam, the family liaison officer, goes across to comfort her. Julian gives me an are-you-happy-now look, which I don't feel I deserve. I stand up.

'So what can we do?' Lisa says, looking at Mac. 'In your experience, how should we proceed from here?'

'As I mentioned, tomorrow we will be moving you to a safe house. This will mean that you won't be able to phone or see friends for a while.'

A great hullaballoo breaks out as Jack and, to a lesser extent, Charlie object to such stringency.

'The most important thing is for every one of us to be aware of safety,' Mac is saying. 'Keep doors and windows locked. Don't invite people home. Report anything unusual, no matter how small or insignificant: a phone call, an email, somebody taking an unexpected interest in you.'

'But that means we're giving in to intimidation,' Jack says.

'Giving in would be handing her the witness,' Julian says. 'We're simply taking sensible precautions.'

Wendy has stopped crying and says, 'I will cooperate however I can.'

Mac smiles at her. 'You won't be confined to barracks, but I would urge extreme caution.'

'The children won't be going out,' Julian says before I can voice the same thought. 'Non-negotiable.'

Jack says, 'Well, I was grounded anyway.' He sighs, then raises his mug of tea. 'Here's to a happy summer, everyone.'

'Any further questions?'

Silence as we all digest what we've just heard.

Bea comes into the room. 'I need a wee,' she says, then, suddenly shy, runs to me and hides her face in my lap.

'I'll take you.' I stand up.

'Let me, Claire.' Wendy comes forward and takes Bea's hand. 'It'll let you get on with the packing.'

I take part in the charade of packing. First I get Jack organised, then Bea. I've told her we're going off on holiday for a few weeks and she accepts this without question. She sits on the bed while I hold up her tops and skirts and trousers and she gives me a thumbs-up or -down. At the moment her toenails are painted a vivid pink. Wendy did it for her. She rubs her heels on the cover and then touches her big toes together. Out of nowhere I get a sudden and overwhelming feeling that this woman will take her. Dizziness creeps up from my feet and fills my head with flashing lights and sickness. I go into the landing and crouch down with my back against the wall.

'Are you OK, Mum?' Charlie sees me from his room and comes across.

I grit my teeth. 'I'm OK. I'm fine. Actually'—I reach for his hands and he pulls me upright—'I'm going to go out for a bit. I need some air.'

'Mummy!' Bea shouts.

'Will you be OK?' he says. 'Do you want me to come?'

'I'll be fine.' I stroke his cheek. 'Would you put Bea to bed for me?'

'Yeah. No probs.'

I give Charlie a grateful smile and head down the stairs. It's after nine. Mac will be home by now. I stop in the hallway to put on my shoes.

'You're going out?'

With a jump, I look up from tying my laces. 'Julian, you scared me.'

He folds his arms. 'Where are you going, Claire?'

I lie to him, barefaced. 'I'm going out for a drive to clear my head. I plan to park at the seafront, sit in the car and listen to music.' I move in closer, holding his eyes. 'I'm dealing with this in the only way I know how and at the moment I need a couple of hours alone before I'm cooped up in a safe house.' I take my car keys off the hook. 'I'm setting the alarm. The code, should you need to go out, is 2949. Charlie's putting Bea to bed.'

On the way out, I speed-dial Mac's number. 'I need to see you.'

'I'm at home.'

I climb in the car. 'I can come to you.'

'OK.' He gives me his postcode and I key it into my sat nav.

'I'm setting off now,' I say, and start the engine.

9

The drive to Mac's house takes about fifty minutes. He lives about halfway between London and Brighton, close to a village on the edge of Ashdown Forest. When I reach his cottage, there's a woman standing at the front door. She's wearing flat leather boots with jeans tucked in, and a camel-coloured suede jacket. Her smile is wide, her teeth perfect.

I climb out of my car and approach the front door just as Mac appears alongside her. 'This is my wife, Donna,' he says. 'Donna, this is Claire.'

'Hi! How are ya?' She holds out her hand. She is American. Blonde and leggy, almost six feet tall, she oozes sunshine and blue skies even on a cold and cloudy night when the wind is whipping through the trees.

'Pleased to meet you.' I shake her hand. 'This is a lovely spot.'

'Even better in the daytime. You must come.' She widens clear blue eyes. 'Mac tells me you two were colleagues once.'

'Yes.' I smile. The skin on my face feels dry and tight.

'Well . . .' She kisses him. She takes her time. It's a hands-off-my man kiss. 'I'll leave you to it.' She strides towards her car and starts the engine.

Mac ushers me into a hallway with exposed stone walls and wooden beams. Just before we reach the large living room at the end, he heads off at an angle into the kitchen. 'Tea? Coffee? Or something stronger?'

'Tea's fine,' I say. 'It's late for Donna to be going out, isn't it?'

'She's doing an all-night yoga session. Breathing. Meditation. It's all going on around here.' He hands me a mug of tea. 'Let's go through.'

He sets off along the hallway, past the front door and into a blokeish den, with a battered leather couch against one wall and a huge pine table, close to ten feet long. There's a flat-screen monitor and keyboard at one end of the table and the rest of the surface is covered in books and papers. But it's the jazz memorabilia on the walls that makes it Mac's space. It's always been his passion, his escape from the dirt and grind of police work.

He gestures towards the couch. 'Take a seat. Tell me why you're here.'

I try to relax into the leather couch, worn soft and accommodating by years of bodies. 'Mac, I need you to give me the witness information because if something happens to Bea, I won't have a life any more.'

'Claire.' He lengthens my name, sounding out the letters. He's standing opposite me in front of the table. He folds his arms and looks up at the ceiling. When he looks back at me, it's with regret. 'You know that isn't possible. It would ruin the chances of bringing Georgiev to justice.'

'It doesn't have to. Think about it. At the moment she's coming after my daughter and you're spending time and money protecting us. What if she does know where the witness is? Protect him instead. Double his security. Lock him up in a cell, if need be. Surely that's fairer than what's happening now, an innocent child caught up in it because of her father's job.'

'The law doesn't look at it that way.'

'But you can,' I say quietly. 'I know you. Your belief in the system only goes so far and in that we're alike.' I pause. 'You know when to break it and when to keep it.'

He looks down at his feet and gives a half-smile. 'Have you tried to get the information out of Julian?'

'Yes. Last night he told me the witness had been moved. And he doesn't know the new address. Do you?'

'Yes.' He sits beside me on the sofa, his body sideways, one leg pulled up. I mirror him so that we're facing each other, our knees almost touching.

'Are you going to tell me?' I say quietly.

'This witness is key, Claire. Georgiev will walk free without him.'

'I know. I've thought it through. I've turned it every which way in my head. But Bea is a little girl. She deserves protection.' I raise my voice. 'I need the witness information and I won't leave until you give it to me.'

His eyebrows lift at this, the look on his face a warning for me not to overstep the mark.

'I won't tell anyone how I came by the information. I'll email it from my own laptop directly to her email address. I can't lose my child and I'm not convinced that we can adequately protect her.' I swallow the last of my tea. 'And if you need any more convincing, then you must know that I will report you for falsifying records that led to Abe Martin's conviction.'

I say all this in a flat tone, feeling calm for the first time since I opened the parcel with the heart in it.

Mac is still eyeballing me. 'Abe Martin murdered Kerry Smith,' he says slowly. 'He was guilty as fuck. You know it and I know it.'

'You're a policeman, an upholder of the law, and yet you broke it. You broke several laws, in fact. And those offences could not only have you sacked but also prosecuted. Maximum sentence five years in prison.'

'You're threatening me?'

'Yes.'

'And here I was thinking you would offer yourself to me.'

I smile. 'Would you like that?'

He looks me up and down. 'Would you?'

'Yes.'

He leans in close and kisses me lightly on the lips. 'I don't believe you.'

'You want me to prove it?' My lips tingle and there's heat in my stomach.

'You have balls, Claire. I'll give you that.'

'Look me in the eye and tell me you wouldn't do the same.'

'For my child?' He leans back and thinks about it. 'By now I'd have you strung up by the heels. I'd torture it out of you if that's what it took.'

My heart stops. 'Then you'll give it to me?'

'Yes.' He's staring right into my eyes. 'But not because you threatened me. I'll give you the details because my gut feeling is that I should.' He stands up. 'You know that people will assume the leak came through Julian?'

'Yes.' I can barely breathe. I hover beside him as he writes a name and address down on a piece of paper. He holds it out to me. I read it and put it in the pocket of my jeans. 'Thank you.' I blink and tears run down my cheeks. 'Thank you so, so much.'

'You're welcome. Now go.' He turns me round. 'Do your worst.'

THE JOURNEY HOME takes twice as long as it should. There's been an accident and an ambulance is blocking the road, and the few of us who are travelling this late are sent the long way round. I drive home as quickly as I can, but I'm dismayed to find that I've missed my midnight deadline. When I arrive back in our street, it's almost one in the morning. There's no movement apart from a dark blue Fiat that pulls away from the kerb. I clock the registration. I even go so far as to write it down on a used parking ticket that's sitting in a hollow in the dashboard. Then I step out of the car and pull my cardigan round me. A freezing wind is blowing. I run up the steps and am at the top before I realise that Baker and Faraway are missing. I look down the street but see no sign of them. And then I hear footsteps and watch as the two policemen who were patrolling the back of the house run into the street. They have their firearms out and are using their radios.

Fear grips my throat. I step into the porch. The lights on the console are unlit because the alarm has been switched off. I push open the inside door and in the dim light see what looks like someone lying on the floor. I run towards it and slide on a wet patch, crashing down hard on my elbow.

Lights! Lights! I say to myself, get up on my knees and then my feet, grope along the wall and switch on the light. I blink. There are fingerprints in red paint on the wall and the light switch. And there's red paint on my hands. I stare at them. It's not paint. It's blood. Ruby-red human blood. There's a gurgling noise behind me. I turn and see that the person on the floor is Julian. His hand clutches at the side of his throat as blood escapes through his fingers. I drop to my knees beside him and place my hands where his are, feel his pulse, each beat sending a further spurt of blood into my hands.

'Help!' I shout. 'Help us!'

Lisa's bedroom door opens and she comes out, gives a howl of disbelief.

'Call an ambulance,' I'm shrieking. 'Now. Quickly.'

She runs to the kitchen for the phone just as the light goes on at the top of the stairs and Charlie almost flies down.

'Get me a towel,' I shout.

He's staring. His mouth open, eyes like saucers.

'Now!' I scream. 'Do it.'

He gets one from the downstairs bathroom and I pull it tight round the cut, afraid that to pull it too tight will mean Julian won't be able to breathe but not tight enough and he will bleed to death. I press some more but still he bleeds. I watch the towel redden. 'No, no, no, no, no.'

Lisa appears at my side and sobs as she and Charlie cling to each other. 'I don't understand,' she says. 'I didn't hear a thing.'

Julian's eyes are still open but only just. His face and cheeks are now a blue-grey colour. He is losing too much blood. He tries to speak—no words, just more blood, coming from his mouth this time.

'Don't talk,' I say. 'The ambulance is coming. Don't be afraid. We have time. You're going to be OK.' And then I see what he's trying to tell me. It's written in his eyes. My hands start to shake, but I don't let go of the towel. 'Charlie, go upstairs and check that Bea's in her bed.'

'Mum.' His voice cracks.

'Do it.' I look back at my husband. 'Julian, you have to hang on.' His eyes are closing. I watch his tears run into the blood. 'Don't you dare die. Do you hear me? Look at me. I will not lose you. I. Will. Not. Lose.You.' His eyes flutter open again. 'Good,' I say. 'You keep looking at me.'

I am split in two. My eyes are with Julian; my ears are with Charlie. I hear him upstairs, going into every room. When he arrives back at my side, he cries out, 'She's not in the house, Mum. Bea's not here.'

I am pitched into a dark and dreadful place. My worst fear has been realised. Bea has been taken. I am too late. The blackmailer has moved more quickly than I thought she would. I have let my daughter down.

Charlie is gulping back uncontrolled sobs, his body shaking so much he can barely stand, and Jack is with him, hanging on to the back of Charlie's T-shirt, looking terrified. I want to join them both and huddle together and let go to the despair inside me. But I can't.

'Boys, put on some warm clothes, then go into the sitting room and stay there.' I turn my head to shout to Lisa, 'Take my phone from my back pocket. Press number two and then the green key. It's Mac's number. Tell him what's happening.' I look down at Julian. His eyes are shut. I don't think he's breathing. 'No, Julian, please.' I put my face close to his. 'You can't leave me. Please, please. Fight. Fight hard.'

THE PARAMEDICS PUSH their way inside. I stand back. One cuts away Julian's clothes and shocks his heart as the other stems the flow of blood. Another two paramedics arrive and three of them work on Julian while the fourth calls back to base, 'Adult male. Serious knife wound to right side of throat. Lost a lot of blood. We're stabilising him now. ETA ten minutes.' He looks at me. 'Do you know his blood type?'

'He's O positive,' I say.

'And you're his wife?'

I nod. 'His name is Julian Miller.' I'm watching the heart monitor. They shock him a third time and his heart starts to beat for itself. Relief washes through me. One second at a time, I tell myself.

Lisa appears at my elbow dressed in jeans and a sweater. 'Are you going to the hospital with Julian?' she asks me.

I nod my head and then immediately shake it as I remember that I still have to send the email. I don't want to leave Julian's side, but I need to let the blackmailer know that I have the details she wants.

Lisa sees my indecision and says, 'I can go to the hospital with Julian. If you want to stay here . . . with the boys . . . and in case Bea comes home.' She holds my wrist tight. 'Mac is on his way.' She kisses me on both cheeks and then goes to stand by the door.

The paramedics lift Julian onto a stretcher. I say into his ear, 'I love you, Julian. I'll get Bea back.' I kiss his waxen cheek. They slide the stretcher onto the ambulance. Lisa climbs in beside him and they close the door.

I run inside and downstairs to Julian's study. I log on to my laptop. My hands and clothes are stained with Julian's blood. Some of it has already dried and flakes onto the keyboard. I hear myself moan. I catch hold of the hysteria building in my chest. *Not now.* The voice inside my head is stern, like a schoolteacher. I make the effort to listen. *Email first.*

I type in the blackmailer's address and write:

I have the witness's name and whereabouts. I will give you the details. Do not harm my daughter.

I add my mobile-phone number and then I press 'Send' and watch the screen change to 'Message sent'.

Right. OK. What now? I run back upstairs and, sidestepping the blood on the floor, up another flight to my bedroom. I strip off my clothes as far as my underwear and go into the en suite. I run the tap. I use soap to scrub my hands and my face, and watch Julian's blood turn pink in the water. I grab a towel and quickly dry myself, back into clean clothes and down the stairs. *Next. What's next?* I go to Charlie and Jack. They're sitting next to each other on the sofa. Jack is completely still, as if he's been placed in a trance. Charlie is agitating his legs up and down.

'Dad is on his way to hospital,' I say. 'Bea has been kidnapped, but we will get her back.'

Charlie jumps to his feet. 'We could go out on our bikes,' he says. 'Cycle around. We might see something.'

'I want you both here,' I say. He goes to protest. 'I promise that if Mac says we need to go out on the streets looking for her, then that's what we'll do. In the meantime we're going to stay here. That's an order.'

Jack nods; Charlie paces.

I remember the dark blue Fiat that was pulling away when I arrived. 'Charlie, go outside to my car.' I tell him where to find the old parking ticket.

He runs off. I sit down next to Jack and hug him. He clings to me, his face buried in my neck, his arms squeezing me tight. I cup my hands round his face and look him in the eye. 'We'll get through this. We will.'

I leave him on the sofa and go back to the front door. The street is teeming with police and the area in front of our house is now cordoned off with incident tape. Mac has arrived. He's nodding his head as two policemen give him details. He sees me and comes running up the steps.

'Claire.' His eyes are full of concern. He catches sight of the blood on the floor behind me. 'Fuck.' He leans forward to touch me.

I step back from him. 'Are Baker and Faraway dead?' I say.

He nods. 'They had their throats cut.'

'Jesus.' I drop my head, then look back at Mac. 'I hope I got to Julian in time. Lisa's gone to the hospital with him.' I say this calmly, as if it isn't a matter of life and death to me. I don't know where I'm finding the strength. 'I've sent the blackmailer an email telling her I have the information she wants.' I take the parking ticket from Charlie as he comes inside. I give it to Mac and tell him what it is. 'It must have been her in the car, leaving as I arrived, otherwise Julian would have been . . . gone.' I take a steadying breath. 'He must have let her in. Apart from me, he was the only one who knew the code.' I think. 'Maybe she was holding a knife to the policeman's throat.'

Mac shakes his head. 'Julian wouldn't have opened the door.'

'So he must have known her.'

'We'll find out. The CCTV at your front door is being checked,' Mac says. Then, 'Is that Julian's phone?'

I follow his eyes. Julian's BlackBerry is lying under the table in the hallway. I pick it up.

'See who called him last.'

I scroll through. 'Megan,' I say. 'At half past midnight.'

Mac's eyes narrow. He takes the phone from me and calls her. It goes straight to the answering service.

'Megan?' My mind tries to engage. 'Has someone taken her too?' A dizzy blindness settles behind my eyes. 'My God! Do you think she was forced to help the blackmailer?' My ears are ringing. 'Julian would open the door to Megan. He trusts her.' I slump against the wall.

'I have the tape.' A policeman comes into the hallway. He's carrying the tape from the CCTV camera. 'We have clear views of the three people who came to the door.'

We watch it in Julian's study. At five minutes before one, the policeman on duty goes down the steps. Thirty seconds later Megan comes to the front door. The front door opens. I can't see Julian's face as he is below the camera, but Megan's is in clear view. It's her. And she doesn't look as if she's been coerced. She seems as relaxed and confident as ever. And then, as she comes inside, two men dressed in black take the steps two at a time and push their way into the house behind her. Two minutes pass and then all three come out. Megan is carrying a sleepy Bea, whose head is draped over her shoulder. I let out a cry and Mac throws me a worried glance. Another minute goes by and then I appear on the steps, looking bewildered.

Megan Jennings is more English than Julian. She outclassed several other ambitious solicitors to become part of his team. She has spent long days working for the Crown, for Queen and country.

Megan Jennings has sat at my dinner table and eaten my food.

And now it appears that Megan Jennings is the blackmailer. She was present while two policemen were murdered. She watched as Julian had his throat cut and was left for dead.

Megan Jennings has kidnapped my daughter.

A POLICEMAN DRIVES me to the hospital. Julian is in theatre and then he'll be brought to the high-dependency unit. I meet Lisa walking up and down the corridor. She runs to hug me and I let her, but only for a second.

'Please look after the boys for me,' I say.

'Of course. I'll go straight home.'

I walk on to the ward, remembering that it was only three days ago I collected Lisa from another part of the hospital. Lisa, who is sick, and is now having to cope with this. I should have let her hug me for longer.

'Mrs Miller?'

'Yes?' I swing round sharply. There's a nurse behind me.

'Would you like to wait in our relatives' room? The doctor will come and speak to you as soon as he can.'

I follow her into a small room, painted magnolia. She closes the door on her way out and I'm left alone. There's a clock high on the blank wall facing me, marking the seconds.

Tick . . . Julian is in a critical condition.

Tock . . . My daughter has been kidnapped.

Tick . . . She is in grave danger.

Tock . . . I don't know whether she has Bertie with her.

I should have checked. Why didn't I check? I start to moan. At first it's a low, monotonous sound and then it rises in pitch and I snap up straight.

Enough.

The clock keeps up its relentless ticking and I know that I can't stay in this room. I haul myself up and walk out of the room and along the corridor, back to the entrance so I can use my mobile. I check my emails—nothing.

I call Mac for an update. The police have been to Megan's flat and it's completely empty. Up in Hertfordshire, her parents have been pulled from their beds and brought in for questioning. They've been shedding light on how Megan could have met Georgiev.

'She worked in Europe during her gap year, in one of the mountain ski resorts in the Alps,' Mac tells me.

'I know about that,' I say. 'She was telling me about it the other day.'

When she returned, she had changed, her parents said. She was more secretive. They thought it was all part of her growing up. She seemed more mature, had a clear sense of direction. Having been disillusioned with life and unsure about what she wanted to study at university, she announced she wanted to be a solicitor. Naturally, they were delighted.

'He was setting her up that long ago?' I say, astonished.

'Seems so,' Mac affirms. 'Georgiev knew that at some point the law would catch up with him. There had already been attempts to build a case against him, but the evidence hadn't been strong enough to support a prosecution. He wanted someone on the inside.'

'Any other updates?'

'The two men with her on the CCTV are known associates of Georgiev. The dark blue Fiat was bought for cash from a woman in Worthing last week. She said the man who bought it was foreign—Polish, she thought.'

'Thanks, Mac. I'm going back inside. See if Julian's out of surgery yet.'

'We'll speak soon.'

'Find her, Mac,' I say quietly. 'Please just find her.'

I end the call and go back to the ward. The duty doctor tells me, with a heartfelt yet measured empathy, that Julian is still in theatre, that he may have suffered brain damage, and that his condition will remain critical for a number of hours. There's nothing I can do except hope and pray.

It's after seven o'clock in the morning now and I risk using both my mobile and Julian's Backberry in the relatives' room. No emails have arrived, and Mac has nothing else to tell me. Bea has been gone for more than six hours and we have no idea where she is. No leads. No clear direction.

I try to hold the tears back, I make great, loud gulping sounds, but there's no catching them. I ache with everything that I am for this to be over, for both Julian and Bea to be safe. I will never again take my life for granted. I will live each day in the knowledge that I am blessed beyond words.

There's a knock at the door—Julian is out of theatre. I straighten my clothes, smooth my hair and blow my nose, and walk out of the room. A tall man with grey hair and large feet approaches me. He's called Mr Murray and he's the surgeon who's just sewn my husband's throat back together. He's still wearing green theatre garb. He takes me aside and asks me about the attack. I tell him what little I know.

'Your husband was lucky,' he says. 'He must have turned his head just as the knife was used. The aim was slightly off and missed completely severing his carotid artery, otherwise he would have bled to death before anyone could help him. As it is, we've managed to repair the damage.' He takes my elbow. 'Come through and see him now.'

He leads me to a bed. I don't recognise the man lying there as Julian. He has a tube down his throat. The ventilator is pushing air into his lungs. There's a constant beeping noise from all the machinery registering his blood pressure, temperature, oxygen saturation levels and heartbeat. One side of his head has been partly shaved. His face is bruised, his eyelids swollen. And then I recognise his left hand. This is Julian. These are his long, slender, pianist's fingers, his freckled skin, blue veins and paler skin where his watch normally is. This is my husband's hand. I bring it up to my cheek, then bend down to kiss the motionless face.

'My darling,' I say, 'the operation was a success. You're going to be OK.'

'Talking is good.'

I look up. A nurse is reading results from one of the machines and jotting it down on a chart. She finishes writing and brings me a chair. 'Hearing is the last sense to go and the first to return. Talk to him as much as you can.'

'Right.' I sit down and I start to talk. At first I feel self-conscious and then I forget all that and just talk about anything and everything: memories from university, what we'll do with the summerhouse, whether we'll go to France this year. What I don't talk about is the trial or Megan. And I don't mention Bea because I can't tell him she's still missing and I'm too afraid that if he can hear me he'll grow agitated and upset.

I stay with him until ten o'clock and then I take a taxi back home. I want to make sure the boys are OK. I want to have a shower. But mostly I want to stand in Bea's bedroom and feel her presence. I want to see whether Bertie's there. I don't know whether him being there or not being there will make me feel worse or better. I just need to know.

Police tape is still cordoning off the area in front of my house. No through traffic is allowed into the street. 'Something happening along there this morning,' the driver says, craning his neck. 'You'll have to climb out here.'

I pay him and step out onto the pavement. It's thirty yards or so to my house and I'm about halfway along when a figure rushes into my peripheral vision. I jerk round quickly, not so much afraid of what's coming, more to get myself in a good position if I need to fight back.

'I'm sorry. I'm not— Oh God.' It's Mary Percival. She puts her hand over her mouth. Her face twists. 'I heard about Julian and about Bea.' She takes a tearful breath. 'I'm so very, very sorry.'

'Thank you.' I feel the weight of her sincerity, but I can't take it on board. 'And I'm sorry to have been rude to you. It was Megan we should have been watching out for. Not you.' I continue walking.

After a few seconds she follows me. 'Megan?'

'She worked with Julian. It seems she fooled us all.' My phone beeps twice. It's the sound of a text arriving. I take it out of my pocket and read the message: *Come to the playing fields on the London Road. Alone.*

My heart starts to pound. I look along the street. I need to get to my car. It's in the cordoned-off area.

'Mary,' I say, 'will you do something for me? I want to get my car out. The police will ask me where I'm going and I need to have a reason. I'm dropping you at the vet. Douglas isn't well, so I'm taking you there.'

Mary looks down at Douglas and then at me. 'OK,' she says. 'But he looks well. Shall we say it's for his vaccinations?'

'Fine.' I walk quickly and Mary follows me. I go into the house. The first thing I notice is that someone has washed Julian's blood off the floor. Mac is in the hallway making a phone call and stops as soon as he sees me.

'How's Julian?' he says.

'He's out of theatre.' I walk past him and lift my keys off the hall table. 'We'll know more later.'

'Are you driving somewhere?'

'I'm dropping Mary at the vet. Douglas is due injections.'

He starts back in surprise. 'What?'

'I need to stay busy.' I go back outside and run down the steps.

'Claire?'

I ignore him. Mary and I climb into the car. The policeman on patrol moves the barrier and I drive off while Mac stands on the kerb and watches.

10

'I'll drop you round the corner,' I tell Mary. 'Thank you for covering for me.' She sits beside me with Douglas on her knee, his tail wagging.

'How is Julian?' she asks.

'He's . . . holding his own.' I think of him lying in the bed plugged into machinery looking both strange and vulnerable. 'They don't know yet whether there'll be any permanent brain damage.'

'I'm sorry,' she says. 'This is a horrible time for you.'

I stop by the kerb. 'Is this OK?'

'Thank you.' As she's climbing out, she turns back and says, 'If you need any more help, please ask.'

'I will. And, Mary . . . About Dad. About you. We'll talk soon. I promise.'

She gives me a grateful smile and I set off. I talk myself through what I need to do. Park the car. Go into the playing fields and wait, and when I see her coming, give her the piece of paper Mac gave me and— 'Shit.' I've left the paper in the pocket of my jeans and they're lying on my bedroom floor. I don't have time to go back and anyway Mac would start questioning me. I rack my brains and find that I can remember the witness's name—Kaloyan Batchev—and he's being held in a safe house in East London, but was it Gordon Place or Gordon Avenue? Number fifteen or number thirteen?

Think, Claire, *think.*

I rack my brains some more and decide the house number was fifteen. If it was thirteen, I'm sure a thought along the lines of unlucky-for-some would have gone through my head. Avenue or Place? I try to visualise the piece of paper. It doesn't work. All I can do is choose one and hope I can secure Bea's release before Georgiev's men arrive at the address.

It takes me ten minutes to get to the playing fields. On one side are the fields, their perimeters dotted with trees. On the other is a row of 1930s semidetached houses. Several boys are kicking a football into the goal in the far field, and there's a man walking his dog along the street, but otherwise it's quiet. I walk onto the field and send a text back: *I'm here.*

I hold my phone in my hand and wait. There's no one in sight. I stand there for a quarter of an hour, until my phone finally rings.

'Walk diagonally across the field.' It's Megan's voice. 'Cross the road and come in the front door of number thirty-nine. If I get so much as an inkling you're being followed, you won't see Bea again.' She ends the call.

I walk at a normal pace, feeling remarkably calm. I walk up the path to number thirty-nine, my shoes scrunching on the gravel. The door is slightly ajar. I push it open and step inside. As I turn to close it, the back of my right knee is kicked. It buckles and I topple back. While Megan's left hand yanks my arm up my back, her right hand comes to the front and round my throat, where I feel a blade settle against my skin. She moves with such speed that I am disabled before I even register the kick.

'You wouldn't lie to me, Claire, would you?'

I can't speak. Her hold is too tight. She twists round and throws me ahead of her into the front room, where I land on the floor with a thud. I automatically rub my throat and then look up at her. 'Where's Bea?'

She's dressed in black—trainers, T-shirt and trousers. Her hair is tied back and she isn't wearing make-up. Gone is the accommodating tilt to the head, the slightly shy, breathless air. In its place there is a deliberate lack of expression. She slides the knife back into the sheath attached to her belt.

'Where's Bea?' I say again.

'Get up.' The room is about twelve feet square and dingy. The only items of furniture are two hardback chairs facing each other in the centre of the room. She points to one of them. 'Sit.'

I do it. I'm not about to argue. I just want to see Bea.

In another part of the house, I hear a phone ring, followed by a man speaking in short, staccato sentences. Then two men appear at the entrance to the room. I recognise them from the CCTV footage. One or both of these men murdered Baker and Faraway, and seriously injured Julian.

My eyes burn as I stare at them. I'd like to make them pay for what they did, slowly and painfully. I know my feelings are showing on my face, but neither of them is looking at me. It's as if I don't exist and it gives me the chance to observe Megan's interaction with them. One stays silent, while the other talks to her. His tone is irritable. Megan replies in Bulgarian, her voice rising and falling with annoyance and then agreement. She is different from her 'English' self. Not only is her voice more forceful, more masculine, but so too is her body language, which is pushy and dominant.

Abruptly, the men turn and leave the room. They go out through the front door, closing it behind them. It seems like a gift. Without the men here, I feel I have more chance of persuading Megan to set Bea free.

She comes towards me, stopping inches from my feet. 'Tell me who the witness is,' she says.

'Where's Bea?'

She cuffs me across the face with the back of her hand. I don't see it coming. My lower jaw takes the brunt of it and is pushed to one side so that an intense pain, worse than any toothache, shoots up the side of my face.

She pulls the chair in close and sits down. 'Tell me who the witness is.'

'Where's Bea?'

She cuffs me again. This time my vision jumps and then blurs. I blink several times until it clears and I'm left with ringing ears and a battered cheek.

'How long do you think you can keep this up?'

'As long as it takes.' I hold my back straight. 'Where's Bea?'

She looks up at the ceiling and sighs. I brace myself, but this time she doesn't hit me. She stands up, grabs me by my hair and pulls me along behind her. We go through to a room at the back. 'If you wake her,' Megan says into my ear, 'I'll knock her out. Is that clear?'

I nod and walk towards a single bed under the window, where I can see the outline of a child's body. I hold my hand over my mouth to suppress a cry of bittersweet joy and anguish. Joy because it's Bea. She's lying on her side, fast asleep, her breathing deep and regular. And in her arms she has Bertie, his soft head resting against her cheek. Anguish because I want to take her in my arms, run out onto the pavement and back to my car.

'That's it,' Megan says, and pushes me ahead of her back to the front room and onto the chair. 'Now tell me.'

'Kaloyan Batchev.'

'Batchev?' she snaps back, and for one heart-stopping moment I think Mac has given me false information. Then she says, 'Pavel thought he was dead.' She nods like this explains a lot and then she laughs and talks under her breath. When she stares back at me, it's with flat eyes. 'And where is he?'

'Fifteen Gordon Avenue,' I say, making a sudden decision that, avenue or place, the important thing is that I buy some time and get Bea out of here before the men return. 'It's in the East End.'

'You're not playing a game with me, Claire?' Her voice is gentle. 'Making up an address to buy you time?'

'No.' I make a point of holding her stare. 'I wouldn't do that.'

'So how did you get the details? I know Julian didn't tell you. He's far too principled for that.' She moves in close. 'Was it our trusty copper?'

I look down.

'So it was.' She thinks about this. 'Why did he tell you?'

'I have something on him.'

'What?'

'Some years ago he made a procedural mistake,' I say. 'I could make sure it comes back to haunt him.'

'I see.' She stares into my face for a few seconds more, seems satisfied and stands up. She pulls her phone from her pocket and makes a call. She talks curtly in Bulgarian, apart from the address, which she repeats in English. When she finishes, she lights a cigarette and goes to the window. She moves the net curtain slightly to one side and looks along the street in both directions. Then she rests the cigarette on the edge of the windowsill and raises a pair of binoculars to her eyes. I have the brief and foolish idea to rush her, grab the knife from her belt and threaten her with it. I'm contemplating doing it when she tunes into my thoughts and says casually, 'Don't even think about it. I won't hesitate to kill you.'

I don't believe her. Despite the blackmailer's assertion that she'd killed before, I'm not convinced Megan is a cold-blooded murderer. But she does have a knife and I don't want to find myself on the wrong end of it.

'Will you let Bea go now?' I ask.

'Not until we have Batchev.'

'Why didn't you wait?'

'Wait for what?'

'I got you the information. I told you I would. There was an accident on the road and that's why I was late.'

'You were the one who'd set the midnight deadline.' She turns to face me. 'We didn't want you moving to a safe house.'

'And were you following us? Did you go to the nursery?'

'If you'd had the sense to check,' she says smugly. 'You'd have soon discovered I was working from home on both those days.'

How well she fooled us all. Not once did it cross my mind that the blackmailer could be Megan, despite the fact that she regularly came to my house.

'And how did you know about what happened at Bea's party?' I say.

'That was Julian.' False regret puckers her eyebrows. 'I spoke to him when he was in the taxi going to the airport and he told me all about it.'

I look down at my feet, feeling sick to my stomach. When Julian wakes up, he will be devastated to know that he unwittingly helped Megan.

'And the magazine at your front door?' Megan says. 'Did you find that?'

I nod. The one I blamed Mary for. 'You left it?'

'I slipped in without anyone hearing me.'

'I have to hand it to you, Megan,' I say, 'you managed to stay under the radar. There was no suggestion that you had any links with Georgiev.'

'We have always been extra careful.'

'You met him when you were on your gap year?'

That surprises her. 'How do you know that?'

'Your parents. They're being questioned by the police.'

She raises a lazy eyebrow. 'Goodness knows how they'll explain that at the country club.'

'You left Julian for dead.' My eyes sting. 'How could you do that to him?'

'He was in the wrong place at the wrong time.' She pauses for thought. 'A couple of months ago I tried to get him into bed, you know? But he was having none of it.' She gives a short laugh. 'Just think, if he had been willing to commit adultery, I could have found out what I needed to know and none of you would be going through this. It's a case of too much virtue.'

Her view of what's happening is so twisted that bitterness fills my mouth and hardens my spine to steel. 'What will happen now your cover's blown?'

'I'm more than just a solicitor to Pavel.'

'But surely he values you in proportion to your usefulness?'

'Poor Claire.' She laughs silently. 'I thought you were smarter than this.' She takes the last drag of her cigarette and sits down opposite me again. 'Pavel has made me everything I am.'

'He's a criminal.'

'Yes.' The edges of her face soften. 'But I see past that. I love him.'

'So this is all about love? My God! Two policemen are dead, Megan.' I look down at my feet and shake my head. 'Faraway and Baker—you were making friends with them just the other day. They didn't have to die.'

'If it was up to me, I would have left them alive.' She shrugs. 'But that's not the way it's done.'

I want to end this. I feel my heart's yearning for Bea, fast asleep, not thirty feet away. 'Did you give Bea a sedative of some sort?'

'It won't cause her any long-term damage.'

Another chink. Another toe in the door that leads to the Megan I know. I have the sure and sudden knowledge that there's no need to physically fight with her. The vestiges of the Megan who has been to my house, sat Bea on her knee, chatted to us all—I think I can talk her round. 'You have to let Bea go before the men get back. You know you do.'

'I've told you. I'll let you both go when we have the witness.'

'Do you want a child's death on your conscience?'

'Nothing will happen to Bea.'

'You sure about that? You sure that the men won't just kill me and Bea? I mean, why not? We're loose ends. And like you say, it's the way it's done.'

'I won't allow it.' Doubt flickers at the corners of her eyes. She looks at her watch. 'It won't be long now.'

I lean forward. 'You really think you can stop those two?' I take a gamble. 'Georgiev is sophisticated, cultured. He keeps his hands clean. Granted, he's a criminal, but he has old-fashioned values. Like for like is acceptable. The policemen, Julian—they were pitting themselves against him. They're fair game. But a child? A little girl? Would he be happy with that?'

I watch her lips tremble and know that she is conflicted.

'I'm going to the bedroom.' Energy and determination thunder through me. 'I'm taking Bea.' I stand up. 'I'm not going to look back. I'm not going to tell anyone about what happened here. I just want my child.'

I don't wait for her reply. I turn. I walk fast. I hold my breath. I reach the bedroom. I gather Bea into my arms. She doesn't stir. I walk back along the hallway. One, two, three . . . ten, eleven, twelve steps. I reach the front door. I balance Bea on my right arm and open the door with my left hand. I step onto the gravel. The sunlight bathes my face. I feel a moment of pure joy and then there's a loud crash, my ears buzz and I'm falling back against the wall of the house. A rough edge of brick scratches along my neck.

'Steady.' A policeman wearing a flak jacket takes Bea out of my arms. 'Come with me, Mrs Miller.' He walks off to one side. As I follow him, I glance behind me, bewildered. Half a dozen men, dressed like him, fill the hallway. I can hear Mac's voice shouting, 'On the ground! Face down!'

I blink. Another policeman lays a jacket on the grass. The one carrying Bea lowers her down gently. I fall on my knees in front of Bea. She's lying exactly as she was in the bed: on her right side, her legs drawn up, Bertie close to her cheek. I stroke her hair and shake her gently. 'Wake up, Bea. We need to go home.' She snuggles further into herself.

There's a commotion behind me. I look round. My eyes focus on Mac. He's on the driveway, pushing Megan ahead of him, her hands cuffed behind her back, shoulders slumped, feet dragging. She is staring at the ground, her expression hidden.

I don't want any more of this. 'Bea.' A sob catches in my throat. 'Please open your eyes.' I shake her more forcefully. 'Wake up, sweetheart.'

And she does. She opens her eyes very slowly and sits up. 'I don't like Megan, Mummy. She gave me pink milk and it tasted funny.'

Without warning, tears spring from my eyes and course down my cheeks. They are huge, hot, Olympic tears running at the sound of the starter's gun.

'Mummy.' She yawns. 'Why are you crying?'

'I'm just so happy.' I bring her onto my knee and hug her tight.

She yawns again, her eyes drooping. She forces her eyes open wide and looks at me closely, leaning right in so that I can feel her breath on my throat. 'You cut yourself.' She sits back a bit and nods. 'You need a plaster.'

'Let's go and find one, shall we?' I stand up and lift her into my arms. 'Let's go home.'

'COMAS LIKE THIS normally last between two and four weeks.'

'And then what?'

'And then he may wake up . . . or he may slip into a persistent vegetative state.' The nurse looks apologetic. 'But his observations are encouraging and he's almost ready to breathe for himself, so let's stay with that.'

One week has passed and Julian is no longer critically ill. He is now just seriously ill. His last MRI scan shows that his cerebrum was damaged by the lack of oxygen. There were complications. He had raised intracranial pressure. The surgeon had to drill through his skull to release the pressure on his brain. If it were a cartoon, steam would escape.

Several times a day I whisper in his ear, 'We found her, Jules. She's safe. Not at all traumatised. Her normal self.' I don't know what's going on inside his head, so I try to keep it simple. For hours at a time I sit beside his bed, hold his hand and talk to him about the little things that Bea's doing and how much we're looking forward to him coming home.

The children visit him every day. Charlie is worried about Julian but manages to act fairly normally around him, chatting about university and politics as he always has. Jack struggles to stay any longer than ten minutes. He bends to kiss Julian but stops an inch from his cheek. His fists clench and unclench. His face flushes. 'I'll get you some coffee from the machine, Mum,' he tells me, and leaves the room, blinking back tears.

After the initial rush of questions from Bea—'Why is that tube in Daddy's mouth?' 'Why doesn't he open his eyes?'—she sits on the edge of the bed and strokes his hair and chats to him. 'And when you're finished your long, long sleep, Daddy,' she says, 'you can see my new puppy.'

With my permission, Mary has promised Bea one of the puppies Douglas has fathered. Mary is becoming a regular visitor to our house. Julian had been in hospital a week when I knew I could no longer keep Mary's revelation a secret. I decided to tell Lisa first. I tried to break it to her slowly, but in the end there was no easy way to say it.

'Dad had another daughter,' I told her, as I sat with her at breakfast. 'It's Mary Percival, Bea's nursery teacher.'

Lisa took a couple of hours to get used to the idea and then we told Wendy, mindful that this would be a reminder of our dad's infidelity. She listened to the news without interruption and then, as ever, she humbled us both with her generosity when she said, 'She's part of our family? Girls! What news! We must invite her round.'

I soon realise that, when she sheds her shyness, this new sister of mine is fun. The boys and Bea think so too, but Bea refuses to believe she's her auntie. 'She's my teacher, Mummy. You've made a mistake.'

'It'll take time,' I tell Mary.

'Of course,' she says. 'I'm just so happy that I've told you at last.'

After ten days Julian is taken off the ventilator and he breathes for himself. He's still unconscious, but it's progress. He's moved out of the high-dependency unit into a side room on an adjacent ward. His wound is healing, and the scans show that his brain is settling down. His pupils are reacting to light. He responds to painful stimuli. These are very encouraging signs that he doesn't have permanent damage. We just need him to wake up.

I lurch between emotional states. My daughter is alive, blessedly, miraculously alive. My husband is unconscious. Home and hospital are two separate worlds. I leave Julian for the night and come home to the family. In my absence Wendy, Lisa and Jem have rallied round and my house is running better than it normally does.

Lisa's cancer is in remission. 'Too much else going on,' she says. It's unclear how long this will last, but I'm thankful that today, now, she's well.

Jem comes round every day. Pete has forgiven her for keeping her prison time a secret. Now that it has come out, she feels a weight has lifted. She's working hard on what she's calling Project Summerhouse, roping the boys in to help and bringing laughter and industry into their lives, the perfect antidote while we wait anxiously for Julian's recovery.

Charlie spends a couple of weeks with a broken heart when he realises that Amy has already moved on. I don't mention meeting her on the pier; I'm simply there for him as he wrestles with feelings of loss and betrayal before managing to file them away somewhere in his heart.

Communication between Mac and me has been strained since I found out that he not only followed me to where Bea was being kept, but the information he gave me was not accurate. The witness's name was indeed Batchev, but he was being kept somewhere in North London. Four of Georgiev's men turned up to the Gordon Avenue address—so I guessed right after all—and were met by a dozen armed officers. But Mac calls me most days to let me know how the case is progressing. The trial has been delayed by three weeks. Batchev is still in a safe house, ready to testify. Megan was remanded in prison, charged with several offences that would see her serving upwards of twenty years. On the tenth day she slit her own throat. How she acquired the razor blade was never established. Mac visited Belmarsh Prison himself to tell Georgiev. He told me Georgiev cried like a baby. It seems that their love for each other, however warped, was genuine.

And then the momentous day comes: Julian wakes up. I'm sticking the latest card Bea has made for him on the pinboard at the side of his bed.

'Thirsty.'

I stand stock-still.

'Claire, thirsty.'

I look down at the bed. His eyes are open. I scream with delight and then I laugh and jump up and down. 'Julian!' I kiss his face. 'You're awake!'

The nurses come running. We give him water and he falls asleep again. We're all grinning like mad. After four long weeks he's come back to us.

His recovery begins in earnest. He has two main areas to work on: a left-sided weakness in his limbs and a difficulty with language. He begins an intensive course of physiotherapy. Walking is tough. He grows tired and cross. It's hard for me to watch. I'm used to the strong, patient Julian, not someone who cries and loses his temper. I feel for him, wish I could save him from the pain and frustration of relearning what was once so familiar.

Speech therapy is even more frustrating for him. He understands what's being said to him, but has difficulty finding the right words when he replies. Nouns are especially hard to pinpoint. The therapist shows him cards and he has to say what the object is. Sometimes he's close. He'll say 'shed' for 'house' or 'dog' for 'cat'. Other times his choice is completely random.

When he's seven weeks into his recovery, Mac comes to visit. He gives Julian the news we've all been hoping for—Pavel Georgiev has been convicted of people-trafficking, drug-dealing and several counts of murder. He's given four consecutive life sentences. He'll never walk free again.

I walk with Mac along the corridor, and stop at the top of the stairs. 'Goodbye, then,' I say.

'It was good to see you again, Claire.'

'Under those circumstances?' I give a short laugh. 'I could have done without it.' He steps forward to give me a hug. I hold out my hand to keep him away from me. 'See you around.'

He briefly clasps my hand, then lets it go. 'Don't be a stranger.'

I walk back along the corridor and into Julian's side room. I see at once that he's in a black mood. He's sitting on a chair at the side of his bed and I sit down opposite him.

'Julian'—I lean forward and look up into his face—'I love you. I'm so glad that you're alive. I can only imagine how hard this is for you.'

'Do you blame me?' he blurts out.

I take his hand. 'For what?'

'For Bea. For Megan.'

'No!' I almost laugh. 'I thought you blamed me!'

'I should have listened to you.' There's a sadness in his eyes that makes my breath catch in my throat. He looks defeated.

'I didn't see that coming, Julian.' I stroke the side of his face. 'I didn't clock Megan. Nobody did.'

I tell him then about my own feelings of guilt. I tell him the whole story: how I took matters into my own hands, went behind his back, went to see Mac. He holds my hands and listens and I can see that he doesn't blame me.

'The responsibility was mine,' he says. 'I don't trust myself. I don't trust my . . .' He gropes for the word. ' . . . law . . . article. . .'

'Judgement?'

He nods. 'I'm no good.'

'Never say that.' I put my arms round him. 'It isn't true.'

We cry. We hug each other, and for the first time in weeks I know I'm going to get him back. The essence of him, the man I love, is coming back.

Finally the day arrives when he's well enough to come home.

'I have to warn you that the children have organised a small party,' I say, as we pull up outside the front door.

I'm about to get out when he stops me. 'Claire?'

'Yes?' I twist round in my seat to face him.

'I always wondered whether Mac might have been the one.'

For a moment I can't speak. Of course he knew. He knew and he said nothing. It makes me feel humbled. 'You, Julian.' I take his hand and look deep into his eyes, hoping he can read the sincerity in mine. 'You're the one.' I smile slowly and then kiss him. 'Now, come on. They're waiting.'

Bea is just inside the door, carrying her new puppy. 'This is Puppy.' She passes the ball of white fluff to Julian. Small enough to sit on the palm of his hand, the puppy's tail wags round in circles like a propeller.

Julian laughs. 'So what are you calling him, Bea?'

'Puppy.'

'Doesn't he need a proper name?'

'Miss Percival says I can take a few weeks to decide.'

'He's lively as a bag of eels, I know that much,' Jem says, walking through from the kitchen. She puts her hand on Julian's back. 'Great to have you home.' And then she gives me a surreptitious thumbs-up.

'Let's go and sit down in the garden,' I say.

Bea makes wide eyes at me. I put my finger over my lips and we follow Julian through to the back. He sees it from the kitchen window.

'What on earth?' He turns to look at me, his eyes shining. A cloth banner—'Welcome home, Daddy!' painted in red and gold—is hanging in front of a brand-new purpose-built wooden summerhouse, equipped with running water and electricity and with a comfy chair for Julian to rest on.

'They've been working hard,' I say. 'Go and have a look.'

With Jem on one side and Bea on the other, he goes down the back steps into the garden. Lisa, Mary and the boys are standing outside, smiling widely, and I watch them take Julian by the arm and show him around.

I've waited a long time for this moment, ten weeks of hope and hard work, and my chest swells with love and with relief that we're all back together again. But nothing in life is certain and I feel like from now on I'll always be on my guard. So that next time I'll see the danger coming.

I'll see it and I'll be prepared.

julie **corbin**

Where did you grow up and what is your strongest memory of that time?

I grew up in a small place called Lasswade, about ten miles outside Edinburgh. My strongest memory is being cosy indoors—it always seemed to be windy or raining!

Can you tell us a little about your life now?

I live in Forest Row, East Sussex, with my husband. I have three sons—Mike is twenty-six and works in Hong Kong, Sean is twenty-four and works in New Zealand and Matt is twenty-one and at university in Portsmouth.

Did you always want to write?

I always enjoyed writing but didn't imagine I could write a novel until about six years ago. I joined a local writing class and was lucky to have an excellent teacher. It took me a couple of years to gain confidence and find my own style but I got there in the end.

What did you do before you became a full-time author?

For thirteen years I worked as a nurse, running the medical department in a local boarding school. I also taught PSHE and Citizenship. It was a job I really enjoyed, but juggling job, family and writing became too much for me so something had to give.

Where do you write? Do you have a writing regime?

I have a small study at home—a male free zone!—that looks out over the back garden. I go in there at about nine in the morning and am in and out like a Yo-yo—unless I have a deadline, in which case I immerse myself in the story until I'm living and breathing it.

***Where the Truth Lies* is your second novel. Was it harder to write than the first?**

It was harder to write—partly because I had an imminent deadline to work to and partly because my dad was very unwell and sadly died, and my sister became ill, and I was still working full time. My editor was great, though, and delayed the publication date so that I could step back and make sure I got the novel right.

How did the premise for *Where the Truth Lies* evolve?

The idea came from a conversation I had with a barrister friend about the possibility of barristers being blackmailed because of a law that was passed in 2008—the Criminal Evidence (Witness Anonymity) Act. I spoke to a couple of criminal barristers who affirmed this possibility and I realised there was great substance for a plot.

What usually comes first, plot or character?

With me an idea comes first, then the central character, and then elements of the plot fall in to place—or not!—as I write the first draft. Sometimes I write myself into blind alleyways, but I'm not a writer who meticulously plots before I begin. I like to feel I'm discovering the story as I write.

Claire is a gutsy character. Did you enjoy throwing problems at her and seeing how she would cope?

Yes, I threw a fair bit her way but I think that for many of us there are times in our lives when we're coping with more than one problem and we're forced to prioritise. Perhaps it's because I was a nurse but, for me, small problems don't really cut it. I think love and death are the main themes in my novels—how we handle both these aspects of our lives.

Do you know how your novels will end before you start writing?

No, I don't. I've finished my third novel now and with all three of them I've had a rough idea of where I'm headed, but have surprised myself with endings that have felt 'right'.

Did you have to do lots of research about macrobiotic food or do you follow this healthy diet?

My husband and I met at a macrobiotic cookery class in Edinburgh many moons ago. We don't eat that way now, but we grow most of our own vegetables and are almost vegetarians. I'm not a paragon of virtue on the food front, however, and often eat whole bars of chocolate and leftover pudding!

Would you ever consider writing genres other than psychological thrillers?

Well . . . sometimes I think I'd like to write straight domestic drama but, as my youngest son pointed out, everything I write has an unnatural death of some sort in it. I'm finding my way into my fourth novel now and I can feel it heading further into crime territory.

What do you love most about living in Sussex?

So much! We live on the edge of Ashdown Forest, which is wonderful for walking the dog and soaking up the changing seasons. I love the proximity to London and to Brighton and the weather is so much milder than in Scotland so the winters are easier to bear.

How would you describe yourself as a person?

I'm quite shy, loyal, determined, hard-working—and I laugh a lot!

What do you like most, and least, about being an author?

The things I like most are the emails I get on my website from readers who have enjoyed my novels. I've always been a voracious reader myself and so it's heart-warming to know that I've evoked a similar experience in someone else. Sometimes writing is a lonely occupation and, depending on what stage of the process I'm at, it can be difficult to get motivated, but mostly I have no complaints. It's a privilege to be paid to do a job that I love.

POLICE
INVSTGN NO. SNI 005681/0056
MONK Jerome / 04632-0009457
STATUS: CONVICTED

The Calling Of The Grave

Simon Beckett

Eight years ago, forensic anthropologist Dr David Hunter was one of a team investigating a body buried on Dartmoor. The identity of the killer—a man already behind bars—looked certain.

Now, Jerome Monk has escaped and, in a nightmare scenario, appears to be targeting those involved in the original police operation. Lured back to the moors by a desperate call for help, Hunter begins to realise that neither the events unfolding now—nor those of eight years ago—are quite what they seem.

1

Eight Years Ago

'What name is it?'

The policewoman's face was cold, in every sense. Her cheeks were chapped and ruddy, and her bulky yellow jacket was beaded with moisture from the mist that had descended like an earth-bound cloud. She regarded me with what seemed barely restrained dislike, as though holding me responsible for the foul weather, and the fact that she was standing out on the moor in it.

'Dr David Hunter. Detective Chief Superintendent Simms is expecting me.'

With a show of reluctance she considered her clipboard, then raised her radio. 'Got someone here to see the SIO. A Mr David Hunter.'

'It's Doctor,' I corrected her.

The look she gave me made it clear she didn't care. There was a squawk of static from the radio and a voice said something unintelligible.

With a last sour look she stepped aside and motioned me past. 'Straight ahead to where the other vehicles are parked,' she said, gracelessly.

'And thank you,' I muttered, driving on.

Beyond the windscreen the world was draped with curtains of mist. It was patchy and unpredictable, lifting one moment to reveal the drab, wet moorland before wrapping white gauze round the car again the next. A little further along, a makeshift police car park had been set up on a relatively flat patch of moor. A policeman waved me on to it, and the Citroën bumped and lurched over the uneven ground as I eased it into a space.

I switched off the engine and stretched. It had been a long drive. Simms hadn't given me many details when he'd called, only that a grave had been found on Dartmoor and he wanted me to be there while the body was recovered. It had sounded routine, the sort of case I could be called out on several times a year. But for the past twelve months the words ‘murder’ and ‘Dartmoor’ had been synonymous with only one man.

Jerome Monk.

Monk was a serial killer and rapist who had confessed to murdering four young women that we knew about. Three of them were little more than girls, and their bodies had never been found. If this grave was one of theirs, then there was a good chance the others were also nearby. It would be one of the biggest recovery operations of the past decade.

And I definitely wanted to be a part of it.

‘Everyone’s always thought that’s where he got rid of his victims,’ I’d said to my wife, Kara, in the kitchen of our house in southwest London that morning, as I was rushing to get ready. ‘Dartmoor’s a big place but there can’t be so many bodies buried out there.’

‘*David*,’ Kara said, looking pointedly at where Alice was eating breakfast. I winced and mouthed *sorry*. Normally I knew better than to mention the grisly details of my work in front of our five-year-old daughter, but my enthusiasm had got the better of me.

‘What are vic-tims?’ Alice piped up, frowning in concentration as she lifted a dripping spoonful of raspberry yoghurt.

‘It’s just Daddy’s work,’ I told her, hoping she’d let it drop.

‘Why are they buried? Are they dead?’

‘Come on, sweetheart, finish your breakfast,’ Kara told her. ‘Daddy’s got to go soon and we don’t want to be late for school.’

‘When are you coming back?’ Alice asked me.

‘Soon. I’ll be home before you know it.’ I bent down and lifted her up. Her small body felt warm and ridiculously light. ‘Are you going to be a good girl while I’m away?’

‘I’m always a good girl,’ she said, indignant.

I gave her a kiss and set her down before gathering up my notes. I tucked them into a folder and turned to Kara. ‘I’d better go.’

She followed me into the hall, where I’d left my bag. I put my arms round her. Her hair smelt of vanilla.

‘I’ll call you later,’ I said. ‘I should have a better idea then how long I’ll be away. Hopefully only a couple of nights.’

‘Drive carefully,’ she said.

Both of us were used to my going away. I was one of the few forensic anthropologists in the country, and it was the nature of my job to go wherever bodies happened to be found. My work was often grim but always necessary, and I took pride in both my skill and my growing reputation.

That didn't mean I enjoyed this part of it. Leaving my wife and daughter was always a wrench, even if it was only for a few days.

I climbed out of the car now, treading carefully on the muddy grass. The air smelt of damp, heather and exhaust fumes. I went to the boot and pulled out a pair of disposable overalls from the box of protective gear I kept in there. When I'd zipped up the overalls, I took out my equipment case. A car pulled up as I began to make my way through the parked police vehicles. The bright yellow paintwork should have been a tip-off, but I was too preoccupied to pay it any attention until someone shouted.

'Found your way, then?'

I looked round to see two men climbing from the car. One of them was small and sharp-featured. I didn't know him, but I recognised the younger man he was with. Tall and good-looking, he carried himself with the easy confidence of an athlete. I hadn't expected to see Terry Connors here but I should have realised when I saw the car. The garish yellow Mitsubishi was his pride and joy, a far cry from CID's usual bland pool cars.

I smiled, although I felt the usual mixed feelings at seeing him. While it was good to find a familiar face among the impersonal police machinery, for some reason there was always an edge between Terry and me.

'I didn't know you were on the investigation,' I said as they came over.

He grinned, cheek muscles bunching on the inevitable piece of gum. 'I'm deputy SIO. Who do you think put in a word for you?'

I kept my smile in place. Back when I first knew Terry Connors, he'd been a DI in the Metropolitan Police, but we hadn't met through work. His wife, Deborah, had gone to the same antenatal clinic as Kara, and the two had become friends. Terry and I had been wary of each other at first. Except for the overlap of our professions we had little in common. He was ambitious and fiercely competitive, a keen sportsman. His self-assurance and ego could grate at times, but the success of the few cases he'd steered my way hadn't hurt either of us.

Then, just over a year ago, he'd surprised everyone by transferring out of the Met. I never did find out why. There had been talk of Deborah's wanting to be closer to her family in Exeter, but exchanging the high-octane policing of London for Devon had seemed an inexplicable career move for someone like Terry. Although Kara and Deborah had made a token effort to keep in touch afterwards, it was a lost cause, and I'd not seen or spoken to Terry since. But he was obviously doing well if he was deputy senior investigating officer on an investigation as big as this.

'I wondered how Simms got my name,' I said.

'I gave you a big build-up, so don't let me down.'

I suppressed the flare of irritation. 'I'll do my best.'

He cocked a thumb at the smaller man with him. 'This is DC Roper. Bob, this is David Hunter, the forensic anthropologist I told you about. He can tell more things from rotting bodies than you want to know.'

The detective constable gave me a grin. He had a snaggle of tobacco-stained teeth and eyes that wouldn't overlook much. A potent wave of cheap aftershave came from him as he gave me a nod.

'This should be right up your street.' His voice was nasal, with the distinctive accent of a local. 'Specially if it's what we think it is.'

'We don't know what it is yet,' Terry told him tersely. 'You go on ahead, Bob. I want to have a word with David.'

The dismissal was borderline rude. The other man's eyes hardened at the slight but his grin stayed in place. 'Right you are, chief.'

Terry watched him go with a sour expression. 'Watch yourself with Roper. He's the SIO's lap dog.'

'Is there some dispute about the body?'

'No dispute. Everyone's hoping it's one of Monk's.'

'What do you think?' I asked.

'I've no idea. That's what you're here to find out. And we need to get this one right.' He took a deep breath, looking strained. There was an almost palpable nervous energy coming off him. 'Anyway, come on, it's this way. Simms is out there now, so you'd better not keep him waiting.'

We reached a cluster of trailers and Portakabins that had been set up next to a track running from the road. Thick black cables snaked between them, and the misty air was tainted by diesel fumes from the chugging generators. Terry stopped by the trailer housing the Major Incident Room.

'You'll find Simms out at the grave. If I get back in time I'll let you buy me a drink. We're staying at the same place.'

'Aren't you coming?' I asked, surprised.

'No. Seen one grave, you've seen them all. I'm only here to collect some papers. Got a long drive ahead of me.'

'Where?'

He tapped the side of his nose. 'Tell you later. Wish me luck, though.'

He clattered up the steps into the MIR. I wondered why he needed luck, but I'd more to think about than Terry's games just then.

Turning away, I looked out across the moor.

Wreathed in mist, the barren landscape spread out in front of me. There were no trees, only patches of dark, spiky gorse. The year was still young, and winter-brown fern and bracken sprouted among the heather, rocks and coarse grass. Looking out from the road, the ground fell gently downhill before rising again in a long slope. Cresting it, perhaps a quarter of a mile away, was the formation of rock that Simms had mentioned.

Black Tor.

Dartmoor had more impressive tors—outcrops of weathered rock that rose from the moorland like carbuncles—but Black Tor's wind-sculpted profile was unmistakable against the skyline: a broad, squat tower, as though a giant child had stacked flattened boulders one on top of the other. It didn't look any blacker than any of the other tors I'd seen, so perhaps the name was down to some dark event in its past. But it sounded suitably portentous, the sort of detail the newspapers would gleefully seize on.

Especially if it was Jerome Monk's graveyard.

After Simms's telephone call I'd searched the Internet for background to the case. Monk had been a journalist's dream. A misfit and loner who supplemented his precarious living as a casual labourer with poaching and theft, he was an orphan whose mother had died during his birth. He was often described as a Gypsy, but that wasn't true. While he had lived in a caravan around Dartmoor for most of his life, he'd been shunned by the local traveller population as well as the rest of society. Unpredictable and prone to outbursts of terrifying violence, his personality matched his exterior. If anyone looked the part of a murderer, it was Monk.

Freakishly strong, he was a physical grotesque. The photographs and footage from his trial showed a hulk of a man, whose bald cannonball of a skull housed deep-set, sullen features. His black button eyes glinted with all the expression of a doll's above a mouth that seemed curved in a permanent sneer. Even more unsettling was the indentation on one side of his forehead, as though a giant thumb had been pressed into a ball of clay. It was the sort of disfigurement that looked as if it should have been fatal.

To most people's minds it was a pity it hadn't.

It wasn't just the nature of Monk's crimes that had been so shocking; it was the sadistic pleasure he seemed to take in selecting vulnerable victims. The first, Zoe Bennett, was a pretty seventeen-year-old, an aspiring model who never returned home from a nightclub one evening. Three nights after that a second girl disappeared. Lindsey Bennett, Zoe's identical twin.

Suddenly the investigation became front-page news. No one doubted that the same individual was responsible, and when Lindsey's handbag was discovered in a rubbish bin, effectively ending any hope that the sisters were still alive, there was public outrage. Bad enough for a family to suffer that sort of loss once, but twice? And twins?

When Tina Williams, an attractive, dark-haired nineteen-year-old, went missing as well, it sparked the inevitable false alarms and hysteria. For a time it seemed there was a definite lead: a white saloon car was picked up on street CCTV cameras in the areas where both Lindsey Bennett and Tina Williams had last been seen.

Then Monk claimed his fourth victim, and forever sealed his reputation as a monster. At twenty-five, Angela Carson was older and plainer than the others. There was also a more significant difference. She was profoundly deaf and couldn't speak.

Afterwards, neighbours described hearing Monk's laughter as he'd raped her and battered her to death in her own flat. When the two policemen who responded to the 999 calls broke down her door, they found him with her body in the wrecked bedroom, bloodied and crazed. They were big men, yet he'd beaten them both unconscious before disappearing into the night.

And then, apparently, off the face of the earth.

Despite one of the largest manhunts in UK history, no sign of Monk was found. Or of either of the Bennett twins or Tina Williams, though a search found a hairbrush and a lipstick belonging to Zoe Bennett hidden under his caravan.

It was three months before Monk was seen again, spotted by the side of a road in the middle of Dartmoor. Filthy and reeking, he made no attempt to resist arrest, or to deny his crimes. At his trial he pleaded guilty to four counts of murder, but refused to reveal either where he'd been hiding or what he'd done with the girls' bodies.

With the killer behind bars, the story faded from the public eye, the missing girls just more victims whose fates were unknown.

That might be about to change.

STANDING OUT like a beacon on the drab moorland was a bright blue forensic tent. It was roughly halfway between the road and the rock formation, a short distance off to one side of the dirt track that linked the two.

I set off along the track towards it.

My boots squelched in the black mud as I walked between the parallel lines of flapping police tape that had been strung from the track out to the tent. The area round the tent had been cordoned off, and a uniformed dog-handler stood guard at the opening. He shifted from foot to foot to keep warm as he and the dog, a German shepherd, watched me approach.

'I'm here to see DCS Simms,' I said, a little out of breath.

Before the dog-handler could say anything, the tent flap was thrown back and a man appeared in the gap. He was in his forties but seemed to aspire to be older. His face was remarkably unlined, and as if to offset the blandness of his features he'd cultivated a moustache that gave him a military bearing. The white overalls he wore somehow didn't look right on him. He'd pushed back the protective hood, and the black hair beneath it had managed to stay so neatly combed it looked moulded.

'Dr Hunter? I'm Simms.'

I'd have guessed as much even if I hadn't recognised his voice. It was peremptory and officious, confident in its authority. His pale eyes flicked over me, and in that moment I felt that I'd been swiftly assessed.

'We were expecting you half an hour ago,' he said, before disappearing back inside.

Nice to meet you, too. I followed him into the tent.

Inside it was cramped and crowded with overalled figures. The blue walls gave a diffused light and the atmosphere was moist and clammy. Beneath the odour of freshly turned soil was something far less benign.

The grave was in the centre. Portable floodlights had been set up, and metal stepping plates surrounded the rectangle of dark peat, framed by a grid of string. A scene-of-crime officer knelt over it, a big man who held his gloved hands poised in the air like a surgeon interrupted in theatre.

In front of him, poking through the peaty soil, was a decomposing hand.

'Dr Hunter, this is Professor Wainwright, the forensic archaeologist who's going to be supervising the excavation,' said Simms. 'You may have heard of him.'

I took stock of the figure kneeling by the graveside. *Wainwright?* I felt my stomach sink. I'd heard of him, all right. A Cambridge don turned police consultant, Leonard Wainwright was one of the highest-profile forensic experts in the country. He had a reputation for being an outspoken critic of what he dubbed 'fashionable forensics', which amounted to pretty much any discipline that wasn't his own, and forensic anthropology in particular. Only the previous year he'd published a paper in a scientific journal ridiculing the idea that decomposition could be a reliable indicator of time since death. 'Total Rot?' the title had crowed. I'd read it with amusement rather than annoyance. But I hadn't known then that I'd have to work with him.

Wainwright heaved himself to his feet, knees cracking arthritically. He was around sixty and a giant of a man. He pushed off his mask, revealing craggy features that might charitably have been called patrician.

He gave me a neutral smile. 'Dr Hunter. I'm sure it'll be a pleasure working with you.' He spoke with the rumbling baritone of a natural orator.

I managed a smile of my own. 'Same here.'

'A group of walkers found the grave late yesterday afternoon,' Simms said, looking down at the object emerging from the shallow grave.

I knelt down to examine the gelid dark soil from which the hand protruded. 'The peat's going to make things interesting.'

Wainwright gave a cautious nod, but said nothing.

'It looks as if rain washed off the top layer of soil from the hand, then animals finished unearthing it,' Simms continued. 'The walkers found the hand sticking out of the ground. Unfortunately, they weren't certain what it was at first, so they dug away some of the soil to make sure.'

'Lord protect us from amateurs,' Wainwright intoned. It might have been coincidence that he was looking at me.

I knelt down on one of the metal stepping plates to examine the hand. Most of the soft tissue had been gnawed away, and the first two fingers, which would have been uppermost, were missing. That much was only to be expected—larger scavengers like foxes would have been more than capable of detaching them. But what interested me was that, beneath the teeth marks in the bone, the broken surfaces of the phalanges looked smooth.

'Did any of the walkers tread on the hand, or damage it while they were digging?' I asked Simms.

'They claim not. Why?'

'Probably nothing. Just that the fingers are broken. Snapped cleanly by the look of things, so it wasn't done by an animal.'

'Yes, I had noticed,' Wainwright drawled.

'You think that's significant?' Simms asked.

Wainwright didn't give me a chance to answer. 'Too soon to say. Unless Dr Hunter has any theories . . . ?'

I wasn't about to be drawn. 'Not yet. Found anything else?' The area inside the tent would have already been picked clean for evidence by the SOCOs.

'Only two small bones on the surface that we think are a rabbit's. Certainly not human, but you're welcome to take a look.' Simms was looking at his watch. 'Now, if there's nothing else, I have a press conference. Professor Wainwright will brief you on anything you need to know. You'll be working under his direct supervision.'

Wainwright was watching me with an expression of mild interest. While the pathologist would have final say over the remains, as a forensic archaeologist, responsibility for the excavation would naturally fall to Wainwright. But I'd no intention of being treated like his assistant.

'That's fine, as far as the excavation goes,' I said. 'Obviously, I'd expect to be consulted on anything that might affect the remains themselves.'

Simms studied me coldly. 'Leonard and I have worked on numerous inquiries together in the past, Dr Hunter. Very successfully, I might add.'

'I wasn't—'

'You came very highly recommended, but I want team players. I won't tolerate any disruptions. From anyone. Do I make myself clear?'

I was aware of Wainwright watching. I felt myself bristle at Simms's attitude, but I kept my own face as studiedly neutral as his.

'Of course.'

'Good. Because I needn't tell you how important this is. Jerome Monk may be behind bars, but as far as I'm concerned my job isn't finished until his victims have been found and returned to their families.' Simms stared at me for a moment longer until he was satisfied he'd made his point. 'Now, if we're done, I'll leave you gentlemen to your work.'

He brushed out through the tent flaps. Neither Wainwright nor I spoke for a moment. The archaeologist cleared his throat theatrically.

'Well, Dr Hunter, shall we make a start?'

Time seemed suspended under the glare of the floodlights. The dark peat was reluctant to relinquish its hold on the body, clinging wetly to the flesh that was gradually emerging. Progress was slow. With graves dug in most types of soil, the grave shape or 'cut' is usually easily defined, as the infill soil is looser and less compact than the undisturbed earth around it. With peat the demarcation is less obvious because it tends not to break up like other soils. The grave cut can still be found, but it requires more care and skill.

Wainwright had both. His sheer physical presence dominated the enclosed space within the gently billowing blue walls. He'd been unexpectedly happy for me to help with the excavation, and once my pride had stopped stinging, I was forced to appreciate just how good the forensic archaeologist was. The big hands were surprisingly deft as they carefully scraped away the moist peat to expose the buried remains. As we worked side by side, I found myself revising my earlier impressions of the man.

We'd been working in silence for a while when he scooped up two halves of an earthworm severed by a spade. 'Remarkable things, aren't they? *Lumbricus terrestris*. Simple organism, no brain and barely any nervous system to speak of, and they'll still grow their tail ends back when you chop 'em off. There's a lesson for you: overcomplicate at your peril.'

He tossed the worm into the heather and set down his trowel, wincing as his knees cracked. 'This doesn't get any easier with age. But then what does? Still, you're too young to know about that. London man, aren't you?'

'Based there, yes. You?'

'Oh, I'm a local. Torbay. Driving distance, thank God, so I don't have to be put up in whatever fleapit the police have found. Don't envy you that.' He rubbed his lower back. 'So how're you finding Dartmoor so far?'

'Bleak, from what I've seen of it.'

'Ah, but you aren't seeing it at its best. Largest concentration of Bronze Age remains in Britain, and the whole moor's like an industrial museum. You can still find the old lead and tin mine workings dotted about like flies in amber. Wonderful! Well, to old dinosaurs like me, anyway. You married?'

I was having trouble keeping up. 'Yes, I am.'

'Sensible man. A good woman keeps us sane. Although how they put up with us is another matter. My wife deserves a medal—as she frequently reminds me.' He chuckled. 'And may I give you a tip?'

'Go ahead.' This wasn't the Wainwright I'd been expecting.

'Never take your work home with you. Detachment is essential in our business. Otherwise it will suck you dry.' He picked up his trowel again and turned back to the remains. 'Actually, I was talking to someone recently who knew you. Said you'd originally trained as a medic?'

'I did a medical degree before switching to anthropology, yes. Who told you that?'

He frowned. 'Do you know, I've been racking my brains trying to remember. My memory's not what it was. I think it was at some forensic conference. We were talking about the new generation making their mark on the field. Your name was mentioned.'

I was surprised that Wainwright would admit to having heard of me. Despite myself I was flattered.

'Quite a leap, anthropology from medicine,' he went on, busily scraping the soil from round an elbow. 'I gather you trained at that research facility in Tennessee. The one that specialises in decomposition.'

'The Anthropological Research Facility. I spent a year there.'

It had been before I'd met Kara, after I'd exchanged working with the living for the dead. I waited for the put-down. It didn't come.

'Sounds like quite a place. Although probably not for me. I have to confess I'm not a great fan of Calliphoridae. Disgusting things.'

'I'm not a big fan myself, but they have their uses.' Calliphoridae was the family classification for the blowfly, whose life cycle provided an effective clock for charting decomposition. Wainwright was obviously keen on Latin names.

'I expect they do. Though not in this instance, sadly. Far too cold.' He pointed with his trowel at the remains. 'So, what do you make of it?'

'I'll have a better idea once the body's at the mortuary.'

'Of course. But I'm sure you've already drawn some conclusions.'

I could see the mouth smile under the face mask. I was reluctant to commit myself, knowing how easily things could change once the remains were cleaned. But Wainwright was nothing like the ogre I'd been expecting, and it was just the two of us there. Given his past antipathy to forensic anthropology, it wouldn't hurt to let him know he wasn't the only expert here. I sat back on my heels to consider what we'd uncovered.

Peat is a unique substance. Formed from partially decayed plant and animal remains, it's an environment that's inimical to most of the bacteria and insects that usually populate the earth beneath our feet. Low in oxygen and almost as acidic as vinegar, it can effectively pickle organic matter. Human corpses buried in peat bogs hundreds of years before can emerge uncannily intact. That can make peat a forensic nightmare. Determining an accurate time-since-death interval is difficult at the best of times; without the natural markers supplied by decomposition it can be all but impossible.

In this instance, though, I doubted it would be such a problem. About half of the body was now exposed. It was lying more or less on one side, curled in a crumpled foetal position. Both the thin top that clung to the torso, through which the outline of a bra could be seen, and the short skirt were synthetic, and contemporary in style.

The entire body—hair, skin and clothes—was caked in viscous black peat. Even so, nothing could disguise the horrific damage that had been inflicted. The outlines of broken ribs were clearly visible under the fabric, and jagged bones poked through the flesh of the arms. Beneath the clinging mat of hair, the skull was crushed and misshapen.

'Not much yet, apart from the obvious,' I said, cautiously.

'Which is?'

I shrugged. 'Female.'

'Go on.'

'It's difficult to say yet how long the body's been buried. There's some decomposition, but that's probably explained by how close it was to the surface.' Proximity to the air would allow aerobic bacteria to break down soft tissue even in a peat grave, albeit at a slower rate.

Wainwright nodded agreement. 'So the right time frame to be one of Monk's victims? Less then two years, say?'

'It could be, yes,' I conceded. 'But I'm not going to speculate just yet.'

'No, of course. And the injuries?'

'Too soon to say if they're ante- or post-mortem, but she was obviously badly beaten. Possibly with some kind of weapon. Hard to imagine anyone breaking bones like that with their bare hands.'

'Not even Jerome Monk?' Behind his mask Wainwright grinned at my discomfort. 'Come on, David, admit it. This does look like one of his.'

'I'll have a better idea once I can see the skeleton.'

'You're a cautious man; I like that. But she's the right sort of age, you can see from the clothes. No one over twenty-one would dare wear a skirt that short.' He gave a chuckle. 'I know, that isn't very politically correct. But unless this is a case of mutton dressed as lamb, we've got a young woman who's been savagely beaten and buried in Monk's back yard. You know what they say, if it looks like a fish and smells like a fish . . .'

His manner grated, but he was only saying what I'd thought myself.

'It's possible.'

'Ah, a palpable hit! I'd say probable, but still. Which leaves the question of which one of Monk's unfortunate paramours this might be. This is more your province than mine. One of the Bennett twins or the Williams girl?'

'The clothes might tell us that.'

'True, but I suspect you already have an inkling.' He chuckled. 'Don't worry, you're not on the witness stand. Humour me.'

He was a hard man to refuse. 'It'd only be a guess, but . . . the Bennett sisters were both quite tall.'

I'd learned that from my hurried research after Simms had called: Zoe and Lindsey had the willowy grace of catwalk models. 'Whoever this is, she's more petite. It's hard to get an accurate impression of height with the body curled like this, but looking at the length of the femur I don't think she could have been more than five foot three or four at the most.'

Wainwright's forehead creased as he stared down at the uppermost thigh bone. 'Blast. Should have seen that myself.'

'It's just a guess. And as you say, it's more my area than yours.'

He shot me a look that held none of the joviality of a moment ago. Then his eyes crinkled. He gave a booming laugh. 'Yes, you're quite right. So, the odds are that this is Tina Williams. Good.' He clapped his hands together. 'Anyway, first things first. Let's finish digging her out, shall we?'

Picking up his trowel he set back to work. Leaving me with the obscure feeling that the conversation had been my idea. We spoke little after that.

Simms returned as we were finishing. 'Good evening, gentlemen. Making progress?'

Wainwright stood back to give him room. 'Nearly done. I was about to hand over to the SOCOs to finish off.'

'Good.'

'The victim's female', Wainwright continued. 'Probably in her late teens or early twenties, judging by her clothes. You can see her injuries. Probably caused by either a clubbing weapon or someone with prodigious strength. As for how long it's been here, if I was pushed I'd say less than two years.'

'You're sure?' Simms asked sharply.

Wainwright spread his hands. 'It's only a guess at this stage, but given the peat conditions and the level of decomp I'm fairly confident.'

I stared at him, unable to believe I'd heard right. Simms nodded in satisfaction. 'So this could be one of Monk's victims, then?'

'Oh, I'd say that was a distinct possibility. In fact if I had to hazard another guess I'd say this filly could well be the Williams girl. The femur's far too short to belong to anyone as tall as the Bennett twins. And the injuries certainly point to Monk after what he did to Angela Carter.'

Carson. Angela Carson, not Carter. But I was too angry to speak: Wainwright was shamelessly stealing credit for what I'd told him. Yet I couldn't object without seeming petty.

'At the very least I think it's worth the pathologist looking to see if this is the Williams girl first,' Wainwright added.

'I agree,' said Simms, looking energised. 'And if Monk buried one of his victims here, it's reasonable to assume the others aren't far away. Excellent work, Leonard, thank you. Give my regards to Jean. If you're both free this weekend perhaps you'd like to come over for Sunday lunch?'

'We'll look forward to it,' Wainwright said.

Simms turned to me as an afterthought. 'Anything to add, Dr Hunter?'

I looked at Wainwright. His expression was politely enquiring, but his eyes held a predatory satisfaction.

OK, if that's the way you want it . . . 'No.'

'Then I'll leave you to it,' Simms said. 'We'll be making an early start in the morning.'

2

I was still fuming later that evening when I pulled into the car park of the Trencherman's Arms, the pub I'd been booked into. It was a few miles from Black Tor in a place called Oldwich.

The pub wasn't much to look at from the outside: a long, low building with peeling whitewash and a sagging thatched roof. First impressions were borne out when I pushed through the scuffed and creaking doors. An odour of stale beer complemented the threadbare carpets and cheap horse brasses hanging on the walls. But I'd stayed in worse places. Just.

The landlord was a sour-faced man in his fifties. 'If you want food we stop serving in twenty minutes,' he told me with poor grace, sliding a broken key fob across the worn bar.

The room was what I'd expected, none too clean but not bad enough to complain about. I was hungry, but food could wait. My mobile phone had a signal, which was a bonus. I pulled the hard-backed chair next to the room's small radiator as I called home. I always tried to call at the same time, so that Alice could keep to something like a routine.

'Perfect timing,' Kara said when she picked up. 'There's a young lady here hoping you'd call before she goes to bed.'

I smiled as she passed the phone over.

'Daddy, I did you a picture of our house, except with yellow curtains because I liked them better. Mummy says she does too.'

I felt some of my anger and frustration slough away as I listened to my daughter's excited account. Being outmanoeuvred by Wainwright no longer seemed so important. Eventually Kara sent her off to brush her teeth.

'So how did it go?' Kara asked, when she came back on the phone.

'Oh . . . could have been worse. Terry Connors is deputy SIO, so at least there's a familiar face.'

'Terry? Well, tell him to give my love to Deborah.' She didn't sound too pleased. 'Do you know yet how long you'll be there?'

'At least another couple of days. They're going to start looking for more graves, so it depends on how that goes.'

We spoke for a while longer, then I washed and changed and went down to the bar. I'd forgotten the landlord's warning that they would be stopping serving food, and the twenty-minute curfew was almost up. He looked pointedly at his watch as I ordered.

'Another two minutes and you'd be too late,' he snapped.

'Lucky I was in time, then.'

Tightlipped, he went off to get my order. There were other people in the bar now, more than a few of them police officers, I guessed. There was only one free table, but a sign said it was reserved. A solitary young woman sat at the next table, absently forking up food as she read from an open folder.

I took my drink over. 'Do you mind—?' I began, but the landlord pre-empted me by slapping the cutlery down.

'You'll have to share,' he declared, before stalking off.

The young woman looked from him to me in surprise.

I gave an embarrassed smile. 'I can find somewhere else if it's a problem.'

She waved a hand at the chair. 'No, it's fine. I've finished anyway.' She set down her fork and pushed away her plate.

She was attractive in an unobtrusive way. Wearing jeans and a loose sweater, her thick auburn hair pulled casually back, she struck me as someone who didn't worry too much about how she looked, but didn't have to.

I glanced at the folder she'd been reading, and recognised what looked like a police report. 'Are you here on the investigation?' I asked.

She pointedly picked up the folder and tucked it into her bag. 'Are you a reporter?' There was frost in her voice.

'Me? God, no,' I said, surprised. 'Sorry, my name's David Hunter, I'm a forensic anthropologist. Part of Simms's team.'

She gave me a self-conscious smile. 'You'll have to excuse me. I get paranoid when anyone starts quizzing me about work. And yes, I am on the investigation.' She held out her hand. 'Sophie Keller.'

Her grip was firm, her hand strong and dry.

'So what do you do, Sophie? Or is that being nosy again?'

She smiled. 'I'm a BIA. That's a Behavioural Investigative Adviser.'

'Is that like a profiler?' I asked.

'There's a psychological aspect, yes, but it's a little broader than that. I advise on offenders' characteristics and motivations, but I also look at strategies for interviewing suspects, assess crime scenes, things like that.'

'How come I didn't see you at the grave today?'

'Sore point. I didn't hear about it until this afternoon, so I'll have to make do with photographs. But that wasn't why I was brought in.'

'Oh?'

She hesitated. 'Well, I don't suppose it's a secret. They asked me here because if this is one of Monk's victims the others might be buried nearby. They want me to advise on the most likely places the graves could be. That's sort of a speciality of mine.'

'How do you do that?' I was intrigued. Even with technological advances, grave location was still a hit and miss affair.

'Oh, there are ways,' she said, vaguely. 'Anyway, now you know what a BIA does. Your turn.'

I gave her a potted outline of what my work involved, breaking off when the landlord arrived with the food. Sophie and I considered the plate of over-boiled vegetables and grey meat on the table in front of me.

'So you decided against the smoked salmon and foie gras,' she said.

'It's the perks that make the work worthwhile,' I said, trying to spear a disintegrating carrot on my fork. 'So where are you from?'

'Bristol, but I live in London these days. I used to come on holidays here when I was a girl, though, so I know Dartmoor quite well. I'd like to move here some day, but with work . . . Perhaps if I ever get tired of being a BIA.'

'I'm reserving judgment on Dartmoor, but I know Bristol a little. It's nice country round there. My wife's from Bath.'

'Oh, right.'

We smiled at each other, knowing that parameters had been drawn. Now we'd established I was married we could relax without worrying about putting out any wrong signals.

Sophie was good company, sharp and funny. She talked about her home and her plans for the future; I told her about Kara and Alice. We both spoke about our work, although the subject of the current investigation was avoided, as neither of us was about to give away too much to a virtual stranger.

But when I looked across the room and saw Terry and Roper heading towards me, I knew that was about to change. Terry looked startled when he saw the two of us at the table.

'Didn't realise you two knew each other,' he said.

Sophie gave Terry a smile that seemed to have an edge to it. 'We do now. David's been telling me what he does. It's really fascinating.'

'Is it,' Terry said, flatly.

'Do you want to join us?' I asked, feeling uncomfortable.

'No, we won't interrupt. Just came over to give you the news.'

'News?' I said.

Terry addressed me as though Sophie wasn't there. 'You know when I told you I'd got to go somewhere? Well, I went to Dartmoor prison to see Jerome Monk.'

That explained Terry's secrecy earlier; no wonder he'd seemed keyed up. But Sophie jumped in before I could ask anything.

'You've been to *interview* him? Why wasn't I told?'

'Take it up with Simms,' he shot back.

Sophie was furious. 'I can't believe you questioned him without consulting me! Why bring a BIA in and then not use them? That's just *stupid*!'

I winced. Tact obviously wasn't her strong point. Terry's face darkened.

'I'm sure the SIO'll love to hear how stupid he's been.'

'You said you'd got news?' I said, trying to head off the row.

Terry gave Sophie a final glare before turning to me. 'Monk claims he can't remember who he buried where, but he's agreed to cooperate.'

'Cooperate how?'

Terry hesitated, as though he didn't entirely believe it himself. 'He's going to take us to the other graves.'

THE UNMARKED VAN bumped along the narrow road, police cars front and back. I watched the distant procession as it made its way slowly past the grassed-over ruins of an old water wheel, one of the remnants of the tin mines Wainwright had told me about.

Beside me, Terry Connors gave a grunt of satisfaction. He lowered his binoculars and glanced at his watch. 'Come on. It'll be here soon.'

We made our way back to the small township of police trailers, cars and vans that had sprung into life round the moorland track. The constant traffic was churning the moor into a quagmire. Duckboards had been set down as temporary walkways, but black mud oozed up through their slats, making them treacherously slippery.

Terry had an intense, overwound look about him that spoke of too little sleep and too much caffeine. It was hardly surprising, since as far as I could tell Simms was delegating everything to his deputy. Except for press conferences, which he insisted on doing himself.

I hadn't expected to be here more than a few days, but the convict's surprise offer to show us where the Bennett twins were buried had changed that. Wainwright would remain in charge of any excavation, but Terry had told me that Simms wanted me on hand when—if—any more bodies were found.

It had taken two days to finalise all the necessary arrangements for Monk's temporary release. I'd spent most of that time in the mortuary. Once the young woman's body had been cleaned of the thick coating of peat, the full extent of her injuries was shockingly apparent. There seemed hardly any part of her skeleton that wasn't damaged. It was the sort of trauma you'd expect from a car crash, not something inflicted by a human being.

'The post-mortem wasn't able to establish a definitive cause of death,' the pathologist, a diminutive man called Dr Pirie, told me. 'Any number of injuries could have been responsible. In fact, the injuries this young lady suffered are so severe that shock alone would probably have killed her.'

Young lady sounded curiously old-fashioned. Prim, almost. For some reason it made me warm to the pathologist.

'How do the injuries compare with Angela Carson's?' I asked.

'The soft tissue was too degraded to distinguish any signs of sexual assault, unfortunately. I'd hoped the peat might have preserved it adequately, but the shallowness of the grave worked against us.' He sniffed regretfully. 'The Carson girl also suffered mainly facial and cranial trauma, although nowhere near so severe as this. Jerome Monk either has a truly terrifying temper or he disfigures his victims for pleasure.' Pirie looked at me over his half-moon glasses. 'I'm not sure which is the more disturbing.'

Neither was I. A fraction of the force used would still have been fatal. Whoever she was, she hadn't just been beaten to death; she'd been pulverised. It was overkill in a very literal sense.

Confirming that the dead woman was Tina Williams turned out to be relatively straightforward. The clothes and jewellery the body was buried in matched those the nineteen-year-old was last seen wearing when she'd disappeared from Okehampton, a market town on the northern edge of Dartmoor, and dental records confirmed her identity beyond doubt.

I'd been able to add little to what we already knew. Tina Williams had suffered horrific blunt trauma injuries. Most of her ribs and the clavicle had simple fractures caused by a swift downward force, as did the metacarpals and phalanges of both hands. The frontal bone of Tina Williams's skull—her forehead—bore a distinctive curved fracture. It was too big to have been caused by a hammer; it looked to me like something that might have been caused by a shoe or boot heel. She'd been stamped on.

The rear of her skull was intact, which suggested she'd been lying face up on soft ground when the injuries had been inflicted. Yet she seemed to have made no attempt to defend herself. Typically, when the forearm is raised to block a blow, it's the ulna that takes the brunt of the force, but it was not the case here. That pointed to one of two scenarios. Either Tina Williams was already dead or unconscious during the attack, or she'd been trussed and helpless while Monk broke most of the bones in her body. I hoped for her sake it was the former.

Terry glanced nervously at his watch again as we clattered along the duckboards. 'Everything OK?' I asked.

'Why shouldn't it be? We've got one of the most dangerous men in the country about to be let loose and I've still no idea why the bastard's suddenly decided to cooperate. Yeah, everything's great.' He passed his hand over his face. 'Sorry. I just keep going over all the preparations, trying to make sure we've not overlooked anything.'

'You don't think he's serious about showing us where the graves are?'

'We'll soon find out.' He stiffened as he looked ahead of us. 'Oh great.'

Sophie Keller had emerged from the trailer that was serving as a mobile canteen. She was bundled up in bulky overalls and carrying a polystyrene container of steaming coffee. A middle-aged man I didn't recognise was with her. She'd been nodding at something he said, but a coolness crossed her features when she saw Terry approaching.

She ignored him as she gave me a warm smile, resting a hand lightly on my arm. 'Hi, David. Have you met Jim Lucas?'

'Jim's our POLSA,' Terry said, blanking her in return. 'He's been trying to keep some order in this three-ring circus.'

The police search adviser's handshake was just the right side of bone breaking. 'Pleased to meet you, Dr Hunter. Ready for the big day?'

'I'll tell you later.'

'Wise man. Still, it's not every day someone like Jerome Monk decides to work on the side of the angels, is it?'

'If that's what he's doing,' Sophie said, looking at Terry. 'I'd have a better idea if I'd been allowed access to him.'

Here we go again, I thought as Terry's jaw muscles bunched. 'We've been through this,' he said. 'You get to accompany the team with Monk, but there's to be no direct contact. If you don't like it, take it up with Simms.'

'But it's ridiculous! I could assess Monk's state of mind, gauge if his change of heart is genuine, but instead—'

'The decision's been made. Monk's not talking to anyone, and for the time being the priority's getting him to show us the other graves.'

'You mean Simms's priority.'

'I mean the priority of this investigation, and last time I checked you were a part of it. You want that to change, then say the word!'

They glared at each other, then Terry walked away, feet clumping on the duckboards. Lucas looked as uncomfortable as I felt.

'Well, I need to get on as well.' He gave Sophie an uncertain glance. 'Look, Monk's a dangerous bugger. You ask me, you're better keeping well away.'

For a second I thought she was going to snap at Lucas as well, but then she gave a reluctant smile. 'I can look after myself.'

Lucas kept his thoughts to himself. He gave me a nod. 'Dr Hunter.'

We watched him walk away. Sophie blew out an exasperated breath. 'God, sometimes I hate this job.'

'You don't mean that,' I said.

'Don't bet on it. I just can't understand why Monk's suddenly so keen to *help*. And please don't say it's his guilty conscience.'

'You think he's hoping to escape?' I asked.

I wouldn't have dared mention that to Terry, not given the pressure he was under to see that didn't happen. But everyone was well aware of what Jerome Monk was capable of.

Sophie thrust her hands into her pockets, scowling in frustration. 'I can't see how he can, but I'd feel happier if he'd at least give us a bloody clue where the graves are. But no, he insists he'll only come out and *show* us. And Simms is letting him! He's so fixated on finding the Bennett twins so he can announce he's got the full set, he's letting Monk dictate his own conditions. That's plain stupid, but I can't get anyone to listen.'

Not for lack of trying. I had the sense to keep that to myself, though.

'I don't care how well Monk knows the moor,' she continued. 'It's still been a year since he killed the Bennett sisters. Their graves will be overgrown, and he probably buried them at night anyway. Even if he wants to, I can't see him remembering exactly where they are. Not without help.'

She fell silent as we saw the convoy of vehicles creeping along the road towards us. Monk was here.

3

A stillness seemed to fall as the procession headed for where Terry was waiting with Roper and a group of uniformed officers. A dog-handler stood with them, the intent-looking German shepherd kept on a short leash. The van and two police cars pulled up well away from the other vehicles. In the silence after their engines died, the sound of the doors clunking open carried clearly in the damp air. The police officers who climbed out were all big, bulky men. Their hands went to the batons clipped to their belts as they fanned out round the rear doors of the van.

'Very melodramatic,' Sophie commented.

I didn't answer. There was movement in the shadowy recesses of the van. Something round and pale solidified into a bald head as it emerged into the light. A crouched figure filled the opening, ignoring the step-board below the doors to jump down. Then it straightened.

There was no mistaking the sheer hulking presence of Jerome Monk. His hands were cuffed awkwardly in front of him, and I realised with a shock that he was also wearing leg restraints. Neither seemed to bother him, and he looked powerful enough to snap the handcuff chain without effort.

'Ugly brute, isn't he?'

I hadn't noticed that Wainwright had joined us. The forensic archaeologist made no attempt to keep his voice down, and his words carried clearly in the still air. Monk's moon head swivelled towards us.

The photographs I'd seen hadn't done him justice. The indentation in his forehead looked far worse in the flesh, as though he'd survived being struck with a hammer. The skin of his face was pitted with scar tissue. A scabbed, yellowing graze on one cheek suggested that at least some of it was recent, while the crooked mouth was curled in the same half-smile he always wore. It seemed to acknowledge and mock the revulsion he provoked.

But it was his eyes that were the most disturbing. Small and unblinking, they were flat and empty as black glass. I felt chilled as they settled on me, but I warranted only a fleeting interest. The dead eyes went to Sophie, lingering on her for a moment before shifting to Wainwright.

'What you looking at?'

The accent was local but the voice was a surprise: gruff and disconcertingly soft. Wainwright should have let it go. But the archaeologist wasn't used to being spoken to like that. He gave a derisive snort.

'My God, it can talk!'

Monk's leg restraints snapped taut as he stepped towards him. That was as far as he got before the two prison guards grabbed his arms, bracing themselves with the effort of holding him.

'Come on, Jerome, behave yourself,' one of the guards said, an older man with grey hair and a lined face.

The killer's black eyes remained fixed unblinkingly on Wainwright.

'You got a name?'

Terry had looked startled at the sudden confrontation, but now he moved forward. 'His name's none of your business.'

'It's all right. If he wants to know who he's dealing with I'm more than happy to tell him.' Wainwright drew himself up to his full height. 'I'm Professor Leonard Wainwright. I'm in charge of recovering the bodies of the young women you murdered.'

'Jesus,' I heard Sophie breathe beside me.

Monk's mouth curled. 'Professor,' he sneered, as though trying out the word. Without warning his eyes flicked to me. 'Who's this?'

Terry seemed at a loss, so I answered. 'I'm David Hunter.'

'Hunter,' Monk echoed. 'Name to live up to.'

'So's Monk,' I said automatically.

The black eyes bored into me. Then there was a slow wheezing, and I realised Monk was laughing.

'Smart-arse, aren't you?'

He turned to Sophie, but Terry didn't give him a chance to say more.

'Right, you've been introduced.' He motioned to the guards to lead him away. 'Come on, we're wasting time.'

'You heard the man, laughing boy.' The other guard, a thickset man with a beard, tried to haul Monk away. He might as well have tugged at a statue.

'Don't fucking pull me,' Monk said, levelling that basilisk stare at him.

The atmosphere was already tense, but now the air suddenly felt charged. I could see Monk's chest rising and falling as his breathing grew more rapid. Then a man pushed his way through the encircling police officers.

'Detective Inspector, I'm Clyde Dobbs, Mr Monk's solicitor,' the man said in a thin, nasal voice. 'My client's agreed to cooperate in the search voluntarily. I hardly think assaulting him is called for.'

'No one's assaulting anyone,' Terry snapped. He shot the bearded guard a look. The man grudgingly let go of Monk's arm.

'Thank you,' the solicitor said. 'Please carry on.'

Terry jerked his head at the guards. 'Bring him.'

'Fuck off!' Monk yelled, as the guards strained to pull him back. His eyes were suddenly manic. I watched, stunned, unable to believe this could go wrong so quickly. I waited for Terry to take charge, but he seemed frozen. The moment stretched on, ready to shatter into violence.

And then Sophie stepped forward. 'Hi, I'm Sophie Keller,' she said easily. 'I'm going to help you find the graves.'

For a second there was no response. Then the black eyes blinked as Monk's mouth worked, as though remembering how to form words. 'Don't need any help.'

'Great, then it'll be a lot easier for all of us. But I'm here just in case, OK?' She gave him a smile, a normal, everyday smile. 'Oh, and let's lose the leg restraints. You won't get very far with those on.'

Still smiling, she turned to include Terry in that last comment. I could see the other police officers exchanging glances. Terry's face was red as he gave a nod to the guards.

'Just the legs. Leave the cuffs on.'

He spoke brusquely, but there wasn't anyone there who didn't realise how close he'd just come to losing control. If it hadn't been for Sophie there was no telling what would have happened.

Sullen and subdued, the convict turned to stare at Sophie as he was led off down the track.

'It looks as though Ms Keller's got a new pet,' Wainwright said as we followed on behind, our breath steaming in the cold morning.

'She did well,' I said.

'You think so?' Wainwright's eyes were unfriendly as he watched them walk ahead of us. 'Let's hope it doesn't decide to bite her.'

THE MOOR SEEMED to do its best to hinder us. The temperature dropped and the rain started to fall. It flattened the stalks of the grass and heather, a dull monotonous downpour that chilled the spirit as much as the flesh.

The forensic tent had been taken down and Jerome Monk now stood by Tina Williams's empty grave, rain running across his bald skull to drip from features that could have graced a medieval church gargoyle. He seemed oblivious. Flanked by the two guards, he just stared down at the shallow pit, which was already filling with muddy water.

'Bring back memories, Monk?' Terry asked.

There was no response. The convict could have been carved from the same granite as the rocks of Black Tor for all the notice he took.

The bearded guard prodded him. 'You heard the man, laughing boy.'

'Keep your hands to yourself,' Monk grated without looking round.

His solicitor gave an exaggerated sigh as the guard bridled. 'I'm sure I don't have to remind anyone that my client is here voluntarily. If he's going to be subjected to harassment we can call this off now.'

'Nobody's harassing anyone.' Terry's shoulders were hunched from tension. 'Time's up, Monk. You've done enough sightseeing. Tell us where the other graves are, or you can go back to your cell.'

Monk raised his eyes from the pit and stared out across the moor. His restraints chinked as he raised his hands and rubbed them over his skull.

'Over there.'

Everyone looked where he'd indicated. It was even further away from the road and track. Except for occasional outcrops of rock, there was nothing to see except a featureless plain of heather and grass.

'Whereabouts?' Terry asked.

'I told you. Over there.'

'How far away?' Terry asked, making a visible effort to restrain himself. I'd never seen him so edgy. 'Fifty yards? A hundred? Half a mile?'

'I'll know when I get there.'

'Can you remember any landmarks nearby?' Sophie asked quickly. Annoyance flickered across Terry's face, but he didn't interrupt. 'A big rock, a clump of gorse, anything like that?'

Monk looked at her. 'Can't remember.'

'What *can* you remember, Jerome? Perhaps if you tried to—' Sophie began, but Terry cut her off.

'All right, let's get this over with. Just show us.'

Sophie looked furious but people were already moving away, a cluster of uniforms surrounding Monk's unmistakable figure.

'This is farcical,' Wainwright grumbled as we trudged after them, boots squelching on the boggy moor. 'I don't believe that creature has any intention of telling us anything. He's making fools of us.'

'It might help if you'd stop antagonising him,' Sophie said, still angry.

'You can't afford to show weakness to creatures like that. They need to know who's in charge.'

'Really?' Sophie's voice was dangerously sweet. 'I tell you what. You don't tell me my job, and I won't tell you how to dig holes.'

The archaeologist glared at her. 'I'll be sure to pass on your thoughts to DCS Simms,' he said, before walking on ahead.

'Prick,' Sophie said under her breath, though not so softly that he couldn't hear. She glanced at me. 'What?'

'I didn't say anything.'

'You didn't have to.'

I shrugged. 'If you want to fall out with the whole task force, don't let me stop you.'

'It's just so bloody *frustrating*. What's the point of me being here if they won't let me do my job properly?' She sighed. 'We shouldn't just let Monk lead us around by the nose, not without pushing him for some indication of where the graves are. How's he going to find them again if he can't remember any landmarks? And it's a hell of a long way for anyone to carry a body.' She frowned, staring at where Monk's pale head stood out among the dark uniforms up ahead. 'I'm going to have a wander round. I'll catch you up.'

She struck off back towards the track that led to Black Tor. I could understand her doubts, but there was nothing I could do about them. The going became more difficult as we headed further into the moor, the rain-soaked peat tugging at our boots. Even Monk seemed to be having difficulties, his balance hampered by having his hands cuffed together.

I noticed that Roper had dropped back and was talking quietly on his radio. As I approached the wind carried snatches of his words over to me.

'. . . not confident, sir . . . Yes . . . Of course, sir. I'll keep you informed.'

He ended the call as he saw me. It didn't take a genius to guess he'd been reporting back to Simms. I wondered if Terry knew.

'Enjoying the walk, Dr Hunter?' The DC grinned, falling in step beside me. 'Turning into quite a marathon, isn't it?' The grin was just a little too ready and too sycophantic for me to trust.

'The fresh air does me good.'

He chuckled. 'A little too much of it for my taste,' he said. 'So what do you think of Monk? He's something, isn't he? Face like a bloody Picasso.'

You're no oil painting yourself. 'How did he get the bruises?'

Roper's grin broadened. 'He kicked off on one last night and had to be "restrained". Almost made us cancel the whole thing. One of his party pieces, apparently, having a tantrum after lights out. That's why the guards call him laughing boy. He seems to find it all very funny. Hello, what's happening?'

There was a commotion up ahead. The German shepherd was being held back by its handler, barking at the group with Monk. At first I couldn't see what was happening for the surrounding uniforms, then two of them moved aside. Monk had fallen. The big man was down in the muddy grass, struggling to get up. Police officers and the prison guards swarmed round him, unsure whether to haul him to his feet or not.

'. . . get off me!' He was clumsily trying to lever himself up in his handcuffs as his solicitor confronted Terry.

'Now are you satisfied? This is unacceptable. There is absolutely no reason for my client to remain handcuffed out here. He doesn't pose any escape risk, and in this terrain it's positively dangerous.'

'I'm not taking them off,' Terry said, sullenly.

'In that case, take us back to the van. We're done here.'

'Oh, for—'

'I will not have my client injured because of police intransigence. Either the restraints come off or he stops cooperating with the search.'

Monk was still lying in a heap, glaring up at them. 'You want to try walking with these on?' he demanded, holding out his cuffed hands.

Terry took a step towards him, and for a second I actually thought he would launch a kick at his face. Then he stopped, his entire body clenched.

'You want me to call the SIO?' Roper asked.

If I hadn't heard him reporting back to Simms I might have believed he was trying to help. His suggestion decided Terry.

'No.' Tightlipped, he gave a nod to a police officer. 'Take them off.'

The officer stepped forward and unlocked the handcuffs. Monk's expression never changed as he climbed to his feet and flexed his wrists.

'OK?' Terry asked Dobbs. Without giving him a chance to answer he stepped up to Monk. They were of a height, but the convict seemed twice his size. 'You want to make me happy? Try something. Please.'

Monk didn't speak. His mouth was still curved in its illusory half-smile, but the black eyes were stone dead.

'I really don't think—' Dobbs began, but he was cut off by a shout.

'Here! Over here!'

Everyone looked round. Sophie was standing on a low rise some way away, waving. Her excitement was obvious.

'I've found something!'

A BURIED BODY always leaves signs. At first the body will displace the earth used to refill the grave, leaving a visible mound on the surface. But as the slow process of decay begins, the mound begins to settle. Eventually, when the body has rotted away to bone, a slight depression will be left in the earth to mark the grave's location.

Vegetation, too, can provide useful clues. As the corpse decomposes, the nutrients it releases feed the flora on the grave, causing more luxuriant foliage than in the surrounding vegetation. The distinctions are subtle, and often unreliable, but there if you know what to look for.

Sophie was standing by a low mound that lay in the centre of a deep hollow, perhaps fifty yards from the track. It was covered in marsh grass, the tangled, wiry stalks rippling in the wind. I went over with Wainwright and Terry, leaving Roper with Monk and the other officers.

'I think this could be a grave,' she said, as we slithered into the hollow.

The mound was about five feet long and two wide, perhaps eighteen inches tall at its highest point. But the grass covering the mound looked no different from that growing elsewhere in this rugged landscape.

'Doesn't look like much to me.' Terry turned doubtfully to Wainwright. 'What do you think?'

The archaeologist pursed his lips as he considered the mound. This was more his territory than mine. Or Sophie's, come to that. He prodded it disparagingly with his foot. 'I think if we're going to get overexcited about every bump in the ground, it's going to be a very long search.'

Sophie coloured up. 'I'm not overexcited. And I'm not an idiot. I know what to look for.'

'Really.' Wainwright put a wealth of meaning into the word. 'I beg to differ. But then I have only thirty years of archaeological experience to draw on.'

Terry turned away to go back. 'We don't have time to waste on this.'

'No, wait,' Sophie said. 'Look, I might not be an archaeologist, but at least hear me out. Two minutes, that's all, OK?'

Terry folded his arms, his face shuttered. 'Two minutes.'

Sophie took a deep breath. 'Where Monk's taking us now doesn't make any sense. Tina Williams's grave was exactly where I'd have expected it to be—not far from the track, relatively easy to get to. And it followed the contours of the land: anyone leaving the track round there would naturally find themselves at that point. It made *sense* for it to be where we found it.'

'So?'

'So Monk won't specify where the other graves are. He's just leading us further out into the moor, which means he'd have carried the bodies all this way across moorland, in the dark. Why would he do that? And he says he can't recall any landmarks to guide him back to where they were buried.'

Terry frowned. 'What's your point?'

'I'd expect him to remember *something* at least. When people hide something they use landmarks to align themselves, whether they realise it or not. But where Monk's heading just seems random. Either he's forgotten or he's deliberately leading us in the wrong direction.'

'Or you could just be wrong,' Wainwright said. He turned to Terry with a supercilious smile. 'I'm familiar with the Winthrop technique that Miss Keller alludes to. The army developed it in Northern Ireland to find hidden arms caches. I've used it myself on occasion, but it's mainly common sense. I find it overrated.'

'Then you're not doing it right,' Sophie shot back. 'I went back to the track to find the most likely spots where anyone carrying a body could have left it. Where the going is nice and easy, not too steep or boggy. I've found a few over the past few days, but this time I tried a little further out.'

She levelled a finger back towards the track, some distance from where we'd left it to go to Tina Williams's grave.

'There's a spot back there where the moor slopes gently away from the track. It's a natural point for anyone struggling with the weight of a body to access the moor. The way the ground runs funnels you past that big patch of gorse and into the gulley that brings you here. To a concealed hollow, where there just happens to be a grave-sized mound of earth.'

She folded her arms, defying them to find a hole in her argument.

'This is nonsense,' Wainwright blustered, no longer bothering to hide his animosity. 'It's wishful thinking, not science!'

'No, just common sense, like you said,' Sophie retorted. 'I prefer it to pig-headedness.'

Wainwright drew himself up to respond but I beat him to it. 'There's no point standing here arguing. Let the cadaver dog check it out. If it finds something, we open it up. If it doesn't, we've only wasted a few minutes.'

Sophie flashed me a smile.

Terry sighed and strode up to the top of the hollow. 'Get over here!' he shouted at Roper and the rest, then turned to Sophie. 'I want a word.'

The two of them moved out of earshot. I couldn't hear what was being said, but it seemed heated. Meanwhile, Wainwright prowled round the mound, testing it with his feet.

'Definitely softer,' he muttered. He was wearing a thick leather work belt, the sort used by builders to hold tools. He took a thin metal rod from it and began opening it out. It was a lightweight probe, a metre-long extendable tube with a point at one end.

Sophie and Terry broke off their discussion as Roper and the others reached us. Terry went straight to Monk and his solicitor, who were standing on the edge of the hollow so they could see the mound.

'This ring any bells?'

Monk stared down at it. His mouth still seemed twisted in a mocking smile but I thought there was a wariness in his eyes now.

'No.'

'So this isn't one of the graves?'

'I told you, they're over there.'

'You seem pretty sure all of a sudden. Not long ago you said you couldn't remember.'

Sophie spoke before Monk could react. 'Excuse me, Jerome?'

She smiled as the big head snapped round. This time Terry made no attempt to interrupt, and I guessed her involvement was what at least part of their discussion had been about.

'Nobody's doubting you. But I just want you to think about something. You must have dug the graves out here at night, is that right?'

Monk's button eyes fixed on Sophie. After a few seconds he jerked his head in a nod. 'It's always night.'

I wasn't sure what that meant. Judging by Sophie's slight pause neither did she, but she covered it well.

'Things get confused in the dark. It's easy to make mistakes. Is it possible you could have dug at least one of the graves here?'

Monk's eyes went from Sophie to the mound. 'Might be . . .'

He rubbed a hand over his bald scalp. For an instant he seemed confused. Then Terry spoke, and whatever I thought I'd seen was gone.

'I don't have time for this. Which is it, yes or no?'

Suddenly the heat and madness were back in the convict's eyes. The curved smile looked manic as he faced Terry. 'No.'

'Wait, Jerome, are you—?' Sophie began, but she'd had her chance.

'Right, that's it. Let's get back over there.' Terry started to leave the hollow.

'But the dog's here now,' Sophie protested. 'At least give it a chance.'

Terry paused, indecision on his face. I think he might have overruled her if it hadn't been for Wainwright, who had been probing the mound while the scene played out. There was a *crunch* as the probe hit something.

The archaeologist stopped dead. He composed his features into a thoughtful expression. 'Well, there seems to be something here.'

Terry went over. 'A stone?'

'No, I don't think so.' Wainwright beckoned to the dog-handler, quickly asserting control. 'Start with the hole I've just made.'

The dog-handler, a young policewoman with red hair and wind-chapped pale skin, took the springer spaniel towards the mound. The dog's ears pricked up almost immediately. Whining with excitement, it began scrabbling at Wainwright's last probe hole.

Wainwright clapped his hands together, his earlier scepticism evidently forgotten. 'Right, let's see what we've got, shall we?'

A CSI brought a holdall containing digging tools into the hollow. Wainwright unzipped it and took out a spade. If this was a grave, I could guess who'd take credit for it. There was nothing for the rest of us to do but watch as the archaeologist used the spade to lever out neat slabs of turf.

'Signs of disturbance to the peat,' he grunted. 'There's been something going on here.'

I glanced at Monk. The convict's doll-like eyes were watching without expression. The only sound was the crunch of the spade as Wainwright began sinking the trench deeper. Suddenly he stopped.

'Pass me a trowel.'

Everyone's attention was fixed on the archaeologist as he took the trowel and squatted down to scrape peat off whatever he'd found.

'What is it?' Terry asked.

Wainwright frowned, peering closer. 'I'm not sure. I think it might be . . .'

'It's bone,' I said.

Something smooth and pale was visible in the dark mulch. There wasn't much showing, but I'd cut my teeth differentiating between bone and stone.

'Human?' Sophie asked.

'I can't see enough to say yet.'

'Certainly bone, though,' Wainwright said, his voice betraying his displeasure at my interruption.

The scratch of the trowel filled the hollow as he began digging away at the surrounding peat. Sophie hugged herself anxiously. Terry stood with his shoulders bunched, hands jammed deep in his pockets as though to brace himself. Monk seemed unconcerned. He wasn't even bothering to watch, I saw, big head twisted to look back over the moor behind him.

Then Wainwright spoke again. 'There's some sort of fabric here. Clothing, perhaps. No, wait, I think it . . .' He bent closer, obscuring whatever he'd found. Abruptly, the tension seemed to leave him. 'It's fur.'

'Fur?' Terry hurried forward to see for himself.

Wainwright was gouging the peat away with savage strokes. 'Yes, fur!' He tugged a paw free of the ooze, then let it drop. 'A badger. Congratulations, Miss Keller. You've Winthropped your way to an old badger sett.'

Sophie had no response. She looked as though she wanted to crawl into the hole herself as everyone moved closer for a better look. The badger was badly mangled, broken bones visible through the bristles.

'We had to make sure,' I said. 'It could have been a grave.'

Wainwright gave a wintry smile. 'Neither Miss Keller nor you are forensic archaeologists, Dr Hunter. Perhaps in future you'll—'

I didn't see what happened next, only heard the sudden commotion. Someone cried out behind us and I looked round to see both prison guards and a policeman on the ground.

Beyond them, Monk was running from the hollow. He'd waited for his moment, when everyone's attention was distracted. The convict didn't so much as pause as another officer lunged for him. He charged right through the man, who was knocked aside as though he'd been hit by a bull.

'Get after him!' Terry yelled, breaking into a sprint.

Brute force and surprise had given Monk a few yards' lead. The air rang with curses as heavy boots pounded after him. Then he jinked and changed direction, and suddenly the men who'd been about to catch him found themselves splashing through a grassy bog. Within seconds they were floundering to a halt.

Monk barely slowed. The clumsiness that had led to his handcuffs being removed had vanished. He ran without hesitation, finding solid ground that looked indistinguishable from the bog around it. I realised now why he'd been looking back at the moor instead of watching Wainwright. He'd been planning his route.

'Use the dog!' Terry shouted, trying to detour round the mire.

As soon as the handler had released it, the German shepherd streaked over the moor towards Monk, closing the distance between them. I saw Monk glance back at it, losing yet more ground as he slowed to shuck out of his coat. *What the hell is he doing?*

A moment later I understood: as the dog caught up he spun round, thrusting out a forearm wrapped in the coat. The animal leapt up at him, its jaws clamping on to the thick padding. Bracing himself, Monk slapped his other hand onto the back of its neck and heaved. A shrill yelp was suddenly cut off, then Monk flung the dog's limp body aside and carried on running.

The stunned silence was broken by a cry as the German shepherd's handler began sprinting towards the dog's unmoving form.

'Jesus Christ!' Roper breathed. He scrabbled for his radio. 'Get the chopper in the air! Don't ask questions, just *do it*!'

Monk was hammering across the uneven moorland as easily as if he were in a park. Most of the police were still struggling through the bog, but Terry had managed to bypass the worst of it. And the dog had cost Monk his lead. I felt my breath quicken as I saw that Terry was going to catch him.

Sophie's hands had gone to her mouth. 'He's going to get killed!'

She was right. Terry could handle himself against most men, but we'd just seen Monk snap the neck of a police dog.

But so had Terry. He launched himself at the convict's legs in a rugby tackle, and Monk crashed to the ground. It didn't even seem to wind him. He twisted round and began clubbing wildly at the man clinging to his legs. Terry ducked his head into his shoulders and held on. Then one of the punches connected, and Terry jerked and let go. Monk kicked himself free and scrambled to his knees, but that was as far as he got before a mud-spattered policeman rammed into him, bowling him away from where Terry sprawled on the ground. Another launched himself onto them, and then uniforms were swarming over the convict like ants over a wasp.

Batons rose and fell as Monk lashed out, knocking his attackers away. But sheer weight of numbers carried him to the ground. Face down, he struggled to rise as his arms were wrenched behind his back. Before he could free himself, he'd been handcuffed and it was over.

After the police had fastened restraints round Monk's ankles, they stood back while he thrashed on the ground, raging and helpless.

Terry was on his hands and knees, still dazed. As we watched he shrugged off the attempts to help him and stood up by himself. We were too far away to hear what he said, but he must have made some quip. A burst of laughter came from the men round him, raucous and slightly hysterical.

Sophie sagged against me. 'Oh, God.'

I put my arm round her automatically. Both prison guards and the policeman Monk had knocked down to escape were back on their feet. The older guard had blood smeared down his face from a broken nose, but he was able to walk. Of the police officers round Monk, there wasn't one who wasn't bleeding or nursing some injury. Terry himself had a grazed lump the size of an egg on his forehead, but wasn't badly hurt. He seemed pumped up by what had happened, adrenaline giving him a manic edge.

'Nice one,' Roper said, slapping him on the back. 'How's the head?'

Terry gingerly touched the bump. 'I'll survive.' He grinned at Sophie. 'Doesn't spoil my good looks, does it?'

'Anything's an improvement,' she said coolly.

Wainwright strode up to where Monk lay trussed in the grass and heather. The convict's chest was heaving, and his face and mouth were slick with blood. He'd stopped struggling, except for jerking against the restraints on his legs and wrists from time to time, testing them.

Fists planted on his hips, Wainwright glared down at him. 'My God, to think society wastes money keeping animals like this alive!'

Monk stilled. He twisted his head to stare up at the archaeologist. There was neither fear nor anger in his eyes, only cold appraisal.

'Oh, leave him alone,' Sophie said. 'You're not impressing anybody.'

'Neither are you,' Wainwright shot back. 'And after your display back there you'll be lucky to find another police force willing to hire you again.'

'That's enough,' Terry said, coming over. The energy that had buoyed him moments ago seemed to have gone. 'We're finished here. We'll wait for the helicopter but the rest of you might as well go back.'

Sophie and I began making our way back to the track. She didn't say anything but I saw her angrily brush the tears from her eyes.

'Don't take any notice of Wainwright,' I said. 'It wasn't your fault. It could have been a grave. We had to check it out.'

Something flickered at the edge of my mind as I spoke, but I couldn't quite pull it into view. I let it go, concentrating on Sophie.

She gave a bleak smile. 'I'm sure Simms will see it that way. God, I made a real fool of myself, didn't I? Offering to help Monk remember, so sure I knew what was going on. And he was playing us. He only said he'd show us where the graves were so he could try to escape.'

'You weren't to know that.'

She wasn't listening. 'I just don't *understand* it. How far did he think he was going to get out here? Where did he think he could go?'

'I don't know,' I said. 'He probably wasn't thinking at all. He could have been just making it up as he went along.'

'I don't believe that.' Sophie looked troubled. She pushed a strand of hair from her face. 'Nobody does anything without a reason.'

SPRING CAME and went. Summer moved into autumn, then winter. Christmas approached. Alice had another birthday, started ballet classes and caught chicken pox. Kara, who worked part-time as a radiologist, was promoted and given a small wage rise. To celebrate, we spent the money in advance on a new car, a Volvo estate. Something nice and safe. I flew to the Balkans to work on a mass grave and came down with flu. Life went on.

And the abortive search for Jerome Monk's missing victims receded further into the past. Simms managed to keep the story of the failed escape out of the press. The operation continued afterwards, but the heart had been taken out of it, and after a few days the search was called off. Wherever Lindsey and Zoe Bennett were buried, they were going to stay there.

I hadn't been sorry to leave. The only thing I regretted was that I didn't get a chance to say goodbye to Sophie. She went before I did, still berating herself over what had happened. I hoped she'd get over it. Incidents like that had a habit of following you around, particularly if the SIO was looking for someone to blame. But Simms had another scapegoat in mind.

I only spoke to Terry once before I left. It was on my last morning, and I was loading my bags into the car outside the Trencherman's Arms when his yellow Mitsubishi pulled alongside. Terry climbed out. He seemed tired.

'You look rough,' I said. 'How did it go with Simms?'

'Well, he's not about to put me up for a commendation, that's for sure.'

'He's blaming you?'

'Of course he is. You don't think he'd take any flak himself, do you?'

'But he's SIO. It was his responsibility.'

'Simms will hang me out to dry if it takes some heat off him.' He gave a bleak laugh, and made an unconvincing effort to shrug it off. 'Look, I didn't get much sleep, that's all. Is Sophie around?'

'She left last night.'

'Last *night*? Why the hell didn't I know about it?'

'I didn't see her go either. I don't think she wanted to hang around. She feels pretty bad about what happened.'

'Yeah, she's not the only one.'

'It wasn't her fault. In her position I'd have probably done the same.'

Terry looked at me; there was no friendliness in it. 'How come you're standing up for her? The whole operation's gone pear-shaped and my neck's on the block, but you're more concerned with looking out for Sophie bloody Keller. Still, I noticed the two of you were getting pretty friendly.'

'What's that supposed to mean?'

'It means—' He stopped himself. 'Forget it. Look, I've got to go. Say hello to Kara.'

He went back to his car and accelerated away so quickly that gravel sprayed over my legs. I stood there for a while, angry and bewildered.

But I didn't worry about it for long. There was too much else going on in my own life to dwell on Terry. Alice seemed to be growing up more every time I turned my back, and Kara and I began talking about giving her a brother or sister. Professionally, I was busier than ever. Then came the mass grave in Bosnia. I went as part of an international team charged with exhuming and, where possible, identifying the victims. It was a gruelling, month-long trip, and I'd never been so glad to be home.

At first I put Kara's quietness down to giving me space to adjust. It was only as we sat with a bottle of wine after dinner on my first night back that I realised it was more than that.

'OK, are you going to tell me what's wrong?' I asked.

She'd been staring into space for several minutes. It wasn't like her. 'Hmm? Oh, sorry, I was miles away.' She smiled. 'Come on, let's clear the dishes.'

'Kara . . .'

She set down the plates with a sigh. 'Promise you won't do anything.'

'Why, what's happened?'

'Terry Connors called round a few nights ago.'

I hadn't seen or spoken to him since Dartmoor. 'Terry? What for?'

'He said he was in London and thought he'd drop round to see you, but . . . Well, I got the impression he already knew you were away.'

I felt something cold spread through me. 'Go on.'

'There was just something . . . *off* about him coming round like that, without phoning first to make sure you were in. I could smell he'd been drinking. I made him a coffee but he made me feel . . . uncomfortable.'

'How do you mean, uncomfortable? What did he do?'

Kara's face had flushed. 'He didn't *do* anything. It was the way he acted. I told him he should leave but . . . Well, he asked if I was sure that's what I wanted. He said . . . he said I didn't know what you got up to while you were away.' She picked up her wineglass, then put it down again without drinking from it. 'Alice woke up then and shouted downstairs, asking if you were back. I was actually *relieved*. It seemed to shake him up, and he left.'

'Why didn't you tell me?'

'You were knee deep in a grave in Bosnia. What good would that have done? Besides, nothing actually *happened*.'

'Jesus! He just came here and . . .'

'David, calm down.'

'Calm *down*?' I pushed my seat back, unable to keep still any longer. 'What he said about me . . . It isn't true.'

Kara stood up and came over. She touched my face. 'I know that. Terry just thinks everyone's like him.'

'How do you mean?'

'You must know what he's like. The affairs?'

'Affairs?' I repeated stupidly.

She gave me a quizzical smile. 'Seriously? You didn't realise? I don't know why Deborah's stayed with him as long as she has. I got the impression that's why Terry had to transfer out of London. He was having an affair with someone he worked with, and it turned messy.'

I put my arms round her. 'Why didn't you say anything before?'

'Because it was none of our business, and I didn't want to make things awkward. Not when you had to work with him.'

Not any more. Kara leaned back to look at my face.

'Promise me you'll just let it go. Please? He's not worth wasting time on.' She slid her hands round my lower back. 'And I really don't want to spend any more of your first night back talking about Terry Connors.'

Neither did I. So we didn't.

But I couldn't forget about it altogether. I told myself not to do anything for a few days, to give myself a chance to cool down.

I lasted until the following afternoon.

I was easing myself back into work after the Balkans trip and had arranged to finish early anyway. The plan was for me to collect Alice from school, but my fury at Terry had been festering overnight. I stewed over it for a few hours before phoning Kara at the hospital.

'Sorry about this, but can you pick Alice up later?'

'I suppose so. OK. I was only staying on for a staff meeting anyway.' Then a wariness entered her voice. 'Why, what's happened?'

'Nothing.' I began to regret calling her. 'It doesn't matter—' I was about to say 'Let's forget it', but there was a commotion in the background down the line. I heard raised voices and the banging of doors.

'Sorry, I'm needed,' she said in a rush. 'I'll collect Alice. Bye.'

She broke the connection before I could say anything. I made up my mind to call her back later and say I'd pick up Alice after all. I left it half an hour but when I tried her line it was engaged.

I phoned Terry instead.

I wasn't even sure he'd answer if he saw the call was from me. But he did. He sounded as cocksure as ever. 'David! How're you doing?'

'I want to see you.'

His hesitation was only slight. 'Look, I'd love to meet up, but things are a bit hectic right now. I'll give you a call when—'

'I can be in Exeter in a few hours. Name a place.'

He sighed. 'I can save you the trip. I'm still in London. I'll even buy you a pint.' His tone was condescending. 'It'll be just like old times.'

I willed myself not to lose my temper as I went to meet him. He'd suggested a pub in Soho, and when I walked in I saw why. It was obviously a police watering hole: most of the clientele had the indefinable swagger of off-duty officers. Terry was at the bar, laughing with a group of men.

He excused himself when I went in. The usual smile was on his face, but his eyes were watchful. 'Want a drink?'

'No thanks.'

'Please yourself.' Glass in hand, he propped himself comfortably against a table. 'So. Where's the fire?'

'Stay away from Kara. I don't want you at my home again.'

He was still smiling, but a flush spread up from his neck. 'Whoa, hang on a minute. I didn't know you were away—'

'Yes, you did. The mass grave was all over the news; it didn't take a genius to work out I'd be over there. That's why you didn't phone first, because then you wouldn't have an excuse to go round.'

'Look—'

'You even tried to make her think I'd been seeing somebody else. Why the hell would you do that?'

I thought something that could have been either guilt or regret showed in his eyes, but it was gone so quickly I might have imagined it.

He shrugged. 'Kara's a good-looker. You should be flattered.'

His grin was mocking. *Easy. Don't let him bait you.* If I lost control he could wipe the floor with me and still have a pub full of witnesses to vouch that I'd started it. I didn't know what I'd done to him, but I no longer cared. And realising that I also realised something else.

'Things not going so well, Terry?'

His eyes narrowed. 'What're you talking about?'

'That's why you're here, isn't it?' I nodded round the pub. 'Recapturing the glory days. Your reputation must have taken a knock after what happened with Monk.'

The smile had gone. 'I'm doing fine. Just having a few days off.'

But his eyes gave the lie to that. There had always been something reckless about Terry. He relied on luck and momentum to carry him through: both had let him down and now he was lashing out in frustration.

There was no point in staying any longer. Kara had been right: confronting him had accomplished nothing. I walked out.

I went straight home, half expecting Kara and Alice to be home before me. They weren't, so I began preparing dinner. I berated myself for going to see Terry, and for making Kara do the school run. I resolved to make it up to them both. I'd take them somewhere that weekend, perhaps the zoo for Alice, and then find a babysitter so Kara and I could go out in the evening.

I was so busy planning it that it was a while before I realised how late they were. I called Kara's mobile but there was no answer. Her voicemail didn't cut in, which was unusual. But I didn't have time to worry about it before the doorbell rang.

'If this is somebody cold-calling . . .' I muttered as I went to answer it.

But it wasn't. Two police officers stood outside. They'd come to tell me that a businessman drunk from an expense-account lunch had lost control of his BMW and hit Kara and Alice's car. It had shunted it in front of a container lorry that had crushed the new Volvo's frame like balsa. My wife and daughter had died at the scene.

And as quickly as that, my old life ended.

4

The Present

I'd just come out of the shower. I swore and grabbed my bathrobe, wondering who would be calling at nine o'clock on a Sunday morning.

The pewter sky cast a cold light when I opened the door. The lime trees lining the road outside my flat had shed most of their leaves, covering the street with a whispering mat of yellow. Although the October morning was cold and damp, the visitor wore a suit without any sort of coat. He turned and gave a thin smile, eyes taking in my bathrobe.

'Hello, David. Not disturbing you, am I?'

What struck me afterwards was how ordinary it felt. It was as though we'd seen each other a few weeks ago, not the eight years it had been.

Terry Connors hadn't changed. Older, yes: the hairline was higher than it used to be, and there were lines round his eyes that hadn't been there before. But while the good looks were more weathered, they were still intact. So was the cockiness that was part and parcel of them. I saw his eyes flick over me, no doubt taking in changes just as mine were doing. I wondered how different I must look myself after all this time.

It was only then that the shock of seeing him hit home. I had no idea what to say. He glanced back down the street as if it led to the past that lay behind us. I noticed that his short dark hair was thinning at the crown, exposing a palm-sized patch of scalp.

'Sorry for turning up unannounced, but I didn't think you should hear it on the news.' He turned back to me. 'Jerome Monk's escaped.'

I was silent for a moment as echoes of the bleak Dartmoor landscape came back to me. Then I stepped back. 'You'd better come in.'

Terry waited in the sitting room while I went to get dressed. I didn't rush. I stood in the bedroom, my breathing fast and shallow, my fists clenched into tight balls. *Calm down. Hear what he has to say.* I pulled my clothes on automatically, fumbling at the buttons, then went back out.

He was standing by the bookshelf with his back to me, head canted at an angle so he could read the spines. He spoke without turning round.

'Nice place you've got here. Live by yourself?'

'Yes.'

He pulled a book from the shelf and read the title. '*Death's Acre*. Not much for light reading, are you?'

'I don't get much time.' I clamped down on my irritation. Terry always had a knack of getting under my skin. 'Can I get you a tea or coffee?'

'I'll have a coffee so long as it's not decaf. Black, two sugars.' He replaced the book and followed me to the kitchen. 'You don't seem very concerned about Monk. Don't you want to know what happened?'

'It can wait till I've made the coffee.' I could feel his gaze on me as I put the percolator on the heat. 'How's Deborah?'

'Thriving since the divorce.'

'I'm sorry.'

'Don't be. She wasn't. At least the kids were old enough to decide who they wanted to live with. I get to see them every other weekend.'

There wasn't much I could say. 'Are you still in Exeter?'

'Yeah, still at HQ.'

'Detective Superintendent yet?'

'No. Still a DI.' He said it as though daring me to comment.

'The coffee'll be a few minutes,' I said. 'We might as well sit down.'

He took a seat opposite me at the kitchen table. I'd forgotten what a big man he was. He'd obviously kept himself fit. *The bald spot must kill him.*

The silence built between us. I knew what was coming next.

'Lot of water under the bridge.' He was looking at me with an undecipherable expression. 'I always meant to get in touch. After what happened to Kara and Alice.'

I just nodded. I'd been waiting for the inevitable condolences, in the same way you tense yourself against a blow. I hoped he'd leave it at that, duty done. But he wasn't finished.

'I was going to write or something, but you know how it is. Then later I heard you'd moved, packed in forensics to be a GP in some Norfolk backwater. So there didn't seem to be much point any more.'

There wouldn't have been. Back then I hadn't wanted to see anyone from my old life. Especially Terry.

'Glad you're back in the traces now, anyway,' he went on, when I didn't say anything. 'Back at the university forensic department, aren't you?'

'For the time being.' I didn't want to talk about it. Not to him. 'When did Monk escape?'

'Last night. Bloody press is going to have a field day.'

'What happened?'

'He had a heart attack.' He gave a humourless grin. 'Wouldn't think a bastard like that had one, would you? But he managed to convince the doctors at Belmarsh to transfer him to a civilian hospital. Halfway there he broke his restraints, beat the shit out of the guards and disappeared.'

'So it was staged?'

Terry shrugged. 'Nobody knows yet. He had all the symptoms. Blood pressure sky high, erratic heartbeat, the works. So either he faked them somehow, or it was real and he escaped anyway.'

Ordinarily, I'd have said both were impossible. A high-security prison like Belmarsh would have a well-equipped hospital wing. Any prisoner displaying cardiac symptoms bad enough to be considered an emergency wouldn't be in any condition to escape: the attempt alone would probably kill them. But this was no ordinary person. This was Jerome Monk.

The percolator had started to bubble. Glad of something to do, I got up and poured coffee into two mugs. 'I thought Monk was at Dartmoor.'

'He was, until the bleeding hearts decided Dartmoor was too "inhumane" and downgraded it to a Category C a few years ago. He was shuffled round to a couple of other maximum-security prisons before Belmarsh drew the short straw. Hasn't mellowed him, by all accounts. He beat another inmate to death a few months back, and put two wardens in hospital when they tried to pull him off. Surprised you didn't hear about it.'

I spooned sugar into one of the mugs and handed it to him. 'Why are you telling me all this?'

Terry took the coffee without thanks. 'Just a precaution. We're warning everyone Monk might have a grudge against.'

'And you think that applies to me? I doubt he remembers who I am.'

'Let's hope you're right. But I wouldn't like to predict what Monk will do now he's escaped. You know as well as I do what he's capable of.'

There was no denying that. I'd examined one of his victims myself. Even so, I still couldn't see that I was in any danger.

'We're talking about something that happened eight years ago,' I said. 'It isn't as if I had anything to do with Monk's conviction.'

'You were still part of the police team, and Monk's not one to discriminate. Or forgive. And you were there at the end, when everything went pear-shaped. You can't have forgotten *that*.'

I hadn't. But I hadn't thought about it in a long time, either. 'Thanks for the warning. I'll bear it in mind.'

'You should.' He took a careful sip from the mug before lowering it. 'You keep in touch with any of the others?'

It seemed an innocuous question, but I knew him better than that. 'No.'

'No? How about Sophie Keller? Ever see anything of her?'

'No. Why should I?'

Terry blew on his coffee to cool it. 'Oh, no reason.'

I was growing tired of this. 'Tell me why you really came here.'

His face had grown red. 'I told you, we're notifying everyone—'

'I'm not an idiot, Terry. You could have phoned, or got someone else to phone. Why come all the way to London to tell me yourself?'

He fixed me with the cold-eyed stare of a professional policeman. 'I had some other business to attend to in town. I thought I'd stop by and give you the news myself. For old times' sake. My mistake.' His chair scraped as he stood up. 'Thanks for the coffee. I'll see myself out.'

He strode to the hallway, then stopped and turned. His mouth was a bitter line as he glared at me. 'I thought you might have changed. I should have known better.' He walked out without a backward glance.

I collected the mugs and poured the undrunk coffee into the sink. I didn't know why Terry had really come to see me, but the years hadn't changed one thing. I still didn't trust him.

MONK'S ESCAPE was the main story on the lunchtime news. An audacious prison escape by a notorious killer would have made headlines no matter who it was. When it was Jerome Monk it was guaranteed.

The story was on the radio as I drove into the lab. I listened to the headlines, then switched it off. I was sorry Monk was free, and sorry he'd hurt more people in the process. But Jerome Monk wasn't my problem. Eight years was a long time, too long for him to care about me. Or me about him.

Still, I couldn't shrug off Terry's visit as easily as that. I was long past apportioning blame for what had happened, but seeing him again had dredged up painful memories. I'd been looking forward to a leisurely Sunday, meeting two colleagues and their wives for lunch in Henley-on-Thames. But Terry's reappearance had changed all that. Knowing I wouldn't be very good company, I'd called and made my excuses. I needed time by myself to come to terms with what had happened, to pack my memories back in their box.

I needed to work.

The past blew round me like a cold wind as I pulled into the Forensic Sciences car park. The building was closed on Sundays, but I often came in to work. I had my own keys, and I was used to being there alone. The forensic anthropology department was in the basement of a former Victorian hospital, and the stairwell still had the original stone steps. My footsteps rang as I descended, their echo emphasising the weekend quiet.

Once through the doors at the bottom, though, I was back in the twenty-first century. There were several labs, all of them modern and well equipped, and my office was attached to one at the far end of the corridor. I unlocked it and flicked on the lights. Before pulling on my white lab coat, I switched on the computer. It chimed as it started up.

I sighed and gave in to the inevitable. *OK, just get it out of the way. Then you can forget about it and do some work.* I sat down and went online to a news website. Jerome Monk's photograph stared from the screen like a still from a horror film. I scrolled down the screen to the photographs of his four victims. They seemed frozen in time. The Bennett sisters would be twenty-six or twenty-seven by now, and Tina Williams twenty-eight or nine. Angela

Carson would be about thirty-five. Old enough to be married, to have children of their own. Instead their lives had been cut brutally short.

And now their killer was free.

I started scrolling back to the story and jumped as my phone rang.

I grabbed the receiver. 'Hello?'

There was a slight pause on the other end. 'Is that David? David Hunter?'

It was a woman's voice, strong and slightly husky, though now with an edge of uncertainty. There was something familiar about it.

'Yes. Who's this?'

'Sophie Keller?' she said, and another part of the past clicked into place. 'We worked together a few years ago. On the Jerome Monk case?'

She phrased it as a question, as though unsure I'd know who she was.

'Sure, of course.' I made an effort to gather myself. 'Sorry, it's just weird timing. I was just reading about Monk.'

'You've heard that he's escaped?'

'Yes, I have.' I wasn't sure whether to mention Terry, so I didn't. The two of them had never got on.

There was an embarrassed pause. 'I got your office number from the university website, but I only called to leave a message. I didn't think you'd be there on a Sunday.' I heard her take a breath. 'I know this is really out of the blue, but . . . well, could we meet some time?'

'Is this because of Monk?'

'I'd rather tell you when I see you. I promise I won't take up much of your time.' She tried to disguise it, but I could hear the tension in her voice.

'That's OK. Are you still in London?'

'No. I'm living on Dartmoor now. A little village called Padbury.'

That surprised me. Sophie had never seemed the rural type, although I remembered she'd said how much she liked the moor.

'You made it out there, then.'

'I suppose so.' She sounded distracted. 'Look, I know it's asking a lot, but if you could spare me a couple of hours I'd really appreciate it. Please?'

There was no mistaking the anxiety in her voice. This sounded a far cry from the confident young woman I remembered.

I told myself not to get involved in a cold case, that digging up the past would be painful and pointless. But now that Monk had escaped, the case wasn't really cold any more. Suddenly it felt like unfinished business.

'How about tomorrow?' I heard myself say.

Her relief was evident, even down the line. 'Great! If you're sure . . .'

'I'll be glad of an excuse to get out of London.'

'Do you remember the Trencherman's Arms in Oldwich?'

The name brought back another blast of memory, not all of it good. 'I remember. Is the food any better than it was?'

She laughed. I'd forgotten what a good laugh she had, unself-conscious and full-throated. It didn't last long. 'A little. But it's easier than directing you to where I live. Can you make it in time for lunch?'

I said I could. We arranged to meet at one o'clock and exchanged mobile numbers. 'Thanks again, David. I do appreciate this,' Sophie said before she rang off. She didn't sound grateful, though. She sounded desperate.

I lowered the phone thoughtfully. Whatever she wanted to see me about, I doubted it was an accident that it coincided with Monk's escape. And it had to be something serious for her to get in touch after all this time. The Sophie I'd known hadn't seemed prone to panicking.

Still, eight years was a long time. People changed. I found myself wondering if she'd altered, if she still looked the same. If she was married.

You can cut that out, I told myself, but I smiled all the same.

A FEW WISPS of purple still clung to the heather, but autumn had already leached the colour from the windblasted landscape. The bracken was dying off, leaving nothing to break the monotony but house-sized rocks and clumps of impenetrable gorse. I felt the past thicken round me.

I'd made good time from London, except for a traffic jam on the M5. It was the first time in years I'd been this far west, but I found myself recalling the route. When I reached the moor itself, it was like driving back in time.

Soon the road curved away, and in the distance I could make out the rocky jumble of Black Tor. I slowed for a better look. Even though I'd been expecting it, the sight brought back the chill mists and snap of police tape vibrating in the wind. Shaking off the memories, I drove on to meet Sophie.

Oldwich was an odd place, apparently undecided as to whether it was a town or a village, and still as drab and unprepossessing as I recalled. The last time I'd been to the Trencherman's Arms it had looked dilapidated and depressing; now the roof had been rethatched and the walls were freshly whitewashed. At least some things had changed for the better.

I felt oddly nervous as I pulled into the car park and turned off the engine. I told myself there was no need, and made my way to the entrance.

The doorway was low, and I had to stoop. Inside the pub was dark, but as my eyes adjusted I saw it wasn't just the thatched roof that was new. The stone flags were a big improvement on the sticky carpet I remembered, and the flock wallpaper had been replaced with cleanly painted plaster.

It took only a moment to see that Sophie wasn't there, but then I was early. *Relax, she's probably on her way.*

A cheerful, plump woman was behind the bar. I guessed the sullen landlord had gone the same way as the flock wallpaper. I ordered a coffee and went to one of the stripped-pine tables.

I took a drink of coffee and wondered yet again what Sophie might want. It had to be connected to Monk's escape somehow, but for the life of me I couldn't see how. Or why she'd contacted me after all this time.

My coffee had gone cold. I looked at my watch and frowned: it was nearly half past one. After the way she'd sounded the day before I wouldn't have expected her to be late. Perhaps she'd been held up, I told myself, or perhaps one of us had got the time wrong.

I gave it another quarter of an hour before calling Sophie's mobile. I listened to the clicks of connection, then I heard her voice: *Hi, you've reached Sophie. Please leave a message*. I asked her to call me and hung up.

Two o'clock came and went with no sign of her. Even if she'd been held up, I would have expected to hear something by now. There seemed little point in waiting any longer. Grabbing my coat, I went out.

Now what?

I'd no idea. I'd driven over two hundred miles for a woman I hadn't seen in eight years, and been stood up for my trouble. I tried to convince myself there was a mundane explanation, but I couldn't quite believe it. Sophie had sounded desperate to see me. Something was wrong.

I went back to my car and took my road atlas from the boot. Sophie had said she lived in a village called Padbury, which the map showed was several miles away. I didn't have her address, but it couldn't be that big. I'd just have to ask around until I found somebody who knew her.

Padbury was well signposted, but each marker seemed to direct me further away from civilisation. The roads grew narrower, until I found myself on a single-lane track, hemmed in by high hedgerows. Within another mile or two, the hedgerows gave way to thickets of stunted oak, which seemed to soak up what was left of the daylight. It was only midafternoon but I had to switch on my headlights. I began to wonder if I could somehow have missed Padbury after all, and then I rounded a bend and found myself in it.

And out of it again, just as quickly. It was more a hamlet than a village. I carried on until the road was wide enough to turn round, then drove back. I'd hoped for a pub or post office where I might find someone who knew where Sophie lived, but other than a few cottages there was only a small church, set back from the road. I pulled up outside and got out of the car.

Ancient gravestones flanked the path. The church door was wooden, black with age and hard as iron. It was also locked.

'Can I help you?'

The accent was pure Devon. I turned to find an elderly woman standing by the church gate. She wore a quilted jacket and tweed skirt, and an expression that was as watchful as it was polite.

'I'm looking for Sophie Keller. I think she lives in the village?'

She pondered, slowly shaking her head. 'No, I don't think so.' Her face brightened. 'There's a Sophie Trask, though. Have you got the right name?'

It was possible that Sophie could have changed it—or married—since I'd last seen her, though she'd made no mention of it. I agreed that I might have made a mistake and asked for directions.

'You can't miss it,' the woman called after me as I got back in the car. 'Watch out for the kiln.'

I realised what she meant soon enough. I followed the road out of the village, passing the point where I'd turned round earlier, and saw the curving shape through the bare trees. It was a squat, inverted cone, built of the same rusty-coloured bricks as the house it stood next to. When I drew closer I saw that it looked on the verge of collapse. A rickety framework of scaffolding clung to one side, either to repair it or prop it up.

I pulled onto the verge in front of the garden fence. The dusk was thickening, but the house windows were unlit. A neat sign was fixed to one of the wooden gateposts: *Trask Ceramics*.

I almost drove away when I saw that. This had to be someone else. Yet Sophie had said she lived in Padbury. *You've come this far . . .*

A vague sense of trespassing mingled with embarrassment as I walked up the stone-flagged path. A small orchard of scrubby apple trees grew at one side. There was no sign of life from the house. If someone was in, I would simply make my apologies; if not . . . Well, first things first. I reached out to knock on the door.

And saw the freshly splintered wood where the lock had been forced.

All the doubts I'd had seemed to congeal in that second. I looked around, half expecting to see someone behind me. But there was only the dark path, and the whispering branches of the trees.

The door creaked as I pushed it open with my fingertips. It swung back to reveal a darkened hallway.

'Anyone home?'

The silence was deafening. If I went inside I could be laying myself open to all sorts of trouble, but I had no choice. I knew that if I called the police I'd be told to wait outside until a car arrived. That might be too late.

I quickly checked the downstairs rooms. They'd been ransacked, drawers and cupboards torn open and emptied, cushions flung off sofas and chairs. I ran upstairs. All the doors were closed, except for the bathroom. It was slightly ajar. Through the gap I could see a pair of bare legs on the floor.

I rushed forward. A woman's body lay behind the door, blocking it. I squeezed through. She was lying on her back, a towelling bathrobe fallen open. One arm was flung across her face, over a tangle of damp hair.

No blood. That was my first thought, but when I knelt beside her I saw that one side of her face was swollen in a livid purple bruise. But even with that, and the passage of eight years, I still recognised Sophie Keller.

I felt her throat. Her skin was cold but the pulse was steady. *Thank God.* I eased her into the recovery position, gently pulling back the bathrobe to cover her. There was no mobile reception, so I ran back down to the phone I'd seen in the kitchen and called emergency.

Hurrying back upstairs, I covered Sophie with a quilt from the bedroom. Then, sitting next to her, I took her hand and waited for the ambulance.

5

It took nearly forty minutes for the paramedics to arrive. All that time I'd sat on the bathroom floor with Sophie, talking to her constantly to reassure her that help was on the way. I'd no idea if she could even hear me, but if she was aware on some level there was a chance.

The paramedics couldn't tell me much. There was no knowing how serious the head trauma was, or if she had any other internal injuries. The police arrived as the ambulance crew were bringing her down the stairs. The blackness of the country night was broken by flashing lights, giving the bare trees in the adjoining orchard an eerie, spectral hue.

I had to stay behind to give my statement. I stood by helplessly as the ambulance drove away, answering the flat-voiced questions of a policewoman. I'd no way of knowing if this had anything to do with Jerome Monk, but I decided to tell the police everything. The policewoman's interest pricked up on hearing Monk's name, and so did her questions. Finally, frustrated with repeating, 'I don't know,' I gave in to the inevitable.

'You need to call DI Terry Connors,' I told her.

I was loath to bring him into this, but I hadn't much choice.

I sat in the back of the police car with the policewoman's partner while she made the call. Finally, she came back. 'OK, you can go.'

It wasn't what I'd expected. 'Doesn't he want to speak to me?'

'We've got your statement. Somebody'll be in touch.' She gave me a smile that wasn't unfriendly. 'I hope your friend's all right.'

So did I.

The ambulance was taking Sophie to hospital in Exeter. As I drove there myself I tried not to dwell on the fact that the last time I'd been on this route, eight years before, I'd been going to the mortuary.

The receptionist behind the Emergency desk frowned as she stared at her computer screen after I gave her Sophie's name.

'No one called that's been admitted tonight,' she said.

I realised my mistake. 'Sorry. Try Sophie Trask.'

She gave me an odd look but tapped at her keyboard. 'She was admitted to intensive care about an hour ago.'

'Can I find out how she is?'

'Are you a family member?'

'No, just a friend.'

'We're not allowed to give out that information unless you're the partner or a relative.'

I sighed, trying not to snap. 'I only want to know if she's all right.'

'I'm sorry. Perhaps if you phone tomorrow morning . . .'

Frustrated, I went back outside and returned to my car. *Now what?*

There was no point in staying here. I hadn't packed for an overnight trip, and if anything happened I'd find out as quickly at home as anywhere else. I started the car engine and began the long drive back to London. The roads were quiet and I made good time to start with, but then the rain increased into a deluge that hazed the road with spray, smearing the windscreen like Vaseline despite the furious efforts of the wipers.

When I finally parked outside my flat, it was after midnight and the rain had eased. I unlocked the door and bent to retrieve the usual assortment of bills and fliers. As I straightened, I felt a sudden sensation of being watched.

I quickly turned round, but the dark street was empty. I realised I was holding my breath, waiting for something to shatter the quiet, and forced myself to relax. *You're tired and imagining things. It's nothing.*

I went inside the flat, switching on lights. It seemed too quiet, as it always did. I switched on the TV and automatically flicked to a news channel, turning down the volume until it was no more than a murmur.

I wasn't tired any more. Adrenaline had washed away the fatigue, and I knew if I went to bed now I wouldn't sleep. I went to the cabinet in the sitting room and took out a bottle of bourbon. I felt I'd earned a drink. I poured myself a stiff measure and took a long swallow. Then I went out of the sitting room and opened the door at the end of the hallway. Technically it was a third bedroom, but a bed would barely have fitted inside. A lot of people have a box room, where old furniture and belongings are stored. But in this case the description was literal. The room was full of boxes.

I switched on the light. They were stacked one on top of the other, an assortment of plain cardboard and document boxes that filled the floor-to-ceiling shelves. Everyone has a past. Good or bad, it's what helps make us what we are. This was mine.

After Kara and Alice had been killed I'd tried to sever ties with everything that connected me to what I'd lost. I'd dropped friends and colleagues, sold or given away most of my belongings, but some things I couldn't bear to let go. I'd put them in storage and tried to forget about them, until I'd felt able to come back and pick up the threads of my old life. Now all that remained of it was in these boxes. Photographs, diaries, memories. Work.

I took another drink and set the glass down on a shelf. The boxes weren't in any order, but at least the document boxes were labelled.

I was dusty and sweating by the time I located the one I wanted. Carrying it into the living room, I set it on the low coffee table and opened it. The files were in alphabetical order, so it wasn't difficult to find the one containing my notes from the Monk case. Taking a long drink of bourbon, I sat down and started to read.

I GUESSED it wouldn't be good news when my doorbell rang the next morning. It had been after three before I'd finally gone to bed, having pored over my old notes on the Monk case until my eyes swam. I'd felt sure I must have overlooked something, some vital piece of information hidden among the dry pages. But they'd revealed nothing I hadn't known already. In the end all I had to show for my efforts was a tension headache and a feeling that eight years was both a lifetime and no time at all.

I'd phoned the hospital first thing to see how Sophie was, only to be told they couldn't release any information. I'd left my number anyway, then debated what to do next. Though not for long. Whatever answers there might be, I wasn't going to find them in London. I called the university to tell them I'd be taking a few days off. I was owed holiday and the department secretary had been telling me for weeks I needed a break. I'd almost finished packing when the chime of the doorbell echoed through the flat. I paused, tension knotting my stomach.

I knew who it would be.

Terry looked as though he'd hardly slept. His face was pouched and sallow, his jaw blued with stubble, and not even the mint of his chewing gum could hide the sour smell of alcohol on his breath.

'Getting to be a habit, isn't it?' he said.

I reluctantly stood back to let him in. 'Any news about Sophie?'

'Nope. No change.'

He went into the sitting room without being asked. My notes from the Monk investigation were still on the coffee table. Terry went over and picked up the top sheet.

'Been doing some homework?'

'Just going over a few notes.' I took it off him, put it in the folder and closed it. 'So what can I do for you?'

'No coffee this time?'

'Just tell me what you want, Terry.'

'I want you to tell me what happened yesterday, for a start.'

I'd been through this numerous times the night before, but I knew there was no point in arguing. I went through it again now, from Sophie's phone call to how I'd found her unconscious on the bathroom floor.

'I thought you said you hadn't kept in touch with Sophie Keller,' Terry said when I'd finished.

'I hadn't.'

'You expect me to believe she just called you out of the blue?'

'That's right.' He stared at me impassively. I sighed, annoyed. 'Look, I've no idea why she called me. Have you spoken to any of the people in the village? Friends, anyone who might know why she was attacked?'

'Are you trying to tell me how to run an investigation?'

I held my temper in check. 'No, but it seems a coincidence it happened so soon after Monk escaped. I don't mean he was the one who attacked her, but there must be some connection.'

'What makes you so sure it wasn't him?'

'Why would he have anything against Sophie? She was the only person who tried to help him. Besides, he doesn't normally leave his victims alive.'

'All right, since you don't think it was him, just remind me what you were doing at Sophie's house yourself ?'

'I've already told you.'

'Oh, that's right! Someone you haven't seen for years phones you up asking for help, so you drive two hundred miles, for *lunch*. And when she doesn't show up you track down where she lives and find her unconscious.'

'That's what happened.'

'So you say. But let's try this instead: you go to her house and force your way in. She's naked underneath her bathrobe; you get carried away. Boom. Then you panic and call it in as if you'd just found her.'

I stared at him, appalled. 'That's ridiculous!'

'Is it? The two of you always seemed pretty close on the search. I always wondered if there was something going on between you.'

I realised my fists were clenched. I opened them, fighting not to lose my temper, knowing that was what he wanted.

'Not everyone's like you, Terry.'

He gave a laugh. 'Oh, I was wondering how long it'd take.'

'If you don't believe me, ask Sophie when she wakes up.'

'If she wakes up.' That stopped me. Terry nodded. 'An injury like that, there's no knowing. Puts you in an awkward position, doesn't it?'

I couldn't believe I was hearing this. Terry took a card from his wallet and tossed it onto the coffee table.

'Anything else happens, call me. My mobile number's on there. Don't bother with the office landline; I'm never there.' He went to the hallway and paused, his expression ugly. 'Don't pretend you're any different to me, Hunter. You're no better than anyone else.'

He slammed the door hard enough to shake the walls. I went to the nearest chair and sat down. I felt stunned by Terry's hostility as much as his accusation. There was no love lost between us, but could he seriously believe that I was capable of attacking Sophie? Apparently.

Anger began to kick in again. I went to finish packing. Brooding wouldn't help, and neither would sitting around here. I almost threw Terry's card away, but at the last minute I tucked it in my wallet. Then I set the alarm on my flat, threw my bag into the car boot and drove away. If I didn't get snarled up in traffic I could be in Exeter by midafternoon.

If I was going to start digging round in the past, an archaeologist was as good a place as any to start.

BY THE TIME I arrived in Exeter, the rain was coming down in a sullen downpour. I booked into an anonymous hotel not far from the hospital. It was cheap and convenient, and had a Wi-Fi connection. Unpacking my laptop, I ordered a sandwich and set to work.

Finding Wainwright proved harder than I'd expected. I didn't have his address or phone number, and Terry had said he'd retired, so I spent a fruitless half-hour searching on the Internet before it occurred to me to try the obvious. Years before, Wainwright had told me he lived at Torbay. There was no guarantee he still did, but I typed his name into an online phone directory and there he was: *Wainwright, Prof. L.* The entry gave both phone number and address. *Genius*, I thought ruefully, massaging my stiff neck.

The phone rang for a long time before anyone answered. 'Hello, Wainwright residence?' It was a woman's voice, clipped and officious.

'Can I speak to Leonard Wainwright, please?'

There was a pause. 'Who is this?'

'My name's David Hunter. I worked with Professor Wainwright several years ago,' I added, not sure if he'd remember me.

'I don't recognise your name. Would he know you from Cambridge?'

'No, it was on a police investigation. I'm in the area, and—'

I didn't get the chance to finish. 'Oh, I *see*. I'm afraid Leonard's unavailable, but I'm his wife. I'm sure Leonard would love to see an old colleague. You must pop round. Are you free for lunch tomorrow? We usually have something light around one o'clock.'

Lunch? It was the last thing I'd expected. 'If you're sure it's no trouble . . .'

'No trouble at all. Oh, jolly good! Leonard *will* look forward to it.'

I hung up, bemused by the invitation and wondering exactly what 'unavailable' meant. The prospect of lunch with the archaeologist and his wife wasn't something I relished. Still, I'd accepted now. That left me the rest of the evening to fill. I was wondering what to do when my phone rang.

It was the hospital. Sophie was conscious.

TRAUMATIC BRAIN INJURY isn't like a broken arm. Its unpredictable nature makes any sort of prognosis difficult, but in general the longer a victim remains unconscious, the more chance there is of serious damage.

Sophie had been lucky. Although the blow to her head had left her with concussion, her skull wasn't fractured and the scans had revealed no sign of haemorrhaging or haematoma—cranial bleeds that could go undetected, only to incapacitate or kill days after the initial injury.

She'd woken up a few hours after I'd left the hospital, and it had been at her insistence that the hospital had called me. Now she was propped up in bed in a gown, her tawny hair tied back with a band. Her skull might not be fractured but her cheekbone was, and the bruising extended from temple to jaw in a startling kaleidoscope of colour.

'Thanks for coming,' she said, absently touching the plastic ID bracelet on her wrist. 'I'm not sure if I should thank you or apologise.'

'There's no need for either,' I said, as I sat down.

'Of course there is. I've put you to all this trouble, and if you hadn't found me . . .'

'But I did. And you haven't put me to any trouble.'

She gave me a wry look. 'Yeah, right.'

I smiled, still relieved that she was all right. 'How are you feeling?'

Sophie gave a wan smile. 'Apart from like I've got the world's worst hangover, about the same as I look, I expect.'

Given what she'd been through, she looked remarkably good. Eight years had barely left a mark. Her face was unlined, and apart from the bruising she didn't appear much changed from the last time I saw her.

She looked down at her hands. 'I suppose I feel more embarrassed than anything. I don't know which is worse, the fact that somebody broke in and did this to me, or that I can't remember anything about it.'

Short-term memory loss is common enough after a head injury, but that doesn't make it any less distressing.

'You can't remember anything at all? Nothing about who attacked you?'

'I can't even remember *being* attacked. For all I know I could have just slipped and banged my head.'

That might have been more credible if not for the broken front door and ransacked rooms. Whatever had happened to her, it was no accident.

'Your memory might come back in a few days.'

'I don't know if I want it to.' She looked vulnerable lying there in the hospital gown, not at all like the Sophie I remembered. 'The police say I wasn't . . . that it wasn't a sexual assault. But it's horrible thinking that someone broke in and I can't even remember.'

'Have you any idea who it might have been? Anyone with a grudge?'

'No, not at all. I'm not in a relationship, and haven't been for . . . well, long enough. The police think it was probably a burglar who thought I was out and panicked when he realised I was in the shower.'

That was news to me. 'Have you spoken to Terry Connors?'

The name seemed to surprise her. 'No. Why?'

'He came to see me.' I hesitated, but she'd a right to know. 'He seems to think it might have been Jerome Monk who attacked you.'

'Monk? That's ridiculous!' She frowned as she looked at me. 'There's something else, isn't there?'

'He told me I was a suspect as well. I was the one who found you and since you can't remember anything . . .'

'You?' Her eyes widened. I felt my stomach dip, wondering if she might believe it herself. But when she spoke again the anger in her voice dispelled it. 'Christ, that's just like him. That's so stupid!'

'I'm glad you think so.'

'Look, I know I owe you an explanation, but I don't feel like talking about it right now. I . . . I just want to go home.'

'Sure. Don't worry about it.'

'Thanks.' She gave another weak smile, then put her head back on the pillow, closing her eyes. 'Sorry, I think I need to sleep . . .'

Her voice tailed off and I stood up. I turned to leave.

'David . . .' Sophie's eyes were on me. 'Are you coming back?'

'Of course.'

She gave a slight nod, satisfied. Her eyelids were already starting to droop again, and when she spoke her voice was slurred and barely more than a whisper. 'I didn't mean to . . .'

'Didn't mean to what?' I asked, not sure if I'd heard right.

But she was already asleep. I watched the steady rise and fall of her breathing, then quietly left the ward. As I made my way down the corridor, I thought about what Sophie had said. And what she hadn't.

I wondered what she was hiding.

THE CLOUDS AND RAIN had lifted next morning, giving way to clean blue skies and bright sunshine that lifted my spirits. I checked out of the hotel and set off for my lunch appointment with Wainwright. There was no real need to see him now Sophie was conscious, but having accepted his wife's invitation for lunch, I couldn't cry off at short notice.

The archaeologist lived near Sharkham Point, a headland on the southern tip of Torbay. It was less than an hour's drive, so I chose a longer route that took in more of the coast. Although it was only twenty miles from Dartmoor, it seemed a different world: brighter and less oppressive.

The house was easy enough to find: a pebble-dashed 1920s villa criss-crossed with black beams, set back from the road.

A bright blue Toyota was parked outside the garage. I parked next to it and went up the steps to the front door. *Here we go.* I pressed the brass bell and straightened my shoulders as footsteps sounded from inside.

The woman who opened the door fitted the voice on the phone too perfectly to be anyone other than Wainwright's wife. Less matronly, perhaps, but the perfectly coiffed grey hair and careful make-up were as I'd expected, and so was the steel-trap quality to her eyes.

They were crinkled in welcome now, though, and her smile was surprisingly warm. 'You must be David Hunter?'

'That's right.'

'I'm Jean Wainwright. So glad you found us. Do come in. Leonard's in the study. He's been looking forward to seeing you.'

That was so unlikely I felt suddenly certain I'd made a mistake. As I followed her along the wood-panelled hallway I wondered if this could be some other Leonard Wainwright after all? *Too late now.* His wife opened a door at the end of the hall and ushered me in.

After the dark hallway, the room was dazzlingly bright. Sunlight flooded in through the huge bay window that ran almost its entire length. Bookcases lined the walls, and a handsome, leather-topped desk stood at one side, bare except for a vase of white chrysanthemums. Their scent filled the room, but it was the view that commanded attention. The window faced out over a lawn beyond which was nothing but sea stretching out to the horizon. It was so breathtaking that I was slow to take in anything else.

Then Wainwright's wife spoke. 'Leonard, David Hunter's here. He's an old colleague of yours. You remember him, don't you?'

She'd gone to stand by a wing-backed armchair facing the view. I hadn't realised anyone was sitting there. I waited for Wainwright to get up. When he didn't, I moved until I could see past the winged sides of the chair.

I wouldn't have recognised him.

The giant of memory no longer existed. Wainwright sat hunched in the chair, staring blankly out at the sea. The patrician features were barely recognisable, cheeks caved in and eyes sunken in their sockets, while the once thick mane of hair was thin and grey.

Wainwright's wife had turned to me expectantly. The bright smile on her face now seemed as transparent as the window itself. I'd stopped dead, shocked, but now I forced a smile of my own as I went forward.

'Hello, Leonard.' I didn't offer my hand; I knew there'd be no point.

'Dr Hunter's come for lunch, dear,' his wife said. 'Won't that be nice? The two of you can talk about old times.'

As though finally becoming aware of my presence, the big head turned ponderously in my direction. The fogged eyes looked at me, then Wainwright turned to gaze back out at the sea again.

'Can I get you a cup of tea, Dr Hunter?' his wife said. 'Lunch will be another twenty minutes.'

My smile felt glued in place. 'Tea would be nice. I'll give you a hand.'

'That's very kind, thank you. We won't be long, Leonard,' she added, patting her husband's hand. There was no response.

With a last glance at the figure in the chair, I followed her into the hall.

'I'm sorry, I should have warned you,' she said, closing the door. 'I assumed when you rang that you knew about Leonard's condition.'

'I'd no idea,' I said. 'What is it? Alzheimer's?'

'They don't seem entirely sure. I never realised there were so many different types of dementia. Leonard's developed very quickly, as these things go. The last two years have been . . . quite hard.'

I could imagine. 'I'm sorry.'

'Oh, these things happen.' She spoke with a breezy matter-of-factness. 'I thought seeing a familiar face might help. Our daughters don't live nearby, and we don't get many visitors.'

Suddenly I felt like a fraud. 'Look, Mrs Wainwright—'

'Please, call me Jean.'

'Jean.' I took a deep breath. 'The thing is, this wasn't just a social call. I was hoping to talk to your husband about the investigation we worked on.'

'Then please do. He can be quite lucid sometimes, especially about things that happened in the past.' She opened the study door again before I could protest. 'Now, you two can talk while I get lunch ready.'

There was no way I could refuse. I gave a weak smile and went back inside. The door closed behind me, leaving me alone with Wainwright.

You're here now. Make the best of it. I moved the chair from the desk until I could see him and sat down, searching for something to say. The point of my visit had vanished, but I couldn't just sit there.

'Hello again, Leonard. I'm David Hunter. We worked together once, on the Jerome Monk case. Do you remember?'

No response. Wainwright continued to stare at the sea. I sighed, looking out of the window myself. The view was spectacular. The archaeologist's deterioration was pitiable, but there were worse places to end one's days.

'I know you.'

I looked at him in surprise. The big head had turned towards me. Wainwright's eyes were fixed on mine.

'Yes, you do,' I said. 'David Hunter. I'm a—'

'Calliph . . . Calli . . . maggots.' The voice was the same bass rumble I remembered, although hoarser now, as though unused.

'Maggots,' I agreed.

'Rot.'

I smiled. I supposed 'rot' could have referred to the blowfly larvae's habitat, but I doubted it. Dementia or not, some things hadn't changed.

His eyes were flicking around now, as though something inside him had started to waken. The broad forehead creased in concentration.

'Roadkill . . .'

I just nodded. His mind had obviously started to wander.

He glared at me and thumped his hand down on the chair arm. 'No! Listen!' He started feebly trying to heave himself up from the chair.

I hurried over. 'It's OK, Leonard, calm down.'

His arms felt thin as sticks as he struggled to get up, but his grip was still vicelike as he seized my wrist.

'Roadkill!' he hissed, spraying spittle into my face. *'Roadkill!'*

The study door was flung open and his wife hurried in. 'Come along, Leonard, let's not have any nonsense.' She eased him back into his seat. 'What happened?' she asked me. 'Did you say something to upset him?'

'No, I was just—'

'Well, something must have set him off. He isn't normally this agitated.' She looked over at me, smoothing her husband's hair as he began to subside. Her manner was still polite but now there was no mistaking the frost. 'I'm sorry, Dr Hunter, but I think you'd better go.'

I hesitated, but there was nothing I could do. I let myself out. The day was still bright and sunny, but the sickly sweet odour of chrysanthemums stayed with me as I drove away from the house.

I DIDN'T BOTHER MUCH with the coastal scenery as I drove back to Exeter. I'd promised Sophie I'd call in at the hospital again, and I hoped that would take my mind off the disastrous visit to Wainwright. Seeing the archaeologist reduced like that had been a shock.

When I reached Sophie's ward, I found her sitting on the bed, fully dressed, a leather holdall open next to her. She still looked tired, and the bruise on the left side of her face was even more livid than before. But for all that she was clearly much better than the last time I'd seen her.

She gave me a smile that held as much relief as anything.

'I'm discharging myself ,' she said. 'The doctor wants to keep me in for another twenty-four hours. But all the tests are OK and I feel fine. And I want to go home.'

'You've had a bad head injury,' I said. 'Another twenty-four hours—'

'I'm going home,' she said with finality. 'Look, it's just concussion. I'll take it easy, I promise.'

I let it go. It wasn't my place to argue, and if the hospital hadn't managed to dissuade her I doubted I'd have much success.

'Sorry, I didn't mean to snap,' she said awkwardly.

'So how are you getting home?'

'I'll catch a train,' she said lightly.

'Oh no, I couldn't let you do that!' I smiled.

For all her bravado, Sophie was far from fully recovered. Her eyes closed before we'd left the hospital grounds, and she slept for the whole journey. Her head lolled against the seat rest, but her breathing was strong and regular. There were a number of questions I wanted to ask, but they could wait.

It was late afternoon when I pulled up outside Sophie's cottage. She woke up when I switched off the engine.

'Where are we?' she asked, sitting up and rubbing her eyes.

'Home.'

'God, don't tell me I slept all the way.'

'Best thing for you. How do you feel?'

She thought for a moment, still blinking away sleep. 'Better.'

She looked it. Her colour was normal, except for the shocking bruise on her face. We climbed out of the car. The autumn sun was low, casting long shadows across the garden like a spreading stain. Behind the small orchard of gnarled old apple trees, standing almost as tall as the house, was the inverted cone of the kiln. Its dilapidation was more evident now, crumbling bricks seemingly held up by the rusted scaffolding. A pile of unused poles lay nearby, overgrown with grass and weeds.

'That's my pride and joy,' Sophie said, as I opened the garden gate for her. 'It's a Victorian bottle kiln. There aren't many of them left. Come on, I'll show you.'

'It's OK,' I said, not wanting her to tire herself.

But she was already following the path towards it. The rickety wooden door squealed as she pushed it open.

'You don't keep it locked?' I asked.

She smiled. 'You're not in the city now. Besides, thieves wouldn't be interested. There's no black market for hand-thrown pots. Unfortunately.'

I followed her inside. There was a damp, dusty smell of old plaster. Light came from small windows set round the circular walls. In the centre was the original oven, a giant brick chimney stack that extended through the domed roof. It was scaffolded off, and parts of it were supported by a makeshift assembly of rusted props and timber joists.

'Is it safe?' I asked, looking at the sagging brickwork.

'Safe enough. It's a listed structure, so I can't knock it down even if I want to. The plan is to get it working again eventually, but that'll have to wait till I get the money. Which won't be any time soon.'

Off to one side stood a modern electric kiln and a clay-spattered potter's wheel. Workbenches and shelves were arranged round them, stacked with an assortment of pots. Even to my unschooled eye they seemed striking: organic shapes that looked as artistic as they were functional.

'I'd no idea you could do this,' I said, impressed.

'Oh, I'm full of hidden talents,' she said, absently running her hand over a large ball of dried clay. It stood on a table littered with half-finished and broken pots. She smiled self-consciously. 'As you'll have noticed, being tidy isn't one of them. Anyway, I hope you can keep a secret.'

Leaving me to wonder what she meant, she went to the kiln's curving wall. Sliding out a loose brick, she reached in and took something out.

'Spare key,' she said, holding it up. 'Always comes in handy.'

Until then I'd not given much thought to the condition of the house, but the sight of the key jogged my memory. *Oh, hell.*

'Wait, Sophie,' I said, hurrying after her as she left the kiln, but by then she'd already seen for herself.

She stopped dead on the path. 'Oh, my God!'

I cursed myself. I should have come here instead of wasting my time at Wainwright's. The police had made a half-hearted attempt to wedge the door shut, but muddy footprints crisscrossed the polished floorboards and there was a rank smell, as if a fox or some other animal had been inside.

Sophie stared at the scattered contents of the open drawers and cupboards.

'It's not as bad as it looks,' I said feebly. 'I thought the police would have told you.'

There was no answer. I realised that tears were running down her cheeks.

'Sophie. I'm really sorry—'

'It isn't your fault.'

She slid to the floor and hugged her knees, shaking with silent sobs. Without saying anything, I crouched next to her. She buried her face against me.

'*Oh, G-God, I'm so scared. I'm s-so s-scared . . .*'

'Shh, it's OK,' I told her. I hoped I was right.

I REPAIRED the front door as best I could, with tools Sophie provided. The lock was broken but I salvaged an ancient iron bolt from the pantry, which would serve until a joiner could get there.

At my insistence, Sophie went for a bath while I cleaned up the the mess. Most of the damage was superficial—her belongings had been scattered but there were few breakages. Once I'd opened the windows to clear the musky animal smell, there was little evidence of what had happened.

It was dark outside by the time she came back down, her damp hair pulled back from her face. Although her cheek was less swollen, the skin was deepening into purples and yellows as the bruising ran its course.

'I made some tea,' I said, as she came into the kitchen.

'Fine. Thank you.'

'You might want to make sure nothing's missing. Any jewellery or valuables.' She nodded, but didn't seem interested. 'How's the head?'

Sophie sat down at the scarred pine table. 'Still aching, but not as much. I took some of the painkillers the hospital gave me.' She avoided looking at me as she reached for the teapot.

Silence descended. The only sound was the slow tinkling of the spoon as she stirred her tea. We both watched the spoon going round.

'You'll wear it out,' I said.

'Sorry.' She put the spoon down. 'Look, about earlier . . . I don't usually lose it like that.'

'Don't worry about it. You've been through a lot.'

'Even so, crying all over you like I did. I must have made a mess of your coat.'

'I'll send you the cleaning bill.'

She gave an embarrassed laugh. 'This is really awkward, isn't it?'

'A little,' I admitted. 'Look, you don't have to talk now if you don't want to. It's getting late and I ought to set off soon.'

'You're driving back tonight?' She looked startled. 'I can't let you do that. There's a spare room here.'

'Really, it isn't—'

She gave me a nervous smile. 'You'd be doing me a favour.'

She was trying hard, but I could see the cracks in her composure. After what she'd been through I didn't blame her for being rattled.

'OK, if you're sure.'

Some of the tension went out of her. 'Are you hungry? I don't have much in but I can rustle something up.' Whatever was on Sophie's mind, she obviously wasn't ready to talk about it yet.

I smiled. 'Starving.'

Despite her protests, I made her sit down while I prepared something to eat. She wasn't exaggerating when she'd said there wasn't much in, but I found Cheddar cheese and eggs that I beat into an omelette, then toasted slices from a stale loaf and slathered them in butter.

'God, that smells delicious,' Sophie said.

But she only picked at her food. The tension edged up between us again as we ate, and it was a relief when we'd finished.

'Let's go into the sitting room,' she said. 'We can talk better in there.'

It was a comfortable room: two big old sofas, soft rugs on the polished floorboards and a woodburning stove, which Sophie insisted on lighting. We each sat on a sofa, facing each other across a low coffee table. In the firelight it felt strangely intimate.

Sophie gave a nervous smile. 'I don't know where to start.'

'How about how you ended up here? Making pottery's a long way from being a BIA.'

She smiled self-consciously. 'Yeah, just a bit. I'd had enough, I suppose. After the Monk fiasco I lost a lot of my confidence, started second-guessing everything I did. So I got out before I burned out.'

Sophie looked around the room as if taking it in for the first time.

'I've been here four . . . no, five years now. God! Pottery used to be a hobby, so when I saw this place for sale I thought, why not? I'd always liked Dartmoor and I wanted a fresh start. Can you understand that?'

I could. Probably better than she realised.

'The first thing I did was burn all my notes,' she went on. 'Every case I'd ever worked on. All of it went onto the bonfire. Except one.'

'Jerome Monk's,' I said.

She nodded. 'Do you ever think about it?'

'Not until Monk escaped.'

'I think about it a lot. We had a golden opportunity to find where Lindsey and Zoe Bennett were buried, and we threw it away. We should have done more. *I* should have done more.'

'Monk had his own agenda for being there. He only wanted a chance to escape.' *And almost managed it.*

'But that's the thing, I don't think he did.' She waved away my objection. 'All right, escaping was part of it. But I don't think it was the *only* reason he agreed to help. The way he reacted when he saw Tina Williams's grave, he wasn't putting that on. I'm certain he was genuinely trying to remember.'

She was looking at me earnestly, willing me to believe her. I chose my words carefully. 'Jerome Monk knew that moor better than anyone. He'd managed to hide out on it for months without being caught. If he'd wanted to, he could have taken us right to the other graves.'

'Not necessarily, not after a year, and not if he'd buried them at night. And people blank things from their minds without meaning to. Painful memories sometimes, or when their brain has too much to process.'

'That might apply to an ordinary man who flipped and lost his temper, but you're talking about a sociopathic killer. He has no conscience.'

'On some level he might,' she persisted. 'He's violent and unpredictable, but that doesn't mean he can't be reached. That's why I—'

She broke off, looking down at her hands. An owl hooted outside.

'That's why you what?' I asked.

'That's . . . why I've been writing to him.'

'You've been writing to *Monk*?'

Her chin came up, defiantly. 'I write to him once a year, on the anniversary of Angela Carson's murder. We can't say for sure when he killed any of his other victims, so I thought . . . Anyway, once a year I write and urge him to say where the graves are. And I offer to help him.'

I stared at her, aghast. 'Sophie, for God's sake!'

'He's never responded, but all I need is a landmark, some clue to where they are! What harm can it do?'

I rubbed my eyes. 'Did you put your address on the letters?'

She gave a guilty nod. 'I didn't know how else he could write back.'

'Do the police know?'

'The police? No, I . . . Well, I didn't think there was much point.'

'Not much *point*? Sophie, you get attacked the day after a rapist and murderer escapes from prison, and you didn't think it was worth mentioning you'd been *writing* to him?'

'I was embarrassed, all right?' she flared. 'And yes, I know how stupid it makes me look, but at least I've tried to *do* something! How do you think the family of those two dead sisters feel? I know how it makes *me* feel, knowing we could have done something about it and didn't!'

There was a tremor of emotion in her voice. I reminded myself she'd been through a lot. This couldn't be easy for her.

'You have to tell the police,' I said gently. 'I'll call Terry Connors and—'

'No!'

'Sophie, you don't have any choice. You know that.'

I thought she was going to argue, but the defiance seemed to drain out of her. 'I'll tell the police, but on one condition. I called you to ask for a favour. That still hasn't changed.'

With everything else that had happened I'd almost forgotten why she'd asked to see me in the first place. 'What is it?'

'I want you to help me find the graves.'

6

As we passed the overgrown earthworks that once housed the old tin mine's water wheel, I realised we were nearly there.

Black Tor.

Where Tina Williams had been buried.

I'd known Sophie was stubborn, but her determination to find the bodies of Lindsey and Zoe Bennett bordered on obsessional. The night before I'd tried to persuade her it was useless, that the two of us couldn't hope to accomplish anything after a full-scale police search had failed.

I'd wasted my breath.

'All I want to do is try to come up with enough for the police to launch another search,' she'd said. 'One day, that's all I ask. Give me one day, and if you still think we're wasting our time you can walk away.'

I should have said no. We couldn't hope to achieve anything in a single day. The refusal was on my lips, but I could see the need in her eyes. She sat with her hands clenched, waiting for my answer. *This is a mistake.*

'One day,' I heard myself say.

Now I was regretting it. I'd slept badly, turning restlessly in the small bed in the spare room, and when I'd finally fallen asleep it had been to wake gasping, convinced Monk was breaking in. But the darkened house had been silent, and the only sound from outside was the cry of an owl.

After breakfast I'd given her the card with Terry's mobile number. She'd promised to tell the police about writing to Monk if I agreed to help her search for the graves, and however much they disliked each other it made sense for it to be Terry. I'd pretended to need something from my room while she made the call, then went back downstairs.

'Voicemail,' she said neutrally, handing me his card. 'I left a message.'

We had to wait for a local joiner to come out to repair the front door, so it was midafternoon before we set off for the moor. The atmosphere in the car was awkward from the outset, and grew more so as we neared Black Tor.

I took the turning without having to ask. It was like driving back in time. I parked at the end of the dirt track that cut across the moor to the tor. The last time I'd been here, this whole area had bustled with trailers, vans and cars. Now, except for a few distant sheep, the moor was empty.

I switched off the engine. 'Now what?'

Sophie gave a weak smile. 'I just want to go and see where Tina's grave was. That's all.'

Resigned, I got out of the car. A cold breeze plucked at my hair. The air was fresh, underlaid with a faintly sulphurous whiff of bog. There was no corridor of police tape now, no distant blue forensic tent. But for all that, the moor felt hauntingly familiar.

Beside me, Sophie stood with her hands jammed in her coat pockets, eyes scanning the wintry patchwork of gorse, heather and dead bracken. 'We'd better hurry,' she said. 'It'll be dark soon.'

She was right: the afternoon was already shading into a dusky twilight. A thin mist was rising from the ground like steam from a horse's back.

We set off along the track that led to Black Tor. About halfway along it she stopped, turning to face the moor off to our left.

'OK, this is where the police tape was strung out to the grave.'

'How can you tell?'

Sophie gave me a sideways glance. She leaned nearer to me, her hand resting lightly on my arm as she pointed. 'The trick is to memorise landmarks that aren't going to change. See that other tor about two miles away? That should be at right angles to where we are now. And then if you look over there . . .' She turned, standing close against me so I turned with her. 'There's a sort of cleft in the ground. If we're at the right place, the end of it should line up with that hummock with the flat rock on top. See?'

I nodded, but I wasn't really concentrating on what she'd said. She was still pressed against me. She brushed a windblown strand of hair away from her face as we looked at each other, then she moved away.

'Anyway . . . this is a natural entry point into the moor as well,' she said. 'There's a steep bank running along most of the track, but it's easier to negotiate just here. Shall we?'

'OK.'

I was glad to start walking again. *Keep your mind on what you should be doing.* The embankment might not have been so steep here, but it was a lot more overgrown than I remembered. My boots alternately squelched into mud or twisted on some hidden rock or hole. But Sophie seemed confident of where she was going, as if following an invisible path. It took me a while to realise that she wasn't just reading the landscape any more.

'You've been here recently, haven't you?' I asked.

She pushed her hair out of her eyes. 'Once or twice.'

'Why?' There couldn't be anything to see, not after all this time.

'I don't know. It feels . . . *sanctified*, almost. Knowing what happened, that someone was buried here. Can't you feel it?'

I felt something, but it was more of a prickling sense of unease. *Like we're being watched*. That was stupid, but I was uncomfortably aware of how alone we were, how far we'd come from the road.

'How much further?' I asked.

'Not far. In fact it's just . . .' She tailed off, staring directly ahead.

The moor was pitted with holes.

They'd been hidden by the grass and heather until we were right on top of them. I counted half a dozen, each one about eighteen inches deep and about twice that long, dug with no apparent pattern or scheme.

I looked at Sophie. 'You didn't . . .'

'No, of course not! They weren't here last time I came!'

I crouched down by the nearest hole. Its edges were marked with clear vertical cuts, and an earthworm coiled blindly in the bottom, its tail end neatly severed. 'These were dug with a spade,' I said, straightening. 'Where was Tina Williams buried?'

'Just over there.' Sophie pointed. The patch of ground was undisturbed. The holes were unevenly spread out all round it.

'Are you sure?'

'I'm sure. The first time I came back out here I brought the original Ordnance Survey map I'd marked the coordinates on. I didn't need it after that.' She came and stood closer. 'It was Monk, wasn't it?'

I didn't answer. I looked back down at the wriggling earthworm.

'I don't understand. Why would he have been digging out here?' Sophie asked, glancing round uneasily.

'You always said he might be telling the truth about not being able to remember where the graves were. Perhaps you were right.'

'But why would he *want* to find them?'

I realised what had been nagging me. Worms don't stay long on the surface. They burrow back underground or they're eaten. This one was still here.

'We need to go,' I said.

Sophie didn't move. She was staring across the moor. 'David . . .'

I followed her gaze. No more than a hundred yards away, a figure stood watching us. It seemed to have appeared from nowhere; there were no bushes or rocks nearby where it could have hidden. In the fading light it was little more than a silhouette, motionless in the rising mist. But there was a breadth and bulk about it that had an awful familiarity. Topping the broad shoulders was the pale globe of a head.

There was an instant when everything seemed frozen. Then the figure moved towards us.

I took hold of Sophie's arm. 'Come on.'

'Oh, God, that's him, isn't it? It's Monk!'

'Just keep walking.'

But that was easier said than done. Heather clutched at our feet, and white tendrils of mist spread across the darkening moor like a vast cobweb. At another time I might have appreciated the sight. Now it made each step potentially treacherous. If either of us fell or turned an ankle . . .

Don't think about that. I kept my grip on Sophie's arm, urging her back towards the track. The car was just visible on the distant road, a tiny block of colour disappearing into the dusk.

We stumbled over tussocks of reedlike marsh grass, boots squelching into the mud and water concealed underneath. I took a look back and saw that the figure wasn't following us any more. Instead, he was cutting across the boggy moor towards the road. He was going to try to beat us to the car.

Sophie had seen him as well. 'David . . .' she panted.

'I know. Just keep going.'

God, we're not going to make it. The ground rose more steeply as we reached the bank immediately below the track. Sophie was struggling now, and I had to help her scramble up the last few yards.

Then we were on the track's firmer surface. We still had to get back to the road. I tugged Sophie into a lumbering run. 'Come on!'

'Wait . . . get my breath . . .' she gasped, her face slick with sweat. She shouldn't have been exerting herself, but there was no choice.

'We need to run,' I told her.

She shook her head, pushing me away. 'Can't . . . I can't . . .'

'Yes, you can,' I said, almost dragging her down the track.

My legs felt like water as we lurched towards the car. The figure was no more than thirty or forty yards away, off to one side and slightly below. But he'd begun to slow. The pale head turned towards us as we stumbled the last few yards. He'd stopped, barely a stone's throw away. I fumbled for my key fob and unlocked the car. Sophie collapsed inside while I ran round to the driver's side, conscious of the figure watching from the knee-deep mist.

He'd beaten us. Why did he give up? I'd no idea and didn't care. Slamming the door, I turned on the engine and stamped on the accelerator. As the car roared away I looked in the rearview mirror.

Both the road and moor behind us were empty.

I didn't slow for two or three miles. Only when I was certain no one was following did I began to relax. Reaction was setting in, leaving me wrung out and clammy as I let the car's speed ease back to normal.

'Are we safe?' Sophie asked. She was still breathing heavily. The bruise looked worse than ever against the pallor of her face.

'I think so.'

She closed her eyes.'I'm going to be sick.'

I pulled over. Sophie stumbled out of the car almost before we'd stopped. Leaving the engine running, I checked my phone. With relief I saw that there was enough signal to make a call. I dialled Terry's number, willing him to pick up. It seemed to ring for a long time before he answered.

'This better be good.' He sounded tired.

'We're at Black Tor. We've—'

'Who's "we"?'

'Sophie Keller. She discharged herself from hospital yesterday and—'

'Keller? What are you doing there with her?'

'Does it *matter*? Monk's here!'

That seemed to get through. 'Go on.'

I kept it brief, conscious of the fading light. When I'd finished I heard a rasp of bristles as Terry rubbed his hand across his face.

'OK, leave it with me.'

'Do you need us to hang around?'

'I think we'll cope.' His tone was heavy with sarcasm. 'If I need you I'll know where to find you.'

The line went dead. Feeling the familiar irritation, I put the phone away and went over to Sophie.

She gave me a wan smile. 'Sorry. False alarm. Did you call the police?'

'I've spoken to Terry Connors. He's getting things moving.'

Her mouth tightened at the mention of Terry, but for once she didn't criticise him. 'Do we have to wait here?'

'He says there's no need.'

I looked out at the moor. The light was dropping quickly, and a haze of mist blurred the edges of the little we could still see. Sophie shivered, and I knew what she was thinking. Monk was still out there.

I put my arm round her. 'Come on, I'll take you home.'

THE MIST had thickened to a full-blown fog by the time we reached Padbury. I had slowed to a crawl, my headlights almost useless against the white gauze. I pulled into the lane at the bottom of Sophie's garden and switched off the engine. I found myself glancing around uneasily as we went up the path, straining to hear. The fog wrapped round us, making everything more than a few feet away all but invisible.

The front door was still intact, the new lock fitted by the joiner reassuringly solid. When Sophie opened it and flicked on the hall light, the house looked exactly as we'd left it that morning. I hadn't realised till then how tense I'd been. From the deep sigh she gave as she shot home the new bolts on the door, it seemed that Sophie felt the same way.

'How are you holding up?' I asked as she tiredly pulled off her coat.

'I've had better days.' Her smile was unconvincing. 'God, I need a drink.'

So did I, but not yet. 'I think it might be a good idea to stay somewhere else tonight.'

Sophie was sitting on the stairs, unfastening her muddy boots. She stopped to look up at me, her face closed. 'No.'

'You could book into a hotel.'

'I'm not going anywhere.'

'You've already been attacked here once. If it was Monk—'

'If it was Monk I'd be dead. You know it as well as I do. If you want to run away you can, but I'm not going to!'

I stared in surprise. *Where did that come from?*

Sophie sighed. 'I'm sorry, you didn't deserve that. It's just . . . if I leave now I'll never feel safe here again. Can't you understand that?'

I could. That didn't mean I agreed, but there was no point arguing. 'OK.'

'Thank you.' She came over and gave me a hug. I held her for a moment, feeling the warm pressure of her body before she stepped back. 'I can be a cow sometimes, but I appreciate everything you're doing. And I wouldn't blame you if you decided to go anyway.'

The opening was there. But I wasn't going to take it.

I gave Sophie a smile. 'You mentioned something about a drink.'

We shared the cooking that night. Dinner was grilled lamb chops from the freezer with minted potatoes and frozen peas: simple and satisfying.

Sophie produced a bottle of wine, and the alcohol took the edge off any awkwardness. I didn't argue when she suggested leaving the dishes till morning. Taking the wine with us, we went into the sitting room. I put more logs in the stove and built up the fire using kindling and old newspaper. Soon bright flames were driving the chill from the room.

Sophie and I sat in comfortable silence at either end of one of the sofas. I took another drink of wine and stole a look at her. She was drowsing, legs curled up, head fallen back to expose the slender line of her throat. Her face was relaxed, the firelight softening the bruising. She was breathing with the slow, steady rhythm of deep sleep, the almost empty wineglass still held loosely in her fingers. I was loath to disturb her but it was starting to slip.

'Sophie . . .' I said gently. There was no response. 'Sophie?'

She came awake gradually, eyes staring at me blankly before blinking as awareness returned. 'Sorry,' she apologised, sitting up.

'Why don't you go to bed?'

'Not much of a host, am I?' she said, but she didn't argue. She stood up and put her hand on my shoulder as she swayed unsteadily. 'Whoa . . .'

'Take it easy,' I said, getting up to support her. 'Are you OK?'

'Just tired, I think. Must have stood up too quickly.'

Sophie was still holding on to me. I had my hands on her waist, standing close enough to feel the warmth coming from her. Neither of us moved. Her eyes were big and dark as she leaned into me. A smile curved her face.

'Well . . .' she said, and something hit the window with a *bang*.

We jumped apart. I rushed to the heavy curtains and yanked them open, half expecting to see Monk's nightmare face glaring back at me. But the window was unbroken and empty. All I could see beyond it was white fog.

'What was it?' Sophie asked, standing close behind me.

'Probably nothing.'

It was an inane thing to say, especially when my own heart was pounding. *Monk can't have followed us back here. Can he?* But he didn't have to follow us. Not when Sophie's address had been on her letters.

'Stay here,' I told her.

'You're not going *outside*?'

'Only to take a look.' The alternative was cowering inside, wondering what had hit the window. If it was nothing, we could relax. If it was Monk . . .

Then it wouldn't make any difference.

I took the iron poker from beside the glowing stove and went into the hall. Sophie hurried into the kitchen and returned with a torch.

'Lock the door behind me,' I said, taking it from her.

'David, wait—'

But I was already sliding back the bolts on the front door and stepping into the damp air. I shivered, wishing I'd thought to grab my coat. The fog soaked up the lantern's beam. Keeping close to the side of the house, I began making my way towards the sitting room. I was already beginning to think this wasn't such a good idea. *What are you going to do if Monk's out here?* But it was too late now. I picked up my pace, keen to get it over with. And something moved on the ground at my feet.

I stumbled backwards, raising the poker. There was another flurry of movement, and then the light and shadows resolved themselves.

Caught in the lantern's beam, an owl blinked up at me.

I lowered the poker, feeling stupid. The bird was ghostly pale, its face almost white. It was hunched on the grass below the window, wings splayed out awkwardly at its sides, making no attempt to move.

'It's a barn owl,' Sophie said from behind me.

I hadn't heard her approach. 'I thought you were waiting inside.'

'I didn't say that.' She crouched beside the injured bird. 'It's lucky the window didn't break. Poor thing. The fog must have confused it.'

'It's probably just stunned. Have you got a blanket or something?'

The owl flapped a little as I cautiously covered it with an old towel, but quickly subsided. Sophie suggested leaving it just inside the kiln, propping the door open so it could fly out when it had recovered.

'What about your pots?' I asked.

'They're insured. Anyway, it's an owl. It can see in the dark.'

The bird was surprisingly light as I carried it into the kiln and set it on the floor. Its pale feathers were almost luminous in the darkness.

'Will it be all right?' Sophie asked as we returned to the house.

'We can't do any more tonight. If it's there in the morning, we'll call a vet.'

I locked and bolted the front door, giving it a tug to make sure.

Sophie shivered as she rubbed her arms. 'God, I'm frozen!'

She was standing very close. Looking at me. It would have been natural to take hold of her.

'It's late,' I said. 'You go on up; I'll see to things down here.'

She blinked, then nodded. 'Right. Well . . . good night.'

I waited while she went upstairs, then went through the rooms, angrily turning off the lights. I told myself I'd done the right thing. Sophie was scared and vulnerable, and things were complicated enough already.

But I wasn't sure whether I was angry because of what had almost happened, or because I hadn't let it.

I lay awake in the single bed, listening to the night-time silence of the house and thinking about Sophie. I finally fell asleep, only to be half-woken by a noise from outside, the sharp cry of either predator or prey. It didn't come again, and as sleep reclaimed me I forgot all about it.

NEXT MORNING I woke early and padded downstairs in the cool and quiet house while Sophie slept. I made myself a cup of tea and sat at the kitchen table, watching the sky gradually lighten.

The morning chorus of birdsong reminded me of the owl. I pulled on my coat and boots and went outside. The fog had lifted, though there was still an early haze, part drizzle, part mist. It frosted the branches of the apple trees, beading the cobwebs with quicksilver as I crossed the wet grass.

The only sign of the bird was a few pale feathers on the floor of the kiln. They could have been dislodged by the impact, but there was a less happy explanation. With the kiln door open, the predator could have become prey.

I wandered round the kiln. The scaffolding and props wedged against the walls had been here so long they might almost have grown out of the structure. I guessed that renovating the kiln would be a big and expensive job. Sophie would have to sell a lot of pots.

Still, she was obviously talented. The bowls and vases on the shelves were all simple yet striking designs. I ran my hand across the mound of hard clay on the workbench. It was made up of unused scraps that Sophie had slapped together and left to dry, but it could have been an abstract piece of art.

I went back into the house, and by the time Sophie came downstairs I'd put the kettle on and had a mug of tea waiting. She was wearing an oversized sweater over her jeans, hair pulled back.

'Morning,' I said, handing her the mug.

'Thanks.' She looked a little self-conscious. 'Did you sleep well?'

'Fine,' I lied. 'How are you feeling?'

'My cheek's still sore, but other than that I'm OK.'

'Can you remember anything yet about what happened?'

'What? Oh . . . no, still blank.' She went to the fridge. 'How about the owl? Is it still there?'

'No, I checked earlier. It's gone.'

She grinned. 'See? I told you it'd be all right in the kiln.'

I didn't mention the feathers on the kiln floor. If Sophie wanted a happy ending I wasn't going to spoil it for her.

'No bread for toast, I'm afraid, but I can offer you bacon and eggs,' she said, opening the fridge. 'Scrambled all right?'

I said it was. 'I thought I'd set off back before lunch,' I told her, as she cracked the eggs into a bowl.

She paused, then continued beating the eggs. 'You're leaving?'

'I might as well. The police'll have to relaunch the search for the Bennett twins now Monk's been digging on the moor.'

'I suppose so,' Sophie said. She had her back to me. The frying pan clattered on the range. The silence stretched and grew heavy.

'I can stay longer. If you're bothered about being here by yourself.'

She slapped rashers of bacon into the pan and the hot fat hissed. 'I expect I'll get used to the idea. I don't have much choice, do I?'

'Everything points to your attack being a one-off,' I said. 'Just a burglary that went wrong, like the police said. Whoever did it can't have really wanted to hurt you, or . . . Well, you'd have got more than a fractured cheek.'

'I suppose.' She looked thoughtful, but there was still a shadow in her eyes. Abruptly, it was gone. 'Right, let's have breakfast,' she said.

After we'd eaten I offered to help with the dishes, but she declined. I got the impression she wanted some time to herself, so I left her in the kitchen and went to shower and pack my things.

The radio was playing when I came back down into the kitchen. Sophie was standing by the sink, her hands motionless in the water.

'Is there anything—?' I began.

'Shh!' She silenced me with a quick shake of her head. For the first time I paid attention to what was being said on the radio.

'*. . . police haven't released the victim's identity, although they confirm the death is being treated as suspicious. In other news . . .*'

Sophie's face was white. 'There's been a murder. They haven't said who it is, but it's in Torbay. Near Sharkham Point. Isn't that . . . ?'

I nodded, realising I wouldn't be leaving yet after all.

That was where Wainwright lived.

IT WAS LESS THAN an hour's drive to Sharkham Point from Padbury. Sophie had insisted on going, and I didn't put up much of an argument. I wanted to find out who the victim was just as much as she did. I'd called Terry straight away, but he wasn't answering his phone. That wasn't surprising: odds were he'd have been called out to the scene. I told myself it might not have anything to do with Wainwright. Murders happen every day, and so do coincidences. But I couldn't quite believe it.

Neither Sophie nor I spoke much during the journey. She sat staring out of the window, as wrapped up in her thoughts as I was in my own. Only when we reached the coast did she stir. We passed a signpost for Sharkham Point. Not far ahead of it we could see strobing blue lights on the road.

Sophie's hand went to her throat. 'Is that Wainwright's house?'

A heaviness settled in my stomach. 'Yes.'

A cordon of police tape stretched across the road. Beyond it police cars and trailers were parked on either side of the gates, along with a few press and TV vans. An ambulance was on the driveway outside the house.

I parked a little way before the fluttering cordon.

'What should we do?' Sophie asked. Her usual confidence seemed to have abandoned her.

'We've come this far. No point going back now.' I climbed out of the car.

A policeman in a bright yellow reflective jacket moved to block us as we approached. 'The road's closed.'

'I know. My name's David Hunter. Is DI Connors here?' I asked.

He regarded us for a few seconds, then spoke into his radio. 'Got a David Hunter here, asking for DI Connors,' he said, then waited. There was a long pause, then a crackling voice. He lowered the radio. 'Sorry.'

Sophie spoke up before I could say anything. 'Does that mean he isn't here or he won't see us?'

The policeman regarded her stonily. 'It means you have to leave.'

'Who's dead? Is it Professor Wainwright or his wife?'

'Are you relatives?'

'No, but—'

'Then you can read about it in the papers. Now, go back to your car.'

There was a flurry of activity from the house. A group of police officers came down the driveway. At their head was a man whose smart uniform and peaked cap marked him as police hierarchy. The hair and moustache were greyer, but the bland, unlined features hardly seemed to have aged.

Simms didn't so much as glance in our direction as he strode towards an unmarked black BMW, but someone else did. One of his entourage was staring at us: middle-aged, overweight and balding. Roper.

He hurried over and spoke to his superior. Simms stopped, his pale eyes turning to us. *Now for it*, I thought as they came over.

The PC who'd stopped us stood to attention. 'Sir, I was just—'

Simms paid him no attention. His eyes touched on Sophie without recognition before pinning me again. There had always been an aura of arrogance about him, but now he wore the insignia of Assistant Chief Constable it was more pronounced.

'Dr Hunter, isn't it?' he said. 'May I ask what you're doing here?'

Sophie didn't give me a chance to answer. 'Who's been killed?'

Simms regarded her for a beat, then pointedly turned to me again.

'We heard about the murder,' I said, 'and wanted to find out if Professor Wainwright and his wife were involved.'

'And that concerned you how, exactly?'

His attitude was beginning to rankle. 'Because I thought Jerome Monk might have killed them.'

The ACC's expression didn't change but his eyes were glacial. 'Let him through,' he told the PC.

I ducked under the tape. Sophie moved to do the same.

'Just Dr Hunter,' Simms said.

The PC stepped in front of her. 'Oh, come *on*!' Sophie protested.

'Dr Hunter's a police consultant.' Simms's gaze lingered dispassionately on her bruised cheek. 'As far as I'm aware you no longer are.'

Sophie drew herself up to argue.

'I'll see you back at the car,' I said quickly.

I knew that Simms wouldn't change his mind. She shot me a furious look, then snatched the keys off me and strode back down the road.

Simms was already heading back towards the house, polished black shoes crunching on the gravel driveway. Roper fell into step beside me.

'Turning into quite a reunion, isn't it?' He motioned with his head back at Sophie. 'Not happy, is she? What happened to her face?'

I was surprised he didn't know. 'Someone broke into her house and attacked her.'

'She needs better locks. When was this?'

'Four days ago.'

The grin left his face as he made the connection: four days made it right after Monk's escape. 'Did they get who did it?'

'Not yet. She can't remember much about what happened.'

'Was she raped?'

'No.'

'Anything stolen?'

'No.'

Roper gave a huff of amusement. 'Bloody lucky, eh?'

I changed the subject. 'Who's SIO here?'

'Steve Naysmith. He's a bit of a high flier, only made Detective Chief Super last year.' Roper's tone made it clear he didn't approve. 'But the ACC's taking a very personal interest.'

Simms had stopped by the entrance to the house, where a trestle table had been set up with boxes of protective gear. He tore open a sealed packet of overalls and I followed suit.

'Need me for anything else, sir?' Roper asked.

Simms didn't so much as glance at him as he pulled on overshoes and gloves. 'Not right now, but stay here until Dr Hunter and I have finished.'

Without waiting to see if I was ready, he went inside.

The genteel quietude of the house I remembered had been shattered. White-suited CSIs were packing away equipment, but evidence of what had happened was everywhere. Every surface was finely coated with fingerprint powder. Glass from a broken window was scattered on the parquet floor among the spilled soil from an overturned potted plant.

'The intruder forced open the kitchen door,' Simms told me. 'No attempt at concealment, as you can see. We've also found several patches of sputum, which should enable a DNA analysis.'

'Sputum?'

'It appears the killer spat on the floor.'

He was walking down the hallway in front of me, blocking my view. Then he stepped aside, and I saw Leonard Wainwright.

Dressed in pyjamas and an old striped bathrobe, the forensic archaeologist lay crumpled near the foot of the stairs, among the shattered remains of a glass-fronted china cabinet. Splashes of blood from where he'd been cut by the broken glass had dried blackly. But there wasn't enough of it for him to have bled to death. His head was twisted impossibly far to one side, almost resting on one shoulder. *Broken neck*, I thought automatically.

'What about his wife?' I asked. There was no sign of Jean Wainwright, and the news report had only mentioned a single death.

'She's been hospitalised. Hopefully only from shock. Their cleaner found them both this morning when she let herself in. Jean was in a . . . confused state. She hasn't been able to tell us much so far, but I'm hoping she'll be able to answer questions later.'

'So she hasn't said who did it?'

'Not as yet.'

First Sophie, now Wainwright. I didn't think there was much doubt.

'Has the pathologist found anything?' I asked.

'He says Wainwright's been dead for between eight and twelve hours,' said Simms. 'That puts the time of death between one and five a.m. His neck's been broken, which seems the most probable cause of death.'

'It would take a lot of force to do that,' I said, thinking how Monk had killed the police dog on the moor eight years ago.

I followed Simms back down the hallway. As soon as we were outside he began stripping off his overalls.

'Are there any other witnesses apart from Jean Wainwright?' I asked, unfastening my own.

'Unfortunately not. But I'm hopeful she'll be able to provide us with a detailed account before much longer.'

'It looks like Monk, though, doesn't it?'

'That remains to be seen. And I'd thank you not to speculate. The last thing I need is for the press to start running with unfounded rumours.'

I understood then. For someone as PR-conscious as Simms, it was bad enough that Monk had escaped. The last thing he wanted was for stories to circulate that the escaped killer was on some sort of vendetta. That was exactly the sort of publicity an ambitious ACC could do without.

'Jean Wainwright called me two days ago,' Simms said. 'She told me you'd been here, and that Leonard had become very agitated. Care to tell me what that was about?'

I suppose I should have expected this. 'I wanted to talk to him about Monk. I didn't know about his condition. If I had—'

'Jerome Monk doesn't concern you, Dr Hunter. And now you've put me in the embarrassing position of having to ask where you were this morning between one and five o'clock?'

But I'd been waiting for that. 'I was in bed at Sophie Keller's house. And no, she can't vouch for me. As for Jerome Monk, you can't seriously think I'm not going to ask questions after what happened yesterday.'

'What are you talking about?'

'When Monk came after us on the moor.' Simms was looking at me as though I were mad. 'Oh, come on. Terry Connors must have told you!'

Simms had gone very still. The only sign of emotion on the waxlike face was the compressed line of his lips.

'Terry Connors isn't involved in this investigation. He's been suspended.'

7

It started raining as I drove out to Black Tor. The water came down in sheets, so that the windscreen wipers were hard-pressed to clear the glass. By the time I reached the overgrown mine workings, the sky had darkened so much that it seemed almost night.

Roper was in the passenger seat. Simms had told me to make him my first point of contact rather than Naysmith, suggesting there was no love lost between him and the SIO. Sophie was still at Wainwright's, giving her statement. At least I assumed she was; I hadn't had a chance to speak to her before we left. Roper had returned my keys and assured me that someone would take her home. Then a procession of cars had set off for Dartmoor.

Up ahead, the blurred taillights of the ACC's black BMW were screened by a fine mist of spray thrown up by its tyres. The press conference had been postponed so that Simms could come out here. He'd demanded to hear everything, starting from when Terry appeared on my doorstep on the morning of Monk's escape. I'd kept nothing back, not even Sophie's letters to Monk. I'd felt guilty about that, but we'd gone beyond keeping secrets.

Simms's pale-blue eyes had blazed, but it wasn't until I described finding the holes dug on the moor the day before, and the scrambled chase that followed, that he became incandescent. 'This was twenty-four hours ago and I'm only just *hearing* about it? God *Almighty*!'

I couldn't blame him. I was still trying to take it in myself. Not only was Terry suspended, he wasn't even a DI any more. Simms had told me he'd been demoted to detective sergeant the previous year. It explained why he'd told me to call him on his mobile rather than at headquarters. *I'm never there*, he'd said. At least that much had been true.

I could almost understand him lying about his rank and suspension; pride had always been one of Terry's sins. What was inexcusable was that rather than admit to his charade he'd thrown away a chance to capture Monk. Now Wainwright was dead, and his killer was still on the loose. There was no going back from that.

Beside me, Roper stared at the rain beating against the windscreen and sighed. 'Bloody Connors. He's shafted himself this time. And us.'

I knew an invitation when I heard one. 'Simms said he'd been demoted.'

'Got caught altering an evidence log.' Roper shook his head in disgust. 'Wasn't even anything important, just got his dates mixed up. If he'd owned up he'd have just been slapped on the wrist, but he wouldn't admit to it.'

'And his suspension?' I asked.

Roper sucked his teeth, as though debating whether or not to tell me. 'He assaulted a policewoman.'

'He what?'

'Nothing violent, thank God. He was just too pissed to take no for an answer. Connors never could keep his fly zipped.'

I realised I was squeezing the steering wheel. *No, he couldn't.* I forced myself to relax my grip. 'So he was drunk?'

'Drunk? He's hardly been sober for years. He was on borrowed time even before he got knocked back to DS, and it was all downhill from there.'

'What'll happen to him?' I asked.

'He could be looking at criminal charges. Bloody idiot.' Roper didn't try to hide his satisfaction. He gave me a sideways look. 'So, tell me more about this attack on Miss Keller.'

I ran through what had happened. Roper listened with his hands folded on his paunch. I was starting to revise my opinion of the man. Whatever else Roper might be, I didn't think he was anyone's fool.

'So the locals think it was a burglary, eh?' he said.

'That's what they say.'

'They're probably right. Single woman, living on her own in the sticks. Asking for trouble, really.'

We didn't have much to say to each other after that, but we were almost at Black Tor. Several cars and a dog van were already waiting by the end of the track when we arrived, close to where I'd parked the day before. A mix of uniformed police and CID stood by them, coat collars turned up against the rain. When Simms got out of the BMW, one of the plain-clothes officers stepped forward to speak to him.

'That's Naysmith, the SIO,' Roper muttered as we went over.

Naysmith was a keen-looking man in his early forties, gaunt and raw-boned. I wasn't close enough to hear what was said, but Naysmith gave a terse nod before moving away. The group was all business now as it prepared to go out onto the moor. The air was split by barking as a dog-handler took a German shepherd from a van.

I hoped it had better luck than the last one.

Roper had gone to talk to a small group of plain-clothes officers, so I stood on my own nearby, rain dripping from my coat hood.

'Been a while, Dr Hunter.'

I looked round at the burly man who'd approached. He wore a reflective waterproof coat, and I had to peer at the face inside the hood before I recognised Jim Lucas, the POLSA from the original search. His handshake was as firm as ever, and his eyes crinkled with the same warmth I remembered.

'I didn't realise you were advising on this,' I said, pleased to see a friendly face.

'For my sins. Have to admit, I'd have been happy not to set eyes on this godforsaken spot again.' He paused. 'Bad business about Wainwright.'

I nodded. There was nothing to say.

'The sooner we get Monk back behind bars the better. I hear you and Sophie Keller had a run-in with him yesterday.'

The memory was already starting to seem unreal. 'I think so. We didn't get a close look at him.'

'If you had you wouldn't be here. Either of you.' He let that sink in for a second, then smiled. 'How is Sophie these days?'

'She's fine.' This wasn't the time to go into details.

'Jacked it in to make pots, didn't she? Good for her. I retire myself next year.' He scowled at the foul weather. 'Can't say I'll be sorry. The job's changed since I started. All bureaucracy now. Speaking of which . . .'

He looked behind me as Simms's clipped voice rang out.

'When you're ready, Dr Hunter.'

The ACC had put on a pair of brand new Wellingtons. Not everyone there was so lucky. I saw Roper looking disconsolately at his thin-soled shoes as we set off along the muddy track. The dog-handler, a swarthy man with a shaved head, walked slightly ahead of the rest of us, feeding out a rope attached to the German shepherd's harness as it snuffled the ground.

We waited as handler and dog searched the area where Monk had stood watching while Sophie and I drove away. They found nothing, and were called back. We continued along the track to about the same point that Sophie and I had the day before and began trekking across the moor. I stared ahead anxiously, searching for any sign of the holes. But the moorland seemed untouched, a sea of drab greens and browns that I began to feel was mocking me. *God, please don't let me be wasting everyone's time.*

Then, just as had happened the day before, the heather and grass around us was suddenly pockmarked with muddy craters.

I felt irrationally relieved. Everyone stopped. The only sound was the patter of rain on our coats, then one of the policemen broke the silence.

'Bloody big moles they've got round here,' he said.

Nobody laughed. Naysmith motioned the dog-handler forward. The German shepherd strained on its line, nose pressed to the ground. Almost straight away it began following something.

'He's got a scent,' the dog-handler called, but even as he did the dog changed direction and began zigzagging aimlessly. 'It's all over.'

'I can see someone's been here. I want to know where he went,' Simms snapped. 'Try to find a trail leading away.'

As the dog-handler moved off, Naysmith squatted by one of the holes. 'Well, looks like the other graves must be somewhere nearby. Wouldn't be much point him digging like a dog for a bone otherwise.'

'We searched this entire area last time without finding anything,' Roper said. 'He could have hidden a stash of cash here. Makes more sense than digging up bodies that have been safely buried for years.'

He had a point, but Simms was having none of it. 'Monk wouldn't have buried money. That'd involve planning ahead, and he doesn't think like that. No, this was about finding the Bennett girls. Dr Hunter, where was Monk when you first saw him?'

I scanned the moor. This was Sophie's speciality, not mine, but in his wisdom Simms had made her stay behind. Still, I felt reasonably confident as I pointed. 'Over there. About a hundred yards away.'

Rain dripped from the rim of his hat as Simms looked dubiously at the unremarkable patch of moor. There wasn't much to see, no tor or hummocks large enough to have concealed anyone as big as Monk.

'He can't have appeared from nowhere. Where did he come from?'

'He was just standing there when we saw him. That's all I can tell you.'

Simms's gloved fingers drummed against his leg, like a restless cat twitching its tail. 'Bring the dog,' he said, and started walking.

The moor became boggier as we headed further out. It was only as we neared the spot where I'd seen Monk that I realised this was where he'd claimed the other graves were eight years ago, before Sophie's discovery of the badger sett had diverted us. I considered mentioning it, but Simms was sceptical enough already. *Don't push your luck.*

I stopped and looked around, trying to gauge how far we'd come.

'Well?' Simms prompted.

'Round here somewhere, but it's hard to say where exactly.' I was uncomfortably aware that everyone was watching me.

Naysmith motioned to the dog-handler. 'See if you can find anything.'

The handler began casting round with his dog in an attempt to pick up Monk's trail. But they floundered straight away, the German shepherd's paws sinking into black mud. The dog thrashed and whined as its handler hauled it out, only for it to become stuck again moments later. Finally, it seemed to catch a scent on a stretch of firmer ground. Its ears pricked up in interest as it began to follow it, only suddenly to whine and back away.

'Now what?' Simms demanded, as the dog sneezed and pawed its nose.

'Ammonia,' the handler said, sniffing with distaste. The pungent smell was bad enough for humans; to a dog's sensitive nose it would be actively painful. He patted the German shepherd, giving Simms a reproachful look. 'Someone was expecting us. We're done here.'

Simms seemed about to insist, but Naysmith intervened. 'It's going to be dark soon. We can bring more dogs out tomorrow, organise a proper search. There's not much more we can do tonight.'

He stared levelly back as the ACC glared at him. Simms's hand tapped impatiently at his side before he gave a grudging nod.

'All right. But first thing tomorrow—'

'*Over here.*'

The shout came from Jim Lucas. He stood on a low hummock, looking down at something on its far side. Simms's Wellingtons slapped against his legs as he went over, leaving the rest of us to follow.

The ground dropped away behind the hummock, so it was lower than it first appeared. The concealed side was camouflaged with scrubby gorse, except for where rocks broke through. In the angle where several rocks leaned against each other was a sheer black hole less than a metre across.

'Christ, is that a cave?' Naysmith asked.

Jim Lucas was studying his map. 'There aren't any caves on this part of the moor. They're all in the limestone further out, like the ones at Buckfastleigh.' He folded up the map. 'No, it's an adit.'

'A what?' Simms demanded.

'An old mine entrance. This used to be tin-mining country until about a hundred years ago. Small-scale stuff, mainly. Most of the tunnels were filled in or sealed off, but not all of them. Some are still there.'

Naysmith bent over the opening. 'Looks deep.'

A CID officer passed him a torch. He shone it into the opening and peered inside. His voice sounded hollow.

'Can't see much. Goes back a long way.'

'Get the dog over here,' Simms said.

The handler brought the German shepherd forward. Its coat was black with mud and steam curled from its lolling tongue, but it had recovered from the ammonia. When it neared the opening its ears snapped up, and it lurched towards the hole. Its paws scrabbled as the handler hauled it back.

'OK, good boy.' He fussed and patted it as he looked up at Simms. 'No two ways about it. Either he came out of here or he went down. Or both.'

There was a silence as that sank in. It was Roper who spoke first.

'Well, now we know why Monk wanted to come out here eight years ago. And why he's so hard to find.' The DI's teeth were bared in a grin that was almost a snarl. 'The bastard's gone to ground.'

THE LIGHTS WERE ON in Sophie's house when I pulled up in the lane. I switched off the engine and sat in the darkness, taking a moment to savour the quiet before I went inside. I'd had no choice but to come back. For one thing my bag was still here, but I wanted to check on Sophie anyway; I hadn't had a chance to speak to her since we'd split up at Wainwright's.

A lot had happened since then.

Naysmith had stationed two police officers at the adit in case Monk resurfaced there, though that wasn't likely. Lucas had told me more about the tin mines as we'd walked back to the cars. The remains of old mines could be found across Dartmoor. Not all the tunnels had survived, and the more accessible entrances were sealed behind locked gates and steel bars.

But adits like the one we'd found still existed, overgrown and all but invisible unless you knew what to look for. Monk obviously did.

'We knew about the mines, but they weren't considered a serious option,' Lucas told me, 'because as far as we knew Monk didn't have any caving experience. And believe me those mines are scary places. You don't want to go down them unless you know what you're doing.'

'So they weren't checked at all?'

'Well, the bigger ones were searched after the girls went missing, in case Monk had dumped the bodies in them. But we didn't go very far down, and after that we just had dogs sniff round the main entrances. We didn't find anything, so that was that.' Lucas puffed out his cheeks. 'If Monk's been using them, Christ knows where he is. I'd bet not all the old adits will be shown on maps. Monk could go down one hole and surface God knows where.'

That was an unsettling thought. 'Are there any mines near Padbury?'

'Padbury?'

'That's where Sophie lives.'

'Let's take a look, shall we?' Lucas unfolded his map, stubby finger tracing a path as he consulted it. 'Nothing nearby. The closest would be Cutter's Wheal Mine, about three miles away, but that's sealed off.'

I was glad of that much, at least. I locked the car, and walked up the path to the house. Taking a deep breath, I knocked on the front door.

Nothing happened for a while, but just when I was about to try again I heard the bolts being shot inside. The door opened on its newly fitted chain and Sophie looked out at me from the gap. The door closed in my face, then there was a rattle as the chain was unfastened and it was opened again.

Without a word, she went back down the hallway. I heard the sound of vegetables being chopped as I closed and bolted the door. *Doesn't look good.* I pulled off my muddy boots and followed her into the kitchen.

She had her back to me. The knife thumped on to the chopping board.

'How did it go? Your statement,' I said.

'As you'd expect.' The line of her back was stiff and uncompromising. She scraped the sliced carrots into a pan and began cutting potatoes.

I took a deep breath. 'Look, I'm sorry. I told Simms about your letters to Monk. I didn't have any choice.'

'I know. I told them myself. I'm not a complete idiot, I know I couldn't keep it a secret. I even printed them copies from the computer.'

'So you're OK about it?'

'Why shouldn't I be? It wasn't against the law to write to Monk.' She didn't turn to look at me. The knife sliced up and down, rapping the board.

'So what's wrong?'

'What's *wrong*?' She slammed down the knife. 'They took me away like a—a *criminal*! No one told me anything! I didn't know you'd gone until some hatchet-faced policewoman said she'd bring me home. I felt *useless*!'

'I'm sorry.'

She sighed and shook her head. 'Oh, I know it isn't your fault. First there was the shock of Wainwright being murdered, and then . . . then I had the door closed in my face. It's the first time it's really been brought home to me that I'm not a BIA any more; I'm just a civilian. I *hated* being left out! But I shouldn't take it out on you.'

'Don't worry about it. It's been a rough day for everyone.'

'That's no excuse.' She put her hand on my arm, and suddenly there was a tension between us. It broke when Sophie lowered her hand, turning quickly back to the worktop. 'So what happened after I'd gone?'

I told her about Wainwright, and the adit. 'The police are sending down a cave team, but Lucas doesn't think Monk will still be there. Once we'd seen him yesterday he'd have realised we'd find the mine.' *That one, at least.*

'So that was why he said he'd take us to the graves. He just wanted to get close to the mine so he could escape,' she said bitterly.

'And there's something else.'

I told her about Terry.

'He's *suspended*?' Sophie looked stunned. 'I'd no idea.'

'No reason you should have. By the sound of things he's in denial himself. He's got a drinking problem and his career's on the skids. Simms wants us to let Roper know if we hear from him again, but after what happened to Wainwright I don't think he'd dare.' I took a deep breath. 'I think you should reconsider staying somewhere else until this has blown over.'

Sophie's mouth set stubbornly. 'We've already been through this.'

'That was before Wainwright was killed.'

'We don't know for sure that was Monk, and even if it was, why would he want to hurt me? I didn't do anything to him.'

You didn't have to. You're an attractive woman. For a behavioural specialist, she could be obtuse when it suited her.

'All Wainwright did was insult him eight years ago, but he's still dead,' I said. 'We don't know what's driving Monk. Perhaps Terry's right and he's going after anyone from the original search team. If not, you still brought yourself to his attention by writing to him. It isn't worth the risk.'

She was still scared, I could see that. But her chin was up again in defiance. 'I can look after myself. No one's asking you to stay.'

God, but she could be infuriating. My bag was packed, and I was under no illusions as to my chances if Monk did turn up. But I knew I wasn't going to leave her there alone. Not because she was attractive, or even because of the spark between us. No, my reason was simpler than that: we have to be able to live with ourselves.

I sighed. 'I'm not going anywhere.'

She gave me a tired smile. 'Thank you.'

Dinner was a vegetable curry, thrown together from what little was left in Sophie's pantry and fridge. The meal was a subdued affair. I was acutely conscious of how isolated we were out there, and despite her bravado I think Sophie was too. The past few days had taken their toll on her. When I told her I'd clear up while she went to bed, she didn't put up much of a fight.

'If you're sure . . . Help yourself to whatever you like. There's brandy in the sitting room.'

I was tired myself, but I knew if I went to bed I'd only lie awake, listening to every creak and bump in the old house. After Sophie had gone upstairs I washed and dried the dishes, then went to hunt down a drink. The brandy turned out to be a fifteen-year-old Armagnac. I poured myself a healthy measure, threw another log into the stove and sank back onto the sofa, staring at the flames. I could smell a faint trace of Sophie's scent on the cushions. I sipped the Armagnac, puzzling again over her stubbornness.

The ringing of the phone woke me. I sat bolt upright, hastily setting the glass aside. I snatched up the handset before it could ring again.

'Hello?' There was no answer. *Please yourself*, I thought irritably, about to hang up. Then I heard a sound down the line. Adenoidal and laboured, the wheeze of someone breathing.

Suddenly I knew it was Monk on the other end. The hairs on my forearms stood up. I found my voice. 'What do you want?'

Nothing. The breathing continued. The moment stretched on, then there was a soft *click* as the connection was broken.

I realised I'd been holding my own breath. I lowered the handset and looked at my watch: two thirty. The house was silent; I'd answered the phone before it could wake Sophie. I hurried into the kitchen, searching for a pen and paper before playing back the caller's number and scribbling it down.

From the code it looked like a local landline. Dazed, I called Roper and left a message on his voicemail. I'd no proof it was Monk. But I knew.

I made sure the front door was still locked and bolted, and went from room to room to check the windows. The old wooden frames wouldn't keep anyone out, but at least I'd hear if they broke in. I went back into the sitting room and stoked the embers in the stove before adding more kindling and another log. I closed the stove door and laid the poker down within easy reach. Then I settled down to wait for morning.

EVEN THOUGH I'd left a message for Roper, he wouldn't have been my first choice of police officer to call, but I didn't have Naysmith's mobile number, and I didn't think the SIO would be at his desk in the middle of the night.

I waited until a reasonable hour before trying him, only to be put through to yet more answering services. I briefly explained what had happened and gave Sophie's number rather than trust the poor mobile reception.

Having done all I could, I set about waking myself up. Despite my best intentions, I'd fallen asleep on the sofa as the chorus of birdsong had begun outside, and now I felt groggy and had a crick in my neck. Leaving Sophie to sleep, I stood under a hot shower until I felt a little more human.

She was in the kitchen, wrapped in a thick towelling bathrobe, when I went downstairs. 'Morning. We're down to cereal, I'm afraid.'

'Cereal's fine.'

She rubbed her eyes. 'God, I feel wrecked. I bet I look it, too.'

I'd been thinking just the opposite. Even with her sleep-tousled hair and loosely tied bathrobe there was a natural poise to her.

The harsh ring of the phone brought me round like ice-water. *Damn*. I'd been hoping to tell Sophie about the call before anyone phoned.

'That might be for me,' I said quickly, but she'd already answered it.

'Yes . . . Oh.' She made a moue of distaste and mouthed *Roper*. 'He is. Just a second.' She gave me a questioning look and passed me the handset.

I was aware of her standing there as I told Roper about the phone call.

'What makes you think it was Monk?' he asked.

'The fact that he didn't speak, for one thing. People normally apologise if they call the wrong number, and . . .' I stopped, glancing at Sophie.

'And?' Roper prompted.

Oh, hell. I felt Sophie's eyes boring into me. 'It was only an impression, but I thought he was . . . surprised. As though I wasn't who he'd expected.'

'All this from a silent phone call?'

I ignored his scepticism. 'His breathing was deep, and I could hear him wheezing, as though he were out of breath or asthmatic.'

'Heavy breathing, eh? You sure this wasn't just a dirty phone call?'

My hand had tightened on the receiver. 'Monk was having a suspected heart attack when he escaped. Perhaps he wasn't faking being ill.'

I couldn't believe even Monk could have escaped if the attack had been genuine, but something must have convinced the prison doctors.

'Can't hurt to check the number, I suppose,' Roper said, after a pause. 'Tell you what, I'll call round and take your statement myself.'

'Don't go to any trouble,' I said, my stomach sinking.

Roper gave his nasal chuckle. 'Oh, it's no trouble, Dr Hunter. I'm in the area. And the ACC wants me to keep an eye on you and Miss Keller.'

Which could be taken two ways, I thought as I hung up. Sophie was glaring at me, hands balled on her hips.

'Monk rang *here*? And you didn't *say* anything?'

'It was the middle of the night. I didn't want to disturb you.'

'Don't you think I might have liked to *know* about it?'

There was no point in arguing. 'Look, I'm sorry. I was about to tell you when Roper called. And I'm only guessing it was Monk.'

'God.' She pushed her hands through her hair, troubled. 'Could it have been Terry Connors?'

'I don't think so. If it was Terry, why didn't he say something?'

'Why does he do anything?' she said dully, rubbing her temple.

'There's more good news. Roper's calling round later.'

Sophie stared at me, then burst out laughing. 'Right, just for that you get to make breakfast.'

It was late morning by the time Roper arrived.

'Thought I was never going to get here,' he grumbled, as he stepped inside. 'Not an easy place to find, is it?'

'I thought you were in the area?'

He bared his teeth in a grin. 'Relatively speaking, Dr Hunter.' The grin flickered out. 'Actually there's been a bit of a development.'

So the visit wasn't just about the phone call. 'What's happened?'

The DI looked uncomfortable. 'Wainwright's wife gave us a description of the man who killed her husband. It was Monk.'

'I'M NOT GOING!' Sophie stood at the kitchen door, arms folded in front of her like a barred gate.

Roper wore the dogged expression of a man at the end of his tether. 'It'll only be for a few days. You can come back as soon as Monk's in custody.'

'Last time it took you three months to catch him,' Sophie retorted. 'If you think I'm going to put my life on hold until then, you can forget it.'

Roper looked as if he could have cheerfully strangled her himself. I couldn't altogether blame him. Jean Wainwright had recovered from shock enough to relate what had happened. She'd been woken in the night by a commotion inside the house. Thinking her husband must be wandering—something many dementia sufferers were prone to do—she'd thrown on a dressing gown and hurried onto the landing. She'd turned on the light to find Wainwright lying at the foot of the stairs. Standing over him was Monk.

She'd passed out, and had still been only semiconscious when the cleaner arrived. Preliminary forensic tests had confirmed her story. Monk's fingerprints were all over the house, and DNA from the sputum found on the floor also matched the convict's. He'd made no attempt to cover his tracks.

The anonymous call to Sophie had been made from a lonely public phone box near Dartmoor prison, where Monk had spent the early years of his sentence. That could have been a coincidence, but there was a more compelling reason why the location might have appealed to him.

There was an old tin mine nearby.

The cave team who had gone down had reported that, like the larger mine at Black Tor, it was flooded and impassable after the recent rains.

'Now we know what he's up to he's on a hiding to nothing,' said Roper. 'It's only a matter of time before he's caught. The question is what sort of damage he can do before then.'

Which was why Simms had arranged for Sophie to stay at a police safe house. Or perhaps 'instructed' was more accurate.

The conversation had gone downhill from there.

'I'm not going to some grubby safe house because of some . . . some stupid phone call you don't even know for sure was *from* Monk,' she said. 'This is my *home*.'

'That didn't stop someone from waltzing in and knocking you unconscious a few days ago.' Roper raised his eyebrows in mock enquiry. 'Don't suppose you've remembered anything about that yet, have you?'

'Don't you think I'd have told you if I had? Anyway, that was nothing to do with Jerome Monk. The police said it was just a burglary.'

'So I gather. Except you haven't reported anything stolen, have you?'

Sophie opened her mouth, then closed it. 'There was some cash I'd left lying around and a few pieces of cheap jewellery. Didn't seem worth reporting.'

That was news to me: she hadn't said anything was missing.

Roper regarded her for a moment. 'Look, love—'

'I'm not your "love". And I'm not leaving. You can't expect me to just drop everything, I've got a business to run!'

'You should have thought about that before you chose a murderer as a pen pal,' Roper snapped. 'To Monk that's as good as an invitation.'

Sophie folded her arms. 'I'm not going.'

Roper sighed, looking at me as though to say, *Well?*

'He's right,' I told her. 'It doesn't have to be a safe house. Like I said, we could go to a hotel for a few days—'

'No.' She turned to Roper. 'Sorry you've had a wasted trip. Now if you don't mind, I've got work to do.'

She banged out of the kitchen and headed for the kiln.

Roper stared after her. 'Well, that's that.'

'Can't you arrange for police protection here?'

'We're not a private security service. She's been offered a safe house, but if she wants to stick her head in the sand that's up to her.' He shook his head. 'The ACC isn't going to like this.'

I saw him out, watching as he drove away, then I fetched my coat and went across to the kiln. I could hear the whirr of the potter's wheel before I opened the door. Sophie sat behind it, wearing work overalls now, intently shaping a bowl from a piece of wet clay.

'I'm not going to change my mind,' she said, without looking up.

'I know. I just wanted to see if you were all right.'

'I'm fine.'

'You didn't say anything before about anything being missing.'

'There was nothing valuable. It wasn't worth mentioning.'

I waited. She kept her attention on the wheel. 'I need to work, OK?'

I headed back to the house. I couldn't understand why Sophie was being so stubborn. But then I didn't really know her. *So why are you staying? Just for her?* That was part of it, but there was another reason, one that had been nudging at me ever since I'd heard about Monk's escape. And perhaps even longer: back to the abortive search on the moor. I wanted answers.

I'd just reached the house when my phone beeped. The signal was unreliable here, but a text message had got through. It was short and to the point.

Trencherman's Arms, 2 p.m.

It was from Terry.

THE DRIZZLE gave way to rain as I neared the higher ground at Oldwich. It was the sort of monotonous downpour that seemed as though it could go on for ever. The Trencherman's car park was empty except for one other car. The grubby paintwork and litter-strewn interior made me doubt it was Terry's. Although the yellow Mitsubishi must have been long gone, he'd always been as fastidious about his car's appearance as he was about his own.

But when I went into the pub and saw he was the only customer, I realised the car must be his after all. He was sitting at a secluded corner table. His clothes were crumpled and unwashed, and he was staring into his beer glass with an expression I'd not seen before. He looked lost.

Then he noticed me and it vanished. His shoulders straightened as I went over. He sat back, regarding me with something like his old arrogance.

'I wasn't sure you'd come.'

I pulled up a chair and sat opposite him. 'Why did you want to see me?'

A sour smell of sweat and unmetabolised alcohol came across the table.

'Aren't you having a drink?'

'I won't be staying long.'

I'd told Sophie I was going to buy food. That was no lie: I'd stopped off at a local shop on my way here to stock up on groceries. I didn't like leaving her alone at the house, but after Roper's visit we both needed some time to ourselves. Still, I didn't plan on being away any longer than I had to.

Terry took a drink himself. 'You tell anyone where you were going?'

'No.'

'How about Sophie?' His grin was vicious. 'Don't tell me you've not got your feet under that table. Sympathetic shoulder and all that.'

'Either you tell me what's going on, Terry, or I'm leaving.'

'OK.' He drained the rest of his beer and set his glass down. 'I heard about Wainwright. Monk doesn't mess about, does he?'

'How did you know?' There had been no mention of Monk being a suspect on the news, so I guessed Simms was still stalling for time.

'I've still got a few friends left on the force.' Terry sounded bitter. 'I expect you've spoken to Simms.'

'He told me you'd been suspended,' I said. 'You let me think you were still part of the investigation. Why?'

'It's hard to explain.'

'Try.'

He frowned into his glass. 'I've made a mess of everything. My marriage, my family, my career. The last time I did anything I was proud of was when I tackled Jerome Monk out on the moor.'

His mouth quirked into a grin at the memory. It didn't last long.

'When he escaped . . . well, it brought a lot of things back. Suspended or not, I'm still a police officer. I couldn't just sit at home listening to the news. And I know how Simms's mind works. He made his name from putting Monk away, and he won't want anything to tarnish that. His first priority is going to be covering his own back. Especially now Wainwright's been murdered.' Terry gave a lopsided grin. 'They were friends. It's going to look pretty bad if an ACC can't even protect his old cronies. Especially if people start asking why Monk went after Wainwright in the first place.'

'Perhaps he remembers how Wainwright treated him.' *To think society wastes money keeping animals like this alive*. 'You said yourself he might have grudges against anybody involved in the search.'

'There's got to be more to it than that. Monk's been locked up for the last eight years.You seriously think he doesn't have more important things on his mind than offing a senile old archaeologist who hurt his feelings?'

'Then why did he kill him?'

'To get back at Simms.' Terry leaned forward. 'Think about it. Simms made it a personal *crusade* to put Monk away. Well, now the boot's on the other foot, except Monk knows he'll never get anywhere near Simms. So he's trying to humiliate him instead, going after easy targets like Wainwright to stir up as much shit as possible before he's caught. What's he got to lose?'

There was a perverse logic to it, but something didn't quite ring true.

'Why are you telling me this? What can I do about it?'

'For a start you can get Sophie away from her house. I'm guessing it's pretty isolated. Take her somewhere safe until Monk's behind bars again.'

'I've tried. I don't know if it's because she doesn't want to leave her home or her work, or if she's just being stubborn. Simms sent Roper to persuade her to go to a police safe house, but she wouldn't listen.'

He seemed distracted, but then his mouth curled in contempt. 'Simms must be running scared to even offer a safe house. He's a politician; he's worried how things *look*. All he can do now is spin the murder as a one-off and hope Monk's stopped before he kills anyone else.'

It sounded plausible, but then Terry was good at that. 'If you're so concerned about catching Monk, why didn't you tell Naysmith that we'd seen him on the moor? This could have been over by now.'

'That was a bad call, I admit. I thought you must be exaggerating.' He sighed. 'God knows, I've been regretting it ever since.'

I shook my head. 'Nice try, Terry.'

'What do you mean?'

'You're not doing this out of concern for Sophie. I don't know what you want, but Simms isn't the only one with an agenda, is he?'

He tried to laugh it off. 'Christ, you're a suspicious sod, aren't you? Come on, everybody deserves a second chance. Even me.'

I didn't say anything, just looked at him. His expression didn't exactly alter, but somehow the angles of his face hardened. He gave a tight smile.

'So that's how it is, eh? I thought you might have got rid of that chip on your shoulder by now. Looks like I was wrong.'

I wasn't going to waste my time arguing. I'd come here hoping for answers, but I obviously wasn't going to get any. I pushed my chair back and headed for the door, but Terry hadn't finished.

'Give my regards to Sophie!' he called after me. 'And don't fall for that vulnerable routine. She used that on me as well!'

It was cold and raining outside but I barely noticed. I drove away from the village without giving any thought to where I was going.

Sophie and Terry? They'd never even *liked* each other. On the search operation they'd barely spoken, and when they had they'd struggled to be civil. *And why was that? Because there was nothing between them?*

I felt as though the world had subtly shifted. It was no good telling myself that Terry was lying. There had been a sneering triumph in his voice, as though he'd been waiting for his moment. Sophie's past was nothing to do with me. I'd no right to judge her, or to feel jealous. But we were in the middle of a murder investigation, and it wasn't just anybody.

It was Terry Connors.

I hadn't been paying attention to where I was going, and I had to drive until I saw a signpost before I realised where I was. I'd been heading away from Padbury, and had to backtrack to pick up the right road.

The mist began to close in again as I left the high moor behind. Soon it had thickened to a blank fog, hazing my vision like cataracts and forcing me to slow down. By the time I reached Sophie's house, twilight was gathering, the windows glowing like lighthouses through the gloom.

There was another car parked behind Sophie's in the lane.

Leaving the groceries in the car, I hurried up the path and banged on the front door and waited, straining for any sound from inside. I heard the bolts being shot back, and then the door was opened.

'There's a car in the lane—' I stopped. The chain was on but it was a man's face that stared at me through the gap.

'That'd be mine. Can I help you?' he said.

Sophie's voice came from behind him. 'It's all right, Nick, let him in.'

The man looked past me, scanning the path and garden before closing the door and slipping off the chain. He opened it and stood back, a fit-looking man in his early thirties, wearing jeans and a faded sweatshirt. As soon as I was inside he closed and bolted the door again.

Sophie was in the hallway, smiling. A pretty blonde woman stood next to her: short, but with the compact muscularity of a gymnast. As the man finished locking up, I saw her hand move away from her hip.

There was a gun holstered there.

'David, meet Steph Cross and Nick Miller.' Sophie's smile broadened. 'They're my bodyguards.'

8

If I hadn't been told that Miller and Cross were police, I'd never have guessed. Both were specialist firearms officers, trained in close protection work, but there was nothing about their appearance or attitude to suggest it. In their casual clothes they might have been teachers or medics.

Except for the guns, of course.

'What made Roper change his mind?' I asked. We were in the kitchen, sitting round the table while Sophie unpacked the groceries I'd fetched from the car and began preparing dinner.

'Roper?' Miller asked. He was the more outgoing of the two.

'DI Roper. He's on the ACC's staff.'

'Bit too high and mighty for us, then,' Miller said. 'Our orders came from Naysmith, the SIO on the case. We were told to pack our bags for a trip to the country, so here we are. Ours not to reason why, and all that.'

At least Naysmith was taking Sophie's safety seriously.

'How long will you be staying?' she asked them, scraping chopped onion into a pan. Their arrival seemed to have lifted a weight from her.

'Long enough,' Miller said, peering at the Bolognese sauce Sophie was preparing. 'Don't worry, we won't get under your feet. Just keep us fed and watered and you won't even know we're here. Although you might want to sauté the onions a bit longer before you add the meat.'

Sophie put down the spoon, mock-indignant. 'Do you want to do this?'

'Naw, cooking's not part of my job description. But I'm a quarter Italian; I know these things. I'd go easy with the salt, as well.'

Sophie appealed to Cross. 'Is he always like this?'

The blonde policewoman was younger and quieter than her partner, but there was an air of unruffled competence about her that was reassuring. 'You learn not to take any notice,' she said.

Miller looked hurt. 'I'm just saying, that's all.'

It was almost possible to forget why the pair were there, which was probably the idea. It would be easier to guard someone if they were relaxed.

And Sophie had certainly relaxed. Her objection to staying in a safe house didn't extend to other types of protection. I was glad about that, but the meeting with Terry still preyed on my mind. I hadn't had a chance to talk to Sophie about it. Miller and Cross must have picked up on the atmosphere, because after a while they made an excuse and left us alone. Sophie was on such a high that even then she didn't notice.

'They're really nice, aren't they?' she said, stirring the simmering pasta sauce. 'Did you know Naysmith was going to send them?'

'No.'

Sophie broke off to look at me. 'I thought you'd be pleased. What's wrong?'

'I saw Terry Connors this afternoon.'

She turned back to the saucepan. 'What stone did he crawl from under?'

'He said he wanted to explain.'

'Oh?'

'I didn't know there'd been anything between you.'

She had her back to me, her face hidden. The only sound was the spoon rattling against the pan. 'There's no reason why you should.'

'Don't you think you should have mentioned it?'

'I don't like to talk about it. It was a mistake. A long time ago.'

I said nothing. Sophie put the spoon down and turned to face me.

'Look, it's in the past, all right? It's none of your business anyway. I don't have to tell you everything!'

She was right: she didn't. But she was wrong about it being none of my business. It had become that when she asked for my help. Whatever game Terry was playing affected us both. The sauce popped and bubbled in the pan.

'You need to stir that,' I said, and went upstairs.

My bag was back in my room. I threw the rest of my things into it. The last thing I felt like was a long drive back to London. But Sophie was safe now with Miller and Cross there. And I'd had enough of feeling used.

I'd finished packing when I heard a noise from the doorway.

Sophie was watching me. 'What are you doing?' she said.

I zipped the bag shut. 'It's time I left.'

'Now?' She looked surprised.

'You've got two armed guards. You'll be fine.'

'David . . .' She rubbed her temple with her fingers. 'I know I should have said something, OK? I'm sorry. I was going to, just . . . not yet. It isn't something I'm proud of. I was going through a bad patch and . . . it sort of happened. It wasn't much more than a fling, really. He told me he was separated, that he was getting a divorce. As soon as I realised he was lying I ended it.' She was watching me nervously, her expression sincere.

'Had you been seeing him recently?' I asked.

'No, I swear.' She came over, but stopped just in front of me. 'Stay tonight. If you still feel the same way tomorrow, then I promise I won't try to stop you. But don't leave like this. Please?'

I hesitated, then put down my bag. Sophie hugged me, her body tight against mine.

'I'm not always a very good person,' she said, her voice muffled.

For once I didn't want to believe her.

DINNER WAS surprisingly relaxed. That was largely down to Miller, whose banter made the meal seem more like a social occasion than guard duty. Cross said little, content to leave the conversational running to her partner. Sophie opened a bottle of wine, but only she and I drank any.

Naysmith had phoned earlier to check on us. The SIO was brisk and businesslike when I took the phone from Miller to speak to him.

'Is there any news about Monk?' I asked.

'Not yet.'

'I just wondered if something had happened to make you put Sophie under close protection. DI Roper didn't seem keen on the idea earlier.'

'DI Roper isn't the SIO; I am,' he said. 'We found Monk's fingerprints on the phone box, which confirms he's tried to contact her. As far as I'm concerned, that justifies taking whatever measures are necessary. You've got two good officers there. Their orders are not to take any chances, so whatever they tell you to do, you do it. No arguments, no debates. Clear?'

I said it was.

Monk wasn't mentioned during dinner, but despite Miller's best efforts the convict's presence loomed over the table like an unwanted guest. When the empty dishes had been stacked in the sink, Sophie reached for the bottle of wine. I shook my head when she made to refill my glass; she poured what was left into her own and set the bottle down with a thump.

'So how long have you two been doing this?' she asked, taking a drink.

'Too long,' Miller said. Cross just smiled.

'Do you always work together as a team?'

'Not always. Depends on the job.'

'Right.' Sophie set down her glass unsteadily. Suddenly she seemed drunk. She must have had more wine than I'd thought. She waved her hand at the guns holstered on their hips. 'Aren't you uncomfortable wearing those?'

'You get used to it,' Miller replied.

'Can I take a look?'

'Best not.' He said it lightly enough, though it was obvious that he wasn't happy. Cross was watching Sophie with her usual Zen-like calm, but the atmosphere round the table had abruptly changed.

Sophie seemed oblivious. 'Have you ever used them?'

'Well, they like us to know which end the bullets come out of.'

'But have you ever *shot* anyone?'

'Sophie . . .' I began.

'It's a legitimate question.' She stumbled over 'legitimate'. 'If Monk walked in here, now, would you be able to kill him?'

Miller exchanged a look with Cross. 'Let's hope it doesn't come to that.'

'Yes, but if he did—'

'Who'd like coffee?' I said.

Miller seized on the opening. 'Sounds good.'

Sophie blinked, as though she were struggling to keep up. 'Coffee? Oh . . . right, sorry.' She stood up but clutched the table as she suddenly swayed. 'Whoa . . .'

I reached out to support her. 'Are you all right?'

Her face had paled but she tried to smile as she straightened. 'God . . . what was in that wine?'

'Why don't you go to bed?' I said.

'I . . . I think I'd better.'

I went upstairs with her. 'How are you feeling?' I asked when we reached the bedroom.

'Just a bit woozy.' She was still pale but looked better than she had downstairs. 'My own fault. All that wine when I've hardly eaten all day.'

Reaction was probably as much to blame as the wine, and I was mindful that she was still recovering from concussion.

'Are you sure you're OK?'

'I'm fine. You go back downstairs.' She smiled tiredly.

I went down to the kitchen. I could hear murmured voices but they fell silent as I approached.

'How is she?' Miller asked. I noticed he had his radio in his hand.

'Just tired. Has something happened?'

'Naw, I'm just checking in. That offer of coffee still on?'

I put the kettle on to boil and spooned instant coffee into three mugs.

'Not for me, thanks,' Cross said. 'Time to do the rounds.'

I watched her go. 'She isn't going outside by herself?' I asked Miller.

'No, just seeing that everything's locked up.'

'I thought you'd already checked?'

'Never hurts to make sure.' He said it lightly, but I realised it was in case Sophie or I had unlocked anything. They weren't leaving anything to chance.

I passed him a mug. 'Can I ask something?'

'Fire away.'

'What happens if Monk does come?'

He blew on the coffee to cool it. 'Then we get to earn our wages.'

'You know how dangerous he is?'

'Don't worry, we've been briefed. And we won't underestimate him, if that's what you're worried about.' Miller took a sip of coffee. 'If it's Steph that's bothering you, don't let it. She can look after herself.'

'I'm sure she can.'

'But you'd have been happier if it was two men?'

I didn't like to admit it, but he was right. 'You haven't met Monk.'

Miller's usual brashness had gone. 'Steph's a better shot than I am, she's faster and she could take me in a fight any day.'

There was a half-smile on his face as he spoke, but I don't think he was aware of it. 'We're not here to arrest Monk; our job's to protect Sophie,' he went on. 'At the first sign of trouble we're getting you both the hell out of here. Failing that . . . Well, he's not bullet-proof.'

He gave a cheerful grin that wrinkled the corners of his eyes. Perhaps because I was looking for it I saw the hardness behind them now.

'Do you want a hand with the dishes?' he asked.

It wasn't much longer before I went to bed myself, leaving Miller and Cross sitting at the kitchen table. The only spare room was the one I was in, but Miller assured me neither of them would be sleeping.

I paused outside Sophie's room. There was no sound from inside, so I guessed she was asleep. I went into my own room without turning on the light, and lay down on the bed, fully clothed. *Christ, what a day*. I was tired but I didn't think I'd be able to sleep. There was too much adrenaline racing through my system. I should have felt relaxed with the two armed officers downstairs, but instead I felt restless and pensive. I stared at the ceiling, thinking about Monk, about Simms and Wainwright. And about Sophie and Terry. As my eyelids grew heavy it seemed there was a connection there I could almost see, a tenuous link that hovered frustratingly out of sight . . .

Someone was shaking me. I woke in a panic to find Miller standing by the bed with a torch in his hand.

'Get up, we need to go.'

The last rags of sleep fell away. Blinking against the brightness, I swung my legs off the bed. 'What's happened?'

There was nothing affable about Miller now. His face was grim as he headed back towards the landing.

'Monk's coming.'

I hurried after him. The torch beam made the landing unfamiliar in the darkness. The door to Sophie's room opened and Cross emerged.

'She's getting dressed,' she told him.

I was struggling to take it all in. 'How do you know he's coming?'

'He called again.'

'I didn't hear the phone.'

'We unplugged the upstairs extension so if he rang we could answer it ourselves. We're trying to get a location but it'll take time. So we're getting you both out. We're leaving in two minutes.'

'Just because he phoned again?'

'No, because he thought Steph was Sophie. He told her he was in Padbury and said he was on his way.'

'Why would he warn her?'

'No idea. Could be a bluff but we shan't stick around to find out.' He handed me the torch. 'Go and get Sophie. She should be dressed by now.'

My mind still felt sluggish. *Come on, wake up!* I hurried into the bedroom, expecting to find Sophie dressed and ready. But I found her sitting on the edge of the bed, the duvet draped loosely round her.

'Come on, Sophie, we've got to go.'

'I don't want to.' Her voice was sleepy. 'I don't feel so good.'

I began searching round for her clothes. 'You can rest later. Monk could be here any second. We need to leave.'

She meekly took the clothes I handed her and began to get dressed.

Cross appeared in the doorway. 'Ready?'

'Nearly.'

She waited for us as Sophie finished pulling on her clothes. Miller was standing in darkness by the front door. I gave him back the torch.

'We're just going to walk out to our car, nice and quiet,' he said as I pulled on my boots and fastened my coat, then helped Sophie fumble into hers. 'I'll go first, then you two. Nice and fast but don't run. Steph'll be right behind you. Get in the back of the car and lock the doors. OK?'

Sophie gave an uncertain nod, leaning against me. Miller slid back the bolts, then drew his gun and opened the door in one smooth movement.

Cold, damp air rolled into the hallway. Outside it was pitch black. The beam from Miller's torch bounced back from the thick fog that had closed in round the house. I felt Sophie's hand tighten on mine.

'Stay close,' Miller said, and started down the path.

Mist blanketed everything. Even Miller was just a dark shape, silhouetted against the glow from the torch. Only the deadened scuff of our footsteps told me we were still on the path. The gate creaked as Miller held it open, and then we were on the lane. The hazy outline of their car took shape in front of us. Its lights flashed with an electronic squawk as he unlocked it.

'OK, get in.'

I slid into the back seat beside Sophie. Cross shut the door behind me and climbed into the front as Miller started the engine. There was a *thunk* as the locks engaged and then we were accelerating away.

No one spoke. Cross murmured briefly into her radio, then fell silent again. Miller sat forward in his seat, trying to make out the road. It was like driving on the sea bed, the fog swirling like plankton in the headlights. After a few miles, the sense of tension in the car began to ease.

'Well, that was fun,' Miller said. 'You OK back there?'

'Where are we going?' Sophie asked. She sounded exhausted.

'We're going to take you to a safe house for the time being. Only temporary, but we can sort out what's happening after that tomorrow.'

I waited for Sophie to object, but she seemed past caring. In the darkness of the car I could just see her rubbing her head.

'Sophie? Are you all right?' I asked.

'I don't—' she began, and then Miller yelled, *'Shit!'* as a figure materialised from the fog in front of us.

There was a glimpse of outstretched arms and flapping coat, then Sophie was flung against me as Miller braked and swerved. But not in time. We hit the figure full on, but instead of the expected *thud* of impact it disintegrated in a blizzard of splinters and cloth. The car slewed, throwing me hard against the side window as Miller fought for control.

He almost made it. Fragments of glass peppered us as he punched a hole through the windscreen. The car briefly seemed to level out, then there was a crunching jolt and everything tipped sideways. The car seemed to hang weightless, then something slammed into me. The world became a tumbling confusion of darkness and noise. I was flung around without any sense of up or down. Then there was stillness.

Gradually, sounds and sensations began to reassert themselves. I was sitting upright but at an angle. Something was constricting my chest, making it hard to breathe. I groped at it with leaden hands. I was coated with a fine powder: residue from the airbags. They'd deflated now, draped out like pale tongues. But the seat belt still held me in place like an iron band. I fumbled to unfasten it, and slid down the seat as it slithered free.

'Sophie?' I tried to make her out in the darkness. Relief flowed through me as she stirred. 'Are you hurt?'

'I . . . I feel sick . . .' She sounded dazed.

'Hang on.'

There was movement in front of us as I struggled with Sophie's seat belt. I heard Cross groan. 'You two all right?' she asked.

'I think so.' I tugged at Sophie's seat belt. 'What did we hit?'

But Cross gave a cry and scrambled over to Miller. 'Nick? *Nick?*'

He was slumped in his seat, not moving.

I hurriedly freed Sophie's seat belt. 'Can you get out now?'

'I . . . I think so.'

The door on my side was jammed. The hinges screeched in protest as I kicked it open. My legs almost gave way when I climbed out of the car. I leaned on it for support, aching all over. The car had come to rest at an angle at the bottom of a shallow embankment, its bodywork scraped and mangled. One headlight was smashed and the other gave only a sickly glow, shining sadly into the ground like a blinded eye. There was no sign of fire.

I limped round to the driver's side. The car was more badly damaged here. The roof had crumpled, buckling the door shut. It would have to be cut away before anyone could get to Miller.

Cross was still inside the car next to him, talking urgently on the radio. She'd propped a torch on what was left of the dashboard, and I could see the blood that smeared Miller's face and matted his hair.

I reached through the jagged hole where the window had been and felt for the carotid artery in his neck. There was a pulse but it was weak.

Sophie had climbed out of the car and gingerly made her way over to me. I could feel her shivering as I put my arm round her.

The car creaked as Cross forced her way out. 'Help's on its way.' She'd regained some of her calm. 'They're going to try to send an air ambulance but I don't think it'll be able to get to us in this.'

Neither did I. The fog was as thick as ever, and even if there was somewhere for a helicopter to land I doubted it would attempt it.

'What happened?' Sophie asked. 'God, did we hit someone?'

In the turmoil of the crash I'd forgotten about that. 'I'll go and look.'

'No.' Cross was firm. 'We wait here for help to arrive.'

I saw with surprise that she'd taken her gun from its holster. But I was already replaying the snatched images of the figure caught in the headlights, recalling how it had come apart when we hit it. Not like there'd been flesh and bone inside the coat, more like . . . branches. A scarecrow.

'She's right,' I said. 'We should stay here.'

'We can't just leave them there!' Sophie protested.

Cross was staring into the darkness, but now she turned to face Sophie across the car. 'Yes, we can. If you want to do something, there's a blanket—' she began, and then a shadow charged at her out of the fog.

Miller hadn't lied about how fast she was. The torch beam spiralled as she flung herself backwards. The figure was almost on top of her but she lashed out with a side kick at the same time as she swung the gun up. I heard a thump as the kick landed but her attacker swung a savage backhanded blow at her face. There was a meaty, bone-on-bone impact, and the policewoman pitched to the ground like a broken toy.

Sophie's scream freed me from my shock. 'Run!' I yelled, scrambling round the car, and throwing myself at the figure.

It was like hitting a brick wall. An arm swung, batting me against the car. The breath burst from me but before I could cry out a hand clamped round my throat, pinning me against the bonnet as stars burst in my vision.

In the light from the fallen torch I found myself looking into the Halloween mask features of Jerome Monk.

He stared down at me with eyes that were dead and black. I flailed at him, but his hand was jammed like a vice under my jaw. I could taste the stink of him, foul as an animal's cage. My head felt about to burst, the fog seeming to thicken round me. Through it I saw him look over his shoulder, heard the snap of branches as Sophie stumbled away.

God, no! I tried to shout out but I couldn't breathe. Monk slammed me back against the car. The air burst from my lungs as something rammed into my stomach. Abruptly the pressure was gone from my throat. I felt myself falling and the fog closed in completely.

I passed out, though only for a few seconds. I found myself in the mud, eyes pulsing with blood and head throbbing. There was a rushing in my ears.

Through it, as though from a long way away, I heard Sophie scream.

I tried to stand, but my body wouldn't respond. *Get up! Come on, move!* I clambered onto my hands and knees. My vision was clearing now, the blood-red mist lifting. I retched as my diaphragm spasmed. Sucking in ragged breaths, I used the car to drag myself to my feet.

I took a step and clutched at the car again as my legs almost gave way. Cross's torch had rolled against a front tyre, throwing a flat white light across the grass. In it I saw the policewoman, sprawled in the same broken posture as she'd fallen. There was nothing I could do for her, or for Miller either. I snatched up the torch, then flung open the car boot and grabbed a blanket. I threw it over Cross. Then I went after Sophie and Monk.

I'd only a vague idea of which way they'd gone. The car had crashed on the edge of a wood, and the gnarled trees hemmed me in as I skidded over moss-covered rocks and bog grass. I shone the torch around and shouted.

'SOPHIE!'

My shout was soaked up by the fog. There was no answering cry. Monk had planned this, I thought bleakly. The phone call had been to herd us away from Padbury, towards where he was waiting. Even the fog had worked in his favour, obscuring the scarecrow he'd set up in the road until we were right on top of it. It was still working for him now, making it impossible to see more than a few yards. I'd lost them. It was hopeless.

Numb with defeat, I began to retrace my steps. In the light from the torch I saw the tracks I'd gouged in the soft moss. I started to follow them before I realised. Heart thumping, I swept the beam back and forth in a wide arc across the ground. Off to one side, another muddy trail had been ploughed.

If it was made by Monk and Sophie, he was making no attempt to hide their tracks. Either he didn't expect anyone to follow them or he didn't care.

I set off along the trail until I found myself on an overgrown path that was obviously used by walkers. The ground was churned to black mud in both directions. I stared at it, panting. *Which way?* If Monk had stolen a car then he would have headed towards the road, off to the left. But I hadn't heard an engine. So I followed the path deeper into the woods.

The torch beam pitched drunkenly as my boots squelched in the sludge. Then, as though the fog were solidifying, a craggy rock face loomed in front of me. The light fell on a barred iron gate. A mine.

Lucas had mentioned an old tin mine a few miles from Padbury, but he'd said it was sealed off. *Not any more.* The rusty gate hung open, a broken padlock half buried in the trampled mud in front of it.

I swung open the gate and shone the torch inside. A tunnel of rock ran down into blackness. The sight of it touched on a primal fear that raised the hairs on my neck. But I had no choice. The blue display of my phone lit up like a beacon: no signal. I took out my wallet and dropped it by the gate so that the police would know where I'd gone. *You hope.*

The shaft was barely high enough to stand upright. The air had the cold, dank smell of an old cellar. Water dripped from the roof and trickled across the steeply sloping floor. My footfalls echoed as I scuffed through it.

I'd been walking for about five minutes when the ground began to level out. The shaft opened up, vaulting to twice its height as the walls drew back on either side. But directly ahead was a tumbled mound of rock and shale, with jagged roof timbers protruding from it like broken bones.

A shallow pool had formed where the rockfall had partially dammed the water trickling down the shaft. I splashed through it, shining the torch over in the hope of finding a way past. There was nothing.

I shone the torch over the blocked shaft one more time. The shadows from the rocks and shattered timbers jerked in the beam, but the fall looked solid. Then I moved the torch again and my breath caught in my throat.

One shadow didn't shift with the rest. It was in the angle where the uppermost rocks met the roof, a patch of impenetrable darkness. I picked up a stone and threw it. Instead of a clatter, it vanished silently inside.

Not a shadow. A hole.

I tested the nearest rock. It didn't budge. Neither did any of the others. I carefully hoisted myself up, then slowly levered myself the rest of the way. Now I could see what had caused the hole. A slab of granite had fractured from the top of the tunnel, leaving a gap high up in the angle between roof and wall. All but invisible from the ground, it was like a toothless mouth, perhaps three feet wide and two high.

Cold as it was, I was sweating as I shone the torch inside. The hole extended for a few yards before the beam vanished into darkness.

I lowered my forehead onto the cold, grainy granite. *I can't do this.* I thought about the weight of ancient rock suspended inches above me. The roof had collapsed once already. Even if I crawled through without being crushed, I might not be able to get back. I didn't even know for sure that Monk had brought Sophie this way. The sensible thing would be to go back for help. Let the police come down here with a proper search team.

And what'll happen to Sophie in the meantime? What's happening to her now, while you're dawdling here?

Giving myself no time to think, I pushed myself into the hole. The granite grated like sandpaper as I wriggled my way inside. My breath steamed in the torchlight as I crawled along the rock's dark length. It seemed an age before I reached the other end. Panting, I shone the beam into the dark.

I'd emerged into a long, low cavern. It sloped away to one side, ending in a drop-off from where I could hear the gurgle of running water. Whatever this was, I didn't think it was part of the mine.

I wriggled round so I could swing my legs free, and dropped down to the slanting floor. The low roof meant I had to stoop.

'Sophie?' I called, holding the torch in front of me. *'SOPHIE!'*

My shout rang out, echoing into oblivion. The only response was the chunter of the underground stream, invisible in the shadows. Aiming the torch into the darkness at the far side, I started across.

According to Lucas, there weren't any cave systems in this part of Dartmoor. *Looks like he got that wrong*, I thought, and as I did I banged my head on an outcrop of rock. I reeled back, more startled than hurt.

And dropped the torch.

It clattered onto the rock, the light flickering as it hit. I tried to trap it with my foot but it pitched past, skittering down the slope towards the drop-off, its beam throwing crazy patterns. Then it reached the edge, and as though a switch had been flicked, I was in darkness.

I didn't move. The enormity of what had happened stunned me.

Don't panic. Think it through. My hand was unsteady as I reached into my pocket for my phone. I took it out and thumbed a key.

A blue glow threw back the dark as the phone's display sprang to life. *Thank God.* It wasn't as bright as the torch but right then it seemed beautiful. I edged towards the drop-off. It was possible the fall had just loosened a connection in the torch; if I could find it I might be able to get it working.

I was almost there when my phone rang. The *beep* was shockingly loud. I felt a surge of hope before I realised that no one could call down here. What I'd heard wasn't the ringtone. It was the low-battery warning. I stared at the flashing battery icon. As though to prove a point, the screen went out. My fingers trembled as I pressed a key. The phone lit up but beeped again. There was no way of knowing how much longer the battery would last, but using the display would drain it fast. There was no longer any question of going on. I needed to get out and fetch help while I still could.

I tried to steady my breathing, and moved back towards the hole. My progress seemed agonisingly slow. The phone's display went out twice more as I crabbed back up the slope. Each time I froze, hardly daring to breathe as I pressed a key to bring the screen back to life.

I was perhaps halfway across when the screen went dead again. I quickly thumbed a key. The screen stayed dead. I jabbed the keypad in desperation, praying for just a few more seconds of light.

But it didn't come. I lowered the phone. I wasn't going anywhere.

9

I started to shiver soon after the phone gave out. Once I'd stopped moving the cavern's chill soon cut through my clothes.

My first instinct was to try to feel my way to the hole I'd crawled through. Once I was back in the mine my chances of making it to the surface would be much better. But I knew that even if I didn't crack my head open on the way, it would be all too easy to become disorientated. And if I found an opening, I'd have no way of knowing if it was the right one; I could end up crawling deeper into the cave system without realising it.

No, like it or not, my only option was to stay where I was. The police would find the broken gate and my wallet, and then it was only a matter of time before they found the opening that led here.

I put my head on my knees, wrapping my arms round them to hug what little heat I could to myself. Now I had time to reflect, coming down here seemed unbelievably stupid. I should have stayed with Cross and Miller, done what I could for them until back-up arrived. Instead I was trapped in a cavern no one might even know existed, while Monk and Sophie . . .

I couldn't bear to think about that. Huddled and shivering, feeling as useless as I'd ever been in my life, I closed my eyes and tried to rest.

At some point I must have dozed. I wouldn't have thought it possible, but I was exhausted and had drifted into an uneasy sleep.

Suddenly, I was awake. For a moment I had no idea where I was. I started to lurch to my feet, and narrowly avoided banging my head. Then, as the bleakness of the situation sank in, I lowered myself back onto the cold rock.

That was when I heard the noise. I froze, listening. It came again, the unmistakable echoing scrape of someone's approach.

'In here!' I yelled. *'I'm in here!'*

I stared into the darkness, relief and adrenaline making my heart thump. It seemed a long time before a light appeared in the blackness.

Thank God. 'Over here!'

The light began to move in my direction, the dancing yellow beam of a torch. It was only as it grew larger that I realised it was coming from the wrong direction, from the far side of the cavern.

The shout died in my throat. A sick resignation spread through me as the torch came closer. Beyond the glare I could make out a bulky figure and the pale dome of a bald head, stooped beneath the bellying rock.

Monk lowered the torch. The filthy combat jacket looked too small across the massive shoulders. The button eyes regarded me as his chest rose and fell, each breath accompanied by a low wheeze.

'Get up,' he said.

THE CAVE SYSTEM was an underground maze, but Monk seemed to know exactly where he was going. He didn't hesitate, squeezing through narrow gaps I'd never have dared risk by myself. But despite his size he never once got stuck. On the surface he might be a freak; here he was in his element.

After that single, terse instruction, he hadn't spoken again. Ignoring my frantic questions about Sophie, he'd simply turned and headed back the way he had come, as though he didn't care if I followed or not. It was only as the shadows flowed back into the cavern, rushing to fill the vacuum left by the receding torch, that I forced myself to move. The thought of going deeper into the caves appalled me, yet what else could I do?

I had to find Sophie.

The passage we were in abruptly opened into a space large enough to stand. Monk started across without pausing. I took the chance to catch up.

'Where is she?' I panted.

He didn't answer.

I grabbed hold of his arm. 'What have you done with her? Is she hurt?'

He jerked his arm free. 'Shut up.'

His voice was a hoarse rumble. He turned to carry on, but doubled up as a coughing fit seized him. He spat a gob of phlegm on to the floor, passed a hand across his mouth, then continued on as though nothing had happened.

As I trailed behind him, I thought about the ragged breathing I'd heard over the phone, and the sputum the police had found at Wainwright's house. Everyone had assumed it was a gesture of contempt. I wasn't so sure now.

Monk was ill. Not that it made him any less dangerous, or slowed him down. I had to push myself to keep up.

Suddenly the light went out. I stopped dead, fighting panic. Then I heard a muted noise coming from nearby, and made out a faint glow coming from one side of the passage. I edged towards it and found myself at a cleft in the rock. The scrape and grunt of Monk's laboured progress came from inside, and I could just make out the flickering beam of his torch.

The cleft climbed at a steep angle. I had to haul myself up, clambering after the receding light, the rough grain of the rock scraping against my coat. Fear and bile rose in my throat. *Stay calm. Just keep going.*

Then the passage kinked in a sharp dogleg, and I saw a glow up ahead. Following it I found myself in a small, natural chamber in the rock. I halted, dazzled after the darkness by the dim light from a lantern on the floor. The air was fetid and sour, a mineral dankness fighting with an animal reek. A hissing gas heater threw out a warmth that seemed stifling after the cold of the caves. As my eyes adjusted, I took in a jumble of bags and cans on the floor. Monk was crouched on a rumpled blanket, looking at me.

Huddled as far away from him as she could get was Sophie.

'Oh, God, D-David!'

She flung her arms round me as I knelt by her. I stroked her hair as she buried her face in my shoulder, feeling the trembling of her body.

'Shh, it's OK.'

It was far from that, but the relief I felt at seeing her swamped everything else. Her face was pale and streaked with tears, the bruise still livid. There was something else about her, something that wasn't right, but I was too overwhelmed by finding her to follow up the half-formed thought.

'Are you all right? Has he hurt you?' I asked.

'No, he didn't . . . I—I'm fine.'

She didn't look or sound it, but I felt my relief edge up another notch.

Monk was still watching us with dark, unblinking eyes. The low yellow light from the lantern made the indentation in his forehead into a shadowed pit. The massive shoulders were slumped with exhaustion, and his mouth hung open as he breathed, a sibilant wheeze sounding with every rise and fall of his chest. He obviously had a serious respiratory infection, maybe even pneumonia, and looked like a man at the end of his physical limits.

Except that Monk wasn't a normal man.

'You don't need two hostages,' I said. 'Let her go.'

'I don't want a hostage.' His mouth twitched in a sneer. 'Think I don't remember you from before? Not so smart now, are you?'

No, not so smart at all. 'So why've you brought us here?'

'I brought her. You just followed.'

'Then why did you come to find me?'

Monk sank back against the rock. 'Ask her.'

I turned to Sophie. I could feel her trembling against me.

'I . . . We heard you shouting.' She gave me a desperate look. 'I told him . . . I—I said you'd be able to help.'

'I don't understand.'

Sophie glanced nervously across at him. 'He . . . he says he can't—'

'No, he doesn't *say*, I don't *say*! I *can't*!' His shout reverberated in the small chamber. 'I try but I *can't*! There's nothing there! It didn't matter before, but it does now!' Monk ran his scabbed hands over his skull, rasping them on the stubble growing there.

His mouth worked, as though the next words were being torn from him.

'I want to know what I did.'

I SAT on a wadded up plastic sheet with my back against the rock, with Sophie curled against me. Monk had subsided after his outburst. He seemed exhausted, slumped forward with his head hung between his raised knees. The steady whistle of his breathing made me think he was asleep.

'What did he mean?' I whispered in Sophie's ear.

'I—I don't know . . .'

I pitched my voice low, not taking my eyes from Monk. 'He must have said *something*. Why does he want help? Help for what?'

She massaged her temples, glancing fearfully across at Monk. 'He says he can't remember killing those girls. Not just burying them, any of it! He thinks I can help, because I said I could help him find the graves, even if he'd forgotten where they were. But I didn't mean I could help him get his *memory* back! Oh, God, this can't be happening!'

I could feel her shaking. I hugged her to me. 'Go on.'

'That's why he was digging round Tina Williams's grave. He thought . . . he thought if he found the graves, saw the bodies again, it'd make him remember. That's why he came after us when he saw us out there; he knew it had to be me. God, I'm so sorry. This is all my fault!'

I held her as she cried herself into an exhausted sleep. I was shattered myself, but I had to stay awake. I stared across at Monk's unmoving form. If he really was suffering from some sort of amnesia, there was nothing Sophie could do about it. Sooner or later he was going to realise that.

I looked around the chamber, hoping to see something that might help us get out of here. The floor was piled with empty water bottles and food wrappers, discarded gas canisters and batteries. Near me was a pile of boxes, ripped open to spill cough linctus, foil packets of antibiotics and small brown bottles I recognised as smelling salts, clearly raided from some chemist's. The smelling salts puzzled me, until I made the connection with the police dog that had tried to track him a few days earlier. Smelling salts contained ammonia.

The only other thing nearby was a bag filled with foul-smelling earth. The musky odour was familiar, but I couldn't place it. Still watching Monk, I tried to see what else was hidden among the debris. I gently moved a box aside and stiffened when I saw what lay behind it, just out of reach.

The black cylinder of a torch.

Careful not to disturb Sophie, I leaned towards the torch, stretching as far as I could. My fingers were only inches away from it when I felt a change in the chamber. The hairs on my arms prickled. I looked up.

Monk was staring at me.

Except he wasn't, not quite. His eyes were fixed on a spot just off to one side. I moistened my mouth, trying to think of something to say. Before I could his head jerked to his right, mouth curling in a sneer.

Then he began to laugh. It was an eerie, phlegm-filled chuckle. It grew louder, until his shoulders were shaking with the force of it. I flinched as he suddenly lashed out with a scabbed fist, smacking it sideways into the rough wall beside him. If it hurt he gave no sign. Still laughing, he thumped his fist into the rock again. And again.

Sophie stirred and gave a restless moan. I put my hand on her shoulder, willing her to keep still, and she subsided, too exhausted to wake up fully.

Monk's manic laughter began to die down, and his breathing slowed back into a raw wheeze. He sat quiescent, blood dripping from the hand he'd been slamming into the wall, mouth hanging slack.

Something Roper had said all those years ago suddenly came back to me: *He kicked off on one last night . . . One of his party pieces . . . having a tantrum after lights out. That's why the guards call him laughing boy.*

Monk was starting to stir, blinking slowly as though he were waking up. Another coughing fit racked him. When it passed he cleared his throat and spat on the floor. He rubbed a hand over his face, then saw me watching.

'What you looking at?'

Trying to sound unconcerned, I picked up one of the foil packs of antibiotics that lay on the floor nearby. 'These won't do your chest infection any good. They're for bladder infections, not respiratory tract.'

'How would you know?'

'I used to be a doctor. '

Monk's dark eyes glittered. He looked down at where Sophie's head lay on my lap.

'What's this?' I asked quickly, nudging the soil-filled bag with my foot.

He seemed to debate whether to answer, but at least it shifted his attention from Sophie. 'Fox piss. For the dogs.'

That explained some of his stink, at least. Monk must have been smearing himself with soil from a fox's den, hoping to mask his own scent. Again I felt a sudden disquiet, that there was something I should remember, but I was too distracted to worry about it.

'Does it fool them?' I asked, knowing it wouldn't.

'Not the dogs. The handler.'

I'd underestimated him. Police dogs would be able to track him regardless of what he used. But if an inexperienced handler caught the distinctive smell of a fox, they might think the dog was on the wrong trail.

'What is this place?' I asked. 'I didn't think there were any caves here.'

'Nobody does.'

Including the police.

He nodded down at Sophie. 'Wake her up.'

'She needs to sleep,' I said. 'She's just been in a car crash, for God's sake. If you want her to help you she needs to rest.'

'I didn't know it'd roll like that.' He sounded sullen. He looked at Sophie again, this time taking in the bruise. 'What happened to her face?'

'Don't you know? Someone broke into her house and attacked her.'

Something seemed to flicker in those dark eyes. He frowned. 'It was all smashed up. She wasn't there. I didn't . . . I can't . . .'

'Can't what?' I pushed, forgetting myself.

'I can't *remember*!' His shout reverberated inside the small chamber. 'I try and try, but there's *nothing*! What's wrong with me?'

This time I had enough sense to stay quiet. Some of the heat seemed to go from him as he looked at Sophie. She hadn't woken, even now.

'You and her . . . She's your girlfriend.'

I was about to say no, but something stopped me. Monk didn't seem to expect an answer anyway.

'I had a girlfriend.' He clasped both hands round the back of his head. His mouth worked. 'I killed her.'

BY THE TIME he was fifteen, Monk's life was set in stone. Orphaned since birth, he'd grown up doubly excluded, shunned for his physical defects and feared for his abnormal strength. The few families that fostered him soon sent him back, shaken by the experience. By the time he reached puberty, violence had become second nature. Then the blackouts started.

To begin with he didn't realise. Most came at night, so his only awareness of them was a feeling of lethargy the next day, of inexplicable bruises or bloodied hands. The problem came to light in a young offenders' institution, when his nocturnal behaviour terrified the other inmates. Monk would throw tantrums, laughing like a lunatic and reacting with frenzied violence to attempts to subdue him. The next morning he wouldn't recall any of it.

The subsequent punishments left him more insular and aggressive than ever. Prison psychologists spoke of antisocial behaviour, of impulse-control disorders and sociopathic tendencies. One look was enough to confirm it. He was a freak, a monster. He was Monk.

As he grew older he took to wandering on the moor. It had a calming effect. One day he came across an overgrown hole in a hillside, an old mine adit, and it opened a new world for him. He spent as much time down in the cold, dark tunnels as he did in the run-down caravan he called home. They made him feel secure. Stilled. Even the blackouts seemed less frequent.

He was on his way to the moor one night when he saw the gang. He'd been away from it for almost a week, labouring on a building site for cash in hand. Now, with money in his pocket, the need to get back made his skin prickle and itch. At first he ignored the hooded youths huddled under a broken streetlight. They had something down on the floor, trapping it like a pack of animals. Monk would have gone on by if it hadn't been for their laughter. Vicious and cruel, it throbbed behind his eyes like an echo of childhood. The gang had scattered after he'd knocked two or three of them away, leaving a lone figure on the floor. The tendons in Monk's hands had ached with the need to hit something else, but the girl on the ground had looked up without fear. She gave him a shy smile.

Her name was Angela Carson.

'You *knew* her?'

The question spilled out before I could stop it. According to reports, witnesses had seen Monk in his fourth victim's neighbourhood before the murder, but it was assumed he'd been stalking her. There was no suggestion that he'd *known* Angela Carson, let alone that they'd had a relationship.

The look in Monk's eyes was answer enough.

After that first, accidental meeting, the pair had been drawn together. Both were lonely. Both, in different ways, excluded from society. Angela Carson was almost completely deaf, but the two of them managed to communicate somehow. In the plain young woman, Monk finally found someone who was neither terrified nor repulsed by him. For her part, it wasn't difficult to imagine that she found his strength comforting. He took to visiting her after dark, when there was less chance of being seen by neighbours. It wasn't long before she asked him to stay the night.

The blackouts had been less frequent after they'd met. He'd let himself believe they were over. Even so, he hadn't meant to fall asleep. But he had.

He claimed to have no recollection of what happened, only that he found himself standing by the bed. There was a pounding on the door. All was noise and confusion. His hands were covered in blood.

He looked down and saw Angela Carson.

That was when Monk lost what little control he had left. When the police burst into the room, he attacked them in a frenzy. Then he ran until his legs gave way, trying to escape the images of that bloodied room.

Without even thinking about it, he'd gone out onto the moor. And gone to ground. That the police would be looking for him didn't really enter his thinking; he was trying to escape from himself, not them. Cold and hunger drove him up after a few days. He'd lost all sense of time, and it was night when he emerged. He stole clothes and food and what equipment he needed and was back in his sanctuary before dawn.

Over the next three months he spent more time underground, beneath the gorse and heather of Dartmoor, than he did in the outside world. The blackouts continued, but down there he was only vaguely aware of them. Sometimes he would wake in a different cavern or tunnel from the one he remembered, with no memory of how he had got there.

Then one day he found himself walking on the roadside in broad sunlight. He felt confused, his thoughts as muddy as his clothes, with no idea of what he was doing. That was how the police found him.

The first time he heard of Tina Williams or Zoe and Lindsey Bennett was when he was charged with their murders.

'Then why did you plead guilty?' I asked.

Monk absently rubbed at a spot between two of his knuckles. 'Everyone said I'd done it. They found their stuff at my caravan.'

'But if you couldn't remember—'

'You think I cared?' He glared at me, then convulsed as another coughing spasm took him. When it passed, there was a sheen of sweat on his face.

'The heart attack wasn't faked, was it?' I said.

'It was charlie.'

I took a moment to catch on. 'You overdosed on cocaine? Deliberately?'

The big head nodded.

It explained how Monk had fooled the doctors. As well as sending his blood pressure sky high, a cocaine overdose would make his heartbeat dangerously fast and irregular. The symptoms could easily be mistaken for the onset of a heart attack, and prove just as fatal. Judging from Monk's condition, I guessed he'd suffered cardiovascular damage at the very least. Throw in a respiratory infection and it was a miracle he wasn't dead. No wonder we'd escaped from him out at Black Tor.

'But I don't understand. You waited eight years, why escape now?'

His mouth twitched. 'Because the bastards stitched me up.'

I'd been on the verge of believing him until then. Even pitying him. But this was pure paranoia. I must have let my thoughts show.

'You think I'm a psycho, don't you?' He was glaring at me again.

Careful. 'No! Why do you think you were set up?'

'I got word that this new con was saying he'd seen someone poking round under my caravan before it was raided. They pulled a warrant card on him and said it was police business. Told him to fuck off, that if he told anyone he'd get banged up on paedo charges. So he didn't. Not until he got sent to Belmarsh and wanted to big himself up to the hard men.' Monk turned his head and spat. 'Like I wasn't going to find out.'

This wasn't the paranoid rant I'd been expecting. It had been the discovery of Zoe Bennett's lipstick and hairbrush under his caravan that had confirmed Monk's guilt. 'This prisoner . . .' I said.

'Walker. Darren Walker.'

'Did he tell you the policeman's name?'

'He said it was some bastard called Jones. A DI.'

The name meant nothing to me. 'He could have been lying.'

'He wasn't. Not after what I did to him.' Monk's face was pitiless. His lips twitched back in a snarl. 'Should've said something sooner.'

Terry had told me about Monk beating another inmate to death when he'd broken the news of his escape. *Put two wardens in hospital when they tried to pull him off. Surprised you didn't hear about it.*

'How does Wainwright fit into this?' I asked. 'Why did you kill him?'

'I didn't kill him.'

'His wife identified you, and your DNA was all over the house.'

'I didn't say I wasn't there; I said I didn't kill him. He fell downstairs. I never touched him.'

It was possible, I supposed. Wainwright's broken body had been lying near the foot of the stairs. Finding Monk in your home would have been terrifying for anyone, let alone someone with dementia.

'Why did you go to their house anyway? You can't have thought Wainwright had anything to do with setting you up.'

Monk looked at Sophie. 'I thought he might know where she was. I tried digging holes on the moor like I saw him do, see if that'd make me remember. Didn't expect you and her to turn up, though.' He gave a death's-head grin. 'You were so scared I could practically smell you. If I wasn't knackered from digging them holes I'd have caught you.'

So instead, frustrated, that night he'd sought out the only other person he could think of. Someone whose name was in the phone book.

'Wainwright was ill. He couldn't have helped.'

Monk's head snapped up. 'I didn't know that, did I? You think I'm sorry he's dead? Bastard treated me like scum. I've not forgotten that!'

'I don't—' I began, but it was as if a switch had been flicked.

'*The bastards stitched me up!* Eight years I thought I was too cracked to remember what I did! *Eight years!*'

'If you didn't kill the other girls—'

'I don't care about them! But if I was set up then I could have been for the rest of it. For Ange!' The dark eyes were fevered and manic. His head jerked. 'The bastards could've tricked me, made me think I killed her as well! You get it? I might not have done it, *and I need to remember!*'

Any hope I'd had of reasoning with him died then. Monk wasn't interested in retrieving any lost memories, only in absolving himself of guilt over Angela Carson. But that wasn't going to happen. Whatever the fate of the other victims, whether he'd intended it or not, he'd killed her himself.

'Look, whatever you did, if it happened during a blackout then you're not fully responsible,' I said. 'There are types of sleep disorders that—'

'Shut up!' He surged to his feet, fists clenched. 'Wake her up!'

'No, wait—'

He moved so fast I didn't see it coming. It was little more than a back-hand cuff, but it snapped my head to one side as if I'd been hit with a plank. I fell to the floor as Monk grabbed hold of Sophie.

'Come on! Wake up!'

Sophie moaned, her body still limp. I lunged at him as he drew back his arm to slap her. He thrust me away and I slammed into the rock.

But Monk made no further attempt to hit Sophie. He was staring at his fist, the one he'd struck against the rock, as if he'd only just become aware of it. He saw the blood and the rage left him. He lowered his arm.

Sophie stirred. 'David . . .'

'I'm here.' This time Monk didn't try to stop me.

Sophie rubbed her head, brow creased in pain. 'I don't feel so good. My head hurts,' she said, her voice slurred, and then she vomited.

I supported her until the spasm had passed. 'Look at me, Sophie.'

'Hurts . . .'

'I know, but just look at me.'

I smoothed the hair back from her face. She squinted, blinking in the lantern light. Shock ran through me. While her left pupil was normal, the right was dilated and huge. *Oh, God.*

'What's wrong with her?' Monk demanded. He sounded suspicious.

I took a deep breath. 'I think it's a haematoma.'

'A what?'

'She's bleeding inside her skull. We need to get her to a hospital.'

'You think I'm stupid?' Monk said, and seized hold of her arm.

'Don't touch her!' I snapped, shoving him away.

At least, I tried to; it was like pushing a side of meat. But he had stopped, and there was the same stillness about him that I'd witnessed earlier, a sense of poised violence barely held in check.

'There's blood collecting inside her head,' I said, my voice unsteady. 'It could be from the car crash or before. But if the pressure isn't released . . .' *She'll die*. 'I have to get her out of here. Please.'

Monk's mouth twisted in frustration, his wheezing breaths growing even more rapid. 'You're a doctor. Can't you do something?'

'No, she needs surgery.'

He slapped his hand against the wall. 'She said she'd help me!'

'Does she look like she can help anybody?'

'She's staying here!'

'Then she's going to die!' I was shaking, but from anger now. 'All she's done is try to help you. Do you want more blood on your hands?'

'Shut UP!'

I saw his fist coming, and flinched as it whipped by my face, his coat sleeve skimming my cheek as he punched the rock by my head.

I didn't move. The only sound was Monk's ragged wheezing. Chest heaving, he dropped his arm and stepped back. Blood dripped from his hand. He'd struck the rock full on this time; it had to be broken.

But if it hurt he gave no sign. He looked down at Sophie. For all his size, there was something pathetic about him. Beaten.

'She couldn't have helped anyway, could she?' he asked.

I tried to think of a safe answer, then gave up. 'No.'

Monk lowered his head. When he raised it again the gargoyle face was unreadable. 'Let's get her out,' he said.

I used one of the bottles of smelling salts to rouse Sophie. She moaned in protest, but I needed her as aware as possible. We didn't have much time.

There was always a risk of haematoma after a head trauma. Some developed quickly; others took weeks, slowly swelling blood blisters inside the skull that put pressure on the brain. Sophie's must have been building up for days. She'd probably discharged herself before anyone could pick it up.

I should have realised. The signs had been staring me in the face, and I'd missed them. I'd put her slurred speech down to alcohol and fatigue, dismissed her headache as a hangover. Now she could die because of me.

Sophie barely knew where she was. She could walk, but not without support. By the time Monk had helped me manhandle her from the chamber, it was obvious we wouldn't be able to go back the way we had come, with its narrow tunnels and crawlways.

'Is there another way out?' I asked as she slumped against me.

Monk's breathing sounded worse than ever. 'There is, but . . .'

'What?'

'Doesn't matter,' he said, and set off down the passage.

The world shrank down to the rough rock above me and on either side, and Monk's broad shoulders in front. I'd brought the torch from the floor of the chamber. I had my arm round Sophie, taking as much of her weight as I could. She was weeping with pain, her voice slurred as she begged me to let her sleep. When she started to flag too much, I held the smelling salts under her nose, trying not to think about what would happen if she collapsed.

The passage opened out into a vaulted cavern, where the sound of falling water was deafening. The torchlight showed it pouring down the walls. Nearly all the cavern was flooded, but Monk picked his way along a bank of shale that skirted its edge. At the far side the rock was split by a narrow vertical fissure, just above the water level. My heart sank as he stopped by it.

'Through there.' He had to raise his voice to be heard above the water.

'Where does it go?'

'Comes out in a passage that goes to the surface.'

'Are you sure?'

'You wanted another way out. That's it.'

With that he turned and started back along the shale bank, sloshing through the edge of the water. 'You're not just going to leave us?' I yelled.

There was no response. The torch beam bobbed as he made his way back across the flooded cavern. The level was still rising.

'David . . . what's . . .'

Sophie was leaning heavily against me. I swallowed the fear that had risen in my throat. 'It's OK. Not much further.'

I'd no idea if that was true or not. But we'd no choice. Shining the torch into the fissure, I hugged her to me and edged sideways into the gap—there wasn't much more than eighteen inches clearance between the rock faces. I fought down a wave of claustrophobia as they seemed to squeeze tighter with each shuffling step.

After a few yards I looked back, but the flooded cavern was lost from view. Not that we could have gone back anyway. There was no room to turn round, and I couldn't back up with Sophie tucked under my arm. And now the fissure was so narrow that there wasn't enough room for us both to get through, not while I was holding Sophie.

I willed myself to stay calm. 'Sophie, I've got to free my arm. I need you to stand by yourself for a few seconds.'

My voice echoed oddly, flattened by the rock. She didn't respond.

'Sophie? Come on, wake up!'

But Sophie didn't move. Now that I'd stopped she was a dead weight against me. If not for the walls of the fissure holding her in place, I doubt I could have held her upright. I groped one-handed for the bottle of smelling salts in my pocket, and opened it with my teeth. I reached round to hold it under Sophie's nose. *Come on. Please.*

There was no reaction. *OK, don't panic. Think.* The only option was for me to squeeze through the narrow section first and pull her through after me. I began trying to ease my arm from beneath her shoulders, but no matter how hard I tried I couldn't prise myself loose. I twisted round to get more leverage and felt the rock faces clamp round my upper body like a vice.

Oh, God! I closed my eyes, fighting for breath. There didn't seem to be enough air. I realised I was starting to hyperventilate. *Don't pass out! Think!* But I didn't have any options left. My arm felt dead. Sophie was unconscious, wedged against me more tightly than ever. I couldn't go any further, nor could I back out, not with her blocking the way. We were trapped.

There was a glow off to one side. I looked over Sophie's head and saw a torch beam lighting the fissure behind us, throwing the irregularities of the rock into sharp relief. I heard the rasp of laboured breathing.

Then Monk edged into view. He was jammed sideways into the narrow gap, mouth contorted as he forced himself towards us.

He didn't speak until he'd reached Sophie. Still holding the torch, a massive hand snaked out and gripped her shoulder.

'Got her . . .' His voice was a strained gasp.

I felt most of her weight lift from me. I slid my arm from behind her, skimming my knuckles in the process, and then I was free.

'Go,' Monk wheezed.

He kept Sophie upright while I squeezed between the rock faces until the fissure widened. I sucked in air, giddy with relief as I shone the torch back onto Monk and Sophie.

His mouth was open in a rictus, his breathing agonised as the rock constricted his massive chest. But he said nothing as I reached back and grabbed Sophie's coat in one hand, protecting her head with the other.

The close walls of the fissure helped us now, holding her in place as Monk propped her up on one side while I pulled her through from the other. Heaving her arm round my shoulders so her head was cradled against me, I took her weight and straightened. Then I shone the torch back onto Monk.

He'd worked his way even further in to help me with Sophie. Now he was wedged impossibly tightly in the narrow gap. He fought for breath.

'Can you get back?' I panted. There was no way he'd make it any further.

It was hard to tell but I thought he grinned. 'Bulked out . . . since last time . . .' It sounded painful for him to even talk.

Christ, he's not going to be able to get out of there. 'Listen, I can—'

'Just get her out.'

I hesitated, but only for a second. He'd survived down here well enough without my help, and Sophie was my priority. I began half carrying, half dragging her along the uneven base of the fissure. I stumbled repeatedly, our coats scraping and snagging on the rock that still pressed in on us.

Then the walls opened out. Gasping for breath, I shone the torch round a low passage, wide enough for us to stand side by side. It sloped up at a steep angle. If Monk was right, then this must be the way to the surface.

I started up the slope, but I was stooped under Sophie's weight, my legs leaden and shaking. I lowered her to the floor and knelt beside her.

'Sophie? Can you hear me?'

There was no response. I checked her pulse. It was too fast. When I checked her eyes the right one was more dilated than ever. It didn't change when I shone the torch into it.

I struggled to lift her again, but there was no strength in my limbs. I took a few faltering steps and almost fell. I lowered Sophie back to the ground. *This is hopeless.* I bowed my head, almost weeping. I'd no idea how far there was to go, but I couldn't carry her any further. If she was going to have any chance of surviving, I had to leave her behind.

I stripped off my coat, gently wadding the sleeves under her head and wrapping the rest round her body. The cold bit into me straight away, but I didn't care. I looked down at her, feeling my resolve weaken. *God, I can't do this.* But I didn't have a choice.

'I'm coming back, I promise,' I said, my voice shaking from the chill.

Then I turned away and left her in the darkness.

The passage began to climb more steeply. Before long I was having to use my hands to clamber upwards. The walls and roof closed in, the torch revealing nothing but a black hole surrounded by rock. It seemed endless.

Exhaustion made me dizzy. My senses began playing tricks on me, so that I began to think I was heading downwards, crawling deeper underground instead of towards the surface.

Then something scratched my face. I jerked away, yelling out as something snagged my hair. I shone the torch at it and saw spiky branches. *Plants?* I thought, dumbly. I felt water dripping onto my face, but it was only when I noticed the cold wind on my cheek that I realised it was rain.

I was outside.

It was dark. In the torch beam I saw that the passage had emerged in a clump of gorse that clung to a sloping rock face. I crawled underneath the spiky, dripping branches, and slithered down the last few yards.

Shivering in the cold, I shone the torch around. The fog had cleared but rain fell in a sullen, steady downpour. I was on the moor, at the foot of a small tor. It was overgrown with gorse that hid the cave mouth. I tried to force my numbed mind to work. *Which way? Come on, decide!*

A faint noise came to me on the wind. I tilted my head, trying to catch which direction it was coming from. It faded, and for a moment I was afraid I was imagining it. Then I heard it again, stronger this time.

The distant whickering of a helicopter.

I clambered up the side of the tor, fatigue and cold forgotten.

'HERE! OVER HERE!'

I shouted myself hoarse, waving the torch over my head. I could see the helicopter's running lights now, bright specks of colour perhaps half a mile away. For an awful few seconds I thought it was going to fly straight by. Then it banked and came towards me. When I saw the police markings on its side, the last of my strength went and I slumped onto the cold stone.

10

Sophie was unconscious when they brought her out of the cave and stretchered her to the waiting helicopter. When it landed at the hospital, a team of nurses and doctors rushed her away.

I was taken more sedately to Emergency, where I was given a robe, put on an IV drip, and had my cuts and abrasions cleaned and dressed. I told my story to a succession of first uniformed and then CID officers. Finally, after I was moved to a curtained cubicle, I was left alone. I can't remember ever feeling so tired. I put my head back and was instantly asleep.

The whisk of the curtains being opened woke me. I sat up, disorientated and aching all over as Naysmith stepped into the cubicle.

'How's Sophie?' I asked before he could speak.

'Still in surgery. There's a build-up of blood on her brain, so they need to release it. Other than that, I can't tell you.'

Even though I'd expected it, the news hit me hard. There were different types of haematoma, but recovery depended on how quickly surgery was carried out. *This is your fault. You should have realised sooner.*

Naysmith fished something out of his pocket. 'You might need this,' he said, setting my wallet on the bedside trolley. 'We were just about to send a search team down the mine when the helicopter picked you up.'

'What about Miller and Cross?'

If he blamed me for abandoning them, he didn't show it. 'Miller's got a fractured skull, busted ribs and some internal bruising. Cross has a broken jaw and concussion. She was already conscious when the back-up arrived, so she could tell them what happened. Sort of.'

I was relieved. It could have been a lot worse. 'And Monk?'

'Nothing yet. We're sending teams down. No one had any idea there were any caves connected to the mine. If Monk's still down there we'll find him eventually, but it's going to take time.'

And if he isn't, he could be anywhere by now. Naysmith pulled up a chair and sat down, a man getting down to business.

'So, do you want to tell me what happened?'

I knew he'd have been briefed already, but I went through my story again. He listened without comment, even when I told him about Monk's claim that he'd been framed by a police officer.

'Well, he was telling the truth about Wainwright, at least,' he said when I'd finished. 'He broke his neck falling downstairs. The post-mortem found carpet burns from the stair carpet and there were patches of his blood and hair on the banister. Either he took a tumble in the dark or missed his footing from the shock of seeing Monk. Can't say I'd blame him.' He sighed. 'How much of the rest of it did you believe?'

I made an effort to focus. 'I believe what he said about the blackouts. And about his relationship with Angela Carson. He was too ill to pretend, and the seizure or whatever it was I saw him have, that was real.'

'You really think he might have killed her during one?'

'From what I saw, I'd say it could have happened like that.'

'What about the other girls?'

'I don't know. He genuinely doesn't seem able to remember anything about them, and he isn't interested in clearing his name. The only reason he escaped was because he's desperate to convince himself he didn't kill Angela Carson. That's what makes me think he's telling the truth.'

'He was found in a locked flat with her body, blood on his hands and her face pulped in. I don't think there's much doubt, do you?'

'Not about that, no. But for the past eight years he's had to live with knowing he killed the only person he's ever been close to, and he can't even remember doing it. Can you blame him for clutching at straws?'

Naysmith was silent for a moment. 'What about this story about him being framed?'

Now we're coming to it. 'I don't think he was making it up,' I said.

'That doesn't mean Darren Walker wasn't. There's no record of any DI Jones, now or eight years ago. Walker could have been spinning him a line, trying to fob him off. If I was cornered by Monk, I'd probably do the same.'

'Why would Walker spread a story like that in the first place?'

'He wouldn't be the first to make something up to bolster his reputation in Belmarsh. Besides, there's nothing to corroborate Monk's story. We've only his word to go on, since he conveniently beat Walker to death. And you'll have to forgive me if I don't believe that a police officer planted evidence on the say-so of a lowlife like Walker. Where would this phantom DI have got anything belonging to the Bennett twins, anyway? There's no way he could have lifted evidence from a high-profile murder investigation without it being noticed. Especially not if it turned up again at Monk's caravan.'

'Unless he didn't get it from the evidence locker.'

The words lay heavily in the small cubicle. Naysmith looked at me for a long while, his eyes lidded. 'You know what you're saying, don't you?'

'Are you telling me it hasn't occurred to you as well?'

He didn't answer. He didn't have to. We'd skirted round it so far, but I knew the same question would be preying on his mind as on mine.

If Monk didn't kill the other three girls, who did?

IT WAS LATE AFTERNOON before I was discharged. I'd managed to sleep after Naysmith left, but only fitfully, slipping in and out of wakefulness in the small cubicle. Still, I felt better for it, more alert, if nothing else.

I'd persuaded one of the nurses to check up on Sophie: she was out of surgery but still critical. I told myself that was to be expected after an emergency craniotomy; the doctors would have removed a flap of bone from her skull to drain the build-up of blood. But the news did nothing to lift my spirits. I sat fretting in the cubicle until a junior doctor told me I could go.

'Where's the ICU?' I asked her.

The intensive care unit was quieter than Emergency, with an air of strained urgency about it. The desk nurse wouldn't let me in to see Sophie, and again I was told that information could only be given to next of kin.

I nodded, beaten. The heavy doors to the ICU swung shut behind me with finality as I headed back to the main wards.

I was batted between wards before I finally found where Cross had been taken. At first I thought the policewoman was asleep. But as I approached her bed, she opened her eyes and looked directly at me.

She looked a mess. The blonde hair was plastered against her head. Her face was even more shockingly bruised and swollen than Sophie's had been, and an assembly of wire and screws clamped her jaw shut.

Now that I was there, I didn't know what to say. We just looked at each other for a moment, then she reached for the writing pad on the bedside table, and wrote, *Looks worse than it is. Morphine great.*

I wouldn't have thought I could laugh, but I did. 'I'm glad to hear it.'

More slow scribbling. *Sophie???*

I chose my words. 'Out of surgery. She's in intensive care.'

The pen scratched again. *Miller conscious. Nurses say making bad jokes.*

I smiled. It was the first good news I'd had in what seemed an age. 'That's great.' I took a deep breath. 'Look, I . . .'

But she was writing again. It was more laborious this time, and as she held it out for me her eyelids drooped. She was asleep before it left her hand.

It was just a short message: *U did right thing*.

My eyes blurred when I read that. I had to pause for a while before I tucked it away. I desperately wanted to get out of the hospital, to breathe fresh air and clear my head, but that would have to wait.

There was something else I needed to do first.

MY CAR WAS STILL at Sophie's with the rest of my things. A receptionist directed me to the nearest taxi rank, but I hadn't walked far from the entrance before a car pulled up alongside. I looked round as its window was wound down. It was Terry.

'Thought I might find you here,' he said.

I carried on walking. The car pulled forward until it was alongside again.

'David! I only want to talk. I heard what happened. How's Sophie?'

'She's in intensive care. I don't know any more than that.'

'Christ.' His face had paled. 'Is she going to be all right?'

'I don't know.'

He looked stunned. 'Where are you going?' he asked, subdued.

'I need to collect my things from Sophie's.'

He leaned over and opened the passenger door. 'I'll give you a lift.'

I didn't want to spend any time in Terry's company, but life was too short to bear grudges. Besides, I was so tired I could hardly stand. I got in.

Neither of us spoke for the first few miles. It was only as the city and suburbs gave way to open countryside that he broke the silence.

'Do you want to talk about it?'

'No.'

He fell quiet again. I stared out of the window as the moor began to swallow us up. Soon I felt myself start to drift off.

'At least we know now who attacked Sophie the other day,' he said.

I sighed. 'I still don't think that was Monk.'

'What, even after this?'

'He admitted going to her house, but she was already in hospital by then,' I told him. 'I thought an animal had got in when I took her home, because he was using soil from a fox den to mask his scent. It was hard to miss. If he'd been there before, I'd have noticed.'

'Fox piss? Crafty bastard.' Terry sounded almost admiring. 'There's lots of rumours flying around. Talk that he was having a relationship with Angela Carson. That he might not have meant to kill her.'

I rubbed my eyes. 'It's possible.'

'You're not serious?'

I didn't feel like talking but I couldn't blame Terry for wanting to know. And there didn't seem any reason not to tell him.'Before I left the hospital I spoke to a neurologist. He told me about a condition called frontal lobe syndrome. It happens sometimes when the front of the brain is damaged.'

'So?'

'That dent Monk has in his skull?' I tapped my own forehead. 'It was caused by a bad forceps delivery. Monk's mother died giving birth and I think his frontal lobe was damaged at the same time. That can cause violent and unpredictable behaviour and difficulty remembering things. It's a physiological condition, not a mental illness. That's why the psychiatrists who examined Monk didn't pick it up. Very occasionally it causes what are known as gelastic seizures, where people laugh or scream, and lash out at things that aren't there. It's a type of epilepsy, but because it tends to happen during sleep it's often undiagnosed. Usually it's put down to night terrors. Or someone "kicking off", like the prison guards said Monk did.'

Terry shrugged. 'Big deal. That doesn't excuse what he's done.'

I fought a wave of fatigue. 'Not all of it, no. But everyone thought he was a monster because he raped a deaf girl and beat her to death. If he and Angela Carson were in a relationship, and if he killed her during a seizure after they'd had sex, it changes everything. Like whether he really murdered Tina Williams and the Bennett twins.'

'He *confessed*, for Christ's sake!'

'He was punishing himself. He'd killed Angela Carson during one seizure; for all he knew he might have killed the others as well. But I really don't think he cared by then.'

Terry gnawed his lip. 'So if he didn't kill the other girls, who did?'

I shrugged. 'Have you ever heard of a DI called Jones?'

'Jones? Don't think so. Why?'

That was something else I'd had time to think about. If Monk—and Walker—were telling the truth, then the policeman who'd planted the dead girls' belongings at the caravan was an obvious suspect.

But I'd said enough. 'It doesn't matter. Just something Monk said.'

Terry glanced at me. 'You look done in. We'll be another half-hour yet. Why don't you get your head down?'

I was already putting my head back and closing my eyes. Jumbled images flashed through my mind: the cave, the car crash, the mangled body of Tina Williams, clogged with oozing mud. I felt the scrape of a spade cutting through wet peat, and then the car went over a bump and I woke up.

'Back with us?' Terry asked.

I rubbed my eyes. 'Sorry.'

'No worries. We're just about there.'

I looked out of the window and saw that the light had thickened to dusk. We were almost back at Sophie's. Then Terry was pulling up at the bottom of the garden, behind where my car was parked.

'Well, here we are,' he said. 'Do you want me to stick around?'

'No, I don't plan on staying.' I paused, my hand on the door handle. 'What about you? What are you going to do now?'

A shadow crossed his face. 'Good question. Take my lumps from Simms and then . . . I'll see. Try to get my act together, I suppose.'

'Good luck.'

'Thanks.' He looked away. 'So. Are we OK, then? Me and you?'

It occurred to me that I probably wouldn't see Terry again after this.

Although I wasn't exactly sorry, there was no need to part on a bad note.

I nodded. He held out his hand. I only hesitated a moment before I shook it. 'Look after yourself, David. I hope Sophie's all right.'

There was nothing more to say. I climbed out of the car and watched as Terry pulled away, his car's taillights disappearing down the lane.

I got as far as the front door before I realised I didn't have a key. I slumped against the door, defeated. Then I remembered the spare that Sophie kept hidden in the kiln. She'd had a new lock fitted but I hoped she'd have replaced the hidden key. *Please let it be there.*

The dilapidated brick tower loomed ahead of me as I crossed the overgrown path. The unlocked door creaked as I pushed it open and felt for the light switch. Nothing happened. The bulb must have blown. *Great.*

Pushing back the door as far as it would go, I went inside. The brick dust and smell of damp plaster tickled the back of my throat as I walked across to where the key was hidden. Another scent mingled with them, sharp and familiar, but I'd only just noticed it when something crunched under my boots. As my eyes adjusted I saw that the floor was littered with broken pottery. My sluggish brain was still trying to process that when I recognised the out-of-place smell. Aftershave.

I stopped dead, the hairs on the back of my neck prickling. I turned round. The dim twilight from the doorway didn't reach far into the kiln and the shadows were impenetrable. There was a rustle of movement.

'Is that you, Dr Hunter?' Roper said. He was peering into the gloom, trying to make me out. 'Lucky escape you had, by all accounts,' he said.

My heart was still thumping as I tried to unscramble my thoughts. 'What are you doing here?'

I heard rather than saw him shrug. 'Oh, I just came to check on things. Miss Keller really should have a lock fitted. Unless she wants people to be able to walk in here, of course.' The notion seemed to amuse him.

'I didn't see your car,' I said.

'It's in a lay-by up the road. Thought the walk would do me good.'

And prevent anyone from seeing he was here. I was starting to think that Darren Walker could have been telling the truth about the police officer at Monk's caravan. DI Jones might not exist, but that didn't prove anything. Whoever he was, he'd hardly have given his real name.

I tried to sound unconcerned, gauging my chances of getting past Roper to the door. 'Did Simms send you?'

'The ACC's got enough on his plate as it is at the moment. No, this was just to satisfy my curiosity, you might say.'

There was a click and the lamp on the workbench came on. The light revealed a scene of devastation. Sophie's bowls and dishes had been swept from the shelves to break on the floor.

Roper looked around. 'Looks to me like someone was searching for something, wouldn't you say?' He was smiling but his eyes were sharp and appraising. 'Mind telling me what you're doing here yourself, Dr Hunter?'

'My bag's in the house. Sophie keeps a spare key in here.'

'Does she, indeed?' He scanned the kiln. 'Good at hiding things, Miss Keller. But then a former BIA like her should be, shouldn't she?'

I lost patience. There was no point playing games. 'Did you find what you were looking for?'

'Me?' Roper seemed genuinely shocked and offended. 'I think we're getting our wires crossed, Dr Hunter. I didn't do this.'

I felt my suspicions begin to recede. 'Then who did?'

'Well, now, that's the question, isn't it?' Roper considered the wreckage, absently. 'How well do you know Miss Keller?'

'Why?'

'Because I'm trying to decide if you're involved in this.'

There was a sudden edge to his voice, and my last doubts about him disappeared. 'Until this I hadn't seen her in eight years,' I said carefully.

'You sleeping with her?'

I bit back the urge to tell him to mind his own business. 'No.'

He gave a grunt of satisfaction. 'Tell me, Dr Hunter, doesn't the timing of all this strike you as a bit odd? Terry Connors crops up out of the blue to warn you you're at risk from Monk. Then Miss Keller calls you asking for help. She turns up unconscious and her house is trashed. Except that the burglar didn't bother to take anything.'

'She said some money and jewellery were missing.'

He waved that away. 'You don't believe that any more than I do. And I'm not convinced by her "amnesia" either. Someone breaks into her house and knocks her out, and she can't remember anything about it?'

'That can happen.'

'I'm sure it can, but she didn't seem too worried about it. So why did she lie? Who is she protecting? Herself or somebody else?'

I opened my mouth to object, but he was only saying what I'd thought myself. I just hadn't wanted to accept it. 'What's your point?'

'My point is I don't believe in coincidences.' He prodded a piece of clay with his foot. 'If you've something valuable, the best way to hide it is to put it somewhere no one will ever think to look. Somewhere so obvious they won't even realise it *is* a hiding place.'

I stared at the workbench where Sophie had built up the mound of clay scraps. I remembered how she'd come in here as soon as we'd got back from hospital, claiming she was looking for the spare key. How she'd run her hand across it, as though to reassure herself.

'I think she was hiding something in a ball of dried clay,' I said. Sophie hadn't even bothered to put a lock on the kiln door, practically announcing that there was nothing of value inside.

Roper smiled. 'I'm less interested in where it was hidden than in what it was. All this started when Monk escaped, so there has to be a connection. And whatever was here, it was important enough for Miss Keller to risk facing Monk rather than leave it untended.'

And important enough for someone to knock her unconscious and leave her for dead while they searched the house. My mind was whirring now, the last cobwebs of fatigue dropping away. 'Terry Connors tried to persuade me to take Sophie away yesterday afternoon,' I said.

'Did he now? Then perhaps Monk did him a favour. Got her out of the way long enough for him to find what he was looking for.' Roper considered the debris littering the floor, a smile playing round his mouth. 'I think it's time we had a serious talk with DS Connors.'

A cold feeling was forming in the pit of my stomach. I'd been too tired to wonder why Terry was waiting for me outside the hospital. But that wasn't what struck me now. He'd claimed earlier that he didn't know where Sophie lived, yet I hadn't told him how to get here. He'd already known the way.

'I've just seen him,' I said. 'He gave me a lift.'

Roper's smile vanished. 'Connors was *here*?'

'He dropped me off and then went.'

'Shit!' Roper reached for his phone. 'We need to go. I should—'

But before he could finish, a shadow stepped through the doorway behind him. There was a sickening *thunk* of metal on bone as something swung against the back of his head, and Roper fell to the ground.

Breathing heavily, Terry stood over him with a short length of scaffold in his hands. 'Bastard had that coming for a long time.'

It had happened so quickly there was no time to react. I stood there, stunned by Terry's wild appearance, his look of fevered desperation, as much as by the sudden violence. Panting, he lifted his gaze to me.

'Jesus, David. Why couldn't you just have got your things and left?'

My mind was starting to function again. I hadn't heard a car engine; Terry must have parked and doubled back across the fields. Perhaps when he saw Roper's car in the lay-by. The policeman lay where he'd fallen, dark blood glistening on his head. I couldn't see if he was breathing or not.

Terry raised the pole as I started towards them. 'Don't try it!'

I stopped. 'Put the pole down. Just think what you're doing.'

'You don't think I have? You think I *want* this?' A spasm of anguish crossed his face. 'You want to blame somebody, blame Keller! This is her fault!'

I thought about what Roper had said. About the ball of clay, now in fragments on the floor. 'What was she hiding that was so important?'

At first it seemed he wasn't going to answer. He shook his head, but his grip on the scaffolding pole seemed to loosen.

'Zoe Bennett's diary.'

I began to understand. Zoe, the extrovert of the two twins, who preferred partying to studying. And Terry, still smarting after being forced to transfer from the Met in disgrace. What better way to salve his ego than with a pretty, vivacious seventeen-year-old with aspirations to be a model?

'Your name was in it,' I said.

His shoulders slumped, the scaffolding pole lowered, almost forgotten.

'I'd been seeing her for a couple of months. She was a real looker. Trouble was she knew it. She'd got it all worked out: how she was going to go to London, sign up with a big model agency. She was impressed because I'd been with the Met, could tell her stories about Soho and all the rest.'

He grinned at the recollection, but it quickly faded.

'Then I saw her with someone else, some cocky young bastard in a flash car. You know the sort. We had a row. Things got out of hand. I hit her and she went mental. Screaming at me, saying that she'd see to it I got sacked, that she'd say I raped her. We were in my car and I was scared people would hear. I just wanted to shut her up, so I got hold of her throat, and . . . and it was just so *quick*. One minute she was struggling, and the next . . .'

I looked down at Roper, dead or unconscious at his feet. I felt sickened.

'Jesus, Terry . . .'

'I know! You think I don't know?' He was still gripping the scaffolding pole in one hand. He ran the other through his hair, his face stricken. 'I'd got a lock-up, so I hid her body in there. I thought . . . I thought if I didn't do anything it'd be treated like just another teenage runaway. Zoe was always saying how she was going to go to London.'

'She was seventeen!'

'Oh, don't start,' he snapped, with a flash of his old temper. 'What was I going to do? Give myself up? That wouldn't bring her back! I'd got Debs and the kids to think about. What was the point in spoiling their lives?'

'Did you kill her sister as well?'

Terry seemed to flinch. There was something like shame in his eyes. 'After Zoe disappeared, Lindsey found her diary,' he said dully. 'There was my phone number, details of when we'd met. What we'd done. She didn't tell anyone because she didn't want to hurt Zoe's reputation. She thought because I was a police officer I might be able to help find her.'

Christ. So she'd gifted Terry with the only piece of evidence that could implicate him in her sister's death. And made herself the only witness.

'Don't look at me like that!' Terry yelled. 'I *panicked*, all right? If that had come out it would've been all over! I couldn't afford to be questioned.'

'And Tina Williams? Why did . . .?' I broke off as I realised. *Another teenager, dark-haired and pretty*. 'She was just a decoy, wasn't she? So it'd look like a serial killer and take attention off the twins.'

A strange look came over Terry's face, as though he was confronting a part of himself he barely recognised. He shrugged. 'Something like that.'

The shock had gone now, replaced by anger and disgust. 'I *saw* her, Terry! I saw what you did! For Christ's sake, you *stamped* on her face!'

'She was already dead!' he yelled. 'I lost it, all right? Jesus, you think I wanted to do it? Any of it? You think I *enjoyed* it?'

It doesn't matter; they're still dead. But it explained a lot of things. No wonder Terry's life had fallen apart.

Through the doorway behind him I saw that it was growing darker outside. I couldn't expect any help. Roper still hadn't moved, and from what he'd said no one knew where he was. Somehow I had to get past Terry.

'Was DI Jones the best name you could come up with?' I asked, stalling.

'Worked that out as well, did you?' Terry actually smiled. He seemed calmer, as though relieved to be finally confessing what he'd done. 'It was either that or Smith. Monk was too good an opportunity to miss. I'd still got some of Zoe's things hidden away, but I had to move fast before his place was swarming with SOCOs. I wasn't as careful as I should have been. Almost fell over Walker. But I flashed my warrant card and put the fear of God into him. Said if he kept his mouth shut I'd look after him.'

And for eight years Terry had been as good as his word, making sure any evidence against Walker was conveniently lost or mislabelled. Only when Terry had been suspended himself, and DI Jones finally let him down, had Walker broken his silence. And Monk had beaten him to death for it.

'How did Sophie get the diary?' I asked.

'Nosy bitch went snooping through my things. It was about a year after the search. Debs had kicked me out so I was renting a flat. Me and Sophie had got together again. I always meant to get rid of the diary, but I never did. Stupid. I'd hidden it, but Sophie always was good at finding things.'

He sounded bitter. Part of me registered that their relationship wasn't the fling Sophie had claimed, but now wasn't the time to dwell on that. I thought I saw Roper's hand moving but kept my attention on Terry.

'How much did she know?'

'Only that I'd been screwing Zoe; the diary made that obvious. She was pissed off because it was while I'd been seeing her. She went ballistic. She wouldn't tell me what she'd done with the diary, only that it was somewhere "safe".' His face turned ugly at the memory. 'It didn't matter so much when Monk was in prison. She couldn't tell anyone without admitting she'd been withholding evidence. But when he escaped . . . That changed everything.'

'That's why you panicked and came to see me. To see if Sophie had told me anything.'

'I didn't *panic*. I just wanted the diary back! And I know Sophie. If she was going to go running to anyone, it'd be you.'

He's jealous? There was a bubbling groan from the floor. Terry looked down at Roper in surprise, as though he'd forgotten him. The policeman twitched, his eyes fluttering.

'Don't!' I shouted, as Terry hefted the scaffolding pole.

He paused, the pole still raised. I thought there might be something like regret in his face. 'You know I can't let you go now, don't you?'

I did. And I didn't know what I was expecting. 'What about Sophie? Don't you even care what you've done to her?'

'What *I've* done to *her*? Jesus! The blackmailing bitch's made my life hell for years!'

'She was scared. And she's in hospital now because of you!'

He stared at me. 'What are you talking about?'

'Monk didn't cause the haematoma. You did, when you forced your way into her house looking for the diary.'

'Bullshit! I don't believe you!'

'It's a contrecoup injury from where she hit her head on the bathroom floor when she fell. She discharged herself from hospital before they could pick it up. She obviously wanted to come home to see if the diary was still safe. And even then she didn't tell anyone what had happened. She was terrified, but she still protected you!'

'She was looking out for herself, the same as she always does!' He levelled the scaffolding pole at me. 'You think you're going to make me feel guilty about her? Forget it, she brought it on herself!'

'And if she dies it'll be just another accident? Like Zoe Bennett?'

The way he stared at me told me I'd gone too far.

'At least tell me where they're buried,' I said quickly.

'What for? You had your chance eight years ago.' Terry shifted his grip on the pole, his face blank of expression. 'Let's get this over with.'

He started towards me. Suddenly he staggered. I thought he'd tripped until I saw that Roper had clutched hold of his leg.

Terry lashed out with the pole as I rushed at him. I ducked back, falling against the kiln's central chimney, and felt something grate beneath my shoulder. Wrenching his foot free, Terry kicked at Roper's head as if it were a rugby ball and Roper flopped limply. As Terry came at me again I grabbed the loose brick where Sophie hid her spare key and flung it at him. It caught him a glancing blow on the head before clumping to the floor.

'Bastard!' he spat, and swung the length of scaffolding at my head.

I managed to get an arm up but the metal pole smashed into my chest. My breath exploded as I felt ribs break. Agony burst through me, and as I crashed to the floor, Terry whipped his foot into my stomach.

I doubled up, unable to breathe. *Move!* But my limbs wouldn't obey. Terry stood over me, gasping for breath himself. He touched his fingers to his scalp and stared at the blood on them. His features contorted.

'You know what, Hunter? I'm glad you didn't go when you'd got the chance,' he panted, and raised the length of metal over his head.

The kiln door banged shut behind him. *Monk*, I thought instinctively. But the doorway was empty. The door flapped loosely in the wind, and, as Terry spun round to face it, Roper lurched into him.

He was barely able to stand, but he caught Terry off-balance. His momentum carried them past me and slammed them into the ancient scaffolding against the kiln's wall. The rickety structure swayed drunkenly from the impact, and for a second I thought it would hold. Then the entire scaffold gave a creaking groan, and collapsed on top of them.

I thought I heard a scream as I tucked into a tight ball, covering my head as planks and steel poles came crashing down. The air was filled with a clamour like insane bells that seemed to go on and on.

Then silence.

My ears rang as the echoes died away. I unwrapped my arms from my head. The kiln was in darkness, the air thick with dust. I coughed, gasping as pain shot through my broken ribs.

'ROPER? TERRY?' My shout died away.

There wasn't anything I could do by myself; I needed to get to a phone. I could just make out the light from the door through the murk. I picked an unsteady path towards it across the tangle of scaffolding and broken timbers. The air outside was sweet and clean. A last faint light remained in the sky as I hobbled towards the house, arm pressed to my injured ribs.

I was almost there when I heard a rumble behind me. I looked back in time to see the kiln collapse. It seemed to sag and then, without fuss, simply toppled in on itself. I shielded my eyes as a billowing cloud peppered me with grit. Then all was quiet again.

I lowered my arm. A skein of dust hung like smoke over what was left of the kiln: a jagged ruin against the evening sky. The section of wall with the door was still intact. I limped back to it, covering my mouth and nose with my sleeve as I peered through the partially blocked doorway. Not a sound, nor any sign of life.

The kiln yawned in front of me, dark and silent as a grave.

THE POLICE found Monk three days later. In the aftermath of everything else that had happened, the search for the convict was stepped up still further. But even then events hadn't quite run their course.

It took the emergency services eight hours to dig out Terry and Roper from underneath the kiln's walls. By the time the remaining structure had been made safe enough to start shifting the rubble, everyone knew it was a recovery operation rather than a rescue.

When the last bricks were removed, Roper was found lying on top of

Terry. The post-mortem showed that he'd died almost immediately. Terry wasn't so lucky. Roper's body had partially protected him from the falling debris, and the brick dust in his lungs suggested he hadn't been killed outright. The cause of death was suffocation. He'd been buried alive.

My own injuries were painful but not serious: three cracked ribs, plus cuts and bruises. For the second time in twenty-four hours I found myself back in hospital. I was told that Sophie was stable but still unconscious, although I wasn't allowed to see her.

When I left the hospital and stepped outside into the daylight, everything felt slightly unreal. I couldn't face going back to Sophie's house, so I booked into a nearby hotel. For the next two days I watched the story break on the news. Monk still hadn't been caught, but I knew from the updates I received from Naysmith that it wasn't for lack of trying. The rain continued to fall, and the teams going down into the cave system were hampered by flooding. For a time it looked as though he might have escaped Dartmoor altogether.

He hadn't. When the flood waters receded enough to allow the search team deeper into the dripping tunnels, they found Monk still wedged in the narrow fissure where I'd last seen him. He'd been dead for some time. The strain of forcing his massive frame into that small space had proved too much even for him, as I think he'd known it would. He'd died alone in the dark, far away from daylight or human contact.

He'd made his choice.

The cause of death was heart failure and pneumonia after a cocaine overdose, as I'd expected. But the post-mortem also found massive lesions in the orbitofrontal cortex of his brain, corresponding to the depression in his skull. The likelihood was that they'd been caused by the forceps delivery that had killed his mother. Monk had been born damaged, a freak but not a monster. We'd made him into one of those ourselves.

News of his death deepened my feeling of being stuck in limbo. Every time I closed my eyes I was back in the caves with Sophie and Monk. Or hearing the awful hollow impact as the scaffolding pole clubbed the back of Roper's head. My thoughts would run off at a tangent, as though trying to pick their own way through my mind. I felt as though there was something I should remember, something important. I just didn't know what it was.

When I finally fell into a fitful sleep that night it was only to wake suddenly in the early hours with Terry's voice echoing in my head.

You had your chance eight years ago.

It was something he'd said in the kiln, but it had been buried along with everything else until my subconscious spat it out. I thought it through, fitting it in with everything else till I was sure, and then I called Naysmith.

'We need to go out on the moor.'

THE FIRST FROST of the season crisped the coarse grass in the hollow as the CSIs began digging into the mound that Sophie had led us to years before. Naysmith and Lucas stood beside me, watching in silence as the dead badger was once again exposed to daylight. Preserved by the peat, the animal was hardly any more decomposed than it had been last time.

'Where do you think Connors got the badger from?' Naysmith asked as a CSI carefully removed it from the hole.

'Roadkill,' I said.

Wainwright had told me as much when I'd visited him, but I'd dismissed it as rambling. I was wrong. The discovery of the badger had appeared to explain both the cadaver dog's reaction and the disturbance to the soil. Its presence had been enough to deter us from digging any deeper.

But no one thought to question why an animal that preferred dry, sandy conditions should have dug its sett in waterlogged ground. Monk's abortive escape had distracted us, but there were other clues we'd overlooked. Animal bones had also been found at Tina Williams's shallow grave, and the coincidence alone should have alerted me. More obvious, though, was the broken bone that Wainwright had exposed. It was a comminuted fracture, a fragmented break typically caused by a fall, or being hit by a car. An animal that had died in its burrow had no business with an injury like that.

It was possible that Wainwright had known for years, and elected to keep quiet to protect his reputation. But dementia sufferers often live more in the past than the present. Perhaps the knowledge was waiting in his subconscious, trapped there until it was brought to the surface by some random misfire of failing synapses.

I should have realised myself. And on some level I had. Even back then, I'd felt the familiar itch that told me I was overlooking something. But I'd let it go, putting the Monk case from my mind as I got on with my life.

We found Zoe and Lindsey Bennett only a little deeper than the badger carcass. Whether from sentiment or convenience, Terry had buried the sisters in the same grave. The pressure of earth had contorted their limbs, so it looked as though they were embracing each other, but the peat had still worked its arcane magic. Both bodies were remarkably preserved.

The police found Zoe Bennett's diary in Terry Connors's car, wrapped in a clay-coated plastic bag. He'd sold the bright yellow Mitsubishi years ago, but even the minor mystery of the white car seen when both Lindsey Bennett and Tina Williams had disappeared was now explained: at night, especially on monochrome CCTV footage, it was almost impossible to distinguish yellow from white. From what Naysmith told me, the diary contained nothing very incriminating, beyond the simple fact of Terry's name, though Terry would have been flattered by some of what the seventeen-year-old girl had written. Perhaps that was why he'd kept it.

'It isn't right, what Simms is doing,' Jim Lucas said, as we left the CSIs to complete their work and headed back to the cars. 'You should be given credit, not treated like you've done something wrong.'

'It doesn't matter,' I said.

The search adviser gave me a sideways look, but said nothing. With no one left alive to corroborate my story, Simms was doing his best to discredit my account of what had happened. Not only had he built his reputation on wrongly convicting Monk, but now it emerged that he'd entrusted the real killer with responsibility for searching for the missing victims. The press were clamouring for blood, and for probably the first time in his life Simms was reluctant to appear in front of TV cameras. He'd seen to it that I'd been shut out of the investigation, and it was only as a courtesy from Naysmith that I'd been allowed to accompany them on the moor that morning.

But I was long past caring about Simms. I'd just arrived back at the hotel when my phone rang. It was the hospital. Sophie was asking to see me.

Even though I'd known what to expect, her condition was a shock. The thick mane of hair had been shaved off, replaced by a white dressing. She looked pale and emaciated.

Her voice was a whisper. 'Bet I look a mess . . .'

I shook my head. 'You're OK, that's the main thing.'

'David, I . . .' She took hold of my hand. 'I'd have died if not for you.'

'You didn't.'

Her eyes filled with tears. 'I know about Terry. Naysmith told me. I—I'm sorry I didn't tell you everything. About the diary. I need to explain . . .'

'Not now. We can talk later.'

She gave a faint smile. 'At least we got Zoe and Lindsey back. I was right after all.' Her eyes were already closing.

I waited till her breathing showed she was asleep, then gently disengaged my hand. She looked peaceful, the stress of the past week smoothed from her features. I sat beside the bed for a while, watching her. Thinking.

It was still unclear whether she'd face charges for withholding Zoe Bennett's diary. Although she'd kept its existence from the police, even by Terry's admission it hadn't come into her possession until after Monk was convicted of—and had confessed to—the murders. There was nothing in the diary to undermine that, so it seemed unlikely she'd be prosecuted.

The doctors expected her to make a full recovery, with no long-term impairment. After what she'd been through, they said she'd been incredibly lucky. Even so, I waited until I felt she was well enough to have the conversation I'd been putting off.

Sophie was sitting up in her hospital room, smiling. The dressings were off her skull and her hair was already growing out to an auburn stubble, blunting the sutured, horseshoe-shaped scar. She was starting to look more like her old self. Like the person I remembered from eight years ago. It was as though a weight had been lifted from her.

'The insurers have agreed to pay out for the stock and equipment I lost when the kiln collapsed,' Sophie announced. 'We're still haggling about the building, but I'll get more than enough to set up again. Great, isn't it?'

'Yes,' I said. I'd only been back to the house once, to collect my car. The sight of the ruined kiln had been depressing. I'd been glad to leave.

Sophie's smile faded. 'What's wrong?'

'There's something I need to ask you.'

'Oh, yes?' She tilted her head quizzically. 'Go on.'

'You knew Terry killed them, didn't you?'

I watched the swift play of emotions on her face. 'What? I don't . . .'

'You knew he'd murdered Zoe and Lindsey Bennett, and probably Tina Williams. I just can't make up my mind if you stayed quiet to protect him, or because you were scared what he'd do to you.'

She drew back slightly. 'That's an awful thing to say!'

'I'm not saying you had any proof. But you knew, all the same.'

'Of course I didn't know!' Patches of colour had flushed her cheeks. 'You really think I'd have kept quiet if I'd known Terry was a *murderer*? How can you even *think* something like that?'

'Because you're too intelligent for it not to have occurred to you.'

That took the heat from her. She looked away. 'I'm obviously not as clever as you think. Why would I have bothered writing to Monk, asking where the twins' graves were, if I knew Monk hadn't killed them?'

'I wondered about that. I think you kept copies of those letters to prove you really thought Monk was guilty, in case something like this happened. You just never expected him to call your bluff.'

'I don't believe this! Look, if this is because of the diary, I've already told the police everything. They know all about it!'

'Then why don't you explain it to me?'

She looked down at where her hands were clasped together on the bed, then back up at me. 'All right, I lied about me and Terry. It was more than just a fling. We saw each other on and off for a couple of years.'

'Were you still seeing him during the search?'

'No, we'd split up before then. We rowed a lot. About him seeing other women.' She didn't seem to notice the irony of what she was saying. 'It wasn't until months after the search that we got back together again.'

'Was that when you found Zoe Bennett's diary?'

'His wife had thrown him out by then. He got called out on a job and left me alone in his squalid little flat. I was bored, so I started tidying things away. Half of his things were still in boxes. The diary was in one of them. God, you can't imagine how that felt.'

No, I didn't expect I could. 'Why didn't you tell anyone? You'd got proof that Terry had been having a relationship with a murdered girl. Why would you keep quiet about something like that?'

'I thought Monk was guilty! Everyone did! What was the point of stirring up a lot of needless trouble? Not so much for him but for his family. I'd done enough to them already without that.'

'Sophie, you were a behavioural specialist! You're telling me you never once thought the diary was important?'

'No! I wanted to hurt him, that's why I took the diary. I knew he'd been sleeping with her, but I never suspected anything else!'

'Then why were you frightened of him?'

She blinked. 'I . . . I wasn't.'

'Yes, you were. When I took you home from hospital you were terrified. Yet you still pretended you couldn't remember who'd attacked you.'

'I—I suppose I didn't want to get him into trouble. You can't switch off your feelings for someone, even if they don't deserve it.'

I passed a hand over my face. My skin felt grainy. 'Let me tell you what I think,' I said. 'You took the diary to hurt Terry, like you say. You were angry and jealous and it gave you a hold over him. It was only after you'd taken it that you realised the danger you'd put yourself in. But by then you couldn't go to the police without getting yourself into trouble. So you hid it and kept quiet, and hoped the threat of it would stop him from killing you as well.'

'That's ridiculous!' But there was defensiveness behind her indignation.

'I think you blamed Terry for spoiling your career,' I went on. 'It must have been hard, helping the police to expose other people's secrets when you had one like that of your own. So you stopped working as a BIA and tried to make a fresh start. Except that takes money, doesn't it?'

For a second Sophie looked afraid. She hid it behind bluster. 'What are you trying to say?'

I'd had plenty of time to think it through over the past few days. Terry had called Sophie a blackmailing bitch, and while I didn't give much credence to what he said it had started me thinking. That didn't mean I liked what I was about to do. But we'd gone too far to stop now.

'The cottage you're living in, it can't be cheap. And you said yourself the pottery doesn't sell. Yet you still seem to make a decent living.'

Sophie's expression was defiant but brittle. 'I get by.'

'So you never asked Terry for money?'

She looked down at her hands, but not before I saw that her eyes were brimming. I didn't say anything. Just waited.

'You don't know what it was like,' Sophie said eventually, her voice cracked. 'You want to know if I was scared? Of *course* I was scared! But I didn't know what else to do. I took the diary without thinking. I—I was just so bloody *mad*! He'd been screwing that . . . that teenage *slut* while he'd been seeing me! It was only later that . . . that I . . . Oh, Christ!'

She covered her face as the tears came. I hesitated, then passed her a tissue from the bedside table.

'I didn't want to believe it was Terry. I kept telling myself Monk really had killed them. That's one reason I started writing to him, trying to convince myself I was wrong.' She wiped her eyes. 'But I was angry as well. I'd given up everything because of Terry. My career, my home. The least he could do was help me start again. I thought as long as I'd got the diary I'd be safe.'

Oh, Sophie . . . 'But you weren't, were you?'

'I was until Monk escaped. Terry phoned then, threatening what he'd do if I didn't give him the diary. I didn't know what to do!'

'So you phoned me,' I said tiredly. Not just to help her find the graves. She'd wanted someone with her in case Terry tried anything.

'I couldn't think who else to call. And I knew you wouldn't say no.' She plucked at the damp tissue. 'Next day I was getting ready to meet you when he hammered on the door. When I wouldn't let him in he . . . he broke it down. I ran upstairs and tried to lock myself in the bathroom, but he forced his way in there as well. I got hit by the door.' Her hand went automatically to the fading bruise on her cheek.

'Why didn't you say something then?'

'How could I? I'd been hiding evidence for years! And I'd no idea Terry had been suspended. And when you said he'd been to see you . . .'

A shudder ran through her. I started to reach out, but stopped myself.

'I didn't really do anything *wrong*!' she blurted. 'I know I made a mistake, but that's why I wanted to find Zoe and Lindsey's graves so badly. I thought at least if I could do that much it might make up for . . . for . . .'

For protecting their killer? For letting the wrong man stay in prison?

Sophie looked down at the shredded tissue in her hands. 'So what now?' she asked. 'Are you going to tell Naysmith?'

'No. You can do that.'

She took hold of my hand. 'Do I have to? They already know about the diary. It won't change anything.'

No, but it'll end eight years of lies.

I set her hand on the bed and stood up. 'Bye, Sophie.'

I walked out into the corridor. My footsteps rang on the hard floor as the clamour of the hospital enveloped me. I felt an odd detachment that even the fresh, cold air outside didn't dispel. I unlocked my car and stiffly lowered myself into the seat, my cracked ribs still painful. I closed my eyes and put my head back. The idea of driving back to London didn't appeal, but I'd been here long enough. Too long. The past was beyond reach. Time to move on.

I reached into my pocket for my phone. I'd turned it off in the hospital and when I switched it back on it beeped straight away.

I had a message waiting. Or rather messages: I'd missed three calls, all from the same number. It wasn't one I recognised. I frowned, but before I could play any of them my phone shrilled again. It was a call this time, from the same number as before. I straightened. *Something urgent.*

I felt the familiar quickening of interest as I answered.

simon **beckett**

Where are you from?

I grew up—and still live—in Sheffield. I had an ordinary working-class background at a time when the city was still dominated by the steel industry. I have lived in other places but I've always gravitated back here. It tends to get a bad press, but it's a good place to live, and a lot greener than most people give it credit for—I mean that in the sense of trees and countryside rather than the ecological sense. I don't set my novels here, because I think it's difficult to be objective about somewhere you know well. But other writers have no problem with that, so it's just a case of different strokes, I suppose.

What did you do before you started to write full time?

After university I somehow ended up doing property repairs for several years. Not much fun in winter, believe me. That was followed by a stint teaching English in Spain, and then I came back to the UK and played percussion in various bands. None of them came to anything, but several musician friends became successful after I'd left, which probably says it all. At more or less the same time, I started writing feature articles for the national broadsheets and colour supplements. I don't have any formal training as a journalist, but I've always found it complements writing novels fairly well. It forces you to be disciplined, and gets you away from your desk, which is no bad thing. And if not for the journalism I would never have visited the Body Farm—a research centre for forensic anthropologists, located in Tennessee—and had the idea for my first book, *The Chemistry of Death*.

How did you first start writing?

It was something I'd always been interested in, but I only started to think of it as a potential career when I went to teach in Spain. I worked in the evenings, so I used to write during the day. It was hardly an overnight thing, though, because it was six years before I was published. I didn't have an agent, so I started touting my manuscript around publishers myself. After countless rejections it was picked out of the slush-pile, and within forty-eight hours I'd got myself both a book deal and an agent. That was a real watershed moment.

What type of crime fiction would you say you write?

I suppose the David Hunter novels fall under the banner of forensic crime, because the main character is a forensic anthropologist. But character and psychological motivation are just as important to me as the forensic aspects. And, although I'm happy to be thought of as a crime writer, I don't like the way crime fiction tends to be pigeon-holed. It tends to be dismissed in some quarters as though it isn't 'proper' writing. That's starting to change now, I think, but I can't see a crime novel being shortlisted for the Man Booker Prize any time soon.

How did David Hunter develop as your main character, and is he based on any real-life forensic scientist?

No, David Hunter is entirely fictional. But the forensic techniques he uses are authentic. When it came to creating a central character, to begin with it was more a case of knowing what I didn't want. There are enough heavy-drinking, maverick tough-guys in crime fiction already. I wanted a character who was more flawed, who was introspective and even quite vulnerable in some respects. Hunter's very human—he doubts himself all the time. But there's also a stubborn streak in him. He's got a strong sense of right and wrong, and he'll stick his neck out for something he believes in. Once I had an idea of the sort of person he was, it was a case of building a convincing background for him. And when you've done that, it isn't long before the character himself starts to take over.

We know a little about Hunter's past, but there's an awful lot we still don't know about him. Do you plan to change that?

Definitely. As the series progresses we'll find out more about Hunter's history—perhaps with one or two surprises along the way. But it'll be a drip feed of information from book to book. I like the idea of getting to know a character more progressively rather than giving away everything all at once.

Do you have a scientific background yourself?

Not exactly, although I did plan on being a biochemist at one point. I was all set to take a degree in Biochemistry at university until I failed Biology and Chemistry A Level, and ended up taking an English degree instead. Funny how things turn out, isn't it?

How important is research in your writing?

It's very important. It shouldn't be allowed to take over the story, but if the scientific and other details are accurate it gives a greater sense of authenticity. Besides which, being a freelance journalist I have a real phobia about getting my facts wrong. So if I don't know something, I'll ask someone who does. There are several forensic anthropologists, both UK and US based, who are good enough to help me with that side of things, and I enjoy tracking down experts in whatever other fields I might need to know about, from diabetic comas to police communications in the Outer Hebrides. And, obviously, I'll visit locations where a book is set, to get a feel for the landscape and area. I might not get everything right, but I do my best.

Taken from: www.simonbeckett.com

GARETH CROCKER

FINDING JACK

After losing his family in a tragic accident, Fletcher Carson joins the flagging war effort in Vietnam and cares little if he lives or dies. But during one of his early missions, Fletcher rescues a critically wounded yellow Labrador that he nurses back to health and names Jack. As Fletcher and Jack patrol and survive the forests of Vietnam, Fletcher slowly regains his zest for life—until the US Army gives an order that Fletcher just can't follow.

A captivating tale based on real-life events.

PROLOGUE

Chicago
January 12, 1972

The wind sulked around Hampton Lane cemetery like a child lamenting the loss of a favourite toy. It stirred the leaves lining the cobbled paths but did little more than slowly tow them along, like condemned souls being dragged to the afterlife.

Standing among the rolling fields of dead in a sea of granite and marble tombstones, Fletcher Carson began to trudge towards the foot of a tree where his life lay buried under two stark stone crosses. His wife, Abigail, had been such a positive person that she had seldom discussed death. Only during the drawing up of their wills did it emerge that she wished to be interred under the shade of a maple tree with only a simple cross to mark her final resting place. Her epitaph was every word as humble as she was. It read:

HERE RESTS ABIGAIL CARSON,
LOVING WIFE AND MOTHER.
MAY HER LIGHT NEVER FADE
FROM OUR HEARTS.

Kelly's cross was half the size of her mother's. It carried only her name and the dates of her short life. Fletcher had been a writer for most of his working life. The right words, he was certain, did not exist.

'Fletcher.' A voice drifted towards him. 'I thought I'd find you here.'

Fletcher recognised the broad Southern drawl. It was Marvin Samuels, his editor and possibly only remaining friend in the world.

'You look good,' Marvin continued, but the inflection in his voice suggested otherwise. At just under six feet, Fletcher Carson was by no means a particularly tall man, but there was a stoop in his posture now that belied his true height. He was blessed with smooth olive skin, thick black hair and hazel eyes. At twenty-nine he was in his prime, but the burden of recent months weighed heavily on him. His athletic build remained, but his face carried the expression of a man who had wandered into a dark labyrinth and had long since abandoned hope of ever finding his way out.

'I read somewhere that the dead can hear you,' Fletcher said, staring at the ground. 'If someone they really loved visits their grave, they can hear that person's thoughts. It can be raining or blowing a gale, but just around their grave, everything becomes still. That's when they're listening.'

'I hope it's true.'

Fletcher slipped his hands into his pockets. 'Why have you come here, Marvin?'

'Why do you ask questions you know the answers to?'

'We've been through this. There's nothing left to discuss. I'm leaving tomorrow.'

Marvin folded his arms and looked up at the sky. 'Sure. I'll just stand around and watch while you try to get yourself killed.'

'I'm asking you to respect my decision.'

'Do you think this is what your girls would've wanted?'

Fletcher snapped his head round. 'You're in no position to ask that. Do you know what the last few months have been like?'

'Of course not. But going off to fight in Vietnam isn't the answer.'

'What if it were Cathy or Cynthia? What would you do?'

'I'd try to find a way to get over their passing and carry on with my life.'

'*Really?*' Fletcher said, swallowing hard, and then pointing to his daughter's grave. 'Kelly was only about to be seven, Marvin. How do you get over that? If you know, please enlighten me.'

'Fletcher—'

'Tell me something,' he went on, his voice faltering. 'Do you know where the line is?'

'The line?'

'Where you end . . . and your family begins?'

'C'mon, don't do this.'

'I'll tell you. There is no line. You're one entity, and when a part of you is cut away, the rest of you slowly bleeds out.'

'Fletcher.'

'Our soldiers are being massacred in Vietnam. Most of them are still kids. They've got their whole lives ahead of them. It makes sense that people like me enlist.'

'People like you,' Marvin repeated. 'You mean, people who want to die. You need help, Fletcher. You need to speak to a professional.'

'A shrink? Will that bring back my girls?'

'It might help you to learn to cope without them.'

'That's just it,' Fletcher said. 'I don't want to cope without them.'

Marvin tried to reply, but could draw on nothing meaningful to say.

'I appreciate you coming and all that you've done for me, but I think you should leave.'

'Just let me—'

'Please,' Fletcher whispered. 'Just go.'

Marvin began to walk away, then stopped. 'Do you remember that piece you did on suicide when you were still covering hospitals? At the end, you wrote that if only the sufferers had been able to see past the moment of their pain, they could claw their way back to life.'

'What I didn't realise,' Fletcher replied, 'is that you can never truly understand things that haven't happened to you.'

Marvin shook his head.'I've stood by you through this whole goddamn nightmare. From the moment the plane went down to the day you were discharged from the hospital. If you leave tomorrow, then I've just been wasting my time.'

'I'm sorry, Marvin, but this isn't about you.'

'Fine. But know that this is the last thing your girls would've wanted for you. You're making a terrible mistake.'

'Maybe . . . but it's mine to make.'

Marvin turned away. 'You're heading into a nightmare. It's hell over there.'

Fletcher nodded slowly and pictured his girls beneath his feet. 'It's hell everywhere,' he whispered.

When Marvin was gone, Fletcher knelt down between the two graves. He reached into his pocket and pulled out a silver frame Abigail had kept on her bedside table. It held one of her favourite photos of the three of them, sitting on a boulder in Yellowstone Park. He gently placed it down on her grave. From another pocket, he withdrew a small wooden box, which he rested against the foot of Kelly's cross. In it was a crystal sculpture of the dog he had promised to buy her. She had died three days before her seventh birthday.

It was the present she would never have.

ONE

Death Valley, Vietnam
July 6, 1972

Only the top half of Fletcher's head was visible. The rest of his body was submerged beneath the mud and thick reeds alongside the riverbank. From his position, he could make out three members of his platoon. Point man Mitchell Lord, radioman Gunther Pearson and their lieutenant, Rogan Brock, were hidden in a classic L-shaped ambush awaiting an enemy patrol. They had been hiking up to a site three miles away to set up a landing zone when they were warned about the patrol.

Fletcher blinked away the sweat around his eyes and checked his rifle. As sniper, his job was to pick out the ranking officer and take him down first. Cut off the head and the body will fall, the army taught them.

Both the North Vietnamese Army and the Vietcong, or Charlie, as US soldiers nicknamed them, were smart and elusive. Their tactics were to attack and retreat—basic guerrilla warfare. Charlie would stab you, then withdraw into the shadows. He was a ghost that never slept. He made traps that intended to maim, not kill. Traps that would slow down platoons and gnaw away at their spirit.

Faint voices.

Fletcher narrowed his gaze to hide the whites of his eyes. He remained perfectly still, the area around him disturbed only by a swarm of flying insects breaking the surface of the soupy water with their wings in an attempt to lure out prey.

It seems everyone's hunting, he thought grimly. The body of his gun was covered with mud to guard against reflections. Only the open barrel—the killing eye—was visible to the trail.

Footsteps and voices. Louder now.

A soldier, barely five feet tall, emerged over the rise. Fletcher curled his finger round the trigger of his M16.

Waiting . . . waiting.

Fletcher flinched at what he saw next. An American soldier wearing the emblem of the First Air Cavalry Division appeared. His arms were bound over a wooden pole behind his back. As he limped forward, he was kicked from behind by one of his captors.

Fletcher looked to his lieutenant for instruction. Through a series of hand signals, Rogan ordered him to take out the two soldiers directly in front of and behind the hostage. This would minimise the chance of the American getting shot in the firefight. He then signalled for the rest of the platoon to switch from automatic to single fire. He looked back at Fletcher and held up his fist, waiting for the right moment.

A bead of sweat rolled down Fletcher's nose, then dropped into the water. With one eye on Rogan and the other straining towards his two marks, he held his breath. *C'mon . . . c'mon . . .*

Rogan dropped his hand.

Fletcher squeezed off two rounds in quick succession. Before the second soldier even hit the ground, the rest of the platoon opened fire. The sound was devastating. As Charlie tried to return fire, point man Mitchell Lord burst out of his hiding place, tackled the US hostage, and dragged him down an embankment. It was typical Lord. He was every bit as brave as he was crazy. In less than a minute, twenty-three Charlie lay dead in the burning sunshine of Vietnam.

After a quick sweep of the area to ensure that there were no splinter patrols nearby, Fletcher's closest friend in the platoon, infantryman Travis Tucker, untied the hostage. He appeared badly dehydrated; his tongue was so swollen, he could barely speak. Only after several generous sips of water was he able to relay some information. He was a helicopter pilot who had been shot down while dropping a platoon into a hot zone. He was the sole survivor. He had been held hostage for more than a week and had been interrogated and tortured. His hands were shaking so badly, he could barely hold the water canister up to his mouth.

'Easy with that,' Rogan warned, throwing Travis a glance. 'He'll bring it all up.' From a physical perspective, few men registered a more imposing presence than Rogan Brock. Although tall and heavily built, he was not the largest man in Vietnam, but there was something deeply unsettling behind his stare. There was a sense of raw aggression lurking beyond the black centres of his eyes. His shaven head and pitted face added additional threat to his appearance.

The pilot wiped his mouth with the side of his torn sleeve. 'I can't tell you how grateful I am. I'm pretty sure they were going to kill me today. One more interrogation, and they were going to put a bullet in my face. How'd you know where to find me?' he asked Travis.

The question saddened Fletcher. In his delirious state, the pilot believed that what had just transpired was a planned rescue. The truth was that the US was having enough of a battle just trying to keep a foothold in the war without having to coordinate rescue attempts for POWs.

'Forget about it. The important thing is that you're safe now. We'll have you back at base tomorrow morning, where you can get some rest. The name's Travis, by the way. Travis Tucker.'

'Will Peterson,' the pilot replied, accepting Travis's hand.

'Let me introduce you to the rest of the Fat Lady.'

'The Fat Lady? I've heard of you guys. You were part of the company that survived that shitstorm outside Kon Tum. The story I heard had you outnumbered eight to one.'

'More like four to one, and we didn't all survive. We lost three men that day,' Rogan fired back. 'You shouldn't believe everything you hear.'

Travis moved quickly to defuse the moment. 'This, as you might've already guessed, is our lieutenant, the charismatic Rogan Brock. The man sitting next to you is probably the third best sniper within a hundred yards from here, Fletcher Carson.'

'Definitely top ten.' Fletcher nodded.

'Radioman Gunther Pearson . . . squad leader Wayville Rex . . . weapons specialist Kingston Lane . . . infantryman Arnold Keens . . . medic Edgar Green . . . and infantryman Craig Fallow.'

More handshakes and nods.

'And this,' Travis continued, 'is the madman who dragged you down the embankment. The finest point man in all of Vietnam: Mitchell Lord.'

'All right, ladies, now that we've exchanged phone numbers, we need to get moving,' Rogan cut in. 'There's still a war going on here.'

They picked up their gear while Fletcher and Travis helped Will to his feet.

'Why do you call yourselves the Fat Lady?' Will asked.

'Because Vietnam ain't over, baby . . . till the Fat Lady sings!'

They all laughed, until Rogan spun round. 'We having fun, platoon? Should we light a few flares to make the VC's job a little easier? I don't want to hear another goddamn word until we hit the LZ.'

THE PLATOON dug foxholes and rigged the area with tripwires linked to mines and flares. Most of the soldiers constructed hooches above their foxholes—makeshift tents created by zipping two ponchos together. Once the work was done and their coordinates radioed in to base for the morning pick-up, Rogan called the platoon together for a debriefing. Afterwards, he turned his attention to guard duty. 'Fallow and Green, you're on watch until twenty-two hundred. Carson and Tucker till oh three hundred. Rex and Lane, you relieve them till sunrise.'

Afterwards, Fletcher shook his head. 'Fucking graveyard again.'

Mitchell Lord stood up and ran his fingers through his long black hair. How he was allowed to keep it that length was something of a mystery. 'I'll take over for you guys.'

'Thanks, Mitch, but if Rogan finds out you're covering for us, he'll piss himself,' Fletcher replied.

Mitchell was hardly ever assigned to guard duty, not because Rogan favoured him, but because they couldn't afford to have him tired in his position as point man. Running point required skill and concentration. It entailed going ahead of the patrol, checking for traps, ambushes, enemy patrols. It was also physically taxing, as he had to navigate and hack his way through long stretches of dense jungle with a machete. One of the reasons they had suffered relatively few casualties was because of Mitchell's ability to sniff out danger.

At their foxhole, Travis removed his boots and sat down next to Fletcher. He pushed his glasses onto the top of his head, which, apart from a sprinkling of wispy brown hair, was largely bald. He had piercing blue eyes and a kind and open face that people responded to. For a while they spoke about Will Peterson and the firefight, but gradually their conversation meandered away from the day's events.

'Fletcher, there's something I've been wanting to ask you for a while now. I know I've got no right to ask it, and I'll understand it if you tell me to shut up and mind my own business, but . . . I—'

'You want to know about the crash?'

Travis nodded hesitantly.

Fletcher propped his rifle against the side of the hole and stared out over the jungle. 'The *Odyssey* was billed as a revolution in air travel. Did you know that it took ten years to design and was capable of holding almost six hundred passengers?'

'I remember,' Travis replied softly. 'It was all over the press.'

'You should've seen her, Trav. She was as big as a ship, with a wingspan as wide as a football field. She was designed to fly supersonic at a range of ten thousand miles. Although,' he said, trailing off, 'they never proved that . . .'

'What brought her down?'

'A design flaw in the fuel system was the last I heard, but it doesn't matter. All that counts is that she came down. There were three hundred and twenty-seven passengers on board its maiden flight, and only nine of us survived.'

Fletcher paused. When he spoke again, his voice was flat. 'As one of the journalists invited to the launch, I was allowed to bring my family along for the ride. We had just reached cruising altitude when the pilot invited all the children to the flight deck. Kelly was about to step into the cockpit when the children were rushed back to their seats. The cabin crew told us to put on our safety belts. About a minute later, an engine on the right wing seemed to stutter—it felt like a cough—and then exploded. Another two on the left wing followed moments later. I held on to Abby and Kelly as the plane fell, telling them that everything was going to be OK, but I knew. And then there was nothing. I woke up still strapped to my seat, lying in someone's back yard. I could see what was left of the plane's fuselage. It was lying in a field. The flames were as high as church steeples. I knew then that my girls were gone.'

'*Jesus*,' Travis whispered, taking a minute to process the story. 'And that's why you decided to enlist?'

'Not right away. The day after the funeral, I decided to kill myself,' Fletcher replied matter-of-factly. 'I threw myself off the sixth floor of the hospital where I was being treated. A passing truck broke my fall, and I survived, but a few weeks later I was back on the same balcony, determined to finish the job. Then a strange thing happened. As I was standing there, preparing to jump, a news broadcast came on the radio about Vietnam and how hundreds of American GIs were being killed every week. A mother who had lost both her sons in the space of a weekend spoke of their deaths. I'll never forget her voice. The report went on to describe how the average age of the dead hovered at around nineteen. Still teenagers, still boys. Suddenly suicide seemed like such a waste. That's when I decided to enlist.'

'Thanks, Fletch. I know how hard that must've been to talk about.'

'That's the first time I've told anyone the story.'

'I'm privileged, then.'

Within a few minutes, Travis was fast asleep, most likely to dream about his own dead wife, Fletcher thought. Travis had lost his wife a year before coming to Vietnam. She was driving to work one morning when a car skipped a traffic light and ploughed into her. She was in a coma for over a month, but died the day after their wedding anniversary. Blood tests revealed that she was pregnant—it would have been their first child.

While Travis slept, Fletcher removed his friend's glasses and placed them in his top pocket. He leaned forward and folded his arms on the edge of the foxhole. The sun was a fiery mirage on the horizon. Vietnam sunsets were beautiful while they lasted, but gave way to sudden darkness—there was little honeymoon between day and night, and the soldiers dreaded the night. They were at their most vulnerable under the cover of darkness, partly because of the enemy's tactics of striking in the early morning hours, but also because it was the one time when soldiers were truly alone with their thoughts and fears.

BY MIDMORNING, Gunther Pearson had confirmed their coordinates via radio and ordered their pick-up within the half-hour. Other choppers would follow to secure and develop the area, but their job, at least for the meantime, was over. Wayville Rex and Kingston Lane were instructed to set up three separate smoke canisters in the jungle surrounding the landing zone that would be deployed once the helicopter was within range. Each canister contained a different colour smoke. The pilot would then have three potential pick-up points, of which only one was correct. Gunther would reveal which one they were positioned next to only at the last moment. If Charlie was nearby, he would have to guess their location and, consequently, the pick-up zone. The helicopter would swoop down and hover just above the ground as the men clambered on board. This was by far the most vulnerable time of the operation. Scores of US UH-1 helicopters—or Hueys, as they were known—had been brought down by rocket launchers as they waited to either pick up soldiers or drop them off.

Waiting anxiously, the Fat Lady listened for signs that its lift was approaching. As usual, Mitchell was the first to hear it. 'Flapping bird. Flying from the east.'

As the helicopter's drone grew louder, Rogan gave the order to deploy the canisters. Ribbons of red, blue and white smoke billowed into the sky.

The command of red was given to the pilot in a simple code. It was an inside joke, as the Fat Lady only ever waited under red smoke. Within seconds, the Huey swooped down over the trees.

The Fat Lady hurried towards the chopper and scrambled on board. As always, Rogan was at the rear, looking for any signs of activity in the trees behind them. He turned round for the last few yards and launched himself up into the cabin. He raised his hand, extended his index finger, and swung his wrist round in a circular motion, signalling the pilot to fly. His hand was still turning when something caught his attention. A flash, smoke, and a series of hollow thuds.

'Shooter at one o'clock!' he shouted, immediately returning fire. Mitchell, Travis and Wayville joined in. They sprayed hundreds of rounds into the trees until they were out of range.

'Is everyone all right?' Rogan asked.

'We're good,' Travis replied, 'but Gunther's going to need a new radio.'

'What?' Gunther frowned, removing the radio off his back.

Smoke wafted out from a burnt hole in the middle of the pack.

'Son of a bitch! I knew there was a reason I signed up for comms!'

TWO

The Strip, as it was known by the soldiers, was located thirty miles north of Dak To in a mountainous area near the Laos border. Situated on top of a hill, it was home to some 600 troops. It contained the usual spattering of tents and prefab buildings, several munitions stores, bunkers, guard towers, a mess and, of course, base headquarters. It was surrounded by barbed wire and protected by mines linked to large oil drums brimming with a lethal combination of diesel and napalm. If Charlie wanted to get up close and personal with them, he would first have to tiptoe his way through the Strip's tricky dance floor.

Fletcher plodded towards the tent he shared with Travis and Mitchell. He slipped off his boots and settled into his stretcher. He made sure he was alone before pulling out a photograph he kept in his back pocket—a picture of his wife and daughter taken in their sitting room a year before the crash. The camera had a self-timer that had allowed him to be included in the photograph. However, in his haste to get into place alongside his girls, he had slipped and fallen headfirst into the couch. Scrambling to his feet, he had literally dived in front of the lens at the last moment. The photograph showed Abigail and Kelly in hysterics, watching wide-eyed as he lunged comically across the bottom half of the frame. They looked so happy, so perfect. Abigail, with her long black hair and sultry blue eyes, and Kelly, with a thick mop of mahogany hair and bright green eyes, were incandescent on the small square of paper.

If only he had known they were living on borrowed time, he would have made more of their days together. He would have held hands longer. He would have pushed Kelly on her swing until it was dark. But most of all, he would have told them both how much he cherished them every single day.

He stared at the photo for as long as he could bear before slipping it back into his pocket.

THAT NIGHT, like most evenings after an excursion, the Fat Lady gathered at the Soup to blow off some steam. The pub was little more than a tent furnished with a few tables and benches, a string of old Christmas lights, and a dilapidated fridge.

Although the tone of their conversation was jovial enough, Fletcher sensed there was something bubbling beneath the surface. Wayville, in particular, had the look of a man who wanted to get something off his chest.

'Hey, Wayville,' Fletcher said. 'What's on your mind?'

'This war is what's on my mind,' he replied, staring down into his glass. 'Am I the only one who sees that we're getting our asses kicked out there?'

'Easy,' Mitchell warned. 'Leave it alone.'

'No, screw it! We're getting slaughtered out there! Every day we get weaker, and the gooks keep advancing. We're losing this goddamn war. I want to know when it's going to stop. When will there be enough body bags before those guys in Washington finally pull the plug?'

'Don't do this to yourself,' Travis said. 'This kind of talk will just drive you insane.'

'So are we just supposed to sit back and take it? I'm sick to hell of—'

'Of what?' Rogan interrupted. He was standing at the entrance to the Soup. 'Finish your sentence, Rex.' He walked over to their table.

Wayville paused, then lowered his voice a notch. 'C'mon, Lieutenant, we're risking our necks, and for what? To delay the inevitable? The war will soon be over.'

'You don't know that.'

'Maybe not, but I don't want to get my ass shot off while the politicians try to figure out how we can get out of this mess with our pride intact.'

Rogan slammed his fist into the table. 'Let me make this clear. We're all part of a bigger machine. Our job is to execute our orders. If Lord's mind begins to wander while he's at point, we die. If Pearson radios in the wrong coordinates for support fire, we die. If Green decides not to be a medic, but instead to scratch his dick, we die. And if we die, the men behind us die! Do you get me, Rex?'

The room fell into a deep silence.

Rogan glared at each of the men, demanding their support.

Finally satisfied, he took a deep breath. 'While you're all together, you may as well know we've got orders for a recon mission the day after tomorrow. We spread our wings early—two hours before first light.' He scanned the room, waiting to be challenged. When no one spoke, he turned and walked away.

FOR THE FIRST TIME that Fletcher could remember, the Fat Lady flew in total silence. Were it not for the sound of the helicopter's rotors and the wind swirling through the cabin, it would have been like sitting in a mausoleum.

They were headed to one of the most dangerous areas in Vietnam: Lao Trung. Their job was to pinpoint Charlie strongholds. The coordinates would then be radioed back to base, and the various camps and compounds would later be bombed with daisy-cutters.

To exacerbate the uncomfortable quiet, tension still lingered between Rogan and Wayville.

'Someone say something,' Gunther eventually called out.

'All right . . . You're an idiot,' Kingston offered.

A smile tugged at the corners of Gunther's mouth.

Even Rogan managed a smile, but it was short-lived. Moments of levity in Vietnam seldom lasted.

They were approaching the drop-off zone.

JUMP, LAND, ROLL and run for cover—basic military training. What the army couldn't equip you for, Fletcher realised, was the sickening feeling that Charlie might be waiting behind you in the trees, his AK-47 trained on your back. It never failed to prick up the hairs on his neck.

As Fletcher hit the ground, he rolled and tried to get onto his feet in one fluid motion, but slipped and fell. The weight of his pack pinned him briefly to the earth.

'Carson, get on your feet!' Rogan yelled, grabbing him by his collar and wrenching him up.

Together they scrambled to a nearby rock. They all held their positions as the Huey climbed and disappeared over the treetops.

The key now, Fletcher knew, was to get moving as quickly as possible. The helicopter would have alerted Charlie to their presence. As of now, they were being hunted.

Rogan called everyone in. 'Fallow, what business are we in?' He always asked the same question at the start of an operation.

'The business of survival, Lieutenant.'

'That's right! Let's remember that. Get your minds focused.' A minute later, they were moving. They usually travelled in the same formation: Mitchell at point, followed by Rogan, Wayville, Gunther, Kingston, Fletcher and Travis. The three teenagers—Edgar Green, Craig Fallow and Arnold Keens—always brought up the rear. Rogan insisted on it. Although he never offered an explanation, Fletcher knew why: the young men were safer at the back, shielded from traps and ambushes.

BY LATE MORNING, they had made good ground. They had moved quickly, encountering nothing more sinister than the jungle's wildlife.

They had just stopped to eat and to tend to blisters and insect bites when Mitchell raised his hand as a sign of danger. Back on the Strip, they had often joked that he was two parts bloodhound, one part human. But there was no laughter now.

Mitchell hesitated, as if reading subtle vibrations in the air, then pointed to a small hillock ahead of them.

Without saying a word, he dropped down onto his stomach and began to crawl up the hill. Rogan and Fletcher followed behind him. Reaching the top, they carefully parted the tall grass, and Fletcher eased his rifle through the gap. There were four men, moving slowly, less than 200 yards away.

'What're they holding?' Fletcher whispered, squinting.

Rogan reached for his binoculars. 'Bow and arrow . . . and a spear . . . They're hunting.' He panned the binoculars away from the men and saw what they were after. 'Wild pig.'

'Soldiers?' Fletcher asked.

'Looks like . . . Montagnards. Jungle people,' Mitchell said. 'Hunters. Not many of them left. Some believe they're also cannibals.'

Fletcher watched as the four men closed in on their prey. With unnerving precision, the man in front drove a long spear into the animal's back. The pig squealed briefly, then fell silent.

'All right, no need to sound the alarm. Let's just get moving,' Rogan decided.

They retreated quietly down the embankment, collected their gear, and moved out. After a few minutes, Fletcher pulled up alongside Mitchell. 'Those men were almost two hundred yards away. How the hell did you hear them?'

'I didn't. I could smell shit in the breeze. When animal crap is that strong in the wind, it's normally because it's been smeared on something, in this case, the Montagnards. They were stinking out the place.'

The jungle was a bouquet of different smells, including plants, herbs, dead animals, mud—yet Mitchell had still managed to discern that something was amiss. 'Unbelievable,' Fletcher said.

THREE HOURS LATER, they were nearing the area where they planned to hole up for the night, when Mitchell lowered down onto his haunches and inspected the path ahead of him. It was covered with banana leaves. He carefully prised them up.

Rogan knelt down beside him. 'What've you got?'

'Possible soldiers on a skewer.'

The leaves had disguised one of Charlie's most devastating traps: a Punji pit. Sharpened bamboo sticks lined a deep cavity in the ground. The rest of the platoon gathered around.

'That's the first one I've ever seen,' Arnold Keens said.

Mitchell shook his head. 'Something's wrong.'

'What is it?'

'Too easy . . . They wanted us to find it. They used banana leaves. Proper Punji pits are concealed with mud, small leaves and bits of roots.'

'*Stop!*' Rogan called out to Arnold Keens, who had wandered round the side of the pit to get a better view. 'Don't move.' He walked over to the young infantryman and knelt down. He gently pressed on the innocuous-looking foliage at his feet. The ground immediately caved in, revealing a second Punji pit. This was the one intended for them.

Arnold slowly stepped back. 'Christ, that was close.'

Rogan leapt to his feet and grabbed the youngster by his collar. 'Who told you to break formation? You need to think about what you're doing!'

'Yes . . . Sorry, sir.'

'What are we in the business of?'

'Survival, sir.'

Rogan pulled him closer. 'Arnold, I'm tired of writing letters to mothers explaining how their sons died.'

'I'm sorry, sir. It won't happen again, sir.'

'It better not,' he replied, letting him go. 'It better not.'

It was the first time Fletcher could remember the lieutenant calling one of them by their first name. Perhaps he was human, after all.

ANOTHER NIGHT IN HELL, another hastily dug foxhole.

Travis had managed to fall asleep with relative ease, but Fletcher was again left grappling with the oppressively dark night.

For his earlier lapse, Arnold Keens and his foxhole-mate Edgar Green were pulling watch between 0200 and 0430. Fletcher listened as the two soldiers quietly discussed topics natural to men of their age—cars, music and women.

After a while, Fletcher tuned out their conversation and turned to his own thoughts. The prospect of the war coming to an end left him feeling conflicted. He was happy that American troops would soon go home, but he felt for the South Vietnamese. Without support, they would succumb to the North within a matter of weeks.

The end of the war would, once again, leave him adrift. The jungles of Vietnam had neither claimed him nor provided him with renewed purpose. All the war had done was darken the nightmares that plagued his nights. If he made it out, what would he do with the rest of his life? Return to Chicago? Not likely. He doubted he would be able to face anything that resembled his earlier life. He would have to relocate. Change jobs. Meet new people. Try to outrun his past. If he couldn't, there was always a balcony he could revisit.

FLETCHER WOKE UP to the sound of rain pelting down.

'Just a week without getting wet, that's all I ask,' Travis said, his eyes still closed. 'Tell me I'm dreaming the rain.' Their hooch was covering their bodies well enough, but water was pouring down the sides of the pit.

'You're dreaming the rain.'

'Tell me the Cubs won the World Series.'

'Sorry, but even dreams have a toehold in reality.'

Travis sat up and rubbed his eyes. 'Did you get any sleep?'

'About an hour, if you count all the blinking.'

'That's pretty good for you.'

'Yeah, but I'm thinking of giving it up altogether. Every time I fall asleep, I keep waking up in Vietnam.'

'I know what you mean. I have the same dream.'

Fletcher paused, then adopted a serious tone. 'What are you going to do with your life when you get out of here?'

'No long-term plans, really. But I do know the first thing I'm going to do.'

'What's that?'

'Fly to Miami. Book into a hotel with crisp white sheets and a view of the beach. I'll spend my mornings swimming in the ocean and my afternoons watching it from my balcony. At night, I'll let the tides lull me to sleep.'

Fletcher smiled warmly. He could imagine Travis sitting on a balcony with a drink in his hand gazing out over an azure ocean.

'What about you?'

For a while, Fletcher was quiet. 'Go visit my girls. Tell them about this place. Remind them how much I miss them.'

'And after that?'

'Who knows? Maybe I'll fly to Miami. Spend some time with a friend.'

'I do need someone to mix my drinks,' Travis said, watching muddy water pool at their feet. 'Come with me, Fletch. We'll stay a couple of weeks, then figure out the rest of our lives.'

Outside their foxhole, the jungle was now a solid grey sheet of rain. 'What? And give up all this?'

THREE

Four days later, the Fat Lady was finally on its way to the extraction point. Drained both physically and mentally, they had gathered information and plotted the coordinates of numerous enemy bunkers, at least half a dozen field bases, and a bridge that, once taken out, would hamper the NVA's supply line. Fletcher was startled at just how quickly Charlie was advancing and how strong he had become. All they could do now was try to slow him down.

They had narrowly missed being intercepted by NVA patrols and had twice been forced to separate. Now, with only two miles left to hike, the men were quiet. Mitchell, still at point, was completely wired and absolutely focused. He seemed to regard Charlie's traps not so much as weapons of war, but more as personal affronts. He would shuffle forward a few steps, then stop, breathe deeply, scan the area in front of him, and then dart forward again. Sometimes he would rub his hands on the ground and lick the tips of his fingers. Fletcher wondered, with genuine concern, how he would ever adapt back to normal life.

As was typical towards the end of an assignment, Rogan dropped to the back of the platoon to shepherd his men from the rear. Within hours, their entire area of operations would be the subject of an intense bombing campaign. Most of the men they had stolen past, laughing and drinking cheap alcohol outside huts and bunkers, would soon either be dead or wishing they were. The thing about war is that you could be on the winning side before breakfast, but still be dead by nightfall.

The thought brought no joy to Fletcher.

'Halt!'

'What is it?' Kingston asked.

Mitchell shook his head as if his eyes were deceiving him. 'A dog.'

Fletcher turned to his right. In the distance, a yellow Labrador, with its tongue lolling out of its mouth, emerged from the trees. The animal was moving badly, favouring its left side. What appeared to be a large cut ran from the top of its back down its front leg. Flies hung over the wound. A swollen mass of what looked like dried blood was caked under its neck. 'What the hell is a dog doing out here?'

Rogan briefly studied the animal, then gestured to Fletcher. 'Take him out.'

'What?'

'You heard me, Carson.'

Fletcher was taken aback by the order. He watched as the dog slipped on the wet undergrowth and then struggled to get back up. He looked weak and hungry. 'What are you talking about?'

'Are you deaf? Kill the dog. That's an order. There's something round its neck, probably a mine.'

Fletcher raised his rifle and looked through the scope. 'It's just blood and a lot of dirt.'

'This isn't a debate. Take the shot.'

Fletcher followed the animal in his sights as it approached them. In his first days in Vietnam, he'd spent some time at a base that had a dog unit attached to it. All the animals there had been German Shepherds, but he had heard that there were Labradors working as scout dogs throughout Vietnam.

'I'm not doing it.'

Rogan placed his palm over the top of his sidearm, but kept it holstered. 'Take the shot.'

'You first,' Fletcher said, glancing down at the lieutenant's hand.

'What is wrong with you? It's just a damn dog!'

'He's one of ours. The only Labradors in Vietnam belong to us. He must've got separated from his handler. Besides,' Fletcher bargained, 'if I shoot, we'll reveal our position—'

'I'm warning you. This is your last chance.'

'I'm not doing it.'

The Labrador was less than a hundred yards away and closing.

'Keens . . . take the shot,' Rogan instructed.

Arnold Keens, who'd been watching their exchange in disbelief, recoiled at the sound of his name.

'Your rifle, Keens! That metal thing strapped round your skinny neck. Use it! Take out the dog!'

Reluctantly, Arnold raised his gun and took aim.

'Don't do it, Arnold. Let him come to us. He's hurt. He recognises our uniforms. He's one of us. There's no danger—'

'Shut your mouth, Carson.'

Fletcher turned to face the teenager. 'Arnold, look at me. Please, don't shoot him.'

'Discharge your weapon, or I'll have you thrown in prison!'

The Labrador, sensing that something was wrong, stopped walking.

'Forgive me,' Arnold whispered, and squeezed off two rounds.

The first shot punched into the dog's chest, and the second into the top of his front leg. He collapsed onto his side and immediately tried to stand up, but his legs buckled under him.

Something unravelled in Fletcher's mind. He threw off his pack and launched himself at Rogan.

'Fletcher, no!' Travis yelled, scrambling towards them.

Fletcher hit Rogan in the stomach. The force of the blow sent him hurtling into a tree. Fletcher charged after him and started swinging his fists wildly, connecting with his face and chest.

Wayville and Kingston pulled Fletcher away. Blood flowed from Rogan's nose. 'Have you lost your mind, Carson?'

Fletcher didn't reply. He couldn't. His mind was teetering on the edge of a breakdown. He had rarely felt such anger, such hatred. He turned away and ran towards the dog.

'No,' Gunther warned. 'There could be traps.'

But Fletcher could think only of getting to the animal's side. By the time he reached the dog, it was clear he was dying. His chest was heaving. Blood had formed a half-moon round his body. Kneeling down, Fletcher carefully placed his hand on the Labrador's side to try to comfort him. As he touched his coat, the dog lifted his head and looked at him. Instead of fear, his eyes conveyed a look of sadness, a glimmer of betrayal. Fletcher felt his stomach tighten. 'You were coming to us for help, weren't you?'

The dog tried to lick his hand, but was slipping away.

Fletcher gently stroked the side of his face. 'I'm so sorry, boy.' He withdrew his sidearm. With his hand shaking and his vision blurred, he took aim. 'Close your eyes.'

Slowly, the dog's tail swept across the ground.

Fletcher was about to pull the trigger when he heard a voice over his shoulder. 'Don't do it,' Travis said softly, pushing the top of the gun down with his hand. 'He deserves a chance to live.'

FLETCHER CARRIED the critically wounded Labrador to the pick-up point. He should have weighed sixty or seventy pounds, but in his malnourished state was little more than half that. Edgar, their medic, applied tourniquets, but the dog continued to lose blood. As they waited for the chopper, Fletcher tried to funnel water into his mouth, but he could barely swallow. 'C'mon, friend . . . just a few sips.'

The dog looked at him, blinked, then closed his eyes. For a moment, Fletcher thought he was gone, but his chest continued to rise and fall in an uneven rhythm. He was hanging on, but only just.

Sitting opposite Fletcher, Travis gently patted the side of the dog's face. 'He's going to make it. I know it. There's something about him.'

Fletcher nodded, but couldn't reply. Something deep within him had given way. He knew his actions would have severe repercussions when they returned to base. There would be a hearing, and he would most likely be court-martialled and imprisoned. But all that concerned him now was trying to save the dog.

Edgar knelt down beside the Labrador and listened to his chest. 'Look, I can't be sure, but I think one of his lungs is punctured.'

'Will he make it back to base?' Fletcher whispered.

'His wounds are very serious.'

The next few minutes limped by.

'Bruno Ship,' Fletcher announced.

'Who?' Travis asked.

'Bruno Ship. He's a chef in the officers' mess.'

'Yeah . . . bald guy. Friendly. What about him?'

'A few weeks ago, we got to talking. It turns out he ran out of money and had to drop out of vet school in his final year. He'll help us. He'll operate.'

'Fletcher,' Edgar said. 'The army's going to come down hard on you for what you've done. I'm not sure Bruno is going to want to have anything to do with this.'

'He'll help. I know it. But I need you to do something for me.'

'What?'

'We need to get the dog into the hospital as quickly as possible.'

'No way. There's far too much activity there, trust me. Your best bet is to set something up in one of the tents.'

Fletcher thought for a moment. 'OK, but what about supplies?'

'That shouldn't be a problem. I have a key to the supply room. No one keeps a real inventory, anyway.'

Fletcher looked down at the Labrador and gently traced his fingers down the length of his nose. Each ragged breath seemed certain to be his last. 'Hold on, boy. Hold on.'

In the distance, the sound of rotor blades whooped towards them.

BRUNO SHIP massaged his temples as if trying to ward off sleep. He was standing at the entrance to Fletcher's tent, where the dog lay sprawled out on a stretcher.

'I've been trying to save animals since I was four years old. Of course I'll help you.'

Fletcher felt his throat constrict. 'Thank you. Once the operation's over, no one will know that you were ever involved. You have my word on that. So when do you want to operate? Tonight?'

'No. Edgar was right. Our friend has a punctured lung, and there's a lot of internal bleeding. We need to drain the chest cavity and do what we can to repair the damage.'

Bruno instructed Fletcher and Travis to boil two large pots of water and find a new mosquito net under which he would perform the operation. To make the environment as sterile as possible, the net would be doused in disinfectant.

'I've got a net I've never used,' a voice said, drifting into the room. 'It's yours if you want it.'

It was Mitchell. And Wayville, Kingston, Gunther and Craig Fallow were standing alongside him. 'What can we do to help?'

Fletcher raised his hands. 'Thanks, guys, but there're enough people in the firing line as it is. And there's nothing else for you to do. Bruno has agreed to perform the operation, and Edgar's organising the supplies. But I will take you up on that mosquito net, Mitch.'

'Done.'

'How's he doing?' Kingston asked, moving over to the stretcher.

'He's holding on, but not by much.'

'If he survives, we'll make him our mascot.'

Fletcher nodded but knew that if the dog somehow did recover, he would soon be reunited with his unit.

'How long do you think you've got before they haul you down to HQ?' Wayville asked.

'Hopefully long enough to get the tent set up for the operation.'

Then Fletcher and Travis noticed Arnold Keens sitting on his own. He had the look of a man at conflict with himself.

'I've got this,' Travis whispered. 'Go talk to him.'

'ARNOLD, ARE YOU ALL RIGHT?'

The infantryman flinched. 'Fletcher . . . I'm so sorry. This is all my fault,' he blurted out, his eyes red and swollen.

'No. It's me who owes you an apology. You were given a direct order, and you obeyed it. You were right to do what you did.'

A sob racked Arnold's body.

'Arnold, listen to me. I'm the one to blame here. What I did placed the entire platoon at risk. I wasn't thinking clearly.'

'What's going to happen to you?'

'I'm not sure, but they'll be coming for me.'

They were quiet for a while as Arnold tried to collect himself. 'How's he doing? Is he going to make it?'

'I don't know, but a few good people are pulling for him. That's got to make a difference, don't you think?'

'I hope so,' Arnold replied. 'Why'd you make a stand, Fletcher? Why risk yourself?'

'I don't know, really. I can't explain it. I just felt a connection to him. I imagined he'd been lost in the jungle for days—wounded, starving, trying to find his handlers, and there we were . . . his salvation. He recognised our uniforms. He was coming to us for help, and we were going to kill him. I just couldn't allow it.'

'Do you know if he's one of ours?'

'I haven't noticed any markings, but I'm pretty sure he is.'

'Let me do something, Fletcher. Let me help in some way.'

'Well . . . there's so many people involved now, what's another name on my conscience?'

Arnold smiled appreciatively.

'I'M READY,' Bruno announced, snapping on a pair of latex gloves. He was standing in front of Fletcher's tent.

'All right,' Fletcher sighed, scanning the area for any signs of his imminent arrest. 'You sure you want to go through with this?'

'Uh-huh.'

'What about you, Edgar? You don't mind assisting?'

'You couldn't drag me away.'

'Enough chat, gentlemen,' Bruno cut in, stepping backwards into the tent. 'Let's get moving.'

'Good luck,' Fletcher offered, walking away.

'Where're you going?' Bruno asked.

'To the Soup. I'll lose my mind if I wait around here.'

At the Soup, Fletcher sat at a table with Wayville and Travis.

'Still not incarcerated, I see,' Kingston joked, entering the pub an hour later. He was followed by Gunther and Craig Fallow.

'Not yet, but it shouldn't be long now.'

'Well, they sure are taking their sweet time.'

'I'm trying not to think about it. Have either of you been past the tent? Are they still operating?'

'Yeah, they're still working on the slug in his chest. They haven't even got to the one in his leg yet.'

'Christ, it's taking for ever.'

'Relax, Fletch,' Gunther said. 'Maybe this'll cheer you up. I got hold of a dog unit in Dak To. Their squad leader is willing to help and has set aside medicine and food for our patient.'

Fletcher's expression brightened. 'That's great, but how're we going to get it here?'

'Remember our pilot friend we rescued?' Craig asked. 'The good Will Peterson? Well, as Lady Karma would have it, he's now based in Dak To and has changed shifts with one of his buddies to run the stuff over to us this afternoon. They're loading up the supplies as we speak.'

Fletcher was visibly moved by the news. 'I don't know what to say.'

'Hey, this isn't your personal crusade,' Wayville replied. 'None of us wanted to see the dog shot. You just showed more guts than the rest of us.'

'Nothing gutsy about it. I saw the dog coming towards us, needing help, and we were going to shoot him. It didn't seem right.'

'At one point, I thought Rogan was going to tear your arms off.'

'If you guys hadn't separated us, he probably would've.'

'You didn't do too badly.'

Fletcher allowed himself a wry smile. 'The lieutenant's not the bad guy in this. He was just trying to protect us.'

'How's Arnold doing?' Kingston asked.

'I had a chat with him. He feels really bad. I explained that he was right to follow orders, and I apologised for what I did.'

'Carson!' a voice suddenly called out. Three armed soldiers were standing outside the entrance to the Soup.

FLETCHER WAS ESCORTED to the officers' pub. Inside, the prefab was deserted save for a single patron occupying the table next to the bar. Having delivered Fletcher, the three officers turned round and quickly strode away.

Fletcher pulled out a chair and sat down.

'Do you know how long I've been in Vietnam?' Rogan asked. 'This is my third tour. Seen a lot of death on both sides. Most of the men out here are terrified and will do whatever they can to get back home in one piece. But the Fat Lady is different. I have witnessed exceptional courage. Everyone looks out for one another. The Fat Lady is special. Something rare.'

'I agree.'

'Then why did you choose to threaten what we have today? What made you decide to jeopardise all that we are?'

'I don't know. I just couldn't let the dog die.'

'Do you understand why I gave the order?'

'Yes, because Charlie has been known to booby-trap animals with grenades and mines,' Fletcher replied. 'But there was nothing tied round his neck, I told you—'

'Not *round* his neck, Carson!' Rogan shouted. 'Inside it! They stitch handmade bombs no bigger than your fist into the skin under their necks. The bombs blow the animal to pieces and send a cloud of napalm fifty feet into the air. I've watched it happen.'

Fletcher thought back to how the dog's neck was caked in blood. 'Lieutenant, I didn't know. I'm sorry—'

'You could've killed us!' he yelled. 'What you did put everyone's lives in danger. Do you think I wanted to have the dog shot?'

Fletcher was at a loss for words.

'I know why you're here. I know what happened to your family, and I'm sorry for what you've been through. But that doesn't give you the right to impose your death wish on the men you serve with. You display the kind of fearlessness that only a man who has nothing to lose can show. Up until now, it's made you a highly effective soldier, but today it could've cost us our lives. I can't have you on board unless you get your head on straight.'

'You're right,' Fletcher agreed, holding up his hands. 'Please, believe me, I never meant to endanger the men.'

Rogan looked up at the ceiling, but did not reply.

For a while they sat in silence.

'What happens now? When is the hearing?'

'There isn't going to be one.'

'Are you telling me I'm not going to be formally charged?'

'Not officially, but I want you to apologise to the men. Especially Keens. You put him in a very difficult position.'

'I've already spoken to him. I feel terrible about it.'

'What I have to know right now is,' Rogan continued, 'are you a liability to us? Can I expect any more bullshit from you?'

'No, sir. You have my word. I won't go against your orders again.'

Rogan took a deep breath. 'All right. This is over. Get out of here.'

Fletcher stood up and made his way towards the door.

'Carson, wait. How's the dog doing?'

'They're still operating.'

'*Operating*? Who is—?' He shook his head. 'Never mind.'

AS FLETCHER left the officers' pub, he began to comprehend just how reckless he had been. He shuddered at his selfish behaviour and knew that in time he would have to find a way to make amends with the men whose lives he had jeopardised. But that time was not now. Running, he turned towards his tent. He saw Bruno step out, wiping his bloody hands with a towel.

'Bruno . . . how'd it go?'

'We pulled out four slugs. Two of ours, and two AK-47 rounds. Theirs were in the back leg and neck. I'm not going to lie to you, Fletcher. He's lost a lot of blood.'

'What're his chances?'

'Two, maybe three out of ten at a push. There's significant muscle and tissue damage. He's got three cracked ribs, a punctured lung, and his front right leg was partially dislocated. My real concern is his breathing and whether or not we've stopped the internal bleeding.'

'So what do we do now?'

'We wait. Gunther tells me the proper antibiotics will be here shortly. The sooner I can administer those, the better. We've got him on a drip, and his breathing is still ragged, but it has stabilised.'

Edgar pushed through the tent flap and shielded his eyes from the bright sunlight. 'This man is a genius. He did a great job. He's given our boy a fighting chance.'

Fletcher, swallowing hard, thanked both men and headed into the tent. Mitchell followed behind. The mosquito net, draped over the stretcher, gave the room a clinical feel. The smell of disinfectant was almost asphyxiating.

Fletcher knelt down next to the dog. A wave of affection swept through him. He felt an almost otherworldly connection to him.

As he stroked the side of the animal's face, Mitchell spoke. 'I can't help but notice that you're not in chains.'

'Rogan's not taking it any further.'

'You're off the hook? What'd he say to you?'

Fletcher briefly took him through their conversation. 'I owe everyone an apology. I'll speak to the men tonight. Rogan and I might not get along, but he was right about today.'

The tent flap parted and in stepped Travis and Gunther, carrying boxes of medical supplies. Travis placed one of the boxes down and pulled out a letter. 'This is for you.'

Fletcher quickly unfolded the note and read it out loud:

Dear Corporal Carson,

Your man has told us what you are doing to try to save the life of what you believe is a US scout dog.

Look inside his ears. There should be a letter and number marking his unit. Once you find it, radio the information back to me, and I'll trace where the dog comes from.

Thank you for what you are doing. Our dogs are saving hundreds of soldiers' lives.

The medicine comes with our thoughts and prayers. Let us know if there is anything else we can do to help you.

Sincerely,
W. Wallace
Squad Leader, Wolf Pack

Beside his name was a stamp of a German Shepherd sitting at its handler's feet. The words IN DOG WE TRUST underlined the image.

FOUR

That night, while Travis and Mitchell slept, Fletcher shifted his stretcher up alongside the dog. He listened as the animal drew one strained breath after another. He reached under the net to stroke the dog's chest every few minutes. His touch seemed to have a soothing effect, or so he liked to believe. Two drips hung from the top of the tent, one fighting infection and the other keeping the dog hydrated.

'How's our patient?' Bruno asked, entering the tent holding a small plastic box. 'I've got a change of dressings and a thermometer. I want to see if his temperature has come down at all.'

'He's doing all right, but he's battling to breathe again.'

Using Fletcher's torch, they changed his dressings and were surprised to discover that his temperature had dropped.

'That's encouraging; it means the treatment's working,' Bruno remarked. He dropped to his haunches and gently lifted the animal's jowls to inspect the colour of his gums. Satisfied, he then pulled down one of his eyelids to look at the tissue lining.

Fletcher took a deep breath. 'How're things really looking?'

'Honestly? Listening to his chest, it's not good. If he makes it through the night, I'm going to have to open him up again.'

Fletcher nodded. 'Have you ever seen a dog make it through worse?'

'Dogs are amazing creatures, especially Labradors. You'll be amazed at what they can endure. He's got the spirit for a fight.'

'I hope you're right.'

Bruno looked up at Fletcher and removed his glasses. 'If I may ask, why are you so attached to this dog?'

'I've been asking myself the same question, but I'm still no closer to an answer,' Fletcher replied. 'He can't die, Bruno.'

'Then we won't let him,' he said solemnly.

TRAVIS WIPED THE SLEEP from his eyes. 'Tell me you got some rest last night,' he said, yawning.

'Slept like a baby,' Fletcher replied.

'Liar,' Mitchell whispered, sitting up. 'How's he doing?'

'Same as yesterday. Just holding on. Bruno was here earlier to check on him. His circulation is improved, and his temperature has come down, but . . .'

'It's his breathing,' Mitchell said softly. 'I can hear it.'

'Bruno wants to operate again today. Doesn't think he'll make it otherwise.'

''Morning, all,' Bruno said, entering the tent with supplies in his arms. 'I take it our boy made it through the early morning?'

'He's still with us,' Fletcher confirmed.

Bruno fished out his stethoscope and placed it on the Labrador's chest. He frowned. 'Fletcher, what're your duties this morning?'

'Nothing, we're off for another two days. Why?'

'I need an assistant. We have to operate immediately. He's drowning in his own blood.'

'All right,' Fletcher said, clearing his throat. 'What should I do?'

'HOW LONG HAS IT BEEN?' Wayville asked, sitting outside the tent.

'Almost an hour and a half,' Travis replied.

'Should it be taking this long?'

'How the hell should I know?'

Kingston stood up and stretched. 'Let's take a look-see at what's going on.'

Wayville quietly lifted the tent's flap. A smell of ammonia wafted out to them. Beyond the mosquito net, Bruno was hunched over the dog. Fletcher, standing alongside him, was holding a clamp that disappeared into the dog's abdomen.

'Can we get you guys anything?' Gunther asked.

Neither man replied; they seemed oblivious to the question.

'Let's leave them be,' Mitchell said, closing the flap. 'If they need our help, they'll ask for it.' He turned away and was about to sit back down when the first mortar hit.

'INCOMING!' a panicked voice issued from the base's northern guard tower.

'No kidding!' Gunther yelled, feeling his face for shrapnel.

Wayville instinctively reached for his gun. 'Anyone hurt?'

Travis's glasses had shielded his eyes from the dust, and he was able to scan the area. 'I don't think so.'

'How the hell did Charlie get so close? It's broad daylight!'

Soldiers, half-dressed, spilled out of their tents. Officers barked orders. Jeeps roared to life. Pilots ran for their choppers.

Another mortar whined towards them.

'Get down!' Kingston shouted.

The missile hit less than fifty yards away, taking out a small prefab supply hold. Another mortar hit, further away this time.

The base took close to a dozen hits before it answered with heavy artillery fire. Mitchell, seemingly unaffected by the chaos, stood up and stared out into the jungle.

'What are you doing? Get down, Lord!' Wayville said.

Mitchell breathed in the caustic smell of cordite. His eyes focused on a distant hillside. 'Show yourself,' he whispered.

His eye caught a puff of smoke. 'I see you . . .'

He ran towards the nearest gun battery. The soldier manning it was firing wildly into the air. 'Move,' he commanded.

The soldier was visibly relieved to relinquish control. Mitchell spun the field gun round and opened fire. The ground shook as the giant rounds tore into the hillside.

Travis crawled up to the tent and threw up the flap. 'Fletcher . . . Bruno, you've got to get to a bunker.'

'We can't. If we leave now, he's dead.'

Suddenly three small holes punched through the side of the tent.

'Jesus!' Travis yelled, diving down.

Both Bruno and Fletcher stood their ground.

'C'mon, Fletcher, this is crazy!'

'If I let go of this clamp, he'll bleed out. I'm not moving. Now, get out of here.'

Gunther, lying behind Travis, tugged at his trousers. 'I've got an idea.' He pointed to a parked armoured vehicle. 'It'll shield them.'

Travis's eyes widened in agreement.

Together, they ran to the vehicle as puffs of dust exploded at their feet. Gunther leapt into the cabin and reached under the steering wheel. He twisted the key and slammed the truck into gear. Moments later, the vehicle skidded to a halt in front of the tent.

'Are you guys all right in there?' Travis yelled.

For a moment, there was no reply; then Bruno swore. 'Damn it . . . We're losing him!'

WITHIN MINUTES, the attack was over. By the time the helicopters had emptied the last of their cannons, it was clear Charlie was gone. A sweep revealed shells and blood at half-a-dozen sites, suggesting the offensive might have involved as many as fifty soldiers.

Despite everything, Bruno and Fletcher completed the operation. At the height of the mayhem, the Labrador's blood pressure had dropped alarmingly, but they had managed to stabilise it.

Sitting outside their tent as the sun dipped over the trees, Fletcher, Bruno and Travis nursed a few cold beers. They had spent the afternoon towing away debris and levelling areas where the mortars had hit.

'How'd they get so damn close?' Travis asked.

'I think the real question is *why*,' Fletcher countered. 'They had no real hope of taking out the base. Why do it?'

'To send us a message,' Bruno said. 'That they can hurt us whenever they want.'

'Just a quick twist of the knife and then gone,' Travis added, running his hands through his thinning hair.

'You have to give it to Charlie, though—he is one gutsy, conniving bastard,' Fletcher remarked, knowing that in the wrong company, his comment would spark outrage.

'In the end, it all comes down to motivation,' Bruno replied. 'All our boys want to do is get back home, preferably with their limbs still attached. Charlie is fighting for his way of life, for his survival. He would rather die than have to march to our tune.'

For a long while, they sat in silence, until Fletcher finally spoke. 'Bruno, why'd you go through with the operation?'

'It just felt like the right thing to do. If we'd stopped, he would've died. Too many people have invested too much in him for me to just give up when things got a little hairy.'

Travis handed out another round of beers. 'A toast, gentlemen. To friends coming together to help one another. And to those among us who commandeer armoured vehicles to protect a crazed surgeon and his deranged nurse.'

Fletcher and Bruno raised their drinks to Travis. 'Some things,' Fletcher declared, 'are still worth fighting for.'

DURING THE NEXT two weeks, the Fat Lady was involved in a company-sized foray into the mountains near the Cambodian border. They operated at point, with Mitchell effectively leading a team of 300 men on another seemingly futile exercise through the sticky mess of Vietnam. During nine days, they were involved in two firefights. Their exchanges claimed thirty-four Vietcong, but eighteen US soldiers would never see their families again. The Fat Lady, however, had emerged intact.

By the time the helicopters arrived to pick them up, Fletcher was desperate to find out how the dog was doing. In the days following the operation, the Labrador's vital signs had shown improvement. His temperature had dropped to normal, there was a steady rhythm to his breathing, and it appeared as though he had fought off earlier signs of infection. But he remained in a coma.

When they touched down, Fletcher jumped from the helicopter and ran towards his tent. Bruno emerged, wiping the back of his neck with a towel. His friend's expression told him the news was not good.

'He's alive, but I'm afraid he's in a deep coma. He hasn't regained consciousness since you left.'

Fletcher let his pack drop to the ground. 'What does this mean?'

'I'm sorry, Fletch. If he hasn't regained consciousness by now, there's a good chance he may never do so.'

Fletcher made no attempt to hide his disappointment.

'I'm afraid the bad news doesn't end there. Wilson has found out about all this, and he's not pleased. He wants you, Travis and Mitchell in his office first thing tomorrow morning. Evidently he's not aware of my role in the proceedings.'

'And that's how it'll stay.'

Despite feeling responsible for implicating Travis and Mitchell, Fletcher didn't care much what Battalion Commander Frank Wilson planned to do. Few punishments carried more threat than remaining a soldier in Vietnam. 'Thank you for everything.'

Bruno nodded and placed his hand on Fletcher's shoulder before stepping aside.

As Fletcher moved into the tent, he was stunned by what he saw. Letters and cards of goodwill covered the inside walls of the tent. On the canvas wall to his right, pinned to the material, were hundreds of dollar bills.

'What is this?'

Bruno shuffled past him. 'There's been an outpouring of support while you've been away. It started when three soldiers asked if they could see the dog. I let them in, and they offered to help in whatever way they could. The next day, there were ten soldiers. The day after that, thirty.'

Overwhelmed, Fletcher moved away from the money wall and turned his attention to the dog. The mosquito net was still draped over his stretcher. Lifting the gauze, he sat down next to the Labrador. The animal's golden coat looked brighter. He had put on four or five pounds.

'He looks so good,' Fletcher said, battling to keep his emotions in check. 'He just needs to wake up.' He lightly stroked the dog's fur. 'How've you been managing with the drips?'

'I was close to running out after the first week, but one call to our benefactor, and another consignment was with us the next morning. We have enough drips for another five days or so, and the men's donations should keep us going with whatever else we need for some time to come.'

Fletcher stepped back and pulled down the mosquito net behind him. Again, he surveyed the walls of the tent. 'I can't believe this. I never knew we had so many animal-lovers.'

'I think it's more what our patient represents. Most of the men associate dogs with their lives back home. It gives them something familiar to cling to. Something normal.'

'Either way, I'm grateful for their support,' Fletcher said, reading the message on one of the cards. 'I hope it's not in vain.'

FLETCHER THREW KELLY into an approaching wave. She shrieked with delight. 'Again!' she cried, wiping the salt water from her eyes. 'Again!'

Fletcher grabbed her and again pitched her into an oncoming swell. She emerged laughing, her long hair plastered to her face.

'Easy, honey,' Abigail warned, joining them in the waist-high water. 'That's precious cargo you've got there.'

'Yes, Daddy!' Kelly agreed. 'I'm very precious, don't you know.'

'Precious? More like *precocious*!'

'*Pre*-what?'

'*Precocious*. It means "fish food".'

Kelly slapped her hands on her hips indignantly, her pink bathing suit shimmering in the sun. 'I'm not fish food. I'm a princess—' she began, before a wave knocked her off her feet. By the time Fletcher had fished her out of the water, she was laughing again.

'All right, young lady.' Abigail smiled. 'That's enough for now. Let's go and get something to eat.'

Abigail reached for Kelly's hand. Fletcher took Kelly's other hand, and together they waded towards the beach. As they trudged forward, Fletcher noticed that the underwater currents had grown stronger. Instinctively, he held Kelly back. Fletcher also noticed that the sky was now overcast. A wind rose up and sprayed sea salt in their eyes.

'What's going on?' Abigail asked above a crack of lightning.

'I don't know,' Fletcher said.

'We're going to be sucked out to sea!'

'Don't panic!' he replied, but his words were lost to a gale that now blasted across the choppy water.

'Daddy, don't let us drown!' Kelly pleaded.

Fletcher looked at the water. What was deep blue before, was now black. He searched for the beach, but it was no longer there.

'Somebody help us!' Abigail cried, clinging to her daughter.

The wind cut up the water's surface, and more lightning fired on the horizon. Then came the rain. Where it greeted the water, it burst into streaks of ruby flame. Then his girls were gone. And the ocean, now a swirling mass of lava, began to pull him under.

FLETCHER WOKE with a pinched-off scream. He sat up and used his sheet to dab away the sweat on his face. As he tried to gather his thoughts, he felt a weight pressing down on his right thigh.

He opened his eyes. The dog, lying alongside him, was resting its head on his leg. Fletcher leaned over the animal. Gently he rubbed the Labrador's face. His heart, still racing after the dream, began to pound even harder. He spoke quietly. 'Are you awake?'

The dog stirred, but remained unconscious.

Fletcher leaned in closer and repeated himself. This time the dog's ears pricked up at the sound of his voice. His front right leg gave a short kick. And then, miraculously, he opened his eyes.

Fletcher felt a surge of warmth rise up in his chest.

The dog's rich brown-and-yellow eyes held Fletcher's stare.

'I never doubted you for a minute,' he managed. 'What took you so long?'

FIVE

'I'll be damned,' Bruno said. 'I truly thought we'd lost him.'

'We should have,' Fletcher suggested, gently massaging the Labrador's neck. 'But you saved him.'

'I think we had some . . . higher help. This dog was meant to survive. Believe me, we're in the league of miracles here.'

The dog lifted his head and tried to sit up. 'Easy, buddy,' Fletcher warned, helping to prop him up. The dog looked down at the gauze patches on his body, then back up at Fletcher. His eyes were heavy with sleep.

'You're going to be just fine.'

He blinked and then nuzzled the side of Fletcher's arm.

Arnold, who had been chronically depressed since the shooting, knelt down next to the Labrador. The dog turned, regarded him wearily for a moment, and then licked his hand.

Fletcher watched as tears welled up in the young soldier's eyes. In a single stroke, he had been absolved of his offences.

Gunther screwed open his flask and poured some water into an upturned helmet. 'Let's see if he's ready to drink yet.'

The dog's ears pricked up. He lapped up the water, splashing it all over Fletcher's legs.

Travis moved towards the dog. 'It's so strange that he's a Labrador. Most of the dogs out here are German Shepherds.'

'There're quite a few Labradors operating as scouts. They pick up enemy tracks and provide early warning of snipers and traps. If he has training, we could actually use him,' Mitchell replied.

As the possibility rattled round in Fletcher's mind, Bruno asked, 'What're we going to call him?'

The question was clearly directed at Fletcher, and Fletcher had the answer. 'Jack. We'll call him Jack.'

'That was quick. Why Jack?' Bruno asked.

'I don't know.' Fletcher shrugged. 'The name just came to me.'

Mitchell cupped his hand over the side of the Labrador's face. 'Well, Jack . . . welcome back to hell.'

HUDDLED TOGETHER, Fletcher, Travis and Mitchell waited to be summoned into Frank Wilson's office.

'What's our plan?' Mitchell whispered.

'Just leave the talking to me. It's my fault that you're both here.'

'If you think we're going to sit back and let you play the martyr, you can forget it.' Travis yawned. 'Besides, what's the worst they can do? Send us to bed without supper?'

Fletcher was about to respond, when the door to Frank Wilson's office opened.

'Inside, gentlemen. Now.' Frank Wilson was rolling up a large map he'd been studying. 'I suppose you know why you're here?'

'Yes, sir,' Fletcher replied. 'Neither of these men—'

Frank held up his hand. 'Rogan told me everything. You found the dog while on tour. I know it was Rogan's idea to bring him back, that you were acting under orders. I'm not happy with the situation, but we have to deal with it. I've been told that the dog has been under your care and that he regained consciousness. Is this true?'

Fletcher could not believe what he was hearing. Not only had Rogan covered up their altercation, but he had also taken the blame for Jack being brought to base. Fletcher felt a sudden sense of gratitude towards him, and, in that moment, every preconceived notion he had of the lieutenant was cast into doubt. 'Uh . . . yes, sir.'

'Well? Is he going to live?'

Sensing Fletcher had been put off his stride, Travis intercepted the question. 'We hope so, sir. He's eating and drinking now.'

'I've heard about your tent, gentlemen. I've also noticed what his presence has done for the men. I won't deny that I'm moved by all the support your patient has had, but I have a base to run. Have you checked the dog for any type of identification? We need to get him back to his unit if he's one of ours.'

'We have, sir. All US dogs serving in Vietnam have coding inside their ears,' Travis replied. 'But there's nothing there.'

Frank sat back in his chair and folded his arms. 'All right, gentlemen. What is your recommendation?'

Fletcher, having regained his composure, recognised his opportunity. 'I suggest we keep him here until he is fully rehabilitated.'

'And then?'

'We could use a dog here to patrol the perimeter.'

'We don't have any facilities to care for dogs here.'

'Sir, we are fortunate enough to have been given the support of a nearby dog unit, who've provided us with supplies. We have all that we need at the moment.'

'You're the senior man, Lord. What do you make of this?'

'I think the dog is doing wonders for morale,' said Mitchell. 'And the base can do with all the good feeling we can muster.'

Frank looked up at the ceiling. 'I want a plan, Carson. On my desk by the end of today. Where he's going to sleep, a schedule to get him moving again—everything.'

'Yes, sir. Appreciate it, sir.'

'Lord's right, Carson. It's about morale at this stage. I'm not blind. I've seen what this dog has done for the men. All right . . . dismissed.'

As they turned and headed for the door, Frank stopped them. 'Carson, wait,' he said, offering a wad of dollar bills. 'For your money wall.'

THE NEXT FEW WEEKS were spent largely rehabilitating Jack. At first, his progress was painstakingly slow. They suspected his legs were permanently damaged, as he could barely stand for more than a minute before collapsing. He was eating and drinking better than any dog living in the back yard of American suburbia, but his lack of mobility was a major concern.

Then Jack tentatively began to take his first steps. As the circulation in his legs improved, he progressed to a sure-footed trot. The men took turns walking, feeding and looking after him, but mostly when Fletcher wasn't able to. The dog may have become the base's mascot, but there were no illusions as to whom he belonged.

Gunther spent hours tracking down dog units in the region, but none of them reported a missing dog of Jack's description. Yet the dog was highly trained. It first became apparent when he reacted to basic commands, but it was even more obvious one morning when he was taken on a patrol of the base's perimeter. Fletcher noticed a change in him the instant he put on his leash. Jack quickly moved ahead of him, sniffing the ground. Then Jack suddenly dropped down and began to make soft whimpering noises.

'What is it, Jack?' Fletcher asked, moving up alongside him.

A low growl issued from the back of Jack's throat. Not sure what to do, Fletcher gently placed his hand on top of his head to calm him, but the growl only intensified.

Suddenly Fletcher understood. Less than a yard ahead of them, buried halfway in the mud alongside the fence, was a live mortar that had failed to detonate. A remnant of the attack they had suffered several weeks before. He tugged at Jack's leash, and the Labrador instantly relented and followed after him.

The mortar was later safely detonated, and the majority of Jack's detractors, if any remained, were silenced. Every morning after that, Fletcher and Jack patrolled the perimeter as part of their daily duties.

It wasn't long before Jack's other talents were discovered. They had received a booklet of basic dog commands from Squad Leader Wallace. It consisted of typical word and hand commands used out in the field. Jack knew every one of them.

As the memory of his injuries faded, Jack's true personality began to emerge. He was surprisingly mischievous. He would steal food out of the men's rucksacks and chew holes in their boots. He joined them in the Soup, happily lapping up any beer that was offered to him. In a matter of weeks, he had worked his way into the affections of all on base. All but one.

Despite taking responsibility for Jack being brought back to base, Rogan seemed uninterested in the dog. Fletcher tried to thank him for what he had done, but Rogan stopped him in mid-sentence. His thoughts were only on the war and the role the Fat Lady had to play within it. This, however, was of little consequence to Jack, who continually sought Rogan out, as if he sensed the lieutenant's indifference towards him. In meetings, he would sit at his feet. To the amusement of the platoon, he even offered Rogan his paw during a briefing session. But it had little effect. Rogan's mind was totally focused on the war.

A war they were losing.

'THIS ISN'T A DEBATE,' Frank Wilson declared, wiping his brow with a handkerchief. 'The dog is highly trained and could save your asses out there.'

'We're not a dog unit, Frank,' Rogan snapped back. 'We're not even sure if he's ever operated out in the field before. He could give away our position.'

'The dog follows voice and hand signals. He seems to share half his brain with Carson.'

'This is madness.'

'No. *Madness* is being forced to send you up the Chi San trail. You're going to be moving through treacherous terrain. The dog could well make the difference. We have three days before you go. Carson, Tucker, Lord and Rex have agreed to do two short patrols with the dog to see how he gets along. If by then there are any concerns, we'll leave him behind. If not, he's going with you. Besides, I don't understand why you're against this; you're the one who rescued him in the first place.'

'This is different. It's a big risk, Frank.'

'Look, I'm only doing this because I truly believe the dog can help you. Lord is brilliant at point. Probably the best I've ever seen, but this dog can sense things. He is a wonder.'

'Frank, you have the respect of every man on this base, myself included. So I'll take the dog with us. But I want you to know that if he does anything to threaten our mission, I will kill him.'

Frank agreed. 'Just get in and out as quick as you can, and I promise I'll organise some time off for your platoon.'

Frank held out his hand, and Rogan accepted it. 'How long, sir?'

'Until what?'

'Until we pull out.'

'Could be as soon as a month or two. That's what I'm hearing.'

A sardonic grin danced across Rogan's face. 'More than enough time to die, then.'

'LET ME GET THIS STRAIGHT,' Wayville said. 'We're going to tiptoe up the Chi San trail into Charlie's heart and pick off two of his top commanding officers, all without any back-up?'

'So you were listening,' Rogan replied evenly.

'And then we quietly sneak out without Charlie seeing us and skip merrily back down the yellow brick road?'

'How far back will the drop be?' Gunther frowned.

'Thirty . . . maybe thirty-five miles.'

'Thirty-five miles? That's a two-day hike!'

'More like three,' Mitchell corrected him.

'There's something else.' Rogan paused, looking at his men. 'This base is underground.'

'A tunnel complex? Why don't we just kill ourselves right now?'

Rogan stepped forward and stared at Wayville. 'I don't like this any more than you do. The bottom line is that we've been ordered to go. We have no choice. Now, we can either sit around and whine about it or we can start planning this thing down to the last detail so we minimise our risk. For most of you, the biggest risk will be making it to the complex.'

'How do you figure that? Once underground, we'll be hunted like rats in a maze,' Gunther insisted.

'Because you're not going in! Only Carson, Lord and myself are. Carson's going in as our assassin, with Lord and myself as his shadow. Our informant produced a sketch of the complex and has shown us where our two targets will be sleeping. We'll infiltrate at oh three hundred and be out within an hour.' Rogan paused. 'One last thing. Our commander feels that we might need Fletcher's dog and his tracking abilities. I will only take him with us if every man is in agreement. If one of you feels that the dog might in any way compromise us, speak now.'

The soldiers exchanged glances with one another, but said nothing.

'All right, then. Fletcher will be his handler, and they'll hike at point with Lord. Gentlemen, we leave in forty-eight hours. As of now, there is no more drinking. We're going to be right under Charlie's nose, and he'll be able to smell the booze on you a mile away.'

SIX

Another week, another tense flight over Vietnam, Fletcher thought as they hovered above the Strip. He knew that if he made it back to the outside world, he would never again set foot in another helicopter.

Holding Jack's leash, he looked down at the Labrador, who was sitting quietly between his legs. He appeared relaxed and at home on board the Huey.

'Where did you come from?' Fletcher whispered in his ear.

Despite the drone of the rotors, Jack picked up on Fletcher's voice. He turned and licked him on the cheek.

Travis smiled. 'There's something about him, Fletcher. He's different. I don't know how or why, but he just is.'

'I know. I feel it, too.'

The helicopter swooped steeply over a column of tall trees, clearing the branches by a few feet.

'All right, men,' Rogan called out. 'Ten minutes to put down. Get your minds on the game.'

OVER THE NEXT THREE DAYS, the Fat Lady's pace was slow, as they were forced to hide from numerous NVA patrols. Their movement was further hampered by traps along the trail. Mitchell had so far uncovered more than a dozen. Jack had already repaid the faith shown in him by sniffing out almost half as many traps.

As nightfall approached, after yet another late-afternoon deluge, they were still almost two miles away from the tunnel complex. 'Lord, Carson . . . we need to get a move on. There's not much light left,' Rogan said, marching up behind them.

Mitchell's eyes were red and swollen from the demands of a long day. 'We can't go any quicker. The closer we get, the more traps we're likely to come across.'

'I understand that, but if we don't make it to the complex soon, we lose another day. We definitely can't afford that.'

'We'll try to shift it up a notch,' Fletcher offered.

'You do that.'

For fifteen minutes, the platoon increased its pace marginally, but the light was rapidly dwindling. Already, telltale streaks of pink and purple stretched across the sky.

Again Rogan pulled up behind them. 'We need to move faster. Fall back. I'll take over point.'

'With respect, Rogan—' Mitchell began.

'This isn't a request, Lord! I'm not asking you to dance. Now fall back. Both of you.' With that, he pushed past them and began to run.

'Lieutenant!'

'He's going to get himself killed!' Fletcher cried.

Together they chased after him. They hadn't covered more than fifty yards when Jack suddenly sprinted ahead after him. His burst of acceleration caught Fletcher by surprise, and the leash slipped out of his hand. 'Wait, Jack!'

But the Labrador had made up his mind. When he was close enough, he leapt up and bit Rogan on the arm. It was enough to send him crashing to the ground.

'Release, Jack! *Release!*' Fletcher shouted.

Jack, growling now, stood over the lieutenant.

'Retreat!' Fletcher commanded as he and Mitchell drew alongside them.

Rogan's eyes were reduced to thin slits as he stared at the dog. His right arm, muddied and bleeding above the elbow, was fully extended, and his gun was only inches away from Jack's face.

Fletcher moved up alongside the Labrador and gently grabbed him by his collar. 'Easy, boy . . . easy.'

Rogan looked at Fletcher, as if disorientated, then began to sit up. Jack suddenly leapt at him. This time he snapped at Rogan's face.

'Pull your dog back! Now!'

Fletcher battled to restrain Jack. Rogan again started to get up, when Mitchell noticed something. 'Don't move. Stop!'

Stretched across Rogan's head was a thin tripwire.

'Slide back slowly and keep your head down.'

Rogan did as instructed. Mitchell carefully took hold of the tripwire and gently returned it to its position.

Jack immediately relented, the fight gone out of him, and sat down at Fletcher's side. The wire was linked to a cluster of hand grenades fixed to the base of a tree. Another length of wire connected a further eight trees down the path, each with their own cargo of explosives. Had the wire been crossed, it was designed to take out an entire platoon.

In his first assignment with the Fat Lady, Jack had saved them all.

IGNORING WHAT HAD just happened, Rogan returned to point and continued to push forward, although this time he moved at a more sensible pace. What little light remained was rapidly disappearing. Within minutes, a cloying darkness would descend over them.

The tunnel complex was now just over a kilometre away. They would soon have to find somewhere to hide until it was time to go in. Once their orders had been executed, they would immediately begin their hike back down the path towards the pick-up point.

As they rounded a bank of trees, Rogan pointed to a slight declivity that would conceal their position. One by one, they filed down the embankment and settled under the dense foliage.

Rogan, Mitchell and Fletcher sat down to go over the plan.

'Pearson, we need to review the sketch of the complex. Get over here,' Rogan instructed.

Gunther crawled over to them and shone his torch down onto the creased paper. 'The entrance to the complex is four hundred yards ahead. It's marked by a short wooden stake. A trap door takes you down twenty feet to a crawl space that feeds the main corridor. This corridor runs some five hundred yards south. Off here, you'll find a supply room, a kitchen, a hospital room and the soldiers' barracks. The officers' dormitory lies behind the barracks.'

'OK,' Rogan began, removing his pack. 'The best time to infiltrate is around oh three hundred. If we're lucky, we should be able to get into the main corridor without being detected. The problem comes after that. We don't know how many soldiers are in that room or how difficult it is going to be to access the officers' dormitory.'

'We also can't rely on the fact that they'll all be sleeping like angels.

Fletch, you're going to have to be pretty sure that none of the soldiers is awake before you go in,' Mitchell added.

'And if some of them are not?'

'You'll have to wait. We've built in a bit of extra time for this, but not much. You've basically got an hour to get in and out. That gives us an hour head start. We can't risk anything less than that,' Rogan insisted.

'Where will you two be?'

'Making sure no one comes up behind you.'

Fletcher knew he was asking the obvious, but he proceeded anyway. 'What happens if someone raises the alarm?'

Rogan rested his arms on two hand grenades that were secured to the front of his jacket. 'We'll take out as many as we can.'

FLETCHER'S CHEEK BRUSHED UP against the side of the tunnel. It felt warm and moist against his skin. Apart from the stench of natural decay, he was able to discern a number of other pungent smells, such as stale tobacco, cordite, urine and sweat—although most of the latter was probably his own, he realised. Despite the size of the complex, the crawl space was minuscule; he had to tuck his elbows in tight just to squeeze through the opening that joined the entrance section to the main corridor. He had expected to encounter some resistance by now, but so far, the chamber was empty.

Lying at the entrance to the main corridor, Fletcher remained still, listening for movement. All was quiet. The corridor itself was twice as wide as the entranceway and would allow an average Vietnamese soldier to walk upright. He, however, had to walk with a stoop. He quietly headed towards the faint glow of a lantern some forty yards away. According to their information, the fourth tunnel off to the right of the corridor was the main soldiers' barracks. Behind this area was the officers' dormitory.

He moved towards the pale light and was amazed by how clean and well constructed the complex was. Thick wooden struts supported the roof. As he neared the lantern, he realised it was hanging on the wall outside the first room. True to their information, it was a supply room. Further down the corridor was the kitchen. Then a makeshift though empty hospital ward. Until finally, almost 200 yards further on, the soldiers' barracks.

Standing alongside the open entranceway, he waited to hear if anyone was talking. Another lantern cast a soft yellow glow over the sleeping soldiers. There were at least thirty men lying on the floor, side by side.

Strangely, not a single one of them was snoring, or even stirring. They hardly appeared to be breathing.

There's no room to walk, Fletcher suddenly realised. It had never occurred to him that they would be lying so close together. Staring at the sea of bodies, he weighed his options. He could see a door at the back of the room, which he assumed led to the officers' sleeping quarters. It was some twenty-five yards away. He debated trying to step between the men, but knew there was a strong likelihood that he would get stranded at some point with his path blocked. Or he might lose his balance and step on one of the men. It was too much of a risk. There remained only one other option.

As part of the support structure of the roof, a steel beam with a narrow inner railing, much like a railway track, ran the length of the room, ending a yard or so to the right of the back door. He studied the beam to ensure that there was enough space for him to grip the bar. It seemed sufficient. He would climb over the men.

He glanced down at his watch: 0323. He'd been in the complex for more than a quarter of an hour already. He took a deep breath, checked that his gun was properly secured, and grabbed hold of the railing. He hoisted himself up and began to swing forward. It reminded him of how Kelly used to hang from the monkey bars at her school. He quickly banished the image.

He had made it almost halfway across the room when the first beads of sweat began to rise up on his forehead. The complex was oppressively hot. A few moments later, he could feel the perspiration dripping off his face. His fingers and hands were showing signs of strain. His shoulders were beginning to tremble.

Below, a soldier stirred and then sat up.

Fletcher lifted his knees to his chest. His fingers were burning with exertion and beginning to slide on the sweat-slicked steel. The soldier looked around the room and lay back down. A few moments later, he rolled onto his side and was back asleep.

Fighting away the cramp and pain, Fletcher continued forward. Every new reach sapped away his strength. His legs felt like concrete pillars. As he closed in on the back of the room, he was convinced he was going to drop down.

Five yards. Four. *Three.*

Suddenly he lost his grip. Instinctively, he opened his stance and landed with both feet on either side of a soldier's head. He immediately pulled out his gun and pointed it at the man's face. Miraculously, the man remained asleep. Fletcher quickly looked round to check that none of the other men had woken up.

They hadn't.

He couldn't believe his good fortune.

He straightened up and carefully stepped over the remaining soldiers. He waited a moment to catch his breath before quietly opening the bamboo door to the officers' dormitory. He withdrew his torch, pulled his shirt over the lens to diffuse the light, and switched it on. The room lit up dimly in a sickly green glow. The chamber was almost as big as the soldiers' barracks, but housed only the two commanding officers. They were sleeping in a bunk bed at the back of the room.

Perfect, he thought.

As he approached the beds, he was gripped by a terrible sadness. In a matter of months, he'd gone from pushing his daughter on a swing to standing over two strangers he was about to murder. Did they have children? Did they deserve to be gunned down in their sleep? Fletcher's world was again threatening to spiral out of control.

He cocked the gun and knelt down next to the man sleeping on the lower bunk. He wrapped a small towel round the barrel to further muffle the sound. His last thought was to wonder what the man was dreaming.

He hoped it was a good dream.

Closing his eyes, Fletcher felt his arm recoil and warm blood splatter up his hand and onto the side of his face. The shot sounded like a heavy book dropping off a table. The second officer shifted in the bunk above him. The sound thrust Fletcher into action. He dived on top of his first mark, pressed his gun into the mattress above him, and fired twice. Blood seeped through the holes.

Taking short, sharp breaths, Fletcher could feel his pulse gallop.

He was now a murderer. What he had just done sickened him. For a moment, he battled to contain a thick, viscous nausea that churned in his stomach. After what felt like a long time, he eventually managed to lower his gun. His arm was shaking violently. Wiping the blood off his hand, he checked his watch.

He was out of time. He had to get moving.

He sat up and climbed off the dead man. With his entire body trembling, he hurried out of the room and slipped back into the soldiers' barracks. Still the men slept peacefully. He looked up at the railing on the ceiling, then placed his fingers into the thin steel groove and hoisted himself up. Surprisingly, his body felt light, and his arms and hands strong—most likely on account of the adrenaline coursing through his veins. He quickly began to swing back across the room.

He was approaching the end of the railing when he noticed something strange ahead of him. In what had been a continuous expanse of bodies covering almost every inch of the floor, there was now an open space about three or four yards from the front of the room.

A body was missing.

Fear prickled up the back of his neck. One of the soldiers had woken up and probably gone to relieve himself. He'd be returning any minute. Fletcher needed to get out of the room and down the passage before the man returned.

His mind urged him forward: *Move . . . move . . . move.*

He reached the end of the railing and dropped down as gracefully as he could.

Still no one stirred—except for the man standing in the doorway.

The soldier blinked and took a step back. He was just beyond Fletcher's reach. The soldier took a breath and was about to raise the alarm, when Rogan stepped into view and punched him on the side of his head. He was unconscious even before he collapsed into Mitchell's arms.

Fletcher exhaled, feeling like a man who had narrowly avoided falling off a cliff.

'Job done?' Rogan asked.

'The marks are down,' Fletcher managed, numb, as if the words were not his.

Mitchell carried the soldier back to where he had been sleeping. If another soldier woke up, it was crucial that everything appeared normal. The Fat Lady needed a head start down the trail.

As they started back down the main corridor, Fletcher felt a fresh wave of nausea pass over him. He cleared his mind and tried to separate himself from his circumstances. After a few seconds, he closed his eyes and swallowed back the sickening feeling.

Within minutes, they had made their way out of the complex. Pushing through the top of the trap door, Fletcher filled his nostrils with the scent of the jungle night.

THE DARKNESS made it difficult for the Fat Lady to progress with any speed down the trail. Although Mitchell had mapped out the traps ahead of them, the terrain itself prohibited anything more than a brisk walk. Whenever they tried to accelerate, someone would lose their footing. There was a danger of one of them getting hurt and hindering their pace even further.

After a while, Travis pulled up alongside Fletcher. 'I'm not sure if this is the time, but how'd it go?'

Fletcher shrugged. 'For me,' he began, still fighting a lingering queasiness, 'OK. For the two officers I murdered . . . not so good.'

'It couldn't have been easy.'

Fletcher stumbled, but reached out for Jack to steady himself. 'Taking a life in open combat is one thing. This was just plain murder.'

'It's not murder, Fletcher. It's war. It's not the same thing.'

'Isn't it?'

'C'mon, Fletch, you know it isn't.'

'All I know is this,' he uttered, raising his arms up to the pale moonlight. The backs of his hands and the cuffs of his sleeves were smeared black with blood. 'This is what's real to me right now.'

'We've all got blood on our hands.'

'I don't recognise myself any more. A year ago, I was a different person. Never even thought of owning a gun, let alone firing one. Now I kill people in their sleep.'

Travis was about to respond, when the darkness was lit up by an explosion of angry gunfire.

'Down . . . *down!*' Rogan shouted.

Bright bursts of light—the distinctive flairs of machine-gun fire—crackled to their right from behind a small rise.

Mitchell and Rogan were the first to react, returning fire.

How the hell had they wandered into an ambush? Fletcher thought as he fumbled for his rifle.

The sound of their exchange was thunderous in the dead of morning. By the time Fletcher had emptied his second clip, he realised they were no longer being fired upon.

'Halt,' Rogan instructed. 'Hold your fire.'

The jungle was quiet, save for the birds that had been disturbed from their nests.

Miraculously, nobody had been shot.

Mitchell and Kingston quickly swept through the area. Once again, and to no one's surprise, Charlie was gone. All that remained in his wake were two small mounds of empty shells.

SEVEN

It was late afternoon the following day when they reached the extraction point. The relief of surviving their assignment was eclipsed by their exhaustion. Jack, in particular, looked stiff and sore from the journey. It was the furthest he had travelled since his recovery.

The welcome appearance of the chopper and a text book embarkation meant Fletcher could finally close his eyes and tune out the drone of the helicopter rotors. He imagined he was sitting on a perfect golden beach, the early morning sun shimmering off the ocean. The image evoked the memory of a holiday he and his girls had shared only two years ago. He remembered Kelly, who had built an elaborate sandcastle too close to the shoreline, working furiously to build a moat to protect her handiwork.

'Mommy . . . Daddy . . . help! The water's going to wash away my castle!'

Abigail rushed over to Kelly. 'C'mon, Fletch, help us defend the kingdom.'

Fletcher had set aside his newspaper and joined his girls. The three of them had dug a moat round the castle, but no matter how hard they worked, the waves kept coming. Eventually the incoming tide overwhelmed the castle, reducing it to a blurred, indistinct mound.

After watching her creation be destroyed, Kelly had looked up at her father. She never said anything, but Fletcher saw it in her eyes. She was disappointed in him. She was upset that he wasn't able to save something of hers. He was her father: he was supposed to protect her.

That innocently conceived but accusing expression had haunted Fletcher since the crash. The sandcastle became a metaphor for her death. Just as he could not protect her sculpture, so he had failed to save her from that nightmarish December morning. Sometimes, just that single thought threatened to consume him.

A familiar weight pressed against his thigh, rousing him from his daydream. It was Jack. In his first assignment, he had performed far beyond everyone's expectations. Fletcher couldn't help but feel proud of how well Jack had fared. As he watched the Labrador doze, familiar questions swirled in his mind: where had he come from? Was he truly a Vietnam war dog? He couldn't shake the nagging feeling that Jack was somehow lost, as if he had been headed elsewhere, but then for some reason strayed from his path.

He felt Jack move away from him. He watched with interest as Rogan fished out two biscuits from his pocket and offered them to Jack. Unsure of the lieutenant, the Labrador edged forward and gently accepted the treats. As soon as they left his hand, Rogan turned away as if the moment had never happened.

THE NEXT TWO WEEKS back at base drifted by without incident. The Fat Lady was rewarded with the entire period off. Fletcher and Travis spent most of their time training Jack. If he was to accompany them on more assignments, it was important he learn additional hand and voice commands.

His progress was unreal. Within a few days, they had taught him twenty commands, including an instruction to detach from the Fat Lady and track them down at a later time. The idea was that if they came under heavy fire, it would be safer for Jack to leave the area and return later.

Jack became as much a feature of life on the Strip as the smell of diesel and cordite. Those who hadn't been dog-lovers before the war now enjoyed having Jack around. Even the commander had become partial to him, ordering a special leather harness for his upcoming patrols.

One morning, a few of the men built Jack a special eight-foot-wide steel bath that he could wade around in to cool off. To get him to use it, Fletcher and Travis climbed into the tub and, while trying to coax him into the waist-high water, found it a most agreeable place to see out the afternoon. The next day, they brought beers with them and remained until well after sunset. They spent their hours sitting on either side of Jack, reminiscing over happier times back home. Their conversations remained light and whimsical, circling away from the darker areas of their pasts. Jack, like all dogs, was just content to be in the company of his owners.

As they approached the end of their R&R, Fletcher and Jack had become virtually inseparable. Wherever Fletcher went, Jack followed.

When they finally returned to duty, the Fat Lady was sent on two short assignments. Jack accompanied them on each occasion and twice sniffed out traps that might otherwise have proved fatal.

Jack was no longer simply a dog they had found, or even the base's mascot. He was a soldier.

Theirs.

GUNFIRE RIPPED THROUGH the jungle.

Fletcher grabbed Jack by his harness and scrambled towards a bank of nearby trees. Glancing over his shoulder, he saw Rogan lying on his back, his M16 bucking against his chest as he returned fire. 'Cover . . . cover!' he shouted, urging his men to safety.

As Fletcher rounded the trees and reached for his rifle, he realised that he was at the top of a steep embankment. There was nothing he could do to prevent himself from falling down the back of it, and the mud and slick grass made it impossible for him to halt his slide. As the sound of gunfire continued to punctuate the air, he realised that Jack hadn't fallen with him. In a wild frenzy, he punched and kicked his way back up to the top of the slope.

The first thing he saw was a soldier lying on his side about fifty yards down the trail. Jack was standing over him. His hackles were raised, and he was growling and snapping in the direction of the onslaught, trying to ward off the attackers. The rest of the Fat Lady had managed to find cover and were returning fire.

All except Rogan.

He was running towards Jack and the downed soldier.

Fletcher immediately joined in the chase. Bullets exploded into the ground around Jack and the soldier, but even when two rounds tore into the man's back, Jack stood firm, refusing to relent. Fletcher's breath caught in his throat when he realised who the soldier was.

'No . . .'

Another volley tore into Travis's legs. Suddenly Jack bit into Travis's shirtsleeve and tried to drag him away.

Fletcher's heart lurched at the sight. He held out his rifle in one hand and, without looking, opened fire into the hill.

A bullet tore through a fold in Fletcher's trousers, grazing his leg. Another pinged off the back of his helmet. He was a natural athlete and was right behind Rogan the moment he reached Travis. The lieutenant swooped down and grabbed the front of Travis's shirt and lifted him up. Fletcher scooped up Jack, and together they scrambled for cover. They had no sooner collapsed to the ground than the firing stopped.

Mitchell called out to them from the hill. He had flanked their attackers and taken them out. 'Hold your fire! All Charlie down.'

'Edgar,' Rogan screamed. 'Get here!'

Fletcher crawled next to Travis and cradled his friend's head in his hands while Edgar checked his wrist for a pulse.

Travis had taken at least five rounds. A thick pool of black blood arced round his legs and waist.

'Travis . . . can you hear me?' Fletcher asked, firmly but gently rubbing the side of his face.

His eyes stirred, but remained closed.

'C'mon, man . . . *please*.'

Slowly, he opened his eyes. 'Fletch . . .'

'Yeah, Trav . . . it's me. It's all over.'

The whites of Travis's eyes were outlined in blood. 'Did you see Jack?' he asked quietly, his teeth coated red. 'Did you see what he did? He tried to save me.'

Fletcher nodded, unable to reply.

Edgar was trying to stem the blood flow, but it was useless.

Travis choked, then looked up peacefully at the sky. 'It's true what they say, you know.'

'What is?' Fletcher managed, feeling his friend's blood spreading under his knees.

'How calm everything becomes before you die.'

'Please, Trav . . . don't.'

'It's all right, Fletch, it's OK. Especially for guys like you and me.'

The comment was lost on most of the men, but Fletcher nodded as fresh tears cut a trail through the grime on his cheeks.

'Look after Jack. He deserves to get out of this place. Take him to Miami. Let him run on the beach.'

Fletcher's chin trembled. 'I will. You have my word.'

'Make sure you have a view of the ocean . . . '

'. . . and crisp, fresh sheets.' Fletcher smiled, but there was no humour in his expression.

'If I see your girls, I'll tell them how much you miss them.'

As Travis took his final breath, Fletcher bent over and spoke into his ear, 'Go to your wife . . . she's waiting for you.'

Travis squeezed Fletcher's hand. Then he was gone.

THE WEIGHT OF TRAVIS'S DEATH pressed heavily on each of the men as they flew back to base. His body was bound in sleeping-bags, but blood still seeped through. Jack was sitting alongside Fletcher with his head perched on his knee, staring at Travis's body. The Labrador's expression projected a deep and primal sadness.

'It wasn't our fault, Jack,' Mitchell called out, recognising the look in the dog's eyes. 'They were downwind of us almost two hundred yards. There's nothing we could've done. We never had a chance.'

Kingston, who had not uttered a single word since the ambush, began to sing 'Amazing Grace'. He closed his eyes and let his baritone fill the cabin. His faith, which had never wavered despite all the atrocities he had witnessed, gave him an inner strength that Fletcher envied. His own faith, which at its most resolute had not held much conviction, had been eroded over the past two years. Every death was another wave overwhelming it. He knew he was on the verge of a final breakdown. There were just too many dead faces to contend with. Too much loss. While he thought of this and other nightmares, he allowed Kingston's song into his heart.

BEFORE THE HELICOPTER even touched down, it was clear something important had happened on base. As they came into land, they could see men running, hugging, and punching the air.

As the Fat Lady disembarked, Fletcher remained behind. He already knew why they were celebrating. There could be only one explanation.

As the pilot cut the engine and the rotors lost their will, Fletcher watched one of the soldiers run up to Wayville and Gunther. Fletcher couldn't hear what he was saying, but the shape of his words was unmistakable. 'It's over!' he cried. 'We're going home!'

Fletcher closed his eyes and shook his head. He felt sick.

In the dying embers of the war, Travis might well have been Vietnam's final casualty.

At least among the dead.

THEY HAD ALL KNOWN it was coming, but few expected the end to arrive as suddenly as it did.

As they disembarked from the helicopter, they learned that a cease-fire had been signed by the United States, South Vietnam, North Vietnam and the Vietcong. The war was over.

Before they could properly process the news, the Fat Lady had to tend to their own. They carried Travis down to their church to pay their final respects. It was little more than a tent featuring a crudely fashioned wooden cross, a spattering of candles, and half a dozen wooden benches, but it sufficed. This was the way they always bade farewell to one of their own.

Entering the tent, they gently placed his body underneath the cross and all lowered down onto one knee. Kingston recited a few psalms as well as a passage from Revelation. After a long prayer, Kingston began to sing 'Abide with Me', but his emotions got the better of him and he could not complete the hymn. Despite the sounds of revelry outside, each of the men remained behind, taking their time to say goodbye. Eventually, one by one, they drifted out of the tent until only Fletcher and Mitchell were left behind.

'I can't believe he's gone,' Fletcher remarked, his voice barely registering.

By his very nature, Mitchell was a man of few words. He normally spoke sparingly, as if dialogue were vital ammunition that needed to be conserved. Thus, his reply surprised Fletcher. 'I know how close you were. You were a very good friend to him. And in this place, that really means something.'

Fletcher smiled, tears stinging his eyes. 'At least,' he offered, his voice wavering, 'he's back with his wife, now.'

Mitchell placed his hand on Fletcher's shoulder, but did not speak again. He had no more words left in his arsenal.

THAT NIGHT, almost every man, woman and dog got drunk. Most indulged not only to celebrate surviving the darkness of Vietnam and returning home to their families, but also to remember those who had been lost.

As Fletcher nursed his beer and looked around the Soup, the soldiers' excitement was plain to see. For so long, the horror of Vietnam had been their lives, and now, within weeks, they would all be back home. He imagined wives running into the arms of their husbands, children into the arms of their fathers. The genuine sense of warmth and happiness he felt for them was tempered by the thought of the thousands of families who would never again be reunited and by the fate that awaited the people of South Vietnam. Fletcher knew the cease-fire would ultimately break down, and, without American support, the South would soon be overpowered. The US and allied effort, despite its enormous firepower, had been brought to its knees. Against such determined and resourceful opposition, the South stood no chance on its own.

'To Travis,' Gunther said, raising his beer.

'And to every other mother's son who died in this hellhole,' Wayville added.

'Hear! Hear!' the room chorused.

The drinking never slowed. Fletcher had hoped the alcohol might numb him to the effects of the day, but it seemed only to fuel his depression. He finally decided he'd had enough.

As he and Jack left the Soup and headed towards their tent, he noticed a man sitting on a rock in the open field. There was no mistaking his frame. He had seen it often enough under the cover of night to know who it was. 'Getting some air?' he called out.

Rogan turned. 'Carson . . . what are you doing out here?'

'The beer tasted off. Want some company?'

'Sure.'

Fletcher and Jack sat down a few yards away from the lieutenant, and for a while, both men were quiet.

'I've been out here for almost an hour. So far, I've counted over five hundred stars. I wonder how long it took to lose our first five hundred men in this place.'

'Forget it, Lieutenant. It'll drive you mad just thinking about it.'

'So many lives lost for a failed cause.'

'I understand how you feel—'

'I'm not sure you do. I really believed in what we've been trying to achieve here,' said Rogan. 'Maybe it's why I've lasted this long.' He slowly began to shake his head. 'We're sending the South to their deaths. You know that, don't you?'

Fletcher shifted onto his haunches and, instead of answering the question, decided to change gears. 'Are you going to stay in the service?'

'I don't know. I can't see myself getting a normal job, like selling cars, can you?'

Fletcher smiled at the thought. 'Look, for what it's worth, thank you.'

'For what?'

'Keeping us alive.'

'You've got to be kidding me.'

'I'm not. Without you and Mitchell, none of us would've survived.'

'That's not true, and you know it,' Rogan replied, fiercely. 'For the most part, we were just lucky. Hell, if it wasn't for Jack here, we wouldn't even be having this conversation.' The Labrador had curled up between the two men and was fast asleep. 'If he hadn't stopped me before that wire—'

'That's one time. How many other times have you saved us?'

Rogan looked back up into the night. 'I wasn't able to save Travis.'

'You did everything you could. What you did today was probably the most courageous thing I've ever seen. How you didn't get yourself killed, I'll never know.'

'If I recall, you were running behind me.'

'That's different. You were drawing their fire.'

'Bull. I'm not the one with the death wish. But as much as it might burn you, the world hasn't had enough of you yet,' Rogan countered. 'So what're you going to do with your life now? Find another war? Put a gun in your mouth?'

'I couldn't. Who'd look after Jack?'

'Is that what it comes down to? Is the line that thin for you?'

'Isn't it for everyone?'

'You tell me.'

'Travis was half an hour away from surviving this place. I'd say that's a thin line.'

'I'll give you that, but the difference is, he wanted to live.'

Fletcher shrugged, but did not respond.

Rogan reached across and rubbed the side of Jack's face. 'You know . . . this damn animal really grows on you. I'm glad he made it. He's going to love America.'

'I think so, too,' Fletcher nodded. 'Do you know when we're scheduled to pull out?'

'There'll be a full briefing tomorrow morning, but the men aren't going to like it. Because of our advanced position, we're one of the last bases to leave.'

EIGHT

When Fletcher reached his tent, he tried to ignore Travis's empty bunk, but his eyes were drawn to it. Some of his personal effects—photographs and books, mostly—were stacked on a small bedside table. The sight of them depressed Fletcher. He knew he would have to sort through them and have them packaged and sent home, just not tonight. He was about to collapse onto his bed, when he noticed a large brown envelope on his pillow.

Lifting the envelope, he immediately recognised the handwriting on its cover. It was the same scrawl that had often blotted his articles. It was from Marvin Samuels, his old friend and former editor. He tore it open and removed its contents. There were three back issues of *The Mirror* inside, with highlighted articles about Vietnam, but there was also a second, smaller envelope.

For no particular reason, he felt his pulse quicken.

The envelope contained a letter attached to a document.

Dear Fletcher,

I hope these words find you, and find you well.

You should know that your efforts are greatly appreciated by scores back here, but equally many are against our nation's presence in Vietnam. It saddens me to tell you that some soldiers returning home are being treated like criminals. I hope it's enough for you to know that cowards like myself are very grateful for what you are doing and are indebted to your sacrifice.

I feel sick about the way things ended between us at the cemetery, and I'm truly sorry for my part. Having said that, I fear I have placed an even greater risk on our friendship by what I am about to reveal.

Attached to this letter are thirty-nine pages of a diary your wife kept. Your mother found it in a box during the sale of your home and came to me. She didn't know what to do with it. She felt that if she sent it to you, it might just make what you are going through all that more difficult to endure. Or it might—please let me be right—raise your spirits.

I've kept these pages in my drawer for months under lock and key. Every day, I've debated sending them to you—and every day, I've found a reason not to.

But they're beginning to burn a hole through my desk, through my heart. Neither your mother nor I have read beyond the first page; its content was never intended for us. I pray that these pages go some way to mending the hurt that you live with. Selfishly, I hope they bring me to a day when I can again be in the company of my friend and tell him how proud I am of him. And how much I've missed him.

May God keep you until that day.

Your friend,

Marvin

Despite the heat, Fletcher felt his hands go cold. He had had no idea Abby kept a diary. With his heart racing, he unfolded the pages. He managed to read the first few words before he was overcome.

Abigail had addressed the diary to Kelly, who, at the time of writing had not yet been conceived. It was a mother writing a diary that she one day intended to give to her daughter.

It began: *Kelly, my angel, today I met the man I know I'm going to marry. Today I met your father.*

THE WEEKS THAT FOLLOWED were all about packing up supplies and loading them onto helicopters. The sound of choppers taking off and landing became a constant background noise, like great mechanical bees cross-pollinating through an industrial meadow. The men whiled away their time playing baseball or touch football. The nights were for drinking.

While under the spell of alcohol, the men often became emotional. They shared photographs of loved ones. They got into meaningless arguments. They told stories of home. They reread old letters. They cried over their children. They planned proposals.

They were all slowly coming to terms with surviving Vietnam and the prospect of life beyond it. The dark cloud that had hung over the Strip for so long was finally beginning to lift.

With just under two weeks to go until their withdrawal, Fletcher was on his way to the Soup when a man called out to him.

'Fletcher,' the voice said behind him. 'This came for you.'

It was the base mailman, and he was carrying a crumpled brown envelope. For a moment, Fletcher wondered if Marvin had somehow come across another part of Abby's diary.

He had savoured every word of the thirty-nine pages he had been sent before. Her entries were all about their courtship, and they afforded him a precious glimpse back into their early life together. The emotion of her writing was difficult to bear, but he welcomed her words.

He tore open the envelope. Inside was a letter. He unfolded it and instantly recognised the name at the bottom of the page.

Dear Fletcher,

My squad and I enjoyed helping you get Jack rehabilitated and have taken pleasure in hearing of his successes out in the field. However, I am the bearer of bad news.

It appears the price of withdrawing troops and equipment from Vietnam is proving too costly for our government. I'm afraid there is no easy way to say this. Fletcher, our dogs have been officially declared 'surplus military equipment' and are not being allowed to return home with us. We've been ordered to hand them over to the South Vietnamese. Those that aren't are being euthanised or just left to die.

It's a nightmare for all us dog handlers. Some 4,000 dogs have been fighting in this war and giving their lives to save American soldiers, and they are now being abandoned by our government.

I'm fighting this with everything I have, but I don't hold out much hope. I've been in contact with other dog units, and they've been forced to leave their dogs behind, on some occasions at gunpoint. Other handlers have been arrested for showing resistance.

If I manage to organise safe passage for our dogs, I'll send for Jack. But it's not looking good. We're due to leave in a few days. If you haven't received word from me by March 13, then I have failed. In which case, I pray you have better luck.

I'll be thinking of you and Jack.

Your friend,

W. Wallace

Fletcher's mind was reeling. How could the government do this? How could they just abandon the dogs?

With trembling hands, he reread his friend's letter. '. . . *If you haven't received word from me by March 13, then I have failed . . .*'

The letter slipped from Fletcher's grasp and floated gracefully to the ground. It was March 15.

'THIS IS WRONG!' Fletcher shouted. 'Everyone knows it!'

'I've been given orders right from the top,' said Frank Wilson. 'I know it's cruel. But—'

'But what? These dogs are soldiers. How can we just leave them behind?'

'I know this is hard for you. It's difficult for all of us.'

'Look, this is the way I see it: Jack is the only dog on base. It'll be easier to smuggle him off than it would be if we had a dog unit.'

'I'm sorry, but I can't go against senior orders. I'm not jeopardising a thirty-year career in the military for this. It's ludicrous.'

'He deserves a chance, Frank. Please . . . let me try.'

'No, Fletcher, it's over. There's nothing more either of us can do. Why don't you focus on the positives? You're going home in a few days. You have the rest of your life to look forward to. Start putting your energies into that.'

Fletcher snatched his hat off the table and headed for the door. 'How can you be so damn weak?'

Frank's expression hardened. 'I've had about enough of your attitude. Do I need to remind you who you're talking to?'

'Don't worry. I know *exactly* who I'm talking to. The sad thing is that up until today, I had the utmost respect for you.'

'We're not finished. This—'

'Oh, we're finished,' Fletcher insisted, pushing through the door, 'and for what it's worth . . . *screw you*.'

FLETCHER SPENT HIS FINAL DAYS in Vietnam trying to devise a plan to smuggle Jack back to America. But there were too many logistical hurdles to overcome. He discovered that the trip home involved four flights and several transfers, and he simply didn't have the contacts to sustain the effort. The obvious temptation was to hide Jack in a crate, but the risk of him freezing to death in the various cargo holds forced him to abandon the idea. He wrote letters, spoke to other dog units, even called old press contacts back home, but one way or another, each avenue soon reached a dead end.

Fletcher spent hours alone with Jack, savouring their time together. How long would Jack survive on his own? What would claim him in the end? Starvation, heat stroke, disease? Or would his life finally draw to a close on the tip of Charlie's knife?

Not since his attempted suicide had Fletcher felt more alone. With only a day left before their withdrawal, he found a secluded place near the base's perimeter, where he and Jack could spend the afternoon together. Sitting quietly, they watched as the sun slowly slid across the sky and then finally dipped behind a bank of clouds.

Fletcher knew that just as he had lost his wife and daughter, he was on the brink of losing Jack. He knew that if that happened, then he, too, would be lost.

'THERE'S NOTHING ELSE we can do?' Rogan asked.

'I'm afraid not,' Frank Wilson replied.

'You know how much he gave to this war. Why can't they make an exception? The man is teetering on the edge.'

'I've sent special requests right to the top. They feel that if they let Jack come back, there would be no stopping the remaining dog handlers. They're just not prepared to set a precedent.'

'This is a travesty.'

'I know, but I've done all I can. Believe me.'

Rogan paused as a helicopter swooped overhead. 'Do you know that the dog saved my life?'

'I didn't, but I'm not surprised.'

'In fact, he saved all of us. And now we're just letting him die?'

'I'm sorry, Rogan. I really am,' Frank said, as he packed away the last of his personal effects. 'Look, I'm scheduled on the next chopper out. Why don't you join me.'

'No. I'm going to stay with Fletcher and do what I can to make this easier for him.'

Frank stood up and held out his hand. 'Something that's always impressed me about you, Rogan, is how much you care about your men. You're a fine soldier and a great leader.'

ROGAN STOOD at the entrance to the tent and watched Fletcher brush Jack.

'He should've died that day,' Fletcher said without looking up.

'Maybe so, but you saved him.'

'No. He survived because he was meant to live. I'm convinced of it.'

'Fletcher, you've done all you can. You've risked your life for him more than once. You have the strength to get past this.'

Fletcher looked up. His eyes were bloodshot. 'Without Jack, I have nothing left.'

'Look, I know you won't be with him, but he might make it out there. He survived before—'

'Alone in this place, he'll be dead in two weeks.'

Rogan thought of a reply, but could summon nothing honest. 'Everyone's gone, Fletcher. It's just us now. The last chopper will be here any minute. I'll give you some time to say goodbye.'

As the lieutenant turned to leave, Fletcher called out to him. 'Wait. Hold on, Rogan.' He lifted Jack up and held him against his chest. 'They're taking a register of everyone leaving, aren't they?'

'Yes, why?'

'Will you help me?'

'Of course.' Rogan frowned, wondering what Fletcher meant.

Outside, like the sound of a dying heartbeat, one last Huey approached.

'FLETCHER CARSON? We're under orders to bring you out.'

Startled, Fletcher looked up at the two men in military police uniform. They were both armed.

'What's going on?' Rogan asked. 'Who ordered this?'

'That's of no concern to you, Lieutenant.'

'What have you been told?'

'It doesn't concern you,' the more senior soldier repeated. 'The bird's waiting. Let's go.'

Incensed, Rogan stood up. 'Listen, son, you better tell me what the hell's going on right now, or every time you swallow, you're going to be tasting the barrel of that rifle.'

The soldier stepped forward, tightening his grip on his MI6. 'We have orders that do not involve you. Stay out of this. If you don't, we'll be forced to restrain you. Now, let's go.'

'Move,' his partner chipped in, feeling the need to assert himself.

Fletcher slowly lifted to his feet. Jack, sensing the tension, began to growl. As they exited the tent, Fletcher instructed Jack to walk ahead of him. The Labrador's hackles were raised, and he was still growling, but he reluctantly followed Fletcher's command.

When Fletcher slowed, one of the soldiers nudged him along with his weapon. 'Hurry up.'

Rogan stopped and turned round. 'Look, we're going to get on the damn chopper, but first this man is going to say goodbye to his dog. That's all.'

The senior soldier shook his head. 'We don't have time for that.'

Rogan's eyes were wide with rage. '*We don't have time?* Just what is the big hurry? What the hell's really going on here?'

The soldiers exchanged looks.

'We have orders to shoot the dog,' the senior soldier replied.

'No . . . please!' Fletcher called out.

'Stand aside, Carson,' the soldier instructed, raising his rifle.

Fletcher knelt down and shepherded Jack behind him. 'You'll have to shoot me first.'

'Spare me the dramatics. It's only a goddamn dog.'

Detecting Fletcher's resolve, the soldiers fanned out to create an angle for a shot. As Rogan stepped forward to help Fletcher, the second soldier screamed at him, 'Stay where you are!'

'Stop this, please,' Fletcher urged.

'Make this easier on yourself, Carson . . . Move aside.'

Fletcher tried to spread himself over Jack, but the soldier fired a shot anyway. The bullet narrowly missed him.

'Have you lost your minds?' Rogan shouted. 'You're going to kill him!'

'Then order your man to move away from the dog now!'

The situation had spiralled out of control. Fletcher knew he had to do something drastic. He grabbed a handful of sand and hurled it in the face of the senior soldier. Instinctively, the man dropped his rifle and brought his hands up to his eyes. The incident distracted his partner, and he shifted his rifle away from Rogan for an instant.

It was all Rogan needed. He lunged forward and punched the soldier, sending him crashing to the ground. Rogan quickly disarmed him and ran across to Fletcher, who was wrestling with the other soldier. 'Let him go.'

The soldier stopped resisting, and Fletcher pulled his rifle off him. He shoved the barrel under the man's chin. 'Why shouldn't I kill you?'

'Because I'll take down your lieutenant,' a voice suddenly intruded from behind them.

It was the pilot. With the sound of the rotors disguising his movements, he had managed to sneak up behind them undetected. He was standing only five feet behind Rogan, with his side arm drawn. 'Lower your weapons, both of you.'

The scene had become surreal to Fletcher. 'I just want you to let my dog go.'

'Return the rifle and get on the chopper.'

'Will you let my dog live?'

'Put down your weapon and get on the fucking bird!'

Fletcher was out of options. Rogan had already sacrificed enough for him; he couldn't endanger his life any further. He took a deep breath and looked at Jack. 'Ruush,' he whispered, fighting back the tears. '*Ruuush*.'

It was the command for Jack to run.

'Ruush, Jack—now. *Please*.'

Jack took two steps back, then stopped.

Fletcher felt as if his heart was being torn out of his chest. 'Run, Jack . . . run . . . please . . . They're going to kill you,' he cried.

Reluctantly, Jack turned and fled.

As Jack disappeared, Fletcher discarded the rifle. The senior soldier, angered and embarrassed to have lost control of the situation, quickly retrieved his weapon and swung it at Fletcher. Blood exploded from his forehead where the butt hit hard.

'Leave him alone, you bastard!'

'Shut up!' the other soldier screamed, reclaiming his own weapon.

The pilot turned away and headed back to the helicopter. 'Get them on board and put restraints on them. Think you two can handle that?'

The senior soldier yanked Fletcher to his feet. 'In the chopper, now!'

As they moved, Rogan turned to Fletcher. 'You all right?'

Blood was streaming down Fletcher's face, soaking the front of his shirt. 'This wasn't supposed to happen. This wasn't the plan . . .'

'What plan? What're you talking about?'

But Fletcher didn't respond. Something in his mind had finally let go.

They were pushed on board and forced to lie down on their stomachs with their arms held behind them. While the soldiers searched for handcuffs, the pilot fired up the chopper.

As they lay together, facing each other, Rogan spoke again. 'What did you mean "This wasn't the plan"?'

Fletcher could only shake his head.

'Fletcher! What plan are you talking about?' Rogan insisted as the helicopter lifted off.

'You said you would help me,' Fletcher uttered. 'Please . . . *help me*.' He lifted his head and stared intensely at Rogan. 'I can't leave him behind.'

Rogan looked at him blankly for a moment, and then suddenly understood what he wanted. 'But you'll die.'

Fletcher shook his head. 'I'll die anyway.'

Reluctantly, Rogan nodded. He held Fletcher's gaze for a moment before turning over and, in one fluid movement, tackling the two soldiers.

Fletcher pulled himself to the edge of the cabin. The chopper was rising steeply. Out of the corner of his eye, he saw movement.

It was Jack. He was running after the helicopter.

Just as Fletcher had stepped off a ledge to end his life months before, he again plunged into another abyss. Except this time, he was falling to save himself. As he plummeted to the ground, he felt himself turning over. He landed on his back. A jolt of pain drove through his spine. He struggled onto his haunches just as Jack reached him. The Labrador launched himself into his arms.

He held him close, and Jack licked the side of his face. 'I was never going to leave you. I never planned to get on that chopper.'

The helicopter hovered above them, and Fletcher watched as the two soldiers battled to subdue Rogan. Before they overpowered him, he managed to get hold of a gun and push it out of the cabin.

Then, just as Fletcher had suspected, instead of landing, the helicopter continued to rise. For them, the war was over. As he watched the helicopter disappear, Rogan managed to stretch his arm out of the cabin. He pressed his thumb into the palm of his hand and extended two fingers. It was one of the many dog commands they had taught Jack.

It meant, Find home.

NINE

Fletcher sat holding Jack until he could no longer hear the chopper.

As his breathing eased and he checked himself to make sure nothing was broken, his mind turned to Rogan. He could barely believe what his lieutenant had done for him. His actions would have dire consequences back home. He would almost certainly face a court-martial, perhaps even jail time. His career in the army was all but over.

'Thank you, Lieutenant,' Fletcher whispered, staring up into the sky. 'For everything.'

Jack shifted in Fletcher's arms and nuzzled his hand. He was just happy that they were together again.

'It's just us now, Jack. Alone in hell.'

Fletcher scanned the deserted base. It was an eerie scene. Half a dozen tents remained, as well as two supply rooms and an empty munitions depot, but without the constant throng of soldiers, it felt like a foreign landscape.

'Surplus military equipment,' he remarked cynically before moving towards the tent closest to them. He walked inside and headed to the far corner, where he knelt down and dug through the soft sand. A moment later, he pulled out a map and compass wrapped in a plastic bag.

'I told you I never meant to get on that chopper.'

Jack tilted his head and tried to bite the bag.

Fletcher had never intended to abandon Jack, although the arrival of the two MPs almost derailed his plan. Unfolding the map, he used his finger to trace a line from their base westwards, out of Vietnam, across Laos, and into Thailand—a country friendly to the United States. The route constituted some 350 miles of hostile territory.

He looked down at Jack. 'I know we can do this.'

They were going to hike out of Vietnam.

THE STRIP HAD BEEN one of the last US bases to pull out of central Vietnam. There wasn't another American for 150 miles. Not that it mattered. Fletcher had no intentions of travelling south. Their journey lay west to Thailand. There he would find a way to get them home. A 350-mile walk on an open road would take upwards of ten days. Their journey was likely to take a month.

With Jack following closely behind, Fletcher began to gather the supplies he had stowed away. He had four water canisters, two boxes of matches, two loaves of bread, sixteen soup powders, and a pile of exactly 157 dog biscuits. The water canisters were important because although there were likely to be numerous water sources along their route, not all of it would be safe to drink.

The biscuits would become their staple diet, by far their most nutritious food source. They could survive on a handful of them a day. If things got desperate, he could always hunt for food using the gun Rogan had thrown out of the chopper, but as it risked bringing unwanted attention to themselves, it would be only as a last resort.

Picking up an old, worn rucksack, Fletcher loaded their supplies. He wondered what their chances of survival were. They would have to negotiate traps and pass undetected for weeks. His navigating would also have to be extremely accurate. Laos was still hostile territory. It was also home to Charlie's largest supply route to the South—the infamous Ho Chi Minh trail—which he would have to traverse in the days that followed.

As he loaded some of the biscuits into a pocket on the side of the rucksack, he felt a small bulge near the bottom. He reached down and withdrew the object. It was a first-aid kit, with scissors, bandages, a needle and three vials of penicillin.

'Let's hope we don't need this.'

THAT NIGHT, Fletcher battled to fall asleep. The Strip, which had been their sanctuary for so long, was now a dangerous place to be. Charlie would be coming soon, sweeping through the deserted camps like scavengers picking at the wet bones of a rotting corpse.

Just not tonight, Fletcher hoped.

'WHO'S THERE?' Fletcher mumbled, startled. He had no idea what had woken him, only that something felt wrong. The flap of the tent swayed gently in the breeze. A shadow appeared on the canvas wall beside him. He snatched at his gun. The figure was stooped over, but the pose seemed exaggerated.

'Jack,' he said as the Labrador poked his head inside the tent. 'Where've you been?'

Jack wagged his tail and flopped down.

'Don't get too comfortable.' He yawned, noticing the darkness beginning to lift on the horizon. 'It's almost time for us to go.'

As the sky lightened, Fletcher's anxiety grew. The furthest he had ever hiked was seventy miles over six days. Their journey ahead was five times that. He scanned the abandoned base and was unnerved at how quiet it was. No Jeeps. No Hueys. No voices.

Just them, alone in the enemy's garden. Forsaken.

THE FIRST FOUR DAYS were mercifully uneventful. With the war over, there were few active patrols left in the area. They had encountered Charlie only once, and even then, he appeared more concerned about being snared in one of his own traps than anything else—a concern Fletcher shared. Twice Jack had sniffed out tripwires that he had missed. On both occasions, it had been late in the day. Fletcher found that his concentration began to waver after about nine hours. Jack's mind, however, seemed never to tire.

They had been walking most of the afternoon when Fletcher noticed an old wooden sign ahead of them. A large part of its message had long since been scrubbed away by the wind and the rain, but a portion survived: LAOS.

Sometime during the day, they had crossed over the border. By his calculations, they had already covered more than sixty miles. He was overjoyed at how quickly they had progressed, but during the last few hours, Jack had developed a slight limp. After checking Jack's paw to ensure he hadn't picked up a thorn, he thought the injury must relate to the shooting and worried what condition the Labrador would be in a week from now, a month from now.

Stopping for a moment, Fletcher laid Jack down and stretched out his back legs. He pressed his hand down gently on the scar above his hip, and Jack yipped in pain.

'All right, Jack, all right. We'll slow down tomorrow.'

Checking the area, he found a well-covered spot near the base of a tree, where they could spend the night. As always, he climbed the tree to get a better look at their surroundings. Satisfied, he opened the rucksack and took out their food for the evening. Three dog biscuits each and a packet of soup to share. The soup would have tasted a good deal more appetising had they been able to heat it, but they couldn't afford the attention a fire would bring.

'I'll never take any food for granted again, that's for sure.'

Jack moved alongside Fletcher and, as always, rested his head on his thigh.

'Get some sleep, Jack. We've got a long way to go. We're barely down the driveway.'

BY DAY SEVEN, Jack's limp had deteriorated from a slight hobble to the point where his back right paw touched the ground only every third or fourth stride. As troubling as it was, it didn't slow him much—not yet, at least.

Over the past two days, however, Fletcher's legs had started to cramp. His calves locked up every few hours. Each attack would force them to stop so that he could massage out the spasm. The whole process delayed them for around ten minutes at a time. A worrying sign was that the intervals between the cramps were getting smaller, their grip lasting longer.

On the positive side, they had managed to safely cross the Ho Chi Minh trail. Fletcher wished the trail led to Thailand. That way, they might have been able to stow away on the back of a truck. But bisecting the path meant that they had covered something in the region of 100 miles. It was an important milestone. But still two-thirds of their journey lay ahead of them.

Nightfall brought with it welcome rain. After days of clear skies, Fletcher celebrated its arrival. Following the natural path of the water as it flowed through the trees and funnelled down leaves, he carefully positioned their water canisters until they were full. Making the most of the situation, they both drank until their stomachs were bloated. The water was delicious.

Using a thin ground sheet to shelter them from the downpour, Fletcher watched as the rain pooled at their feet. He had been truly grateful for the shower, but now his thoughts turned to where they would hole up for the night. The prospect of sleeping in the mud was becoming more and more likely by the minute.

Whether it was the driving rain or just a lapse in concentration, Fletcher didn't see the animal until it was right on top of them.

He stared straight into its eyes, less than ten feet away, but still couldn't believe what he was seeing.

The animal was stalking them. Hunting them.

It seemed impossible. *Am I hallucinating?* he wondered.

The predator's orange stripes, like licks of flame, lit up the gloom.

Fletcher slowly withdrew his side arm, mindful of making any sudden movements. The tiger crouched down, the muscles in its shoulders writhing like snakes coiling under a silk sheet. Its variegated coat appeared almost fluorescent in the pouring rain. The last thing Fletcher wanted to do was shoot it. Tigers were not known to hunt humans, but this one was clearly hungry. Jack let out a low, threatening growl. Fletcher grabbed his collar.

The tiger, as big as a small car, took a half-step forward. It was now within striking range.

Fletcher cocked his gun. 'Find something else, friend,' he said in a deep, steady voice.

The animal took a step back. Fletcher waved the pistol in a slow arc. 'That's it . . . move away.' The tiger slowly backtracked through the trees. Then, just as suddenly as it had appeared, it vanished.

'Did that really just happen?' Fletcher asked, easing his grip on Jack's collar. The Labrador's hackles were raised like quills.

'I think he's gone. I hope so.'

But for how long? he realised. Would he return later while they slept? They would have to find somewhere safe to rest. This meant a tree. But most of the trees in the area were unsuitable. Soon it would be too dark to continue their search, and they would be forced to spend the night awake.

'Come on, give us a break,' Fletcher pleaded, scanning the trees.

Thoroughly dejected, he took a deep breath, and, as he did so, something flickered in the bottom of his vision. What was it? Metal? Glass?

At first, he thought his eyes were deceiving him, but as he moved closer, his doubts evaporated. A small truck, stripped of its wheels and engine, was wedged between two trees.

'How the hell did that get here?' He laughed, striding towards it. He stepped up to the driver's door and was about to open it, when he realised it might be booby-trapped. After satisfying himself that it wasn't rigged to anything, he carefully clicked it open.

He felt like crying. The windows were intact, and the front seat bench was big enough for both of them to stretch out on. 'It's like the Ritz!' he cheered. 'C'mon, Jack . . . get in.'

Once inside, Fletcher stripped off his wet clothes and used a small towel to dry Jack's coat. Within minutes, all the windows had misted up. The harder it rained, the less likely it was that they would be found. They were dry and warm, and Fletcher couldn't help but feel that they were safe.

Day fifteen. Fletcher removed his socks and wrung out the sweat, which was now tinged red with blood. The coppery stench made him feel nauseated. He looked down in dismay at his feet. They were covered in thin cuts and blisters. He had lost two toenails, and his right heel was cracked.

Jack wasn't faring any better. His back right leg was now a useless appendage. He was reduced to dragging it behind him, no longer able to hold it up. The hair on top of his paw had been worn away and replaced by a thin, wet scab.

Infection had already set in; Fletcher could smell it. He decided to administer two vials of their precious penicillin to Jack. After he was done, he strapped up the paw with a torn section of his shirt. 'There, Jack. That should help.'

They were both in some pain, but of more immediate concern was their food reserves, which had dwindled far quicker than Fletcher originally calculated. They were down to just three soups and fifty-seven biscuits.

Not nearly enough, given the energy they were expending.

Fletcher forced his boots back on and winced as he tightened the laces. Standing up was always the worst. The pain brought on a wave of nausea, which he had to contain at all costs. If he vomited, he would lose the little food he had just eaten.

Jack waited patiently until Fletcher started moving again before trotting up to point. As ever, he began searching and sniffing for danger.

The more they walked, the better Fletcher felt. Each step was closer to Thailand—closer to home.

The pain seemed to numb after an hour, until all that was left was a sense of heaviness at the bottom of his legs. That, and the sensation of sweat and blood squelching between his toes.

By nightfall, Fletcher calculated they would have covered over 250 miles.

Only 100 miles to go. He was starting to believe.

TEN

Day twenty brought another impossibly dark night in Laos. Fletcher had become used to functioning without light and was no longer perturbed by the insects that occasionally wandered over his body. For the most part, they were harmless. Even snakes barely factored on his list of things that were likely to harm them.

What was of growing concern, however, was a painful and disturbing throbbing that had burrowed into the lower half of his legs. His feet had become so swollen that to take off his boots, he had to remove his shoelaces.

Jack was in worse shape.

Using the canvas sheet to conceal the light, Fletcher shone his torch onto Jack's bandaged paw. He needed to change the dressing. As he unfurled the dirty rag, the smell that emerged made his eyes water. The wound was covered in a thick, murky layer of slime and blood. The skin around the area was tight and swollen. Fletcher unscrewed the lid from one of the canisters and poured water over the wound. As he gently prodded the area, he could feel there was a build-up of fluid under the skin. He unpacked his knife and a box of matches and began to burn the tip of the blade. After a few seconds he tightened his grip around the top of Jack's leg.

'This is going to hurt, but I promise you'll feel better afterwards.'

He pushed the knife into the middle of Jack's paw, and a thick wave of pus splashed up onto the blade.

Jack whimpered and tried to withdraw his leg.

'I know it hurts, buddy, but we have to do this.'

IN THE MORNING, Fletcher was relieved to see that the swelling in Jack's paw had gone down. Fletcher mixed a bowl of soup and gave it all to Jack. He needed the energy to fight off the infection.

'C'mon, Jack. Another week of this crap, and we'll be in Thailand. From there . . . somehow I'll find us a way home.'

Jack rose slowly and wagged his tail. He stepped forward and managed to touch the ground with his injured paw. He quickly lifted it up, but it was a sign of improvement.

As the afternoon shadows lengthened, Fletcher felt increasingly detached from their situation. His head felt light and dizzy. He had also begun to lose sensation in his legs. But that wasn't the worst of it.

Paranoia, like an insidious disease, was starting to creep under his skin. Suddenly Charlie was everywhere: hiding in the grass, waiting behind bushes, stalking him from behind. Twice, he almost shot at trees, convinced soldiers were hiding behind them.

The lines between reality and delirium were starting to blur. And then the dead started showing up.

He saw the two officers he had assassinated in the tunnel complex sitting in a tree, fresh blood seeping from their wounds. Then the first man he had killed in Vietnam—a young, barefoot soldier—appeared through the jungle ahead of him.

He couldn't take it any more. He stopped walking and dropped to his knees. His tongue was thick and swollen. He was barely able to swallow. He opened one of the water canisters and took a sip. He poured the remaining contents into Jack's bowl. As he listened to him drink, Fletcher lay down.

'I have to rest, Jack,' he whispered. 'I'm just so . . . *tired*.'

He was exhausted. He just needed to stop for a while.

To close his eyes. Just for a minute.

A KICK. Fletcher tried to open his eyes, but the late-afternoon sun was blinding. There were several dark figures crowded around him.

Was he still hallucinating?

He tried to talk, but one of the figures rammed something into his face. This was no dream; the pain was excruciating. As he struggled to his feet, voices shouted at him.

Another strike to his head. Then one against his back.

The onslaught took his breath away. He tried to raise his arms to defend himself, but the back of his hand was violently swatted down by the butt of a rifle. He felt, and then heard, the bones crack.

As his vision narrowed, he heard Jack attack one of the men. From the sound of the man's cries, he was being torn to pieces.

'Please leave my dog. Please!' Fletcher shouted. 'Jack . . . *ruush* . . . *ruush* . . . get out of here!'

Fletcher felt his world begin to recede. But just before the blackness was drawn over him, he was afforded one final sight. It would break him in every way that a man could be broken.

A soldier smashed the side of his rifle into Jack's face, spun it round, and as an early twilight carried Fletcher away, two shots were fired.

TWO DAYS LATER, Fletcher woke up with a start.

'Easy, mate,' a voice issued from behind him. 'You're pretty banged up. Been out for some time now.'

He was lying on a hard mud floor. His head was wrapped in a strip of green material, and he was sweating profusely.

'You're bloody lucky to be alive.'

'Where am I?' he managed.

'The end of the line, I suppose.'

Fletcher absorbed his surroundings. The prison was no bigger than six or seven square yards and made entirely from thick bamboo struts bound together by wire. Through the space between the bars, he could see five or six bungalows in the distance. There was a lookout tower some eighty yards away, on top of which two guards were sharing a cigarette.

'What's your name, friend?' The voice belonged to a tall, bearded man with a mane of curly blond hair. His accent was unmistakably Australian.

'Fletcher,' he offered. 'Where are we?'

'We're in a prison camp about forty miles out of Cambodia.'

'Still in Laos?'

'Yeah.'

'How far from—'

'Thailand? About fifty-five miles, I reckon,' he said, then laughed. 'But we may as well be on another planet.'

Fletcher thought of Jack. He recalled seeing the Labrador hit in the face and hearing two shots. The image scalded him like a branding iron. Had Jack been killed?

'Tell me . . .' Fletcher said, clearing his throat. 'When they brought me in, did you see if they were carrying a dog?'

'A dog? What . . . yours?'

'Yes.'

'Why would they bring your dog back with you?'

Fletcher's reply was barely audible. 'For food. Please, do you remember seeing anything?'

The man stared at the ground. 'I saw them bring you in, and I'm pretty sure they weren't carrying a dog.'

A vague hope lifted Fletcher. If Jack had been killed, there was a strong likelihood the soldiers would have brought his body back to camp.

'Look, I know it's none of my business, but I've got to ask you something,' the Australian said. 'The war ended weeks ago, but you've only just arrived here. Where the hell have you been?'

Fletcher looked down and noticed that his legs were tied to one of the thick bamboo struts. 'We were on our way home.'

IN THE DAYS FOLLOWING his capture, Fletcher forged a comfortable bond with the Australian, Matthew Summers. They debated different ways of escaping, but had not yet come up with a plausible plan. Fletcher learned that there had been another soldier in the cage, but shortly before his arrival, the man had been dragged down to the river and shot in the head.

Fletcher spent much of his time replaying the moment of his capture over in his mind. Was it possible that Jack was still alive? Had he maybe been shot, but escaped? Was he lying in the jungle somewhere, slowly bleeding to death?

As these dark thoughts continued to plague him, a soldier in his early twenties approached their cage carrying two tin cups. The man had been surprisingly kind to them. He had given them extra food and warm soup.

The soldier carefully pushed the cups inside the cage and backed away. 'Drink tea. Get better. You see. You see!'

It was the same four sentences from the day before.

'War over. Soon you go home.'

This was new.

'No,' Matthew replied, pressing his finger against his temple. 'We dead.'

The young soldier shook his head. 'No . . . war finish . . . no more dead! Home soon for everyone!'

'Thanks, mate, but they're going to kill us. Trust me.'

The soldier knelt down and tried to get Fletcher's attention. 'You feel better? Is tea help?'

Fletcher nodded. 'Tea help. Thank you.'

A smile dawned on the man's face. He was pleased to finally draw a reaction from Fletcher.

'I bring more tea?'

Fletcher held up his hand. 'No. We have enough.'

'More food?'

The soldier's keenness to help was a mystery.

'More food is good,' Matthew offered.

The soldier quickly rose to his feet and ran off. Within minutes, he returned with a large wooden bowl brimming with rice.

It was more food than Fletcher had seen in days.

As Matthew accepted the bowl and began scooping handfuls into his mouth, Fletcher reached out through the bars and gently grabbed the young man's arm. 'What's your name?'

The man regarded Fletcher warily. 'My name Lee. Lee Tao.'

'I'm Fletcher, and this is Matthew. Why are you helping us?'

The soldier leaned in closer to the cage. 'You not remember?'

'Remember what?'

'Small village near Suang. You save us!'

For a moment, Fletcher had no idea what he was talking about, but then a gossamer memory—flimsy and delicate—floated across his mind. During one of their assignments, they had come across a small village that Charlie was tormenting. Several of the young girls had been raped as the Vietcong continued to intimidate and forcibly recruit able-bodied young men into their army. Those who refused were murdered and their wives and children beaten. As it happened, the Fat Lady decided to wait for this particular band of soldiers who were due back the following morning to recruit more men. As Charlie marched into the village shortly after daybreak, intent on more bloodletting, the Fat Lady was waiting for them. The firefight had lasted less than a minute. It was the only time Fletcher had ever extracted any joy in taking other men's lives.

'More men returned after we left, didn't they? That's why you're here.'

'They very angry. My wife . . . they were going kill her,' Lee explained.

'I'm sorry. How long have you been here?'

'Five months,' he answered. 'Please tell me . . . is my village OK? Is my wife still alive?'

'I don't know. I'm very sorry, Lee.'

Lee's expression darkened. 'Eat, Mr Fletcher. I see you tomorrow.' With that, he stood up and ran towards the bungalows.

THE NEXT MORNING, Fletcher woke up with a fever and a debilitating headache that bordered on a migraine. He was sure it wasn't malaria, but rather a nasty dose of flu. Rubbing his eyes, he tried to swallow and discovered that he could add a raging throat infection to his list of ailments.

'You've been out since early last night,' said Matthew. 'I was beginning to think you'd never wake up.'

'I've been conserving my energy. I was thinking of crawling to your side of the cage today.'

Matthew smiled. 'And why would you want to do that?'

'Change of scenery. Maybe I'll have better luck on your side.'

'I thought you said you were a writer, not a comedian.'

Fletcher managed a smirk. 'Any idea what time it is?'

'Must be around eight. I wonder what's keeping our friend this morning. He's late.'

'He might be in trouble for yesterday.'

Matthew carved his initials in the sand with a small stick, then the Australian flag. 'I hope you're wrong.'

'Yeah, me too.'

'It's a good thing you helped out his village. These things all happen for a reason, you know.'

'Lucky coincidence, that's all.'

'You think so? I think it's karma. You defended him and his wife, and now you're being repaid.'

In the distance, a group of soldiers headed towards them. Their rifles gleamed in the morning sun. Matthew strained his eyes. 'This doesn't look good.'

The soldiers were all highly animated. As they came closer, yelling and gesturing with their hands, the man in front raised his rifle and pointed it at Matthew.

'Wait. Wait! You can't do this,' Matthew began, backing into the corner. 'Your government has signed a treaty. This is not—'

But his words were cut short by a single bullet that tore through his face and blew a hole out of the back of his head.

Fletcher closed his eyes and waited for his bullet. The thoughts that ghosted into his mind were no different from the ones that kept him from his sleep.

His girls and Jack.

THE SHOT NEVER CAME. In its place was callous laughter.

By the time Fletcher wiped the blood from his face, the soldiers had already opened the cage and were removing Matthew's body. One of the men made a comment, and the others laughed. Fletcher felt like lunging at them and clawing out their throats, but had little strength to draw on.

The shooter tapped the barrel of his rifle and blew a kiss at Fletcher. Then, one by one, the soldiers filed away, dragging Matthew's bloodied body behind them.

Although they had known each other only a short while, Fletcher had grown fond of Matthew. He was a kind and warm man and had managed to remain upbeat despite their circumstances. He had a young son back home in Perth of whom he spoke sometimes for hours on end. In letters to him before his capture, Matthew had planned a month-long camping trip with the boy. The prospect of which, Fletcher knew, had kept him going.

And now he was gone, his child for ever lost to him.

As the morning progressed, Matthew Summers quickly assumed his position in Fletcher's psyche as the latest inhabitant to prise at his sanity. It was becoming a crowded space.

FLETCHER STARED OUT through the bars and noticed Lee Tao heading towards him. He was carrying something in his arms, but it was hidden under a dark cloth. Fletcher was relieved the young man was still alive.

As Lee approached the cage, he bowed his head as a mark of respect at Matthew's death. 'I sorry about your friend, Mr Fletcher,' he offered quietly. 'You no hurt?'

'I'm all right.'

'I bring soup and special food.'

He removed the cloth and presented a bowl of rice and soup.

'Lee, I'm very grateful for this, but they'll kill you if they find out what you're doing.'

'I don't care. I hate this life. I rather . . . be dead.' His optimism from the previous day had all but evaporated.

'Listen to me,' Fletcher said, shifting closer towards him. 'The war is over. You could return to your village now. They wouldn't go after you. You can find your wife and start over.'

'No more village left. My wife gone. I saw in your eyes.'

'You saw nothing in my eyes! I really don't know about the village. It could still be there. Your wife might still be alive.'

Lee ignored him. 'Must eat, Fletcher, please.'

'Why are you doing this? They're going to kill me anyway!'

Lee shook his head. 'No. I help you. To . . . go away.'

Fletcher marvelled at how this relative stranger was willing to risk so much for him. 'No escape, Lee. This is the end.'

'No, you still have far to live.'

'It's all right, Lee. I should've died a long time ago.'

'No, you must live.'

'Why? What makes you say that?'

'I was part of patrol when we find you sleeping. I watched. You must escape. He need you. He hurt badly . . . but is still alive.'

Fletcher felt his face go numb.

'Yellow dog. I saw him last night at river. He been following you.'

Fletcher couldn't believe it. Was Jack really still alive? 'Are you sure, Lee? How do you know it was my dog?'

'Yellow,' Lee replied. 'It's your dog.'

'But he was shot!'

'No. Soldier tried to shoot him, but missed. Your dog run away. His legs hurt, but he still able to walk. He walks for you, Mr Fletcher.'

Suddenly a voice called out from the distance, and Lee leapt to his feet. A brief but intense look washed over his face. 'I wish I live in your country. In America, you are free.'

Fletcher didn't know how to respond.

'No hope here, just death,' Lee said, then spun away. 'Please . . . must eat. Food save you.'

And then he was gone, running towards the voice that had summoned him, every inch a prisoner himself.

Fletcher's hands were trembling. His skin tingled with energy. Jack was alive. It was a miracle.

When he had calmed down sufficiently, he looked at the food. He grabbed handfuls of rice and forced it into his mouth. He was nearing the bottom of the bowl when he felt something cold and hard. He quickly fished out the foreign object.

He stared at it disbelievingly and then slowly heard himself laugh. Was he losing his mind? Was it all a dream?

Food save you . . .

It was a long, thin strip of metal. It was a blade.

ELEVEN

That night, Fletcher used the blade to saw through a dozen of the bamboo bars. He was tempted to try to escape right there and then, but knew it was too risky. It would soon be daylight. He would wait until the following evening to break out. He only hoped Jack could survive another day without him.

He was massaging his hand to try to relieve some of the cramp that had set in, when he heard movement at the back of the cage. It was Lee, his face etched with concern. 'You must go now, Mr Fletcher!' he urged.

Fletcher scrambled towards him. 'Lee, what's going on?'

'They going to shoot you! I heard. Did you use knife?'

Fletcher nodded.

'Hurry . . . *Hurry*.'

'All right, Lee. But first answer one question. Do you want to leave this place? Do you really want a life in America?'

Lee's eyes widened, and a glimmer of hope flickered across his face. 'Must . . . hurry.'

Fletcher had his answer. 'I'll come back for you, Lee. I'll take you to America. You have my word. Stay alive, and I'll find you.'

Lee pulled a sack from under his shirt. 'Food. Now go!'

Fletcher crawled across to the far side of the cage where he had sawed through the bamboo struts, and he kicked them out. He squeezed through the gap and replaced the bars behind him. If he was lucky, they wouldn't come for him for another hour or so.

As he turned round, Lee was standing in front of him. Instinctively, Fletcher embraced the young man.

'Your dog under trees over there,' Lee said, pointing to an area across the river. 'He waiting for you.'

RUNNING HARD, Fletcher hunched over as he approached the trees. '*Jack . . . Jack . . . Jack*,' he whispered loudly. There was no sign of him. Fletcher scrambled from tree to tree. 'Jack!'

Had he died during the night? A feeling of dread gnawed at him. He called out again, louder this time.

A faint whimpering issued from somewhere behind him.

He spun round. 'Jack! Where are you?' he pleaded.

The Labrador emerged from between two trees. His back legs were buckled uselessly under his body, and he was using his front legs to drag himself into a patch of moonlight.

Fletcher dropped down next to him and scooped him up in his arms. He buried his face into the fur round his neck, partly to drown out the sound of his own crying and partly because he needed to feel Jack, to make sure he was real. 'I thought I'd lost you.'

After holding him for a few moments, he sat up out of the embrace. Beyond Jack's pain, he could see the happiness in his eyes. 'You tracked me, buddy. I'm so proud of you! Well done.'

Jack lifted his head and licked the side of Fletcher's neck.

'What's wrong with your legs?' he asked.

Jack's back paw, still bandaged, had swollen up like a baseball, but his other hind leg looked all right. Why wasn't he able to walk? As his eyes followed the curve of Jack's legs, Fletcher realised what the problem was. His right hip had dislocated. He had no choice. He took hold of his dog's leg and gritted his teeth. He kissed Jack on the head and then twisted the leg and forced it into the joint. Jack bucked at the sudden explosion of pain and then collapsed onto his side.

'Sorry, sorry, boy. It's over. I think it's back in. Just rest for a minute,' he said, gently stroking his head.

As he allowed Jack some time to recover from the shock, he weighed their options. The night sky was beginning to peel away from the horizon. They had the little bit of food Lee had given them, but still had at least fifty miles to travel just to reach Thailand. They had no map, no medicine, and would soon be hunted by their captors. That, and Jack couldn't walk.

Fletcher knew they would have to run. He rose to his feet and lifted Jack in his arms. Taking a breath, he looked up at the sky. 'You've taken everything from me. Just help me this once . . . *please*.'

BY THE TIME THE SUN had risen above the mountains, Fletcher estimated they had made six or even seven miles. Jack had felt light initially, but now weighed heavily in his arms. The worst headache of his life wasn't making matters any easier. On a positive note, his feet had healed over the past few days. All that remained was a distant ache as his boots fought for purchase on the slippery ground. His immediate concern was water. He was desperately thirsty. The sky overhead was clear, and they had not yet encountered a single water source.

By running, he knew he was taking a risk of crossing a wire or falling into a trap, but prudence was not an option any more. He had to put as much distance between himself and his captors as possible. To further compound matters, the infection in Jack's paw had clearly spread to the rest of his body. He needed medical help if he was to survive.

Despite this, however, Fletcher had to stop to rest. His back was aching, and his throat was burning. He still felt feverish. He laid Jack down and took a moment to catch his breath. He untied the knot of the food sack Lee had packed.

Inside were two loaves of bread, a jar of rice, and a canister of water. Unscrewing the lid from the canister, he carefully funnelled the water into Jack's mouth. 'That's it, Jack. Drink.'

Then Fletcher took two long sips of his own and replaced the lid. He wished they could have more, but he knew they could afford to drink only enough to stay alive.

Survival was now a race.

FLETCHER PUT ONE FOOT AHEAD of the other and tried to remain upright. His arms had become ungainly leaden weights, and his back ached as if his spine were a column of burning lava. He kept peering over his shoulder, expecting to see soldiers behind him, but each time, there was nothing in his wake.

As the sun dipped over the trees ahead of him, he began to search for a place to spend the night. He needed to give his body a few hours to rest.

He noticed a slight vale under some heavy foliage some fifty yards to his left. It looked perfect.

He carefully stepped down, parting the branches ahead of him. The hollow was just wide enough for both of them. He lowered Jack down gently onto his side and stretched out his arms. His biceps felt thick and swollen.

Looking down at Jack, he could see he was hurting from all the jarring. Fresh blood seeped through the bandage on his paw. Fletcher sat down, removed the sack from his shoulder, and fished out one of the loaves of bread. He broke off a piece for Jack and gave him some water. Fletcher took a few sips himself and then quickly ate half the loaf. He was relying on the carbohydrates to give him the energy he needed for tomorrow—for one final push. He tried to get Jack to eat more, but he was not interested.

As the jungle's nightlife began to stir, Jack fell into a deep sleep. As if joined by an invisible tether, Fletcher followed after him.

AN INTENSE CRAMP in his shoulder plucked Fletcher from his sleep. At first, he thought something was trying to grab him, and he instinctively swung out, connecting only with the rough bark of an adjacent tree. As he regained control of his senses, he realised what was happening. He reached for the inflamed joint and massaged away the cramp.

It suddenly occurred to him that Jack had slept through the entire incident. Normally the slightest sound would wake him. Something was wrong. Fletcher pressed his hand against Jack's chest and felt for a heartbeat.

'Jack. Wake up, boy.' Nothing. 'Jack . . . hey.' He grabbed the skin around the Labrador's neck and pulled. Jack swallowed heavily, but his eyes remained closed. 'Jack! Stay with me. Do you hear me?'

Fletcher quickly sat him up and tried to feed him. He got down two pieces of bread and a sip of water. When he was done, he rested the Labrador's head on his thigh. He put one hand on his chest and the other two inches in front of his nose.

Jack's condition was deteriorating by the minute. For the rest of the night, if by sheer will alone, Fletcher was going to make sure Jack kept breathing. 'Don't give up, Jack. Our journey's almost over.'

THE MORNING took for ever to arrive. When it finally did, Fletcher wasted no time. He carefully lifted Jack up and climbed out of the vale. Jack had slept peacefully enough, but his condition was dire. In the hours before sunrise, he had picked up a worrying tremor and his breathing had become laboured. He remained in a half-sleep.

All that mattered now was moving quickly. Fletcher estimated they had at least twenty miles to travel just to reach the Thailand border. From there, however, there was no way of telling how much further they would have to hike to find help.

Despite protests from his arms and shoulders, Fletcher began a slow jog. As he trundled forward, he realised that his mind no longer seemed capable of complex thought. It appeared to process only basic needs and functions. Time, distance travelled, food reserves, potential water sources, traps and changes in Jack's condition were the only real items considered high priority.

There was, however, one exception.

Like a continuous movie reel, images of Abigail and Kelly never totally escaped him. Favourite memories would be broadcast over and over again. The day he met Abigail, the red dress she was wearing. Their wedding day. Kelly's birth. Her first day at school. As the memories drifted inexorably towards the crash, Fletcher tried to suppress them. But in the end, he was always left with the shell of a burning plane and the tortured screams of its victims.

By midday, Fletcher was carrying Jack over his shoulder. His arms could no longer take the weight. Unfortunately, it meant a more painful ride for Jack. Each jarring stride was transferred through Fletcher's shoulder and into the Labrador's body. Thin rivulets of blood from Jack's wound ran down Fletcher's chest.

He kept searching for signs that they were no longer in Laos. Several times he stopped, believing he could hear activity from a nearby village, but each time, he was mistaken. Once, he thought he had heard a child's voice, but it was only a bird.

His mind was starting to play tricks on him.

THEY HAD BEEN HEADING west all day, and still there was no sign that they were in Thailand. Fletcher felt as though the jungle had become a giant conveyor belt, and they had been drifting around in circles. He half expected to turn a corner only to discover the Strip ahead of them. Was he finally losing his mind? Were they even heading west? Was he still locked up in his bamboo keep?

He had large welts and blisters on his shoulders and arms from carrying

Jack. His left knee had locked up, the subsequent compensation in his stride had caused his right ankle to become swollen. Still, the most pain stemmed from the infection in his throat—he was now starting to taste blood.

But this was all background noise. Jack was dying.

What little life he had left was ebbing away. In Fletcher's mind, Jack's remaining hours had become dry sand; the more he tried to hold on to it, the quicker it slipped through his fingers. Soon it would all be gone.

Fletcher was becoming frantic. He had blacked out twice, and his sense of paranoia was growing again. He was convinced that a helicopter was doing sweeps over the area. It would swoop down low and hover above him. Each time he heard the swish of its blades, he would scramble for cover, but the chopper seemed determined to hunt him down.

Was it real? As the thought infected his mind, he suddenly stopped walking. Through the trees, a bright orange glow reflected on the leaves. He rubbed his eyes, then slowly moved towards the light. Carefully, he parted the branches ahead of him.

What he saw was madness.

His own.

His wife and daughter were walking through the jungle ahead of him. Their bodies were engulfed in flames.

'Abby . . . Kelly!' Fletcher cried out, his voice raw and hoarse. He had to get them on the ground to douse their flames. Their clothes, their skin, their hair—everything was ablaze. He could smell their burning flesh. But the harder he chased after them, the further away they moved. 'Abigail . . . Kelly . . . stop . . . it's me! Please, we have to put out the flames!'

But they kept walking, gliding away from him. They headed down a steep slope, thick with trees and bushes, but somehow it didn't impede them at all. Fletcher, clutching on to Jack, plunged down the embankment after them. Branches clawed at his face. He was running as fast as he could, but still couldn't close the gap between them. They reached the bottom of the slope, then quickly ascended another hill.

'Why are you running away? Please . . . stop!' he pleaded.

They finally drew to a halt. Abigail was holding Kelly's hand, but still their backs were turned to him. Fletcher scrambled up behind them. 'Yes! Yes . . . Abby . . . Kelly!' He got within ten feet of them, close enough to feel the heat from the scalding flames, when they both vanished.

'No!' he screamed, collapsing on the spot where they had stood. The earth was cool under his hands. He stared down at Jack. The Labrador blinked wearily, then closed his eyes.

'I'm sorry. We're lost, and I'm falling apart. There's no . . .'

But his words trailed off as something ahead of him caught his attention. In the distance was a cluster of huts. Next to them were three old buildings. On the roof of one building was a flagpole.

The colours of Thailand flapped gently in the warm breeze.

Fletcher stared at the scene. Twice he turned away, praying that when he looked again, the village would still be there.

It was.

This wasn't a cruel apparition drawn from his imagination. The Thai flag seemed to beckon him forward.

Summoning the last of his reserves, he cradled Jack in his arms and broke into a run. Tears streamed down his face. He began to scream. His throat was burning with each breath. Shielding Jack's face with his free arm, he charged headfirst into the branches of a row of trees that separated them from possible salvation.

The Thai people heard his strained screams and stopped what they were doing. It was a typical village day. There were people manning food stalls, carrying baskets, riding bicycles. Children were playing. As one, they waited and listened.

Suddenly Fletcher burst into view. He took a few steps, then slumped onto his knees. What strength remained in his arms drained away, and Jack rolled gently onto the ground. The villagers watched as Fletcher shouted, 'Please help me . . . my dog is dying!'

The villagers, stunned, did not move. All except one.

A young girl let go of her mother's hand and ran towards him. Lying on his side now, Fletcher watched through half-closed eyes as she approached him. She was beautiful. Her long black hair framed big brown eyes. Her smile warmed his heart. She knelt down beside him and placed her hand gently on the side of his face. She rested her other hand on the top of Jack's back. Fletcher tried to speak to her, but could feel himself slipping away. His body was shutting down.

The sound of a man's angry shouts punctuated the air. Fletcher saw two Vietcong soldiers running through the crowd. As they reached him, they raised their rifles and shouted for the child to move. The mother quickly scooped up her daughter and disappeared into the crowd.

The soldier closest to Fletcher pressed the butt of his AK-47 into his shoulder and widened his stance.

Fletcher tried to lift himself up, but couldn't. He felt paralysed, empty. He had nothing left.

But Jack did. He lifted up on his front legs and dragged himself towards the soldiers.

'No,' Fletcher cried. He stretched out his arm to try to stop him, but Jack was already beyond his reach.

The soldier curled his finger round the trigger and took aim.

Jack snarled and tried to lunge at the man—but fell short, collapsing onto his chest.

Tears burned Fletcher's eyes. 'Jack!' he screamed. '*Jaaaack!*'

A helicopter, flying fast and low, roared over the treetops. The two soldiers immediately swung their rifles up at the chopper as it churned up a tumultuous cloud of dust and grass. As the Huey hovered above them, its blades cutting up the late-afternoon sun, a loud voice issued from the chopper's broadcast system.

Fletcher recognised the message. It was in Vietnamese. It was a phrase they had often used during their missions. It meant 'Put down your weapons or die.'

He felt himself first laugh, then he sobbed like a small child.

How could it be? How was it possible? The voice belonged to a man from another world, another time. It was unmistakable.

It was Rogan.

TWELVE

By the time Fletcher regained consciousness, two days had passed. He found himself lying on a mattress on the floor of a small wooden hut. As he surveyed the room, he noticed that the thatch roof was draped in a ghostly veil of spiderwebs.

'I leave them up there to keep out evil spirits,' a woman's voice offered. 'They don't bother me, and I don't bother them.'

Fletcher rubbed his eyes. 'Excuse me?'

'The spiderwebs. They insulate the room against unwanted spirits. At least, that's what the locals believe.'

'I'm sorry, but who are you?'

'A friend of a friend.' She smiled. She was an attractive woman, probably in her early thirties, and she appeared to have some Asian blood in her, although her accent was distinctly American. She was thin, with long black hair and a kind face.

'My dog,' Fletcher said. 'Do you know what happened to him?'

She stared at him and her smile faded. 'I rather think your friends should speak to you about that.'

Fletcher felt his stomach tighten. 'I just want to know if he made it.'

The woman knelt down beside him and gently placed her hand on his shoulder. 'Everyone's very happy that you made it.' With that, she stood up and walked away.

'Please, I need to know—' Fletcher began, but stopped when he saw shadows gather on the wall alongside the doorway.

Will Peterson was the first to enter, followed by Mitchell and Rogan. They were carrying Jack on a stretcher.

Fletcher's breathing stalled.

'Just tell me one thing,' Rogan said. 'How in Christ's name, did you do it?'

'Lieutenant . . .'

'Please, Fletcher, it's Rogan. The war's over.'

'Mitch . . . Will . . .'

Will smiled. 'We thought you might want to see this fleabag.'

Fletcher was unable to speak.

'We don't know how he does it, but he does seem pretty determined to hang around.'

As they lowered the stretcher, Fletcher could no longer hold back his tears. 'Jack,' he whispered, gritting his teeth. 'It's over. We made it.'

The Labrador opened his eyes and, as he saw Fletcher, barked softly.

Fletcher pulled himself to the edge of the mattress and threw his arms round his friend. Jack licked away his tears until Fletcher was able to reign in his emotions. 'How,' he asked, looking up. 'How did you know where to find us?'

'Later,' Rogan suggested. 'Right now you need to rest. We'll talk through everything tomorrow.'

EARLY THE FOLLOWING MORNING, Fletcher staggered out onto the wooden deck that surrounded the hut. All three men were sitting on rickety cane chairs waiting for him.

'Some coffee?' Will offered, handing Fletcher a mug.

'Sure thing. Thank you.'

The mug felt heavy in his hand, but its contents tasted heavenly. After a few sips, he looked up and noticed they were in a small clearing in the middle of a jungle.

'I didn't dream the last few months, did I? There was a war in Vietnam?' Fletcher asked quietly.

'I've heard of it,' Mitchell confirmed.

'And we took part in it?'

'Against our better judgment.'

'All right, that's a start,' he said, bringing the mug back up to his lips. 'So Jack and I really did hike out?'

'Close to three hundred and eighty miles,' Will replied. 'You made it to a village called Moyan in southeast Thailand.'

'Where are we now?'

'Officially?' Rogan asked. 'Nowhere. Lost. Missing in action.'

A smirk skimmed across Will's face. 'We're twenty-five miles north of Moyan. How much of your ordeal do you remember?'

'Flashes, mostly—pieces of a puzzle that don't quite fit together.'

'Well then, let's at least tell you what we know,' Rogan stated, pulling out a chair. 'You may as well get comfortable. This might take a while.'

For the next hour, Fletcher listened intently as the story unfolded. He learned that after the incident on the Strip, Rogan had been arrested, but after pressure from various quarters, he was released. He found out about an American soldier being captured in Laos and his subsequent escape. Suspecting it was Fletcher, Rogan managed to get hold of an out-of-service Huey that he had had repaired and set up for flight. When Mitchell and Will caught wind of what he was planning, they insisted on being involved. And so it began.

Without authorisation, they started brief flights between Thailand and Laos, searching around Laos's western border. Rogan was convinced that Fletcher would head for Thailand. It was the only logical move. After ten days, their breakthrough finally arrived.

'It was blind luck in the end. We were on our way back from a sweep when Mitchell saw you, carrying Jack, running towards the village. By the time we turned the chopper round, two soldiers already had their rifles trained on you, but we managed to distract them before they could do any damage,' Will explained.

'I remember hearing Rogan's voice through the helicopter's speakers, but that was it. What happened afterwards?'

'We picked you up and brought you back here. The lady you met yesterday is Shayna Sykes. She's in the Red Cross here in Thailand. She also happens to be a doctor. She operated on Jack using a combination of Western medicine, voodoo, and God knows what else to fight the infection in his leg.' Will paused, reluctant to break the bad news. 'But, Fletch, she doesn't believe he'll ever be able to walk properly again. We'll have to wait and see how he recovers.'

'I guess I can live with that.' Fletcher nodded, just grateful that Jack was alive. 'How'd you find out about Shayna? Why'd she agree to help?'

'Let's just say our commander had a hand in things,' Mitchell replied. 'He spent some time in Thailand several years ago.'

'Wilson helped us? He knows about all this?'

'Officially, no.'

'Wilson had something of an attack of conscience when he heard about what you did,' Rogan explained. 'So he made a few calls to some people he knows, and Shayna is the result of that.'

'Unbelievable,' Fletcher remarked, getting to his feet and shuffling to the edge of the deck. He rested his hands on the wooden railing. 'I have a memory of a helicopter doing sweeps over the Laos jungle. I spent hours hiding from it.'

'You realise that was us?' Will said.

Fletcher nodded. 'If only I had known it then.' He turned round and folded his arms. 'Why'd you guys do it?'

'Personally, I couldn't get enough of Vietnam,' Rogan replied.

'Weather's great this time of year,' Mitchell added.

Rogan stood up and walked over to Fletcher. 'What you did for Jack might be the most remarkable thing I've ever witnessed. How could we turn our backs on that?'

'I'll never be able to properly thank you.'

Rogan shook his head. 'You don't have to. At some stage, we've all played a part in keeping each other alive. The point is, it's over now. I've made arrangements to fly us back home—Jack included. Three days from now, this will all be a memory.'

Fletcher turned away and gazed out into the jungle. 'I'm sorry, but . . . I can't leave yet. There's something I still have to do.'

'What the hell are you talking about?' Rogan demanded.

'Look, I'm sorry, but I made a promise to someone.'

'What promise? What could possibly keep you here?'

'When I was captured, a man helped me escape. I would've died were it not for him.'

'So? What's that got to do with you staying here?'

'I'm going back for him.'

The group was quiet as each of them digested Fletcher's statement. 'I gave him my word that I would return for him and bring him to America.'

'Are you out of your mind? You can't be serious,' Rogan said. 'We didn't risk our lives so you could throw yours away based on some ridiculous pact you made with one of your captors!'

'Who is this man?' Mitchell intervened.

'His name is Lee Tao. He was forcibly recruited from that small village near Suang we helped defend about five months ago. That's why he helped me—he recognised my face. He gave me a blade, which I used to escape. Without it, I would've died. I can't just walk away. I couldn't live with myself if I didn't at least try to help him.'

Rogan paced across the deck. 'How far into Laos is this camp?'

'Fifty-five, maybe sixty miles.'

'What's the protection like?'

'Pretty lightweight. No perimeter fencing. Three guard towers.'

'Soldiers?' Mitchell asked.

'Maybe forty, but there could be more. Why?'

'Well, you better be sure. We'll need to know before we go.'

'Before *we* go?'

'Gentlemen.' Rogan sighed, looking to Mitchell and Will. 'How do you feel about one last dance in our little slice of hell?'

Will thought for a moment. 'I'll fly you wherever you need to go.'

'One final twirl on the dance floor? Thought you'd never ask,' Mitchell responded, bowing.

'No, forget it. I won't endanger—'

'The decision's made, Fletcher. We're playing this thing out together one way or the other. But before we take this any further, is there anything else we should know? Is there an orphanage in Saigon you'd like us to rescue?'

Fletcher looked up at the sky. 'Actually, there is something. Lee has a wife in that same village we helped protect. We don't know if she's still alive, but if she is, we need to get her out as well.'

THE REMAINDER OF THE WEEK was spent planning the rescue.

Mitchell got his hands on an aerial shot of the camp, which showed the three guard towers. Apart from the river, which guarded its western perimeter, its remaining boundaries appeared exposed.

Rogan said, 'It's too easy. What kind of camp doesn't raise a proper perimeter? There must be mines. How'd you get out?'

'I crossed the river. Jack was waiting under the trees on the other side.'

'Then that's how we'll go in. No one leaves their front door open like that . . . even if the war's over. We'll infiltrate at around two in the morning; that should give us enough time to make it back.'

Fletcher stroked Jack, who was sleeping on the stretcher alongside them. He was concerned that the Labrador hadn't yet stood up. The prospect of him never being able to walk again filled Fletcher with dread. But Jack had recovered before.

'How close can you drop us?'

'Probably about three or four miles out,' Will calculated.

'Let's keep it at five to be safe,' Rogan said, still studying the photograph. 'I'm confident we can fly in undetected.'

Fletcher agreed. 'When do you think Mitchell will be back?'

'I don't know, but if the woman's alive, Lord will find her.'

They had woken up two days earlier to discover that Mitchell had disappeared. He'd left a note: *Gone for the wife*. He made no indication of what his plan was or when he expected to be back.

'I hope he makes it,' Fletcher said.

Will clapped his hands and rubbed them together. 'All right, then, everything's set. When do we dance?'

'Tomorrow night,' Rogan replied. 'Let's finish this.'

THE WATER WAS SURPRISINGLY COLD. Fletcher and Rogan waded halfway across the river and waited by a patch of reeds. The camp was quiet. A lone soldier sat on the guard tower closest to them, but he appeared to be sleeping.

In fifteen minutes, they hadn't seen any signs of a ground patrol; the area separating the bungalows appeared deserted.

'You ready?' Rogan asked, scanning the camp with binoculars.

Together they crawled up the embankment and ran across to a large tree less than twenty yards away from the first bungalow. There were still no signs of activity.

'What makes you think he's in this one?'

'I saw him come in here at least twice a day.'

Pressing the butt of his rifle into his shoulder, Rogan ran towards the front of the bungalow. Fletcher shadowed behind him. They stepped quietly up onto the wooden deck and listened. Only the sound of water, dripping into pools at their feet, detracted from the silence.

'The door,' Rogan whispered.

Fletcher stepped forward and quietly turned the handle.

The door opened with a slight creak.

Rogan moved through the doorway, swinging his M16 in a wide arc. He was able to make out two rows of soldiers sleeping soundly on the floor.

Fletcher immediately began to look for Lee. Using a torch that he had taped up with black cloth to diffuse the light, he quickly searched the first row and was halfway through the second when he found him.

Rogan knelt down beside him. 'On three.'

Fletcher raised his thumb. 'One . . . two . . . *three.*'

They both threw themselves on top of Lee. Fletcher cupped his hand tightly over the soldier's mouth while Rogan held down his legs.

Lee immediately tried to struggle free.

'Lee . . . Lee,' Fletcher urged, trying to calm him down. 'It's me. Look.'

Lee's eyes locked on to Fletcher, and the fight immediately drained out of him. Fletcher removed his hand.

'Mr Fletcher . . . how . . . what you doing here?'

'We've come for you.'

'For me? I don't understand.'

'To get you out of here,' Fletcher explained, and then smiled. 'I told you I'd come back for you.'

Lee sat up and threw his arms round Fletcher as if they were old friends.

'All right, you two,' Rogan interjected. 'Let's go.'

They quickly stood up and moved towards the door.

Back out on the deck, they surveyed the area for signs of danger. There was still no indication of a patrol. But Rogan noticed a change on top of the guard tower. The soldier was now having a smoke. 'We're going to have to wait this out. Hopefully he'll finish his smoke and go back to sleep.'

Sitting with their backs against the bungalow, they watched the guard. The man finished the cigarette and flicked the burning stub over the side of the tower. Then, without warning, he turned on his search lamp and ran it across the bungalow. The light washed over them before they had a chance to react. The guard hastily reached over to raise the alarm.

'We have to go . . . now!' Rogan said, scrambling to his feet.

As they ran, the guard opened fire. They threw themselves into the river and swam for the embankment. Fletcher glanced over his shoulder and watched as soldiers streamed out of their bungalows.

'They're coming! *Move!*' Rogan insisted, reaching the bank. Together they hurried into the bowels of the jungle.

'Where we going?'

'There's a helicopter waiting for us,' Fletcher gasped, sucking in large mouthfuls of air. 'Not far from here.'

'We never make it. These soldiers very fast.'

AK-47 fire ripped through the branches above them.

'Just run!' Rogan called back.

ROGAN REALISED the soldiers were gaining on them. 'Those trees,' he gestured, pointing ahead. 'Get up them.'

With the soldiers only a hundred or so yards behind, they each scrambled up a tree. As Fletcher hurried to get into a shooting position, his M16 slipped from his grasp and fell to the ground.

Lee jumped down and hurried towards it. Just as he reached down, the first soldier rounded the corner. The man lifted his AK-47 and pointed it at Lee. But before he could pull the trigger, Rogan shot him twice in the chest.

Lee grabbed the rifle and threw it up to Fletcher.

'Down, Lee!' Fletcher shouted as the other soldiers appeared.

The second man tripped over his dead compatriot, bunching up the group. They never stood a chance.

From their elevated position, Rogan and Fletcher cut down the entire group within seconds. Their automatic fire obliterated them.

As the smoke filtered up through the trees, Lee stood up and walked over to the pile of bodies.

'War,' said Lee. 'Terrible war.'

'This is the end,' Fletcher said. 'It's all over now.'

'In America, there is no war?'

'Not like this.'

'We leave this place?'

'Yes . . . we leave this place.'

THE HELICOPTER FLIGHT back to Thailand was an edgy affair. As long as they were over Laos, they were still at risk of being shot down. But as the first signs of morning lifted the gloom, they crossed over into Thailand and put down in a small open area, barely wide enough to house the chopper. They jumped out and quickly hauled a green-and-brown tarpaulin over the Huey.

'Over here,' Shayna called out. She was parked in an old Jeep under a nearby tree.

'Where we going?' Lee asked.

'Somewhere safe,' Fletcher said.

After a short drive, they pulled up in front of Shayna's hut. A tall, dark figure was standing in the doorway, waiting for them.

It was Mitchell.

'Mitch! You made it!' Fletcher clapped his hands together.

'Of course. I see you did, too.'

Rogan swung his rifle over his shoulder and climbed out of the Jeep. 'What took you so long, Lord?'

'Stopped to admire the shiny bullet shells on the side of the road, Lieutenant.'

As they approached, Mitchell looked towards Lee and said. 'Fletcher tells us you're to blame for saving his life.'

Lee missed the joke. 'Only after you all save my village. I very grateful for your help.'

As they congregated together, Lee turned to Fletcher. 'I want to thank you for coming to me, Mr Fletcher. You sacrifice very much to help, but . . .'

'What is it, Lee?'

'I sorry . . . I can't come away with you,' Lee explained. 'Not until I know for myself. Maybe my wife still alive. She mean everything to me. I cannot leave not knowing what happened to her.'

Mitchell leaned forward and placed his hand on Lee's shoulder. 'We thought you might feel that way.' He stepped away from the door, and an attractive petite young woman appeared behind him. She kept her head down, seemingly afraid to look up.

Lee's eyes widened in surprise. 'Tay?' he managed.

'Lee,' the woman replied, breathless, still reluctant to look up.

'Tay . . . Tay!' he repeated, and ran towards her. They embraced and collapsed to their knees, crying. Lee said something to her in Vietnamese, and she sobbed back her reply, repeating her answer over and over.

Fletcher, taken by the moment, glanced across at Shayna, who was fluent in several languages. 'What did she say?'

Shayna dabbed her eyes with her shirtsleeve. 'What we all dream our partners would say of us: "I never stopped believing in you." '

After Lee and Tay had finally ended their embrace, Mitchell explained how he had tracked down her village and paid an old Vietnamese informant of theirs to go in and get her out. After a day of walking and two days of driving, the man delivered her to a village on the outskirts of Saigon.

Mitchell looked up at Fletcher. 'There's also some good news for you.' He pursed his lips and whistled loudly.

Jack emerged in the open doorway, his tail wagging.

'Jack . . . you're walking!'

As if to prove it, he slowly weaved towards Fletcher.

Shayna shook her head in disbelief as the Labrador brushed past her. 'This is impossible. He shouldn't be able to stand, let alone walk. The bone density in his leg should not be able to support his weight.'

'Jack has remarkable powers of recovery,' Will said.

'No, you don't understand. Recovery is one thing—this animal shouldn't be mobile. I knew he would never walk again; I just didn't have the heart to tell any of you. Him walking is medically impossible!'

'When it comes to Jack, anything's possible,' Mitchell corrected her. 'If you knew his past, you wouldn't be surprised. He's a survivor.'

'Where did he come from?'

Fletcher looked up at Shayna, and a knowing look eased onto his face. 'You wouldn't believe me if I told you.'

Mitchell bent over to pat Jack as he passed. 'What do you mean, Fletch? Did you find out which unit he was attached to?'

'No, he was never part of any unit in Vietnam. Although I've no way of proving it and you're probably going to think I've lost my mind, I know it's true. Jack didn't come from Vietnam. He came from somewhere . . . *else*.'

Will frowned. 'You've lost us.'

Fletcher knelt down as Jack reached him. He rested his forehead against the side of the Labrador's neck. 'Travis was right. He said Jack never belonged here—something about the look in his eyes. I believe I now understand why. My daughter, Kelly, died in a plane crash three days before she would have turned seven. She kept begging my wife and me for this one special birthday present. She was adamant about it. She wanted a Labrador. She even had a name picked out.'

Will closed his eyes. 'Jack?'

Fletcher nodded in return and then raised his head. 'I've never been more certain of anything in my life. My daughter sent Jack to me.'

EPILOGUE

Chicago
Ten years later

More than a decade had slipped by since Fletcher first passed through Hampton Lane's front gates, but still the cemetery appeared the same.

As their cavalcade wound towards the southern end of the cemetery, Fletcher cast his mind back to the war and their last days in Thailand. He recalled how they had all agreed to keep in touch, but despite everything they had endured, he always knew their friendships could not be sustained on the outside. Their bonds had been forged in another world.

Stepping out of his car, Fletcher headed up the embankment towards the large maple tree that still regularly haunted his dreams. As always, he lowered down and gently placed a white rose across each of his girls' graves.

Every visit still hurt him deeply; the wounds had never quite healed. He knew they never would. They were now just a part of his life that he tried to deal with as best he could. As he waited for the rest of the group to join him, he tried not to look at the newly dug grave alongside him. He knew that if he did, it would drain away what little courage he had summoned for the burial.

'You all right?' Marvin asked, joining him at his side.

'No, but thanks for coming. I really appreciate it.'

'Nothing could've kept me away.'

Marvin had been a loyal friend to him over the years, both before the crash and in the wreckage after it. Following his return to America, Marvin persuaded him to go back to journalism. He got him to freelance for the newspaper and, after a while, to compose letters to his girls. It was almost impossible in the beginning, but after a few weeks, the words came a little easier. Eventually, Fletcher was able to write freely. He told them about the horror of Vietnam—but also how hope can exist in the darkest of places—and of how much he missed them. He wrote about his attempted suicide and confessed that for a long time after the crash, thoughts of taking his own life never strayed far from his mind. But that had slowly changed. A year after returning from the war, Shayna Sykes arrived unannounced on his doorstep. In the months that followed, they became friends and, eventually, lovers. He had found a safe space in his heart where he could love Shayna without tarnishing Abigail's memory. He finally accepted that it was OK to give himself to another woman. Just as she had brought him back from the brink of death in Thailand, Shayna gradually taught him how to live again. She would even accompany him to the graves of his girls sometimes, but decided not to join him on this occasion. This was their day.

Lee and Tay were next to reach the gravesite.

For them, their first taste of America had been difficult. There weren't many people prepared to welcome Asians into their neighbourhoods after the war. But like everything, things improved with time. Prejudices softened; hatred dissipated. When the time was right, Fletcher helped them open a small art gallery in Miami, which was now turning over a tidy profit. They were both talented artists, and their work was becoming highly sought after. The free life Lee had always dreamed of was now a reality. If that wasn't enough, they were blessed with two wonderful children: a boy and a girl.

Fletcher looked back and watched as Mitchell, Will and Rogan came up the hill. It occurred to him that Mitchell was still walking in front, ever the point man. He still had his long black hair and a look of madness lurking deep within his eyes. After the war, he had joined a government agency. He was not permitted to talk about his job, and Fletcher had no desire to ask.

Will Peterson followed with a slight limp—a keepsake from his time as a hostage in Vietnam. During the day, he ran a successful charter airline with over a dozen aircraft under his control. At night, he drank. More than he ought to. He married twice, but both unions had failed. Vietnam, it appeared, continued to cast its dark shadow over him.

Walking slowly at the back was Rogan. Fletcher had never quite come to terms with what his lieutenant had done for him. From the day on the chopper and the rescue in Thailand to travelling back into the war to save a stranger. They had come a long way together. In the outside world, Rogan lived alone in a small flat in Detroit, working as a night-shift security guard at a chemical factory. Fletcher wondered what kind of dark thoughts plagued his mind in the small hours of the morning. The hostile reception Rogan received upon returning from Vietnam was too much for him to bear. He was a patriot who believed wholeheartedly in what they were fighting for. He considered their cause honourable and just. The American public's lack of appreciation of his and his fellow soldiers' efforts affected him more than most. It was a betrayal. It stripped away his spirit.

Yet another casualty of Vietnam.

Fletcher stepped forward and took a deep breath. As he looked at the people around him, he struggled to contain his emotions.

'Before we left Thailand all those years ago, we made a pact that regardless of where we were, we would all come together one last time. It means a great deal to me that you've each kept your word and made it here today. After Vietnam, I flew to Miami, initially to honour a promise I made to Travis, but, as it turned out, I could never find a reason to leave. The city has not only become my home, but it is also home to Lee and Tay, who are now close friends.'

Fletcher took a moment to compose himself. 'When we made this pact, I always prayed that today would be a great many years away. As it turned out, I was given ten full years. But you always want more. Each morning, Jack and I would go down to the beach. Jack loved to swim and run after seagulls. His exuberance never waned. In his last few months, when his hips began to fail, I would carry him to the beach and we'd stare out over the ocean together.' He paused, his voice faltering. 'It was a beautiful, warm morning when he died. Just as I had carried him in Southeast Asia . . . so he slipped away in my arms. I must've sat on that beach holding him for hours, stroking his face. It was Lee who eventually found us. He prised Jack from my arms, and Tay helped me to her car. I can't tell you where we drove that day, just that I cried all the way. I take great comfort in the last years of Jack's life. I know that he loved each and every day we shared—God knows I did. But,' Fletcher said, no longer able to restrain his grief, 'it doesn't make his passing any easier. I . . . I guess I just miss my friend.'

The group crowded round Fletcher, and Rogan placed his hand on his shoulder. Fletcher rested his own hand on top of his lieutenant's, but kept his head bowed. For a while, they were quiet as Jack's coffin was moved into position.

Mitchell walked across to a basket that was filled with a dozen white roses. He chose one, kissed it, and gently placed it on top of Jack's coffin. Marvin, Lee and Rogan each followed suit. Fletcher could hardly see any more. His tears had blurred his vision. He wanted to say more, but he knew the words would fail him. He stumbled up to the grave and placed Jack's leash on top of his coffin. 'I wish we could spend just one more day together,' he managed. 'Just to watch you run, Jack . . .'

Tay ran up behind Fletcher and wrapped her arms round him. Together they watched as Jack was lowered down. When the coffin had come to a stop, each of the men shovelled a measure of sand into the grave until there was little of his coffin left to see.

Fletcher felt exhausted, drained, his head reeling. He felt on the verge of passing out. As Lee and Tay led him away, he looked back and saw that both Rogan and Mitchell were kneeling next to Jack's cross.

They were reading his epitaph.

Fletcher closed his eyes and read along with them.

JACK

I NOW KNOW THAT VIETNAM COULD NEVER CLAIM YOU.

SOME SOULS BURN TOO BRIGHT TO BE LOST TO THE DARKNESS.

YET, AS WE PART, KNOW THAT OUR JOURNEY IS NOT AT AN END.

JUST AS YOU FOUND ME, I WILL SEEK YOU OUT AGAIN.

RUN TO HER, JACK, SHE'S WAITING FOR YOU.

I'LL BE ALONG IN A WHILE.

RUUSH

FLETCHER

gareth **crocker**

Gareth Crocker was born in Johannesburg, South Africa in 1974. He has a degree in English, Psychology and Communications and has worked as a journalist, copywriter, news editor, public relations manager, publishing editor and, most recently, head of communications and spokesperson for a multinational corporation.

He is married to his high-school sweetheart and the couple have two girls, Jordann and Jennifer, as well as four dogs and three cats. 'My wife and I adopted Jennifer from a Children's Home in the south of Johannesburg. She is coloured and has the wildest, most rock-star-like extravagant mop of curly blonde hair the world has ever seen. We fostered her for two years before finally adopting her in 2006.'

Gareth Crocker has been writing since he was nine years old and his initial literary creations were love poems that he sold to love-struck boys in the playground, each of whom, in turn, would present them to the girl of his dreams. Crocker jokes that it was one of the more lucrative periods of his writing life.

His adult writing career began after college, when he spent several years as a young reporter for a community newspaper. However, he soon realised the miniscule pay would be a problem should he ever want to support a family, so he turned to the corporate world. In 1997 he joined a top South African public relations firm, where he says he learned that 'the terms "PR" and "fake" should sit smugly beside each other in the dictionary.' After a few years he was responsible for hundreds of annual reports and company magazines. Eventually, though, he tired of the PR world.

Gareth Crocker began writing fiction and, armed with numerous manuscripts, he headed to London to find an agent. He spent eight days going door to door, dropping off copies of manuscripts with all the agents he could find. Although he quickly realised that finding an agent was much harder than he had naively imagined, luck was with him. He had dropped off a manuscript on the patio of an agent who happened to have locked herself out of her home that day. While she waited for the locksmith, she began reading *Finding Jack* and liked it. She called Crocker and invited him to her office the next day. The author realised how lucky he was when he arrived at her office and saw mountains of unread manuscripts piled up—and she explained that it was only a month's worth.

After securing an agent, the next hurdle was finding a publisher, which took years. The problem, says Crocker, was that his story was something of a hybrid—a war story that was really more of a love story between a man and his dog. Therefore, publishers felt it did not fit into any specific market. Finally, though, they found one. 'I received the publishing contract on the one day it snowed in Johannesburg in something like twenty years. Unforgettable.'

Gareth Crocker wrote *Finding Jack* as a tribute to the real Vietnam War dogs who worked with American soldiers. Approximately 4,000 dogs served, but the US government refused to bring them home at war's end. Only 200 made it back to America. The rest were abandoned. He had stumbled across the story while visiting the Vietnam Memorial Wall in Washington several years ago. 'I was standing next to a Vietnam veteran, dressed in full military gear, when I noticed he had come to place a dog harness at the foot of the wall. Recognising this was a profoundly personal moment for the man, I stood quietly beside him for a few minutes, before politely enquiring about the harness. He replied that he was forced to leave his German Shepherd behind in Vietnam at the end of the war, despite the fact that his dog had saved his platoon from tripwires linked to mines on three separate occasions,' Crocker explains. 'He then took me through the basic story of the Vietnam War Dogs and, when he was done, he wept openly. He cried like a man who had just lost his child. And this, almost thirty years after the incident. I remember being extremely moved by the man's utter despair at the loss of his dog and resolved then that I would write a book as a tribute to the dogs. I'm not particularly interested in judging the politics behind the decision that was taken to leave the dogs behind. All I'm dealing with is the fact that these dogs were abandoned after saving the lives of so many soldiers, and that, is a great tragedy,' says Crocker.

'My hope is that Finding Jack *will endure as one of those great animal stories that people will remember for many years and hopefully pass on to their children.'*

The plight of the Vietnam War Dogs remains relatively unknown, particularly outside the United States. 'My hope is that *Finding Jack* will endure as one of those great animal stories that people will remember for many years and hopefully pass on to their children. Because if they can remember Jack, then they can remember all the Vietnam dogs and what happened to them. And that, as least, is something,' says Crocker. 'After all, as the famous saying goes, if we do not learn from our history then we are doomed to repeat it.'

COPYRIGHT AND ACKNOWLEDGMENTS

THE LION: Copyright © 2010 by Nelson DeMille.
Published at £12.99 by Sphere, an imprint of Little, Brown Book Group,
An Hachette UK Company.
Condensed version © The Reader's Digest Association, Inc., 2011.

WHERE THE TRUTH LIES: Copyright © Julie Corbin 2010.
Published at £19.99 by Hodder & Stoughton, an Hachette UK Company.
Condensed version © The Reader's Digest Association, Inc., 2011.

THE CALLING OF THE GRAVE: Copyright © Hunter Publications Ltd 2010
Published at £12.99 by Bantam Press, an imprint of Transworld Publishers.
Condensed version © The Reader's Digest Association, Inc., 2011.

FINDING JACK: Copyright © 2011 by Gareth Crocker.
Published at £17.99 by St Martin's Press, Inc., New York.
Condensed version © The Reader's Digest Association, Inc., 2011.
Originally published as *Leaving Jack*. Johannesburg, South Africa:
Robert Hale Publishers, 2008. Condensed version of *Leaving Jack*
© The Reader's Digest Association, Inc., 2009.

The right to be identified as authors has been asserted by the following in accordance with sections 77 and 78 of the Copyright, Designs and Patents Act, 1988: Nelson DeMille, Julie Corbin, Simon Beckett, Gareth Crocker.

Spine: Shutterstock. Front cover (from left) and page 4 (from top): www.trevillion.com; Darren Hendly/www.istockphoto.com; Neil Robinson/Getty Images; TJ Scott/Cinematic Pictures. Page 5 (top) © Matt Carr/Contour by Getty Images. 6–8: image: Shutterstock; illustration montage: Rick Lecoat@Shark Attack; 178 © Sandy DeMille; 179 © Getty Images News. 180–2 illustration: Kate Baxter@velvet tamarind; 324 © Bruce Corbin. 326–8 image: Shutterstock; illustration montage: Rick Lecoat@Shark Attack. 472 © Hilary Beckett. 474–6 illustration: Darren Walsh@velvet tamarind. 574 © Kerry-Anne Crocker.

Printed and bound by GGP Media GmbH, Pössneck, Germany

020-272 UP0000-1